THE WATERS OF CHAOS

The Ancient Saga • The Modern Quest

By

Jeff Dobson and Jerry Dobson

ISBN: 978-1480072176

LCCN: 2012918979

Cover design by DAMONZA

Admiralty Press

thewatersofchaos@gmail.com

Dedication

This book is dedicated to our mother, Margaret, who taught us geography, and our dad, J.L., who loved the earth and deserved to see more of it.

Other Works by the Authors

The Waters of Chaos: The Ancient Saga
By Jeff Dobson and Jerry Dobson
A Novel, Sold Separately

The Waters of Chaos: The Modern Quest
By Jerry Dobson and Jeff Dobson
A Novel, Sold Separately

O Brothers, Let's Go Down!
By Jeff Dobson
A Screenplay
A prequel to *O Brother, Where Art Thou?*
By Joel and Ethan Coen

About *The Waters of Chaos*

The Waters of Chaos is a science mystery tackling the greatest puzzle of all: How did human society evolve from the Ice Ages to today? In short, how did we get to be so smart? The *Saga* and the *Quest* take readers on an unconventional romp through science covering vast spans of time. *The Waters of Chaos: The Ancient Saga*, set at the end of the last Ice Age, brings to life a cast of heroic characters living in that long ago time and coping with the imminent global catastrophe of sea level rise. *The Waters of Chaos: The Modern Quest* follows twin brothers Jared and Rick Caisson as they search for evidence of a lost civilization beneath the sea, employing the most advanced technologies available. Both stories invoke Egyptian mythology and universal flood myths to connect science and lore. The modern book proposes new and radically different theories, while the ancient book illustrates how those theories may have worked in the real world. Check out the evidence, and you'll find that almost all of it is true and convincing enough to challenge conventional wisdom. Meanwhile, the two brothers meet head-on the hidebound resistance of fellow scientists, and a close-knit clutch of youngsters grow to adulthood 10,700 years ago in a surprisingly advanced world facing certain disaster. Two youths fall in love and ultimately lead the exodus of their people from the flooded coast to refuge above. Mystery, high- and low-tech adventure, action, romance, sunken pyramids holding the Secrets of the Ages; *The Waters of Chaos* has them all.

The Waters of Chaos consists of two books strategically combined or sold separately. The books are: *The Waters of Chaos: the Ancient Saga* and *The Waters of Chaos: the Modern Quest.*

[Color images available at **www.thewatersofchaos.com**]

Table of Contents

. . . and Yahweh said to the sea:

Hitherto shalt thou come, but no further;
and here shall thy proud waves be stayed. (Job 38: 11)

Prologue

The Grandest Tombstone of All

February 27, 1993

"Insha' Allah," Metwalli mumbled, *Allah's will*, and his stomach heaved with a taste of oil and whiff of gas sucked from the filthy rag crammed in his mouth. *Fahima will miss me*, he thought, *and it's my own damned fault.* He breathed deeply through his nose again and again until his lungs cleared, then calmly resumed contemplating life's great irony. *The hint of death horrifies. The certainty of death soothes. How can that be?*

He had faced danger many times before and knew the fear that comes with not knowing. Now, with the surety of a captain who truly understands his ship and his sea, he waited dispassionately for the sound of death. *Ah, here it comes.* But that first metallic whisper never grew into the screeching, rumbling clamor that he expected. *That's just soft coral brushing against the hull. There's hard stuff underneath. We'll strike it sooner or later . . . on this reef or the next.*

Tape bound his arms and legs. Ropes lashed his body to pipes running along a bulkhead. His wrists and ankles ached and bled from hours of straining against unyielding bonds. *These bunglers don't mean to kill us, but they will. They'll kill us all . . . out of pure ignorance.*

Another faint swish, and only he could hear it, his ear flattened against the iron deck. *Are my affairs in order? Have I left enough money to see our children through? Will Fahima know how to manage? Yes, she has a good head on her shoulders. They'll be alright. Yes, they will make it without me. Our boys are good boys. Our girls are strong. They'll help Fahima.*

Soon, the scrape of hard coral was loud enough for all to hear. *My sailors know what's coming, but they're as helpless as I am, and the fools on my bridge don't have a clue.* In the remaining moments, he calmly reviewed every misstep that had brought him to this sorry end.

* * *

Earlier that night, his rust-red freighter had heaved sluggishly from a makeshift port on Israel's rugged coast. Captain Metwalli set a rhumb-line course across open sea to the first landfall beyond Egypt's heavily guarded shore. The warm winter night's calm would have favored a leisurely passage except for the threat of first Israeli then Egyptian gunboats. The boat chugged through the night, its running lights damped to pass unseen by occasional merchantmen. On or off, the lights mattered little to military patrols. Nothing could keep their radar from detecting a chunk of iron like the *Tress of Berenice*.

Metwalli was accustomed to hauling cargo, not passengers, but this time his clients had insisted on boarding with their load. They were a small band of hill and plains fighters, neither experienced seamen nor trained terrorists. One of the young men sat at the helm and shared a cigarette. The boy soldier carelessly discussed his whole mission, omitting only the truth about the cargo.

"My people must have medicine . . . spare parts," he said, "very bad, very bad. Our men . . . they come to Israel. They make deals."

Six weeks earlier, rebel buyers had contacted merchants eager to exchange rifles and ammunition for hard currency. Certain officials turned a blind eye knowing the arms would be used against an Islamic fundamentalist regime. Even better, the fighting would be distant, across open sea beyond the entire expanse of Egypt, and thus would entail little danger of spreading to Israel itself.

Naive soldiers in a naive war, the rebels understood the danger of betrayal among gunrunners but little else about smuggling at sea. They chartered Metwalli's freighter under the pretext of smuggling parts and supplies out of Israel, a routine haul in this part of the world. As luck would have it, they chose one of the few skippers in the region who had made a personal vow not to carry tools of war. "My family and village have suffered too much from these fanatical, careless revolutionaries," Metwalli once told a would-be arms agent. But, this time the sellers had dismantled and camouflaged the guns so completely that even he, with all his experience as smuggler and trader, mistook the cargo for harmless contraband.

A hundred miles out, his watchman sighted two patrol boats far astern. *Israeli, no doubt*, Metwalli judged, *but why aren't they closing faster on a slow, suspicious freighter like the Tress?* Then, he realized, *They don't want to catch us. Still, we must get out of their waters as fast as possible.* "Full speed," he ordered. Soon, the Israeli boats fell behind, and Metwalli sighed relief. Once inside Egypt, he ran a narrow, treacherous course between shallow bottom and open sea. A second watchman scanned for Egyptian patrols beyond the bow, and a third checked shoreward.

A new set of lights appeared astern, and Metwalli quietly sent his first mate below for a closer look. Five minutes later, the mate's frown said *Guns and ammo!* as clearly as the words that followed.

"Get your stinking shit off my ship!" Metwalli growled to the rebel at his side. "Overboard . . . every last crate."

"May Allah condemn your soul to Hell," the rebel commander replied. Then to his men, "Seize them!" Better disciplined than Metwalli had guessed, the rebels snapped to action, quickly overwhelming his crew. They tied the captain and his men with ropes and took command. Rashly, the commander picked a crewman, without regard for rank or experience, jerked him to the helm, and pointed an old British pilot's pistol at his head. "Follow my orders, driver," he yelled. The mutineers had no idea what risk they brought on themselves as the battered revolver bestowed authority without knowledge.

"I see land. Head for it, then run beside it just out of gun range." Together the helmsman and commander could read the shore well enough to recognize the final cape ending Egyptian territory.

"Steer for open sea!" Metwalli pleaded, and a rebel slammed his head to the deck.

"Round the point. Head for that bay," ordered the commander. "It marks the border. It is the quickest way home."

"No! Not there," Metwalli said. "There are seccas, jagged shoals, everywhere, just beneath the surface! It means sure death!"

"Piss on you, old man. Your pilot says these waters are 30 meters or more. You are trying to get us caught to save your own stinking ass."

"You didn't let my pilot finish. Yes, the bottom is deep, but it's scattered with reefs that touch the surface. You'll kill us all," he said, his grizzled beard turning crimson where his cheek rubbed against a jagged flake of rusted metal.

"You can't trick us," the leader snapped. "We've seen maps."

One highjacker pulled a tattered shred from his shirt pocket. It was the sort of map Metwalli recalled from classroom walls. With quick nods all the rebels agreed that from this coast the sea spread unbroken for leagues. But Metwalli knew what lay ahead. "Your maps are for children, you fools. The scale is too coarse. Look at my navigation charts. They show rocks awash—fouls. This place is infamous for its shoals, so many the bay itself is named for them."

"Shut up, infidel." He grabbed a dirty rag and handed it to a soldier. "Help our brave captain hold his silence." Gagged and subdued, Metwalli ended his last watch. *It's my own fault,* he cursed a seventh time in silent regret.

* * *

A swish . . . a screech . . . then a sickening, grating wail made Metwalli's case for him. All chatter ceased as the rebels, too, heard roaring, rushing water below.

"Insha' Allah," Metwalli whispered, this time without inhaling the fetid fumes.

Within minutes the ship listed to starboard, its bow dipping beneath the waves. No one survived as the *Tress of Berenice* slid forward and down to its final resting place more than a hundred feet below. No one saw the broken block of coral-encrusted stone that joined her in descent.

Then captain, crew, and soldier alike lay together, forever unaware of the massive triangular wall that stood beside their common grave like the grandest tombstone of all.

CHAPTER 1

Search Log 1: A Question of Time

An automatic timer started coffee brewing at 6:15 on a cold Tennessee morning. Ten minutes later, the aroma wafted upstairs just as music erupted from the clock radio beside the Caisson's king-size bed. The radio, set at low volume, was perched on a piece of refinished furniture, appreciated more now as a nightstand than ever before as a school desk. Jared reached for the "off" button, thought just in time, and pushed "snooze" instead. He was not a morning person. Neither was Ellie, but when the radio sounded again she had the willpower to rise, put on a warm gown, and trek downstairs.

When Ellie returned with coffee, they both propped against pillows and slowly came to life. A few minutes later, she dressed while they caught the news and weather on the *Today* show. At 7:15, Jared sprang out of bed, this time with a bit more bounce than usual. After years of silent deliberation, he had decided to confide in a friend, and he looked forward to the debate that would follow.

"Are you sure you want to do this?" Ellie asked, concern showing on her face.

"Ellie, I've gone as far as I can without help. I need someone to talk with, someone who'll give real feedback."

"What about Rick. You could talk to him. He'd understand."

"Not yet. He may be my brother, but he'll claim I'm going off half-cocked. I'll start with Ed."

"Alright, but you know how it went last time."

"I'll be careful," he called back as he bounded down the stairs. "Ed has more data than anybody else on the planet."

He stoked the woodstove; she made a light breakfast; both left for work before daylight. During 25 years of marriage, they had learned to make the dreaded routine pleasant except for the essential fact that each would have preferred to sleep longer and spend more time together. The familiar pattern was at its best for a few weeks in the fall and spring when the trees were bare and sunrise came with the coffee. On clear mornings they could lounge comfortably in bed and view one of the great panoramas of the eastern United States. Rising two thirds as high above the Tennessee Valley as the Rockies rise above the Great Plains, the Great Smoky Mountains each morning form a rich blue wall that blocks the sun and turns the sky red, gold, or, on a good day, Tennessee orange. Often, in winter, the blue wall itself is capped with a smooth blanket of deep white, the highest peaks layered with more than a hundred inches of snow.

Descending the twisting driveway, Caisson glimpsed distant mountains and closer valleys backlighted by the faint glow of dawn. Lake

Loudoun's fog lay white and heavy in mid view. He stopped his Pathfinder at the paper box, where private drive met public road, and grabbed the newspaper, regretting as usual that he couldn't pay much attention to it until evening when every news item would be nearly a day old. He glanced at the headlines while he made his way to the main road. Skimming the front page a few column inches at a time, he took a mile or so to reach the headline: "FREIGHTER SINKS IN MIDDLE EAST–Sabotage Suspected, No Survivors"

It meant nothing to him at the time, just another senseless act in a part of the world where senselessness has become a way of life, but the name of the ship, the *Tress of Berenice*, caught his eye momentarily. He tossed the paper into the passenger's seat and glanced at the hills. Then his mind drifted back to the question that had troubled him so as he pondered the secrets of the ages. He tried to imagine how human intelligence and civilization itself could all have come about.

CHAPTER 2

Chronicle 1: Tales Around an Ancient Fire
The Induction: 10,700 BP

Atop the Sacred Pyramid, aged men circled a glowing fire. They were the Elders, the Wise Men, the Tellers of the Tales. Beneath their solemn glare were gathered the finest young men of their clan, engaged in the most sacred ceremony of their age. The boys stood in silence and awe while tellers told their ancient tales. And so it had been for millennia, repeated anew as each generation passed its knowledge to the next. They told of ancient lives, ancient men, ancient gods. They told of science, some known to the youths, some unknown, and they told of an alien world too strange to be believed.

Above them all, Anbaht, the High Priest of Egia, spoke, "My children, tomorrow is the day of the lowest sun and longest night. Tomorrow is the day our god has chosen to end all that is old and to be remembered. It is the day to begin all that is new and to be discovered. Tomorrow, you shall commence your struggle to become men in the eyes of our people. You are specially chosen from among your peers and now become part of the Divine Right Order, which we also call the Order of the Ma'at. You are to know the ways of our world and its seasons and cycles. The earth was not always as we know it. The land has not always been nor shall it always be the same.

"The ancients told us many things which I now repeat to you. We believed them as we were told, and so must you believe as you are told, for the day shall come when the earth will change. The sea will test your knowledge and your strength. The land will test your faith and endurance. The sky will test your wisdom and love. The time will come when the Midland Sea shall rise and devour our land. Some of our people will find safety because they know and understand; others will perish because they do not. Our King will board his sacred barge and start a new life in the land above." He paused and glared at his charges. "What I now say, you must never repeat to anyone not among the Chosen; else you and your family will perish by the hands of your own priests and fellows of the Chosen.

"All men know the Slow Rise of the world's waters. Yet few generations have known the Fast Rise. When the waters rise slowly, our people plan for the survival of large numbers of our kind. But the waters do not always rise slowly. Three times in this, the Rising Age of the Fourth Kalpa, our people have seen the waters rise many times the height of a man in a single generation. When the waters rise quickly, we can only hope to save a few of our Seed for a new beginning. You are that Seed."

Young Osi shuffled as the revelation hit home. The boy knew well the voice of the High Priest of Egia. He often delivered prayers on their most important ceremonial occasions. Once, in the company of a distinguished fellow priest from another land, the old man even visited Osi's home. The two had spoken privately with his father.

Our King is a mortal man, Osi mused. *How can this tale be true? Can a man fly like a bird to a new land in the sky? Where is this land? Why would this sweet earth and these calm seas choose to wreak havoc on us, its loving children? Our lives are good here. Our land is bountiful. Our sea is beloved. Do we not call ourselves the Beloved People because of our special bond with this land and sea? Will the world we know suffer such a catastrophic end? Why do our trusted Elders tell such fanciful tales,* he questioned. *Surely this is their way of frightening us in some cruel rite of passage.* But no, he had heard whispers of what was to come.

Older boys, on three or four occasions, had taunted Osi and his friends about the secrets they knew. They joked about the sea and the lands around it. The jokes were obscure beyond Osi's comprehension, but he had laughed along to save face. On another occasion, when Osi asked older boys about the Lands of the North, they laughed at him and told him he should build a boat and visit there while its islands were still afloat.

And there were insults that Commoners had hurled at his father and uncle when Osi accompanied them one day into the surrounding countryside, seeing to the King's affairs. Osi's father had seemed disconcerted by the jeers of a rowdy crowd of strangers they met along the road. "Keep your secrets, you highborn fools," a burly local yelled.

"We know the mysteries of how to eat and sleep and bed our women!" shouted another.

"That's knowledge enough for any man!" chimed yet another.

On one occasion youths had taunted him and his friends, other sons of the Chosen. "If you'd like to trade places for the Manhood Ceremony, tell me now. For a small fee, I'll find a willing fool," one had said.

"No, thanks!" the boys had replied with a laugh, not getting the joke but going along with it all the same. Anything called the Manhood Ceremony had to be important, but the young boys could only guess what might make it so. All they had learned for sure was that the occasion was a night they would remember the rest of their lives.

Osi's father told him only this morning that he would soon learn of strange and shocking things to come. Geb had tried to prepare his son for the news while faithfully guarding the Secrets of the Ages. It had been an awkward conversation. Osi knowing not to ask more than his father had been willing to volunteer. Geb knowing that to say too much or too little would only confuse and frustrate his impatient adolescent son.

"Be patient, be attentive, believe what you are told," Geb told his son, "for the day will come when your life and the survival of our King will depend on your strength and wisdom. You have been chosen to serve and to survive. This is the greatest honor and privilege our Elders can bestow."

"How were we chosen?" Osi asked.

"The priests of the temples seek out the best and the brightest of each generation. They go to each home in the land. They meet with the children and converse with them to test their minds and their hearts. They observe their strengths and their weaknesses."

"But I don't recall such meetings." *I only recall the two priests—the High Priest of Egia and another—and they asked no questions.*

"You were specially chosen by Toth, the Chief Priest of the Realm," Geb replied. "He saw your face in a vision and learned of your birth under the sacred sign of Sahu-Orion, our guiding constellation in ages past. He required no further confirmation, as one is so chosen from each generation. He came from Punt to tell us privately that you were chosen in this special way and to witness your consecration. But there is more. Toth prophesies that you have a special destiny. You above all will one day save our King . . . and you will live to save our people as well."

Later, as he stood with his peers in the solemn ceremony, Osi felt the gravity of the situation. The young boys surrounding him were now becoming Chosen Ones, and most were sons of the Chosen. Someday, however, certain ones would slide, as many had before, into disbelief, despair, or sloth. He had known of Chosen Ones and Commoners all his life, but now, for the first time, he would be privy to the knowledge that separated the two castes. The cadets finally would understand what it meant to know the truth, and they were disturbed by the prospect of such newfound knowledge.

The Chief Priest of Egia again spoke, "You are the wisest and most knowledgeable young men of your generation. Just as my fellows and I were selected from our generations and your fathers were selected from theirs, thus are you selected to be the vessels of all knowledge, science, and truth. You are chosen to survive the Chaos to come. You are chosen to become the guardians of our King when the waters rise and our beloved sovereign must be placed aboard the Royal Barge and transported to the land above. You are to be his oarsmen, his navigators, his defenders. You, and the finest young women of your generation, shall be the Seed of new life. You are to be the nobles, merchants, Geometers, priests, and physicians who populate our new land. You are to carry in your minds the knowledge of our world and the wisdom of our age. You are to pass that knowledge along to your children and your children's children so that the wisdom of our world will not perish along with our people.

"You are to know the ways of the Divine Right Order, and its custodians will monitor your progress in this learning. You will learn the Book of Truths by heart, for the Divine Right Order must be preserved if our way of life is to be preserved. The Order is the foundation upon which you must build the remainder of your lives, but not, as some believe, a set of immutable laws to slavishly follow. The Book of Truths is a living creed kept by the Chief Priest of the Realm. It is changed with each generation, for the Order must be remolded continually to fit the realities of our lives and times as long as our people thrive. Not all agree in this, but it is as it must be.

"Different beliefs about the Divine Right Order threaten our heritage—there are those who believe too little in the ways of the Order, and there are those who believe too much. Beware these extremes. There will be among you some who believe that unchanging laws of the Ma'at must be strictly observed in every word and deed. The most devout of these will endanger themselves and others with their foolish actions. An even greater threat lies in those who believe too little.

"You will be scattered among our people and serve in many walks of life. But, when the Chaos comes, you shall gather together by a signal that will be known to all the Chosen. The cry of 'Ma'at!' shall be your sign. Upon that cry, the Chosen shall unite. Upon that signal, the Chosen will come together to seize the lands above, and the masses will be left behind." Anbaht ended as abruptly as he had begun.

Osi quaked as he considered the terrible responsibilities these old men were conferring on him and his peers. It was frightening and almost beyond comprehension. He was especially saddened to learn of the fate of his land and his people. Still, Osi felt a surge of pride that he had been among those chosen for such honor and a sense of relief that, if he performed well, he and his future wife and children would be among those surviving the Chaos.

"Here, take this drink of sacred wormwood in consecration of your vows," Anbaht said, lifting a chalice high above his head. From an amphora on the stone altar, acolytes filled similar vessels, then handed them to the nearest boys. Each took a shallow draft from the cup and passed it on. One by one, the youths swooned, then righted themselves. Osi waited anxiously as the cup approached. He sipped modestly. His first sensation was the familiar taste of anise, with a taint of hard metal. Then the effect of the strong liquor began to swirl about his body like a writhing serpent. First his tongue, then his throat, then his stomach felt the warm glow of the enchanting liquid. His temples, his ears, his fingertips flushed with its curious effect. Senses were disabled one by one. Reality itself became oddly unreal. As the effects of the sacrament diminished, he felt heightened awareness of his surroundings.

Faint daylight vied for Osi's attention. He traced the outline of the terrace on which they stood. Stairs led from the topmost platform to the one below. As the black of night brightened to the purple of dawn, he saw the dim outlines of his father's generation assembled two levels below. During the night, amid the singing of the songs and the chanting of the chants which had preceded the Elder's speech, Osi had pondered briefly the whereabouts of his father and his father's peers. Now that he understood the purpose of this gathering, it came as no surprise that they would be standing guard. At daybreak, Osi was reassured to see his father, Geb, standing near the stairs leading to the pinnacle.

Osi's mind drifted from the ceremony to the panorama unfolding about him. Never having been allowed atop the pinnacle, he couldn't have imagined that the low light of dawn would reveal such spectacular vistas. To the north, a vast expanse of ocean stretched as far as he could see. Its rolling waves faded into an indistinct blend of gray-blue water and violet sky. To the south, a line of steep, green-clad bluffs rose like a fortress, vanishing in the far distant eastern and western horizons. The escarpment was broken only by a dramatic gaping notch through which flowed the mighty river that warmed and nourished his homeland. Between the cliffs and the sea lay a narrow strand where crops, pastures, and orchards painted broad swaths on a backdrop of rich brown soil interspersed with irrigation canals.

As the disk of the morning sun mounted the new pyramid that stood between the High Priest of Egia and the eastern horizon, the old man suddenly transformed as if possessed by a spirit not his own. Osi snapped from his reverie. He shook his head trying to break the wormwood's spell. With first a shriek, then a silent shudder, Anbaht's face contorted into the visage of a being more animal than man, more wizard than mortal, more spirit than substance, more prophet than priest. Bright red rays of sunrise reflected in his eyes like embers. It was an unforeseen departure from the age-old ritual. The transformation, or illusion, seemed profound, one not likely to be seen in the course of a hundred generations.

As the old prophet slowly surveyed the assembled youths, his fiery eyes cast a piercing glance into the face of each young man. "Mark my words," he wailed. "We have seen the skies. The waters of the world will not wait. You are the generation that will meet the test. You are the ones who will lead our Seed to refuge." His eyes widened, his gaze intensified. Suddenly, he peered into the eyes, or rather pierced into the very soul, of the young Osi. Red beams blazed from the prophet's deep sockets as they met Osi's glare. "Heed me, heed me! There is among you one who will lead our Seed to salvation, one who was born under the sign of Sahu-Orion, the Swordsman, principal god of the eastern sky. One who alone will save our King and lead our people to salvation in the lands above."

The old man suddenly ceased his revelation. Instantly, his face relaxed to its rightful form. Osi looked about, expecting to find each of the boys staring at him. To his surprise, the others shuffled about as if they had no inkling the priest's revelation had been aimed toward any particular individual in their midst. Had Osi only imagined the purposeful gaze of the priest? Had he perhaps fantasized the entire transformation from priest to prophet to priest again? Perhaps the wormwood sacrament, the lack of sleep, and the strange morning light played tricks on his mind. Could the priest's potion have heightened his own perception? Or dulled the minds of those about him? Still, the import of the event, whether real or imagined, had indelibly impressed the young cadet. Never again would he think of himself or his world in the same manner as just one short night before. Never could he forget his sacred vow to save the King.

CHAPTER 3

Search Log 2: Missing Link

Jared Caisson's drive to work was almost as scenic as the view from his ridgetop home. Crossing Beaver Ridge on the main highway, he could see the steep face of the Cumberland Plateau no more than ten miles ahead. Three-quarters of a mile from the I-40 overpass, he glanced up at the familiar escarpment. *Ah, there they are,* he thought, *the Petite Tetons*—two gently rounded, identical knolls, their tops peaked by highwalls. The recumbent Cumberland maiden, viewed from best vantage, her perky nipples the only blessing strip-mining ever brought to East Tennessee.

The next valley held a narrow arm of Watts Bar Lake and the manicured grounds of Melton Hill Dam. Beyond the river, the road entered the reservation and curved through several miles of hardwood and pine forests unspoiled by stores, houses, or other signs of human occupation. Eight-and-a-half miles from home, he entered the East Portal of Melton Valley Laboratory. Arriving before 8:00 a.m., he could park at the outer reaches of the main lot. Latecomers would face a long walk from overflow lots. This morning, he took his favored space, walked briskly through the cold clear air, and entered the guard station.

Guards were rotated on an erratic schedule designed to foil any conspiratorial attempts to breach security. Some guards were friendly, others stern, others indifferent except to their uncompromising duty to view each badge, physically touch it, and establish that photograph indeed matched face. This morning the guard was Officer Tom Washburn, one of the few whom Caisson knew by name. They had served together in the Tennessee National Guard 20 years back.

"Good morning, Tom."

"Good morning, Junior." Caisson registered no surprise at being called Junior. That's what Tom had called him for the past two decades. He wasn't a "junior" in any sense of the word. Close friends and family called him Jerry, and many acquaintances mistook him for his twin brother, Rick, but no one else had ever called him Junior. Yet somehow, sometime in the annals of their casual, cordial friendship Tom had adopted "Junior" as his God-given name. There was no explanation and no turning back. Thus, as it happened, the one person on earth who had his name indelibly wrong was among the few people on earth paid to confirm it officially on a regular basis.

Caisson clipped his badge to a front belt loop and stepped into the securely fenced grounds of the Laboratory. A few yards of tree-lined avenue brought him to the Flagpole Lobby of 4500-North, the Laboratory's main administration and research facility. His office, upstairs almost directly above the lobby, offered one more daily fix for his addiction to scenic vistas. A large window, comprising most of the rear wall, faced a hillside covered with a proper mix of oak forest, grassland, and scattered fruit trees—a poignant reminder that the MVL reservation once held farms, churches, and communities like others throughout East Tennessee.

Caisson settled in, drank his first cup of coffee, and waited for Edison Field's usual morning drop-by. He stared at three maps on the wall across from his desk. One of them showed projections of global sea level change modeled by MVL scientists. Another showed similar estimates for the United States in greater detail. The third was a satellite image of actual land cover changes throughout the Chesapeake Bay region over the past five years. Jared and Ed Field were the authors of the third map. *How odd,* he thought, *everybody nowadays is obsessed about projected rises that would amount to less than 30 feet in the worst case, yet hardly anyone mentions the enormous rise that has been stealing the world's land steadily since the Ice Ages.*

There was the usual perfunctory knock as Ed opened the door and slipped inside. "Morning, Jer," he said, "How the heck are you?"

"Fine, Ed." Caisson gazed at his coffee mug as Ed cleared some papers from a chair.

Ed sensed something was up. "What's on your mind?"

"It's a big one, Ed—and it may be too big."

"Not again. Not another twist on Continental Drift, is it?"

"No." He laughed. "They almost went postal on that one, didn't they? Same thing on lake acidification."

"'Fraid so."

"Most folks will choose bad theory over good evidence any day of the week. I understand, though. Geologists and ecologists think they own the earth, and I'm an outsider to them. They forget that geographers have been studying this old orb longer than any other discipline."

"Look, Jer. You've made your reputation. Solid as a rock. You should be floating toward retirement, but you're steering for whitewater again, aren't you? That's what you're about to tell me. Right?"

"I'm afraid so, Ed. I've got enough years left to solve at least one more big mystery. It's just not in me to hold back and rest on my laurels."

"If whatever you're talking about becomes too controversial, you could lose the funds you already have to study global change."

"That's a chance I'll have to take."

"So what is it, Jer? What mystery is worth risking all?"

"It's human evolution, Ed."

"Well, it's about time. Did you know they had a trial on that very subject several years ago down at Dayton?"

"Yes! I haven't read the book, but I did see the movie."

"Human evolution? Where did that come from? Last week we were studying changes in coastal land cover on Chesapeake Bay. I thought that was intriguing enough. Now you want to head off in a new direction. Surely you don't plan to take on Charlie D."

"No, but something's not right about standard Darwinian theory, and it's not just evolution. It's the whole prehistory package. Even as a boy, I couldn't buy it. I accept evolution. I accept natural selection. I can believe that gradual evolution, or more likely punctuated evolution, got us from microbe to human, but common sense tells me one key premise is dead wrong."

"And that is .. ?"

"Why would natural selection drive human intelligence to a level of sophistication thousands of times more advanced than conditions warranted at the time of the selection? Archaeological evidence strongly suggests our brain was fully developed more than a hundred thousand years ago. Yet, agriculture is only supposed to have come along about 10,000 years ago. Why would humans, challenged by nothing more stimulating than hunting mammoths and gathering wild grain, somehow develop a brain capable of exquisite artistry, profound philosophy, advanced physics, complex mathematics, high technology, space travel . . ."

"I get your point, Jer. It's a classic case of being overqualified for the job. Go on."

"Natural selection simply can't account for such a leap."

"So, are you going to test Von Daniken's hypothesis . . . Earth colonized from space? National Science Foundation should go for that, no problem." Ed shook his head dubiously.

"Well, they've funded worse, but that's not what I have in mind. Von Daniken's space travel was a bit over the top, but I really do believe Armstrong made it to the Moon a few centuries later."

"And you suspect . . ."

"I suspect the mystery could be explained by one modest event requiring neither supernatural intervention nor extraterrestrial visitation." Jared paused. "I suspect human culture may have reached at least one other peak of development in some way similar to the one occurring today. The more I look at the evidence, the more I think I'm right."

"Hold on, Jer. Lost civilizations? Don't you think you ought to stick to something more believable. Cold fusion? Perpetual motion?"

"I'm sticking to straight science. No harmonic levitation, no Edgar Cayse visions. I've pondered this for three decades. Then a few days ago I stumbled across what may be the key. I've discussed it with Ellie, of course, and I'm ready to talk with you, but I won't go public until we find the right data, and everything checks out."

"Out of the map closet, eh?"

"You might say."

"You know this won't set well with other scientists? The tabloids will eat it up, but archaeologists and paleontologists will eat you alive."

"You're right. No question. The sad truth is that scientists are no more tolerant of new ideas than they were four centuries ago when they persecuted Galileo. Or, worse yet, when they ridiculed Wegener about continental drift for half of *this* century. Today, science has become a pyramid scheme, a sort of chain letter in which each new "discovery" *must* confirm existing theory. Ideas that challenge accepted theory are labeled heresy just as they would have been in the Dark Ages."

"Well preached."

"You know it's true, Ed. It's both productive and destructive. The system produces lots of new findings, and most of them are true. Collectively, they offer a lot of insight, but the system prohibits challenges that might root out bad theory. Modest, reasonable questioning or wildly controversial scientific heresy—either one gets the same hostile reception."

"Come on, Jer, professors routinely urge their students to ask questions, challenge dogma."

"Yes, but the same guy who tells his class there's 'no such thing as a stupid question' will crucify a fellow scientist for testing 'heretical' hypotheses. And what is a hypothesis? Just a stupid question posed to seek an objective answer."

"Maybe we're worrying too much. You've handled these things before. It may not be easy, but you can survive professionally as long as you don't venture too far out on an evolutionary limb."

"I'm human, Ed. I'm willing to face ridicule if I have to, but it's painful wondering who snickers and who doesn't when they meet me in the hall."

"Where do we start?"

"The real answer to human evolution must lie somewhere here on earth, and I have some rough ideas where to look. The culture may not have been as technologically advanced as our own, but it must have faced some of the same challenges to natural selection. Or, maybe it was more advanced than ours. Even today, we only tap part of our potential brain power."

Ed paused, then asked, "How do you figure the timing?"

"Well, from what I've read, the human body approximated its current form, except for brain size, about two-and-a-half million years ago. That's about when the Ice Ages began. By roughly 120,000 years ago the brain was fully formed. And there's clear evidence of human culture as early as 36,000 years BP. . . 'before present,' that is. So, I'd peg it sometime before 120,000 BP with possible recurrences right up to the dawn of recorded history."

"Wouldn't a technological society leave some physical trace that would have been found by now?" Ed asked.

"I've thought a lot about that. If it came early in the two and a half million-year time frame, nature might have wiped out practically every trace. Even metals would have corroded away by now. Erosion and sedimentation would have destroyed or hidden most sites. But I doubt it was that early, because brains were still pretty small in the early years.

When brains finally did reach current size, it may have been a long time before they were organized to run an advanced society. A modern-size brain doesn't necessarily imply modern intelligence. Probably, the high-performance brain was a refinement that came fairly late in the process. So let's bracket our search between 120,000 BP and, say, 11,000 BP when the first cities appeared," Jared replied.

"So, *where* is it?"

"That bracket coincides with the last major episode of Pleistocene glaciation. I first thought the most likely time was a warm period like today, thus pointing toward high-latitude sites later obliterated by glaciers. This new evidence sparks a different thought, however, and I can't get it out of my head."

"Out with it!"

"Do you realize where sea level was just 18,000 years ago? It was 400 feet lower than today! Even at the end of Pleistocene glaciation, just 10,000 years ago, it was 325 feet below the current level. I probably heard those numbers before, but it didn't occur to me how dramatic the rise was until I ran across an article in *Discover* magazine. Did you see the one about Tasmania?" Jared asked.

"No."

"The topic had very little to do with the Ice Ages, but the author casually mentioned that Tasmania was connected to Australia as recently as 10,000 years ago when sea level was 400 feet lower. His figure may be off by a few feet or a few thousand years, whichever way you want to look at it, but the exaggeration may have been good, for it started me thinking. I was struck by the magnitude and timing of the rise. Even with the more accepted figure of 325 feet in 10,000 years, that's a hell of a lot of water."

"Must be a lot of land, too! Have you been able to determine where it is, worldwide?" Ed asked.

"I've consulted every map of the sea floor I can find. Not one has a 400-foot bathymetric contour or anything close to it. Most of them have a 200-meter contour. Let's see, that's about 650 feet. I would guess, from the 100- and 200-meter lines I've seen, that the area exposed must have been enormous in certain parts of the world, especially the tropics."

Ed ruminated for a few seconds and then replied, "Well, we can check that part easily enough. I have NOAA's world elevation and bathymetry database on my workstation downstairs. I'll plot the 0 to 400 foot depth. Be back in an hour."

Search Log 3: The Forgotten Land

Caisson had begun his second cup of coffee when Ed reentered and spread a crisp plot of the globe across his cluttered desktop. The colored-wax image was still warm to his touch. "This matches what I expected.

Look at that. The Nile Delta, the Persian Gulf, flanks of India, huge expanses off Southeast Asia! It's all above water."

"Why did you expect those particular areas?" Ed held the map up and pondered the areas Jared had noted.

"Because all of their adjacent land areas are known today as early cradles of civilization," Caisson said, "but there's one surprise. I wouldn't have guessed the Adriatic Sea. Greece and Rome were early by current standards, but much later than Egypt, Mesopotamia, India, and Southeast Asia. Of course, no one knows for sure where the Etruscans came from. They were early occupants of the region but not that early."

"You're ignoring the Western Hemisphere," Ed said, pointing toward patches of yellow in the Caribbean Sea and off the coast of Argentina. Neither man mentioned polar regions. It went without saying that these cold lands were covered with ice and could have been significant only in the interglacial hypothesis.

"If the Western Hemisphere contained advanced cultures, they must have been peripheral to the main areas of civilization in the east. At any rate, they didn't leave a lasting legacy that resulted in later cradles of civilization like those in the east. The Mayas and Aztecs and even the Olmecs and Toltecs are late bloomers compared to the people of Egypt and Asia. My money is on this submerged area off Southeast Asia as the oldest and most advanced culture, with major offshoots in the Persian Gulf, the Mediterranean, and maybe the Red Sea. All we have to do is figure out where to look for ruins. What do you think?"

"I think you're crazy," Ed replied, "but you're right about one thing. If any such civilization actually did exist, the only place worth looking for it is under the sea."

"Agreed," Jared said, "except for one problem. If there was a civilization down there, what would have kept them so totally confined to the seashore? How could they be so geographically limited that they wouldn't leave a single trace in the lands that are now above water? Any viable theory will have to resolve that puzzle, and no critic will give us an inch of slack."

"Good point. You'd think there would be an outpost or a trade center or a fort or a monument or something left over. That's one to ponder. I don't think the answer will come easy."

Jared returned to his earlier argument. "Right now I know very little about archaeology and marine biology, but surely we can make some assumptions that will hold with or without a truly advanced civilization. First, let's stipulate that the submerged zone must have contained populations no less numerous and cultures no less advanced than the Ice Age cultures already known from terrestrial archaeology."

"Agreed. That's a no brainer."

"In fact, those tropical lowlands should have been the most habitable zone on earth. Oceans would have moderated temperatures, and the land would have collected water flowing from uplands even if it didn't get much rainfall of its own. It would have had the highest carrying capacity for human populations because it would have had food sources from both land and sea. Conservatively though, let's just assume that the populations were average for the time. Now, if these people lost vast territories to rising oceans they either had to die in place or move to higher ground. Okay?"

Ed nodded, and Jared went on. "A rapid rise would have favored dying in place, but we know it wasn't that fast. A fellow would have to be an awfully slow walker to be overtaken by water rising 125 feet in 8,000 years."

"Unless it happened in spurts."

"Well, that seems unlikely. In fact, I remember seeing some graphs that showed a fairly gradual rise, some ups and downs but nothing precipitous enough to drown large areas overnight. The only people who might be trapped would be those living on large, flat lowlands where a few feet of vertical rise or a sudden storm surge might wipe out a huge horizontal area."

Ed pointed toward the world map on Jared's wall. "Isn't that the situation in Bangladesh today? A yard or so would cover half the country." He switched to the U.S. map. "Florida and the Delmarva Peninsula would be devastated at 30 feet."

"Good point. The worst situation of all would be a low island where a yard or two would cover almost everything, and there would be no place to escape except by boat—think Maldives today."

"Or Tangier Island!" Ed pointed to the image of Chesapeake Bay. "You recall what we saw when we did our fieldwork there . . . graves in the front yard . . . water lapping at the back steps."

"Yes. Now, let's assume that some forced migrations occurred. If both areas, origin and destination, were occupied at or near maximum carrying capacity, the newcomers most certainly would not have been welcomed with open arms. In fact, there must have been a battle royal every time a group moved inland. Generally the home team had the advantage, so the visiting team would have won only when they held some major advantage— like technology or sheer numbers. A population expansion like that should show up in traditional archaeological literature, probably with uncertainty and speculation as to where the aggressors came from. Do you know of any cases where that happened?"

"As I recall, there are lots of cases like that, but it's been a long time since I took world history and one lone course in archaeology. Come to think of it though, I read in *Discover* magazine that seafaring people of unknown origin invaded Cyprus, overwhelmed the local population, and ate the pygmy hippopotamus into extinction."

"When was that?" Jared asked.

"The March issue, I believe," Ed replied with an ever-so-slight glint in his good eye.

"No, dammit! What year did they invade?" Jared shook his head.

"Ten thousand years ago. But you know archaeologists tend to round off to popular numbers."

"Maybe so, but 10,000 BP seems more popular than most. For instance, there has been a big argument about *where* agriculture originated, but practically all of the contesting archaeologists claim circa 10,000 BP as the time of origin in their favored regions. A truce of sorts has been reached in most textbooks through the claim that agriculture was independently invented in three different forms at three different places at the same time."

"But you don't buy that?" Ed asked.

"Realistically, independent invention is rare. Triple independent, simultaneous invention would be like winning three state lotteries in the same year. My guess is that agriculture must have originated in one place, diffused and diversified along the old seacoast, then spread to the uplands through forced migrations as the water rose about 10,000 BP. That could explain wheat in the Middle East, root crops in South Central Asia, and rice in Southeast Asia all appearing about the same time. It could also explain a few outliers such as some disputed evidence of rice in upland Southeast Asia as early as 15,000 years ago."

"But what would be left as evidence, and how will you find it in 325 feet of water? Huts or houses would have been torn apart by wave action or covered with sediment. Anyway, we won't find them with the bathymetric data we have now. Only one data point about every five miles. It's good for landforms several miles across, but any reasonable building would have been much smaller than that. It's like looking for a micro-needle in a mega-haystack."

"Where can we get more detailed bathymetric data?" Jared asked, as he stared at the global map.

"This is the finest available for the whole globe. If anything better exists, it must be in the Intel community. A few years ago, they classified some U.S. coastal data that NOAA had already digitized. I doubt it exists for most of the area you're interested in. It would have been hopeless as recently as a year ago, but Vice President Gore is pushing all the intelligence agencies to release information that may help study global change. Maybe we can convince someone that bathymetry falls in that category."

"Alright, but we can't put all of our eggs in one basket. Old habits are hard to break, and the spooks have never had much respect for people who sell data . . . even less for people who give it away. Let's sketch a plan of attack that will give us the answers we need."

Jared went to the board. Together they listed more than 20 different lines of research. The first item was bathymetric data combined with a better understanding of the continental shelf. The second was a better understanding of the evolution of the human brain. Other items ranged from Ice Age climate to language to mitochondrial DNA, always with an emphasis on geographical distribution as well as process. Paleoculture and demographics headed the second column.

"Most items should be tackled by a *bona fide* expert, but that takes money. It's the inevitable Catch 22 of groundbreaking research. There's no funding to test the hypothesis and no way to get funding without first proving the hypothesis." Jared marked a final item on the list–funding sources. "Until we get some funding, most of my time is going to be nights and weekends."

"I can wedge in some hours between projects," Ed said, surveying the list. "Other Lab or university experts are out of the question."

"Yes, and even if we get some funding, we can't solicit collaborators without letting them know what we're up to. There aren't many experts who'll risk joining if they know we're questioning accepted theory. A handful in each field might be willing, but neither you nor I know them by name."

"Yes, and searching for them will have its own risks. If even one of the final team turns out to be a kook, it will doom our effort and probably brand every member of the team for life."

"We need help, but it will have to come from people we know and trust. That's a pretty short list."

Search Log 4: Too Deep for Treasure

The Seagate team met in the same conference room at Berkeley National Lab continuously for two solid days, and Jared was anxious to leave. The schedule called for a free afternoon, but the dedicated professors and project scientists spent several more minutes wrapping up loose ends and making last minute arguments. Then, more time was lost deciding who wanted to go where and how to share the limited vehicles available.

"Jerry, let's run up to the Muir Forest. We can make it up there in an hour or so, spend a couple of hours knocking around in the forest, and still make it back here for dinner."

"Not me, guys. Thanks anyway, but I'm going to head over to Barnes and Noble." He had spotted a promising bookstore on a nearby street corner and was anxious to check its shelves for books that might shed light on the Ice Ages, human intelligence, or early cultures. "I'll head over there and meet you folks later for dinner."

"You spend enough time in libraries during work hours. It's a beautiful drive."

"I know, and ordinarily I'd join in a flash, but I need something to read on the plane home."

"We'll be back in plenty of time for Barnes and Noble."

"I'll go on one condition. Promise me you'll get us back to Berkeley by early evening. The store closes at 11:00 p.m., and I need at least a couple of hours before they turn out the lights."

The afternoon gradually slipped away as the friends strolled leisurely among giant redwoods. Caisson gently nudged them to move along. As the group moved slowly from vista to vista, he doubted that they would make it back in time. When twilight came, however, they were out of the hills and approaching the north end of the bay. For several minutes they were lost in Mill Valley, and he recalculated his projected arrival time at the bookstore across the bay. Then someone asked, "Anyone up for dinner in Sausalito?" Apparently Barnes and Noble had been forgotten.

"But . . ." Caisson started to protest, then decided against imposing his personal quest on the others. The seafood dinner was excellent, spoiled only by his secret impatience. When it was over, he calculated there was still time to reach the bookstore an hour or so before closing. But the car headed toward Chinatown, and it was not to be. He tried to muster some enthusiasm as they walked the lively old streets, but that was hard for he desperately wanted to be across the bay.

In what Jared later came to think of as divine providence if not an actual miracle, he and his colleagues reached the front of their hotel at 10:30. "Please drop me off at the bookstore before circling to the hotel's parking lot, if you don't mind," Jared said. He rushed through the front door and headed for the Science & Nature section.

Caisson wasn't sure why he had such high hopes for this particular bookstore; perhaps it was its proximity to the large university so widely known for its intellectual style. Even so, he was slightly astonished when his eyes focused immediately on a book entitled *Ice Age Climates and the Evolution of Human Intelligence*. Titles often mislead, but this book surely must have something to offer on the topic that so intrigued him. He would buy it without even looking inside. Skimming through rows of titles, his gaze passed through a section marked "ANTHROPOLOGY & ARCHAEOLOGY."

His thoughts turned toward ancient civilizations, but what caught his attention was something even more pertinent, *Marine Archaeology*. The book would devote most of its text to sunken treasure; that was clear from the cover. Caisson bought it anyway for what it might say about underwater search technology. Maybe it would contain a few tidbits of insight on his quest, as well. At 10:56 Jared stepped to the checkout counter with these two plus a third, less promising, text on the evolution of the human brain.

* * *

On Good Friday morning, the Caissons indulged in one of their favorite pastimes. Propped on pillows piled against the wooden headboard, Ellie and Jared each held a book in one hand and a cup of coffee in the other. Occasionally the coffee hand would deposit its burden on the closest nightstand and reach for a shortbread cookie. When the cookies were gone, they drank coffee, and, when the coffee was gone, they took turns going downstairs for more. Once in a while, they sat quiet, simply gazing at the mountains and savoring the solitude of Beaver Ridge.

Caisson had chosen the place and designed the building himself. From the circular drive in front, the house looked formal and traditional, Federalist-style, with tall windows facing the Cumberland Plateau. The rear, however, was mostly glass facing southeast toward the Great Smoky Mountains. Between mountains and plateau lay the Tennessee Valley, where the winding river carves a thousand-foot-deep gash more than 100 miles wide and curving 600 miles from its Appalachian headwaters to its confluence with the Ohio. But the valley itself is broken by dozens of knife-sharp ridges, including the Caissons' own Beaver Ridge and others with telling names like Copper and Black Oak. Most homes lie in the narrow valleys, and their occupants pass each day unmindful of what lies beyond. But, Caisson carefully chose this ridge and this knoll so that every window of the house captured either the morning spectacle in the east or evening spectacle in the west.

In summer, a curtain of leaves blocked their view of the Smokies, but the Cumberlands were clear year-round. Ellie preferred summer when foliage guaranteed total privacy. Jared preferred winter with its full panorama, especially on weekends when the two of them could wait for sunrise and enjoy the view for as long as they chose. This morning, the big poplar tree just outside the window and the oaks around the backyard were at that tender stage of greening when husband and wife both had their way.

The old poplar shouldn't have been left in the backyard when the house was built 11 years before. Too close against the eaves, it now had grown too large for comfort. He knew it should be cut but dreaded taking that step. The man who makes his home in the forest naturally balks at removing the forest from his home. Perhaps he would cut it in the fall or winter when its finest attributes were no longer on display.

Jared considered himself a slow reader and felt hampered whenever his work called for an in-depth search of scientific literature. Yet, thoroughly engrossed in a topic, he would read voraciously. Since late March he had spent every spare moment on one of the books purchased in California, others found in local bookstores, and still others borrowed from MVL's Central Research Library.

"What's the latest?" Ellie asked as they sat in the poplar's budding shade and admired "their" mountains.

"No smoking gun, but I've learned a lot. There's circumstantial evidence connecting the rise of human intelligence with Ice Age climates. I'd hoped to get a decent understanding of the process, then talk with specialists in each field. I'm nearing that point. Some of what I've found may even be solid enough to include in a scientific article."

"Worthwhile. That's good."

"You know my philosophy. A reader is fortunate if he can read a book and come away with one good idea worth remembering a year later. Two of these authors have earned their keep by that measure."

"Any hint yet as to location?"

"Early on, I asked 'How deep?' This marine archaeology text says even professionals rarely go below 160. Even for gold worth millions, treasure hunters rarely venture deeper because it's too damned expensive and too risky. This invisible barrier practically guarantees that ancient settlements below 160 feet would go unnoticed even in modern times."

"But what about the big question that bothered you so?"

"The evolution of human intelligence and its connection to the Ice Ages? I can't answer that just yet." He picked up another book, this one by a fellow named Calvin, and began reading.

Search Log 5: Vestiges

In mid-May, Jared and Ed headed out for fieldwork on Chesapeake Bay. Here, the Seagate project was almost complete, and they went for what they hoped would be the final check of their results. Before leaving MVL, Ed plotted satellite data on paper maps and printed transparent overlays of the road network. These custom maps helped orient them, but still the work was demanding. On one particularly fine afternoon, they drove into a fishing village on the Eastern Shore. They had been rushing from site to site since 7:30 am and were exhausted, drained by the mental effort of constantly locating themselves on the ground and on the map and then checking to see if what they found on the ground matched what they had prophesied on the map.

Jared spotted a quaint tavern by the water and insisted on stopping for a beer. Its walls were made of weathered wood, and the parking lot was paved with oyster shells. Jared parked up front in the nearly empty lot, and the two went inside. They breezed by the bar and asked for seating on the deck. Without delay, a waiter escorted them to a choice table overlooking fishing boats in a tiny harbor framed by the broad bay beyond. Jared ordered a Bass Ale and was pleasantly surprised to find they had it. Ed, a teetotaler, ordered his usual glass of sweet iced tea. Soon enough, Jared's main purpose for the leisurely stop became clear.

"I want to update you. Calvin's book on human evolution during the Ice Ages is a good piece of thought, but there's a gaping hole. He ignores the submerged land . . . entirely . . . to the detriment of his own argument. I've seen the same thing in everything I've read. Most don't even mention that more land was available for settlement back then. Of those who do mention it, most speak only of a 'land bridge' as if ancient people scurried across, single-mindedly aiming for where the seacoast would lie 10,000 years hence. Let's call it the 'Wallenda Vector'–a tightrope from one place we value today to another place we value today with hoards of ancient people skittering across." Laughing, Jared took a deep draught of his ale.

"But you did get something out of the book?"

"Oh, yes. First, no one knows how or why the human brain advanced so much so fast. The step by step progression is mostly outside the archaeological record. Second, the main growth in cranial capacity coincided with the Ice Ages. It grew to four times its pre-glacial size in that 2,500,000-year period. Calvin's field is neurobiology, so he's as qualified as anyone to speculate. He addresses two aspects: physical size and mental organization. Of course, it's easy enough for anthropologists to measure physical size since the main artifacts are skulls, but mental organization is quite another matter. There's no direct measure; organization can only be inferred indirectly from the activities the hominids engaged in. For most of that time, tools are about the only indicators, and they just don't provide enough to go on."

"I understand there are some cultural artifacts–sculptures, ornaments, things like that–in the later periods."

"Yes, Calvin mentions art. He says the mind must have advanced a lot about 37,000 to 20,000 years ago because that is when carved ivory and cave paintings first appear. Geographer Jared Diamond calls it the Great Leap Forward. But, evidence of the advancement itself is pretty sparse. It's entirely possible that earlier people were just as artistic, and we haven't yet found their artifacts. Maybe, for instance, they painted outside walls instead of cave walls, and rain washed it all away. It could be that simple."

"What's the earliest time it could have happened?" Ed asked.

"The great physical expansion couldn't have been much earlier than about 118,000 BP. That's the beginning of the most recent Ice Age, and there's no evidence of *Homo sapiens sapiens* before then. Calvin thinks the timing is more than a coincidence. He suspects a causal link between climate and human evolution."

"Okay. How does he think they're connected?"

"The development was remarkably fast by ordinary standards of evolution–so fast that Calvin thinks it can't have been a normal evolutionary process. On the other hand, I'm not sure what normal evolution is. Darwin assumed a slow process, later called gradualism. Since the early '70s there's been a tilt toward the idea that species remain static for long periods of time, then change rapidly in response to some new stimulus."

"Like climate change."

"Exactly," Jared responded, "or new competitors, things like that. Eldredge and Gould originated the idea. They call it 'punctuated equilibrium.' Some scientists think changes almost always occur in response to catastrophic events. In regard to human evolution, Steven Stanley, for instance, propounds what he calls the 'catastrophic scenario.' Climate change brought down the forests, forcing Australopithecus out of the trees and onto open plains which enabled him to use his hands more freely. If Eldredge, Gould, and Stanley are right, fast change is the norm; it just doesn't happen very often. Most important, Calvin proposes a "Darwin machine" that depends on precisely the sort of geographic catastrophes that you and I have been talking about. He thinks the territorial expansion and contraction of glaciers creates boom and bust cycles that amplify the cycle of innovation. The same principle should apply to sea level change and the boom and bust that would accompany it, too. And that's what Calvin forgot to mention."

"How does his Darwin machine differ from plain old natural selection?"

"Natural selection assumes a gradual advantage for the organisms best adapted to a particular environment. It works ploddingly when conditions are stable and may be accelerated when conditions change rapidly," Jared said. "Keep in mind, however, that evolution has both a negative and positive side. Poor adaptations die. Good adaptations survive. But where do the innovations themselves come from? As Calvin sees it, when glaciers retreat, new territory opens up and innovations occur rapidly. To put it simply, any mutation, cultural or physical, has a far better chance of surviving and spreading when there's plenty of food for everybody."

"When glaciers retreat, what they leave behind is bare rock and gravel."

"Good point. It takes a while for soil to accumulate and forests to grow. But when that happens, in Calvin's view, the whole world becomes *underpopulated* because of the additional available land. People gradually migrate into the new land and enjoy a kind of golden age for many years before new population growth exhausts the resource. The new land becomes a crucible for innovation."

"And in the tropics . . ."

"Calvin's Darwin machine is a powerful mechanism periodically ratcheting development upward. He only mentions glaciers, but a similar crucible would operate in the Tropics, where enormous quantities of productive coastal land would be gained at precisely the same time his colder, smaller land is lost in the far north. And, the reverse would be true when glaciers retreat. Thus, we've turned his single-action pump into a double-action pump generating innovations at both ends of the climatic cycle."

"Anything else?"

"The most useful part is what he says about the distinguishing characteristics of humans– language, throwing, concealed ovulation, toolmaking, and our unique way of thinking. Our most advanced capabilities, such as space travel, are just refinements of his basic categories. A Saturn-5 rocket, for instance, is just a really big, complex tool. I am especially intrigued by his point that we humans have an unusual attraction to swimming and shorelines."

"Rising sea level?" Ed ventured.

"It's called the Aquatic Theory. We have quite a few odd characteristics in common with aquatic mammals."

"For instance?"

"Subcutaneous fat, meaning that layer of pork beneath your skin. Kidneys designed to get rid of both water and salt. Even the tears that roll down our cheeks when Bama plays UT. But it's mostly those kidneys that force us to stay near sources of freshwater and eat salt with our food. In fact, a physiologist named Alister Hardy specifically proposed that humans must have foraged along shorelines at some time in their evolution."

"That fits your theory to a tee. But I'll bet the shoreline episode was long ago since those characteristics are so basic to our body design."

"Maybe it started early and persisted for a long, long time. Maybe through the Ice Ages," Jared said. "There's also a Savanna Theory that says we lived in open grasslands and ate a lot of seeds. Some people think that's how we developed upright posture. Calvin also propounds a temperate episode in which the trials of winter were a major driving force. The three theories are complementary and perfectly consistent with ours if the phases happened over and over again rather than in a neat, one-time shift from aquatic to savanna to temperate."

"Seems to be something missing, though. Aren't we in a boom time right now? This one isn't because of new territory. It's because of technology."

"Right. Technology . . . and better cultural organization. Calvin says the same thing may have happened to a lesser degree when our ancestors invented big game hunting, boats, cooking by fire, baskets, pottery, and, of course, agriculture itself."

"Yes," Ed replied, "but your original question was, 'Why did the human brain advance beyond the demands of the Ice Ages?' I see lots of pressures to advance, but nothing that would have required high technology, symphonies, great works of literature, or any of the other things you mentioned."

"Exactly! There had to be something more demanding than simply running back and forth between glaciers and tropical seas. I was especially intrigued by Calvin's view that certain climatic changes, such as the Allerød warming event from about 14,000 to about 13,000 years ago and the warm-up following the Dryas event about 11,000 years ago, would have been abrupt enough to disrupt stable civilizations. He estimates that, in all recorded history, only about 20 cultures were advanced enough to build cities. The odd thing is that, except our own modern society, each of them showed most of its innovation in its earliest years and then later settled into technological stagnation." Jared paused, and his gaze intensified. "Could that be because they weren't innovators in the first place? What if all the civilizations from Sumer through Rome were just vestigial survivors of something once truly magnificent."

Search Log 6: Return to the Ice Ages

"Talk about dumb luck!" Ed exclaimed as he entered the office. "Just when you want to return to the Ice Ages, we get a trip to Alaska."

"Alaska! Why? When?"

"It's NOAA. They want to tackle Alaska next in the Seagate Program. K Kinski will be their project manager. He wants us to fly up as soon as possible."

"That's great," Jared responded, "but they can't mean the whole state. That coast would take dozens of satellite scenes. Did they mention any specific area?"

"It's just one place that covers a big fiord and a big glacier. I told him we can't do more than one scene this summer due to our current workload, or rather overload. It sounds manageable unless we run into the four-corner rule."

"Yep. No matter how small an area may be, it always falls on the corners. Maps, air photos, satellite scenes. Always works the same."

"Kinski says a few years ago one of Alaska's galloping glaciers formed a temporary ice dam," Ed explained. "Now they think it's happening again. They want us to monitor land cover changes as the glacier advances, water rises, and the saltwater fiord turns into a freshwater lake. He said something about a new river forming at the opposite end of the fiord."

"He must mean the Hubbard. Remember the news back in '86? As I recall, the glacier advanced across a narrow strait and blocked the mouth of Russell Fiord for about four months. Water level rose 80 feet. When the ice dam broke, it released the largest discharge of freshwater in recorded history." Then Caisson went silent as the significance of his own words struck him.

"Since the Ice Ages, you mean?"

"Yep, let's get there as fast as we can. But first some legwork. Otherwise it'll be little more than a sightseeing tour...not that I'd mind sightseeing up there." Jared looked at the list of research topics he and Ed had compiled on the whiteboard. Old items had been altered and new ones inserted, but few had been crossed off.

"NOAA can tell us everything we need to know about the Hubbard itself–dimensions, rate of advance, probable impacts on terrain and fisheries."

"Yes, but if we're going to make the most of this for our own purposes we need climatic trends for the past 120,000 years."

"Then we better move fast."

"I know where we can get some help." He pointed back at the board. Scribbled at odd angles were the names of tentative contacts. Beside "Ice Age climates and sea levels" was the single name "Caisson." He tapped the board sharply with his index finger, smudging the two middle letters.

"Yourself?" Ed asked.

"A close second," Jared quipped.

"Rick? You mean Rick? He heads a computer company. What does know he know about the Ice Ages?"

"Not much about human intelligence, but early in his career he taught physical geography at the University of Alaska."

"…where every hill and valley says 'Ice Age.'" Ed seldom waxed poetic, but when he did, he did his best, God bless his heart.

"Right. Rick acquired a respectable knowledge of just the sort of information we need about the Ice Ages."

"And he went from geography to high-tech business? That's quite a switch."

"Not really. It wasn't as dramatic as it sounds. He did about the same thing most other geographers did as the discipline moved toward computer mapping, satellite image processing, and GIS. He just delved deeper into the technology than most."

* * *

That evening, the two brothers sat on Rick's back porch savoring a damp twilight and good cigars. Their wives were inside the spacious Victorian home. Jared intended to extract as much information as possible without revealing much himself. Later he would explain, but now he felt guilty harvesting such valuable knowledge with so little in return.

"It seems we'll be doing some work in Alaska. Does that take you back a few years?"

"Surely does. I like working here in 'Silicon Holler,' but I'd give anything for a chance to go back for a while. I even like the long winter night that drives so many newcomers crazy."

"I called NOAA this afternoon and confirmed it. They want us to monitor the Hubbard Glacier."

"That's fantastic! Even if it is Baja Alaska." Rick set his jab.

"Oh, that's right. Fairbanks is the *real* Alaska with real winter and all."

"I never got down to Russell Fiord. But you're in for a treat, no doubt about that. The ice dam incident happened several years after I left Fairbanks. But I read about the rescue efforts."

"Rescue efforts! I didn't know anyone had to be rescued. I assumed they had plenty of warning."

"Oh, the people were okay. It was the wildlife that needed rescuing. Marine mammals were the greatest concern. A lot of seals and sea otters were trapped behind the dam. They all would have died as the water turned from salt to fresh, if some humans hadn't hauled them across to the sea. The airlift was worthwhile, but it didn't save them all. Multitudes of saltwater fish perished, too."

"How come this particular glacier is advancing when everybody is so worried about global warming? Wouldn't that cause retreat?" Jared began his subtle interrogation. Of necessity, he had become a master at such tangential probes.

Rick responded, "Actually, that fits the pattern. Globally, Arctic glaciers are advancing while alpine glaciers are retreating. Why? Nobody knows for sure. A good case can be made for alpine retreat caused by global warming, but Arctic advance takes more imagination. Some people think it comes from warmer oceans with increased evaporation in the Tropics. Global circulation then carries more vapor to the poles, hence heavier snowfall in high latitudes, thus feeding the buildup of ice. Back in the '70s, there was even some talk that continental ice sheets might have happened during unusually warm periods rather than unusually cold ones. A handful of scientists believed that greater snow and ice accumulation might occur simply because melting in summer couldn't keep up with heavier snowfall in winter. Back then, they didn't have enough evidence to say one way or the other. Later, biologic indicators, independent of the glaciers themselves, convinced practically everybody that glaciation coincided with cold spells, not warm spells. Still, the earlier reasoning wasn't as crazy as it sounds, and warm cycle glaciation may explain part of what's happening today."

This was just the opening Jared needed for his next tangent. "How precise are the temperature curves for the last 120,000 years or so?"

"Depends on who's talking. Lots of people write as if they know for certain, but there are too many different answers for much confidence on my part. Try this little experiment some time. Take a look at temperature graphs for a given time span from several different sources. First, count the number of warm and cold phases. You get a different count with each source. Next, pick a date at random, say 41,000 BP, and search for the temperature. Most sources are so vague they won't give you a precise number, and the ones that do will vary widely. Collectively, they agree on a general trend over each 10,000 or 20,000 years. Beyond that, you have to interpolate where your date falls and hope for the best."

"Isn't sea level a surrogate for temperature? Each warm or cold phase should follow a predictable relationship between the amount of water locked up in glaciers and the amount left in the ocean." Jared continued his probe.

"Sure, if you trust sea level curves. Except for a bit of a lag and some smoothing, the same thing works with sea level, ice volume, or glacial advance and retreat. They're all quantitatively related, but I find the same uncertainty as with temperature. No two sources agree, and hardly anyone gives a precise answer."

"Is there any particular study that you trust more than the others?"

"Not really, but there's one that gives a fairly precise temperature curve for the last 17,500 years. I don't know whether to trust it more than the others, but I use it to lessen my own confusion about the dates. It's good enough for most purposes if you don't believe it too much." Rick's explanation showed both commonsense and critical thought. Listening to the discourse, Jared reflected how little his brother's curiosity had diminished since his teaching days. In fact, Rick seemed to enjoy science more than ever. Company business could have his long, demanding day, but, whenever he had a free moment, something inside insisted on following the topics that had intrigued him two decades ago at three different universities.

"This particular study is based on measurements of coral growth at Barbados in the Caribbean Sea. The curve starts with extremely low sea levels, about 400 feet lower than today. Most of the rise, about 325 feet, occurred from 11,000 BP to 5,000 BP. Several other sources say it got a few feet above current levels about 6,000 years ago, but nothing like that shows up in the Caribbean data. Maybe that's because there aren't any live corals to measure above sea level, but the curve doesn't seem to indicate any trace of an upward blip."

"You're speaking of change over time. What about geographic distribution?" Jared asked. "I assume sea level change is uniform all over the world, except for some minor differences caused by the earth's bulge at the Equator."

"Depends on whether you're talking about absolute rise or relative rise. The water surface responds pretty much the same all over the World Ocean, but the rise or fall relative to local landforms can be highly variable. Water is an extremely heavy substance. When a coast is flooded, the water itself can push the inundated land downward, and that can cause other, adjacent lands to rise. The same thing happens in reverse when ice melts and lightens the load. It's called isostacy. It's a local phenomenon highly influenced by the geologic structure of each stretch of coast. It can happen catastrophically in structurally weak areas, but it usually progresses very slowly. Some areas like the Gulf of Bothnia, between Finland and Sweden, as well as the Hudson Bay are still bounding back even today. Of course, some areas are geologically stable, and the relative rise there is about the same as the absolute rise of the water itself."

"Back to temperature. What's your best guess as to the timing of warm and cold periods over the whole 120,000 years?" Jared asked.

Rick stared into the thick night for a moment, his face strained in recollection. "Counting just major peaks and troughs, most sources show about four cycles. Of course, you can get any number you want by counting smaller fluctuations. The initial slide began around 92,000 years ago. The first major trough was about 55,000 BP, the second about 43,000 BP, third about 30,000 BP, and the most recent about 18,000 years ago. In America, we call them the Wisconsin Advances–Early, First Mid-, Second Mid-, and Late Wisconsin."

Jared took one last puff and tossed his cigar into the bushes. "Thanks for the overview."

"What's behind this?" Rick asked. "You seem awfully interested in historic sea levels."

"Gotta go," Jared said with a devilish smile.

"It is getting late out on Beaver Ridge," Rick said. *Something's up, but no need to push*, he thought. *He'll open up sooner or later.*

Search Log 7: Forces of Nature

As they discussed arrangements by phone, Kinski offered to hire a bush pilot to fly them over the glacier. The flight service at Yakutat was the nearest jump-off point for the Hubbard and Malaspina Glaciers. Kinski assured them, "Pete's the best pilot between Glacier Bay and Valdez, and he's known for not taking unnecessary chances. I've flown with him many times before."

On a Wednesday night, Caisson and Field arrived over Juneau in the long twilight of summer. "Look at those mountains!" Jared exclaimed as their commercial flight circled the runway.

"And those islands! Absolutely spectacular," Ed added.

"This is even more beautiful than the interior."

"You've been here before?"

"Oh, yes. I thought I told you. Back in '79 when Rick was leaving Alaska, our younger brother, Kent, and I flew up to Fairbanks. The three of us drove the entire length of the Alaska Highway . . . in winter, no less. Ever since, I've dreamed of visiting the southeast coast, but this is better than I had imagined." Caisson stared at the glacier looming outside his window. He was impressed, most of all, that an everyday flight into an ordinary airport would offer such a close, personal view of a glacier as massive as Mendenhall.

Kinski had arranged a motel and would meet them next morning for the flight to Yakutat. After a good night's sleep, Caisson and Field drove back to the airport, arriving at the departure gate a few minutes ahead of

Kinski. A contingent of mountain climbers filled the small waiting area. They busied themselves strapping and unstrapping, checking equipment, and quietly discussing plans.

"What's going on here?" Ed asked.

"I don't know," Jared said. "Must be a bunch of climbers from the Lower 48. I guess ice climbing is really popular here, but they surely are fastidious about it."

As they spoke, K Kinski cut his way through the crowd. He had a pained expression on his face.

"Guys, I have some sad news. Pete's been killed."

"Killed, how?"

"He flew down to pick up some rafters on the Alsek River. They didn't show. Pete flew up and down the river looking for them till he had to give up. On his way back to Yakutat, he hit a cloud bank, turned the corner too early, and crashed into a mountain. Happened yesterday. I got the word this morning. I've made arrangements with another pilot. She was my next choice all along. We'll be in good hands."

"So these climbers . . ."

"Rescuers heading up to take Pete's body off the mountain."

* * *

The single engine pulled a heavy load up Disenchantment Bay. In typical Alaska fashion, the four-seater carried five people even when weather conditions, better than average for southeast Alaska, would have prohibited flights in the Lower 48. As the plane droned toward the narrow strait at the mouth of Russell Fiord, what had seemed so complex in news articles gradually shifted to a simple, dramatic truth. Entering from a side valley, the Hubbard Glacier was poised to dam the strait and turn Russell Fiord into a freshwater lake.

Caisson occupied the seat next to the pilot. It was comfortable and had a clear view. Ed took a cramped rear seat with a good view out the opposite side. Jared felt guilty taking the best seat, but his job was to direct the pilot while Ed scanned the land below with a trained eye for what a satellite passing overhead might see. *Which features would be large enough to show in Landsat's 30-meter pixel, and which would not? Which patches of light or dark ice and soil would mark the glacier's movement? Which colors of vegetation highlighted depressions where water would spill or pool when the basin overflowed? Which patterns of light and texture would trick the analysts and lead to false conclusions? Ludicrous mistakes would be easy to spot, subtle ones quite difficult.*

The land inundated in 1986 was unmistakable, even from high above. A band of light green rimmed the shoreline where shrubs had died and leafy sprouts had regrown to take their place. Gray-brown patches marked the quick kill of high water where forests once had stood. *Will satellite sensors distinguish these two patterns of water-induced change reliably and consistently? In most terrain, that would be no problem. Here, however, steep slopes might render the swatch of shoreline too narrow for the satellite's gaze. Plus, shadows would hide some north-facing terrain.*

"How about a loop over the Hubbard before we head up the fiord?" Jared asked over the din of the engine. He expected a quick turn and was surprised how long it took. "Seems slow," he said to Kinski.

K shouted over the engine noise, "Those ice cliffs at the face of the glacier are about 400 feet high. Think about it! That's the height of a forty-story building."

"Are you kidding? I'm really off scale. We're way higher than I thought."

"8,000 feet," the pilot said.

"That means this glacier is far bigger than I realized." Jared was awed anew by the immensity of the scene. The effect was mesmerizing as he stared down into the eerie aquamarine glow of Hubbard's crevasses. Cliffs of ice cracked and bent toward the sea. Tiny black specks, he suddenly realized, were seals riding huge ice floes all about.

Three cameras clicked continuously as the aircraft passed into the fiord and southward. "Most of the fiord's water enters from Nunatak Glacier east of here. The drainage divide at the south end is crucial," Kinski said. "The Geological Survey predicts a better than 90 per cent chance that Hubbard will close with Gilbert Point in the next ten years."

"For how long?" Ed asked.

"This time it may last for decades, even centuries. The wall of ice is much steeper and higher than before. Russell Fiord will become a freshwater lake about 130 feet higher than its current level. It's walled in by mountains on the east and west, so the new lake will eventually discharge across the southern divide and flow to the sea through a new river system of its own making. The changes will be catastrophic to wildlife in the fiord and in the bogs and streams displaced by the new river."

"How does that compare to '86?"

"Back then, the ice dam burst when the water got to a little more than half the tipping point." Kinski gestured. "There's Gilbert Point where the outburst occurred. It was spectacular. You can see where it scoured the shore."

"Does that happen a lot with glaciers?" Ed asked.

"Oh, yes. All the time. 'Jökulhlaup' is the technical term for the outburst of an ice dam or from beneath the glacier itself. This one stands out only because of its size," Kinski said.

"It looks devastating."

"It is. Last time, NOAA worried about endangered marine mammals trapped behind the wall of ice. This time, if it fills completely, we're worried more about a unique stock of salmon in the Situk River below the divide. I've been studying the Situk sockeye for years. Its life strategy is more efficient than any other salmon. Other stocks spend their first year or two in freshwater streams before moving out to the rich feeding grounds of the open ocean. This one heads directly out to sea only weeks after hatching. Five years later, spawning adults return as ocean-fed salmon, making the Situk one of the most productive fisheries in the world. We want to propagate the species elsewhere, but, instead, we may lose its habitat through natural events beyond our control."

Leaving a clutter of ice-capped peaks behind, the plane flew lengthwise over Russell Fjord. A glacial tarn perched high on Mt. Tebenkof reflected like a piece of beveled glass. Dodging clouds, the pilot winged over the low divide into the Situk's headwaters, mainly vast bogs just below the divide. Jared tapped her shoulder and pointed downward. The plane's nose dipped and circled so everyone could get a better look at the mat of willowy shrubs. A moose charged out of the trees and suddenly stopped in its tracks like a cartoon. The river broadened, and salmon skiffs appeared. The last reach coiled through sandbars and beaches scattered with shanties of men and women whose ancestors had fished these waters since the end of the last Ice Age.

Completing its grand circle, the plane headed home. They had witnessed the power and beauty of nature. The final leg testified, instead, to the destructive power of man. From Situk to Yakutat, some 13 miles, less than one tenth of the forest remained standing. The fifth passenger was Forest Service, and it was his turn to explain. "These lands were logged after the Alaskan Native Claims Settlement Act returned huge tracts to indigenous people. The act came from plenty of good intentions, compensating for centuries of greed and abuse, but it's turned into an environmental disaster. Native corporations were desperate for income, so they sold their timber as soon as the titles transferred. Unaccustomed to business dealings of this sort, they sold it all at once. Glutted the market."

"Maximize net present value," Kinski said. "That's what hired-gun economists advised all over Alaska."

"They should have been shot," the forester said. "They didn't have a clue about the cumulative effect. Every corporation along the coast simultaneously followed their stupid advice. In the end, the natives got only a fraction of what their timber would have brought in a phased release. Once the timber companies got contracts, they held off until the market rose again, then they butchered the land and made a fortune. The only trees left are in a few ragged stands along stream banks where Federal regulations prohibit cutting."

"Over there, toward the east," Kinski said, shaking his head in disgust. "Look at those bulldozers advancing through the last stands of taiga between Yakutat and the Situk."

Search Log 8: Step by Step

The huge mound of salmon steaks dwindled, as ten good friends sat around the Caissons' long trestle table. Rick and the others raved as Jared beamed over his catch.

"Thanks for having us over," Garrett Shepherd said, toasting the salmon a second time.

"You've broken a long-standing family tradition," Rick said. "Dad would be proud. One of his sons finally shook 'The Caisson Fishermen's Luck.' First time anybody in our family ever presided over a feast of fish that he, himself, caught."

"When I got to SeaTac Airport yesterday, I called Ellie and told her about my catch. We both agreed we wanted to share the bounty with our closest friends." He paused, "But they couldn't come, so we invited all of you." *Lame joke*, thought Jared. *Nice of them to laugh. I guess they know what I'm getting at. It's great to be among such good friends.* He told about the plane crash and the loss of their intended pilot and ended saying, "So we had to fly with the second-best pilot in Alaska."

"No," Ellie said. "Now she's the best. That's how pilots get to be *the* best."

When a few scattered morsels remained on the platter, when the coffee was gone and the dishes cleared away, when all of the friends had departed and only family remained, Jared motioned Rick to the patio. He opened the lid of the Kimado cooker where the salmon had smoked. Only the slightest hint of salmon and lemon and garlic escaped. He poked at the coals. They were fine, but his real purpose had been deeper anyway. Jared had decided it was time to let Rick in on his suspicions. He produced a couple of cigars, clipped the butts, lit a stick from the remaining coals, and touched it to Rick's Hoyo de Monterrey.

"Have you ever wondered what human culture really amounted to during the Ice Ages?" he began, then lit his own cigar. He took a deep draw. Quickly, concisely, he laid out his own questions before giving Rick a chance to respond.

When he got to the part about rising sea levels, Rick stopped him. "Don't you remember what I said about the Persian Gulf four or five years back?"

"Yes, that's been in the back of my mind ever since I started this crazy quest, but I'm afraid to say anything about it. You know any sort of Biblical discussion will hurt more than it helps in a scientific forum."

"It was handled well enough in the *Smithsonian*."

"Yes, but some newspapers reported it factually–'Archaeologists Speculate Biblical Garden of Eden Located Beneath Persian Gulf'–while others made it sound more like 'Elvis' Face Seen on Mars.'"

"As I recall, the author believes the entire gulf was dry land during the Ice Ages and may not have filled until as recently as 4,000 BP. He thinks the most productive land was in the lowlands rather than on the dry slopes above. Makes sense." Rick paused for a puff. "That was the first time I realized the extent of inundation at the end of the Ice Ages. Before, it seemed so remote, but finally it meant something to me. There were people around! They knew what happened! Some survivors may have been savvy enough to pass it along as lore. Hence, the Garden of Eden."

"Why stop there?" Rick had asked back then. "Wouldn't that inundation make an even better explanation for Noah's flood? Can't you imagine a ridge slowly becoming an island? Sea level climbing gradually up its slopes. But then, as it neared the top, even a few inches became crucial. One lone man recognized the disturbing trend while everyone else ignored it. Neighbors laughed as he built his boat, but laughs turned to cries when the final surge came. Then he loaded every type of domestic animal living on the island and headed for the mainland. Imagine the story growing as his descendants asked, 'How long did it rain? How high did it rise? How far did he sail? How many animals did he bring?' What started out as a fact no more remarkable than many of today's news stories became a legend, then later a thread in the fabric of a global religion.

He continued, "I recall being fascinated by the Persian Gulf, but neither of us realized how much other land was inundated at the same time. Or how long it went on. Did we?"

"No, we didn't. But, you know how it is. No scientist can cite the Bible even as a source of secular, historic information without being dismissed as a religious zealot. I'm no better than the others. When someone claiming to be a scientist starts quoting scripture, I become suspicious. It's ironic! We scientists treasure documentation above all else, yet we'll trust a scrap of pottery found all by its lonesome in the middle of a desert more than the Bible, one of the best authenticated, eye witness accounts from antiquity. Otherwise, your explanation isn't outrageous in the least. If we dismiss the exaggeration that came with retelling, the rest only requires that the ancients had a better corporate memory than we previously assumed. I'll keep it in mind, but believers would make too much of it, and nonbelievers would belittle it. Not to mention the fact that I'd be casting secular, skeptical aspersions on one of the most revered traditions of our own Judao-Christian heritage."

Rick could barely see Jared's face in the muted light emanating from the kitchen.

"But keep this in mind," Jared continued. "That flood didn't happen just because the Persian Gulf is a shallow sea. It was a worldwide event, and the loss was staggering. An area as big as North America, the best land on earth, simply disappeared, most of it within a 5,000-year period."

"That much in 5,000 years? I've seen the graphs again and again but no maps."

Jared stepped inside and returned with a copy of Ed's new map.

Rick whistled as his brother held it facing the glow of a window. "I didn't realize how much land was involved. When I was at the University of Alaska, however, a fellow professor, Don Lynch, told me he thought the 'land bridge' between Asia and Alaska was much more extensively settled than the term implies. He used the proper name, Beringia, to describe a land that may have contained a sizable population of its own. Don also predicted that some dates of settlement eventually would be pushed back tens of thousands of years. Some recent findings support him. In all my reading, I found only a handful of scientists who said the inundated areas may have held people as advanced as those in the areas we can still see today. An anthropologist named Brian Fagin from the University of California at Santa Barbara is notable among them, but even he didn't say coastal areas might have been *more* favorable and contained *more* advanced civilizations."

"That's how I see it, too. They just missed the boat, and it's hard to understand why. Have you read any hints in the literature?" Jared asked.

"Ice Age studies show a heavy bias toward ice, or at least toward cold climates. There's hardly any interest in the tropics during the Ice Ages. From an archaeologist's perspective, of course, Pleistocene lowlands are off-limits due to subsequent inundation."

"If advanced settlements existed in tropical lowlands, wouldn't we have stumbled across hard evidence on land by now?" Jared asked, playing Devil's advocate.

"Not necessarily. Why? First, because no serious scientist has been looking for it. Second, because a lot of what was found has been dismissed or misclassified. Of course, any theory you generate will have to explain what binds a species so tight to the sea that they wouldn't spread to adjacent interior regions."

"In retrospect, did you find *anything* that *might* suggest a higher culture existed in the submerged zone?"

Rick contemplated for a moment. "It's plausible. We've long known of remarkable similarities in ancient cultures scattered around the globe. Creation legends from widely separated places often speak of rising or parting waters and sometimes seas of mud. And what about pyramids? They're found around the world . . . not just on one continent."

Rick paused, then added coolly, "Actually sea level rise *could* explain step pyramids."

"Step pyramids. How do you figure?"

"When most people think of pyramids, what comes to mind is the smooth-sided variety found in Egypt. They're called true pyramids. But step pyramids were popular architecture in the ancient world. They circle the globe. Even the true pyramids of Egypt are just step pyramids with angular limestone blocks filling every notch to make a smooth, white plane. The earliest known pyramids in Egypt were step pyramids with large steps and no cladding. And, to make things more confusing, some true pyramids are thought to have older step pyramids deep inside."

Rick paused to make sure Jared understood the distinction, then continued, "Suppose you lived on a low island or coastal lowland with a great view of the sea. You might pave an area for some purpose, say religious ceremonies or rock concerts . . . whatever . . . to take advantage of the sight and sea. If later you faced a rising sea with occasional surges due to storms, earthquakes, or other natural events, you might build a good solid platform, higher and more substantial than the original pavement. Then, suppose the sea level rose again. If you wanted to keep the site, say because of its strategic importance or religious significance, the next thing you might do is build another platform on top of the first, with waves lapping at its base. Of course, you would make it slightly smaller than the first for the sake of stability. As the water level continued to rise, again and again, you might build smaller and smaller tiers until finally there would be no space left. Ultimately, you'd have a step pyramid, whether you started out to build one or not. You could live on it, worship on it, or be buried in it; but finally your descendants would have to abandon the site when the last tier was inundated.

"Why do we find them on dry land today? Perhaps the style of architecture became established and each new generation repeated it again and again in place after place as they resettled to higher and higher ground. If so, the last settlement should be above the waterline and should look pretty much like the lower ones because the refugees had no way of knowing where the sea would stop."

Jared followed every detail of Rick's argument. "So there'd be pyramids beneath the sea, and they'd look pretty much like the ones we know in Egypt and elsewhere. That's good. Until now, I thought we would be searching for field patterns or house foundations, faint evidence at best. Pyramids would be much easier to find and recognize."

"Yes, it makes sense. Almost any other type of architecture might have been eroded or washed away by now, but a hefty stone pyramid should last forever. So now you're looking for haystacks instead of needles. Question is, can you find them?"

"Where do you think they'd be?" Jared asked.

"The mouth of the Nile would be one likely spot. I envision a remnant delta backed by high cliffs cut by the Nile as an extension of its gorge. Giza would overlook it all. The old delta would have been ideal for human occupation, just like the modern one. But don't you suppose sedimentation would have covered the evidence by now?"

"I don't know. We'll just have to see," Jared said. "I've pondered this same question for months. Until now, I assumed the settlements would have been one or two stories at best. Pyramids undoubtedly would be higher, and stone masonry would be more durable than the mud and stone construction of cities like Jericho, which is above water today, but existed simultaneously at the end of the ice ages. This could be the key we've been looking for."

The two brothers stood for a while in hushed contemplation and stared into the warm Tennessee night. The Big Orange moon was barely visible behind a silhouette of mountain oaks that formed the summer horizon. Occasionally a draft from the breezeway refreshed the night air. For a moment, they listened to the rhythmic chirping of invisible crickets or katydids or silver tree frogs. Both had lived their lives in the South without ever learning which of these nocturnal creatures was responsible for the incessant noise. Not knowing, somehow made the nighttime special.

"Can you imagine?" Rick said.

CHAPTER 4

Chronicle 2: Training

High Priest Anbaht paused in silence as the sun disk broke free above a nearby pyramid. Prayers pierced the morning air as throngs of the Chosen gathered in the plaza below. Osi, tired but exhilarated from the all-night vigil, shivered in awe at the grandeur of the True Pyramid, the Temple of the Sun God, and the surrounding temple complex–symbols of prosperity and tranquility for his nation. He gloried in the accomplishments of his people, their King, and their Geometers. He was filled with pride for his people and love for his land.

The King's Agent was ushered onto the portico of the grand palace adjacent to the Temple Square to see and be seen by all. From a nearby terrace, royal musicians played martial music on horns and drums. A giant earthen cauldron of scented oil boiled slowly over a fire of aromatic wood selected from the banks of the Great River.

Anbaht spoke in a sonorous voice as, from the Temple's ceremonial balcony, he prayed the prayer of the ancients. "Praise be to Rahn! Protect us, O Rahn, from the ravages of the sea. May the tales of the ancients be told. May the vessels of knowledge be full. May the mothers of our children be wise. May preparations for the ascension of Rahn Mennon, our King, be wisely made. May the King's oarsmen row swiftly and well. Save our Seed from the Waters of Chaos." The cadets joined in with the chants, responding in unison to the unfamiliar words spoken by the priest. And so it went, as Anbaht alternately prayed and chanted until the sun's disk was fully one hand of time above the horizon.

How strange is life and the passage of time, Osi reflected as the High Priest held his hand skyward. *Today I learn the Secrets of the Ages, but it seems like only yesterday that I learned to count time in the manner of our people. Yet it must have been years ago that Mother took me to the plaza and said, "Osi, my child, you must learn the meaning of the hand of time." Then she showed me how to hold my hand at full length against the sky. "Now move your hand in an arc, my son, and you will see that 12 hands span the sky from one horizon to the other. Just as you move your hand, so moves the sun from horizon to horizon. Six hands make the morning, and six hands make the remainder of the day." How many hands have crossed the sky since that day,* Osi reminisced. *Now here I am, nearly a man, and learning the greatest secrets of the earth and its ages.*

Following prayers, the boys marched to a barracks adjacent to the Temple Pyramid. The barracks adjoined a kitchen and dining hall where mutton roasted and lamb shanks sizzled on spits. They ate a morning meal of braised meat, dried fish, boiled grain, fruit, and seaweed broth, then retreated to their quarters in the communal chamber. Finally, they would sleep, the first time in his life that Osi had slept outside the safety of his own home, away from the mother who nurtured him from birth. Still, he felt profoundly secure in his new home and new life.

Osi studied the chamber—three rows of stone columns supporting a thatched roof. Each of the four aisles contained a row of simple stone beds, each covered with a mattress of fluffed straw. A fur drape lay across each boy's bed. Beneath sat two small clay pots, one empty and one filled with water. A thin opening above the wall just beneath the roofline admitted fresh air and light. It was pleasant, clean, and quiet. *I'll learn to like this harsh life*, Osi told himself as he slipped into peaceful slumber.

He awoke in the afternoon and watched as his fellow cadets came alive. One by one, the boys stirred, then shook their heads or yawned and rose. There was an unexpected sense of normality, but this was no ordinary day. This was the beginning of a new era for Osi and his fellows. It was the commencement of their journey to manhood, a truly momentous occasion after which their lives would be irrevocably altered.

"Osi," whispered a friend, "what do you think? Can this be true? Do you think our world will end?"

"Surely it's true, Busah," Osi said. "Why would the Elders lie? Father said to believe everything the Wise Men say. Yes, I believe, and so must you, else you will perish and so will our King."

"Maybe, Osi, but it sounds too fantastic, unreal. Can the sea really rise and fall like bathwater in a basin? Where does the rising water come from? Where does the falling water go? It's all too strange."

"Maybe so, but it must be true. You *must* believe," Osi said.

"I'll wait until I hear more. But I won't be easy to convince."

"I understand. What you say makes sense, but don't jump to the wrong conclusions. I want to see you in the land above after the Chaos comes."

"Fine, but enough of this. Let's get ready for dinner. We must get ready for tonight's celebration," Busah said.

Directed by an orderly, Osi and Busah stepped into the passageway behind the barracks where a small stream of water coursed beside the building. There, along with other boys, they relieved themselves. The orderly pointed toward a nearby pavilion containing an open-air bath where the entire troop assembled. On cue, the boys jumped in. They welcomed the cool, salty water and were pleased to be cleansed of the grime and dust of the long night and the sweat of their afternoon sleep. It reminded Osi of the pleasant days when he and his friends would spend half their day swimming along the shores of the Midland Sea. The boys rinsed their faces and necks with freshwater from basins arranged on a ledge along the room's limestone outer wall, then dried with sponges. When they finished, attendants stepped forward with lush linen towels and dried their charges.

"Come share the bounty of the Beloved Land," beckoned a steward from the galley in a nearby building. Hearing this familiar, welcome call, the boys filed in for their evening meal.

Busah gawked at the food. "This is a feast compared to any meal my family has ever served."

"I've never seen so much food," Osi agreed diplomatically. On the banquet board, which occupied the ledge along the outer wall, sat large wooden trays. Steamed oysters, clams, crabs, and smoked fish were the main fare. Porridge filled a large earthenware tureen. Freshly cut fruits piled high. Each boy was issued a saucer made of shell and a spoon expertly carved from bone. Glass bowls and cups held food and drink. The boys ate and drank their fill under the watchful eye of Parthus, the major domo, who joined them as they ate. His role was a curious blend of sergeant, caretaker, steward, and surrogate mother to homesick youths.

Parthus took over as master of ceremonies, first introducing himself and then the others of his staff. At his invitation, each boy stood in turn, told his name, and described his lineage. Parthus recounted the basic rules of the dormitory, then closed with inspirational words for the coming months of training and discipline. "You are the Chosen Ones," he said, "Your lives will be hard. You will face many dangers and demands, but the outcome will be worth all your sacrifice. Your Seed will survive, and you will preserve our way of life."

Morning came too soon. There would be no rest before training commenced. "Up, up on your feet, cadets! To the field! No straggling!" Parthus yelled. Osi grimaced, then shook his head to test reality, to be sure he was not asleep. Up he shot to the sound of drums filtering in through a portal facing the training field, the dreaded specter confronting the young cadets. It would haunt them day in and day out for the duration of their training. There, they would suffer in the morning, sweat at midday, and bleed in the afternoon. Exercise and swimming in the morning, running in the noon sun, mock battles at day's end. Day after day, week after week, month after month, the regimen would continue until they learned the art and science of warfare.

* * *

"I can't do it, I just can't!" Osi heard one of the boys cry during a grueling scrimmage. He turned to aid his classmate but then realized he had to handle his own predicament. Soon one boy held his feet; another pressed his back to the ground.

I'm not sure I can free myself, thought Osi, *much less help someone else, but I can't give in.*

"Take that!" Osi said. He twisted sharply to his right, then used the stronger muscles of his sides to dislodge the larger boy from his shoulders. With a quick jerk of his legs, he threw the other opponent off balance and freed his lower body as well. Osi next propelled himself into a seated position, then to a low squat from which he exploded to an upright, victorious stance. Arms extended, head held high, Osi yelled, "Victory!" He turned to help the other youth, then chuckled as he saw who it was.

"Get off me, you brute," the familiar voice yelled.

"Who's that wimp?" asked Banda, one of the tougher boys.

"That's Ketoh, a friend of mine," Osi said, "...my neighbor. The big house. You know the one."

"Oh, a rich kid, eh. A pampered mama's boy. He won't make it, not in this man's game." Banda shook his head.

"I know Ketoh's weaknesses all too well, but I also know his strengths. He'll do the right thing in the end."

Finally, the opponent released Ketoh and shrank from his cross glare.

"Why should I endure this?" Ketoh muttered to Osi as he stalked off the field. "It's beneath me. Let the others fight. I'll do my part . . . by leading, not by fighting. Leaders lead. They don't need to fight."

* * *

On the following afternoon, as they rested between mock battles, Osi was amused to see Ketoh and three other troublemakers making their way among the trainees offering water from heavy skins strapped over their shoulders. *That's the discipline I fear most*, Osi thought. *I'm prepared for physical punishment or loss of privilege, but to lose face among my peers would be the most painful and enduring punishment of all.*

"Ketoh!" Osi called. The boy ignored him. "Ketoh!" Eventually, Ketoh glanced in Osi's direction, pretending he couldn't pick out the voice from the crowd. Osi rose, walked over to his friend, and placed a hand on his shoulder. "Hello, my friend, good to see you found exercise more to your liking."

"Oh?" Ketoh said. "I surely didn't want to rejoin you as a water boy, my friend."

Osi laughed at Ketoh's frown. Finally, Ketoh cracked an almost undetectable smile.

"Don't question the wisdom of the Elders, Ketoh. They know what it takes to survive the Chaos. Only a few will make it. Each survivor must do his part if we are to rebuild our world."

"Our world? The King isn't even here. He's a world away in the land of the Valley Sea. No Egian has been chosen for duty there since our fathers were young. All this talk of being the King's oarsmen is inspiring, but what are the chances of such glorious service for us, even if we do our best?"

"Better than you think. If what they say is true, we may be more 'employable' than our fathers' generation. Think clearly. Act wisely. That's how we'll be selected."

"Maybe, but for now all I want is to shed this water bag and get on with my training. It's hard to see any further than that."

"Don't worry, my friend, you'll soon rejoin us in the quest!" Osi consoled the young man. "Where did you spend the night?"

"In the guard tower down by the Great Canal. We stood watch all night long...Water?" Ketoh asked as one of the trainers approached.

"Yes, thanks." Osi took a big gulp of the cool water. "Eight hands of hard work," he said, shaking his head.

"Later, I hear, we will run or swim all night and then do battle," Ketoh said, "that is, if I'm allowed to rejoin."

"Don't worry, Ketoh, you'll be allowed, and only too soon, for it isn't so easy as carrying water."

"By then I'll have to work even harder to catch up. It may be a week or longer before I'm allowed back. The rest of you will be stronger by then."

"Then your struggle will make you all the stronger in the end, Ketoh. You will survive, and you will thrive," Osi said over his shoulder as he headed back to his ranks. *Yes,* he thought, *Ketoh won't like it. Ketoh will moan, but Ketoh will prevail, if for no other reason than that he cannot endure failure.*

* * *

The afternoon of the Manhood Ceremony arrived with surprisingly little fanfare. The boys were marched onto the parade ground that lay beside the main courtyard across from their barracks. In their hearts, this field, used mostly for public events, was distinctly different from the training ground that dominated their daily regimen. Osi himself had attended ceremonies here on important occasions when the King's Army or the Cadets of the Realm had presented themselves formally to the people. The celebration of renowned victories, the birth of a future king, or the death of a King's Agent or Regent were such occasions. Tonight's unusual ceremony, however, would be closed to all but the military community.

The Army unit charged with training inductees and maintaining the Divine Right Order was a world unto itself. Some cadets would serve for only a few years, then form a ready reserve of citizen soldiers in all walks of life. Others would spend their whole careers as officers and soldiers, a caste apart from the rest of the Beloved People. Upon induction, every man swore an oath of allegiance to King Rahn Mennon, and every career soldier swore never to take part in the pursuits of commerce, land ownership, wealth, or political position. "A soldier for a breath, a soldier until death!" was their motto, and there had been few transgressions or exceptions in the collective memory of the Beloved People. In exchange for this loyalty and sacrifice, the kingdom assured its forces they would never want for material comfort, much less for the necessities of life. The compound at Egia thus included a thriving community of military families, cadets, and apprentices.

Camp followers–cooks, servants, groomsmen, and artisans–saw to the feeding, lodging, and other needs of the Army in garrison and on campaign. Most of them lived and worked beside the gates of the compound. Only the top civilian leaders were granted quarters inside its walls.

On this semi-secret occasion, the entire population of the compound turned out to celebrate the beginning of manhood for a new class of cadets. The ceremony consisted of games and contests at the outset, then music and marching, followed by close-order drill. Cadets sat on the sidelines until time for their participation. Martial music filled the air as they formed at center field. The commander of the Army of Egia, ruler of the compound, spoke words of praise and congratulation as he stood atop the reviewing stand. Behind him spread the distant skyline, its center dominated by the giant Sacred Pyramid. A fire burning brightly on the highest level of the partially completed pyramid accentuated its massive construction.

The boys were reordered into a single row facing the jubilant crowd. Then, to the sound of trumpets blaring and drums rolling, each cadet marched to a station at centerfield where he was issued an ornately carved staff that would be his standard for the rest of his life. Acceptance of the staff was, in effect, a contract with the King to a dedicated life of military and civil servitude. This moment was, for each cadet, a point of no return.

The Priest of the Corps stepped forward beside the commander. Four other chaplain priests proceeded to pre-assigned positions, one at each end of the row and two in the center. Prayers were said, and the cadets were ordered to disrobe. In time with a drum roll, each boy was directed to place the staff across his shoulders, his arms extended back and over it. So positioned, the cadets then were ordered to focus on the fire atop the pyramid while chanting the solemn oath of servitude.

As each completed his oath, he was shocked to feel the rough hand of the priest on his genitals. With a deft flick of the wrist, the priest removed a ring of flesh from the cadet's penis and tossed it into a pottery jar that dangled from his elbow. As the pot filled and the beacon dimmed, the crowds dissipated and the boys stood silent. Not one man had shrieked or whimpered or even registered his surprise. The ceremony had been too sacred, the occasion too profound, for such childlike behavior. Tomorrow they would suffer, but tonight they would dream of the life that lay ahead and rejoice in their new status.

Chronicle 3: The City

Osi and Busah had known it was coming, but in the midst of their training such freedom seemed hardly more than a dream. Earlier, as an incentive to perform well, the major domo had told his cadets they could look forward to the last day of each month when the worthy would be allowed to visit the city. Ketoh, for his part, wasn't so sure he would be counted among the worthy. But when the day arrived, Ketoh joined his friends as they stepped from their barracks into the sun and shadows of late afternoon.

"Let's head to the market. My treat." Both companions stared at Osi. "We have to hurry. Shops close before dark, so we don't have long."

"What's the special occasion?" Busah asked.

"I have a surprise, something to celebrate, but not yet. Wait until we reach the market."

"What is it?...What is it? Don't keep us in suspense."

"This news is worth the wait," Osi said. He smiled. "Besides, we have the city before us. Let's enjoy ourselves."

"That should be easy with no parents along to make us behave," Ketoh said.

"They wouldn't let us go into the city alone, but I don't think it was *our* behavior they were worried about. Do you, Osi?" Busah asked.

"I agree. It was our *safety* and somebody else's behavior." Osi said. "My parents often speak of a time, not long ago, when the city was safe. Now, children can't wander about on their own, not even in daytime, and adults must take care at night."

"Yeah, well, a month ago they may have called us 'children.' But not now. We've been through the Manhood Ceremony. We've earned our first liberty. That's sign enough for anybody that we've come of age. We may not be men yet, but we certainly aren't children. Not after what we've been through," Ketoh said.

"That's right, Ketoh. No one can doubt that childhood is behind us. But it's a long journey from the Manhood Ceremony to manhood, I'm told. The greatest step will come a year and a half from now, when, on the eve of the summer solstice, we'll officially be designated men. Young men, to be sure, but men."

"Yes, and after that, we'll still have two more years of training before we get adult privileges," Busah said.

"I'll be an old man by then," Ketoh said. "I'll have almost 18 years behind me. And, in the meantime, we have all this training to go. Are you sure it's worth it?"

"No doubt in my mind. I don't want to be left behind when the Chaos comes. Besides, training may be hard, but it isn't all bad," Osi said. "Action. Challenge. I sort of look forward to it."

"And we can look forward to liberty once a month...plus furloughs on religious holidays."

"Our challenges begin again tomorrow at daybreak, so let's make the best of tonight."

The direct route into the city was through the central courtyard of the barracks and its ceremonial colonnade, but novitiates were not allowed to take that path on their own. Instead, the three would have to find their way through back streets. The first turn brought them to a narrow alley lined with small apartments inhabited by artisans and laborers. Servants' quarters and the homes of carvers, stone masons, potters, weavers, and tailors gave a uniform look to the street. Dwellings were single-story— some constructed of sun-dried bricks, others of wooden slats and clay daub. Some roofs, called "seccas" in Egia, were ridged or pointed. Most, however, were flat and topped with patios bounded by low walls of wooden posts and beams. A vast assortment of drying vegetables, seafood, seaweed, freshly laundered clothing, and newly tanned hides hung from the rails. The scent of charcoal fires and searing meat permeated the air, for residents typically cooked their meals on top, when the weather was fair as it was this night. Still full from their earlier feast, the boys wished they were hungry again.

The street broadened near its intersection with the grand boulevard. Shouldered against the street, a huge apartment building filled the first block. A small, majestic chapel occupied the opposite corner. Beside it sat a single house, modest in size but quite elegant.

"That's Wintar's and Becha's. Let's go in." Ketoh said. "They recently finished their training. Now that we're cadets, Wintar can tell us about the manhood training and Becha can tell us about the women." It wasn't a bad idea, but the others were anxious to reach the heart of the city.

"Maybe on our way back," Osi replied.

"*If* they're still up," Busah added, hoping their return would be late indeed.

They turned the corner and proceeded eastward past the Agent's palace with its manicured lawns. Each boy stared through the metal grate as they strolled beside a protective fence, reminded of the awesome responsibility they would soon share, for they would protect not only the King but his Agents and their noble class, as well. Osi took special note of the small, fortified compound where the King's soldiers garrisoned. Soldiers, he had heard, took little interest in the affairs of ordinary men, for their defense of the King was paramount even above their own lives. These were the guardians of the law, the protectors of the King. Someday, Osi and his friends would be among them.

Adjacent blocks were lined with mansions belonging to the wealthiest and most powerful men and women of the Realm. Next came fancy shops where furniture, cooking utensils, foodstuffs, and household supplies could be seen by all, yet purchased by only the wealthy few. Finally, they came to the simpler, affordable shops of bakers, tailors, copper smiths, embalmers, tattoo artists, physicians, barbers, and dentists.

Busier and busier the street grew as they neared its end. Straight ahead lay the Great River. Before reaching its mighty surging waters, however, the boulevard widened into a massive expanse encompassing the market plaza on their left and the temple complex on their right. The Sacred Pyramid dominated the whole scene, and cast its shadow across their path.

"Soon you will be men . . ." Ketoh chanted, imitating Anbaht, as he danced about on the tip of the pyramid's shadow.

"Stop it, you fool," Osi said, grabbing Ketoh's elbow and pulling him aside. "Don't you realize what will happen if someone tells the High Priest. You'll get us all killed."

"Oh! Oh, you're right. I wasn't thinking," Ketoh said, and the three of them quickly bolted into the din of the marketplace.

Buyers surrounded an army of peddlers on the central pavement. Farmers stood in the fading light beside their carts half-full of vegetables, grain, or meat. Surely each cart had arrived early that morning, overflowing with goods hauled directly from the countryside or from boats docked nearby. The best salesmen with the best produce and most prominent stalls had sold their goods long ago and were now back at their farms, resting and enjoying their own well-supplied tables. Gradually during the afternoon, their vacant stalls had been filled by the burgeoning merchant class, flaunting their prosperity with elaborate tents covering stores of manufactured items–clothing, utensils, cutlery, weapons, inks and dyes, papyrus, and ornaments. Enterprising youngsters filtered among the stalls and carts offering smoked fish, jerky, dried seaweed, dried fruit, cooked meat on skewers, and honeyed breads.

Beyond a massive breakwater, small boats moored in a man-made channel connected not to the river but directly to the sea. Nearby, fishmongers displayed the morning's catch on permanently mounted tables built into the seawall. Their stocks, too, were low and, like the farmer's carts, would be replenished by morning. Occasionally, a laborer hefted a bulging skin and dashed saltwater over the merchandise. The water gushed over the edge and drained into the river. The scent of fish was strong, yet no one objected for it was the smell of the sea, and the sea was their home.

Small shops and cafes bordered the plaza on two sides. Beer parlors were the most popular among them, especially as the sun set and nighttime revelry began. Although the boys had been allowed to drink beer with their meals at home, they knew this was not the time to try their first taste of the stronger brew served in parlors. They would need all their faculties when they returned to duty. "Better wait," Osi said, and the others nodded in agreement.

"Here, good man!" yelled Busah to a passing vendor with a basket slung over his shoulder. The man reeled around and tilted the basket to display its contents. "Two measures," signed each boy as he scooped up a handful of sugared fruit. Each one then handed over a small coin engraved with a likeness of King Rahn Mennon.

The sky darkened, and daytime vendors departed. "Okay, Osi. It's time to tell us your big news," Ketoh said.

"Let's find a quiet place so we won't be interrupted."

From an alley, the boys heard raucous shouting and laughter. Music from flutes and drums poured out like a gush of air as they turned the corner and peered cautiously down the narrow passage. The music itself was intoxicating, not to mention the excessive drink that obviously flowed in the taverns. Warily, they advanced.

"This one should do," Ketoh said with a laugh.

"That's what the older boys call 'Temptation Alley.' " Osi whispered. "We surely won't find a quiet spot there."

"Come!" beckoned a lady outside a cabaret, a young woman, barely older than the boys themselves, beautiful and shapely in the red-yellow glow of late sunset. Fading light revealed the delicate lines of naked breasts, a brass armband, a beaded necklace, a flowing skirt of finely woven fabric split at the waist.

From the boasts of older youths, the boys knew what brought such young ladies to the streets of the city. A Commoner, she sought the company of highborn men whose offspring would be eligible for service to the King. She knew nothing of the coming Chaos, but she understood the social privilege that fell to those who served the King. "Where are you going? Don't you find me beautiful?"

"I suppose my news can wait a little longer," Osi said to his companions. "A little stroll can't hurt. When will we get another chance to see Temptation Alley?"

Trying to avoid eye contact, the boys walked purposefully on down the crowded sidewalk, alternately glancing at her, at the street ahead, and into the cabarets. As they passed her, she spoke to them in a soft bedroom tease. "See me, touch me! I can be yours." Osi couldn't resist a savoring glance. As he looked, with a flip of her hand, she casually parted her skirt revealing herself to the boys. Osi was tantalized by the sight but did not yield. Following his lead, they all moved on.

"Thank you, ma'am," Busah said as he passed by, then blushed when the others laughed.

The boys stopped in front of one particularly loud establishment, pretending to discuss plans for the evening. Inside, men sat on patches of carpet scattered with coins and marked sticks in what appeared to be high-stakes gambling. Gamblers intensely tossed carved sticks then raked in piles of coins. Each time a particular stick landed on top, the tosser was declared victorious. A shout went up, and the lucky gambler seized his winnings as if they were alive and soon would take flight.

Suddenly, a man appeared in the doorway. "Come into my humble hall," invited the portly proprietor, wiping his hands on a leather apron. "I would be honored to have such handsome youths as yourselves grace my business with your presence."

"Sir, I'm afraid your stakes are beyond our means," Osi protested. "We are mere cadets and have no money for the games."

"I would be pleased to have you join us anyway," the man said. "You are novitiates, eh, and so you must be my guests. I may be a worldly man, my sons, but I am one of the Chosen. You are welcome to watch, even if you have no money to wager."

"Shouldn't we head back to the plaza?" Busah whispered.

"And miss a chance like this?" Ketoh said.

"Just a moment," Osi said, nudging his companions out of earshot. "Do you think this man is really one of the Chosen? What if he's just saying that to lure us inside?"

"But what sinister motive could he have for that? He knows we don't have much money."

"Still, it's tempting. Besides, what if he's sincere? It would be an insult to refuse." Cautiously, the boys stepped inside the poorly lit barroom.

"Looks safe enough to me."

"Me, too, but watch your step."

"Surely we can handle whatever comes our way. We are cadets, after all, with a full month of training behind us."

The stench of stale beer rose from the gaming carpets. Gamblers took note as the cadets entered, but no one said a word to them. Finally, the boys claimed an empty carpet and folded their legs beneath them. When hands began to clap, the youths turned to see several young women step from the crowd onto a flat stage in the center of the room. As music welled up, hands clapped wildly, and the women began to dance.

Drinks flowed nonstop. Each time the proprietor passed, he generously offered the cadets a free cup, and they politely declined. They soon felt comfortable and joined in the merrymaking as enthusiastically as any sober man could. Eventually, a patron, flush with victory and drink, offered to buy a round for the whole house. As the proprietor circulated, the boys politely waved him away again as they had several times before. His brow wrinkled, and he whispered, "Take it. Later, you can pour it on the floor."

Experienced men would have caught his meaning, but Ketoh replied loudly for all, "No, thank you. Not tonight." The damage was done.

"Perhaps these Chosen Ones don't believe in strong drink," the offended patron growled. Unfriendly laughter broke out at his table and spread through the room as others retold the cadets' affront.

The boys rose quietly to leave, but the patron, a crude man, apparently a newly-rich merchant, wouldn't let it be. "Wait, young Chosen Ones," he yelled. "Don't leave! Come be my guests on the stage. Perform for us, and we will clap for you." The man pointed toward the stage at the center of the room where naked women danced. The crowd yelled and chanted for the boys to step forward, but they headed for the door. Suddenly the music stopped, and a wall of men blocked their exit. Others stepped back, clearing a path to the stage. The patron burst from the crowd, sticks and coins scattering across the floor. He grabbed Ketoh, the smallest of the boys, and jerked him roughly to the stage. Osi rushed forward to assist Ketoh, while Busah, surrounded by riled patrons, struggled desperately to reach the door. Osi grabbed Ketoh's arm, attempting to break the merchant's hold.

"Stop!" boomed the proprietor. The unruly crowd froze as if they had been physically constrained. "Let the youths go!" he ordered in an authoritative, hoarse whisper. "You have no quarrel with these innocent young men. Let them drink or not drink as they will." The men relaxed their bristled stance, some out of caution, some out of shame. "Come, my sons! Be gone."

"I apologize for these brutes," he said as they passed. *Maybe my judgment of this man was too harsh,* Osi thought. *Perhaps he is among the Chosen after all.*

Stunned, the boys rushed from the alley, sped across the plaza, and walked briskly up the boulevard. Clinging to the circular glow of street lanterns, they said not a word until they passed the Agent's palace. But they were young men, soon rejuvenated by the night air and the relative safety of the street. By the time they reached the narrower stretch of road in front of the grand estates, they were ready to joke about the incident.

"You two must thank Rahn that I kept a cool head," Ketoh said. "I saw nothing but cold fear in your eyes."

"I wasn't afraid. You and Osi were the ones who panicked."

"Why would I be frightened by a fortress wall of angry Commoners?" Osi asked. *We made a foolish mistake,* he thought. *It's over and no longer cause for fear, but this is a lesson to remember.* The evening was still young as they turned the corner heading toward their barracks.

"Look," Ketoh exclaimed. "The lights are still on at Wintar and Becha's. Let's go in."

Osi started to object, but then remembered that it was he, himself, who had suggested they might drop in if their return were not too late. The front door remained open, a signal that guests were welcome. "Alright," he said, "I'm for it."

"Can't hurt as long as we follow all customs and remember our manners," Busah added, remembering that the young residents were considerably more affluent than he. And so, in the custom of the day, they removed their shoes at the entrance and quietly stepped through the open door.

The house was actually one large room with individual nooks for sleeping, cooking, bathing, and entertaining. Compartments were separated by gilded archways, each one open between its marble columns, except for one low wall at the base of the archway separating the kitchen from the far end of the bedroom. Politely, the three boys took seats on a cushioned platform recessed into the outer wall. It would be unforgivable to disturb the occupants until their own presence was acknowledged. Between the sitting area and bedroom, water cascaded over a fountain, taking divergent paths so that some fell in showers and some collected in pools. Beyond the fountain, Wintar and Becha disengaged from tender lovemaking.

"Ah, my good friends," Wintar fairly shouted as he rose from the bed. "How good of you to drop by."

"My compliments and appreciation for your good manners," Becha added. "We'll be right out." Together they stepped into the fountain. They bathed in the cool shower and drank from its trickling flow. Soon they were refreshed and ready to meet their guests. Wintar wrapped himself in a tunic. Becha donned a stylish gown.

She was a bright young woman, a year or two older than the boys themselves, and she was stunningly beautiful in the torchlight. Her petite breasts were uplifted by a fashionable bodice that draped from her shoulders across her midriff. Brass armbands circled her biceps, and beaded necklaces draped loosely across her chest. A diaphanous skirt cascaded over the graceful lines of her hips, thighs, and legs. In the style of the northern islands, her breasts were bare, and, in the style of the southern coasts, the dress, itself, was nearly invisible.

Osi couldn't resist a long, savoring glance. He was tantalized by the sight, but not tempted. As for Becha, she thoroughly enjoyed the attention from all three boys, as might any virtuous woman with nothing to fear.

"Well now, how is your training going?" Wintar asked as he took a seat facing the boys.

"You know what we've been through, and we know what we've been through. We were hoping you would tell us what to expect in the future," Osi joked.

"And Becha, we were hoping you would tell us about the women," Ketoh blurted.

"Uh, he means what the women are going through in their training," Busah quickly added as he blushed redder than the torch. Everyone laughed.

"I'll tell you as much as I'm allowed to tell, but there is much I can't reveal. It has to come in stages as you prove yourselves at each level," Wintar replied, first sounding like the friend he had always been and then like an officer who might someday lead them in battle.

"And I'll tell you as much as I can about the women, but there is much you will never know," Becha laughed.

* * *

"What must it be like, being with a woman?" Busah asked as the boys walked home.

"They say there is nothing like it," Osi said.

"It's truly wonderful," Ketoh said smugly. Osi and Busah wheeled about to face him.

"Do you mean to say you've been with a lady?" Busah asked. "Tell us all."

"Stop, my friends! A true gentleman never discusses his conquests," said Ketoh, clearly relishing the curiosity he had aroused. "Besides, Osi has something to tell us, remember?"

"It had better be big news, after this long wait."

"It is."

"Go on…"

"At the time of the summer solstice, I'm taking a trip with my father," Osi confided.

"Land or sea?"

"Land."

"West or east?" Ketoh asked, registering disappointment. "There isn't really that much to see in either direction."

"South!"

"South?"

"Yes, south. Beyond the forest, beyond the great falls…into the Land of the Second Sunset…"

Ketoh and Busah stared in stunned silence.

Chronicle 4: The Land of the Second Sunset

Twice each year, the cadets returned home—two days following winter solstice and three days following summer solstice. These were religious holidays, uncounted and apart from the 12 months that made up their calendar. Every fourth year, the winter holiday was increased by one additional day, making it three days, like the summer holiday. Otherwise, each 30-day month was divided into five weeks of six days each. Through these conventions, meticulously reckoned and monitored by the priests, the calendar of the Realm had remained constant for thousands of years. Only a few times in the recorded history of the Beloved People had their calendar required an adjustment to synchronize with the movements of the sun, earth, and stars.

On the last day of their sixth month, after early morning drill, the boys were free to pack and leave. Osi tried to remain calm as he stuffed his clothes into his pack, a loose fold of sheepskin with a wide strap, which he slung over his shoulder. "What will you tell your parents about that first week of training?" he teased Ketoh.

Busah jumped in with feigned sincerity, "Tell them you didn't have to work because all the girls asked our trainers to keep you rested."

Ketoh smiled. "I made it, didn't I!"

"Of the six who were punished, you're the only one who made it. Now you're as strong and ready as anyone in our class."

"It was tough, but it's worth it. Let's admit it...we're young gods now." He laughed.

"I can't deny a touch of pride," Osi said. "If we continue to perform well, we'll surely be among the candidates for betrothal next year—and service to the King as well."

"Of course, you don't have to wait for adventure. You're going to the Land of the Second Sunset."

"Nobody else our age has ever gone beyond Twin Falls."

"It's true. I'm the luckiest guy in the world."

Packing complete, the cadets picked up their belongings and headed out the main door. They entered the courtyard, which had been off-limits before, and turned down the street toward the great boulevard, the same street they had caroused on their first night of freedom. Back then, they had walked the carefree stroll of youth, today, the swagger of would-be men. This time, before reaching the ceremonial plaza, they turned south.

They passed the grand colonnade marking the city's official boundary and continued into the countryside. Within a few hundred paces, the pavement gave way to a broad, dusty road. Farmers bringing goods into the city, carts filled with produce, and soldiers and messengers of the King comprised its main traffic. Most travelers were locals on foot; some led asses with heavy burdens. Occasionally they met a rider on camelback or a large cart pulled by a camel. From time to time, farmers herded clusters of sheep and goats along the roadway.

On the left was the Great River with a single row of fine estates. The road itself followed the inland shoulder of a natural levee, its crest forming a continuous line of home sites. Manor houses—single or double story—lined the riverbank, each site occupied for so long that the house sat on a tall mound built up from the debris of former structures over the ages, and hence was touched only by the highest floods once every few centuries. Rich vegetation, primarily fruiting shade trees, hid the lower portion of each house from view. Brick walls punctuated by entrance gates stretched beside the roadway. Between the walls and houses lay gardens abundant with vegetables for the family table. On the opposite side of the main road lay lush fields separated by low berms and canals. In each field grew dense crops of two-row barley, oats, rye, grain sorghum, rice, buckwheat, or other staples for sale in the city. Morning fog clung to distant fields, and the horizon was obscured in haze. Workers bent low, tending young plants.

"What will everyone think of us now?" Busah said they walked along. "Surely they must view us as men, even if we aren't quite yet. I'm anxious to see my brothers' and sisters' faces."

"Yes," Ketoh said. "They'll look up to us as never before."

"Don't be disappointed," Osi warned. "We've only been away six months, and we have twice that to go . . ." He paused, then added with a glint, "so they may see us as smaller gods than we really are." The boys laughed.

"What will you do during the break?" Busah asked Ketoh, betraying subtle envy.

"No plans. How about you?" Ketoh responded, making uncertainty sound like an asset rather than a liability.

Busah hesitated, then admitted. "I . . . well, I plan to help my father." No one responded, for it was well known that Busah's family had suffered personal and financial calamities over the past two years. Busah's parents once owned a large farm, inherited from her family. The estate was quite prosperous until farm workers fell ill and several died. Believing the deaths were due to sour water, other workers panicked and left the estate. When the harvest failed from lack of care, his family lost most of its land to the Realm to settle the tax debt. Now, Busah's proud father worked as overseer of his former lands.

Busah's family was able to keep its home, due in part to intervention by Osi's father. At his wife's urging, Geb had appealed to the good graces of King Rahn Mennon. Life was hard, for the King's share was substantial, and workers still shunned the estate. The labor shortage grew even worse when Busah went away.

Training had distracted Busah, but now he would face again the reality of their diminished circumstances. Their only hope was to tend the land well and earn back, however slowly, some of what they had lost. With good luck and a newly-dug well, ten years of hard labor might restore a semblance of the family's earlier status. Busah's father and mother were known to be good managers and hard workers, so Busah's hopes were well founded.

Ketoh on the other hand was one of the privileged few. His family's estate was among the most prosperous in Egia. His parents were legendary for their ability to turn fruits and grains into coins of the Realm. Ketoh wished he could share a fraction of his family's wealth with Busah, but it was impossible. The venerable code of Egia demanded that every person make his own way.

Osi's father, Geb, was an Emissary of the Realm, a role that included managing all the King's estates. Far and wide he ranged throughout Egia minding the King's enterprises. His absence was felt at home, but Nuuti, his wife, was a good manager in her own right. Their personal estate, though smaller than most neighboring farms, was among the most prosperous.

Geb's exploits were famous throughout the land, and Osi was certain to join him at every opportunity. Earlier, Osi had taken day trips through the delta or along the coast. Now, he was granted special leave to accompany his father on a major excursion upriver, a coup that earned the envy of all the other cadets. Starting with summer break and extending into the new training period, the adventure would take nine or ten days. Getting special leave for such an adventure had proven no problem for Osi. He could hardly wait for the next morning's departure.

"Goodbye. I'll see you in two weeks," Osi said to Ketoh as his friend split away and headed down the lane. A short while later he said the same to Busah and turned into his own estate grounds. Osi's pace quickened as he approached the house. At first there was silence, then a loud yell as his brother, Thalan, sighted the returning "hero."

"Osi! Osi!" shouted the ten-year-old. "Come see my new stones." Stones were rare on the delta, and it was a special event whenever any boy was able to acquire new specimens from the interior. On his last trip, Geb had brought Thalan a new agate from cliffs beyond Twin Falls. Once, he even brought a topaz from farther south.

"A beautiful stone," Osi said with hushed admiration. He was happy for his younger brother, but anxious to see his parents and the others. "You must be very proud."

"It's my best!" Thalan beamed.

"It must have come from the Land of the Second Sunset," Osi said.

"That's what father said," Thalan replied. "Why is it called the 'Second Sunset?'"

"Because of a strange sight that occurs when our soldiers climb the long trail to the lands above. If they travel at the right time of day, along the trail they see the sun set just as we see it here in Egia. Soon after, as they continue up the hillside, the sun appears to rise again. When they reach the top of the plateau, the sun goes down a second time. Few have seen it."

"Are you just teasing me? Does that really happen?"

"Our Geometers proved it's true. They say it's perfectly natural. Of course, travelers have to move fast to catch both sunsets."

The two boys locked arms and covered the remaining distance. Osi was pleased to find the entire family assembled in the living area. Osi's mother sat beside a wooden table on which a servant had spread an array of food—oat porridge, almonds, dried fish, and a variety of fruits and drinks—melon juice, milk, and barley water. "Welcome home, my son," she said with disciplined reserve. Never again would Osi be her child. Now he was almost a man, and she would try to remember to treat him as such.

"Welcome, my son!" Geb said heartily. He was joined by a chorus from eight-year-old brother Hammon, six-year-old brother Rannah, and four-year-old sister Imea. The priests had chosen Osi's twin sister Isas, many years ago. He didn't expect to see her, of course, but now another was missing.

"Where is Mira?" Osi asked anxiously.

"She also was chosen by the priests. She's in the temple dormitory." Geb's pride was obvious. To have first a daughter, then a son, and now a second daughter among the Chosen was a rare honor for Geb's family. After all, few families could boast of having more than one child so elevated. Despite his sadness in losing his beloved 12-year-old sister, Osi was overjoyed at this news. Someday, he and both sisters might help regenerate their nation. It was a sobering thought, but it was good to know that they, too, would survive the Waters of Chaos.

After two hands of conversation, Geb announced that he must attend to the work of the estate. With the older children following reluctantly, he left the family compound and walked to the fields across the road. Nuuti turned to Osi, "It's good to have you home, son. You're so grownup now. Without me, you've become . . ."

"I've never been without you, Mother. The strengths that carry me through are the ones you gave me."

"You'll need all my strengths, and your father's, plus any your trainers can spare, my son, for troubled times lie ahead."

"What makes you say that?"

"I see the signs. Your father tries to hide his worries, but I see through him. A visitor came last week and spoke privately with him for many hands. Afterward, Geb was a changed man."

"But that could mean many things, Mother."

"Mark my word. I see worry in old man Anbaht's face as well. I sense it in the marketplace, especially among the traders arriving from Berenicia. Change is in the wind or, perhaps I should say, in the waves. The Waters of Chaos are coming. I feel it in my soul. No one will be safe, and you will be in the eye of the storm. Take care, Osi." Nuuti shifted in her chair and stared out the window.

"I will, Mother, I promise." The rest of Osi's day was spent in preparation for the coming trip. Long after sunset, the family ate a sumptuous meal. Osi went to bed, uncertain as to the meaning of his mother's warning but certain of its importance.

* * *

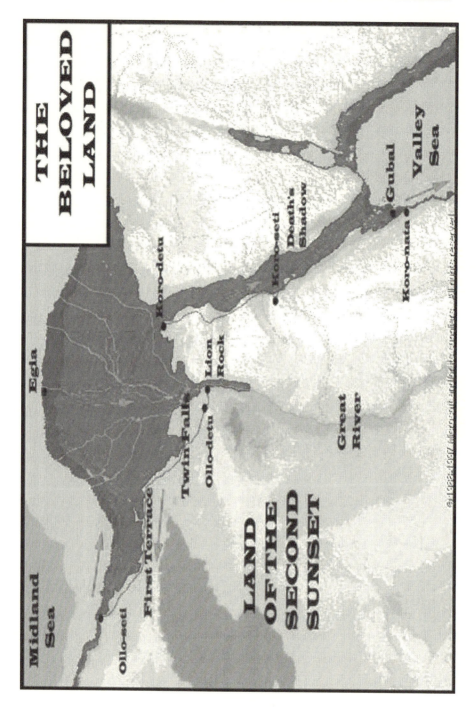

[Color images available at **www.thewatersofchaos.com**]

The morning sun shone brightly through columns surrounding the chamber Osi shared with Thalan and Hammon. Here and there, beams of light filtered among the leaves of surrounding trees. Osi felt a special fondness for this quiet place. He liked the coolness. He liked to watch the birds and lizards in the trees. He savored the soft mat that formed his bed and the scent of mown hay that came from its stuffing. Often, he wished the whole chamber could be his alone, fantasizing of a time when he and a lovely young lady might lie on his soft bedding entwined in each other's arms. For now, the maiden was but a faceless form shrouded in shadows, then lost in the rising sun. Someday he would find a face and a name belonging to that perfect visage.

"Come!" Geb barked over his shoulder as he headed out the portal. "Sun's up! No breakfast. We'll eat on the way. Dockside. Now!"

Osi jumped to his feet, threw on his tunic, and grabbed his pack. "Coming, father!" he yelled out the kitchen door as he reluctantly paused to sip hot, parched barleycorn tea from the cup his mother forced into his hand. Her meaningful glance sealed the pact they had made the day before. After a few gulps, to the river he ran, catching up with Geb on the bank. The two clambered down the steep, well-worn path to the floating dock. The shortcut crossed over a broad, ramp-like trail used by workers with farm carts hauling the year-round harvest of fruits and grains that fed the colony of Egia.

The dock was a deceptively flimsy affair designed to ride up and down with day to day ebbs and flows as well as annual floods. Anchored to wooden pylons driven deep into muck and tied to trees along the shore, it rode more like a tethered boat than a fixed dock. A sturdy ramp stretched from its wooden platform to firm ground above. Moored on the water side was a small cedar wood vessel about four manheights long with a gaffed mast three manheights tall. The boatman stood forward in the felucca tugging a hawser looped over a wooden cleat on the dock.

"Welcome aboard, young man," said the weathered sailor, Ashran, who remembered Osi from previous trips along the delta. He had been Geb's boatman for years, and he enjoyed introducing a new generation to his domain. The snaggle-toothed old man now commanded one of the smallest crafts in the King's Navy, but he was a decorated veteran of the open sea. "You start life out in a skiff, and you end up in a skiff," he said philosophically. "Throw everything aboard, lad," he growled. "Step here. Then take that seat at the stern." Osi jumped to follow Ashran's instructions. "We've provisions aplenty, lad, and all the gear's aboard."

Geb tossed his pack aboard, then moved to the bow where a larger, comfortable seat awaited him. Two stout porters climbed onboard, pushed off from the mooring, and unfurled the boat's triangular sail.

Osi was content to lean back and take in the rain-gorged river and its banks. Everywhere the waterway bustled with barges and boats, heavy-laden with building stones, lumber, firewood, cattle, and grain. In mid-channel, vessels under sail parted or dragged loose green masses of lily pads and hyacinths, characteristic of the Great River in flood. Rafts of bound logs floated passively downstream where, at one port or another, they would be retrieved, dismantled, hauled ashore, and planed for construction. On the near bank, orchards and fields bulged with fruit, vegetables, and flowers. At estate after estate, floating docks served as bustling crossroads of land and water. He could barely make out similar features on the far bank as well.

"Look alive, lad!" yelled Ashran, as he unfurled the boat's triangular sail. "You'll earn your keep aboard this vessel." He tossed Osi the opposite end of a coiled rope held gingerly, almost lovingly, in his hand. Placing that now-free hand on the rudder and, with the other, guiding the boom past his face, the skipper barked orders. The young cadet had heard them all before but never in such rapid fire. "Coming about, lad, look alive, look alive! Haul that sheet. Hoist the gaff! Cleat the main! Stand amidships!" Osi jumped from mast to cleat to mast again in futile attempts to comply.

"What?...where?" Osi spun round and round looking for identifiable parts. *How can a little skiff need so many actions to stay afloat?* he wondered. Then he saw the crack of a grin on Geb's face. All had a good laugh at Osi's expense. Belatedly, he laughed as well.

"Now, lad, you don't think I'd play a trick, do you?" Ashran said with a smile, and Osi smiled back.

"I want to learn your vessel, sir," Osi said, and Ashran silently motioned the boy to his side. Soon, Osi had his bearings and was ready to come about in earnest. Ashran calmly told him where to stand to clear the boom. Grasping the line in his hand, Osi listened as Ashran instructed him to loosen, then chinch again once the boom had passed. Pulling on a second sheet, Osi tightened the gaff, and the felucca was under full sail on a long tack. Ashran then invited the boy to take over the tiller. Step by step, he explained to Osi what had just been accomplished and what would be next.

"We can't go into the wind, you see, lad, so we must dance with her first one way and then another. Treat the wind like a beautiful lady, and she'll take you where you want to go." Osi felt a sudden thrill as the felucca accelerated, and the tiller began to vibrate solidly in his hand. Wind lofting off the sail blew flush into his face. The sensation of speed without reference to solid earth was exhilarating. This was the fastest he had ever moved.

From a vantage point beside the mast, Ashran directed his pupil as they traveled upriver, tack by tack, into a strong headwind blowing straight down the river. "Just wait," Ashran advised. "We'll have a tailwind soon. There's a hot day ahead." He spoke as one who knew the river like an old friend. On calm days along most of the coast a navigator would have to reckon only for sea breezes in the morning and land breezes in the evening, but the Great River was so massive it made its own weather.

Farther up the main channel, after leaving the cultivated delta, Osi saw mostly pastureland. By late morning, orchards and vineyards supplanted the pastures, creating a buffer zone that protected livestock from predators living in the surrounding forests. Soon, signs of human habitation grew sparse, and he saw a grand display of wildlife. In deep water, riverine porpoises cavorted playfully under and over the surface. In the shallows, elephants bathed; hippopotami fed on water hyacinth; crocodiles slithered in and out of the water. Flocks of colorful shorebirds and waterfowl rested at the water's edge. On the embankments, giant turtles lazed in the sun. Herds of giant deer drank from shallow pools or grazed on low grasses along the narrow flood plain. Dholes and dire wolves, normally creatures of the night, occasionally appeared for a quick run to the water's edge, then disappeared into the thin patch of forest lining the river.

Overhead, migrating birds blackened the skies in flocks so dense their shadows provided a fleeting shade for the travelers. Cawing and cackling occasionally drowned out conversation aboard the felucca. An elephant trumpeted. *This must be paradise,* Osi decided.

By noontime, they reached the headwater diversion of the West Bank Canal. "We should be at the garrison by now," grumbled Geb. "Not your fault, lad. It's this headwind. We'll have to make up time. Eat aboard. Keep moving." With a nod from Ashran, a sailor opened a chest mounted on the afterdeck and, rummaging about, retrieved several dried fish strips, bread, olives, and a goatskin of rich wine which he passed around to the passengers and crew. Osi kept a firm grip on the tiller and ate with his free hand.

Abruptly the wind and the land changed. The Great River's broad delta gave way to a gorge flanked by towering cliffs, growing ever deeper toward the south. The morning's gusts yielded to a single force of misty cool air rushing toward the gorge. The steady tailwind forced Osi to tack more frequently as crosswinds dissipated and the channel narrowed. Awestruck, Osi panned upward to the pinnacles and spires that formed the upper lip on either side of the canyon. Occasionally, mulia ibex and wild goats appeared on the craggy ramparts to look down on these aliens invading their domain.

Rounding the first bend of the chasm, Osi heard a deep rumbling that shook him to his soul. What can *that be?* he wondered, too proud to ask. The sound deepened till his chest vibrated with the pounding roar. The boat breasted a second huge bend, and his heart leaped, as before him loomed the most magnificent display of untamed nature he had ever seen, heard, or felt. The gorge opened to a large circular theater above which the walls of the Great Gorge stretched heavenward. Near at hand, a gigantic column of rock, soaring upward as far as the eye could see, defined the west bank. Far in the distance, a buttress of equal grandeur bounded the east bank. Monumental pillars of stone seemed set in place by the gods, and beside each one, a monstrous waterfall, fed by its own upland river—each a great river in its own right—plunged in suicidal frenzy to the enormous pool below. Dashing on boulders and outcrops into an amphitheater of torrid rapids, the waters spread into twin rainbows that reached far out over the placid river beyond the rapids. Even at this great distance, a cool spray pelted the boat. Upstream, the river itself rose slightly and churned enough to discourage any small boat such as theirs. The craft, which had seemed ample just moments ago, quickly became tiny and insignificant. Osi almost relaxed his grasp on the tiller for a moment.

"Quite a sight, eh, son?" Geb exclaimed. He had told his family about Twin Falls before, but no one could describe their scale or their impact on mortal souls. For that reason, he had elected to let Osi experience this wonder unannounced. It had been a good strategy, and the boy stood speechless before the natural marvel.

"Who could have imagined that two lesser streams can eclipse the majesty of the Great River itself?" Osi finally said.

"Reclaim your senses," Ashran prodded. "Come about and set sail for that point between the river and the column." Osi complied. Deftly he guided the craft to a soft impact with the natural dock. Two huge boulders defined its margins, and between them nestled a large flat rock. Nearby, a crocodile sought refuge in deep brown waters along the bank.

Seven of the King's soldiers waited at the landing. "Welcome to our humble outpost," yelled their captain, a seasoned officer with stiff military bearing. "We are honored by your visit." Old Ashran poised at the stern and caught a tossed line. Steadying the craft, he secured it to a cleat on the bulkhead, and, one by one, the passengers jumped to the waiting grip of a soldier. Camels, saddled and ready, stood nearby.

"This must be your son. Please meet my swordsmen Phanus, Ateela, and Kon. They will accompany us to the interior."

Awed by the size and swagger of these robust specimens of manhood, Osi managed only a courteous nod.

"Yes, captain, my eldest son, Osi, a Cadet of the Realm," Geb proudly announced. "He's anxious to see the interior and learn more about the kingdom he's sworn to protect."

Geb then faced his son. "Osi, meet Captain Hano, commander of the King's garrisons in this sector. He and his men will accompany us to the fort at Ollo-detu." He turned again. "Captain, I must inform you of changes in your mission. My purpose is to determine the needs of Ollo-detu and prepare for increased traffic. Osi and I will leave you at Ollo-detu and return by way of Ollo-seti to inspect the western fortifications, as well."

On a ledge beside the river stood a barracks of baked bricks where the men ate boiled crabs, olives, bread, grapes, breadfruit, and wine. Afterward they began the steep ascent from the river's edge to the main plateau, more than 60 manheights above. The path at first led westward on an incline along an old fault in the rock face. For the remainder of the afternoon, it twisted and turned up a narrow, sloping trail. The final stretch rose into friendlier terrain, parted from the channel, and emerged on gentle slopes.

Eventually, the tiny caravan entered the gardens and terraced vineyards of the last settled outpost of the Beloved People. Afterward, the terrain steepened, and all signs of habitation ceased. The trail was well trod, but the land was covered by thick virgin forest. Pines, cedars, and junipers stood high above. Occasional rock outcrops punctuated the wooded slopes. Osi, who had never before seen a natural landscape, found the wilderness at once beautiful and frightening. Around him towering trees cast long dark shadows, no doubt concealing dens of the most ferocious beasts ever faced by man.

"Father, will we see Hill People along the way?" Osi asked.

"No, son, they're farther west. Hano's soldiers have forced them away from the military trail to Ollo-detu. They have plenty of land and will not be seen here."

"I've heard so many stories."

"We'll traverse a corner of their territory on our return trip. They try to conceal themselves, but they're not always successful. Occasionally, our soldiers report seeing one or two at a distance. I myself once saw a small troop from afar."

The trail steepened, leveled, then steepened again as the column wound higher and higher above the valley floor. All the while, the steady rumble and roar of the falls gave a sense of grandeur that transcended fear and made Osi appreciate the experience all the more. The continuous shaking of the ground, the resonance in his chest, the sights, and even the silence of the forest itself constantly reminded him how fortunate he was. In a single day, he had seen more of the world than most would see in a lifetime. Yet Osi sensed this was only the beginning. He yearned to experience the greater world, the whole world, to grasp the earth in his hand and see and smell and hear as much of it as his senses would bear. This brief foray awakened a burning passion that could only be quenched through exploration.

"Attention!" yelled Ateela, then riding vanguard. "Ahead! There's something beside the trail." The column slowed as they neared a dark bloody carcass.

"What is it?" Osi asked.

"Fallow deer," the soldier said.

Osi stared at the gnawed remains of a once-proud stag, its enormous rack blocking their path.

"Dirktooth cat!" warned the soldier in a woodsman's whisper. "Those are the marks of a dirktooth cat." A hush fell over the entire entourage. Before this moment, Osi had never seen in his father any sign of fear.

"But don't be scared, lad," Captain Hano said with bravado, "We can handle that kitten! You men, toss this careless beast off the trail." Three men dismounted.

"Be alert, son," Geb whispered to Osi. "All men fear the dirk. No weapon can stop him. He lurks nearby. He won't retreat until he's had his fill."

Osi noted fresh slashes across the hapless animal's neck and haunches. One shoulder, savagely ripped from the body, was missing, but erratic twitches of exposed muscle showed the animal was not yet dead. As the men moved closer, Osi sensed their fear. With each step they silently, reflexively swept the forest for any sign, any movement, any hint that the terrible cat lurked nearby guarding its prey. Even the seasoned veterans of the frontier trembled as they approached the inert body.

The giant rack spanned fully two manheights, and the body was more than that in length. It must have stood one and a half manheights at the shoulder before it fell.

"Hack off the head. Roll it aside."

Phanus, the largest and strongest, drew his sword and assumed an executioner's stance beside the massive withers. As he swung, the beast shuddered its final spasm of death. Neck muscles flinched one last time, and the massive head turned as if to face the swordsman eye to eye. In so doing the giant rack lurched, striking Phanus squarely in the chest. The antlers hardly seemed to move yet they flattened Phanus' ribs to his spine. One spike punctured his side, releasing a hiss of air and gush of bloody froth. Osi could scarcely believe he had seen his first violent death.

As quickly as Phanus had fallen, another took his place. Kon's vengeful blow severed the deer's spine, and his second and third strikes completed the task. Both soldiers then seized the giant rack and on Hano's signal shoved the head over the edge then down the steep slope, snapping tree tops as it rolled and bounced.

Captain Hano directed Ateela to cut a large slab of fresh meat from the flank. To disguise the scent, Ateela carefully wrapped the flesh in a tarp lined with aromatic leaves.

Captain Hano walked reverently to Phanus' body. Bending down as if to embrace him, the officer instead untied the colorful sash at his waist. With solemn steps Hano approached the unarmed Osi and handed him the sash, scabbard, and sword. "The weapon of a brave and honorable soldier brings unearned honor to you," he said, "You must, in turn, bring honor to the sword and the man." It was a soldier's blade comprised of the best metal the craftsmen of Egia could forge. It was strong yet brittle, for the armorers of Egia had not yet learned the secret of turning iron into glistening steel. Simple in design and devoid of ornamentation, it was hardly the sort of weapon Osi had dreamed of wielding in battle, but he would wear it for the remainder of this mission. When he returned home, the sword would be placed in safekeeping, but custom demanded that someday he must find an opportunity to use it in battle to honor the slain Phanus. Acceptance of this sword implied no less than a debt and an unspoken promise to the dead soldier. As an officer he hoped one day to wear a blade of fine Berenician steel, but for now he would bear the iron with pride.

The soldiers took positions and lifted the fallen man. They proceeded slowly to the cliff edge and laid their comrade face-up beside the path.

"Shouldn't we take Phanus' body to the fort?" Osi asked naively.

"No," Geb said, "the sea will someday claim him here, and the sea is a fitting grave for any man. He shall thus be laid out for the sea." It was a saying Osi knew well, but never before had events forced him to face its real meaning.

"Here," the captain said, handing the riderless camel's reins to Kon. "Let's get out of here before the dirk returns to finish his meal." The party remounted and filed past the grotesque hulk. Each camel in turn stepped over the withers and proceeded up the winding trail. Dusk fell.

Surely each man is aware he could have been the tiger's prey, Osi mused. *Surely each knows the same danger lurks at every step. Yet no one shrinks from action or shirks his duty.*

"Look out!" screamed Kon. A thunderous roar shook Osi. He wheeled about in time to see a flash of gold as the huge cat leapt from rocks above. Flashing talons sank into his camel's haunches. Instinctively, Osi drew Phanus' sword and swung with all his might. The brittle blade strained on impact. Like metal on metal, the shaft reverberated till his hands stung. A chip of iron as big as a thumbnail flew by his face, but the blade remained intact. A severed ivory tusk fell to the ground.

The dirk instantly recoiled but held to the camel's flank, first stunned, then outraged. Finally, the tiger released its grip, turned as if to leave, then spat and skulked to a nearby mound. Osi rebounded into a strike-ready pose—elbow bent, sword raised, eye to eye with his attacker. The dirk lunged. Aiming just above its collarbone, Osi used the monstrous cat's own momentum to drive the sword home. The flailing cat knocked both rider and mount to the brink of the precipice. Osi broke free in the nick of time as his camel plunged into empty space. Striking hard ground, he felt a sickening, steady slide toward the brink, now less than one manheight away. It had taken much of the afternoon to climb from the base of this very cliff to their present height. In an instant, he would fall as far. Loose gravel rolled under his thighs, belly, chest, and elbows. Frantically he grasped for anything that would arrest his slide toward certain death, but his fingers felt nothing more than pebbles. With his legs stretched over thin air and his fate apparently sealed, suddenly his body jerked. His heart sank as he eased on over the brink, but looking up, he laughed. His new, bright-colored sash had snagged on an upthrust rock.

"Geb, have you not taught this boy how to ride a camel?" Captain Hano said as he peered over. The others then gathered and gawked while Osi swung helplessly. Pride turned to embarrassment as the seasoned soldiers roared in laughter. Geb's sash was off in an instant, the loose end dropped down within reach. Soon Osi was back on his feet atop the ledge.

Across the path, lay the slain beast. Ateela and Kon stared in amazement as Osi hurried to survey his kill. He counted aloud. Five strides from tail to head. Straining with all his might, he withdrew the bloody sword.

Geb approached, holding the broken tooth. "Of all our people, no man has ever killed a dirktooth alone. Troops of men have done so, but no boy has ever taken part in a kill. You will be a legend among us . . . forever. It is a blessing...." He paused and turned. "Or is it a curse?" he said as he stepped away, lost in thought.

Kon handed the reins of the slain soldier's camel to Osi. They rode in silence as the sun set over the western horizon. To Osi's delight, however, the golden sphere soon reappeared as they crested the ridge, and it remained high as they ascended a broad upland. *The Second Sunset!* Ahead, the trail continued to a line of low hills on which Ollo-detu, meaning "West, the First," was situated.

A sandy terrace marked the final approach to a dome-like knoll. So this is the renowned First Terrace, Osi thought. Only the boldest merchants and best-armed soldiers dared venture beyond it. According to tradition, this was the highest beach line that existed in the Topping Age of the Third Kalpa, thousands of years earlier, before the sea fell and turned to ice in the Northern Lands.

"There, son. That's the famous 'Lion Rock.' It's just now coming into view up the trail. It marks the edge of the mount of Gizah on which Ollo-detu stands."

"Wow. It looks just like the head of a lion."

"Yes. As if it's guarding Ollo-detu. No wonder the ancient Westerners worshipped here."

"They did? I thought they were afraid of this place."

"Today, yes. But long ago, it was a sacred place. They came here to celebrate the new sun and anoint each new shaman. That is, until the seasons changed, the land dried, and fires consumed the land. They thought their gods had abandoned them, and they in turn abandoned Gizah. Somehow, the men who then lived where Egia stands today learned of the Westerners' taboo. They brazenly occupied Gizah, and the Westerners have never reclaimed it."

"Why do we call them Westerners when they live south of Egia?"

"Because our ancestors in Berenicia named them," Hano answered.

"If our people lived in the delta hundreds of years ago, why didn't they themselves name the primitives?"

"Oh, the people who carved this lion weren't our ancestors. They were a separate people who occupied the lowlands near the mouth of the Great River early in the Rising Age of this Kalpa. They were modern people like us, and they were prosperous for thousands of years. The Lion People, they called themselves. From prosperity came pride and from pride came arrogance, so they carved this lion rock—a colossal monument to themselves. They believed the lion's crouching body extended beneath the surrounding ground. In their lore, it was said that greatness will come to those who liberate the beast from its burden of earth. There at the base of the lion's neck, you can see the scars of their feeble attempts to free the lion within. Eventually, they were flooded out. Because they wasted their efforts in ostentatious projects like this, they had no refuge. Now all that's left of their civilization lies at the bottom of the Midland Sea, sunken in the muck offshore beyond our own modern day settlements."

"...and up here," Osi added, pointing toward the partly finished sculpture.

"You have a good point. The only visible sign is this silly, half-carved cat, so I suppose it does have some value. Even the primitives respect it six thousand years after it was cut."

"Did all those people perish?"

"Most of them. Legends say a few wise men among them survived by turning to the sea. It is said that these Sea People sailed outside the Midland Sea, beyond the Outer Pillars of the Gods, across the Western Ocean. There, on a large island that blocks passage to the Opposite Continent, they are said to have founded an ideal kingdom called Aztlan. It isn't clear in the stories whether they founded it or simply *found* it. That is to say, there may already have been a great civilization there which accepted them into its fold. Who knows," said Geb.

"No one knows for certain?"

"No. My dear friend Captain Hervov . . . you've heard me speak of him many times . . . has sailed the world's seas. He has never been to Aztlan, but he's heard credible accounts from seamen who claim to have been there. They tell of a beautiful, well-ordered place filled with wonders."

"When did the Beloved People claim Egia?" Osi asked.

"Our ancestors were the People of the Living Sun who came from the Valley Sea and claimed the new land about 1,000 years ago. Before that, the delta had remained unsettled for 2,000 years while its land re-formed at the new sea level. Eventually, we renamed ourselves the Beloved People, but we are still part of the Realm of the People of the Living Sun."

Osi turned westward. "Look, the sun now kisses the horizon a second time," he said. "This is truly the Land of the Second Sunset."

"Tonight you are fortunate indeed," Geb said.

* * *

Near their destination, a breathtaking view unfolded. To the north, the cliff-rimmed sea presented a magnificent panorama. To the west, low hills etched the face of the setting sun. To the east, the Great River crossed like an unbroken ribbon between phalanxes of south-running ridges. Where the river stretched southward, low forests marked the near ridge bordering the plain. Farther off, rows upon rows of ever-fainter ridges–purple, then violet, then blue–competed to define the ambiguous line where earth met haze and haze met sky.

By the time they reached the highest point, twilight had cast its soothing veil. The river was in flood and, through the dusk, silver light from a full moon sparkled beneath the galleria forests crowding its banks.

On a hillock overlooking the tree-speckled plain, stood a frail fortification of sunbaked bricks. A simple foursquare design enclosed the compound where Captain Hano and his men would soon rejoin their comrades. Despite the waning light, its outline was well defined against the sky, its golden folds turned pale blue as the moon rose.

Hano took the lead. He gave a low whistle like a night bird in distress, then quickly whispered, "Halt!" The tension in his voice sounded loud and clear despite his attempt to remain calm. He whistled again, sniffed the air, then led them all to shelter behind a rock outcrop less than 50 paces from the fort. Without further instruction everyone quietly dismounted. Ateela and Kon handed their reins to Osi, then crept toward the fort.

"No sentry," the captain said. Gliding from shadow to shadow, his men advanced. The stout wooden gate swung freely on its massive stone base and iron hinge.

"Ateela...to the left...Kon...with me...to the right...toward the quarters," Hano ordered. "Mind the ramparts," he said. "Find torches." The three men disappeared. For Osi, the wait seemed unending.

"Come in, but prepare yourselves," the captain finally shouted from the gate. Geb and Osi led the camels inside. Halos of torchlight revealed a garrison gutted by fire. Smoke curled upward from fallen timbers. "Twenty-four soldiers, that's the full roster, plus camp women, of course," the captain said. "Most of their bodies are in the magazines below. They must have held out, even though fires were set."

"What happened?" Osi asked.

"Westerners!" Captain Hano said. "Must have attacked early today. Secure the gate, then follow me. We'll sleep on the ramparts tonight. Kon, gather wood and coals; we'll roast our venison up there."

Osi awoke the next morning to find Ateela still on watch. An acrid smell of death rose to the ramparts. The fort's interior courtyard was strewn with hacked and charred bodies. The captain arose and bellowed orders. Four hands later, all the victims had been laid out respectfully to await the coming of the sea. Captain Hano called the name of each victim by heart as Osi and the others stood in silence.

* * *

"I will tell you things known by no man outside the inner circles of the King," Geb said, pulling the captain aside. The two walked to a quiet spot overlooking the valley. Each chose a rock and settled down for serious conversation. "You are to tell no one unless ordered by me. Is that clear?"

"I hear and will obey. By my solemn honor and my allegiance to the King!" Captain Hano swore.

"The skies! They are changing! Our Geometers have seen the signs."

"Rise or fall?" the captain asked.

"Rise!" Geb said.

"How soon?"

"Too early to tell."

"And the attack on Ollo-detu?"

"Already our settlements push against the cliffs that wall the Valley Sea, and so we must seek a new land. The king has decreed that a refuge must be established, and he is considering the Land of the Second Sunset."

"The Land of the Second Sunset?" The captain gasped. "Among the Westerners?"

"Already they feel the pinch, and so they fight back."

"So be it. The King is wise!" Hano replied loyally but unconvinced. "I tell you, Geb, longer perhaps than any other man of our time, I've lived in this Land of the Second Sunset. I know its dangers, its desolation, and its dearth of prospects for human enterprise. Most of all, I know the Westerners. Leave them alone and they pose no threat. Barbarians yes, but peaceful hunters. Challenge their domain, however, and they become merciless killers. Even with crude axes and spears, they can easily destroy the small armies that our nation, the strongest and most advanced, can muster."

"You're right, Hano...I know you are. Westerners can't assemble massive forces, but they can be everywhere our armies are not. They rule the Land of the Second Sunset just as cats rule the forests and sharks rule the seas."

"This site is vital to our merchants and emissaries who travel the Great River," Hano said, waving his hand toward the river, the valley, and the plains. "Yet never in this Rising Age have we attempted to settle the Land of the Second Sunset—not even a thousand years ago when the Waters of Chaos suddenly swallowed vast portions of our coastal land."

Geb understood the captain's warning. "If the Geometers are correct, we'll soon be desperate for land, and we'll have no place else to go."

"I'm a soldier sworn to serve. And the search for land is already underway, you say?"

"Yes, Geometers and soldiers were dispatched from the capital under secret orders. They followed the trade route from Berenicia to Kom Ombo, thence north along the Great River toward Ollo-detu. As they took instrument readings less than two days' walk upriver from here, they were attacked by Westerners."

"And all were killed?" Hano asked.

"Three soldiers escaped overland to the Valley Sea. They were rescued by a freighter, and word reached Egia less than two weeks ago."

"No wonder the Westerners are enraged."

"Yes, and sadly it has cost the lives of your men."

"No matter! When the final count is taken, these deaths will be no more than the first gust of a mighty gale. But the Land of the Second Sunset extends far inland. How will our people live without the blessings of the sea?"

"The rise may be great. No Geometer can predict how high, but the waters may increase for centuries, perhaps millennia! They believe someday Ollo-detu may be near the sea or even beneath it."

"That's inconceivable! We've watched the seas change many times, and never in thousands of generations has the water been as high as the base of Ollo-detu's mount, much less its summit. You, yourself, saw the First Terrace far below Ollo-detu."

"The Geometers fear that all the ice in the world may melt."

"How can that be?"

"You and I know the workings of the world no better than Geometers know how to wage war. We must accept their wisdom and their understanding of the Secrets of the Ages."

"But there are as many opinions among Geometers as among soldiers in the Army."

"Not this time. They differ on how fast and how high, but the signs of rise are unmistakable."

"What does the King ask of me?"

"Your orders are to enlarge your garrison here at Ollo-detu and establish additional garrisons, seven in all, with 200 men each, along the Great River."

"And your Osi? What role is he to play? You brought him along for a reason, I'll wager."

"Osi and his fellows will be deployed to Berenicia. Any cadet who distinguishes himself may secure a post close to the King. Osi will be one of the few who has ever ventured here. I don't deny that I seek to prepare him for good service to the King."

When the two men returned, the soldiers had cleared the garrison. Food and supplies had been retrieved from hidden larders, and the noon meal was underway. Osi sat down by Hano, "Your men say the Westerners have broken the truce of Ollo-detu. No one understands why."

"Who knows? It's probably that cursed lion rock," Hano said. He pointed condescendingly toward the huge stone outcrop. "After 3,000 years, you'd think its evil powers would have diminished."

Chronicle 5: The Hill People

Geb and Osi rose early to set out for the next Garrison.

"Your orders are firm," Geb reminded Hano. "I appreciate your offer of an escort, but what difference would three men make? The Westerners slaughtered a full garrison behind stone walls; an escort would do little more than attract attention. No, Osi and I will rely on stealth and good fortune. Your place is here at Ollo-detu." He laughed, "Besides, I have a dirk killer with me."

Geb was anxious to report the debacle at Ollo-detu, lest the second garrison be caught off guard as well. Ollo-seti, meaning "West, the Second," was a smaller outpost in a more secure region overlooking the sea, accessed by open plain. It was normally a six-day journey away, but traveling light and pushing the limits of exhaustion, they could save at least one day. Immediately on arrival, a runner would be dispatched to Egia to request reinforcements. Geb would inspect the fort; then he and Osi would continue their circuit along the western crest of the First Terrace, down to the seaside strand, and back to Egia.

Osi was enthralled with the grandeur of the wide southern plateau. The uplands surrounding Ollo-detu consisted of lush, grassy plains dotted with animals hunting or grazing in the sun or lazing in the shade of scattered trees. Lions, tigers, hyenas, and dirktooth cats were the predators. Antelope, wildebeest, warthogs, and zebra were the prey. Isolated copses punctuated the grasslands where springs gushed from the plain. From these clusters of oil palm, mampato, and acacia came howls of monkeys and wails and cackles of wild birds. A large bowl-like depression, brimming with a rain-swollen lake, lay to the southwest.

Soon, they turned northward and trekked speedily toward the coast. The ever-changing seascape occasionally was revealed beyond the cliffs. By sunset, the trail settled in to a comfortable niche along the First Terrace.

The rolling terrain was like the plain surrounding Ollo-detu except where forested slopes encroached from ravines below. Tongues of forest thus spread across the plain. Eventually, low hills running parallel to the coast blocked the view of the lake, now well to the south. Geb and Osi stuck to the open plain, occasionally detouring half a day's journey to skirt around the broader ravines. A direct route would be out of the question due to predators that posed an even greater threat than Westerners, whose crude settlements they sometimes saw in the distance. As the moon rose and a chill set in on the fifth night, the welcome silhouette of the fort appeared. Geb whistled the proper signal, and from atop the fortress came a friendly reply. Tonight they would eat soldier's rations and sleep in cozy quarters.

* * *

At first light, Geb surveyed the skies. Joining him at the rampart, Osi understood his father's distress. White swirls of mist swept past the cliff. Silhouetted against a dark sky, storm clouds gathered over the Midland Sea, a cold sea chilled by melting ice on its far side.

"A fearsome sky, like never before," Geb muttered. It seemed the sky would burst, and the gods would cast their bolts at defenseless travelers. Surely, Geb thought, this must be a sign of change. "A fearsome sky, indeed," he said.

The travelers ate breakfast with the garrison's officers while soldiers harnessed and loaded their camels. Most of the provisions and both bedrolls were heaped on Osi's camel to equalize their respective loads. Father and son then mounted and left for Egia.

A thunderstorm rolled in as they reached the cliffs beside the Midland Sea. Thick oiled-leather cloaks protected all except hands and faces from the sting of hard-falling rain. Osi shivered as a rivulet of rainwater streamed down his neck and soaked his linen singlet. Maneuvering carefully from crag to crag, the two could barely discern path from cliff, and progress was slow. One slippery misstep could mean a plunge of 20 manheights or more.

Halfway down, they broke through the clouds and paused on a small promontory overlooking the roiling sea. Geb hitched his camel to a tree limb on the upslope side of the trail. Osi did the same and followed Geb to the edge. He welcomed the respite to discuss the events of previous days. He knew his father carried important orders, some of which he would not be able to discuss. So, he stuck to safe topics, attempting to lift his father's mood. Ketoh's misadventures led the list of suitable topics.

Geb's eyes flared suddenly as a flash of mottled brown zipped past on the trail. Then came another and another. Osi turned just in time to watch his camel fall, clinched in the iron jaws of five short-faced hyenas. As large as lions, their soundless stalk and lightning leap made them even more fearsome than those big cats. Soon they sniffed the carcass to confirm their kill. Snarling, they competed to rip flesh from its flank and gulp blood from its neck. Then the proud animals posed and postured, hind feet on the ground, forelegs on their victim. Victory complete, the hunters howled and snarled in celebration. Beneath their drooling, blood-dripping muzzles lay food and bedrolls Osi and his father needed for the journey home.

Father and son stood back to back, swords drawn. "Will they turn on us?" he whispered.

"They've chosen their prey and sated themselves for now . . . presumably," Geb said. The lead animal yelped to warn the humans away, and the pack held its position. After pausing to affirm their mastery, the hyenas resumed devouring the spoils. Geb and Osi inched slowly toward the low-hanging branch where Geb's camel was tied. The pack leader turned an icy stare, then growled but took no action. Stealthily, Geb loosened the reins and led his camel down the trail away from the site. A few hundred steps down the path, he paused to mount.

"What about our food and equipment?" Osi asked.

"A small sacrifice to the 'short-faces,'" Geb answered. "We'll survive. Here, take my hand." Fore and aft, they gripped the hump and resumed their cautious descent.

The terrain changed abruptly as they neared the plain. First there were outcrops covered completely with bushes and trees, then sizable ones with rock faces showing. "There, those caves," Osi said, "up along the scarp. Is that where the Hill People live?"

"Perhaps. The ones with water trickling from their mouths are likely prospects." Lush vegetation painted each stream bank with a rich coat of green tracing downslope. Numerous small streams crossed the path, causing Osi to suspect more caves higher up the bluff. Game animals, especially roe deer, could be seen from time to time darting across the trail or standing like statues farther away. Once, a lumbering cave bear crossed the trail only a few paces behind them. Startled, their lone camel stumbled under the weight of its two riders and the awkwardness of the narrow trail. Gravel rolled under its normally sure-footed, padded step. At first a slight limp, then a noticeable hobble, affected his gait. Finally, he dropped to his haunches and balked as they neared a particularly hazardous bend–more corner than curve–around a huge boulder dislodged from the cliff long ago.

Clucking anxiously, Geb prodded the animal. "Get up, get up, you lazy beast."

"Ha, ha!" rang out from the crest of the rock. Geb and Osi jerked in unison, scanning upward till their eyes met other eyes. Three Hill People pointed, slapping their thighs in hysterical laughter, tears streaming down their faces.

Hill People had no need for camels, and no respect for camel-hauled lowlanders who occasionally passed through their territory. In fact, human legs really did work best in their vertical world, and no self-respecting Hill Person would put himself at the mercy of a dumb animal. Ordinarily, they kept to the high slopes or deep forest and avoided interaction with passersby, but the scene before them was too funny to ignore. Just the sight of two men on one camel was enough to make them chuckle. The added effect of the balked animal and tousled riders was more than they could resist.

Fear gave way to humor as Geb and Osi envisioned how ridiculous they must appear from the onlookers' perspective. Laughter soon relaxed the tension that separated their worlds. The leader of the party climbed down from the perch, followed by his men. With outstretched hand, a universal gesture of peace, the two men approached. Unintelligible greetings were exchanged. Osi followed his father in a friendly handclasp with each of the Hill People.

The long black hair and dark features of the Hill People contrasted sharply with the trimmed hair and red-bronze tones of the Beloved People. Dressed in carefully stitched hides with exquisite beadwork, the men appeared more civilized than Osi expected. Even in the most favorable accounts in schools back home, the Hill People were depicted as crude, dirty tribesmen. Seeing the care with which garments were made and the artistry of their beadwork, Osi concluded these were not the mindless primitives of Egian lore.

"Come!" the leader suddenly said, in the language of Egia. "Come!" he repeated. Geb and Osi's eyes met in surprise. *Could this be a trap or was it an unprecedented invitation to socialize with the Hill People?* With more gestures, the man made it clear he wanted Geb and Osi to follow straight up the bluff. Pointing to one of his men and then to the camel, he indicated that a guard would be left behind. Osi handed over the reins, and a tribesman lashed the line to a tree branch overhanging the trail. The man then stood guard while the rest of the party moved upslope.

The natives passed with ease up the steep hillside, a grueling climb for the Egians. Along the way, the group passed rock faces marked with painted silhouettes of human hands, circles, coils, and snake-like symbols. Above them, Osi saw an overhanging cliff and later, beneath it, a shelf-like landing. The ledge stretched many paces in each direction, its flat floor furnished with chunks of fallen rock which served as seats and tables. At the eastern edge of the shelter was a tunnel, its mouth surrounded by columns and spires of rock that continued up the hillside. A tiny stream issued from the cliff face a few steps downslope from the end of the ledge.

On the well-worn surface of the ledge, men, women, and children moved about in feigned indifference to the approaching strangers. Only a few toddlers, not yet trained in community etiquette, turned to stare. At the back wall, a fire burned. Around it, wooden poles leaned in a circle, and sides of meat were drying. Strips of jerky in the making were suspended above the fire, reached by wisps of smoke but not by flame. Little smoke issued from the fire despite its size and intensity.

The chief motioned to his people, and the little settlement came to life. Geb and Osi were accorded a place of honor at his side on a throne-like boulder. "Eat," barked the chief. Chunks of venison, clusters of wild grapes, a mash of forest tubers, and a beer-like drink comprised a poor man's feast worthy of the finest tables in Egia. Osi ate heartily but didn't care for the beer, preferring to drink spring water instead. The chief smiled as Osi passed the bowl untouched a second time. Geb politely pretended to sip and passed it along as well. Pointing to the beer and venison, then to his own stomach, the chief proudly signaled that the beer was brewed from the fermented contents of a slain deer's stomach. Summoning his courage, Osi reached for the bowl and took a lengthy draught. The hosts laughed and beamed, and Osi knew he had endeared himself to them.

The meal ended when the chief stood. He beckoned to Geb and Osi, then walked, almost as if in a trance, toward the mouth of the cave. The shaman advanced to his rightful place beside his tribal leader. Tribesmen grabbed torches, and the entire community proceeded toward the tunnel. Adult males shuffled out of the crowd and lined up behind the chief and his guests. Bearing torches, two of the younger men led the column inside. First, they entered a wide corridor that served as common sleeping quarters. Next, the path led through a narrow crevice into a series of passageways and small chambers and finally to a large chamber, the center of which was cleared of all rockfalls and debris. The men took positions on the floor, cross-legged, facing the shaman, who now stood beside a small bier of lighterwood and kindling at the center of the circle. At his command, one of the volunteers ignited the fire and the chamber blazed with yellow light.

Geb and Osi marveled at the artwork, delicate and beautiful, painted on cavern walls. Roe deer, fallow deer, and ibex spread upward as far as firelight shone. The old Shaman chanted, solemnly invoking the powers of the earth from the darkest reaches of it.

"Tonight we beseech the Darkness for blessings on our hunt," Osi recited beneath his breath as he recalled the mocking chant of Egian boys pretending to be savages. *Perhaps,* he thought, *these are the very words the weathered Shaman is uttering as I sit in this real cave. The chant is much as I imagined it, but the cave is not. My childish dreams had smelly old carcasses lying about in a musty cave. No grand works of art in my fantasy. No. We thought the Hill People too primitive. Why, these paintings are more artful than half the murals in Egia.*

The shaman directed a phalanx of young hunters to stand beside the great mural. On his order, each man placed one hand on the cave wall. Another command, and each with his other hand dipped powder from a shallow bowl. More commands step by step, and each man chewed the red pigment, forcefully spewed the slurry across his hand, and then withdrew. An indelible, negative imprint was left for eternity. Stark witness to the healing power of the earth, it was a solemn vow that he would play his part in the age-old struggle for survival.

His chant completed, the shaman shifted into a litany showing the hoof pawing of the deer, the startled leap of the antelope, the rooting of the wild boar, the bleating of the mulia ibex. With each characterization, he pointed his staff toward the respective animal on the wall. He then engaged in a serious dialogue with the hunters and commanded each one to rehearse his part in the upcoming hunt. *This is no pagan ritual,* Osi thought. *This is a thoughtful, business-like discussion of tomorrow's hunt.* The ceremony ended when the altar fire waned. The chief and his men lined up and exited the cave. Out in the open, women spread fur-covered hides as bedding for their guests.

Well before daybreak, the cave community came to life with startling suddenness. Two strong young men with leather packs approached Osi and Geb. The chief pointed down slope. Osi was confused, then appreciative as he understood the chief's kind offer—packs and enough provisions for their journey home.

Reaching the rock overlook, they were pleased to see watchman and camel alive and well. They were surprised, however, to see the same guard just where they had left him the night before. Looking tired and forlorn, he appeared greatly relieved by the Egians return. After an exchange of mutually unintelligible expressions of thanks and goodbyes, the lowlanders headed down the last sloping trail to the valley below.

"An eventful passage," Geb remarked as they reached the outskirts of civilization. "We took an entire day to descend less than a hundred manheights."

"But what an adventure," Osi replied.

* * *

The Great River and Midland Sea created the Beloved Land. Its outer reaches, remnants of earlier deltas, had survived the erosion of intervening ages when sea level had dropped even lower. The change from slope to plain was abrupt. Toward the city, vegetation patterns changed gradually, first appearing lush and disordered like the land of the Hill People, then sparse and well organized near lowland settlements. Finally . . . a clearing beside the dusty trail, a diminutive mud brick hut, a fruit gatherer and his family homestead. Beside the hut was a lean-to with several goats and an ass to pull a rickety cart now parked beside the house.

"Hail, Beloved Brother!" Geb greeted his countryman.

"Hail!" said the farmer.

"May we pass your land?" Geb asked. He nodded courteously as he spoke.

"All may pass. Chosen Ones may pass with special blessing!"

"Then we shall pass with your blessing!"

"Have you no camels to ride?" inquired the man, nodding toward the lone camel in tow.

"We've lost two mounts to creatures of the forest. This poor beast is injured and unable to bear the two of us. Can you help us, friend?"

"I'll take you to a camel merchant. Men of your esteem should not be seen afoot."

"We're grateful for your kindness."

"Your packs are exquisite. Flawless workmanship. But, what strange design! Is there a new craftsman in the city?"

"They were given to us along the way," Geb said. A quick glance signaled to Osi that he intended to keep secret their encounter with the Hill People.

"Unusual design, very useful," the farmer muttered as he harnessed the ass.

Osi removed the packs and placed them on the cart. Geb led the camel to a shaded spot beside the lean-to and strapped its reins to a branch. "If we prod this poor creature any further, he'll never be able to work again. May we leave him in your care?" Understanding Geb's intention to make a gift of the animal, the farmer fell at his feet and gushed his appreciation.

"That's a fine animal. Once healed, he'll double my yield. How can I ever repay you?"

"No need. Your help today is payment enough," Geb said.

For the remainder of the afternoon, the three men rumbled along in the old cart, creaking with every bump. Eventually the trail merged with a road that ran parallel to the coast, occasionally allowing glimpses of the sea through trees on their left. For a short distance they passed through more orchard country. Later came vineyards, and at dusk they reached green pastures. Here small herds of sheep, goats, and cattle pastured on fertile grasslands that spread down to the seaside. Finally, they reached a livery stocked with camels, and Geb purchased two.

"We can't reach home tonight, son. There's a crude inn a short distance from here. We'll stay there for the night. Not much choice."

"You seem to dread the prospect, father. Have you stayed there before?" Osi asked.

"I've seen it in passing. It's an unruly place, and the accommodations aren't up to my standards, but we're not yet near the estates where we would be welcomed for the night. We'll need protection for our camels as well as for ourselves."

The inn was little more than a peasant's cottage. Raucous locals sat at tables outside the tavern drinking beer or wine in the twilight. A few ate olives or munched pieces of dry bread dipped in olive oil and wine vinegar. A portly matron shifted from table to table serving the revelers. Three pretty peasant girls moved among the tables flirting with the men. A livery boy led their camels to a pen while Osi and Geb made their way to an empty table. A waiter served food and beer to the famished pair and booked their lodging for the night.

Talk at surrounding tables was of two incredible reports that had just come in from the wilderness. First, a runner from Ollo-seti had told of a massacre at Ollo-detu in the Land of the Second Sunset. No survivors. Soon after, however, his tale was overshadowed by greater news from Ollo-detu itself. A traveler who visited the fort only a day after the massacre had reported a fantastic tale of a young boy who single-handedly killed a dirktooth cat. The patrons scoffed and refused to believe such a ridiculous story.

"However," said one, "if true, I would dearly love to behold the boy capable of such a deed."

"I'd love to hold him dearly, too!" joked one of the girls, igniting a round of laughter.

Geb winked at Osi. "Your exploits may soon outshine the Telling of the Tales."

"The Telling of the Tales?"

"You'll learn all about that in Berenicia."

"Berenicia? That's in Punt. Going there is just a dream."

"You may be surprised."

"Now, Father. What are the chances my class will be chosen? Hardly any Egian has gone to the Valley Sea since your own passage."

"I have reason to believe that will soon change."

"You know something, don't you, Father?"

Geb nodded. "But don't be mistaken, Osi. Getting there can be more nightmare than dream."

"I've weathered this trip well. Surely seasoned soldiers will guide us."

"Perhaps so. But there is no safety past the First Terrace. You've seen what it's like here. The trail to Berenicia is fraught with more danger than any man can imagine in a lifetime."

"Surely it can't be worse than what we've encountered."

"Son, here you find names like 'Ollo-detu' and 'Lion Rock.' There you will find 'Hell's End' and 'Death's Shadow.'"

CHAPTER 5

Search Log 9: The Unknown Zone

Ed Field's back was barely visible behind a rack of outdated computer tapes that served as a room divider. He stared at the workstation screen as Jared came into the office, moved some papers, and took a seat. At his next stopping place, Ed turned around.

The usual, "What's up, Jer?"

"Young Ed. We may have something concrete to sink our teeth into."

"Sounds painful, but we all have to suffer for our science."

"First, I cataloged what I know about ancient settlements. Then, I tried to imagine how their three-dimensional shape would translate into bathymetric contours. Here's how it goes. A small Middle Eastern city like Jericho shows up as a broad, circular mound a few yards high. An urban site occupied for thousands of years rises considerably higher as the city is repeatedly rebuilt on its own debris. Mounds like that are called 'tels,' and hundreds are known throughout the Middle East. This shows what we need to look for in the sea floor profiles. A tel might show up with high-resolution bathymetry but not with the coarse data available for most of the World Ocean. Most early cities were sited on hills, usually with defensible slopes leading up to them. A submerged hill of that type could be detected with fairly coarse data, but there's no way to distinguish civilized hills from plain old uncivilized seamounts. But . . . if we find a seamount of that description with something distinctive on top, then we might zero in on some candidates."

Ed thought for a minute, imagining the contours. "Okay, so a hill would appear as a series of nested circles, or almost circles, kind of spread out at the center and bunched at the slope. Hill or seamount, topographic map or hydrographic chart, land or water, it's all the same. Now, what might indicate that a town was there?"

"My brother suggested a fantastic possibility. He reasons pyramids may go back that far. The step form found in the Middle East is called a ziggurat. They're large blocky structures, usually built at the top of a town hill. That should easily distinguish between a tel and a seamount."

"Yes, but the largest pyramids we know about are way too small to show up in the digital data. If the data were fine enough, you'd see a small spike in the middle of all those nested circles. You need sea floor maps with more detail."

Jared eyed the mounds of maps and data that cluttered Ed's office, stacked with a certain topographic quality of their own. "I checked the map section of our Central Research Library. The best hydrographic charts here are 1 to 1,000,000 scale. They only show bottom contours every few hundred feet."

"A lot of big ships would bump into a lot of small islands if they didn't have better charts than that," Ed said in his practical way.

Returning to his office, Jared automatically stopped to refill his favorite coffee cup–the colorful one Rick had brought him from New Orleans. Today, it held 100% Colombian, but its bright French Market theme reminded him of the savory French roast with chicory that had come along with it. Back at his desk, he stared at the mug and planned his assault on the maze of confusion that usually surrounds geographic information of any kind. He mulled his options before starting the calls. Question: If NOAA is responsible for charting the sea floor in U.S. coastal waters, who's responsible in foreign waters? It would be logical for the same agency to handle the same topic all over the world . . . probably too logical. Of course, the "powers-that-be" would also consider the purpose of the information. Domestic charts are mostly intended to improve commerce, so they fit logically under NOAA, part of the Department of Commerce. Foreign maps, on the other hand, are primarily for military planning and usually fall under the Department of Defense. The two communities are so different they can't even agree on what to call a piece of paper with lines drawn on it. The seafarers–NOAA and the Navy–call them charts, but just about everybody else calls them maps. In either case, the people who make them are called cartographers and the field itself is called cartography after the "charts" of early seafarers.

After a minute or two, Caisson was as uncertain as when he had begun. Impatient, he dialed the Navy's Oceanographic Office. He knew the first stop is never the right one, but this was as good as any place to start. Jimmy Dione, a civilian employee, quickly confirmed Jared's suspicion. "No, I'm afraid our office has nothing more detailed than NOAA's global E-TOPO 5 database," he said.

"I don't necessarily need the whole world. I know the United States and most European countries have precise hydrographic charts. What's the best source for countries in the Tropics?"

"Paper charts or digital data?" Dione asked.

"I'd prefer digital, but I'll take anything with good detail."

"How detailed?"

"I'd prefer a horizontal resolution of 100 feet or finer, but I know that's unrealistic. Again, I'll take whatever I can get, but I hope for something better than the five-mile resolution of E-TOPO 5."

Dione paused for a moment and said, "Only a few tracks exist, mostly on approaches to harbors. Even then, many of those databases are classified according to agreements with foreign governments."

"I need to search large stretches of open, shallow water. Will it help if I explain why I need it?"

"Maybe."

Jared embarked on a cover story that would explain his interest without revealing the full story and without lying. "Everybody's concerned about global change, especially global warming and sea level rise. The science policy community has decided the most important zone on earth is tropical rain forest because of its effect on the atmosphere. I've suggested to my sponsors that an even more revealing zone may be the one where sea level rise has already occurred over the last 10,000 years or more. Do you realize that the first 400 feet of the continental shelf was dry land less than 20,000 years ago?"

"Wow, that much," Dione replied, "but Defense agencies won't have that sort of data."

Jared was surprised. "Why's that?"

"We've been playing cat-and-mouse with the Russians for 45 years, but the hunt for Red October was a Blue Ocean war. Anything above 650-foot depth has been out of bounds because those big boys can't maneuver in tight spaces. Plus, there's a technical reason. If you're like most people, you'll be surprised to know it's easier to measure deep water than shallow water."

"How so?"

"With sonar, we're limited to a 45-degree angle of incidence. That means the swath measured beneath a research vessel can't be wider than twice the height from the vessel to the sea floor. In other words, in water one mile deep, we can scan a swath two miles wide and cover a big chunk of ocean pretty quick. In water 100 feet deep, each pass covers only 200 horizontal feet, and it takes forever to scan even a small part of a small sea. Roughly, it costs about 100 times as much to survey a given area in 100 meters of water as it does in the deepest ocean."

"Well, Mr. Dione, you've opened my eyes. I'll keep looking, but at least I know the limitations. Can you name someone who may know about foreign waters?"

"Yes, just a minute." Dione searched his files. "Try Lieutenant Commander Loreen Kelsey in Denver. Here's her number. She's assigned to the folks who keep the data. You might also check with Matt Lockridge at the National Geophysical Data Center. NGDC's data are mostly domestic—40,000,000 coastal soundings in the U.S—but Lockridge is president of the International Hydrographic Organization; he can help if anybody can."

After several attempts, Jared finally connected with LCDR Kelsey. She was helpful but not as familiar with the data as he had hoped. "Sir, what you need is GEODAS. That's a database available on CD ROM that tells where the track lines are for all the existing bathymetric data in the world. It sells for $200. I'll send you the order forms. We also have digital contour data from the General Bathymetric Charts of the Oceans, but the source charts are at 1:10,000,000 , no more precise than E-TOPO 5. You might also want to check with the British Oceanographic Data Center. Let me see. Yes, here's a contact. Pauline Weatherby." She gave a number in England and started to sign off.

"Before you go, may I ask if you know anything about hardcopy hydrographic charts for foreign seas. I'm not sure whether to check NOAA or the Defense Mapping Agency."

"I don't know much about the charts themselves, but I believe they're held by NOAA's office in Riverdale, Maryland. Here's the number. Good day, sir." The conversation would have been described as curt, almost rude, if she had been a civilian. Considering her rank and service, however, Jared judged it "smartly done."

Jared tried for two days without finding Lockridge. He was able to reach NOAA Riverdale, but the news there was as confusing as the rest. "The charts you want are made by the Defense Mapping Agency alright. We used to keep them here along with our own domestic charts, but they've relocated to DMA's office at the Federal Center in Denver. Give me a second and I'll come up with a name and number. Here it is. Robin Warntz."

Warntz was willing to help, but she wasn't the right contact. "You'll need to speak with Joe Gillette at the U.S. Geological Survey's Distribution Center here in Denver. His number is . . ."

Caisson carried his frustration to the next call. The number was for the main desk of the big distribution center. "I'm sorry, sir," the receptionist said, "there is no such person working here."

"Are you certain? I was given this number by someone who knows him well."

"Yes, sir. I have a list and his name isn't on it. Perhaps if you....no, that wouldn't work. Wait just a moment...let me check. No, there's no Gillette on staff here."

"Well, perhaps someone else could help me." He described his target data.

"Let's try this number." She rang.

"Mr. Gillette's office. How may I help you?" answered the secretary.

"Mr. Gillette, please."

"I'm sorry, sir. He's in the warehouse."

"I'd like to leave a message."

"I'm sorry, sir. I can't take messages. Can you please call back?" Jared patiently made four more calls.

"Well, yes," the secretary finally admitted, "Mr. Gillette's job does keep him in the warehouse most of the time."

* * *

That night, Jared called Rick to report his meager progress and one major finding. "Rick," he said, "the sea floor we're interested in is the least known zone on the planet. In surveillance terms, it's the darkest place on earth. Divers routinely visit down to 160 feet, and military services cover everything below 650, but the middle zone falls between the cracks. With a glacial maximum depth of 400 feet, we've got a crucial band of Ice-Age land 240 feet thick that is less known than the surface of Venus. This reinforces my suspicion that even some fairly obvious evidence of human settlement might have been missed, especially since no one has really been looking for it there."

"So it's up to us," Rick said with a heavy sigh.

Search Log 10: The Pyramids of Kush

"What do you have?" Ed asked Jared, after a week's search.

"I've only been able to resolve a few questions, and I've received only two pieces of useful information."

"Ever hear from the data warehouse guy?"

"No. But his secretary sent me an index of all the DMA hydrographic charts. That and an order form for GEODAS from LCDR Kelsey are all I have in hand. I still haven't seen any actual data, and I still don't know how much detail to expect in the charts or digital databases."

"So we really haven't learned a thing."

"I've always said: Total confusion is SOP for geographic information. It's nothing like the orderly image data providers would have you believe. In government, industry, or academia only a few data sets are well documented, much less indexed and available. Only a few can be ordered as if from a catalog. Most require custom searches and personal requests to their proprietors. Exploring data today is about as frustrating as exploring the real world used to be."

"So where do you go from here?" Ed asked.

"I'll try a different tack. Up to now, I've focused on data providers who sell comprehensive high-quality data sets. Now I'll settle for viewing data anywhere I can find it, then evaluate the quality and decide whether it's worth ordering. I spent the summer of '66 digging through the Library of Congress on a research internship—came to know their Map Division well. I'll check out their hydrographic coverage. I gave them a call this morning, and they may have what I need. They say they have the best collection of DMA and British Admiralty charts in Washington. I'll soon find out; Seagate is scheduled to meet there before the end of the month."

* * *

The Seagate meeting tentatively scheduled for Washington in late July was finally set for August 5. Out-of-towners would fly in on Wednesday evening. Proceedings could begin early Thursday morning, and Jared would leave for a field trip on Saturday morning. The first day's meeting was scheduled to finish at noon. As usual, it didn't end on time. Afterward, there were informal conversations as well, so Jared felt fortunate to leave at 2:35 p.m. He'd lost his only shot at studying sea floor maps, since budget cuts had slashed evening hours at the Library of Congress. He barely had time to visit his second choice, the National Geographic Society, which was closer.

Jared quickly left the building and hailed a cab. "National Geographic on 17th," he said. The driver turned a fast U on E Street, and six minutes later Caisson hopped out in front of Explorer's Hall.

Entering the white marble building, he was uncertain which lead to pursue first. He suspected the Red Sea was the most promising region, but which topic? Historical accounts of early peoples of Egypt and Sudan would be extremely helpful; explanations of reef biology would be helpful; Rick's suggestion about pyramids intrigued him along with related topics like ziggurats and villages. What he needed most, however, was the three-dimensional form of coral reefs. Ironically, a straightforward eye-witness description of a reef was, he discovered, most difficult to find. Written descriptions were useless because divers typically focus on fine details. Photographs were his only hope, and National Geographic would have them if anyone did.

Caisson was eager to start the search, but, for a few minutes, vanity got the best of him. The first sight greeting him in the grand hall was a huge display announcing a special exhibit on Chesapeake Bay. Months before, National Geographic had requested Seagate data. He had helped compile and proof the map. Anxious to see the final result, he rushed through the exhibit to find a copy on display. To his dismay, the magazine article, so obviously pertinent to the topic, was not included in the display. *How bizarre,* he thought. *Right hand must not know what the left hand is doing.*

The exhibit rounded Explorer's Hall and ended at the NGS Bookstore only a few paces from the entrance *cum* exit. Even this commercial nook evoked the image of faraway places. The impression came partly from the English bookstore facade and wood-grained interior—quiet and a bit too dark for easy reading—still more from the beasts and other wonders staring from every shelf. Animals, hills, canyons, lakes, and seas! That's what most people think geography is, and the imprimatur of the world's most famous geographical society, "proved" them right. Most geographers objected to this simplistic view of their often highly technical discipline, some so strongly they refused to join the Society. Of the professional geographers who were members, only a handful considered the organization respectable enough to list on their professional resumes.

Caisson, as much as anyone else, disliked geography's shallow image, but still he appreciated the Society's contribution. Even the magazine's shallowest articles offered a sense of place found nowhere else. Since college, he had listed the Society on his professional vita, in defiant tribute to the service they performed. Now, as in so many times past, he would look first to NGS before reading more specialized journals.

How can I stick to my mission with all these temptations? he asked himself. Books on volcanism, tropical rainforests, and exotic cultures caught his eye and captured his imagination. Finally, *Splendors of the Past* came into view. It was a big coffee-table book with huge photographs and plenty of text. A few quick passages suggested serious history, hidden in a popular style aimed at a broad audience. The subtitle said, "Lost Cities of the Ancient World," but the theme actually covered mysterious ancient civilizations, those known to have existed but still "lost" because so little is known about them. The stony Hittite capital of Asia Minor, the towering Temples of Angkor, and the charred remains of Pompeii crossed its pages in pageants of color and speculation. Photographs showed what is known; drawings showed what might have been. Sumer, Kush, and Khmer marched through time like vast armies glimpsed through shadowed forests. What interested Jared most, however, were maps showing where these strangers lived and how they organized themselves into working cities, nations, and regions.

He found no books specifically on the Red Sea and no books on coral reefs, at least none that focused on what he needed. That left the magazine itself as his final hope. He approached the desk and paid $19.95 for *Splendors of the Past*, cheap for a coffee-table book and a real bargain if it met his personal criterion of one good piece of information worth remembering a year later.

"I need to search your collection," he told the clerk. "How do I go about that?"

"Oh, that's easy," she replied, "Just use the index at the end of the counter. If you need any of the old issues, we can sell them to you right here."

"Do you have all past issues?"

"Not every one of them, but enough to fill most requests."

"Red Sea." The name appeared in bold font followed by seven citations. He recorded them in abbreviated form, "Nov 1987 July 1983 Nov 1978 Sept 1975 Nov 1974 Nov 1972 Apr 1964." He was pretty sure he had them all at home. Only the '64 issue gave him some concern. If not, he could always go to a library. He would keep the clerk's offer in mind but would pass on it for the time being.

* * *

Thirty minutes later, a tired Jared Caisson boarded an escalator for the lofty climb from the Red Line subway up to Q Street. He stood to the right, in proper fashion, as others rushed past him toward the semicircle of light at the top. With no reason to hurry, he gazed upward, fascinated yet again with the optical illusion of the Metro escalators. Years ago, he had discovered that focusing directly on the apex of the incline, about where the moving handrail disappears from view, causes the entire escalator to appear vertical, truly vertical. The convincing illusion reminded him of Spiderman climbing a skyscraper, except that ordinary people in everyday clothes glided up and down with ease. Unlike the pajama-clad hero, these citizens walked upright. The illusion was easy to summon in deep stations like Rosslyn and Dupont Circle, and it could be conjured with effort on moderately deep ones, as well. He had shared it with friends and fellow travelers. Many were able to experience it; others were not. Somewhere along the way, he questioned whether the pleasure that came to those who experienced the illusion was worth the occasional mocking by those who couldn't make it happen. Ultimately, he decided it was.

Hot evening air added to the burden of luggage as the weary traveler trudged up Connecticut Avenue. Today had been rewarding, but tomorrow's prospects seemed bleak. He winced at the thought of spending a second day in meetings and leaving D.C. without seeing any sea floor maps. His spirits rose only slightly as he entered the cool lobby of the Pullman Highland.

After his usual nightly regimen of CNN, Jared propped up in bed with the oversize *Splendors of the Past* and skipped to the map of the Red Sea coast. He stared at it for a moment and began reading. Scanning the index, his eye fell to the chapter on the Kingdom of Kush, but he failed to connect Kush with his own memory of biblical "Kushites," a vague recollection from Sunday School classes long ago. Reading on, he learned that Kushites were also called Nubians, whom he remembered well from art and history. What boy hadn't fantasized about Nubian maidens due to confusion between "Nubian" and "nubile"? Still, if asked before tonight, he would have guessed Kushites lived east of Israel, and Nubians lived south of Sudan. He was surprised to learn they were the same mysterious, dark-skinned people.

The text was fascinating, but the photographs were more revealing. There in vivid detail was an array of nearly 20 pyramids in a style he had never seen before. The caption explained that most of the world's pyramids are in Sudan, not Egypt, despite what most people might assume. The cemeteries of Meroë, just 500 miles southwest of Foul Bay, in fact, contain the largest single collection of pyramids in the world. Too good to be true, he thought, for that might imply a common heritage for Egyptians and Sudanese. Architecturally, Sudanese pyramids are smaller and steeper than Egyptian pyramids and never quite reach a point at the top. Their most distinctive feature is an offertory chapel that forms a portico extending from the face, always on the eastern side of the pyramid. From the front, it appears flat like a wall, but from the side it looks like a column connected by a beam to the sloping wall of the pyramid.

Could this be the style of pyramid that sits on the floor of Foul Bay? Jared asked himself. Even more significantly, did Egyptians and Nubians share a common heritage? Were they perhaps separate fragments of a single ancient culture uprooted by rising sea levels? Were Egyptians the nobility who claimed the prime land of the Nile valley following the Chaos, relegating their common cousins to shabby lands upriver? Perhaps, Jared thought. I surely wouldn't rule it out.

The text explained that Sudanese pyramids came later and were crude copies of the imposing structures in Egypt. Under normal circumstances one would expect a crude form to precede a refined form, but archaeological dating placed these buildings several centuries after the Great Pyramid of Cheops. Here Caisson took special interest. Timing would be crucial, so he read carefully to learn how the dating had been done. Ah! In the early part of this century, an astute American archaeologist assumed that each king would place his tomb on the most imminent site and the next king would follow on a lower site. Roughly speaking, elevation then became a surrogate for time, and the chronology of kings became a timeline for the history of the nation and its architecture.

"Bullshit!" Caisson mumbled in the quiet of his hotel room. *Those lazy rapscallions dreamed up this silly rule of thumb because it's easy. Now they've fooled everybody, including themselves, into thinking it's fact.* What if, for example, a really powerful king decided to tear down or build over an earlier pyramid in order to usurp a favored site? What if kings had individual tastes in siting? Any number of factors might determine a different order of construction. Conventional wisdom said the theory must have been right because it had not been disproved in seventy years. From the sound of it, he suspected there was too little information to confirm or deny.

Regardless when Sudanese pyramids were built, the Nubian people existed before Egyptian pyramids appear in the archaeological record. According to Egyptian records, warfare was underway between the Pharaoh and his southern neighbor as early as 4900 BP and went on for nearly 3000 years. After 3550 BP, Kush was occupied by Egypt. Yet strangely, Sudanese soldiers were loyal to the Egyptian Pharaoh, and their nobles were pacified, not by military force but by two Egyptian promises: One was a commitment to provide the children of Nubian nobility an Egyptian education, and the other was a plan of temple construction that would provide better Nubian access to the state religion of Egypt. Finally, about 3000 BP, Kush regained its independence, and three centuries later, the tables were turned as Kush conquered Egypt. Oddly enough, when the Nubian King Kashta began his campaign to conquer Egypt, he said his purpose was to restore Egypt to its former glory. *Egypt? Not Nubia?*

None of this made sense if Egyptians and Nubians truly were separate cultures. Nations that fight each other for thousands of years don't suddenly capitulate out of respect for the superiority of their foe. In recent history, that would be like China submitting to Russia in exchange for a good Russian education and better access to Marx and Lenin. Most societies view themselves as superior and resist assimilation by another culture, even if it really is superior. To Caisson, the story of Kush and Egypt sounded more like class warfare with the poorer class being mollified by a grant of envied privileges. He was especially intrigued that Kush would care about restoring Egypt to its former glory. Caisson could more easily imagine a rebellious working class leader saying to his superiors, "Now, see what a fine mess you've made of things," then seizing the reins to make things right. Perhaps the usurpers had taken over for a few decades and then, predictably, retreated home in failure.

He reached for the phone to share his findings with Rick. Then he checked himself. *Rick won't like these cultural arguments,* he thought. *He may not reject them outright, but he doesn't embrace them either. We've had these discussions before. It's not worth the fuss.*

On and on he read, fighting to keep his eyelids open until, finally, he could no longer resist. It seemed only minutes later that the phone rang and a pleasant voice wished him good morning. "Good morning," he replied on the off chance that it was a human being. It wasn't, and another day began with all the comfort a machine could provide. After cradling the phone, he noticed the blinking red message light. He called the front desk. It came from Wade Onover, manager of Seagate. "Friday afternoon session canceled."

Search Log 11: Places of Ascension

Fatefully, Friday morning's session ended precisely at 12:00 o'clock. Jared gathered his belongings, said a few quick goodbyes, and headed for the Library of Congress. Inside the Madison Building's big glass doors, he passed through the congested lobby, acknowledged the guard, and headed inside. One floor below, the elevator deposited him beside a huge revolving globe in front of the Geography and Map Division.

Everything went well except for the awkwardness of carrying his briefcase and heavy suit bag through several sets of doors. Finally, scores of map cabinets loomed beyond a counter with waist-high swinging door. The flimsy gate creaked as he charged through. Then, "Pardon me," a whispery voice said, "please sign the register." Never in previous visits had there been such a requirement, but the imposition was no surprise. All of Washington was more and more security conscious nowadays. Plus, even low-risk offices required signatures to prove they had customers, purely to justify their funding. Jared dropped his load, took out his glasses, and scanned the register. He complied without complaint even though the form was long, and he was anxious to get underway.

Form completed, he charged through the gate again. "Pardon me," the young clerk said again. "Bags are not permitted inside the work area."

Jared was shocked. Every office in Washington was accustomed to an army of visitors working on the run with bags in hand, particularly on the first and last day of each visit. Most offices were accommodating, though some insisted on examining bags on departure.

"Where can I leave it?" he asked.

The courteous but disinterested young man handed him a numbered key. "There are lockers behind you, sir."

Caisson's mood shifted from indignation to embarrassment as he turned and saw two solid walls of lockers. He shoved the bag inside, closed the metal door, then tried every possible way to insert the key and close the latch. Nothing worked. So, back to the desk for a different locker and key. Placing the bag in its new home, he inserted the key and turned the latch with a sigh of relief.

Again he headed through the gate, and again the clerk said, "Pardon me, sir, bags are not permitted inside the work area."

"This isn't luggage. This is my briefcase."

"I am sorry, sir. Briefcases are not allowed inside the work area."

Caisson was stunned. In Washington briefcases were body appendages. Never in his entire career had he seen anyone treat them otherwise. This time, he had carefully packed the briefcase with ruler, calculator, magnifying glass, and other necessities to ensure efficient use of the precious little time available. He couldn't afford to run back and forth fetching materials from the locker, but neither could he afford the time to argue. Seething with growing frustration, he placed the briefcase on the counter and carefully inventoried its contents. When he was reasonably sure he had every necessity, he tossed the briefcase into the locker and headed for the work area. He listened for the still, small voice, but heard not a peep as the gate swung shut behind him.

His quest was nothing less than to discover the oldest cities on earth. His heart told him to start with the Mediterranean. *That's where the action is.* His head said, *No, start with Southeast Asia. That's where it all began.* First, he would follow his head.

The hydrographic charts were not up front. He would have to depend on library staff to retrieve them from the stacks. He wasn't certain which would serve better, British Admiralty Charts or DMA Hydrographic Charts. He would start with DMA purely because he was already familiar with the index booklets and maps sent by the agency following his telephone call. Indexes would greatly accelerate the work and enable him to focus directly on places with greatest potential. He wrote six numbers and handed the chit to a staff assistant. Not till then did he allow himself to be consumed with the anticipation befitting such an enterprise. He tried to stay calm, telling himself the charts might contain little of interest or perhaps nothing at all. Yet his instincts told him something was there, and he was about to find it.

Most of the Southeast Asian DMA sheets were at 1:500,000 scale with a contour interval of 50 meters. That would show landforms, not buildings. But there were lots of individual soundings between contours, as well. They might indicate high points just beneath the surface. Scattered symbols also contained numbers that looked like depths, but there was no legend to explain them.

Caisson's mind took flight. *Scheherazade must have been a geographer,* he thought. *Only she and her boy Aladdin and every blessed geographer who ever lived can turn a flat map into a magic carpet. Fly over the whole earth. Zoom in. Zoom out. See every land as if you were there. Hover. Spot some fetching place. Dive. Climb its mountains. Swim its oceans. Raft its rivers. Hear its sounds. Smell its scents. Reject. Rise up. Zip to the next spot. Start over again.*

His *flight* over the Straits of Sunda passed quickly in spite of its vast territory between Southeast Asia and Borneo. *Move on, folks,* he imagined himself barking to Scheherazade and the crowd. *Nothing to see here. Move on.* Most charts showed shallow seas with hardly any noticeable features. Whole sections were easily dismissed with a single, rapid scan. *No, wait. What's that over there?* A couple of shoals and rocks appeared on Chart #93280, but they were in shallow water and appeared to be natural. *But, look there!* Only one map was well endowed with candidate sites. Chart #93020, covering a patch of the China Sea off the coast of Vietnam, was sharply divided by a break from shallow to deep water at the 100-meter contour. *There, right below us, those promontories look just like a seacoast town perched on the edge of an old coastline.* Some reached the surface, some lay just beneath it, others peaked at 30 to 40 meters down. He *swooped down* for a closer look. More than 20 sites, including Îles Catwick, were regularly spaced about four miles apart. He *rose* again. Northward near the present-day Mekong Delta lay numerous sites in a similar pattern. *Doesn't look natural to me.* The height of some features approached 60 meters. *Jeez, that's' taller than most Middle Eastern ziggurats and all but the tallest Egyptian pyramids.*

Ranging farther south, he spotted more candidates on Vanguard Bank and Prince Consort Bank where numerous peaks rose to within 26 meters of the surface from a bottom of uncertain depth but in all cases less than 200 meters deep. *Looks promising, Sher, don't you think?*

Next he *flew* over the Persian Gulf. *Your old stomping ground, Sherry Baby, and prospects are improving all around. Almost the entire gulf is shallow enough to have been exposed at glacial maximum. Still, shoals are scarce.* On Chart #62530 at 26°55' N, 51°00' E, two peaks tipped the surface from a bottom of 45 to 50 meters. *Look down there, Aladdin, my lad. Those peaks must have been a coastal promontory. That Sambarún Bank is even more promising. The little rise on top precisely matches the ziggurat profile.* And it did, with two tiny peaks at ten meters on a rocky platform at 22 meters atop a broad base at 50 meters surrounded by general depths of 60 to 84 meters. Thirty-six miles farther south a similar feature matched, too. *That's a tel with ziggurat on top, if I've ever seen one . . . which I haven't . . . unfortunately . . . of course.*

Not far away was a cluster of possible sites in shallow water. In the middle was an array of shoals spaced at regular intervals of 20 to 44 miles. *Just like the arrangements of modern-day cities on a plain,* he mused. *Mental note. Add new item to the list on my wall: Check sea floor features against Central Place Theory.* Typically, geometric patterns look about the same for large cities or small villages, but distances vary according to settlement size and mode of transportation. Usually, in societies that travel on foot, the distance between market centers is about an hour's walk. *The interval here, however, implies about a full day's travel on foot. Of course, low-order markets usually don't have buildings as ostentatious as the ziggurats implied here,* he thought, *and key ceremonial centers are likely to be spaced at a full day's walk–20 miles or so.*

Caisson felt satisfied as he finished the last Persian Gulf chart. It was gratifying to know that some of the predicted patterns really did exist. As statisticians might say in their backhand way, "the hypothesis could not be rejected" on the basis of what the maps had shown. Settlements appeared to be sparser in the east, denser toward the west. Perhaps more significant, the information suggested an age gradient from east to west as well, with deeper, and therefore older, settlements in the east.

What then may lie even farther west? Later? More advanced? He turned anxiously to the Mediterranean and Red Sea. *First, I've got to find the symbol for "sec" or "secs."* The book on marine archaeology mentioned jagged peaks, called secs, in certain parts of the eastern Mediterranean, often rising directly from a level sandy bottom to within a few feet of the surface. The author touted them as hazards to shipping, therefore good places to search for shipwrecks and treasure. Caisson was interested for a different reason. The description, as far as it went, might well fit a pyramid or temple surrounded by open ground. In glossaries and map legends, however, he hadn't found the word.

Jared had found the same term on U.S. hydrographic charts, but there it always had a number before it and a period after, as in "20 sec." Friends at NOAA explained that was the frequency of revolution, in seconds, of lighthouses on land or light buoys at sea. *That's so each light can be identified, and that helps with navigation. Can it mean the same thing here,* he wondered, *only nobody cares how fast the light turns. Just a warning? No good for navigation? Or,* he reasoned, *since light buoys often are placed over shoals and other hazards, perhaps the abbreviation might have evolved into a nickname for the pinnacles themselves. Or, maybe it had a different meaning entirely and a different origin.*

Map series usually come with legends in separate booklets, and usually the booklets get lost. *Surely the Library of Congress doesn't lose them like I do at home,* Caisson mused. He approached an assistant, "May I have the legend for the DMA Hydrographic Chart Series?" He was relieved when she immediately reached under the counter and handed one over. "Thank you," he said politely. *Yes, he thought, my culture drives me just as theirs did them, way back when.*

Surely "sec" will appear in the legend. He searched diligently. *Not here,* he concluded. Later, however, turning to a separate legend of local place name terminology, he found something suspiciously similar. The word "secca" was defined as an Arabic term for shoals. *That must be the answer! I'm not interested in all shoals, of course, just the ones that rise abruptly from depths. Secca can mean any shallow area regardless of surrounding depth, so it may be only a vague indicator.*

Scanning the legend, Caisson soon found "Rocks awash" routinely noted because of their danger to shipping. *First time I've seen the term. The maps I've been using were too coarse for such small features. These DMA charts, however, are intended for navigation, and they take their hazards seriously.* The symbols for rocks awash usually were surrounded by depth soundings. Thus, he could distinguish abrupt peaks from other shallows. *This will be crucial for locating inundated pyramids.* He ordered a selection of maps.

Sailing high above the central and eastern Mediterranean, Caisson spied little worth recording. *The Nile Delta drops off to impossible depths much too quickly. It couldn't have been a sizable platform for human settlement.* Within a seaward arc no more than 35 miles from the delta's northern tip, the bottom reached 200 meters, well below sea level at glacial maximum. Near Alexandria, the drop was even more precipitous, reaching 200 meters within ten miles. Aside from numerous wrecks and a vaguely labeled obstruction, the chart showed uniform contours and hardly any rocks awash. Any pyramids that might have been present likely would have been covered by new sediments, which account for the smooth contours today.

After an hour or so of searching the island-dense Aegean Sea, the shallow Adriatic Sea, and the deep Mediterranean itself, he found only one site of possible interest. Near the shore of Turkey, a cluster of peaks rose to within 16 to 120 meters of the surface from a bottom of 360 to 600 meters. He duly jotted them in his notebook. *But, these surrounding bottoms are so far beneath the surface, even at glacial maximum, I doubt the features themselves can be of human origin.*

"Red Sea, please." He handed over a new list of chart numbers.

Several minutes later, the assistant returned and graciously handed over six large map sheets. Caisson felt a brief shiver of excitement as he pulled the first sheet from its folder and stared at the southern end of the Valley Sea. *Nothing strikes me at first. How about you, fellow travelers,* he said to the imaginary throng of geographers onboard his flying fabric. First, he would have to make sure he understood the scale, contour interval, and legend. He settled down with Chart #62100 and began scanning carefully for key bathymetric contours, rocks awash, and telltale depth soundings. He stopped searching just long enough to confirm that the depths indeed were in meters, then resumed, oblivious to the genteel hustle and bustle of the room.

Suspicious sites appeared quickly, but convincing ones would not come easily. He recorded each location. Parkin Rock peaked within three meters of the surface in 38 to 44 meters depth. Conspicuously labeled, it would be easy to find again. At 12°25' N, 42°45' E, a circular feature reached 74 meters in 142 meters depth and another reached 82 meters in 177 meters depth. Both were about 1,000 meters across and marked "coral." *Nope, their bases are too deep for pyramids.*

Caisson finished scanning the first map and pulled Chart #62290. Soon his eye fell on Abu-el-Cosu, an oblong feature submerged at 3 to 20 meters in a general depth of 27 to 73 meters. Just east of it lay two rocks awash and a patch of exposed coral. In his notes, Jared also highlighted a patch of coral and two rocks awash at 18°40' N, 38°20' E. *That site looks promising.* Three shallow features stood in 35 to 84 meters depth on a triangular point. *That point clearly was a promontory, now submerged.* It would have overlooked the sea next to a precipitous drop of 322 meters. *Say now, that would have been a dramatic site for a ceremonial pyramid or temple . . . defensible site for a military post . . . or simply a good spot for a lookout tower scanning the coast.*

He had expected rocky sites to be scarce, and in the south they were, but everything changed as he *flew* farther north. Where coarser maps had shown open water, these maps showed scores of submerged rocks, the first at 20° N, 37° E, about two-thirds of the way up the western coast. *Wow!* The pattern extended northward onto the next sheet, then narrowed and grew sparse again. *Finally, the mother lode.* His notes read, "Chart #62230. Foul Bay (Inset Map). Rocks all over. Some regular geometric patterns in 30 to 64 meters of water." *Dense. Impressive. No doubt why sailors dubbed it "foul" for shipping. Is there any other patch of sea on earth,* he wondered, *so plagued with hazards lurking just beneath the surface?*

"Whoa! That's got to be it!" he gasped, almost loud enough to disturb nearby patrons. *My God, there's a whole city down there, encased in coral!*

The possibility was staggering. Inconceivable at first, the revelation gradually came clear. *If all those rocks awash hide ancient structures, the city in Foul Bay was almost as big as Los Angeles today.* He measured to scale. *70 kilometers long! 30 kilometers wide! Far greater than anything Rick and I imagined! Even in our wildest dreams a city the size of tiny, ancient Jericho would have seemed extravagant.* Jared could hardly contain his excitement as he stared at the massive array of symbols. *He strolled its streets, visualizing the texture, color, and thickness of the shroud covering every building on his way downtown. He spotted an open plaza at the end of the boulevard and, stepping inside, found a massive, triangular pyramid encased in living coral. See, Strabo, look here. This place was ancient even in your day. Did anyone talk about it anymore? Hank, will ya' look at that,* he said to the Navigator. *Check out these piers, half a mile long, poking into the harbor like a triple trident.*

Regaining control, he cleared his mind and disciplined himself to think deliberately, cautiously, skeptically about the startling information lying before him on the table. He conceived several arguments, some positive, some negative. *Some of those formations are straight lines like buildings spaced along a boulevard. Many run to the sea like streets in beach towns everywhere. Others run parallel to the coast as might a coastal highway . . . or a natural reef. Most clusters could have been physical or cultural.* Long fringing reefs that seemed natural were scattered about, interspersed in shallow water. On balance, the evidence looked promising but far from convincing. The only true test of this wild hypothesis would be to go there himself and find actual masonry. No amount of reasoning, nothing short of physical artifacts would sway any legitimate scientist. Even so, the rocks of Foul Bay showed how an entire civilization could escape notice for thousands of years. Perhaps the greatest secret of the ages lay right under modern noses, enshrouded in coral.

Exhilarated, Caisson *dismounted his magic carpet. Oldest, silliest cliché in the geographer's lexicon,* he reflected, *but nothing in the real world operates like our minds. Planes are too fast. Helicopters too slow . . . and too disruptive. Now, back to some real world technology.* He took Chart #62230 to the oversized copier, inserted coins, and copied the Foul Bay inset. As he stared at the map, he heard the familiar booming baritone of Walde Peplies, right down to the distinctive Germanic lisp. "No bags inside? What's this about?"

"No, sir. Bags are not permitted inside the work area."

"Where can I leave it?" Walde asked, in exasperation.

The clerk tossed a key on the counter. "There are lockers behind you, sir."

Jared chuckled as Walde stashed his carry-on in a locker and returned, briefcase in hand.

"Pardon me, sir, bags are not permitted inside the work area."

"This isn't baggage. It's a briefcase."

"Give it up," Jared called out, pointing toward the locker. *Yet, another victim ensnared,* he thought until Walde finally made it through.

"Professor Peplies," Caisson said, motioning for Walde to join him at the worktable. "What brings you here? I knew you were coming to D.C. this week, but I didn't expect to see you here."

"Arranging a conference, a joint effort between the ETSU Geography Department and the Mapping Division of the Library. You know I can't stay home in East Tennessee very long at a time. Sometimes my colleagues wonder whether I'm chairing a geography department or serving a term in Congress."

"Well, your timing couldn't have been better. I've just discovered something startling, and I'll burst if I don't tell somebody."

"Why don't you just shout it out. If it's worth saying, it's worth saying loudly." Walde stroked his stubby goatee.

"Properly Wagnerian, I'm sure, but I can't broadcast this one loudly. You're one of the few people on earth I would confide in at this stage of the game."

"Come now. You're just saying that because I happened by."

"No, it's true. Ellie . . . Ed Field . . . my brother Rick . . . and you. That's about it. I've already written your name on my to-do list back at the Lab."

"I'm honored, but what on earth for?"

"Geographic literature about early cultures."

"Fascinating. You know that's one of my favorite topics. If I can be of help . . ."

Caisson quickly summarized his suspicions regarding sea level rise, then spread the chart in front of Walde. "Look at this map of the Red Sea floor. It's a place called Foul Bay. What do you see?"

"Sea floor. Sea mounts. Rocks awash."

"Anything of human design?"

"Could be structures. Nothing to indicate that they aren't. Hard to say."

Caisson grabbed an atlas. Leafing through its heavy pages, he searched for a map of the Red Sea. Finally, the turn of a page brought him to the one he had hoped to find. There in shades of antique gold sat Egypt and its neighbors. Foul Bay conspicuously marked the Egypt-Sudan border. The map contained no more than a few place names, national boundaries, seacoasts, and prominent meanders of the Nile. "Note Foul Bay's relationship to the valley of ancient Egypt," he said. "History has focused primarily on the Nile, but I'm struck by the central position of Foul Bay. It's only 300 kilometers overland from the First Cataract at Aswan. When sea level was low, that would have been a much shorter land crossing than Suez."

"Mein Gott, Jerry. Of course, of course. That place would have been a marvelous location for a port, if indeed any commerce existed."

"How could anyone reading these maps avoid that conclusion? And look at these charts of the Persian Gulf. Do you see what I see?"

"That's as good a Central Place distribution as I've ever seen. It looks like Iowa."

"So maybe we aren't crazy." Jared went on to describe Rick's theory about step pyramids.

"But that would mean...millennia before we...but then.... It...it's just too revolutionary to contemplate."

"But we *have* been contemplating it, Walde. For years now, I've wondered how mankind became so smart so fast. It just didn't make sense. Now here's an answer that does."

"But now we'll have to reevaluate everything we thought we knew about the first few thousand years of human culture."

"Now you know why your name is on my whiteboard."

Walde nodded appreciatively, then momentarily lost himself in thought. "Oh, no," he said suddenly, then paused in deep contemplation. Finally he continued, "You realize, of course, what this means?" Characteristically he posed his question, then waited as if expecting an answer. After a proper delay, he resumed as if Caisson had said, "Why, no, Professor. Please tell me."

"More than anything else it means that much of what we took for myth may have been real."

"Mythology? Egyptian mythology? I don't know much about it myself."

"Well," Walde answered, "start with the most fundamental myth of ancient Egypt. Egyptians believed Atum, the god of creation, rose from *the waters of chaos* to create the universe. Not only that! They believed he ascended *from a pyramid*. In fact, the Egyptian word for pyramid means a 'place of ascension,' not a tomb. The word for 'tomb' means a 'castle of eternity,' an entirely different concept. Anthropologists claim this rising from the waters of chaos was symbolic—just another creation myth to explain mankind's emergence from the unknown.

"It's a lot like the Old Testament account of creation," he continued. "If the objects on this map actually represent pyramids and palaces, we have to consider the possibility that both legends were secular, historical accounts. No theological hocus pocus. And, a literal reading would square with Rick's suggestion that step pyramids may have resulted from repeated flooding. Another point in favor of your flooding hypothesis is that the word for pyramid, meaning a place of ascension, also applies to other natural features that emerge from receding waters, like the hummocks that disappear and reappear during the Nile's yearly floods."

"Is there anything indicating Egyptians expected all their pyramids to face eventual flooding?" Jared asked. "Rick thinks one of the primary reasons for the design of true pyramids may have been to make them waterproof. The masonry that makes them smooth would seal them, too. Just about every reference mentions the tight fit of stones. 'Can't slip a sheet of paper between them,' and all that. Refugees fleeing from rising seas would have no idea how high the water eventually would go. They would have to view every new plateau as a temporary home even if the waters never reached it, as in the case of Giza."

"Oh, yes," Peplies responded. "Arab legends of the Middle Ages are sensational on that point . . . if you take them literally, that is. As late as the 1300s, a famous Arab geographer named Ibn Batuta insisted the pyramids were built to house the Secrets of the Ages, specifically to protect them from the returning waters of chaos. He claimed an ancient Pharaoh foresaw the Great Flood and built pyramids to preserve contemporary knowledge of geography, geometry, astronomy, physics, and technology. Batuta mentioned books of science and knowledge and a vague collection of other matters worthy of being preserved from oblivion and ruin."

"Secrets of the Ages! That fits with our theory to a tee."

"Apparently, this same Pharaoh was able to predict the flood based on the appearance of the stars. Come to think of it, that could be a reference to changing climate. It stands to reason that atmospheric conditions, even in the Tropics, must have fluctuated dramatically between glacial and interglacial periods. When the water released from continental ice sheets evaporated, for example, it might have made the whole atmosphere more opaque, thereby reducing the brightness of stars. Or it could mean clouds were increasing over lands that had been dry."

"Rick will be interested in that story. He says the northern Sahara was much wetter about 10,000 years ago than it is today." Jared contemplated for a moment and added, "Burying secrets! That hints at how old their culture must have been."

"How so?" Herr Professor Doktor R. Waldemar Peplies asked with genuine curiosity.

"Caching valuable items of any sort, especially the deepest secrets of their culture, would mean they expected the rising water to recede someday and once again expose the inundated buildings. Only an incredibly ancient culture would have known it was a cycle!"

"Yes. Yes. I see what you mean," Walde replied.

"That would require a corporate memory reaching back to the previous glacial maximum when sea levels really did fall," Jared said.

"And, that might explain their curious habit of storing boats in the desert. You know, of course, that several chambers containing boats have been excavated near major pyramids. One was found beside the Great Pyramid at Giza. Myths say the boats were there to ease the Pharaoh's ascent so he could accompany the Sun God on daily excursions around the earth. Anthropologists have assumed this was a heavenly voyage after death, but a secular interpretation would match your theory nicely."

"Think for a minute. Can you remember any other hints that the ancients may have known about the rise *and* fall of the sea?"

"Yes, now that you ask. Most of the early cultures from Southeast Asia through the Mediterranean–Buddhists, Hindus, Greeks–divided history into four epochs. Buddhists were especially clear that endless cycles were composed of Great Periods, called kalpas. Each kalpa was composed of four ages, the first of which was an Age of Destruction by water, wind, and fire. The other three represented a gradual resettlement of the earth as the primordial waters receded and dry land slowly reappeared."

"Four epochs! That's a long time. Four glacial cycles would go back at least 60,000 years, maybe even 70,000 if you count the implied creation of the world destroyed in their First Kalpa." Jared described Calvin's Darwin machine.

Walde delved deeper into his memory and visualized a graph he'd seen in *Science Magazine*. "Actually, there were seven cycles of rise and fall over the past 120,000 years, but some of them weren't very pronounced. There was a quick drop between the 2nd and 3rd cycles around 90,000 BP, but then the 3rd returned to almost the same height as the 2nd had been. Same thing happened between the 5th and 6th."

"Blips? Between cycles?"

"Just a moment." He ambled over to the old-fashioned card catalog, scribbled some notes on a chit, and returned.. "I'll be back shortly," he said, strolling off toward the stacks. Fifteen minutes later he returned. "Here," he said, handing Jared a photocopy of a chart with a sinuous curve coursing from side to side. "Does this help?"

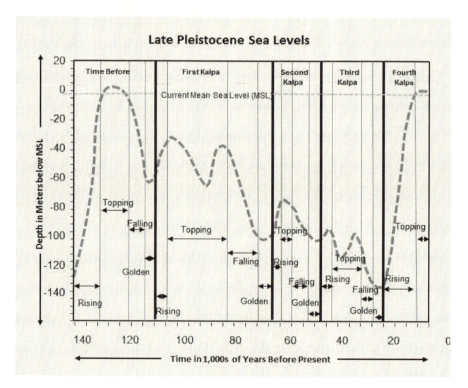

"I'll say it does. And, I see what you mean. It's hard to guess whether the ancients would have considered each of those sets as one kalpa or two. If one kalpa per set, then four kalpas would go back more than 100,000 years."

"Oh yes. You can see on this graph why there's a tendency to round off some of the smaller peaks and troughs into a single kalpa. It's not unlike what we do today with economic data to simplify recessions and expansions of the economy. And you will note that this fellow has finessed the kalpas by referring to the previous Ice Age as the 'Time Before,' If you think about it, that's not a bad way to look at it, because the most recent Ice Age has certainly obscured a lot of evidence of previous glaciations." He paused. "You know, Jerry, in the context of glacials and interglacials, one might interpret the four ages of each kalpa to be (1) rising water, (2) topping out, (3) falling water, and (4) a steady period of low water, a Golden Age when land and resources would have been plentiful."

"But a Golden Age in addition to the one Calvin envisioned! And precisely opposite to his in time and space!" Jared exclaimed. "Still, I'd be shocked if humankind's corporate memory went back that far. One argument in favor, however, is that human brains reached their current size about 120,000 BP, which would have been in the previous cycle. But let's not put too much stock in such speculation. The ancients could have been referring to minor ups and downs, fluctuations too small or too brief to show up in the current data record. For now, let's assume that the people who built the pyramids remembered one major fall and one major rise. Even that would require a lost civilization three times older than any known civilization." Jared halted, then resumed.

"One more thing. I'm curious how the Egyptians built the pyramids. There's been some pretty wild speculation. I'm looking for a practical explanation, nothing so outrageous as anti-gravity or harmonic levitation. Looking back with this new perspective, can you see any other possibilities? Rick and I think they may have preserved the technology from an earlier building phase. Of course, several millennia may have passed before they regained the stability and material wealth to recreate what they left behind…Or should I say *below?*"

Peplies stared absently at a nearby globe, one of a dozen or more stationed about the room. He blinked his eyes in recognition and said, "Yes, as a matter of fact!" Excitement showed as he lingered over the last word, "fact," with a long Germanic "a."

You'd never know he grew up in Chicago, Caisson thought.

"Everyone raves about the mathematical precision of pyramid engineering, but I'm impressed with the timing of it. Do you realize they reached that level of perfection in just 100 years from start to finish? In all human history, only a handful of societies have advanced so fast: Egyptians from 4,700 BP to 4,600 BP, Europeans in the 15th Century, Western Civilization from the Industrial Revolution to the present. Of course, we've outdone the Egyptians technologically, as far as we know, but keep in mind that they were notoriously non-innovative in every other aspect of their lives. Egyptian art, for example, changed less in 3,000 years than our own art changes in a single decade. Certainly their national psyche seems better attuned to preserving technology than inventing it."

"Any ideas as to how they might have preserved architectural technology and employed it with such precision after a millennium or so?"

"Jerry, I don't think you're ready for this. Not even you."

"Try me."

"Perhaps we shouldn't make too much of this. I hesitate to mention it." He hesitated.

"Come on, Walde."

"Okay, but don't say I didn't warn you. Egyptians used binary mathematics, just like modern-day computers. And, I might add, that's extremely difficult without a computer."

"Whoa! You're right! That's more than I can deal with. Let's put that one on ice, at least for a while."

"I concur, but in the final analysis don't let skepticism hide the truth. Once you embark on this revolutionary course, one revelation is just as believable as the next. That is both the blessing and the curse of science, my good friend. Believe too much, and you are a fool. Believe too little, and you are no less a fool, but society will treat you far more kindly.

"But," Walde continued, "do keep in mind that pyramid technology wasn't always perfect. One of the earliest attempts, a true pyramid near Meidum, collapsed because its angle, a full 75 degrees, was too steep. Archaeologists know exactly when it happened because the Bent Pyramid, 28 miles away, was being erected at the same time, and engineers corrected its angle in mid-construction. The angle shift from 54 degrees to 43 degrees is still visible today. A computer, one might think, would have preserved the correct angle."

"I'd prefer a more conventional explanation anyway. Any idea how they might have maintained such complex technology and culture for hundreds or thousands of years when it wasn't even being used?" Jared asked.

"It's not outrageous to think that there might have been some written records or, perhaps, some illustrations or models that preserved the precise information," Walde suggested.

"Sort of a *Time-Life* Series?"

"Yes, or perhaps, the *Idiot's Guide to Pyramiding.*"

"That might take care of a few key technologies, but not an entire culture."

"Well," Peplies replied, "how about Ma'at? Ma'at, as we understand it, depended solely on human memory and transmission of an oral tradition."

"What's Ma'at? I'm not familiar with the term."

"It means the 'Divine Right Order.' Egyptians were slaves to Ma'at. Every human activity was prescribed in excruciating detail and instructions were followed without question. The lowest peasant and the Pharaoh himself had to know and obey the rules of Ma'at. To illustrate how complete the instructions were: Everyone, including the royal couple, had to follow precise rules as to when and how they bathed, used the toilet, or made love. Art remained unchanged for all those thousands of years because Ma'at decreed every component even down to the proportional height and width of a human figure. When you think of Egyptian art, you think of that flat, side-looking face, right? You take that strange perspective for granted. Well, that's because Ma'at said all faces had to be drawn that way."

"You mean Egyptians didn't really walk that way? Wow. We do have to reassess our long-held beliefs."

"You know, Jerry, this theory may explain something that has puzzled me for a long time. Ma'at is a cultural oddity, the most self-restricted society ever invented. Yet, unquestioning adherence to a preexisting Divine Right Order might make perfect sense if the original authors foresaw a collapse . . . and wanted to maintain all customs and technology through the lean times they knew were coming. They could have anticipated the collapse for a long, long time and organized their whole society for the single-minded purpose of preservation. Now, that makes sense! Yes, I like that very much. I can't imagine a more effective way to transfer a whole culture. Nor can I imagine a more reasonable response when a whole culture is imperiled. It's odd some scholar didn't think of this possibility long ago.

Walde cupped his beard in his hand. "And one more thing! Pharaoh Amenhotep III is quoted as saying the primary obligation of every Pharaoh was to make Egypt flourish as it had in primeval ages. He was supposed to accomplish that goal by following the designs of Ma'at."

"That's too good to be true!" Caisson said. "Anything else I need to know?"

"Not really, but there *are* some things you would find quite interesting."

"Such as?"

"Well," Walde said, "try this one: Ancient Egyptians often wed brothers or sisters to keep their blood lines pure."

"Like Hawaiians. I recall reading about that in Michener's *Hawaii.* Seemed pretty weird to me as a teenager."

"Actually, it was fairly common among early cultures. In fact, the words for 'wife' and 'sister' often were used interchangeably, whether or not the wife was really a sister. King Tut's parents were brother and sister, and he married his half-sister. Cleopatra married first one of her brothers and then the other. Incestuous marriage was practiced by whole dynasties, in vogue at times and not at others. Who knows how it got started."

Prompted by a scurry of closing time activity, both men simultaneously checked their watches and agreed to be on their respective ways. Ten minutes later Jared stacked the last chart and gathered his belongings. He charged out the gate, unimpeded by the still, small voice of security. *Apparently the powers-that-be fear something dangerous may be smuggled in,* he thought, *not that priceless maps and documents may be smuggled out. How odd!*

* * *

Knee propped on a low windowsill overlooking Connecticut Avenue, Jared dialed his brother's number. Waiting for an answer, he visualized Rick standing before a similarly tall window in his home. "Rick, I think we've got it!" he said. "You won't believe what I found over the past two days."

Earlier, Rick had favored the Nile Delta as the birthplace of Egypt. Jared had been intrigued with the greater Mediterranean Basin, especially the Adriatic Sea. What he now described clearly favored the Red Sea, but Rick, in particular, was not ready to give up on the Med, especially the Nile Delta. "I understand," Jared conceded, "but, even if there is something in the delta, it will be a lot harder to find. Let's agree to keep looking up there, but Foul Bay must be our top priority."

"Okay, I suppose that makes sense. At least we won't be hampered by heavy sediments. Now, let's think this through. How did they migrate from Foul Bay to the Nile?" Rick's voice trailed off in contemplation.

"I'm guessing there would have been two movements. If their societies were as stratified as most ancient cultures, the aristocracy would have traveled in style and settled in the most favored refuge. Commoners would have had less choice in the matter. If their homeland was attached to the mainland, they probably waited until the last minute, then struck out overland. Alternatively, if the homeland was an island, many commoners may not have made it ashore. The unwashed may have found themselves awash, you might say. Surrounded by mainland, the inhabitants of Foul Bay, of course, could have escaped overland. There would have been nothing to stop them from spilling over the mountains to the west."

"Don't assume that land was unoccupied. I'll bet they fought for every step they took," Rick said.

"Probably right." Jared paused and stared at the high ceiling. "But, I'll bet the aristocracy planned ahead and pacified their refuge, undoubtedly the fertile Nile Valley. In fact, they probably built cities and moved in stages well before they finally abandoned Foul Bay."

"Don't assume the same land was fertile then as now," Rick admonished. "In that region the name of the game is water. Occasionally, the climate was pretty wet, but timing would have been crucial because most of the time, Egypt was a desert. In certain epochs, the refugees could have moved without difficulty. In others, the higher land would have been dry as a bone. I have some doubts about water availability even in the basin beside your Foul Bay. For the time being, however, let's assume Foul Bay had water, possibly based on an extensive irrigation network. That's much easier to accomplish near sea level than at higher elevations. Even 100 meters might have made a big difference. If the whole nation relocated, they probably had to schedule the siting, pacification, building, and agricultural development very carefully before relocating."

"That makes sense, but still it's hard to imagine a time when the Nile Valley itself wasn't well watered and fertile." Jared rebutted. "How do you suppose they kept commoners from cutting out early?"

"Probably kept them in the dark about what was happening," Rick surmised.

"Next, let's try to figure out the migration routes," Jared suggested.

"I'll bet the aristocracy went mostly by boat up to Suez. From the gulf's north end they would have had two choices. The shortest route would have been directly west overland to the lower Nile; the other would have been overland to the Med pretty much where the Suez Canal is today. From there, boats could have delivered them anywhere, the delta or even as far upriver as Aswan."

Now it was Jared's turn to admonish. "That's impossible. The Gulf of Suez didn't exist until Foul Bay was flooded."

"I didn't mean they could sail all the way. Caravans have been standard transport for thousands of years. The elite most likely sailed to the Suez Valley, dry in those days almost to the southern tip of Sinai, then mounted camels and headed north."

"I doubt it," Jared replied. "Land travel was miserable before trains and automobiles. 'Travel' is derived from the 'travail,' and caravans must be the prime reason. People chose water anytime available, especially for cargo. My money is on a direct overland route from Foul Bay to Aswan, then downstream by boat or barge to Thebes, Giza, whatever delta existed, and all points between. Either way, through Suez or Aswan, would involve a caravan, but the Foul Bay to Aswan route would minimize the overland part."

Suddenly, his own statement rocked him with a revelation so profound he sat down to compose his thoughts before repeating them to his brother. "My God, Rick, do you realize what this means? Foul Bay would have been THE PORT CITY . . . THE CROSSROADS . . . not just for Egypt but for the entire Atlantic/Mediterranean realm *and* the entire Indian Ocean/Pacific realm? There's nothing like it today! Every item of trade between two completely different realms, one mostly tropical and the other mostly subtropical, would have passed through a single city. An entrepôt for the whole world! No wonder it was so huge." Then he stopped and reminded himself it was just a theory. "I mean, if the place existed at all."

Rick, too, was struck with the awesome possibilities of such a central place, but he insisted the Suez route was still a viable alternative. "Besides," he said, "we don't know what conditions were like at the mouth of the Nile. I still think there may have been another cataract there, or even a waterfall, that would have blocked the way and required a second major portage. And there may have been other crossings directly from the Nile to the Red Sea."

"Good point," Jared said. "I'll check for other crossings as soon as I can find a good map of the terrain. I'll also look for maps of ancient trade routes. Probably a lot of them would have stayed the same from prehistoric to early historic times. Only the Suez Valley route would have changed, due to inundation."

"Okay. Back to the poor folks. Where did they end up? I can't imagine any place other than the Upper Nile. There isn't much good land because the valley is so narrow, but it's mostly desert for hundreds of miles in every direction." Rick was slightly embarrassed to realize he was making the same mistake he had chastised Jared for. "I mean, if the conditions haven't changed."

Jared recalled what he knew about the climate and terrain. "Yes, it's dry and rough outside the valley . . . except for the southern headwaters of the White Nile, where swamps and marshes extend for hundreds of miles in each direction. But that's a long, long way. Even if refugees from Foul Bay reached the Sudd, they would have to invent a whole new lifestyle. I'll go with the Upper Valley from Aswan into Sudan as far as the confluence of the White and Blue Niles."

"But I keep imagining pyramids beneath the Nile Delta, unknown to the Alexandrians flitting above them today. Why don't I do some preliminary checking? Then we can decide whether it's worth pursuing."

"Sounds okay, Rick. But don't let your imagination drift too far down the Nile. I know you want to go digging, but I think we've found the main site. Anything in the delta would be just an outlier."

"Maybe so, but you can't blame a guy for trying."

Search Log 12: The Land of Punt

Jared despised the heat and humidity of summer in the sunbaked South. "You've heard me say it a thousand times," he growled to Ellie, "'if you want a perfect year, scratch August and replace it with an extra October.'"

August is mostly miserable, but, on rare occasions late in the month, a Canadian air mass, cool and dry, dips south and oozes across the ridges of East Tennessee. His second day home from DC was as close as he would get to that extra October he craved.

"Feels like fall," Ellie said, "let's cook a special supper tonight, something wintry." Together they discussed options and decided on a Southern meal straight out of their childhood, one they both enjoyed immensely.

Ellie and Jared grew up in North Georgia at the southernmost tip of the Blue Ridge Mountains where Southern food was prepared daily with no less care than gourmet dinners in fancy restaurants elsewhere. They recalled the tastes of everyday meals and relished fond memories of families gathered around long kitchen tables. The handmade, plank tables disappeared long ago, and families were scattered thither and yon. Only the food itself remained as a wistful token of the dwindling Southern heritage they loved so much. Sadly, the swill still served in "Southern-style" restaurants made such a poor substitute that they hardly ever patronized the popular chains.

August's only saving grace is the harvest of fresh vegetables essential for Southern cooking at its finest. It is the month of green tomatoes, fresh ripe red tomatoes, okra, and peas. It is the month when sweet corn and white half-runners, the only green beans worth stringing, can be picked from the garden or bought from tailgates of pickup trucks parked beside the road. But those good things would have to wait as cool, clear air brought to mind the heartier, simpler meals of fall.

Columns of steam and wisps of pure flavor wafted from pots on the stove. Fresh cabbage was sliced thin and cooked tender yet crisp, perfect except that it lacked the distinctive sweet, nutty taste that comes with the first harvest of early spring. White onions were cut in quarters so each crescent would hold a sprinkle of salt. Jared gathered a few hot, green Cayenne peppers from the garden beside the breezeway, and made cornbread, one of the few items he could cook on par with Ellie. Its crust was crisp and brown, its inside tender and yellow. When it was done, he cut two wedges, sliced each one, and inserted pats of butter. Steam rose from each piece as the butter melted inside. Ellie's iced tea, a staple at every meal except breakfast, was fresh, mild, and sweet but not sugary.

Jared had sliced country ham almost as thin as prosciutto, its Italian twin, and Ellie fried it precisely halfway between chewy and crunchy . . . dry and salty on the outside, moist on the inside. But, the meat would not be central as in most American meals; here the starring role belonged instead, to a huge steeping pot of "soup beans" -white beans, cooked for hours and flavored with hambone or salt pork, much like the famous Senate bean soup, only thicker and tastier. The aroma brought to mind football Saturdays and snowbound windfalls when Jared liked to mind the pot and adjust the flavor all day. The beans had to be soft with a delicate taste. Given the couple's predilection for Georgia food, the beans on their table might almost be considered an exotic import to East Tennessee where "beans and cornbread" more often meant pintos. Jared took his first bite with onion and bread and contemplated the proper name of white beans.

"Ironic, isn't it, that our favorite Southern food is the Great Northern bean." Jared reflected, "Suppose Nubians ate Great Egyptian beans?"

"What? Why on earth would you say that?" Ellie had heard a lot about Nubians and Egyptians and Jared's suspicion that they came from the Red Sea coast. She understood that he was speaking hypothetically. She was accustomed to such discussions and often helped him clarify important points. Her main contribution was common sense.

"Oh, it's just that their relationship with Egypt seems a lot like our South's relationship with the North. Both post-bellum and both what you might call grudging subservience."

"From what you told me, I wouldn't be surprised. But don't rush to conclusions. Rick thinks you may be making too much of these cultural connections."

"He just thinks it's been too long since the last rise for them to be meaningful. Plus, he says scientists don't generally accept cultural arguments. He's right about the acceptance part, of course. But cultural affinities do last a long time in that part of the world."

"So why does Rick disagree?"

"Oh, he doesn't disagree. He just doesn't yet agree. It's a fine, yet meaningful, distinction." He smiled impishly.

After clearing the dishes, Ellie grabbed a book and headed for the deck. Jared stopped by his study, then rejoined her a few minutes later with a stack of *National Geographics.* "This is great. I had all seven issues with articles on the Red Sea, even April '64. It's a wonder I found that one; I only have two or three months from the mid-'60s."

First, he skimmed them, looking for Foul Bay. *Interesting, he thought, most of the Red Sea articles are by the same person and focused entirely on one place, Ras Muhammad at the southern tip of the Sinai Peninsula. Only one article features the western shore, and that's the 1964 article by Jacques Cousteau.* He opened it and began reading.

Cousteau told of Conshelf Two, an undersea laboratory in which his crew set an endurance record for undersea living. In 1963, five of the captain's good men spent a month aboard Starfish House. The main laboratory was only 36 feet down, but Deep Cabin, a smaller chamber, housed two men at 90 feet for a full week. *Good. Good. The depth range coincides with what I saw on the maps of Foul Bay . . . but the location, Sha'ab Rumi, is farther south near Port Sudan.*

On the maps, Caisson had found suspicious reefs all along the west coast, especially near Port Sudan itself, but from there southward they mingled with others more likely natural. A map in the *National Geographic* article showed other Cousteau dive sites along the route to Sha'ab Rumi. Two were in Foul Bay, and others were scattered along promising stretches of coast, but the article itself focused on the site of Conshelf Two. The text dealt mostly with undersea technology rather than the reefs themselves.

Jared turned pages in deep concentration. Then suddenly, "Holy crap!" he muttered under his breath. Ellie looked up and smiled.

Nothing had prepared him for the impact of page 494. "Look at this," he said, handing the magazine to Ellie. He pointed to the blue-toned photograph. At his fingertip stood the exact form of a Sudanese portico.

"It looks like a column, partially covered with coral."

"Look there." He pointed to the top of the column. "It looks like a capital free of coral on its outward side." From this rounded, stony disk, a lintel-like beam spanned to the slanting face of the pyramid itself. "That looks awfully familiar." Jared dashed inside to retrieve *Splendors of the Past*. "See. It looks a lot like these Sudanese pyramids. Cousteau's photo shows just a fraction of an entire pyramid, but for that portion it looks exactly like a coral-encased portico."

Scanning the text, Jared blurted, "This whole damn article is about hardware. Not a word to explain the scene itself." He forgave the captain as he read on, still about hardware, but this time a "diving saucer" for extremely deep exploration. Suddenly, Jared was stunned. At about 325 feet, Cousteau observed a "well defined horizontal ledge from six to 30 feet wide, running continuously along the vertical reefs." The feature, never reported before, was made of hard coral and appeared at that depth everywhere the saucer probed. Cousteau called it a hard, level "Andean highway" and speculated about its geologic origin. He guessed it might have been a former sea level. Jared reasoned that a sea level feature should be almost perfectly level, but Cousteau wasn't clear what he meant by "level."

"That 325-foot contour is no accident," he said to Ellie. "That's the depth of the straight that separates the Red Sea from the Indian Ocean. It's called the Bab al Mandab, 'the Gate of Tears.' The Red Sea shoreline would have hit that level anytime the World Ocean dropped by 325 feet, but then everything depended on rainfall. If there was plenty of rain in the Red Sea watershed, the basin would have filled and seawater would have flowed out through the Bab al Mandab. As sea level fell even lower, there could have been a waterfall as tall as 75 feet dropping down to the Indian Ocean. If rainfall was low, however, the Red Sea could have fallen far below the ocean. Then, when the oceans again reached the sill, seawater would have flowed inward and the waterfall would have been on the Red Sea side of the Bab al Mandab."

No doubt Cousteau's line was related to sea level. Maybe the thin shelf was an old beach ledge. Eons of crashing waves may have carved the shore into a distinctive erosional feature with a fringing reef extending along its cliffs. Cousteau, however, called it an "Andean highway" because it reminded him of a road. *What if it really had been a highway?* Jared knew it was a long shot, but images of present day coastal highways came to mind and wouldn't let the notion die. Jared reasoned that a road, a beach, and a reef would behave very differently wherever stream channels crossed, but the article said nothing about such crossings. Apparently the crew intersected the line many times but never followed it. Caisson calculated that the last opportunity to build a road at this depth would have been sometime between 12,500 and 10,500 BP. After that, the Indian Ocean would have breached the sill, and the Red Sea's waters would have risen in sync with the World Ocean.

"What do you think?" Jared asked Ellie after half an hour of reading and thinking.

"About the underwater 'pyramid'? It looks pretty convincing. But I wouldn't get my hopes up about the road."

"I agree. It isn't worth much on its own, but it is intriguing, nonetheless. Oh, well, look at that sunset."

"Feel that cool air."

"All we need now is some rustling leaves, and I'd have my extra October," Jared sighed.

"You'll have to settle for a flutter."

* * *

At work the next morning, Jared sat at a library terminal searching again for material on the Red Sea. "*Key Environments: Red Sea,*" the title read. It would probably focus on ecological issues. Perhaps it would have good information on physical features—reefs, ledges, and such. Probably, it wouldn't say much about culture, ancient or modern. Jared determined to pull it from the shelf himself rather than trust the computer again, but it was in the Environmental Sciences Library outside the security fence and more than a mile away. He would stop on his way home that evening, departing earlier than usual to catch the librarian before her quitting time.

Jared spent the intervening hours searching, yet again, through the gray metal cabinet that housed the Central Research Library's entire map collection. After several minutes of unfolding and refolding, he found the sheets that covered the Red Sea. DMA's terrestrial map series was considerably more detailed than its hydrographic series. At 1:250,000 scale the maps showed terrain and roads but not individual buildings. He focused immediately on Foul Bay, and the map scale was ideal for a broad view of its surroundings.

First, he wanted to know the character of the terrain separating Foul Bay from the Nile. Would the passage have been easy or difficult? Map #NF 36-8 indicated a relatively gentle rise from Marsa Sha'ab, on the Bay, up Wadi Ibib to the main divide. The legend defined "marsa," literally meaning "anchorage," as an Arab word for "coastal inlet." Beyond the divide, the route descended on a similar slope through Wadi Fiqu to Aswan just below the First Cataract of the Nile. He couldn't calculate the actual slope because elevation was shown as imprecise "form lines" rather than numerical contours. A flat pass less than six miles wide separated the east-

and west-draining wadis. In wetter times, this would have been the only streamless stretch. So far, so good! He guessed the traverse would have been fine in wet eras and passable in dry eras, especially if water storage pits were dug at strategic points along the way. The map showed that a modern road does indeed follow a similar course up Wadi Hawdayn to Aswan. Two stops on the road were marked "good water" and "drinking water."

Second, he wanted to compare this crossing with other possible ways to the Nile. *No use looking above the First Cataract where the river curves far to the west.* Scanning all sheets from Foul Bay to the Med, he found no other crossings as passable as the one from Foul Bay to Aswan. Modern roads confirmed it. All were longer and steeper, and none had "good water" along the way. *FB to Aswan wins hands down.*

Would Foul Bay ever have had enough fresh water to support such an immense city? The map noted two "good water" sites on the shore, but a huge city would need more than springs like the ones there today. In wet times, Wadi Ibib would have supplied some water, but its drainage area, extending little more than 50 miles into the hills, seemed too small. Wadi Hawdayn's was even smaller. He searched farther along the perimeter and finally came across Wadi Oko, terminating near the south end of Foul Bay. Following it "upstream", he turned sheet after sheet. The watershed was impressive, extending more than 225 miles inland, dry today but big enough to have once fed a mighty river. More important, the Oko's headwaters lie in high mountains far to the south where the slightest northward shift of the Intertropical Convergence Zone–a band of uplifting air always hovering near the equator–generates continuous clouds and steady rainfall. A map of ancient climates confirmed a rainforest there 12,000 years ago.

Jared closed the drawer and headed back toward his office. On his way out, he passed the reference section and remembered another source. He pulled the Columbia Lippincott Gazetteer from its shelf. Hefting the tome to a counter, he thumbed his way to "Foul Bay." *Not much there.* He turned to "Berenice." *A tiny stick of dynamite.* Berenice had been a major trading port between Egypt and India during the days of Ptolemy II. *Confirms my port theory. If Foul Bay made even a little sense when sea levels were up, surely it made a lot when sea levels were down.*

What about other coastal towns with roads leading across the Red Sea Hills? He checked each name. None showed up in the gazetteer until he came to Quseir, listed as "Kosseir." Yes, Quseir had been an important coastal town in the Ptolemaic period, an industrial center based on mining in the Eastern Desert. A route connected it to the Nile, but the gazetteer made no mention of a port function for goods other than the city's own production of phosphate, lead, and zinc.

Yes, he thought, *old Berenice-Beneath-the-Sea is looking more and more like a real city, maybe the most crucial port city the world has ever known!*

Energized by his new findings Caisson returned to his office and tackled some Seagate work, interesting but hardly exhilarating. A little before 4:30, he packed his briefcase quickly, grabbed his laptop, and headed for the Environmental Sciences Library. He found a space in the crowded lot and rushed in just before closing time. The librarian was helpful and pleasant, even though his last-minute request for *Key Environments: Red Sea* would cause her to leave late. He took the green-backed book home as quickly as the usual traffic jam allowed.

Over the next two nights, Jared spent all his spare time painstakingly studying the book, the first he had found that was focused completely on the Red Sea. Early on, he was pleasantly surprised at the content, both physical and cultural in scope and very thorough. Ultimately it revealed more information than any other source he had found except the hydrographic charts.

On the weekend, Jared visited Rick to report his findings. He parked in the driveway, walked to the porch, and knocked at the front door of the Victorian home. Rick's silhouette appeared behind etched glass as the double door opened. A few minutes later, they settled in the den surrounded by books, magazines, and photocopies. Jared was anxious to tell what he had found, but Rick had a few surprises of his own. "After you called the other night, I ran across a *Smithsonian* article on the Nubians. It agrees with what you found in Washington plus a few more details." The brothers compared what Rick had found in the magazine against what Jared had found in *Splendors of the Past.* "The magazine says Nubia has been called by many names. Ancient Egyptians knew it as Ta-Seti, Yam, and Wawat. Later Egyptians called it Meroë, after its most accomplished city. Greeks and Romans called it Aethiopia, but it wasn't coincident with today's Ethiopia. To Hebrews, it was the fabled land of Kush," Rick said as he turned through the magazine. "Nubians copied Egyptian style in almost everything, except that Nubians were much less formal."

Jared responded from his own reading, "Maybe Egyptians and certain Nubians really did come from the same culture. The common hearth could well have been from that stretch of coast. Even today, Foul Bay's sovereignty is contested between Egypt and Sudan. Egyptians were esoteric, like intelligentsia; Nubians were much more practical. For example, Egyptians claimed Nile floods were caused by gods; Nubians blamed heavy rains upstream. Egyptians were self-disciplined to a fault. Nubians were playful pleasure-seekers who enjoyed their wine and just about everything else. When I read about Egyptians, I think of the upper crust sipping tea in proper style. But when I read about Nubians, I think of blue-collar workers enjoying a night at the pub."

Rick thumbed a few pages to stir his memory. "Oh, and Nubia *started* with a written language composed of hieroglyphs identical to Egyptian ones. Much later, during the time of Meroë, they abandoned hieroglyphics in favor of an alphabet." He flipped a few more pages. "Egyptians fairly loathed Nubians while Nubians revered Egyptians. Egyptians couldn't find words vile enough to describe their southern neighbors. They even had images of Nubians imprinted on the soles of their shoes so they could insult them with every step. Yet, Nubians went out of their way to revive the lost learning of Egypt, rebuild its temples, and remind Egyptians of their glorious past. And one more thing! This article may explain why no trace has been found of outlying settlements near Foul Bay. It says pyramids were built to last, but houses were built of perishable stuff, mostly wood and thatch. The pastoral settlements of the hills may have been so perishable they disappeared completely, perhaps thousands of years ago."

"Yes, same thing in *Splendors of the Past*. The author says that many mud brick settlements known in historic times have vanished in only a few thousand years."

They methodically finished the first two sources; then Rick pointed toward the book at his brother's side. "Now, what have you got there?" He knew Jared was anxious to tell what he had learned, but they had chosen to cover the common ground first.

"Well, this is the most complete, scholarly source I've found. It even shows the old caravan and sailing routes. Of course, these are the ones known from recorded history, but they're probably a good indication of where prehistoric routes lay too. Apparently, the Red Sea has been one of the busiest and most crucial routes of world commerce for as long as anyone knows. More to the point, an important caravan route between Aswan and Berenice definitely existed. Its main function was to connect Egyptian settlements of the Lower Nile with the main port for the India trade. Only one other crossing shows up. It's a short, steep connection directly from the Lower Nile to a Roman port on the Red Sea, called Myos Hormos. The Egyptians must have followed a similar route to reach Wadi Gawasis, an earlier port nearby."

"Why would they have used those ports even after the Gulf of Suez was filled with seawater?" Rick asked. "They could have sailed almost to the Mediterranean, and the terrain looks friendly enough,"

"It really isn't a question of sailing versus walking. It's a question of sailing on the Nile versus sailing on the Red Sea. The portage distances are about the same. This book says, in no uncertain terms, that the southern route was preferred because sailors dreaded every minute spent on the Red Sea. One early traveler called it an 'infamous region of rocks, reefs, and shoals.' Given a choice, they would put in as far south as possible and make up the difference by river. In later years, big ocean-going ships put in at

Suakin near present-day Port Sudan where goods from the Orient were transshipped to smaller coastal vessels or to camels for the overland trek."

"I know the coral reefs are treacherous, but what's so dangerous about the open sea?" Rick asked.

"Wind and water currents are fierce, and they move in opposing directions most of the year. That stirs up a tremendous roll. Plus, early navigation wasn't precise enough to hold a steady course up the middle. Longitude was far more difficult than latitude in the days before sailors had an accurate, reliable chronometer. Since the Red Sea runs north-south, errors of longitude favored drifting to one shore or the other. At any rate, most early shipping was coastal. Only the boldest captains ventured out on the open sea, even on the Mediterranean itself in Greek and Roman times. Red Sea ships sailed only in daylight, and the sailing day was sometimes as short as five hours because sailors were unwilling to pass a known, safe anchorage late in the day. Shippers could easily beat that on the Nile. Even caravan travel stacked up pretty well compared to a five-hour day at sea. From a shipper's standpoint, the southern ports simply made good economic sense."

"Shifting monsoons must have provided fast sailing to and from Southeast Asia. Is there any evidence of that?"

"Yup! Very specific," Jared replied. "A Roman captain named Hippalus figured out monsoon winds in the first century AD and kicked off a surge in east-west trade. Maybe the earlier moguls of Foul Bay knew it, too, and the knowledge was lost. I can understand why they would lose navigational skills if the collapse were followed by a significant period without ocean commerce. Of course, it's also possible that it wasn't really lost and that Hippalus himself was merely reviving or even continuing an ancient tradition."

"Does your book say what trading partners the early Egyptians had, besides India."

"Ah, very interesting, indeed! There was major trade with a nation called Punt, but it's all too mysterious. Scholars can't agree on the location of Punt even though it appears prominently in Egyptian records. Speculation has ranged as far as India and down the African coast to Somalia, but consensus today leans toward the Red Sea coast of Sudan or northern Eritrea."

"Those are precisely the areas we suspect! When was this trade?"

"Best guess is that it started around 3,550 BP and ended abruptly about 3,150 BP."

Rick searched for a moment, pulled a sheet from the stack, and checked his chart. "Sea level would have been down about 16 feet at that time. Could have been the last remnant of a once-flourishing Red Sea culture. Do you know where a plateau or island of that depth can be found today?"

"Not without going back to the hydrographic charts. But there's a clue here. Look at this quote. Back in 1948, a fellow by the name of Thomson speculated the Red Sea got its name from a mythical red island on its west coast that sank into the sea. Maybe it wasn't so mythical after all."

"Any information on what the people of Punt were like?"

"Egyptian paintings portray them as red skinned, neither black nor white. In no small coincidence, Nubians were portrayed in two colors, one red like Punt and the other black like Sudanese pastoral clans of today. The red color may suggest a link between Punt and certain Nubians."

"And what were their exports to Egypt?"

"Short-horned cattle, wild animal skins, ivory, ebony, gold, and incense. Sounds very Biblical, doesn't it."

"What happened to Punt?" Rick asked.

"It just disappeared from the record. Notice, however, that the people who founded Meroë appeared from nowhere just shortly after Punt disappeared. My guess is that they were the same people, forced inland by rising water, and pyramids at Meroë aren't copied from Egypt but rather from their common cradle in Foul Bay. Of course, that wouldn't have been the only forced migration, just the last of many over several thousand years every time the sea inundated a populated area."

"Did you find adequate water for a city the size of Foul Bay?"

"Yes, I checked the terrain as soon as I got back from Washington. The drainage basin is big enough to collect lots of water whenever precipitation falls, and this book says rainfall was high on the African side from about 12,000 BP to 8,000 BP. That matches the general dates you mentioned earlier."

Rick considered the dates. "I suspect we can bracket the Foul Bay culture from the beginning of the wet period to the final migration, let's say about 12,000 BP to 3,150 BP. That makes 9,000 years in which a culture could have grown, roughly equal to the time of our civilization since the founding of Jericho."

"Well, our society has managed to rise and hasn't fallen yet, but I doubt we're prepared to survive the sort of catastrophe they faced."

"The big difference is they knew it was coming. We aren't prepared because we haven't agreed on what the real threat or threats may be."

"Scary, huh?"

"Sobering, to say the least," Rick said.

"By the way, there was another wet period from about 24,000 BP to 18,000 BP," Jared said before closing the book.

"It's possible there were several sequences of rise and fall of Ice Age cultures based on the convergence of wet-dry cycles with sea level cycles. I've been toying with an idea that may relate all that to the evolution of human intelligence."

"So, we're back to my initial question."

"Yes, I think so. I call it the Platform Pump model. Remember that book on Ice Age intelligence you read in the spring? Calvin suggested a 'pump' that kept ratcheting human development upward."

"So what are you saying about a platform?"

"Well, if you apply the pump model to each continental margin, you should find specific elevations, let's call them 'platforms,' where the leading innovations would have occurred as sea level dropped. That's also where you would find the fiercest competition as sea level rose. Sunda, the Red Sea, the Indus Valley, China, Greater Florida, the Yucatan, Chesapeake, each would have had its turn. Each would have contained specific platforms at which biological and cultural traits were encouraged or tested depending on which way sea level was moving."

"I envisioned something like that when I saw the depths of those suspicious features in Foul Bay, the Persian Gulf, and Sunda, but I hadn't put a name to it. Do you think we can quantify the stages?" Jared questioned.

"Yes, I think so. We'll need to match the flood dates of the known platforms statistically with the appearance dates of new peoples, ideas, and technologies in adjacent uplands."

"I don't think it's that simple. Most scientists aren't impressed by spatial correspondence. They'll argue the locations and timings are purely coincidental."

"Maybe so, but it *will* mean something to geographers. They understand how unlikely a series of such spatio-temporal coincidences would be. The odds against more than a few accidental matches are astronomical!"

Search Log 13: Seed Money

An alarm sounded, and a voice blared outside Jared's office. *Another routine drill,* he thought, *but more annoying than most.* He worked feverishly to complete his review of a manuscript submitted by some unidentified scholar to the *Journal of Remote Sensing and Geographic Information Systems.* Now, due to the drill his response would miss the afternoon mail and arrive past the editor's deadline. *Somewhere an author, his name concealed for blind review, will spend an extra, agonizing day or two wondering if his paper has been accepted or rejected.* It was tempting to ignore the warning and stay at his task, but the Department of Energy was deadly serious about safety. Anyone who ignored such an alarm would risk dismissal or, worse yet, an endless hell of paperwork and interrogations. He hopped up, without even closing his computer, and joined the line of employees edging down the corridor and out to a parking lot.

By tradition, MVL had always been a democratic sort of place. Among hundreds of PhDs, many famous in their fields, only a persnickety few insisted on being called "Dr." Class distinctions among workers, scientists, and managers were almost nonexistent. Evacuation drills threw everyone together with the jostle and good humor of sports fans leaving a ball park. Jared's hall held an especially diverse mix of employees ranging from the Laboratory Director to the operators who ran the Laboratory's big computers. Some people called it "Mahogany Row," a ludicrous term considering that the furniture was mostly gray metal. If any real mahogany or wood was there, Jared hadn't found it. Even the walls were metal, a legacy of the days when science was mostly done in laboratories. *So they could blow the roof off without killing each other, he often thought.* Every item on the wall–every photograph, calendar, scrap of paper–was held in place by screws or magnets.

Soon they reached the designated parking lot. He reported to the rally point, then ambled through the crowd conversing briefly with familiar "evacuees." *Like working the crowd at a conference,* he thought. By chance, he bumped into one of the Lab's Associate Directors.

"Hi, Jerry. Enjoyed your presentation," Walt Carlos said.

"Thanks! I thoroughly enjoyed giving it. Thank you for coming. I hope I answered your question."

"Yes, you did. I sensed tremendous interest throughout the Laboratory. That was the largest attendance we've ever had at a Showcase Presentation?"

"I heard, but I don't think it has much to do with me. It's just a reflection of the general interest in GIS and geography."

"Maybe, but you held their attention once they got there."

"You're very kind. Thanks again." But Jared's memory was bittersweet. The audience had indeed been wonderful. They applauded wildly at one high point and again at the end. They laughed when he wanted them to laugh. They appreciated his deft use of information technology, his innovative theories about continental drift, and his declaration of a new geographic revolution in science. But the excitement he felt that morning was tempered by the frustration of holding back. He had enjoyed showcasing past work but yearned to explore new ideas on Ice Age culture. He wanted desperately to reveal just a hint of his thoughts, enough at least to see if anyone would offer new evidence or volunteer to help.

Foolhardy, he thought! *If I had given the slightest hint of such heresies, they would have torn me to shreds. Worse yet, they would question everything else I've done for the last 20 years. Maybe when I have more evidence? No, not even then. Not until I can walk to the podium with physical evidence—actual artifacts—of massive underwater ruins. Carlos' compliment brings back the feelings I had onstage. I was like a young pup, frisking and prancing and having a grand time until I reached the end of my leash and felt the jerk.*

"What's next?" Carlos inquired.

Jared wasn't expecting the question, a standard one for students but seldom asked of research scientists for fear of getting an answer. *Was Carlos just being courteous? No, he seemed genuinely interested.* He was asking, and Jared was anxious to tell. *Why not tell just enough to tweak his interest?* "Everyone is talking about global change," he began, "including sea level rise. I'm intrigued by the fact that sea level has already risen about 400 feet in the last 17,500 years and hardly anyone ever mentions it in the global change debate. I'd like to study the submerged zone where that rise occurred and see what it says about environmental conditions at the time."

"400 feet! That's most of the continental shelf. 400 feet. Are you sure?"

"Definitely. Numbers vary a little from author to author, but the gist is well established in geologic literature. I want to study the biophysical evidence to see what it tells us about trends."

"Sounds great! How'll you go about it?"

"First, I want to map the inundated zone to see where it lies and how extensive it is. Then do fieldwork with corals. Certain corals are excellent indicators of water depth and ambient conditions. We can link conditions and depths to specific ages. I'm especially interested in certain Red Sea reefs."

"Who is sponsoring the work?"

"That's the problem. No sponsor. I think we could interest parts of NOAA, maybe even DOE, but not without doing some work up front."

"Why don't you submit a proposal for internal Seed Money?" Carlos asked. "It's there precisely to give a little front-end boost to worthy ideas with funding potential."

"I know, but I haven't had any luck with the review committee in the past. The members are heavily skewed toward hardware. They might support R&D on a new sensor designed to measure the health of corals, for example, but not to study corals in the context of global change."

"How much do you need?"

"Probably $20,000 to establish some minimal credibility."

"Is there any way you could cut that down to $15,000?"

He ran some figures through his head. "I could map it, but I couldn't do any fieldwork." Then he figured some more. "Fieldwork is essential. Maybe I can do both if I combine the travel with another funded trip."

"Okay. Now we're in business!" Carlos said as his eyes searched from face to face. "Mack!" he called and led Jared through the milling crowd. "Jerry, this is Mack Reed, head of the Seed Money Committee. Mack, this is Jerry Caisson. He's in the GIS section, and he's interested in research on global change. He was just telling me that sea level has risen 400 feet since the Ice Ages without attracting much attention in the global change community. What he's proposing is good science, and it may have some potential for future funding. How is your Seed Money budget holding up?"

"Not well this late in the year. Can you wait till the new fiscal year begins?"

"Well, yes," Jared replied, "but I haven't had much luck with the review committee in the past."

"If it's a good idea, I can approve up to $15,000 on my own signature without committee review. Just send me a proposal in October. I'll see what I can do."

"Fantastic!" Jared said as an "all clear" sounded and evacuees headed back toward their offices. Alone again in the crowd, he asked himself if what he had done was ethical. *Yes,* he decided, *everything I told them is true, and the study I proposed, even in its reduced form, is worth far more than $15,000 to the Lab and to the taxpayers who'll foot the bill.*

Plus, if Rick and I are right, they'll get the bargain of a lifetime.

CHAPTER 6

Chronicle 6: Overland to Punt

The high sun glared through a clear blue sky. The camp was ablaze with anticipation. Today the cadets would begin their arduous journey to Berenicia in the Land of Punt. First came a solemn, private ceremony at sunrise, then a glittering public spectacle in late morning to celebrate completion of the first phase of training. Families and friends watched as commanders presented cadets front-and-center. Osi's award as top cadet surprised no one, and he was privileged to lead the pass-in-review before the King's governor, the High Priest of Egia, and other dignitaries. Nuuti and Geb were among the honored guests on the balcony of the nearly completed Grand Pyramid, and they beamed as their son marched by. Osi's military bearing and strong self-discipline would not allow him to face them. Still, he glanced in the corner of his eye the pride that every child hopes one day to see.

Protocol was suspended for a last goodbye from family and friends. At noon, they would reassemble and depart for their next duty post, Berenicia, on the shores of the Valley Sea. Osi's family edged toward the parade ground as the cadets were released. Osi ran to his mother. "Thank you, Mother," he said. "This is your moment as well as mine." He hugged her with as much warmth as his new status and public setting would allow. "And to you too, of course, Father." He leaned to hug his father as well; then thought better of it and extended a manly handshake. Thalan ran to him, then caught himself too and slowed to a dignified walk as he approached his now-renowned brother. "Do you know something you aren't telling?" Osi asked, spying Thalan's mischievous glint.

As the family watched, Osi's father turned to an aide. "The package, please," he ordered, motioning toward a bundle wrapped in chamois. Geb theatrically unfolded the soft suede in an obvious attempt to heighten suspense. When the contents finally emerged, Osi saw the most splendid sword he could imagine. "Go ahead. Take it. It's yours," Geb said.

"It's...it's...unimaginable. . . most beautiful ...better than the highest officers' swords. I thought, perhaps, it would be the sword of Phanus, newly burnished. Nothing so grand as this."

"Look again, son. It *is* the sword of Phanus. I sent it to Berenicia to be reworked by the King's armorers. They made a mold of the old iron sword, then re-smelted the metal. It's now the finest steel Berenicia's craftsmen can make . They recast the blade, tempered its steel, and added the golden hilt."

"Spectacular."

"Look closely at the grip."

"The tooth of the dirk, isn't it?"

"I told them to etch the cat as you last saw it–jaws wide open and ready to attack. Now you can honor your pledge to Captain Hano while bearing a sword befitting your rank." To Osi's delight, the blade, despite its perfection in every other detail, still bore the thumb-size nick from its fabled encounter.

Thalan stepped forward beaming a broad smile. "And don't forget this," he said, raising a smaller bundle toward Osi. From folds of chamois, Thalan extracted an ivory handled dagger. Its hilt and haft were identical to that of the sword, only smaller and finer, but Osi gasped when Geb pulled the dagger from its sheath. "I've never seen anything like this," he said. The gleaming iridescent blade glowed brightly with an eerie red light that emanated from deep within its metal. "What is it?"

"It's a strange metal… orychalcum. . .redsilver. You'll see more of it in Punt. It has remarkable qualities. Use this weapon only when all else fails." Osi placed the sword in his sash and lashed the dagger to his thigh at this, the proudest moment of his life.

Festivities completed, family members embraced and said goodbye. "May Rahn be with you, my son," Nuuti said, tears welling. "May we live to meet again." Osi couldn't suppress a tear as his family rejoined the well-wishers and revelers. He donned the fine pack of the Hill People and readied himself and his troop for departure.

* * *

Osi led the 200-man regiment. Cadets who distinguished themselves in training served as platoon leaders under his command. Standard duties included hunting, foraging, preparing food, pitching and breaking camp, caring for injured cadets, tending pack animals, and scouting. They were trained to move and fight as a single, coordinated unit. An honor guard of regular soldiers of the Army of Egia accompanied the expedition as far as the Great River. After that, the cadets would be on their own as far as the first fort, Koro-detu, where they would meet a score of King's Regulars. Then, under the watchful eyes of such veterans, the cadets stood a good chance of getting most of their men through to Berenicia. To be sure, they would learn much along the way.

The journey to the southeast coast was part training, part essential travel, and part final examination. By this time, each cadet was proficient in methods of combat, the art of the hunt, the science of overland navigation, and physical skills needed to defend himself and his King. This journey would be the final test of the entire unit's physical conditioning, mental and emotional preparation, and ability to apply knowledge and skills to real-world situations. Most of all, it would be a test of their officers' ability to coordinate 200 rambunctious young men under constant threat of violent death.

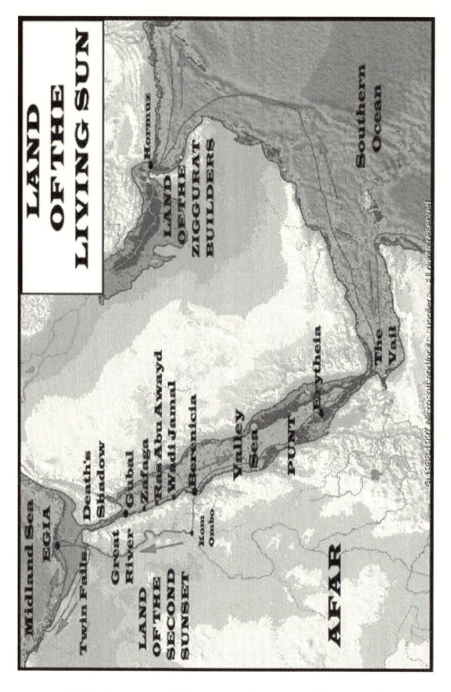

[Color images available at **www.thewatersofchaos.com**]

Vessels ferried all 200 across and upriver to the Eastern Road. Orderly reassembling on the far side, the full contingent set out on the infamous eastern route to the Valley Sea. The main trunk road ran atop a levee beside a principal canal serving the delta. The first week's march was four abreast in churning dust, their only relief a cleansing swim in the canal at day's end followed by a brief snooze in close formation on the road itself. On the seventh night, they reached Koro-detu, meaning "East, the First," at the delta's edge. Here they would leave the canal behind and pitch their first real camp.

Koro-detu was one of seven new garrisons established in compliance with the King's order conveyed by Geb a year and a half earlier. The commander of the King's Regulars met Osi and briefed him. "From here to Koro-seti, you'll be in steep rocky terrain. You'll march two abreast at most, single file at times. After that, you can sometimes go four abreast, but usually not."

"Two abreast," Osi said. "At four abreast half my men can relax their guard at any given time. Two abreast will deny them that luxury."

"That's right. Each man's survival will depend on constant vigilance through every hand of every day. Only at night can some relax while others stand guard."

Osi addressed his troops, "Do not depend on the Regulars," he ordered in closing. "They're here to advise and observe, not to protect. Now rest while you can. Dismissed!"

"I don't care how rough the trail is, this is the most exciting time of my life," said Ketoh, commander of the hunting platoon, the most prestigious of all billets. Training had been a struggle for him in the beginning, but his second year had been exemplary. He worked hard to develop physical stamina. Archery, tracking, and hunting became second nature. Long hours in the forest with veteran hunters, even a foray west of the Great River into the Land of the Second Sunset, had taught him the ways of prey, knowledge that would be essential for the regiment's survival. Independence and inventiveness had caused some trouble, but they would be his strongest asset in the unpredictable wilderness. In the end, all agreed that he deserved the appointment.

"I trust you'll keep us well fed, my friend," said Busah, who led the platoon in charge of logistics. It was a thankless task that demanded efficiency. His men worked harder than any others and were exposed to special dangers since they were the first to arrive at each campsite and last to depart. His platoon controlled the only beasts of burden allowed on the trek. Eight camels transported food and gear for the entire regiment. It was a blessing and a curse. They would protect these creatures with their lives.

"I'll fill the larder so long as you provide me a soft place to sleep." Ketoh said. "And you, Osi, how are you planning to squander your time, since you have no platoon to lead?"

"My job will be to help the hunter climb down from trees when he's chased by hyenas," Osi said.

"I've never lost my mount to a pack of hyenas," Ketoh said.

"Nor have you slain a dirk," reminded Busah.

"Come now, that little pussycat? Show me where he sleeps."

"Okay, but be warned, brave heart. Cats sleep a lot, but sometimes they wake," Busah said to the laughter of the others.

"So, where do we go from here, my captain?" Ketoh asked.

"We'll hike at dawn up a long easy grade, but don't let that fool you. The way beyond is rugged and fraught with danger. By mid-afternoon, we'll reach higher ground, just below the First Terrace. We'll camp tomorrow night close to the first garrison, then cross the Land of the Second Sunset for the next six days. Next, we'll camp beside the second garrison, which lies at the head of the Gorge of the Suas. Then, we'll spend another ten days descending the gorge down to a tongue of the Valley Sea. Our twenty-fifth night, we'll reach Koro-nata, the third garrison. Another three days and we'll be at Gubal. If luck is with us, we'll catch a passing ship. Otherwise we'll rest for a couple of days, then march three more to Zafaga."

"Are no ships scheduled to meet us?" Busah asked.

"If ships of Berenicia are patrolling off Gubal and happen to spot us, they may take us onboard. Otherwise, they'll meet us at Zafaga on our sixth day after reaching the sea."

"And the boat ride on from Zafaga?"

"Two-and-a-half days if all goes well. We'll lay over at Ras Abu Uwayd the first night and Wadi Jimal the second."

"So. . .forty days. . .if we're lucky. Why didn't we take the Great River trail instead?" asked Urgan, another platoon commander.

"Sailing upriver is the reasonable choice for merchants hauling freight, even with the long portage from the First Cataract to Berenicia, but not for soldiers afoot. This eastern trail is long and rough but not bad enough to arouse pity among our high command. Were you under the impression, Urgan, that we would be granted passage on the Royal Barge?"

Urgan laughed with the others. "No, but our people have taken the Great River route to and from Berenicia for generations. The Suas route is more dangerous . . . unless there's something you're not telling us."

"Yes, there's trouble, but we can't discuss details. Westerners are increasingly hostile. Now, only trading fleets with heavily armed escorts use the river route."

"What's upsetting the Westerners?" Ketoh asked.

"State secret. Don't ask," said Osi.

"Are there Westerners along the Suas route?"

"The new forts have secured most of it, but there's still a threat of ambush."

In the evening, cooks under Cadet Tanta's command prepared a hot meal, mostly meat but with travel-hardened bread dipped in a salty black seaweed sauce plus a tiny portion of dried fish and a splotch of boiled bitterleaf greens. "More than welcome after a week of cold rations," said many a man with his mouth full of meat and bread. Starting with the meal and continuing into the night, they sang and laughed as young men do.

Busah and his crew neatly laid out the camp. Each cadet spread his sheepskin bedroll beneath the sparkling night sky. The hide roll given to Osi by the Hill People stood out conspicuously, though all alike were waterproof and warm enough for any type of weather. Tonight, however, the air was warm, and the cadets lay placidly atop their bedrolls.

At dawn, they rose for another hot meal—bread, dried fish, and boiled tubers—then went on their way while Busah broke camp. The trail continued on the level, and Osi recognized the same pattern of land use he had seen farther west a year and a half earlier. Tilled, irrigated fields formed the core, followed by successive bands of pastureland, vineyards, orchards, wild fruit trees, and cutover forest.

By noon, the column reached the slope. First came a short rest beside a cool spring for the midday meal. Then, they advanced upward in single file. As they climbed, Osi recalled his first experience with steep terrain, the massacre at Ollo-detu, and his encounter with the Hill People. But no Westerners or Hill People would appear today. The King's soldiers had scoured these slopes for a full year and eliminated them from a wide swath covering two days' hike on either side of the trail. Today, the main concern would be the animals that stalked the hillsides, for no amount of soldiering could eliminate that constant threat. Seldom did a caravan pass without at least one attack by a predator. Constantly roaming ahead, scouts searched for likely dens, hiding places, and points of attack. Nonstop noise was the best defense, since most predators knew to avoid large troops of men. The worst incidents occurred when animals were caught off guard.

This day they were lucky. No animals attacked. No friends or comrades were lost, no beasts of burden. The night might be different. For now they would accept good fortune with thanks, day by day.

Chronicle 7: The Garrison at Koro-seti

Koro-detu, meaning "East, the First," stood on a ridge above the First Terrace. Would the fort be manned? Recalling the tragedy of Ollo-detu, Osi anxiously ordered a cadet to hail the gate. The whistle sounded, and moments passed with no response. The King's Regulars began to murmur, knowing that frontier guards traditionally prided themselves in distinguishing a caller and responding instantly. His man whistled again, and finally the response came. As they approached the fort, the sentry was silhouetted against a dusky sky. The cadets uttered a collective sigh, and the column snaked up the final stretch.

"Was no one on guard?" Osi asked as he entered the wide-swung wooden gate.

"Yes, my guard was awake, young man," answered the garrison leader sarcastically. "Your call, however, sounded more like a dying peacock than a noble swallow. Not long ago, a Westerner gave such a feckless call at Ollo-seti, and the fort was overrun. All because a guard ordered the gate open without first arming every man on post as we did here tonight."

"How many were lost?" Osi asked.

"Only two men lived to tell the story. They escaped into the forest and made their way to Ollo-detu but later died of their wounds."

"I knew the men of Ollo-seti. How sad. I've stayed among them. I know their faces."

"It's tough out here. Western warriors have killed 300 men in the past year. We have better weapons and tactics, but their numbers overpower us. The new forts protect the eastern trail, but it will take a huge army, perhaps larger than the Realm can muster, to secure the western passage along the Great River from Berenicia to Egia. Whistles we have; it's men and arms we need."

"It's late, captain. We must make camp," Osi said, ending a conversation that unnerved the cadets within hearing.

Busah's men unloaded camels and distributed bedrolls, vessels, and provisions. Cadets gathered firewood from the surrounding hillside and lit safety fires. Tanta's men made a hearty stew of sun-dried mutton with vegetables, dried fruit, bread, and olives. Then the exhausted soldiers retired for the night. Osi inspected the camp and later joined Ketoh beside his campfire. He probed its coals with a stick.

"Everything is going well. You must be pleased," Ketoh said.

"I am. But we still have so much to learn. Look at these safety fires."

"What's wrong ? I've never seen better."

"You would if you had visited the Hill People."

"So that's where your pack and bedroll came from. I thought you got them at Ollo-detu."

Osi nodded. "It will take months to train our city boys to handle the wilderness."

"We've done well so far."

"Yes, but an easy passage gives false confidence. The day will come when some of us will die in the line of duty. The odds against a totally safe passage are far too great. Even a short march without casualties is a rare blessing in this strange land."

In the shadow of Koro-detu, they passed the night uneventfully. Cadets and King's Regulars rose together. "Hit the trail," grumbled the King's commander after half a hand.

"We can't leave yet," Osi said. "Master Urgan's platoon hasn't finished breaking camp."

"Your men are green, Master Osi, lolling around and losing daylight like this. My troops are restless. We'll head out and scout the trail. Get your men in shape and catch up. There's a prominent outcrop about five hands from here. You'll know it when you see it. Be there by noon."

"Yes, sir," Osi said. "No problem, sir."

Half a hand before noon, Osi spotted the outcrop. Undoubtedly, the soldiers had passed the landmark and were resting at the spring on its south side, but he would take no chances. As his column neared the rocks, Osi hailed. "Yei, Yei!" he called. No response. "Yei!" he yelled louder, signaling for caution and silence.

"Ketoh, circle the rocks. I'll lead a unit over the top. Busah, Urgan, Takkan, watch for my signal to attack or hold."

When Osi reached the crest, he gave the signal, and the three-pronged column quickly converged on the spring. "Oh, oh, oh," Takkan said, looking into the low terrain beside the spring. "Another massacre! They're all dead."

"Westerners," Osi said in disgust, looking down on the mutilated Regulars. He bolted back to the top to survey the surrounding terrain. "Ketoh, fan out 500 paces. Sweep the area. Then return here!"

"Busah, lay these soldiers out for the sea. There's a good site just off the trail not a hundred paces back." Osi called an emergency meeting of his platoon commanders.

"Now it's up to us..." Osi said.

"How can we proceed without seasoned soldiers?" Urgan asked. "We must return to Koro-detu for replacements."

"The garrison has no one to spare," Osi said.

"Then we must go back to Egia and start over again," Urgan urged.

"We wouldn't reach Berenicia in time for the solstice," Ketoh argued.

"Our orders are clear. Forward is our only choice," said Busah.

"But we don't know the way," Urgan said.

"Soldiers briefed me on the course," Osi said. "I am prepared to lead."

"We must return," Urgan said again.

"I will march forward as long as men follow," Osi said, ". . . or by myself," he added. "Who joins me?"

Ketoh, Busah, and five other commanders stepped forward immediately. One by one, the others advanced as well, all except Urgan. "Will you return alone?" Tanta asked, and Urgan finally joined them.

In orderly fashion, every man drank from the spring. Tanta's men distributed the midday meal, and soon they were underway. The trail lay on open ground, and the regiment easily reached the next campsite on schedule. Busah's men readied camp, and Tanta's men cooked. Gradually the men gathered in clusters around fires throughout the camp. Eating. Murmuring about the day's tragedy. Speculating on prospects for the remainder of the trip. Facing unspoken fears. Eventually, they quieted and turned in for the night. Osi inspected the camp to see that all fires were lit and guards posted at every station. Assuring himself of their readiness, he retired to his bedroll.

* * *

Osi sprang from his bed in pre-dawn darkness as frantic screams awakened the camp. Stars twinkled over fog in the valley as he took command in the ensuing chaos. "Ketoh, arm your men! Archers, Swordsmen! Fall in! Follow me!" he yelled on the run. Scanning from fire to fire, he reached the tragic scene with armed guards close on his heels.

"My worst fear," Osi said looking at six torn bodies. "Who let this happen?"

"I...I guess I fell asleep on watch, sir," a dying cadet moaned. "My fire...went out. Good men are dead because I failed." The six had died in a flash; four others managed to wake and defend themselves. Now they too were dying.

"They're gone now, sir, but it was giant cats. I swear it was giant cats. A pack of them," a quivering cadet said. Finally a torch arrived.

"Those are dirk tracks, alright," Osi said, "at least three sets, and dirktooth punctures on these bodies. Was no one able to respond? What about others at fires nearby?"

"Two more men slept here around our dead fire, sir. But they were able to run and save themselves."

"Saved themselves?" Osi stared angrily into the man's face. "No one in my command saves himself while his comrades die. Where are these brave self-saviors?" he asked. "Bring them to me. Their punishment shall be swift." Two cadets stepped into the torchlight.

No, not Banda. Not my old friend Banda. I've known him since our first mock battle.

"Return to Egia!" Osi commanded. "Surrender your weapons! Depart this instant!"

"But, sir," begged Banda, "that's a death sentence. Unarmed men cannot survive the walk back to Egia."

"You heard my judgment. My order stands. Be gone." Two silhouettes slowly disappeared into the night, and the dead were laid out for the sea.

"No man in my command will ever again cower from an enemy, man or beast!" Osi declared. Silence was their consent as young men returned to their bedrolls. "Medical, give these men something for pain. It's the least we can do to ease their final hours." Osi stalked angrily back to his own campsite.

Did I do the right thing? I believe my duty was clear. At least, I think I did the right thing. It's so hard to know. Is there anything I could have done...should have done...to prevent this?

After stretching out on his bedroll, Osi arose again, then paced from station to station, checking fires. Silently, he vowed to make extra rounds each future night to ensure the guards' alertness. Never again would his men fail to protect themselves in the night. He wandered about until near dawn, then returned to his bedroll for a hand of needed rest. But there was no more sleep for him that night.

* * *

A sentry signaled the dawn with a howl that woke the whole camp. Cadets stirred, then rose for their morning routine–urinate, drink water, fold bedroll, eat, muster, depart.

As they marched, Osi was reminded of the view from Ollo-detu and scenes along the route to Ollo-seti. Broad expanses of grassland interspersed with scattered copses of acacia, oil palm, mampato, and a mix of upland trees. Wildlife was abundant. Playful green monkeys chattered in the oil palms or scampered on the forest floor picking fallen fruit and digging for tubers. Brown monkeys waded in puddles of shallow streams trickling from oases. Red monkeys scurried about the branches of enormous mampato trees or ranged the plain digging for grass shoots and grubs. Osi was amused by the antics of the potbellied little creatures but wisely gave them a wide berth.

For most of the crossing, the main force stuck to the open plain where ambush, by man or animal, seemed less likely. Here, surrounded by broad vistas and grass or low brush, a man could see a day's walk in every direction. Bitter experience, however, had warned the Beloved People that cats, hyenas, and Westerners alike had perfected the arts of stalking and hiding and sometimes waited days for the moment to attack.

Today would be a time of watching and hoping. And wonder! Not a man passed long without commenting on the magnificent sight. "Look at that! What are those? Have you ever seen anything like it?" A whistle here, an "Ahhh!" there, or a sudden breathless silence. From horizon to horizon, massive herds of elephant, rhinoceros, gazelle, and wildebeest grazed across broad swaths of open plain.

"We're lucky you're such a great hunter," Tanta said to Ketoh. "These conditions must really test your skills."

"Yes, Ketoh. With game in such abundance, you must be cautious when you aim. Otherwise you'll bag more antelope than we can eat," Busah said, "and what a waste that would be."

"A careless hunter could get a hernia from trying to bring back so many carcasses," Sareem added.

"We shoot only the small ones...that are headed in the right direction," Ketoh retorted. "But have your fun at my expense. Today we faced two prides of lions and several lone leopards on the prowl."

"We saw them lying in the sun. Those lazy bastards didn't want any part of you or your kill."

"Maybe we didn't suit their appetites today, friends, but tastes change."

"These are savage beasts, Ketoh. They've hunted the greatest prey on the plains and killed the finest hunters among the Westerners. Don't expect them to lower their standards just to satisfy your quest for adventure," Sareem said.

"I'll gladly forgo the privilege, my friend, of being eaten alive by such connoisseurs. Anyway, it's for their own good. If I don't make it to Berenicia, the ladies of the town will rush out here and take revenge. There won't be a cat left standing."

Chronicle 8: Death's Shadow

Osi made sure no lax guards would repeat the earlier, tragic mistake. At twilight, he assigned staggered shifts of officers to walk in pairs all night. They watched every fire and checked every guard station. Osi himself rose several times to check on officers, guards, and fires alike. Thankfully, there were no more encounters with Westerners or dirks.

Across the plain at last, on their fifth day out of Koro-detu, the cadets frolicked in a big upland lake. They camped and drank and swam. Each man missed his usual seafood and pitched in to add a little variety to the succulent, yet somehow unsatisfying, upland game. They trapped fish and gigged frogs and delivered them to the cooks. On the sixth night, they made camp on the brink, just below the First Terrace, from which they could view the Gorge of the Suas. Half-built columns marked the site of a new fortress to be called Koro-seti, meaning "East, the Second," but recent hostilities had halted construction.

By sunset next day, they would reach the gorge. "We made our schedule in spite of mishaps. We must be better than the King's Regulars," Urgan boasted.

Busah stared blankly at him for a moment, then countered, "No need for arrogance. Misfortunes are built into the schedule. No one passes this way without them."

"For your part, we wouldn't be here at all, Master Urgan," Tanta said.

"I only presented an alternative for your consideration. I never really wanted to turn back," Urgan said. The others glared skeptically.

"If you plan to change your mind, now is the time to do it," said Tanta pointing toward the fearsome canyon that lay ahead.

The morning opened bright and clear, auspicious signs for safe passage. As they moved down the first ragged slope, two dirktooth cats lurked on the canyon's east rim and a lone cat patrolled the west, but, due to the cliffs, their movements gave no cause for alarm. Below the first ledge, it became impossible for scouts to guard the column. For days, they descended single-file into a steep gravel-strewn streambed with endless opportunities for ambush among its cliffs and caves.

Osi was far ahead when, through orderly repetition by every third cadet, the rear column sent word of an attack. "Dire wolf. Side canyon. One man down. Left the column. Wrong turn. Vicious attack. Rescue attempted. Medicine given. Likely to live."

Yes, but his remaining days on the trail will be miserable. In this place, to lose sight of the column is suicide. He may not think so now, but he's a lucky man.

Late on the fifth day below the rim, a hush along the column confirmed their arrival at Hell's End. A rocky precipice overlooking the deeper gorge presented the only spot halfway suitable for bivouac.

"Busah, let's see what you can do with this site," Osi said.

"What site?" Busah asked, staring at the rough ground.

"Everyone camps here," Osi said. He looked up at rock laid down by early seas wrinkled and folded by forces within the earth.

"There's hardly a spot smooth enough and large enough for a man to lie down," Busah said. The platform was actually a circular ledge bulging to the edge of the escarpment that marked the break from upper to lower gorge. Steep rock faces protected three upslope sides of the ledge, and the end plunged off into oblivion. "But there's no shortage of narrow ledges suitable for cats to approach their pr.... I mean 'us.'"

Busah deployed his men in the central trough where they could use the rock shelves for opening, sorting, and dispensing equipment and supplies. Later Tanta's men would use the same ledges as cook sites. And later still cook fires would be converted to watch fires. Bedrolls were scattered over two sizable mounds on either side of the trough wherever each man felt he would be least uncomfortable. Like it or not, the rumpled site would have to do for the night.

"I hate to do it," Busah said, looking toward his line of fine draft camels.

"They're troopers, alright," Tanta said. "Hate to see them go. But every camel learns sooner or later that Hell's End is...well, the end."

"Do you think the trail below is really that narrow? It's hard to believe a single camel can't pass. They're sure-footed creatures, too. And, it would be good not to have to take up their burdens," Urgan said.

"We have no choice," Osi said, and Urgan went silent.

Cooks slaughtered the animals and roasted large hunks on spits over brushwood fires. The meat, richly flavored by the aromatic smoke, was a suiting feast of passage for cadets on their way to Berenicia. While they ate, long strips of flesh were stretched over coals to dry. This jerky would sustain them on the trail until they reached the Valley Sea. Cadets tossed the carcasses and skins over the ledge at a point sure to avoid fouling the trail below, a further safety measure that would lure predators out of reach from camp.

* * *

Beyond Hell's End, the trail descended steadily into a deep ravine that stretched for another five days' travel until finally it met the Valley Sea. This lower gorge, known by all as "Death's Shadow," was, in places, little more than a narrow slit barely wide enough for one man to sidle through. Often the sky disappeared above the crenellations of steep canyon walls. Long before, in wetter times, the bottom had been an impassable torrent, a veritable flume. Fifty generations ago, the weather turned drier, and the trail could be traversed year round. In Osi's lifetime, however, it had been passable only during the dry season.

"Over the past two generations, only a handful of storms have occurred during the month preceding the solstice," he had been advised on departure. "Still, once you're in the Shadow watch constantly above for three killer clouds. Blanket clouds will bring slow, steady rain; keep your men moving; they'll wade up to their middles, but most will be saved. Clouds that billow just above the horizon will bring heavy rains; seek high ground and wait out the flood. Tall clouds will bring a flashing torrent of water; there will be no survivors in Death's Shadow."

"I won't enter the Shadow under threatening skies," Osi had said. "But what if they come swiftly?"

"Low clouds and blanket clouds come slowly. You'll know their warning in advance. High clouds come quickly, and there are stretches where you will not see the sky for whole days. There, you are at the mercy of the heavens," his advisors had said.

Two scouts climbed to a vantage point above the encampment, a promontory legendary for its uncanny resemblance to a distinguishing feature of male anatomy. Their purpose was to view as much of the skyline as possible. "Not high enough," a scout called down, and they scampered higher toward the tip.

"Careful, careful," Ketoh yelled. "Tickle that scamp too much, and you'll never make it to the top." A wave of laughter swept across the regiment.

"Clear in all directions," came the report from the top. In three hands, the column was ready to move. Osi called on the young chaplain to issue prayers for safe passage.

I'm not superstitious, and I don't believe everything the priests tell us, but many of these men are sincere believers. They need this priest and his prayers. As for my own faith . . . well, it never hurts to add a prayer or two just for good measure.

All his life, Osi had heard horror tales of the Shadow. Never in his most impressionable youth, however, had he imagined the helplessness that possesses men as they inch through the dark crevice. The gorge funneled hurriedly to a tube barely the height and breadth of a man, and for hundreds of paces at a time the skyward slit above their heads narrowed to the thickness of a man's hand. Seldom did the light of day penetrate its depths. For thousands of paces at a stretch, the abyss was more cave than chasm, and Osi's men used torches of resinous desert brush to light their way. Frightful crooks and turns sometimes led to false avenues. Precipitous drop-offs surprised them often. Pits or deep grooves sometimes lay on either side of the trail. Twice, Osi narrowly avoided injury, catching himself as a foot slipped over the edge. A syncopated marching rhythm kept the cadets carefully paced and properly distanced from one another. Torches were essential for more than a day's march; then, for three days they walked mostly in sunlight. Some parts of the channel were broad enough for a comfortable bivouac and high enough to avoid flash floods, others so narrow the cadets napped in their tracks.

On the fourth morning they entered a darkened tunnel, this time without torches, now in short supply. Osi sent scouts ahead to search for higher ground for their next encampment. Finding none and knowing it would be foolish to dally in this worst part of the Shadow, he ordered his men to march day and night . . . no sleep, not even naps, no rest, no stops except for water whenever springs were found.

Despite its darkness, the last reach of the chasm was reasonably safe, because it had no quick turns, drop-offs, pits, or grooves. Using his staff to feel for rocks, Osi seldom stumbled, and the regiment made good progress. Regular reports from the rear, 2,000 paces behind, said all was well throughout the column.

A chamber called the Gullet was the last stop before the gorge's mouth, and it opened broad enough to house a small army. Here the men rested briefly before the final push for the exit. A sloping ledge led up to the canyon's rim where a narrow slit opened to the heavens. *Tempting to explore,* Osi thought, *but not now, not when we are so close to the end.*

Shortly after midnight by Osi's reckoning, a muted glow silhouetted the tunnel-like exit from Death's Shadow. Two hundred paces later, he emerged gratefully and triumphantly from the darkened chasm. Before him, bathed in moonlight, lay the enchanting shore and gleaming waters of the Valley Sea. One by one, his men emerged and stood with him in awe at the scene.

As the crowd parted to make room for emerging cadets, the surf suddenly blazed with reflected light. "Look! In the northwest sky!" a man yelled.

Osi scrambled up the bluff that blocked his view. Joining cadets at the end of the ledge, he too surveyed the night sky and there saw the looming tower of a high cloud with flashing core. He wheeled toward the tunnel and issued a terse command, "Double-time!" Then, more thoughtfully, "Get out as fast as you can, but take care. Keep good order. Don't panic." Immediately, the men in front quickened their pace and filed into the growing cluster on the ledge. "Make way, make way!" the officers ordered, and the crowd stepped aside, spilling to the rocky beach below.

Inside the tunnel, each cadet relayed the emergency orders and every man took heed. Osi climbed to a rock above the outlet and counted as men ran out.

"Step to the side, to the side!" he yelled to gawking men below. Suddenly a gust of air burst from the opening and fairly blew the cadets along, its eerie roar dousing any hope of communication. Cadets stumbled in its wake; then the water gushed. Osi lost count as exploding water spewed men like leaves from a gutter pipe. Ten or 12, maybe more, washed into the sea.

Orders followed in rapid succession, "Post watches . . . Line the shore . . . Tend the wounded . . . Collect the dead!" In moments, the cadets were deployed and reports filtered back. "Two injured . . . three dead . . . seven unaccounted for." *Some will never be found,* Osi thought. *The sea has claimed them.*

"Search all the night," he ordered, but no more cadets were found until daylight when three more walked in, injured but alive, and two more bodies washed ashore.

"Two remain unaccounted for at roll call," came a lieutenant's report. By midmorning, the search was discontinued. Cadets strapped the wounded on litters for the journey to Gubal, laid the dead in the surf to be reclaimed by the sea, and grimly marched on.

Chronicle 9: The Valley Sea

By noon, the regiment was well on its way. The shoreline–crystal clear water dashing on pebbles, stones, and boulders–took a gentle curve as it followed the narrow tongue of the sea stretching from Death's Shadow to the coastal fortress of Koro-nata. The third garrison on the eastern route was a welcome sight when they finally spotted its prominent outline early on the third day. Picking up the pace, they reached the fort in midafternoon The Commander welcomed them and offered bivouac space beside the fort. Quickly setting up camp, they finally had time to indulge in their favorite recreation, swimming. They dove in the shallow waters and gathered shellfish and seaweed for a sumptuous evening meal.

"It's good to be back in the sea again," Osi said at his nightly gathering of officers.

"Indeed it is," came the unanimous reply. "And eat real food again," someone added, and the others cheered.

"Now, if only some ships will find us in Gubal and haul us to Berenicia," Tanta said.

"Here's to a quick sail," Busah cheered with his cup held high.

For the first time since leaving the Land of the Second Sunset, the cadets enjoyed a secure night's sleep. Guards were posted, but the threat was minimal beside the high walls of Koro-nata. With the next day's dawn, they broke camp and headed for Gubal, encountering along the way their first signs of civilization on the Valley Sea. Seasonal huts used by fishermen, lobstermen, crabbers, and other watermen were scattered along the shore. Families worked in shoddy, temporary shanties to clean and dry the harvest. Later they would haul their products a short distance into Gubal and sell them at a modest profit. Most of the fleet was out, but sand scars proved that scores of fishing boats had berthed the night before.

In late morning, Gubal's imposing mountain and massive seaside fort came into view. By early afternoon, the regiment had reached Koro-reni, the fourth garrison of the east. The mighty fortress was larger and better supplied than any Osi had seen. It sat beside a protected cove on the northwestern arc of the bay. High canyon walls at first blocked Osi's view of the open sea, giving one last impression that there was no escape yet from the lingering specter of Death's Shadow.

The seaport itself consisted of large stone docks and storage shelters. Almost as big as the main harbor at Egia, the wharf could accommodate as many as three seagoing vessels at a time plus 40 or 50 smaller craft. Adjacent to Koro-reni, a village crowded the strand. Sailboats loaded with fish lined the pier. Working skiffs plied the channel or clustered in the natural harbor. Nearby, naked children swam in shallow waters, and, farther out, young women dove for mollusks. Except for its prominent mount, Gubal looked like Egia many years ago. No fields, Osi reflected as he surveyed the harbor town. Here, the people made their livelihood entirely from the sea, as all the Beloved People had done before they learned the Geometry of the Earth's Living Things.

"Welcome to Gubal," the captain said coldly.

"We are honored by your kindness," Osi said.

"I am Captain Arrak, Commander of Koro-reni, Fortress of Gubal. Keep your men in order during their sojourn here, and all will be well," the captain said. "They may enter the town, but they must obey my rules and honor the customs of our people."

"My men always obey rules and honor the customs of our people," Osi responded.

"That's my concern, boy. They follow the customs of your people, not ours."

"What do you mean, sir? Are we not one people?"

"Ha! Young man, you have much to learn. Berenicia is the greatest port, and Punt the greatest land on earth. Egia is but a sleepy outpost and your Beloved Land a pitiful little colony of our empire."

"I will order my men to be on their best behavior and to observe the ways of Punt," Osi promised, his pride shaken.

Our "sleepy outpost" has to be just as busy as Berenicia. The cargo that passes through Berenicia must also pass through Egia, as well, if it's heading across the sea. If he weren't an officer, I'd give him an earful.

After a swim to refresh themselves and a dinner of fresh shellfish garnished with fruits shipped north from Berenicia, the cadets went to see for themselves the supposed wonders of this northernmost outpost of Punt. "This little town doesn't look much different from Egia, if you ask me," Sareem said. "Same dusty streets, houses, apartments, poor men's hovels, city market…but no fine estates like Egia's."

"Looks pretty scruffy to me."

"Not even a pyramid standing above the plaza."

"What plaza? Nothing more than a fort and a market, if you ask me," Osi said, looking at the lineup of imported trade goods in stalls lining the square. "It's busy enough. . .but nothing to brag about."

"It does seem to have a lively side," Ketoh said, spotting a procession of revelers stumbling from a side street.

"Looks like some heavy bargaining over there," Busah said. Occasionally, a shout rang out, and two men would clasp hands to signal agreement.

"You'd never see this sort of thing going on at midday in Egia," Osi said. He watched a buyer surrender a handful of coins, then walk to the open door of a nearby apartment. A sensuous teenage prostitute greeted him, and they disappeared inside.

"Maybe in the side streets. Certainly not on the main plaza," Busah said.

"Holy Rahn!" Tanta said as two girls ran by in a playful game of chase. They were naked except for jewelry—necklaces, anklets, earrings, bracelets, and bangles. Seductive music, like the sounds Osi and his pals had heard in Egia's Temptation Alley, wafted from nearby buildings. Gamblers wagered, won, lost. Fights broke out along the seawall where deals were being made. No one seemed to take note of the goings on except for the cadets who stood in stunned silence.

"Osi, do you suppose people behave like this in the capital?" Busah asked.

"This is a remote fishing outpost, even if Captain Arrak won't acknowledge it. Surely, the people of Berenicia aspire to higher standards," Osi said.

"This *is* the height of my aspirations," Ketoh shot back with a mischievous glint.

"Your aspirations are well known and seldom equaled...even in your own real exploits," Osi said. "Perhaps you should rush on to Berenicia tonight. We'll join you later."

"Now, why didn't I think of that myself? Goodbye, my friends!"

"Perhaps you might wait to see if ships arrive. We may pass you on the way."

"You're right, as always, but I must warn you that the ladies of Berenicia may hold you personally responsible, Master Osi, if I arrive late."

Three cadets standing nearby summoned up the courage to approach Osi. "Master Osi, sir!"

"Yes, men?"

"May we partake, sir?"

"Of course. It's your right and your duty," Osi said seriously. "Take your liberty. Stay as long as you need, but be back in camp by daybreak. Just don't embarrass Egia by behaving crudely as the natives do." Word spread quickly, and fresh lines soon formed outside the establishments.

* * *

Next morning, Osi slowly awoke to sunlight filtering through heavy eyelids. Suddenly, an imposing shadow broke the beam. As he gathered his wits and opened his eyes, he saw Arrak's dark silhouette. Beside him stood four of Osi's men—eyes blackened, faces bloody, bodies bent in pain. "Is this how you control your men, Master Osi?" the officer asked, blending question and accusation.

"Captain Arrak, sir! They are my men, and I take full responsibility for their actions. What have they done?"

There must be some mistake, but I'm shaking like a leaf. Why am I so frightened by this man?

"They insulted a lady of this city, and they shall be punished."

"Can this be true? Sikmet? Sareem? Is this true? Did you insult a lady of Gubal?"

"Yes, Master Osi. It was an accident."

"And how did such an accident occur?"

"We approached a girl who was drinking in the streets near the brothels. We mistook her for a lady of the night and asked her to share her favors. She was wearing only a little jewelry and no clothing. We had no way to know she was a highborn lady, daughter of a garrison officer."

"Captain, if what my men say is true, they can hardly be blamed for their behavior." He turned back to the four cadets, "And all you did was ask? You didn't force yourselves on her?"

"No, Master Osi. The men of Gubal were touching her at will. We asked politely."

"And did you fight? How did you receive these bruises?"

"We didn't fight. We were beaten by these soldiers."

"But you did offer money," Arrak insisted.

"Yes. That we did, and we are sorry," one of the erring cadets replied.

"Captain Arrak, I will see that this does not happen again."

"You will see that these men are severely punished, or you will suffer the consequences, young sir."

"They've already been punished. Your men did enough damage. This matter is closed," Osi said.

"Your schoolboys are ignorant rubes from the colonies. They must learn to distinguish a lady of rank from a lady of the streets. If you won't discipline your troops, I will."

"They are my men, and I forbid it." *I'm talking tough, but what can I do to stop him?*

"You know the rules of command, cadet. On the trail, you're on your own. Encamped at my garrison, you're under my command. To disobey me is to defy the authority of the King. I can revoke your commission for insubordination or your life for disobedience. Guards, seize these yokels! Ten lashes!"

"You'll not whip my men while I stand free. Take me as well."

"Very well, colonist." He turned to his men, "Take this one, too! Line them up. Strap them to the wall! Ten lashes for every man...30 for this impudent punk." Soldiers stripped the cadets to the waist, and five of them stood with martinet in hand. Other troops poured from the garrison eager to watch. A methodical countdown commenced at Arrak's signal.

The first blow was unbearable. How can I possibly stand 29 more lashes? Listen to the screams of my men. I can feel their pain almost as well as my own...but...I cannot scream. I must not yield. Twenty-eight to go. Can I endure? Twenty-seven. Twenty-six.

And so went the count until none remained. The twentieth lash was only a blur in Osi's memory. The rest he could not recall.

The crowd scattered, leaving only the Egian cadets. Finally the others were cut down, and only Osi remained. "Did I yield?" Osi asked upon regaining consciousness.

"No, Osi. You did not."

"How long must I remain here?"

"Arrak will not relent until you've been sufficiently humiliated," Ketoh sneered, hatred dripping from every word.

At high noon, Ketoh received the order, cut the straps, and lowered Osi to the ground. Four men carried their leader to the bay and revived him in its cool salty waters. Yet something important had changed.

"That was a remarkable deed," Ketoh said. "The men have always respected you, but now they hold you in awe. You've grown immensely in their eyes."

"Any man...would have done the same," Osi said.

"No, Osi, few men would have done what you did," Busah said in confidential tones. "No man who followed you through Death's Shadow or saw you at the wall will ever doubt your destiny."

"Any man would have done what I did if he were in my position. I only hope Captain Arrak learns the error of his ways . . . before I again visit Koro-reni," Osi said, while unconsciously reaching over his shoulder and gingerly touching his injured back with the tips of his fingers.

"Perhaps it would be best not to pass this way again, Osi," Busah said.

"At least not until you outrank that bastard," Ketoh said.

* * *

"We can't wait another day," Osi declared.

"Two days in port, and not a single ship big enough to haul passengers. That just doesn't seem right. I thought the fleet follows a strict schedule." Busah paced impatiently on the dock.

"Not now, lad," an old ship's chandler said. "Used to be regular stops—here, Zafaga, Ras Abu Uwayd, and Wadi Jimal. Now with the war, we're not high enough on the list. If you wait just a few more hands, one may show up; 'course you could wait a month and still be standing here." The old man smiled wryly.

"Our only choice is the long march to Zafaga," Osi said.

"If they're still following the old schedules, a ship should be in Zafaga right now. But you'd have to make record time to get there overland. She'll berth for two days, three at most." The chandler winced.

"At least three days, by my count," Busah said.

"You'll move faster if you don't lug gear," the chandler added. "No boat here can accommodate 200 men, but they can haul your heavy equipment and bulk supplies."

"That would help," Osi replied.

"Amand, these boys...I mean men...want to bargain with you," the chandler shouted across to an adjoining pier. The boatman came over and commenced haggling. The price started high but ended reasonable, thanks to Busah's stubborn negotiation.

"Agreed. I'll drop your load with the harbormaster in Zafaga. He'll pay me, then release the goods on your signature. That's the way the military does it for troops in transit. He'll get paid the next time a Ship of the Realm docks."

"Okay, let's get out of here!" Osi said as cadets stacked their packs on the deck of the scruffy scow. Hearing an approaching runner, he wheeled around.

"Return to the garrison!" the runner yelled.

"Why?" Osi asked.

"Arrak's order. No need to question. Leave everything here and follow me."

"Why would he interrupt our departure?" he asked Busah without expecting an answer. "We need to hit the trail."

"And the boatman is leaving with the tide in two or three hands," Busah reminded him.

"Fall in, fall in!" the call came again.

"I won't fight Arrak again—if I can avoid it," Osi said.

"Leave everything here, including weapons," the runner said. Osi reluctantly laid his dirktooth sword on the rough wooden deck.

It's hard to part with it even for a short while.

As he laid the gleaming blade on the deck, he thought better of it, reached into his pack, and retrieved the chamois wrap Geb had used to conceal it back in Egia. Wrapping the sword, he handed the bundle to the boatman and sternly charged him with protecting it. He then slipped the ivory dagger inside his tunic–his only hedge against Arrak's whim, which he faced soon enough.

"What's the meaning of this?" Osi asked, barely able to contain his anger. Then, remembering protocol, "Sir," he added curtly.

"Just a little training drill. I sense that your boys have grown a bit rusty in the art of water combat. How long has it been since they drilled?"

"Sir, we've been crossing overland for nearly two months; there was little opportunity to practice any skill involving water, much less waves. I plan to renew their training on the way to Zafaga. We'll be near surf every night and day."

"Foolish boy, that's why you train them now. They must be prepared if a water attack comes."

"I'll train them tonight at our very first stop before we're out of sight of your own watchtower. If you'll excuse us, sir, we must be gone."

For the first time Arrak gave a direct order to Osi's men, "Into the water now, colonists." Arrak's own men were already in the water, congregated around a buoy in the middle of the harbor. Osi nodded, and the men complied. "Don't fret, Master Osi. My quartermaster will oversee the loading of your equipment. For now, you'd best take charge of your men. Some may get hurt. But first, stand beside me, and let's see how they do on their own."

Osi wheeled about to view the mock battle. Swimmers coursed toward the buoy. Dark forms streaked underwater in unpredictable patterns, some converging, others darting across. Arrak's Regulars, coordinated as if in close-order drill, vastly outnumbered Osi's leaderless men. The cadets were tentative at first, then too aggressive. When finally the two forces met, it was a disaster. One by one, the youths disappeared beneath the surface, always struggling valiantly to no avail. To his horror, Osi realized that clusters of Regulars were converging beneath to hold each captured cadet down.

Some of Arrak's men fought the surviving cadets at the surface, while those on bottom took turns coming up for air. It was a brilliant tactic, which would have earned Osi's admiration under any other circumstance. Here it was being used to kill innocent young men . . . his men.

"You heartless bastard!" Osi yelled, charging Arrak, until two soldiers grabbed him. Looking around he saw that all his officers–Ketoh, Busah, Tanta, even Urgan–had reacted similarly, and they, too, were being held.

When every Egian was down, Arrak signaled. Suddenly, five hundred men came to the surface, including every last one of the cadets. The cadets gasped for precious air. "Surely you don't think I'd kill off a regiment of future soldiers, even provincials like these. I'm not a selfish man. My amusement can wait till they face real war and die for good cause. My men weren't gulping air for themselves alone. You're such a novice. A well-trained commander would have calculated that we were gathering twice as much air as any man needs. Your inexperienced troops owe their lives to those extra mouthfuls of air."

"Thank you, captain. . .You've taught us a lesson we won't forget." Osi said.

"Regroup and try again. This time show some leadership of your own," Arrak commanded.

Five times the attack was repeated, and five times the Regulars won. Each bout, however, Osi exercised firmer control, and the cadets improved remarkably. After three hands, when the session ended, Osi felt his men could handle anyone except highly trained Regulars. The cadets, too, were in high spirits as they dressed and returned to the harbor.

Osi stared at the dock in disbelief. "Empty. Nothing," he said.

"Not a single item! Weapons, packs, staples, emergency gear. All gone," Busah said in dismay. The overloaded freighter was well on its way to Zafaga.

"This is no accident," Osi said. "That bastard deliberately lured us away to deceive us."

An orderly arrived with a message from the bastard himself. "Young Master Osi, you are to begin marching toward Zafaga this instant. We'll see what you provincials are made of."

"Assemble!" Osi ordered. "Forward march." He turned to Ketoh as they tramped out of camp, "I swear to you, Ketoh, never again will I allow myself to be outsmarted like this. But enough. We have a long march ahead of us. . .and we have to survive it." Osi slapped his side where the famous sword should have been. *I feel naked, he thought, but I will retrieve the Sword of Phanus in Zafaga. I will.*

He pulled out the dagger and lashed it in place. "Our only weapon for so many men," he said. *Father said to use the dagger when all else fails,* Osi thought. *Maybe he knew such a day would come.*

"We'll be fine," Ketoh said. "This lowland has been pacified for hundreds of years…we can live sumptuously off the bounty of the sea . . . the weather's warm . . . bedrolls won't be needed."

Night came soon, and Ketoh's predictions proved true. The men ate well, mostly shellfish, and slept warm and dry above the seashore. Their first full day was an easy jaunt along a serpentine beach. Late in the day, however, they encountered a recent landslide, sprawling with huge boulders, that blocked the strand. The rock fall lay at the base of a mountain, jutting out from the cliff like the horn of a huge charging rhinoceros. "Maybe we can swim around it," Sareem suggested.

"Check for currents," Osi said. "It looks rough."

Sareem swam out a short distance from shore and returned. "Unusually strong currents, swirls, waves, heavy chop," he reported grimly. "Too risky."

"We'll have to climb over, but we can't make it before dark. Set up camp here. Wasting a little daylight is better than spending the night in a boulder field."

At daybreak of the second day, the column formed for the difficult scramble. Walking, crawling, climbing hand over hand, they made their way across the jumble. The massive mound turned out to be much broader than they had suspected. Half a mountain, it seemed, had fallen. By late afternoon, the last of the cadets negotiated the boulder field, and the unit was on its way at full march again. The barrier had put them half a day behind schedule.

Making up for lost time, Osi marched them all day with hardly a break. "Shouldn't we make camp, Master Osi?" Urgan said, looking at the rising moon. "The sun has set and the men are exhausted. It's too dangerous to continue in darkness."

"We have no choice, Urgan. The dangers of moonlight are nothing compared with those of the overland route if we miss our rendezvous at Zafaga. Tell your men to summon their strength. We'll need every man's best effort to make it through in time. The ships won't wait."

"But the men object, sir. They can't keep moving. They haven't had a full meal since yesterday."

"Is it they who object, Master Urgan, or you? You are a leader. Inspire your men to greater effort."

"But this is more than great effort. It's impossible."

"Sometimes, soldier, you must inspire your men to do the impossible."

"It isn't wise."

"You may question my wisdom if you wish, but you will not question my orders. Keep your men on the march, or surrender your appointment."

"I will do as you order, sir."

When the moon went down, fog obscured the scant light of the stars. Total darkness meant slow progress for men walking two abreast between beach ridge and waterline. They found their way by following a faint yellow-green luminescence of small sea creatures churning in the roiling surf. At times, they waded through shallows to skirt rocky headlands. For most of the night, however, the strand was unobstructed, a veritable highway compared to the terrain already traversed.

Near daybreak, word of a slowdown at the rear of the column filtered up to Osi. Sareem ran up from the rear. "It's Master Urgan, sir; our unit is falling behind. He says we are exhausted and must hold up."

"And how is it that you are able to run when they are unable to walk?" Osi asked.

"It is my duty, sir."

Osi followed Sareem rearward to the malingering troops. "Urgan, what is your condition?"

"My men are beyond exhaustion."

"Yet, Sareem was able to run forward to summon me?"

"I did as you suggested and inspired him to the effort."

"Then could you not also inspire other men to keep pace?"

"It is impossible, sir. I have the welfare of my men at heart."

"You are unfit to lead, Urgan. You are relieved. Sareem, assume command."

"But, Osi, I am high born, and Sareem is barely more than a peasant!"

"That is all. Say no more! Assume your position in the ranks."

"You are too harsh, Osi. You let your rank rule your head."

"That's enough, Urgan! You are fairly warned."

"It's unfair," Urgan groused to his men as Osi walked away.

"Return to Egia, Master Urgan," Osi said calmly. Urgan gasped at the severity of the sentence. But there was no recourse. He turned and, with heavy steps, began the long walk into darkness and certain death. Sareem and his troops double-stepped to catch up with the column. Osi ran back to the front.

At daybreak the cadets found themselves at the base of a cliff rising abruptly from the water. The sea filled the entire cove leaving no room for passage. "We have no time to hike around," Osi said. "Into the water, men!" He led the column into the surf. His cadets set the cadence—each stroke syncopated with the movements of the unit. Progress was good, but the distance was long. For three hands of time, the regiment plowed through surging waves.

Finally, they reached a muddy flat. They rested in the soothing ooze for more than a hand, finding a clam here and there, then washed themselves and moved on. Bodies refreshed and legs rested, they quickened their pace except when crossing deep mud or shallow channels that drained back toward the sea. Ketoh found a promising spot, and Osi allowed the men to dig clams in earnest with bare hands and seashells. They gobbled the sweet, salty meats and filled their pockets with whole clams wrapped in seaweed. These they ate on the run as the afternoon wore on. By alternating double time and regular cadence, they covered the final leg in two-thirds the expected time. Night fell as they rounded the last stretch of open beach and saw the welcoming glow of Zafaga's light.

"Surely we'll fare better here," Osi said. "This place looks more civilized than Gubal. Maybe we'll finally get a suitable welcome and some decent lodging. My father says that Zafaga has been known to hold celebrations in honor of arriving cadets."

Chronicle 10: The Port of Zafaga

"No ships in port," Osi said, eyeing the signal staff atop the lighthouse. He surveyed the bustling port and military stronghold.

"Stay here," he ordered his troops. "Busah, find provisions and fetch our belongings from the harbormaster. I'll arrange our stay in the barracks. Ketoh, go with Busah. Ask about ships and report back to me at once. If they've already come and gone, we'll have to march overland to Ras Abu Uwayd, maybe even Wadi Jimal."

Osi headed for the fort. "I am Osi, Commander of the Cadets of Egia," he announced on arrival.

"Yes?" responded the fort's commander without a hint of interest or welcome.

"We seek accommodations in the barracks of Zafaga."

"We are full."

"Full? Why?"

"King's Regulars. Top priority. Colonials have to fend for themselves."

"Surely there is some way...something we can work out."

"You must think more highly of yourselves than we do, lad. There's a war going on. We have no time for children's games. Why don't you try the harbor? Maybe you can find work there to earn your night's keep." He laughed as he slammed his office door in Osi's face.

Ketoh soon rejoined Osi in the plaza.

"The harbormaster was out of his office, but good news anyway. The ships haven't arrived yet, but the merchants say they may show up anytime. They were expected two days ago."

"The commander says we are at war, Ketoh. Have you heard talk of it? Did he mean the war with the Westerners? That's old news."

"No. The Westerners are a great fear, but there's war to the east as well. It's all I heard about from one merchant to the next. They say that rebels across the Valley Sea have formed an alliance against the Realm. Already they've taken land in the eastern regions of Punt. Now there's fear they may be staging in readiness to cross the Valley Sea and attack our ports north of Berenicia."

"Surely the Realm can fend them off. What do the merchants think?"

"They're more concerned with commerce than war. No one believes the threat is real."

"And who leads this little rebellion?"

"That's the strange part, Osi. No one knows who leads or why they fight."

"But there are traders in the streets. Busah was able to buy provisions, was he not?"

"He found food but only at a very high price. With no currency and little status, we Cadets of the Realm hold no sway in this time of crisis, Osi."

"Are our belongings with the harbormaster?" Osi asked.

"Yes. Busah spoke with his quartermaster, but he will not honor our Rights of the Realm. He wants hard currency or a portion of our goods. He was a difficult man to deal with, Osi," Ketoh said in despair.

"This place is in turmoil, Ketoh. We'll have to solve this problem on our own . . . and quickly. . . for the sake of the men."

"So many people," Ketoh said. "Every open space is taken, and the shore is stripped of food. The people don't welcome us here. They're running vagrants out of town. What can we do?"

"I'll speak with Busah and revisit the harbormaster if I can find him. Surely a reasonable man will deal with us."

At the base of the massive ramp rising to the lighthouse sat a quaint cottage occupied by the harbormaster. Hard knocks on the lintel finally brought the old man to the door.

Drunk, Osi thought. The room reeks of stale alcohol, and his breath smells like fresh barley beer.

"Yes!" the man answered crossly.

"I am Osi, commander of the Cadets of Egia. This is Busah, my quartermaster. We seek provisions and lodging till a ship arrives."

"Colonials, eh? How much are you prepared to pay?"

"We have no money. As Cadets of the Realm, we are entitled to be fed and sheltered by the garrison or city whenever necessary."

"Can't you see what's happening, son? We have enough soldiers here to found a colony of our own, though we'd need a few women to make it last. We can't care for every colonial who passes through. Pay for your stay, or sleep in the fog. That's your choice."

"The captain of the next vessel that arrives will gladly pay for our lodging. I'm sure of it."

"Ha! You colonials don't keep up with the news, do you? Ships may come, but not for you. The Army has commandeered all vessels to serve the construction of new roads at Wadi Jimal, Ras Abu Uwayd, and Zafaga. They're busy moving laborers, supplies, and real soldiers, not boys in training like you."

"What roads?" Osi asked. "Where will they go?"

"To the Land of the Second Sunset, of course. Come daybreak you'll see the beginnings on the hillside."

"But that's a violation of our age old truce with the Westerners. It will mean all-out war."

"How much worse can the fighting be?" the old man stammered

"But we must be in Berenicia before the solstice. We'll have to go overland if the ships aren't here within three days."

"Overland? You won't make it in time, even if you depart tonight, young fellow."

"Why not, sir? I am told the march is 13 days."

"Because you'll be dead in two or three. The Westerners have slaughtered every man who's topped the First Terrace since hostilities began."

"Back to the business at hand. We're willing to work for our stay," Osi said.

"Egians working in ports of the Valley Sea? That's a good one! What would do you? Row my tugs about the harbor? Ha! If you have no money, our chat is finished!" With that, the harbormaster drew back to slam the door.

"Wait, sir! We must reclaim our belongings from your lockup. The ship's captain will pay when he arrives," Busah said.

"So you're the owners of that pile of rubbish. I should have guessed."

"May we reclaim our rubbish, sir?" snapped Osi. His response brought just the hint of a smile on the old man's lips.

"Let's have a look," the harbormaster said, pulling a ringed set of keys from a peg behind his door. Shuffling and stumbling, the drunken man led them along the dock to a commodious storeroom beside his office. There in rough heaps on the floor lay the cadets' possessions. Osi's pack had arrived in good condition.

My sword, Osi thought. *Where's my sword?* Dropping to his knees, he shuffled through the pile. *There. Thank Rahn, it's here.* Hurriedly he peeled back the chamois. *Perfect condition.*

Oblivious to what was going on, the harbormaster said, "Damn officials. Payments don't come. Arrogant sons of bitches. Never pay a man." He rambled on. "Are you really cadets? I get all sorts through here, you know. Everybody begs a free stay. Everybody wants…beautiful sword…" he said as his beer-clouded vision suddenly focused on the magnificent weapon.

"Now if I had something of value to hold as security, I might be willing to advance your men their food and lodging until the ships arrive," the old man said smoothly, a sly glint in his eye.

"Such as my sword?" Osi asked.

"Such as that sword . . . no matter who owns it!" the old man said. "Of course, it wouldn't bring much of a price, what with that old broken-tooth handle and that big nick. Practically broken in half, it is," he said.

"That sword was the gift of a Captain of the Realm," Busah said indignantly. "This man swore a solemn oath to bring it honor in battle?"

"These are hard times, young man. Honor in battle is a noble cause, but it won't put fish on my table or shelter this tired old body. Your men must pay, and your leader has the collateral to guarantee it." He faced Osi, "What is your choice, lad? The sword, or the welfare of your men?"

"My men will not suffer."

"But Osi, what if the ships don't come? What if the captains refuse to pay? Don't let this man take advantage of you," pleaded Busah.

Osi faced the harbormaster. "Here is my sword and with it my honor. Take care that it is not damaged or lost or dishonored. I will reclaim it when the ships arrive. If we must go overland to Berenicia, I will return after the solstice. You will not sell it until the equinox. Is that clear?"

"Fair enough. Yes, I agree! You will have food and lodging for your men until the ships arrive."

"Plus 20 days' rations and release of essential equipment should we be forced to go overland!"

"Agreed, agreed . . . if you decide to be so foolhardy." His voice betrayed his eagerness. He would gladly trade 20 days' rations for such a prize. Knowing the dangers of the inland trail, he was certain the sword would be his. "Now bring your men to the harbor. We'll find them a palatial place to sleep."

Chronicle 11: Aboard the *Ruby*

The third morning passed, and their "palatial" quarters in the hold of a sunken freighter reeked from its burden of human occupation. Still no ship in sight, and conditions grew worse each day. The people of Zafaga were a self-absorbed, contentious lot who callously discriminated against "colonials" and daily swindled the trusting youths. Stories of crimes against their own kind abounded as well. On more than one occasion, fights broke out among townspeople and cadets. Three of Osi's men were seized by local authorities on trumped-up charges and held until Osi could coax more funds from the harbormaster to purchase their ransom.

"It's high time we move on to Berenicia!" Ketoh said as they scurried from the market after yet another encounter with locals.

"If the ships don't come, we march at daybreak tomorrow," Osi said. "Meanwhile, confine our men to the harbor. I don't want any problems. Assign extra guards."

Before dawn, Osi assembled his regiment on the dock. "Men, the time has come. I've made arrangements with the harbormaster. Gather your weapons, packs, and bedrolls. We leave in one hand."

When the time came, Osi took his position at the front of the column, and the long march began. "The new road makes the going easy, but not for long, I'll wager," Osi said to Ketoh as the column headed up the steep, half-finished roadway. Laborers cleared obstructions and notched the hillsides to straighten an ancient trail. Soon the regiment passed the foremost construction teams, and the unimproved path wound through deeply incised meanders of an upland valley. Reaching the cliff top by late afternoon, they turned southward along the First Terrace

Osi occasionally glimpsed the Valley Sea on which he had hoped to sail that morning. Sometimes he saw the lighthouse spire, but no flag unfurled to signal a new arrival.

* * *

"Ships! Ships! Master Osi. Incoming ships, headed for Zafaga." Bracon, serving as scout, was charged with scanning the eastern horizon, and the precaution paid off. With luck and a fast walk back to port, the cadets might sail at the next morning's light. Even at this great distance, Osi saw three tall masts of the greatest ships that sailed the World Ocean. The mighty barquentines of Berenicia dwarfed all other vessels.

Three hands later, Osi stood before the *Ruby of Berenicia* and shouted to the sergeant-at-arms, "I am Osi, Commander of the Cadets of Egia." The magnificent crimson barquentine stood high and proud. "Ships of stone," she and her sister ships were called after their rock-hard, gleaming-red cladding that rang like a bell against a dock or enemy vessel. *Redsilver,* Osi thought, *just like my dagger. Father said I'd see more of it in Punt.* Osi relished the steady tolling of the *Ruby's* metal hull as each wave gently nudged bow against berth. The other two lay silently at anchor just outside the harbor.

"Yes?" a junior officer said.

"We desire passage to Berenicia." Osi spoke with less surety than in previous dealings.

"We have no bunks. Our holds are bulging with cargo to supply workers at Gubal. We'll offload some here, then proceed to Gubal. After that, we return directly to Berenicia. We have no time to stop for colonials. You'll have to wait for the next convoy."

"And when will that be?"

"Perhaps three or four weeks."

"We must arrive in Berenicia before the solstice."

"That's only a ceremony, lad. We're preparing for war. Our schedule allows no time for boys hitching rides to graduation."

"It's our duty to train for service to the King," Osi said, his exasperation showing.

"Except for our captain, we're merchant seamen, hired to man the vessels of Berenicia. We are paid to haul cargo. If you want bunks, you'll have to pay. Find yourself a coastal freighter."

"What's going on here?" the ship's captain demanded when finally the heated conversation rose to his ears.

"This colonial thinks we should stall our mission to ferry a troop of cadets to Berenicia."

"And who are you to demand such service?" the captain asked.

"I am Osi, Commander of the Cadets of Egia."

"Egia, eh? Tell me, lad, do you know Geb of Egia?"

"He is my father, sir!"

"And your father is well?"

"When last I knew," Osi said. He choked at the words. *It's been so long already,* he thought. *Never again will I know my family's fortunes or misfortunes until months or even years after each turn of events.*

"I am Captain Hervov of Berenicia. Your father and I sailed together many times when he came to the Valley Sea for training. I myself was born in Egia and spent my youth there. I too was chosen for duty here in Punt. I was given to a ship, and Geb was given back to Egia."

"My father has spoken of you."

"You must be the young man who killed the dirktooth. Single-handed. Is that true?"

"Yes, sir. It is true."

"Then show me your sword, young man. I heard reports of it in Berenicia."

"I will be happy to do so," Osi said with a smile, "if you will join me on a visit to the harbormaster."

On hearing Osi's story, Captain Hervov readily agreed to ransom Osi's sword. "My officer spoke the truth, Osi. We have no room for men aboard the *Ruby.* But stay here in Zafaga for a few days. We'll offload in Gubal. The *Blaze* and the *Pearl* can take the crucial cargo directly to Berenicia. I'll run the *Ruby* in at Zafaga and pick you up. With good winds, we'll reach Berenicia in two days."

* * *

"Swiftly sailing on an open sea! It's even better than the Great River! Here there are no bounds." The only measure of movement was the rush of wind past his face and the shush of water beneath the metal bow. The ship was under full sail and well-heeled into a high wind. No other vehicle on earth could move as fast as a ship, no other ships on earth could sail as fast as the barquentines of Berenicia, and no other barquentine could catch the *Ruby.*

Captain Hervov approached Osi as he stood at the bow staring out to sea. "Geb knows a fine sword," he said, eying the Sword of Phanus proudly hanging from Osi's sash. "How would you like to take the helm?" Snapping from his reverie, the young man wheeled about and faced the captain.

"You're too kind. It's much too great a ship for me to handle."

"Have you ever held a tiller before, lad?"

"Yes, when I was a boy. But only a felucca."

"Then it's settled. A ship's a ship. You must try the helm of the *Ruby.* It's my honor. If a man can kill a dirktooth cat, he certainly can handle the whipstaff of a mere barquentine."

"My pleasure, sir." They walked to the steerage deck where Osi surveyed the strange contraption that controlled the rudder. It was a long stick jutting up through the deck like an inverted pendulum. Notches were cut in the frame that lined the whipstaff's well. They were spaced at regular intervals so that the whipstaff could be held in place with little effort once a course was set. If a correction were required, the whipstaff could be wrenched quickly from one notch to another. The well-worn grip told Osi where to grab hold.

"Take her to starboard until you feel the weight of a spring lamb, then set her in the notch. Get the feel of the vessel. If you want more speed, add more weight. Not too much or you'll take us under." The captain spoke casually as if the possibility of capsizing were only a minor concern.

"I'll happily maintain the lesser setting," Osi said, at first visibly nervous. For the first two hands or so, his helm was unsteady. The big ship lumbered to port and then to starboard, faster, then slower, then faster again.

"You'll get the hang of it. Just treat her like a lady."

Old Ashran's precise words. I guess the captain's right. A ship is *a ship.*

With that he settled down and in no time was fully at ease with the helm. "Tell me how to speed up without capsizing."

"Pull until you feel the weight of a man and her sails groan. Much beyond that might make her sound like a whale." Osi laughed at the unexpected pun. He soon reached full speed, heeling the vessel well into the wind like a veteran helmsman. He couldn't resist pushing the whipstaff a notch farther. To his delight, the proud ship coursed still faster but held steady in the water. "Under your hand, we'll be in Ras Abu Uwayd by late afternoon," the captain said after three hands at sail. "With such instincts, you could become a decent sea captain."

"Perhaps, when I finish my training in Berenicia, I will elect naval training."

"There is another choice. By the rules of your service, you may join me now as an apprentice. You could avoid one year of soldiering. It would be my honor to teach you all I know. After two years at my side, you'll become captain of your own vessel. An apprentice from my command can choose the best assignments on the best ships in the entire fleet. What do you say, Osi?"

"Sir, are you suggesting that I resign my commission as a Cadet of the Realm to become a ship's apprentice?"

"Yes, lad, many a cadet has done so. There's no dishonor. I chose that course myself. Cadets serve only by their own commitments."

"I would be pleased to accept your offer, sir, but, the choice is not mine. I've sworn my allegiance to the King, and I must continue. I will await my assignment at the completion of training."

"That's a wise decision, lad, but I would treat you as my own son if you chose to serve with me."

"Rahn Mennon, our King, is wise. I'll place my fate in his hands."

Hervov smiled dubiously.

The rest of the leg to Ras Abu Uwayd was ripe with instruction by the captain, the helmsman, and the first mate. Osi absorbed most of the information but was nearing saturation when the vessel approached the harbor. The captain ordered the sails struck, and the ship slowed to a snail's pace.

"Take her to port, lad," the captain said when Osi stepped aside for the regular helmsman.

"But, sir!" Osi, the first mate, and the helmsman said in unison.

"Take her in," the captain said firmly. "You can do it. You have a gift."

Osi jerked the whipstaff and felt his way into port. He soon had the ship under control and headed straight for its assigned berth.

"Steady as she goes," Captain Hervov said. "Now take her down to a crawl. Slower. Now bring her alongside. Longshoremen will gaff us dockside. Slower . . ."

I'm not going to make it. Should I surrender the helm? No, I can make it.

"Ease up. Let her drift...." Hervov dashed for the whipstaff. "Too late...." Clang! Redsilver struck hard stone. Osi was thrown against the capstan as the *Ruby's* bow rammed the city dock.

"Are you alright, sir?" Osi asked.

"Oh, I'm fine. Let's hope no one noticed." Hervov laughed as he pointed to throngs of gawkers onshore. Every eye in the port was focused first on the *Ruby's* bow and then its youthful helmsman. "Don't worry about the *Ruby,* son. That's why we use redsilver—just in case a crazy captain turns his command over to a wild cadet."

Ras Abu Uwayd was larger and more vulgar than Zafaga. Otherwise, with their massive lighthouses and stone wharves, each town could easily have been mistaken for the other. Remembering Zafaga, Osi denied shore liberty.

At the earliest glint of day, the *Ruby* cast off, and she was under sail in open water by sunrise. Skies were overcast but rainless, and winds were light. Osi's instruction continued throughout the day as the ship raced toward Wadi Jimal for its nightly anchorage. Seas were calm and waters deep near shore, so Captain Hervov held a course close to land.

Osi watched the coast. "I'm surprised there are so many towns. Some seem larger than Egia!"

Hervov chuckled, recalling his own youthful "discoveries." "After leaving Egia, I came first to Jobal Erba, a small town south of Berenicia. I thought it was a major city. At 16 years I went to Bur Sudan and was shocked by its size. A year later, Berenicia exceeded my wildest dreams."

"I know Berenicia is a splendid place."

"It is indeed, lad! But Berenicia is much more than you've been told. It's one of the largest cities the world has ever known. It has hundreds of pyramids and a magnificent lighthouse with a pinnacle of redsilver."

"I can't imagine such a sight. This dagger and the *Ruby*'s bow are the only redsilver I've ever seen. Where does it come from?"

"You'll see the mines this afternoon before we reach Wadi Jimal. They are guarded well."

As the noon hour passed, Osi spotted coastal settlements and fishing villages but little industry. A head of land with barren banks jutted far out into the sea. Gradually its slopes redefined themselves as sheer cliffs rising more than 30 manheights above the billowing waves.

"That's Redsilver Point," Hervov said, "the place I told you about. It's a major landmark for navigators and the main source of redsilver ore. There's another big mine east of the Valley Sea."

At last, Osi saw a bustling anthill of activity in and out of scattered holes perched high on narrow ledges.

"Now look over there." Hervov pointed to the juncture of the cliff base and a thin strip of beach. A tiny hole just large enough for a man to squeeze through hung like a painted dot on the slick rock face.

"So that's what you mean by 'well guarded.'" Osi gestured toward the hundred or more troops along the base of the cliff, flanking the tiny opening, and surrounding a large building a few hundred paces away.

Hervov winced. "That tunnel is the only access to the mine, and its only approach is through the surf in that cove. So, come by sea, and currents and crosswinds will bash your ship unmercifully against the rocks. Come by land? Well, the Land of the Second Sunset is blocked by cliffs just as high and steep as these."

"Those workers must be the most trusted men in the Realm."

"The least trusted, I'm afraid. No one who mines or smelts redsilver is trusted. Hundreds of men go in each year, but only redsilver comes out. Once a man enters that tiny portal and climbs inside the mines, he's there until he dies."

"I think I've learned all I want to know about redsilver," Osi said.

Chronicle 12: Passage to Berenicia

Captain Hervov made certain each cadet had a few coins to enjoy Wadi Jimal. "Here, take this small sum. Go. Explore the city, lad!" the captain said with a wink. Osi hesitated for a moment, his hand open with the coins centered in his palm. "Go ahead, it's not a gift. It's your due!" the captain said.

Should I? Osi thought. Then he firmly grasped the coins and nodded thanks.

Wadi Jimal was a bustling metropolis of more than 20,000 inhabitants. Drunken men roamed the streets, but so did the King's Army. Men could revel as they pleased, but, if their rowdiness troubled others, soldiers herded them off to jail. Osi, Ketoh, and Busah had been friends since their earliest memories, and each had, at times, confided his dream of the day when he would taste the delights of a beautiful woman. By custom, they had become eligible on completion of training in Egia, but there had been no time to indulge before leaving Egia. Later, the difficulties of Gubal and Zafaga kept all the officers too busy for such diversions. Ketoh, by his own, somewhat questionable, admission, was the only one who had indulged. Now Osi and Busah would have an opportunity to catch up with their comrade.

Sex was encouraged in the culture of the Realm for the great duty of the People of the Living Sun was to spread their seed. After becoming eligible, it was considered selfish of a young man, a Chosen One, to conserve his seed, and few cadets were inclined to do so. By morning, Osi reckoned, there wouldn't be a virgin cadet left in the entire regiment.

Finding the courage to approach a prospective partner, however, was quite another matter for Osi, Busah, and several others. They shared the obligation to multiply, but their high birth had sheltered them from many experiences common among their friends. To Osi and Busah, it was remarkable, if true, that Ketoh had found the courage to seek out a sexual partner in Egia, especially since he had done so "on the sly" before reaching the age of eligibility. Osi had fought a dirktooth cat and bravely led his troops through untold dangers in unknown lands, but still this particular unknown territory made him quake. Busah had been at his side through all but the first adventure, yet he, too, was worried.

"Ketoh," Busah said, "you must advise Osi and me. We've never bedded a woman before."

"It's nothing, my friends. Everything happens so naturally. Have no worry."

"Perhaps Ketoh doesn't want to share his success," Osi said to Busah, dismissively.

"No, no. It's easy. Women will be grateful for your favors. At least they were for mine."

"But Ketoh, we need to know everything there is to know. We don't want to embarrass ourselves," pleaded Busah.

"Yes, Ketoh, tell all, so we won't be nervous."

Cornered, Ketoh's cockiness subsided. "Truth is, I'm just as nervous as you, friends."

"But why? You have experience. You know the ways of women."

"No one knows the ways of women, Osi."

"Perhaps not, Ketoh, but there's no substitute for experience."

"Actually, Osi, there is one." Ketoh's brow wrinkled and his voice wavered.

"And that is?"

"Lies, Osi, lies!"

"What do you mean?"

"I mean I lied. I've never had sex. I'm just as new to this game as you are."

"Well then, there's level ground among us. Let's go make fools of ourselves together," Osi said with a laugh. With that, the trio headed out to conquer their own fears and a lady or two. For Ketoh and Busah, the matter was clear. For Osi, however, there was that vague specter of a beautiful, unnamed maiden. Someday he would meet such a woman...wed and build a life with her. No woman of the streets could fulfill that desire, but for now he would put dreams aside. He would fulfill the expectations of his people. He would share his seed.

* * *

The noisy street reminded Osi of Temptation Alley. The smoky tavern was familiar too–stale beer, strong tobacco, gambling men, raucous yells. A provocatively dressed young lady handed Osi a beer.

"What's your price, pretty one?" he asked as directly as he met any new challenge on land or sea.

The girl impishly recited a well-rehearsed line, "A coin of the Realm buys the brew. Two more buy the night."

"Here, take these coins to your master." Transaction completed, the couple walked out the back door through a narrow alley to nearby lodgings. In the glow of a bright window, Osi saw that she was perhaps a year or two younger than he and even prettier than he had realized in the dim light of the tavern. "You're very lovely," he said. "You look so soft...so innocent." The girl cringed at his last word.

"I may be soft, and you may think me lovely," she said, "but I am no longer innocent, not since I was brought to this evil place."

"What do you mean, 'brought'? Aren't you here of your own accord?"

"I am the youngest daughter of a poor fisherman from a village near Ras Abu Uwayd. My father died at sea. My brothers sold me to the whoremongers of Wadi Jimal."

"That's...that's horrible. How could they do such a thing?"

"They needed money. My bondage brought as many coins as a good season's catch of fish, dried and sold at market."

"They sold you into sex servitude for so little?"

"Oh, that's not so little. It put a full year's rations on our family table. I've been in Wadi Jimal for nearly a month, but my younger brothers and sisters eat well at home."

"Maybe it's best that we just talk. You're held here against your will. It would be wrong for me to force you to...share yourself."

"But, no, young master," she responded. "You are the kindest man I've met in this city. It would be a shame to lie with so many vile men and let one who shows kindness go unrewarded. Take me, and we'll share our joy. It will be my only real pleasure in this place they call a 'house of pleasure.'"

With that understanding, Osi and the girl engaged in something close to love, an intimate encounter at once both tender and unconstrained, however temporary it might be. Their passions lasted the night, and Osi returned to the *Ruby* at dawn.

I was indeed fortunate to encounter such a girl, he thought. Perhaps someday I'll help right the injustice of involuntary servitude. Now that I've benefited from its corruption, he chided himself. *But guilt is no match for the pleasure I'll remember for a lifetime.*

Every man in Osi's command returned smiling that night. *No arrests or floggings,* Osi thought. *Now, I suppose they'll all want to boast of their exploits.* "This will make the Telling of Tales look like child's play, Ketoh," Osi said on hearing the first bravado.

"Everyone speaks as if virgins by the score eagerly surrendered their maidenheads to our charms," Sareem said to the crowd.

"Let's admit, fellows, our charms were no greater than the number of coins we held," Osi said.

"And your 'coin' is no bigger than ours, Master Osi!" responded Busah with a timid laugh, obviously referring to hard currency not minted by the Realm.

"No one has a bigger 'coin' than I!" laughed Ketoh.

"No bigger, perhaps, but undoubtedly of a higher denomination!" Busah said, gesturing toward his own tunic.

"Tell us of your evening, Master Osi," a platoon leader interjected.

"Silence is my story," Osi said with a laugh. He was not above idle talk, but the experience of the past evening was too intimate to discuss so openly.

"Ah, so there's still one virgin among us!" shouted Ketoh.

"Think what you will, Ketoh."

"So tell us your story, Osi." Ketoh demanded mischievously.

"Which is better? Not to tell of things that *have* happened . . . or to tell of things that have *not* happened?" Osi peered into Ketoh's eyes.

"So, Master Osi, when will we sail again for Berenicia?" Ketoh asked, wisely changing the subject.

"At three hands past sunrise," responded Osi, mercifully allowing his friend an easy escape.

* * *

"Aweigh. Aweigh. Aweigh the *Ruby*. Aweigh the *Ruby of Berenicia!*" shouted the coxswain. "Winds strong at two hands past sunrise."

At three hands past noon, Ras Banas loomed high on the *Ruby*'s starboard. "These bluffs verging the Valley Sea are draped in lush vegetation unlike any I've ever seen," Osi said as they rounded the cape. "I thought Egia was green, but this makes our little delta look like dry steppe." A hand of time later they entered the harbor channel, and Osi saw before him the broad sloping piece of ground on which the miraculous city stood.

Seaside slopes supported rich grain fields on irrigated terraces reaching almost to the distant cliffs. Osi took pride in this innovation first perfected in Egia and then disseminated throughout the Realm. As the Ruby drew close to land, Osi spotted irrigation channels emanating from storage basins carved into the hillsides just below the First Terrace. Cave dwellings with ornately carved entrances dotted the hillsides. Reaching the inner harbor, he saw the grand city laid out before him. Not a word did he say, for he, like every other cadet on deck, was dumbfounded by the sight.

A city like no other! The massive lighthouse, its graceful spire sheathed in gold and crowned with redsilver, dominated the skyline. In waters along the shore and on land stretching to the upper slopes were thousands of buildings. Hundreds of pyramids spiked the city's skies. Structures of every description stretched across the plain, up the hillsides, and north and south as far as the eye could see. On the higher slopes half-finished pyramids, temples, and lesser buildings, like beehives, swarmed with workers. Inland a few houses and shops neared completion where the city spread up a broad canyon toward the First Terrace. A grand tree-lined highway led northwest, the overland crossing to the Great River. Southward stretched the Coast Road, its broad surface elevated above the alongshore marshes. Northward along the beaches stretched a scenic, shaded pathway studded with parks. Scores of shadufs—counterweighted devices used to raise water from one level to another— pumped fresh water from canals to parks and fields.

One enormous edifice, a true pyramid like the one in Egia but even larger, was under construction above the city. "They're using a building technique I've never seen before," Osi said, pointing toward an open tunnel near the harbor. Into it floated a long narrow barge, a single massive stone on its deck.

"They've cut a tunnel all the way to the base of the pyramid, haven't they?" Ketoh marveled.

"They deliver building stones beneath the hillside directly to the building site. How clever!" Osi said.

"Then they float stones to the top," Ketoh added. He pointed to a line of shadufs that stretched from a wide canal all the way to the pyramid's highest tier of construction.

"There, atop the pyramid, see that shaft head where the stones emerge." As they watched, a rafted stone slowly rose into view. *This site must be foreseen as the center of a new Berenicia to replace the current city as the waters rise someday. Good idea, but even it will be inundated if the worst predictions of the King's Geometers come true.*

Gold-clad pyramids graced the old city center where the Royal Military Academy stood beside the main garrison. Nearby, row after row of piers spread their tentacles into the harbor, crowded with every type of seagoing vessel. Berenicia was a hundred times the size of Wadi Jimal. No wonder it held such sway. Great naval vessels, a mighty harbor fortress, and 10,000 men at arms guarded the city.

A skiff approached the *Ruby*, whose ensign was struck, ceremonially folded, and handed to the skiff's first mate, who then headed off toward other incoming vessels to collect their flags as well.

"Did I not tell you this city is beyond anything you have imagined?" Captain Hervov asked.

"Yes, Captain. It is the most beautiful spectacle anyone could possibly imagine," Osi said, still in awe. "But what of the war? I had expected the city to be on war footing. It looks so peaceful and prosperous."

"The Westerners are always acting up. That's nothing to be concerned about, lad."

"In Gubal they spoke of an uprising in the east. Is there no vigilance against an attack from the sea?"

"Oh, that pesky little war. Don't worry, young fellow. Our military leaders in Berenicia say the rebels have no ships worthy of such an attack. They claim no power on earth can touch the bastions of the Realm. Those imps may pester the likes of Zafaga and Wadi Jimal, but not Berenicia or the Red Island. They wouldn't dare. Even if they tried, they couldn't scrape together a dozen galleons to float their fight. They strike our struggling outposts, and we strike back." Then, Hervov's feigned smile transformed into a frown. "At least that's what Commander Ortilon says." His furrows deepened, "One day he may learn otherwise."

"Who leads these rebels?"

"No one knows. They began as a secret order, and they've kept it that way. Perhaps one day we will know...after it's too late."

"When will we be allowed ashore?"

"We'll anchor here until a berth is free. Perhaps we'll be in port before sundown, perhaps not. Not long ago, we could have gone right to the dock. Now, military traffic alone exceeds capacity, and the wait has grown longer and longer. I know you're anxious to land. Your men have a busy night ahead. Watch the lighthouse for the flag of the *Ruby*. When it flies, we'll land."

Presently the ensign of the *Ruby*, a bright red stone on a deep blue field, appeared above the lighthouse. Captain Hervov gave orders, and the crew hoisted anchor. "No room to maneuver under our own power," explained Hervov when, at sunset, a tugboat rowed by 60 oarsmen materialized from the confusion of the harbor and approached the *Ruby*. Lines were tossed, and the stout vessel muscled the *Ruby* into port. Through rows of vessels, moving barges, tugs, and tows the *Ruby* wound its way to the appointed berth, proudly marked by its own flag sent down from the lighthouse.

"Berenicia at last!" whooped Osi as the ship's prow rang against stone. He went amidships and assembled his men on the *Ruby*'s broad deck. "Our time has come, men. We've arrived, but night is approaching, and tomorrow is the solstice. We'll march directly to the barracks, take our evening meal, and bed down for a few hands. We must return to the seashore by midnight. There'll be no liberty in Berenicia until granted by the commanders of the King's Guard."

He turned to Captain Hervov. "Thank you for your help, sir. Without it, we would never have made it here in time. Goodbye for now. May our paths cross again and again."

"That they will, lad, but not before you've learned many a lesson atop the Sacred Pyramid of the Six Moons."

"So I am told, sir," Osi said.

"And don't forget the First Betrothal," Ketoh said.

"If anyone will have you," Osi said with a laugh.

* * *

Four abreast in darkness, the cadets assumed their familiar cadence and marched the winding street toward the barracks of the Royal Guard. When the column reached the temple, ushers led them to its outer sanctuary, a huge central hall lined with four rows of enormous columns. This was the public vault where any citizen could come to express and experience the majestic faith of the People of the Living Sun. Flaming sconces lighted the cavernous chamber. High above, massive stone lintels spanned from pillar to pillar. Stealing peeks at the surrounding walls while they stood at attention, Osi saw magnificent drawings and writings all about. As best he could make out, the walls contained scenes from everyday life in the Land of the Living Sun.

The cadets stopped momentarily before the free span that opened to the middle sanctuary, and Osi read on its gigantic lintel: "FOR THESE ARE THE AGES OF MAN." The boys advanced through the portal and entered an auditorium formed beneath two rows of columns, smaller than those in the outer sanctum, yet massive still. Finally, in the privacy of the sanctuary the boys were allowed to break ranks and stroll about. On its walls were religious texts and many scenes from the history of the People of the Living Sun.

Osi marveled at huge murals depicting great events. A noble savage led his people running before a raging fire. A leader pointed westward. The Secrets of the Ages lay abandoned inside a dank cave. Seas parted. A roving band of ancient men discovered a wonderful red island. On another wall he read:

"Listen...

FOR THESE ARE THE AGES OF MAN
The tales of the ancients tell us,
  200,000 years before our time,
  our people lived as savages,
  and then the Seas fell below the First Terrace.
And in the Golden Age of that unknown Kalpa,
  140,000 years before our time,
  the Ancestor Queen ruled,
  and iron thunderbolts rained from the sky.
And in the Topping Age of the First Kalpa,
  84,000 years before our time,
  the Ancestor King ruled,
  when blue seas washed the First Terrace.
And in the Falling Age of the First Kalpa,
  59,000 years before our time,
  the Ondwan, the Star King, ruled,
  and the Seas fell to forty-six manheights below the First
  Terrace.
And in the Rising Age of the Second Kalpa,
  46,000 years before our time,
  the Sindwan, the Water King, ruled,
  and the Seas rose to twenty-four manheights below the
  First Terrace.
And in the Topping Age of the Second Kalpa,
  45,000 years before our time,
  the Wirawan, the Wonderful King, ruled,
  and the Seas did not change.
And in the Falling Age of the Second Kalpa,
  37,000 years before our time,
  the Ketawan, the Seeking King, ruled,
  and the Seas fell to thirty-six manheights below the First
  Terrace.
And in the Golden Age of the Second Kalpa,
  36,000 years before our time,
  the Morowan, the Sea Floor King, ruled,

and the sea's land revealed its bounty.
And in the Rising Age of the Third Kalpa,
> 31,000 years before our time,
> the Tirowan, the Rival King, ruled,
> and the Seas rose to twenty-eight manheights below the
> First Terrace.

And in the Topping Age of the Third Kalpa,
> 27,000 years before our time,
> the Darowan, the Conqueror King, ruled,
> and the Seas did not change.

And in the Topping Age of the Third Kalpa,
> 17,000 years before our time,
> the Rindwan, the Great King, ruled,
> and the Seas did not change.

And in the Falling Age of the Third Kalpa,
> 16,000 years before our time,
> the Latawan, the Claiming King, ruled,
> and the Seas fell to sixty-four manheights below the First
> Terrace.

And in the Falling Age of the Third Kalpa,
> 13,000 years before our time,
> the Nellawan, the Shy King, ruled,
> and the Seas fell to sixty-nine manheights below the First
> Terrace.

And in the Golden Age of the Third Kalpa,
> 10,000 years before our time,
> the Moltawan, the Golden King, ruled,
> and the Seas did not change.

And in the Golden Age of the Third Kalpa,
> 7,000 years before our time,
> the Tattawan, the Bold King, ruled,
> and the Seas did not change.

And in the Rising Age of the Fourth Kalpa,
> 5,000 years before our time,
> the Erawan, the Red King, ruled,
> and the Seas rose to fifty-five manheights below the First
> Terrace.

Do not forget...
FOR THESE ARE THE AGES OF MAN."

After reading the texts and studying the murals, Osi reverently passed, along with the other cadets, into the inner sanctum. It was a chapel, smaller than the middle sanctuary, and older by far. Sheer walls of cut stone, darkened with age, replaced the grand colonnades that defined the other two chambers. Here they assembled for prayers and a devotional delivery by Toth, the Chief Priest. He blessed the cadets and impressed upon them the importance of betrothal and the sacred institution of marriage that it sanctified. He reminded them of the Ages of Man.

At the close of the ceremony, the boys formed two files and departed the great hall through the aisle opposite where they had entered. In military regimen, they were to look forward at all times. As they left the chamber, however, Osi, from the corner of his eye, caught one brief glimpse of a most wonderful sight. In the opposite aisle, two rows of ladies dressed in white entered for their own tour of the building.

Why do I feel so elated? Osi asked himself. *My heart is pounding. My temples pulse with excitement. It is as if within their ranks there is a light I cannot now see—like a star barely seen that disappears when viewed straight on.*

FOR THESE ARE THE AGES OF MAN

KALPA/AGE	YEARS BEFORE PRESENT (BP)		BEFORE OSI's TIME (BO)		RULERS	MEANING	REIGNED (BP/BO)	
Perspective:	Modern Perspective		Ancient Perspective				Modern/Ancient Perspective	
Time Before	From	To	From	To	Ancestor Queen		150,843	140,143
Rising	>140,000	128,000	>129,300	117,300				
Topping	128,000	117,000	117,300	106,300				
Falling	117,000	112,000	106,300	101,300				
Golden	112,000	107,000	101,300	96,300				
First Kalpa								
Rising	107,000	103,000	96,300	92,300				
Topping	103,000	79,000	92,300	68,300	Ancestor King		95,048	84,348
Falling	79,000	68,000	68,300	57,300	Ondwan	Star King	69,476	58,776
Golden	68,000	62,000	57,300	51,300				
Second Kalpa								
Rising	62,000	57,000	51,300	46,300	Sindwan	Water King	57,119	46,419
Topping	57,000	54,000	46,300	43,300	Wirawan	Wonderful King	56,189	45,489
Falling	54,000	47,000	43,300	36,300	Ketawan	Seeking King	47,776	37,076
Golden	47,000	42,000	36,300	31,300	Morowan	Sea Floor King	46,833	36,133
					Utawan	Stone King	46,804	36,104
					Kondwan	Wise King	42,826	32,126
Third Kalpa								
Rising	42,000	40,000	31,300	29,300	Tirowan	Rival or War King	41,742	31,042
Topping	40,000	27,000	29,300	16,300	Darowan	Conqueror King	37,914	27,214
Falling	27,000	22,000	16,300	11,300	Latawan	Claiming King	26,932	16,232
					Nellawan	Shy King	23,712	13,012
Golden	22,000	17,000	11,300	6,300	Moltawan	Golden King	21,033	10,333
Fourth Kalpa								
Rising	17,000	5,000	6,300	Osi's Day	Erawan	Red King	15,567	4,867
Topping	5,000	present						

CHAPTER 7

Search Log 14: Underwater Search

On Labor Day, the whole Caisson clan gathered at the family home place in Georgia. Even Kent, the youngest brother of the Caisson trio, and his daughter Meghan flew in from Camp Lejeune, North Carolina, where Kent was serving as a Lieutenant Commander in the Navy. By 1:30 p.m., everyone was home and the table was spread with a typical feast. The big round oak table wouldn't hold it all, and an antique meal chest against the kitchen wall was loaded with food, too. Margaret Caisson was in her element, cooking, darting here and there, giving orders to her kids and grandkids, to anyone who dared appear in the kitchen near mealtime. It was a happy time, reminiscent of many such meals when J.L. was alive.

Shunning the bustle, Jared walked out the back door and stared at the familiar green hills, burnished with the faintest hint of fall. The place stirred memories of his father, and he was overcome with a sad emptiness for those places J.L. once had been. He looked over the grasslands and thought of his father plowing those same plots when they had been gardens and fields. He reminisced about the summer of '54 when they spent J.L.'s entire vacation fencing the four-acre "flat patch," signaling the end of an era as crops became pasture. He looked at the forests and remembered cutting firewood with his father and brothers. He looked at the barn and thought of tending cattle together. He remembered back even to a time when he was too little to help, and his parents tended the whole place on their own.

On the asphalt drive at the rear of the house, Jared, oldest son by a mere 22 minutes, remembered how the backyard looked years ago. *I would have stepped onto the back porch, opened the screen door, and strolled beneath that giant willow on the stone walkway my grandfather, Monroe, laid with his own hands.* Now the porch was enclosed, and most of the backyard was sheltered by a carport holding two cars with extra room for a picnic table and an old church pew. *What I miss most is the old well curb, which I myself demolished in a regrettable fit of progress three decades ago, now lost beneath the concrete slab of the carport.* He missed the willow tree that shaded most of the backyard and imparted a homey look to the whole house, front and back. The spot where he stood once had been a farm road running from the potato house and garage above to the barn and chicken houses below. Long before he was born, it had been a public road. In his youth it was merely a firm path for moving equipment around on the farm. Now it would take an archaeologist to find any trace of it. The rustic smokehouse beside it had been replaced years ago by J.L.'s woodworking shop, painted white and topped with shiny galvanized metal.

Interrupting Jared's reverie, Rick stepped out to call him to lunch. "What are you thinking?" he asked, but the memory was almost too intimate to share.

"Oh, I was just thinking how much things have changed out here since we were kids. Item by item we've altered this place from a country home in the old Southern style to something that almost would fit in a modern subdivision anywhere in America. We remodeled not just a house but a whole landscape. We thought each step was good at the time, but now I'm not so sure. I really miss the old willow, the well curb, and all the stone paving that used to be out here. This whole neighborhood has changed the same way. Hell, the whole countryside has changed, all so gradually that nobody realized what was happening."

Rick scanned the carport and yard for a moment, remembering himself how it used to be. "You're right. It slipped up on us, but the difference is like night and day. So much has disappeared, and so much has been added. Reminds me of our search. If this place we know so well can change so much in a single lifetime, imagine how much the world has changed in thousands of years. No wonder it's so hard to find traces of ancient cultures, especially any that may have existed as long ago as the Ice Ages."

"My thoughts exactly."

Suddenly the wind gusted, and a vivid flash brightened the southern sky. "Look at those black clouds!" Jared exclaimed.

"Did you read about the boy who was struck by lightning over on the Cumberland Plateau last week?" Rick asked. "Ran under a tree in a thunderstorm. Common mistake. That's absolutely the worst place to be."

"You'd think a thirteen-year-old boy would have known better?" Jared said.

"Oh, I don't know. I can't remember our parents warning us about that when we were kids."

Jared leaned toward Rick as if he were revealing an embarrassing secret, a long held burden on his soul. "Well," he said, "they told me. But they said they'd whip me if I told you."

Rick responded with mock anguish. It had been a game between them for many years to "one-up" each other with such barbs. Once, introducing his twin at a conference, Rick had said to the audience, "People often take me for a fool, and here's the fool they take me for." Over the years, Rick had dominated the competition, but today Jared was the clear winner. The two brothers laughed, then stepped inside to eat far more than they should. Jared walked into the crowded kitchen with a satisfied grin on his face.

As the meal ended, Margaret's sons and grandchildren toted a few dishes to the sink and made token offers of help. She quickly dismissed them from her domain, as they knew she would. She preferred Ellie and Anna, partly because the three of them worked together well, and partly because, subconsciously, she wanted to preserve the old way—women in the kitchen, men in the fields. The fields were gone, of course, and it was only for old times' sake that she pretended the men had work to do or needed special rest. But the end of custom was evident as, without a thought, she dismissed granddaughters and grandsons alike.

The grandkids hopped in Matt's car and headed for a prearranged rendezvous with their favorite second cousins who lived nearby. Rick, Kent, and Jared repaired to the front porch to recover from lunch. The sultry afternoon air made eyelids heavy.

"By the way, did you finish reading that book about underwater archaeology? The one by Marx." Rick droned.

"Yes, weeks ago. I thought I told you about it."

"No, you never mentioned it."

"Maybe I told Ed and just thought I had told you. Are you sure we didn't discuss it?" Jared sluggishly struggled to recall.

"Enough. What did you find?" Rick said with more than a hint of impatience.

"Okay! Okay! Hold your horses. Marx is a treasure hunter turned archaeologist, so his focus is primarily on shipwrecks. Still, he did some good work and deserves credit for it. He gripes too much about professional archaeologists, though."

"Can't be worse than you two," Kent said drowsily.

"Well, yes. I realize we grumble a bit, but it's hard not to . . ."

"We can talk about that later," Rick interrupted. "Was anything relevant?"

"I'm not sure. He says he's searched the world over, but most of his findings are from the Bahamas. Some of it's interesting, though. For instance, a tiny clay head in a Phoenician style recovered from the Caribbean Sea. Does that mean anything? It's impossible to say because the date can't be established. Dropped from a wagon 10,000 or 12,000 years ago, it could be a crucial piece of evidence for us. Dropped from a cabin cruiser forty years ago it doesn't mean a thing. Dropped from a ship, say 2,000 years ago, it would mean a lot to people like Barry Fell who advocate pre-Columbian contact. You remember Fell, don't you? He claimed Phoenicians and Iberian Celts traded regularly in the Americas 2,000 years ago."

"Certainly. He made a fascinating argument supported by lots of physical artifacts, translations of ancient inscriptions, and a rationale that sounded pretty reasonable. I'll grant the inscriptions are debatable since ancient Celtic script amounts to little more than scratches, but the rest of the stuff is impressive."

Jared took over, "Either the man's a charlatan, or he's right."

"Fell's not alone. I read *Kon-Tiki* when I was a kid. Thor Heyerdahl made a strong case for transpacific navigation in prehistoric times. Even took to the sea in a balsa raft to prove it," Rick said.

"I should have thought of Heyerdahl myself. He took a similar voyage across the Atlantic in a reed boat modeled after boats in ancient Egyptian murals. Later he excavated pyramids at a place called Tecume in Peru. Turned up some murals that showed reed boats similar to the Egyptian craft."

"Okay, what else does Marx say about the Bahamas?"

"He presents air photos of walls and building foundations under the sea. Back in the late '60s someone spotted several structures from an airplane, some west of Bimini and others north of Andros Island. Geologists and archaeologists later investigated them, with the usual arguments and inconclusive results. Again I can't tell how important they are because Marx doesn't even say how deep they are. They're substantial features, though. Two of the walls are more than a fourth of a mile long, in the megalithic style so characteristic of early cultures. He claims 5,000 BP, but that's purely speculative. He also says some ancient sea charts show small islands on Little Bahama Bank that now lie beneath the sea. He even found some tree stumps still rooted to the bottom at one site."

"And the rest of the world?" Rick asked.

"I don't know what to make of it." Jared recalled his earlier struggle to trace Marx's reference to "secs." "He claims that in the eastern Mediterranean there are jagged pinnacles that rise almost to the surface. Surprisingly, the sea floor surrounding many of them is flat and covered with sand. I'll bet coral won't grow in sand, so there has to be stone underneath. Again he isn't specific about where they are or how deep the bottom is. He says they're called 'secs,' but I'm still confused about the term. My best guess is that it's either divers' slang that hasn't made it into official glossaries or a misinterpretation of the map abbreviation for 'seconds' that always accompanies a lighted buoy on shallow shoals or a shortened form of the Arab word 'secca' meaning a shoal."

"It's curious that someone would write a book about underwater archaeology and offer so little about archaeology," Kent said.

"He does mention one piece of intriguing evidence. In a Florida sinkhole, a human skeleton and some skillful artifacts were found under 230 feet of water. That depth hasn't been exposed since 12,000 years ago," Jared said. "Throughout, he earnestly attempts to correct a grievous wrong that he believes others are perpetrating *against* underwater archaeology. Apparently, land archaeologists concede that valid archaeological sites exist underwater, but they object to spending research money there, mainly because underwater exploration costs several times more per site. They see one water guy eating up the funds for a hundred or more land guys."

"But there *are* underwater archaeologists, some well respected. I've read their stuff," Kent said.

"Marx said there are fewer than a hundred, and most of them have learned by the seat of their pants, or wetsuits as the case may be. He named only eight universities and declared Texas A &M as the best of the lot. But, then again, he lives in Texas."

Jared paused to watch a blue jay harass a much larger crow high above the tall pine trees, now standing where pastures had lain when he headed off to college. "Some underwater settlements have been excavated, but most of them sank in recorded history due to earthquakes. The best known is Port Royal, Jamaica, which sank in 1692. Some less famous sites could be victims of sea level rise. A priest named Poidebard found an ancient settlement in the Mediterranean near Tyre in 1934. It's got port facilities, jetties, and stone walls. You remember the Biblical connection between Tyre and Sidon. Well, they found a similar settlement near Sidon in 1946. A single British archaeologist, named Fleming, claims to have checked out more than a hundred sunken settlements in the past 35 years. Edwin Link documented the sunken city of Caesarea in 1960 and tried to investigate two other cities off Greece."

"I'm convinced direct fieldwork is our only option. We don't know the technology, and we don't have the money, but we'll just have to find a way," Rick said with his jaw set. "Does Mr. Marx have any advice for us?"

Jared laughed, "Yes. Don't undertake any exploration without proper experience, plenty of money, competent divers, and top notch equipment— everything we don't have. He also says don't go near the water 'til you know what you're looking for and where to look. We're in pretty good shape on that account. It's the lack of experience and equipment that does us in. Looks like the odds are about a thousand to one against us."

"Odds be damned, we'd better start planning. We'll get there one way or another," Rick said.

"The obvious answer is to hire a boat and dive, but that won't be easy. Fortunately, depths in Foul Bay are mostly within scuba range. Unfortunately, neither of us dives. Hell, I don't even swim well, and that could be a real drawback," Jared laughed. "Plus, Foul Bay must be an extremely hazardous place to dive. It's one of the most remote places on earth. There probably aren't any diving services in the vicinity, maybe not even any boats to hire. Berenice is a tiny place. Worse yet, maps show the southern half of the bay is contested territory between Egypt and Sudan.

"How will you recognize pyramids, even if they are there?" Kent asked.

"First, there's general form—the 3-D shapes of the mounds and the 2-D patterns of their locations. Regularity might suggest a city, while randomness might suggest a natural, physical cause. But I doubt we'll get an overview. We'll be lucky to see a whole mound of coral at one time, much less a meaningful cluster."

"Suppose we can document Sudanese pyramids like the portico in *National Geographic?*" Rick asked.

"Oh, that would be great, but don't count on anything that perfect. I still don't understand why coral hasn't grown enough to conceal that portico. Must be something unique about the current, light, or nutrients at that particular spot. We need something more conclusive."

"Mortar joints," Rick said. "Mortar joints will prove they're man-made. The ideal would be lots of carved stones and joints. But let's assume the worst case...all buildings completely covered with thick coral."

"And the masonry blocks themselves are made of coral. And real buildings are mixed with natural formations on natural rock bases...," Jared interrupted.

"Right! Let's assume we have at least a 50-50 chance of hitting natural rock instead of building stone. In that case, I see no choice but to get under the coral somehow."

"But you can't just go around blasting coral. A little drilling maybe, but *no* nitro."

Rick's brow furrowed as he considered the matter. "The end might justify the means, but I agree. Damaging coral is absolutely our last resort. So how do we check the underpinnings?"

"First, coral has to have a hard foundation," Jared replied. "Second, vertical growth must outpace horizontal growth. If so, then there should be a vulnerable edge just beneath the base of each reef. That's where we may get a peek at the foundation. We'll have to find coral columns that rise directly from sand and then remove some of the sand to see what lies underneath—masonry or natural rock. Marx describes technologies for that type of excavation."

"Tools of the trade, huh? What are the choices?"

"We'll have to use remote video. Diving is expensive, and we have a lot of territory to cover. At depths of 80 feet or so, a diver can go down only twice a day for a little more than an hour on the bottom. That just isn't enough time. Treasure hunters face the same problem. They use sensors to locate likely sites; then dive to map and retrieve artifacts."

"Sensors?" Rick questioned.

"Oh, anything from video cameras to highly specialized sonar gear, magnetometers, radar, metal detectors. Usually they're towed behind small workboats on sleds that control depth. Some are remote-controlled and self-propelled, but they're expensive to buy *and* to operate."

Kent had been patient, dozing in and out of the conversation. Now he was awake and interested again. "I haven't worked undersea myself, but I understand side scan sonar yields the most detail, especially for bottom profiles. Even a small object shows up on the image."

"That agrees with what I've read," Jared replied. "They used side scan to find the *Titanic* and the Civil War ironclad *Monitor*. More to our point, they successfully used side scan to find a ship, named the *Defense*, when only small artifacts remained."

"You guys will just have to go down and see what's there. Too bad you can't swim! Okay, you can swim, but you can't scuba dive."

"Maybe we're getting too fancy for our own good," Rick countered. "How about those cheap little depth finders they use for bass fishing nowadays. We should at least check them out."

"Sounds possible," Jared answered. "Might be able to locate the larger structures, but how do we check them out once we find them?"

"What about submersibles?" Rick asked Kent.

"Expensive to buy . . . rent . . . operate . . . maintain. Definitely out of your range. Besides, one wrong move, and I'm a Sole Surviving Son. The best you can do is tow a waterproof video camera, maybe with spotlights attached, and send divers down when the serious probing begins."

"So you think we should *hire* divers?" Jared asked.

"I was purposefully vague."

"I've read that amateur divers help with digs just for the pleasure of diving, but that raises another big question. How can we maintain ownership of the discovery? It's like Sir Edmund Hillary and Tensing Norgay. Hillary felt he had to give equal credit to the man who took him to the top of Everest. For us it will be worse. There wouldn't be any question who saw it first. I say we have to do the diving ourselves."

"Ultimately, one of us will see it first, and the other will have to take second place anyway," Rick said.

"Not necessarily. No one can tell you guys apart. Why don't you do what Hillary and Norgay did?"

"Kent's right! We can claim equal credit and never reveal who saw it first."

"Okay. Let's make a pact." Rick stuck out his hand.

"Done." Jared shook it firmly. Kent extended his hand too, but his brothers rejected the offer with a laugh.

"Now the big question: What do you hope to find? Other than stone buildings and pyramids, I mean," Kent asked.

"There was a time when I dared not hope for anything more than field patterns or irrigation ditches. As for buildings, I was just thinking of long-gone wooden huts, straw houses, maybe some mud brick houses. Even if they were stone, who knows how much sediment would cover them. I wasn't optimistic."

"Pyramids really turned the whole thing around, huh?"

"Yes, but sediment may not be such a problem after all. This part of the Red Sea is pretty clear."

Kent thought for a moment, "What about marine borers? That's what does wooden ships in."

"Right, Bro! *Teredo navalis*, the notorious shipworm! We won't find much wood. Shipworms are active down to 600 feet or so. Wood survives only under special circumstances, say, in a place with a tremendous influx of fresh water. Even if borers didn't get to the old home place, Marx says most buildings disintegrate from wave action soon after inundation."

"How much natural light can we expect?" Rick asked.

"Oh, I think the threshold for total darkness is usually about 400 feet."

"Just our luck," Rick said.

Search Log 15: Illegal Immigration

Ed Field and Walde Peplies met outside Jared's door.

"Come on in." Jared called when he spied their silhouettes through frosted glass. "Have a seat. Look at this!" He handed out copies of an article from *Science Magazine*. Thick, black letters proclaimed, "Demic Expansions and Human Evolution."

"For once, they published some good geography," Jared exclaimed. While they read, he skimmed through and reexamined its maps. "It shows the trend lines of genetic dispersal over time. What do you think?"

Walde went first. "Yes, it is good geography. Three scientists from different fields took a measure of migration and applied an appropriate statistic. Principal component values . . . isopleths . . . good scientific geography. Then the authors interpreted the results spatially and reached a conclusion based on spatial logic. The maps are coarse but suited to the level of detail inherent in the data. General maps for general findings. I like it."

Ed nodded. "I agree. Mitochondrial DNA is a reliable indicator of migration. That's the DNA in the cell wall, which passes only down the female line. It's constant from generation to generation except for the occasional mutation, and mutations are assumed constant over time. The amount of difference between observations tells how long it's been since the individuals or species diverged from a common ancestor. The maps indicate several dispersals out of Africa."

"Careful," Jared said. "Don't let shading fool you. The actual direction of migration can go either way. The one from Scandinavia to Spain, for instance, may actually run from Spain to Scandinavia."

Ed searched for a particular paragraph and pointed toward it. "They also considered archaeological and cultural factors. They've done their best to give the right direction to each dispersal."

"Okay, now what do you see in the data? I see something vital that the authors either missed or didn't want to admit."

Ed and Walde stared at the maps for a moment; then Walde began. "Let me guess. I know how you feel about land bridges, 'Wallenda Vectors,' and all that. You're probably upset over the treatment of Japan. After complimenting archaeologists on their demographic history of Japan since the Ice Ages, the authors acknowledge that it's only for areas above current sea level. You're probably annoyed that they didn't go further."

"Actually, what disturbs me most is that they remain mute on something that is brazenly obvious in their data."

Then it was Ed's turn. "They declare America the last continent settled, and they accept the standard theory–Africa to Asia then across the Bering land bridge to Alaska. That's right according to some of their data, but other parts only make sense *if* some of the migrations occurred directly across the Atlantic between Africa and South America."

"Right on the money, Ed. They may have missed it, or they may have been afraid to say it, but the pattern is undeniable," Jared said.

"My goodness! You're right," Peplies exclaimed. "This far exceeds what anthropologists have accepted. There's certainly no land bridge between Africa and the Americas. It would mean ocean voyages long before standard theory says they happened."

"We have to take this map seriously, and it says people migrated across the Atlantic," Jared declared.

Search Log 16: The Shroud of Tourin'

In mid-September, Jared and Ed returned to Alaska. Ed had worked feverishly for two months so they could reach the field before first snowfall. K Kinski and Chris Ojala, both from NOAA's Auke Bay Laboratory near Juneau, met them in Yakutat. 'Training samples' would be identified on the image and used to determine a characteristic spectral signature for each type of land cover–forest, grassland, beach, wetland, and so forth. It was demanding work, but Alaska offered wondrous compensations–mountains, glaciers, lakes, and other glacial features more spectacular than most people would see in a lifetime. The Yakutat Foreland, despite its butchered forests, was undoubtedly one of the most beautiful places on earth.

"Where do we put our gear?" Jared asked.

"That's our ride," K proclaimed proudly, pointing toward a pea-green Chevy Suburban parked beside the landing strip. "It's on loan from the U.S. Forest Service. Up here, it's in everyone's interest to share equipment and, especially, to help one another out of tight spots."

"She's seen better days," Chris said, "but none the worse for wear." He paused thoughtfully and kicked a knobby, battered tire. "Hop in. I'll drive." The scent of fuel oil, spilled in the rear, permeated the vehicle. Chris peered between cracks in the windshield, one high and one low, that somehow failed to obstruct his vision. The rear door handle was stashed conveniently up front next to the steering column. Still, the old Suburban was no shabbier than most other Yakutat rides.

Jared laughed. "Here we are, depending on a 20-year-old junker to transport the latest advances in geographic information technology." He pointed to a powerful laptop computer nestled in an oversized cardboard box and, next to it, a hand-held GPS unit.

"What does it do?" K asked.

"It's a new concept that combines GPS, GIS, and satellite imagery on a mobile computer. It processes satellite imagery and displays it in color onscreen. Each scene can be overlaid with roads, streams, or other digital data. It's linked to this handheld unit that continuously receives signals from the Global Positioning System satellites. As we drive along, it continuously calculates our precise coordinates and plots every move right on top of the image."

"Whoa, that's a long way from the old theodolites and colored pencils cartographers used before," K said.

"We used to spend hours looking for long-lost USGS benchmarks," Jared said.

Kinski placed the apparatus in his lap and watched closely as the satellite signal registered on the GPS screen.

"It's a beta unit we're testing for the developer," Jared added. "We've had a lot of input into the final design."

"Is that why you cover it with a cardboard box?"

"Oh, you mean the Shroud of Tourin.' No. There's a problem with laptops. The best and brightest screens are great in the shade but useless in sunlight. This box shades the screen."

"How well does it work?" Kinski tilted the assemblage, looking for the start button. Jared reached over and pushed it for him. Kinski watched wide-eyed as the PC slowly came to life.

"Our current position shows as a blinking white dot. See there?" Ed said, as he leaned over from the back seat.

"Oh, oh, there. Yes, I see it. Now, what are these red cross marks?"

"The system updates our coordinates every two seconds. Each time the white dot moves, it leaves a plus mark behind. That trail of breadcrumbs shows our path since we activated the system back in Yakutat."

"Okay. Now, what am I seeing here on the rest of the screen?"

"It's a satellite scene processed to depict land cover. It shows data for every 30 meter by 30 meter pixel on the ground. The dark green pattern represents coniferous forest. Red represents forested wetlands, and magenta represents marshes."

K watched closely as the digital landscape drifted across the screen while the real landscape floated past his window. Within a few minutes, he had a pretty good feel for the color scheme of land cover types.

"We're about to run off the edge of the screen. What should I do?"

"Slam on the brakes!" Jared joked. K looked to Ed for a serious answer.

"Nothing. It'll automatically pan and reposition the window, placing us in the center again." Moments later, K watched the screen shift. "We can zoom out to see the whole satellite scene or zoom in to see a tiny patch of ground. Mostly, we just try to pick a good level of detail and let the software pan along."

"Gee, this is terrific," K said. "There's that patch of trees. You've nailed it. I can even see the difference between full-grown forest in dark green and scrubby second growth in olive. And there's the marsh. I can see precisely where it shifts from grass to low shrubs. The breadcrumbs show us right on the road, beside this marsh. It's like the arrow that says, 'YOU ARE HERE,' at a Seattle mall, only it follows everywhere we go."

"The whole system is jury-rigged and finicky, but it's still the greatest invention since the accurate chronometer."

"Accurate chronometer? Isn't that just a clock?"

"Yes, but that was a big deal centuries ago. Before it came along, seafarers could determine latitude by observing the sun or the stars, but they practically had to guess longitude. GPS is a modern replacement for the old chronometers. It's a refinement that allows us to calculate our position continuously and with ease."

Search Log 17: Solid Foundation

Washington, D.C. was almost a second home to Jared, for his work took him there often. This time he was attending a conference in Georgetown, but he chose a hotel near Capitol Hill hoping to spend a few hours each morning or afternoon at the Library of Congress. Finally, one afternoon he was able to break away and grab a cab downtown. On the way, he pulled a DMA index from his briefcase and noted charts covering the Bahama Islands plus a sizable area off the coast of South America. His entry to the Map Library was downright efficient now that he understood the procedure. Once inside, he handed a scribbled list of chart numbers to the librarian. Five minutes later, he spread the Caribbean charts across a huge table and scanned for rocks awash.

The *Science* article had aroused his and Rick's belated interest in the Caribbean. If people really traveled the Atlantic in pre-Columbian times, it would blow the lid off standard theories of human history. Subsequently, they had combed a vast body of scholarly literature. One of the founding cultures of Central America was the Olmec of Mexico. Their arrival coincided with major migrations of the enigmatic Sea Peoples in the Mediterranean and also with Egypt's last mention of Punt. If such migrations were caused by sea level rise, the brothers reasoned, there might be a submerged Olmec homeland somewhere in the region. Maybe they used stone in construction as they did in sculpture. If so, their buildings would have formed a solid foundation for coral reefs to form.

Jared took stock. *Ed's data show vast submerged platforms surrounding the Bahamas...Florida... Yucatan...Honduras...Nicaragua. Start with the Bahamas. Olmecs claimed they came from an island called Aztlan that sank into the Eastern Ocean. Their Eastern Ocean must be the Egyptians' Western Ocean— the Atlantic. That coast where the Olmecs settled, near today's Veracruz, is one of Central America's few stretches without much continental shelf. Other lowlands would have been taken by neighbors pushed inland as the sea rose, but that stretch would have been available for invasion from the sea. Islanders would have no place to go except by sea, and the Veracruz lowland would be a godsend.*

Leaning over Chart #27005, he began searching as he had before in the east. Soon his notes read: "Silver Bank 20°30'N, 70°30'W; Caicos Bank 21°30'N, 72°00'W; Great Bahama Bank 22°30'N, 77°00'W." They were shallow banks scattered with rocks awash like the ones at Foul Bay, 16 of them on Silver and 41 on Caicos. Between them lay several smaller banks— Turks, Mouchoir, and nameless others–with a few rocks each. But the mother lode was on Great Bahama Bank, more than 150 rocks, all in water less than 20 meters deep, especially at the southern end surrounding a dramatic channel known as Tongue of the Ocean. *Waves would have lapped at their bases about 7,000 years ago.* By contrast, the next chart revealed only a few scattered singles and doubles mostly along island shores, none of them in suspicious locations. After viewing Chart #25000 his final note said simply, "Not much to go on." As soon as he wrote it, a librarian announced closing time and nudged him out the door.

Back on Independence Avenue, Jared deliberated his next move. He was pretty sure the Main Reading Room stayed open until 9:00 p.m. The most important missing piece was a better description of coral formations. He crossed the avenue, directed by a motorcycle cop controlling the rush of bright young staffers leaving Capitol Hill. Once inside he found his way to the Main Reading Room and settled into an elegantly carved desk beneath the cavernous rotunda, then ambled over to a foyer filled with terminals connected to the house computer. It didn't take long to figure out the online catalog, by far the best he had encountered. The first screen asked what sort of search he preferred. By the third screen, he was sorting through dozens of references. To that point the only keys he had punched were the five letters: "coral." Everything else was handled through touchscreen menus. He marked several dozen items and printed full citations, then returned to the reading desk and skimmed the hits.

After a few minutes, he paused to reflect. Glancing upward, he saw the library's tall columns and fanciful dome towering above. Yellow marble and gilded scrolls crowned the Main Reading Room–a neglected relic of a bygone age when grownups worshipped knowledge and housed it in gilded temples. He stared at the balcony above, where, as an intern in the library's Map Room, he had first seen the wondrous dome. He and other interns would climb to that balcony just to gawk. Rick, working high-rise construction elsewhere in D.C. that summer, had joined them on more than one occasion. At 21, and still at 48, he thought himself fortunate to know this private nook that ranked among the most magnificent sights in all of Washington.

Awestruck as before, Jared opened his briefcase and removed a green highlighter. Item by item he read the printout's annotated references and marked the ones he wanted. Then he transferred the required information to tiny order forms, wrote his name over and over (*Repetitive tedium, the thing computers do best, is left to the human,* he noted) and handed the completed slips to a librarian. Items ordered this time of night would be delivered to the desk in 45 minutes or so, she explained. Or, he could have the items collected overnight, and they would be waiting next morning at the circulation desk. Jared recalled his schedule for the next day and decided he could make it back for an hour or so when the library opened at 8:00 a.m.

Search Log 18: Travel Info

Four weeks later, on a follow up trip, Jared's plane landed at National Airport in midafternoon on a miserable November day. He darted through lines of taxis, only to stand and wait while the dispatcher and drivers argued. Cold rain dripped from his city-style Stetson. Finally, he tossed his bags into the winner's trunk and jumped inside. "Egyptian Embassy on Decatur Place," he said.

"Sorry, sir, so sorry. I do not know where this Place is," the driver replied in a clipped Indian accent, driving determinedly, nonetheless, up George Washington Parkway toward downtown D.C. "I will call to find this information."

"Thanks! I know it's somewhere northwest, probably near Mass Ave. but I've never been there."

After several inquiries and crackling radio replies, the driver felt confident he could find Decatur Place. He turned to face Jared, with no apparent need for forward vision. "I have this correct information, sir. Do you have the street number?"

"Twenty-three hundred."

When the taxi arrived at 2300 Decatur Place, Jared slung his laptop over his shoulder, grabbed his bag from the trunk and started walking. Finally he spotted a small brass plaque that said "Embassy of the Arabic Republic of Egypt" in English and, presumably, in Arabic. But the door was locked. Thinking there might be a compound of several buildings, he walked along the street and soon came to a tiny courtyard. A low wall separated the overgrown lawn from the sidewalk, but the wrought-iron gate was open. A cracked walkway led to a brick building at the rear where a plaque said, "Consular Affairs." This door, too, was locked, but a handwritten sign directed visitors back to the main building he had just left.

Lugging baggage and dripping with rain, Jared finally found a plain glass door leading to a cramped stairway. Uncertain, he ascended, bumping his bag against the walls as he climbed to an equally narrow hallway, on its left a transom door. The room brought to mind the old optometrist's office, already aged in his childhood, where he used to wait forever whenever his mother bought new glasses. Counters crowned with tellers' windows reminded him of the old, hometown bank 40 years earlier. Two young women, both American, sat behind the counter. "May we help you?"

"Yes, I need travel information. May I use your library?"

"A library! No, sir. No library."

"How about travel brochures?"

"Yes, I believe so. You will have to speak with Mr. Fawzi."

Jared waited for instructions, but the woman said nothing. "Where is Mr. Fawzi, and when may I speak with him?"

"Oh, that's his office, but he's at prayers." She pointed toward a door ten feet away. "If you will be so kind as to wait, he will be available in a few minutes."

"Certainly," Jared replied, chagrined that he hadn't already grasped the situation. *Just shows how much I have to learn before I start bumbling around the Middle East,* he thought. *There, I'll need to remember constantly the custom and the hour.* He laid his baggage in a corner and ambled about the room. The wait was considerably longer than she had indicated and awkward without chairs. He thoroughly familiarized himself with the wooden floor and a calendar printed in Arabic, the only adornment on the aging plaster walls. He was unsurprised to see that the days of the lunar months failed to align with the Gregorian calendar, but he was surprised that the numbers ran left to right. He'd always assumed that just as their writing runs right to left, so would the days of the month. The door to Fawzi's office was slightly ajar. Through the crack he saw a man, younger than he expected, kneeling, barefoot, on a mat. Jared consulted his own internal compass and concluded the gentleman's capped head was, indeed, facing east. The placid ritual seemed strangely out of place in bustling D.C.

"Mr. Fawzi will see you now," the young woman said as she detected movement inside. Fawzi smiled as Jared entered.

"Hello, I'm Jared Caisson from Melton Valley Laboratory," he said distinctly and proffered his card. In scientific, academic, or government circles, the Lab's name usually brought instant respect, seldom distrust. Elsewhere some people were impressed, others were hesitant, most were indifferent. Many foreigners know of the Lab's historic contribution to the dramatic ending of World War II, but Fawzi's reaction was a blank stare.

"How may I help you, Dr. Caisson?" he offered in halting but correct British-style English.

"I'm interested in your Red Sea coast. I want to go diving there and would like information."

"Yes, yes. Many Americans dive there. You will have many choices. In Cairo, there are many tours that will take you there."

"I'm especially interested in the coral reefs of Foul Bay. Is there a diving service nearby?"

"That I do not know, sir. You must go to Cairo. There you will find many tours. Perhaps some of them will take you to this bay."

"Do you have any literature describing your Red Sea coast?"

"Yes, certainly. I will be right back." He stepped out to the counter and said something to one of the women. Jared heard just enough to know that he was speaking English.

Fawzi returned empty-handed, then spent several minutes explaining visa requirements and limitations on visits to Egypt. Finally, one of the "tellers" knocked on the door and deferentially handed over a stack of brochures. Fawzi ceremoniously passed the stack to Jared, one item at a time without explanation. Jared examined each as it entered his hand. *Glitzy propaganda distributed by the Egyptian Tourist Authority.*

"I was hoping for something more specific about Foul Bay," he said.

"And where did you say this Foul Bay lies?"

"Your Red Sea coast on the border with Sudan."

"Oh, then, sir, this document should tell you what you want to know." He politely touched one of the pamphlets in Jared's hand. It was a list of excursions covering the Sinai Peninsula and Red Sea coast. The southernmost destination was Hurghada, far north of Foul Bay. Berenice rated only two sentences. One said it was a good place for "remedial tourism," and the other said nothing of substance.

"I was hoping for a more complete description of the land and especially the reefs of Foul Bay."

Fawzi looked embarrassed, almost ashamed. "I am sorry, Dr. Caisson. For that, you must go to a library. We have no such information here." *Leave now*, Jared thought; *you'll only embarrass him more if you persist. There's little hope anyway.*

Back in the rain, Jared appreciated his Stetson and wondered why hats had fallen into disfavor. Only a superman could carry two bags *and* an umbrella. His next stop was the Sudanese embassy, but the hour was late, and he was discouraged. *What the hell*, he thought, *I'm already wet. And it's only a couple of blocks over on Massachusetts Avenue. I'll walk that direction and stop if it's open . . . unless I spot a taxi on the way.*

He found a slightly frayed townhouse with a tarnished brass plaque by the front door. Nearly 5:30. *Probably closed*, he thought, but an aging butler answered his knock. Jared introduced himself, presented his card, and stated his purpose. The old gentleman motioned toward a formal living room. Jared was content to wait but not at all certain what he was waiting for.

Ten minutes later, the mystery was solved as a man about Jared's age entered with the smile and jaunty stride of someone in charge. The reason for the delay was clear, for his pants remained unzipped. Obviously, he had been in the restroom and rushed to meet his guest, more courteous than cautious. The man carefully read Jared's card and presented his own. "Ah, my dear Dr. Caisson, my country welcomes persons traveling as you suggest. You must come to Khartoum."

"I would like very much to visit your capital city, but I am especially interested in diving the coral reefs of Foul Bay. Will I find diving services there?"

"There are excellent diving services in Port Sudan. It is a modern industrial city. There are many commercial diving companies."

"I want to visit Port Sudan, but I would like very much to dive in Foul Bay. Do you have any information on that portion of the coast."

"No, nothing here, but I am sure you will find all the information you need in Khartoum."

"Do you have any tourist brochures?"

"No, but there is a tourist bureau in Khartoum. They will assist you in every possible way."

Suddenly it was clear that this meeting would yield even less than the one before it. *Well,* he pondered, *what can I salvage?* Then he remembered how little he knew about traveling to Sudan. His question provoked a recitation of rules, regulations, and fees like the one he had just endured about Egypt.

"Is it safe now for American nationals to travel in your country?"

"Yes, we welcome Americans. You may travel anywhere you like, but what you will like most is Khartoum."

"How do most visitors come to your country?"

"Many people fly to Cairo and then travel overland to Khartoum."

"Is there any difficulty crossing the border from Egypt?"

"No, no. We have friendly relations with Egypt."

"Is there a good road from Khartoum to Foul Bay?"

"Yes, yes. There is a railroad from Khartoum to Port Sudan."

"But what about Foul Bay? Its location is far north of Port Sudan."

"I am not familiar with this place you call Foul Bay, but I am certain someone will know about it in Khartoum."

"Can I reach Port Sudan by water?"

"Well, let me see. Certainly. Yes. You can sail from Jiddah, but it is very expensive. You may prefer to enter from Khartoum."

Caisson apologized for keeping his host late and thanked him for his help. The official escorted him to the foyer and said, "Goodbye," at the front door. Jared left him standing in the doorway, underwear still showing. *I doubt many a Fortune 500 CEO could exude such eminence with his drawers thus exposed.*

After dinner, Jared strolled Connecticut Avenue in the rain. At Dupont Circle, he noticed a large bookstore, newly constructed, half exposed at street level, lights beaming on shelves filled with colorful offerings. It was enticing in the same way that basement cabarets are most seductive when viewed from sidewalks above. He descended the half flight of stairs and ambled roundabout so as to reach his objective last.

Finally he approached the section marked "TRAVEL" and found "AFRICA." Nine different guidebooks on Egypt! He was surprised to find so many.

Searching alphabetically, he found not a single Sudanese guide. Apparently, no one goes there, he thought. Returning to the Egyptian shelf, he pulled them one-at-a-time. The third pick said, "Egypt and the Sudan." Twenty minutes later he was back in his room, dry and in bed, skipping from page to page in both countries. Beside him lay the brilliant red cover of a Michelin map labeled "AFRICA (Northeast) AND ARABIA 1:4,000,000." As he spread the map for a better view, Jared noticed the blinking red message light on his room phone. "Call Mr. Tom McCord," responded the automated attendant. *Too late tonight.*

Late next morning, after several tries, he caught Tom between meetings. Competent, intelligent, devoted to his work, Tom McCord was the exact opposite of what government bureaucrats are rumored to be. Jared had known Tom for years, and the two had become fast friends. In precise terminology, Tom was "The Geographer of the U.S. State Department and Director of the Office of the Geographer."

"Oh, hi, Jerry. Thanks for calling back." They chatted for a minute exchanging pleasantries and a memory or two. "We're beginning to get serious about GIS here at the office. The UN has been doing a little with it, but they want to do more. We're interested in exploring how GIS and remote sensing can be used to improve economic development, especially for the poorer countries and the newly emerging democracies of Central and Eastern Europe. I just wondered if you could help me put together some information."

"Certainly. I'll do whatever I can. From my own experience in Liberia, back in '82, I know I could have accomplished a lot more if GIS had been available."

"What about GPS?" Tom asked.

"Most definitely! Now we can plug a GPS unit directly into the laptop. That single innovation doubles our productivity in the field."

"Well, I'm going to organize a little symposium here in Washington in the next month or so. If you're interested, I'd like you to come. Help me organize it if you have the time and interest."

"Count me in," Jared assured Tom. "If you've got a minute, there's something else I'd like to talk about."

"I can talk for another ten minutes or so. Shoot!"

"I need to know about travel conditions in Egypt and Sudan. What are you telling your diplomats these days?" Jared inquired.

"Egypt isn't too bad for official travel. It's worse for tourists. There have been some attacks on tourist buses, things like that."

"So I may actually be safer off the beaten track?"

"Yes, you'll probably be alright once you leave the main tourist attractions along the Nile. Now, Sudan is a different story. Things can get dicey down there. The southern and western regions are out of the question. You'll probably be alright in Khartoum and Port Sudan, but you'll have to check out the countryside on a case by case basis."

"How about the border between Egypt and Sudan?"

"No active hostility, but relations have been testy for years. Mind telling me where you really want to go?" Tom asked.

"To Foul Bay. It's on the Red Sea smack dab on the border between the two countries."

"I seem to recall that's a problem area. Let me check on it and get back to you. Okay?"

Search Log 19: The End of the Earth

Jared returned to MVL after a Seagate meeting at project headquarters in Beaufort. "That's 'Bofort,' North Carolina, not 'Byewfort,' South Carolina," he had cautioned Rick before his departure. A memo from Mack Reed said, "Seed Money approved. Account established. Funds immediately available."

He dialed Tom McCord.

"Hello, Tom. My funds came through. Were you able to find anything about Foul Bay?"

"Christ, Jerry! You couldn't have picked a tougher place."

"I was beginning to suspect that. Guidebooks mention Berenice but don't really say much about it. And they don't say anything about the surrounding area. One actually says, 'If you go south of Berenice, write us and tell us what you found.'"

"I'm not surprised. Berenice served as a staging area for the U.S. Rapid Deployment Force. The first U.S. troops to reach the Persian Gulf in Operation Desert Storm came from there. But I doubt any GIs are still there. The real problem is Egyptian coastal defenses! Security is an overriding concern in that whole region. As far north as Hurghada, the shore is mined except for designated tourist beaches."

"Mined!"

"Yes, and it gets worse as you go south. If the Egyptians lay mines close to a resort like Hurghada, you know they'll mine a place as strategic as Foul Bay. In fact, travel is severely restricted anywhere south of Marsa Alam," McCord continued.

"So I can't just drop in without an invitation? I'll have to contact Egyptian officials, or at least someone with good connections. How about the Sudanese portion of the bay?" Jared asked.

"The whole bay is now Egyptian. In fact, the Sudanese government never did really own it. The official border lies south of Foul Bay. Always has."

"I wondered about that. Some maps show two lines. One runs as you say, while another angles north to the middle of the bay. Between them it says, 'ADMINISTERED BY SUDAN.' What's that all about?"

"It's called the Hala'ib Triangle. The maps you saw are out of date. Years ago, the two countries agreed that a fixed border would be bad for the Bedouin tribes who had roamed the area for thousands of years. They mutually agreed to let Sudan administer the triangle so nomads could reach traditional grazing grounds and wells. It worked pretty well for a while, but they started bickering in the '50s. When Sudan started exploring for oil, Egypt hit the roof."

"So Egypt took the land back? Then, I'll only have to deal with one country, and it's the better of the two for Americans."

"Not so fast!" Tom warned. "The Egyptians are developing something down there, and nobody knows what. They've closed the whole region to foreigners."

"Oh, no! Any chance of getting special permission?"

"Don't know. Certainly not without good contacts and an even better justification. What do you need to do there anyway?"

"I need to see the coral reefs," Jared said.

"Scuba dive in Foul Bay? Not a chance! You'd have to be crazy. I'm not just talking about run-of-the-mill 'NO TRESPASSING' signs. There'll be 'signs' alright. Mines on the beaches, for sure, and in the water, too!"

"What about nearby islands?"

"Mines? Probably not. Patrols? Most likely. The primary mission is to defend the mainland."

"How about farther south in Sudan, say around Port Sudan?"

"Maybe a little safer, but not much easier to get authorization. Foreigners have to have a permit for every place they go outside Khartoum. Listen! If you're still tempted to go anywhere on that coast, stop by, and I'll let you read some internal documents. You really ought to know what you're stepping into. What's your clearance level?" Tom asked.

"Top Secret, plus some levels I can't discuss over an unsecure line."

"Good. That's more than enough. Just stop by next time you're in town. Oh, and bring your badge."

"Thanks for all the good news."

"What are friends for?"

The next call was to Rick. Jared recounted what he had learned from Tom and the guidebooks.

"Tom was adamant about the risks, but he doesn't know the stakes. He thinks I just have a yen to see the most beautiful reefs on earth."

"So what are you saying? Should we go or not?"

"The price is high, but the prize is still worth it."

Rick mulled it over for a minute. "I agree. We've got to find a way in, even if it means being devious as hell."

"Okay. That's settled. Foul Bay is our first choice, Port Sudan second. Agreed?"

"Agreed!"

Jared hung up, then checked his voicemail back at Melton Valley. The third message was from Ed Field: "Jer, I've been thinking, and I guess I should warn you. I'm afraid you'll run head-on into Atlantis. People are bound to connect your lost lands with the lost continent myth. You'll be labeled a kook."

Jared dialed Ed's extension. "I see what you mean, but that's a stretch," he said. "The Atlantis myth deals with a huge landmass that sank in a single cataclysmic event. I'm just talking about continental shelves that we know exist and long-term sea level rise well established in science."

"Makes no matter! You may not be claiming a lost continent, but you are claiming a lost civilization. People will make the connection."

"Well, maybe you're right. I haven't studied Atlantis. I'll check on it."

CHAPTER 8

Chronicle 13: Lessons of the Sacred Pyramid

The Chief Priest sailed at midnight. His ceremonial reed boat carried firewood, incense, food, bedding, and essentials for a ritual that would begin at Solstice and last for two days. Toth, Chief Priest of the Realm, Keeper of the Book of Truths, was bound for the most sacred pyramid in the history of his people. Before launching, he gave concise directions to the cadets crowded along the shore. "Take the north pass through the near-shore reef. Veer northward where the sun rises three days before the end of summer. You will see then where my pyramid stands. Begin when my boat leaves your vision in the darkness of this night." The boys listened, knowing that each life depended on how carefully they followed the directions, but heeding even more because of their absolute reverence for the venerable Chief Priest. They watched as the old man ascended to his boat and oarsmen strained to launch it through the reef's stout current. The richly decorated craft plied out to sea, pausing at regular intervals for prayer and ritual. As each boy judged that he could no longer distinguish boat from sea, he waded into the surf and began swimming.

It would never have occurred to them that a boat might be offered for this journey of three leagues or more. Magnificent swimmers all, many spent more than half each day in water, and all were accustomed to swimming distances far longer than this. Boats were for hauling cargo and crossing seas. Each boy swam in darkness carrying only a single stick of firewood for Toth's ceremonial fire.

* * *

Osi swam in the deepest dark before dawn as Toth and his solemn audience listened for approaching swimmers. *I'm tired and cold*, he thought. *I must succeed. To succeed is to live. To fail is to die. I must not fail.* He timed each phrase with the rhythm of his one-handed stroke. *Keep to the course. Keep the wood dry. I must succeed.* Finally, the dim glow of a signal fire blinked over the cresting waves. Steadily he urged his body onward to the foot of the mighty pyramid. A hand reached down, and Osi joined the growing cluster of cadets on the pyramid's base.

Soon another father stepped down to welcome his son. The Chief Priest met them on the first step and felt the firewood. "Dry. Well done. Place your offering on the sacred bier," he said. Five other boys stepped up, and five more sticks were added to the fire. The next boy, son of a Royal Guardsman from Berenicia, stood trembling by his father as the Chief Priest felt moisture at one end of his stick. "Go back," the Chief Priest calmly ordered as he tossed the wood into the sea. The father watched in sorrow and shame as his son slid back into the black water and headed home. There would be no second chance for this failed youth in any sacred order.

When all but one boy had reached the pediment, the fire burned with nearly 500 sticks, and 12 boys, no longer cadets, were on their way back to shore. The last lad, also the son of a Royal Guardsman from Berenicia, had missed in the darkness and lost precious time retracing his course to the sacred pyramid. Finally, he crawled onto the step and laid his dripping wood before the Chief Priest. "There's dry wood on the Eastern Shore of the Valley Sea," the old man said flatly. "Go fetch a piece for my fire. Perhaps, your father will help his untrained son." The exhausted boy and disgraced father obediently swam to the open sea, condemned to death by Toth's polite command.

Six hundred men and boys climbed to the top tier and gathered around the flame. After a thanksgiving prayer and blessing, the Chief Priest instructed every man and boy to lie on the warm stone and sleep for the few remaining hours of this auspicious night. Minutes before dawn, he woke them all.

Osi, slow to rise, wiped his eyes to determine whether the morning haze was fog or weariness. The dim horizon revealed nothing, but the glowing fire still lighted the whole pyramid. Soon, a row of boys and men stood on the bottom leeward step, relieving themselves into the water. Others bathed in waves lapping on the other three sides. Osi joined them, then quickly returned before the first rays of morning light struck the summit. At sunrise, the sky glowed red, not just in the east but everywhere. A plane of light slowly cut the clouds above and settled downward to the pyramid's peak. On the topmost step, the cadets were bathed in light, and Osi was surprised to see that the elders had retreated below. The Chief Priest, too, had disappeared.

Wisps of cottony red fog dissolved before their eyes, and another step pyramid emerged between them and the sun. Within seconds, another spike appeared and grew into a pyramid, then another, and another. As sunbeams slowly worked their way down the sacred steps, scores of structures materialized.

When light finally reached the waves below, throngs of pyramids, temples, and natural outcrops broke the flat surface of the sea as far as they could see in every direction. Most were step pyramids like the sacred one beneath his feet; some barely pierced the surface; some were tall because of their own massive construction, others because they stood on what once had been high ground. Some were sprawling temples and palaces, others obelisks no wider than a swimmer's common stroke. Tombs and granaries aligned with water-covered roadways. Pyramids and palaces lined canals that once had been grand avenues. Temples and palaces formed a quadrangle surrounding a flat green sea.

Next, fathers brought food from tethered vessels that would serve as larders for the duration of the vigil. The Chief Priest then reappeared in their midst and began the ancient ritual that would last until the next day's dawn. From beginning to end, Osi sat in rapt attention, but his eyes often wandered to the awesome scene behind the dais. *A city someday to disappear beneath the waves*, he thought, *not to be seen for 10,000 years or more. An eerie beauty. A danger that will grow century by century. Already, submerged rooftops are hazards to ships that recklessly venture beyond marked channels. How many men will someday die with the cry of "Secca!" on their lips?*

Chronicle 14: The First Moon

On his first excursion to the Land of the Second Sunset, Osi had envied the physiques of Captain Hano's soldiers. *Now, my own body looks like a warrior's, and my muscles feel like stone*, he thought. A month had passed since the cadets' first swim to the sacred pyramid. Now, it was time for another monthly test of physical endurance and mental ability. In the light of the full moon, they returned to further their training.

Osi looked forward to the intense mixture of education and self-denial they would face on the stone steps. In most respects, the ritual would be like the earlier one, but this time, for several days and nights, they would hear lectures delivered by the Chief Priest and his subordinates.

Near dawn, swim-weary cadets were roused and led again to the top of the sacred site. At sunrise, the Chief Priest took his place on the crest and began with simple words, "Young men, you have been chosen to serve your people. Listen...I will instruct you in the Secrets of the Ages.

"The Ages of Man are numbered in four kalpas, each divided into four ages. The first age of each kalpa begins when the Waters of Chaos rise and destroy the civilized world; it is called the Rising Age. The second age comes when the sea nears the First Terrace and holds steady for a while; it is called the Topping Age. The third age occurs when the waters fall and fires ravage the uplands; it is called the Falling Age. The fourth age is the time of low water when land is plentiful and our people thrive. It is called the Golden Age. The Falling Age and the Golden Age are blessed years when our people flourish, for land and food are abundant. Afterward, the Waters of Chaos return. The cycle repeats itself forever.

"We don't know when the Waters of Chaos first began to rise, but it must have been long before our tales began. In those days men looked like men but thought like animals. We know little about those days, and so we call them the Time Before. The ancients suspected a time even earlier when our ancestors looked *and* thought like animals, but we have no name for this time. In every kalpa, the Rising Age is a hard time when men look like men and think like men but live like animals. The Waters of Chaos take land and destroy what people accomplished in the Golden Age.

The Rising Age of the Time Before

"Ancient scholars believed the rising waters of the Time Before began more than 130,000 years ago. In the Topping Age that followed, our ancestors lived in the Land of the Second Sunset on this continent of Afar. We are descended from our great Ancestor King who was born near Suas. He was born under the Sign of the Leopard 84,300 years before our present King, Rahn Mennon. His life came at the end of the Topping Age just as the Falling Age began. We do not know the name of this ancestor, but we know from legend that he was a wise man and trusted leader. In our history, he is called 'The Ancestor King of the Time Before.'

"The earth in those days was a strange place, unlike our world today. The ocean was much higher than today—higher than this pyramid on which we stand; higher than the islands of the Midland Sea; higher than the new True Pyramid of Berenicia; higher even than the First Terrace. Most of the world was a hostile place ill-suited to our people. The Lands of the North were warm in summer, and, except in the very far north, no ice could be seen. The Land of the Second Sunset was a barren desert, hot and nearly uninhabitable, not forested and fertile as it is today. The Lands of the East likewise were dry and inhospitable, but farther east, several weeks' journey beyond the dry lands, stood the Eastern Forests with lush plants and ample game.

"Our Ancestor King was a man much like our people today, and his people looked much like our people. Still, they had not learned to think and create and build as we do today. They lived among the Apemen who inhabited the Land of the Second Sunset. In the span of a single generation, our kind were cast out from their homeland, driven by famine and hostile tribes. They fled to the east where many perished in the desert. Our people were in chaos until the Ancestor King took command and led them to the Eastern Shore of the Midland Sea, a nourishing place with prosperous people. In this new land, they met the primitives of the north for the first time and learned to live peacefully among them. By observing their ways, our people learned skills needed for survival in their new land. In those days, our Ancestor King began the Telling of the Tales."

In daylight, Toth spoke in his familiar voice, masculine and strong. He was their teacher and spiritual leader. The first day was filled with pragmatic advice about their mission and conduct. Osi, Busah, and Ketoh were disappointed when Toth's first 12 hours of instruction revealed no more of the Secrets of the Ages than they had heard already in Egia.

That night, however, Toth appeared again in his underworld form, and the stunned cadets learned more secrets than their young minds could bear. Raising his arms and looking to one side and then the other, the sage old man beckoned the Elders with a nod. His cohorts filed by a stack of consecrated wood, each taking a branch and bringing it to the burning mass. In unison, they tossed their branches on the ceremonial fire and stood back to marvel at a constellation of flying sparks. The swirling plume of heat and flame was an extravagant display intended to impress each youth with the singular importance of this night.

While the fire raged, the Chief Priest told stories of their ancestors, speaking in voices they had never heard before. As he guided them through the ages, he *became* the Ancient Ones by skill and faith, for all things are possible in the hearts and minds of true believers. His appearance changed from verse to verse as he assumed first one identity and then another. Even when several Ancient Ones argued among themselves, his voice and visage shifted so quickly and completely that the cadets never had to question who said this and who said that. Neither was there any doubt when the Chief Priest became himself again at the end of each story.

The Falling Age Begins

In the glow of the ceremonial fire, the old priest seized the soul of someone more animal than man. Yet, his audience could not decide how or why he seemed less human. His body was like theirs, but something in his movements said he couldn't possibly think and act as they did. Then he spoke in grunts and cries, and they knew he *was* an animal. He gestured apelike with his hands. In epic rhymes, strained in translation from an ancient tongue, he told of a time 84,000 years earlier on a grassland in the northeastern corner of Afar. He told of strange, unthinkable things when fires fell from the sky, the earth burned, and seas boiled.

Speaking drums called. Baata, baata, baata spoke the high-pitched calling drums. Boola, boola, boola spoke the low-pitched answering drums. To their haunting sound, a chorus called, and the old priest answered. He brought to life their Ancestor King.

> "*Listen...*
>> *Who is he?*
>>> He is the Ancestor who will not bend,
>>> Broad shoulders squared to hot dry wind.
>> *What says he, this Ancestor King?*
>>> Words are few, gestures many, in discourse with kin.
>>> Watch his words, Listener. He beckons again.
>> *What asks he then?*
>>> "People must go!" he signals to all.
>>> "Where?" from darkness his kinsmen call.
>>> "Toward rising sun, where oceans fall."
>> *Where stand they, these rustic men?*
>>> In this corner of Afar, beside this humble hut,

Where springs once nourished acacia, mampato, and nut,
Dead now, for rains have failed this once lush land,
This grassy plain, this home of our ancestral band.
What say others, these rustic men?
"Ask Queen Mother," demands only one,
Who dares to challenge the Queen's wise son?
No other fears death more than son-leader's ire,
Since first he joined this council fire.
What pains them, these rustic men, these men in pain?
Plants are dead and game are gone.
Children starve in every home.
Bone-dry trunks now spear the sky,
Where apes once yowled from canopy high.
What ask they now, these hunters without game?
"Guide us, our Queen!" they humbly plead,
"Where next to plant our people's Seed.
East or West? Go or stay?
Lead us, Queen Mother. Show the way."
What warns she, this wise old queen?
"Sea coast calls, as death clouds rise.
Birds drop dead from haze-dim skies.
Clouds drift in. Firebursts flash.
Raging flames scorch earth to ash."
What yields this fire, this cloudborne fire?
"Death," she calls. "So many kin."
Her fingers flash . . . again . . . again.
Old hands flail as she speaks to explain,
"Never so many in a single day slain."
What answers he, this king to be?
"Must go!" repeats this eldest son.
"Must go toward land of rising sun!
Must leave Lion's Rock behind,
Else fire and famine will kill our kind."
What rules she now, this mother queen?
"Tomorrow you go, but I must stay,
Son now leads; he'll show the way."
Accepting her words as law to keep,
They stoke each hearth and try to sleep.
What now befalls this ancient tribe?
Night winds shift, and flames loom high,
Lighting the night like daytime sky.
Eerie screams awake the night,
Of homes ablaze and kin alight.

What do they, this rustic clan, facing fire?
> They flee the hills where death fire reigns.
> They seek the cool, wet coastal plains.
> Pointing east, the old ones die,
> Too feeble to run, too noble to cry.

What does he, this Ancestor King?
> He leads a small survivor band,
> From hill to plain to find new land.
> With staff he hails, he grasps a stone,
> He marks its haft on leaving home.

Do not forget…"

* * *

Toth, Teller of Tales, Keeper of the Book of Truths, Chief Priest of the People of the Living Sun, thus spoke until dawn of the Time Before.

Chronicle 15: The Second Moon
The Falling Age of the First Kalpa

On the Second Moon, the cadets swam a third time to the Sacred Pyramid of the Six Moons where Toth resumed his telling of the Tales:

"After the time of our Ancestor King came the Falling Age of the First Kalpa. The Eastern Forests turned cold, much too cold for unclothed bodies to endure. For a time our ancestors took shelter in caves like the primitives of the north. Their old homeland grew colder still and farther from the sea. They sought refuge where the midday sun was high, where the air was always warm and the sea provided food. Thenceforth, each new generation followed the retreating sea.

"The world changed," Toth resumed. "The waters of the World Ocean receded even faster than before, and new lands were uncovered. First, our land was unveiled by the retreating Valley Sea. Then, the Sea of Hormuz became but a tiny tongue of the Southern Ocean. Finally, the Plain of Sunda, the greatest land on earth, appeared in all its lush glory. For 100 generations, our ancestors moved farther and farther east to Sunda and even to the lands of Cha on the shores of the Eastern Ocean. There they anointed new kings and became new peoples while others occupied the lands we ourselves now call home.

"For 500 generations, our ancestors prospered in peace. They learned to use stone tools in ways never known before. They learned to use their voices in new and wondrous ways to speak and chant and sing. They learned to pass the Tales of the ancients from generation to generation. They led simple lives, harvesting food from the sea and hunting game in nearby lands. They swam daily and dived in shallow waters for fish and shelled creatures and seaweed. They gathered grain from coastal marshlands. Their numbers grew, and again the world changed.

Toth stared at his charges. "In the midst of this vast eastward movement, 58,800 years before the birth of King Rahn Mennon, a legendary King was anointed. His name was Ondwan, which means 'Star King.' He ruled the land at the mouth of the Great River of the Indus, which grew steadily as the seas fell but sometimes was plagued by fires that came from earth and sky. In the generations of the Falling Age of the Time Before, his sons and their sons spread to every river that flowed into the Southern Ocean."

When the night was darkest and the flame brightest, Toth portrayed the history of his people. Possessed again by ancient spirits, Toth changed, or so his listeners believed, into the Ondwan, who settled the delta formed by the Great River of the Indus. Again the speaking drums spoke. Again the chorus called and the old priest answered.

> *"Listen...*
>
>> *Who is he?*
>>> He is the Ondwan, who roams new shore,
>>> Named for that which guides before.
>>
>> *What do they now, this Star King and his heirs?*
>>> Foraging far, they pray for luck.
>>> They prowl the marsh and dig the muck.
>>
>> *What find they?*
>>> Oysters and clams in seabed ooze,
>>> Foul-sweet air and ground to choose,
>>> Winners' choice for those who lose.
>>
>> *What lose they, these winners again?*
>>> They lose good land along old shore,
>>> Crowded now with kith and more.
>>> Forced away by hunger's knife,
>>> They wander east to seek new life.
>>
>> *What says he, their chief?*
>>> "The sea has fallen! Our Seed will grow!
>>> Abundance awaits in seabed low.
>>> Follow the sea, or fight the horde.
>>> Seek new land, and sheath the sword."
>>
>> *What does he now, this chief of old?*
>>> Grasping a shell, he points his shaft,
>>> Then carves a sign beneath its haft.
>>> "Eastward ever, as winds turn cold,
>>> Seek new land, when sea strand's old."
>
> *Do not forget..."*

The Golden Age of the First Kalpa and Tales of the Time Before

"The Golden Age of the First Kalpa began at the end of that Falling Age, 57,000 years ago, and ended more than 51,000 years before our day. It was a prosperous time when our ancestors became men and women who could think and talk and plan like people today.

"Our people then lived on the Plain of Sunda between the Southern and Eastern Oceans. They learned to eat its fruits, gather its grains, hunt its game, and harvest its fish. Their numbers multiplied, and the bounty of the land increased. Our people learned many uses of their hands. They spoke new words and fashioned new tools. They made clothing and built fine shelters to protect themselves from the winds and rains. Their wise men came to understand the cycles of days and seasons and years. They learned the changes of the heavens and the ways of sun, moon, and stars. They learned the monsoon cycle of the Cool Dry Wind and the Warm Rain Wind, which ruled their land for half each year. They learned to plan and store foods during wet seasons so more would survive dry seasons.

"In that Golden Age, our people learned the power of the Sun. They worshipped the Sun God Rahn by another name, which in their belief could not be spoken. They sacrificed animals to obtain the Sun God's favor. They prepared their living for death and their dead for the afterlife. They sang songs to the heavens and played drums to the glory of Rahn. All this they learned, but they did not learn the Cycles of the Sea, for theirs was a blessed time without chaos.

"These things we know for certain, but the Tales passed down from that age describe a much earlier Golden Age in the Time Before, and what they describe seems like fantasy to us today. They tell of marvelous inventions too wondrous for belief and cities that flourished far beyond our dreams today. They tell of Vimana chariots that flew and iron thunderbolts that rained from Vimana like brimstone from the sky, and other fanciful things you are not ready to hear."

Generations passed, and Toth transformed yet again into something totally unexpected. He told of the Ancestor Queen who lived 140,143 years before his own time. The speaking drums spoke. The chorus called. The priest answered.

"*Listen...*
> *Who is she?*
>> Ancestor Queen of unknown line,
>> In pearl white robes of shimmering shine.
> *What says she?*
>> "Must end all war, or all is lost."
>> She warns her world of holocaust.
> *What be they, these Tales of the Time Before?*
>> The secrets of old were far more immense,
>> Than any ever imagined or learned of since.

Sciences won from mind's first waking,
Consumed by fire of man's own making.
From whence came this fire, this Secret-burning fire?
From battle's sky, where Thunders dwell,
Ten thousand strong, the Iron Bolts fell.
Eighty thousand years the Secrets waned,
By Sindwan's day, were part regained.
Who stands beside this woman, this woman of peace?
A celestial choir now chants and sings.
Voices rise till heaven rings,
Yet never reach their earthly kings.
What sights surround this angelic choir?
Domes of red, and streets of gold,
Smoke and light of dreams untold.
Silver shadows pierce the sky,
Streamers trailing white and high.
What final act does she perform?
Engraving the bar with symbols terse,
She notes the end of song and verse.
Her redsilver staff reflects the rays,
Of iron bolts strewn from Vimana's bays.

    Do not forget..."

Suddenly, Toth's fire erupted in booms that knocked standing men to the ground and bowled seated boys onto their backs. A searing flash of light blinded each one so that no one saw smoke rise from the hearth in crowned columns higher than the clouds themselves. When the echoes faded, Toth raised his hands and resumed his narrative until all the Tales of the Time Before were told.

Then Toth again became Toth. "In the latter days of that same Golden Age of the First Kalpa, the ancients faithfully recorded the Secrets of the Ages as we do today. Then the world changed and a new kalpa began. A new king was anointed, and his name was Sindwan, which means the Water King. He promised the people that their heritage would never be lost, but his words were empty. When his reign ended, the Secrets of the Ages were lost to the rising Waters of Chaos for he had no Pyramid and no Trove. Only the Tales survive."

Chronicle 16: The Third Moon
The Rising Age of the Second Kalpa

On the Third Moon, atop the Sacred Pyramid of the Six Moons, the old man continued his telling of the Tales. He told of a time long before his own when the Waters of Chaos destroyed the world. The Rising Age of the

Second Kalpa was a terrible and frightening time for people who had no memories or Trove to tell them that the sea could rise.

"In the year of our people 51,300 years before the birth of Rahn Mennon, a great sadness was wrought when the World Ocean devoured the land. Coastal valleys became sea floor; mountains became islands. Apemen ruled the uplands and so were saved, but our kind had chosen the sea, depending on its waters not just for food, as a camel depends on grass, but for its elements as birds need air and trees need soil. The Waters of Chaos thus brought death into every family of our kind.

"First to vanish was the Plain of Sunda, the very heart of the Realm. Next went the hearths of our people in the Sea of Hormuz and finally the Valley Sea. In our continent of Afar, a few tribes survived along the shores of the Southern Ocean, but their numbers were exceedingly small. Only after hundreds of generations, when the waters fell again, did their numbers grow sufficiently to allow them to claim the Land of the Second Sunset from the apemen. They became the Westerners who now make war on the People of the Living Sun."

"In the Sunda, many fled to mountains that became islands, but the lowland, which had been great, became small, and most of the people perished. Strong men died, but clever men survived. They found refuge and discovered new ways to gather food. Some even built dwellings in the tops of tall trees where they were safe for a little while when the Fast Rise came. A few fled to the north. Some escaped toward the rising sun and became the Tribes of Cha on the Eastern Ocean. Some sailed to the Islands of the South.

"By their wits, a few Tellers were spared and their Tales passed on, but the Secrets of the Ages were lost forever to the Waters of Chaos. For thousands of years, our ancestors lived again like primitives, gradually advancing toward knowledge and reason in the next Falling Age. But still they did not understand the rise and fall of the sea. Finally, in the Golden Age of the Second Kalpa when prosperity and knowledge returned, ancient scholars set out to find answers to questions that chafed men's minds."

Toth squinted for emphasis as he reached the high point of his narrative. "It was then that the Geometry was conceived; the first Sacred Pyramid was begun; the Sacred Trove was consecrated; and the Secrets of the Ages were preserved for all time." Toth paused and stared into the crowd as if to burn his words into each and every mind. "Make note, young men. Take heed! The Pyramid, the Trove, and the Geometry are the Trinity of the People of the Living Sun, and no man or woman can survive the coming Chaos without full knowledge of the trinity!"

Many stories were told of the Second Kalpa, among them a wonderful story about the Water King whose end marked its beginning.

* * *

In darkness deep and firelight dim, Toth again assumed the souls of his forebears. He told of that time 46,419 years before his own when the World Ocean first swallowed the homeland of his people. He told of a place in the east where the Plain of Sunda once stood above the sea. The drums spoke. The chorus called. The priest answered.

"Listen...

Who is he?
He is the Sindwan, aged and grand,
Named for that which steals his land.
What says he, this Water King?
"Move quickly," he calls to men who slave,
Hauling stout loads to nightdark cave.
What carry they, these men of yore?
Secrets of the Ages, legacy wise.
Slogging through mud, they carry the prize,
To seal for the ages against sea-rise.
Where keeps the Sindwan these Secrets found?
Wherever residing throughout the land,
In libraries small or temples grand.
In youthful reign, he knows not why,
To seal the vaults and build them high.
What asks he, the Sindwan, while he is yet young?
"Waters of Chaos? How can this be?
Our land rose for ages, but never the sea.
Will it continue, or will it arrest?
Battles now rage for shores to our west.
What answers he, the young Sindwan?
When first the oceans start to rise,
The Sindwan knows where duty lies.
"Collect the Secrets. Stack them high,
In upper halls of palace nigh."
What says he, this Water King in middle age?
"Sea waves lap on palace walls.
Secrets quake in high-borne halls.
Our coastal plain has no high ground,
We'll raise our own. We'll build a mound."
What does he, this Water King in his late years?
Each time the sea turns mound to mire,
He widens the pile, and builds it higher.
He raises the storehouse at its top,
But seas still rise. They will not stop.
What says he, this Water King, when he is old?
"Line these banks of dirt with stone,"
We'll hold this spot when land is gone,"

But storms erode and breach the hill.
The storehouse slumps. The Secrets spill.
What happens when Waters of Chaos prevail?
Buildings crumble and levees breach.
Panic spreads from home to beach.
Masses contend to stay afloat.
Secrets sail on westbound boat.
What happens to the Secrets, sailing west?
Some are lost, but some remain.
Some are soaked by spray and rain.
Invading the coast, they find a cave.
Their shouts discover its echoing nave.
Where go they, these Secret saviors?
To Echo Trove, this pristine vault,
They spiral up. They seldom halt.
Swaddled and cradled, the cache arrives,
Saving some knowledge that yet survives.
What does he, this ancient Water King?
Leaning on his staff, he gauges the sea,
In one moon risen the height of his knee,
He pulls a knife and, cursing the mud,
He cuts a notch to mark this flood.
What says he, the Sindwan?
"All is lost. The sea has won.
All able must follow my trusted son.
For the old and weak, it is too late.
This Echo Trove will seal our fate."

Do not forget..."

"And thus the Trove was lost throughout the Rising Age of the Second Kalpa," Toth said. When the Chief Priest ended his narrative, the youths breathed sighs of exhaustion and relief. The Elders bowed their heads and receded from the glow of the flames. Thus the lessons continued for four nights and five days until the old priest had described all the important events of the Rising and Topping Ages and Falling Ages of the Second Kalpa. He told great legends of the Wirawan, the Wonderful King, the Ketawan, the Seeking King, and others lost to the ages.

Chronicle 17: The Fourth Moon
The Golden Age of the Second Kalpa

With the rising of the Fourth Moon, the ritual swim to the Sacred Pyramid was repeated and the Telling of the Tales resumed. Toth stood before the cadets, his arms outstretched in darkness, and each cadet felt the passing of ages as the sea rose and fell again in the Second Kalpa. "The Golden Age of the Second Kalpa began 36,300 years before the birth of King Rahn Mennon, when the sea floor was revealed as never before. Generation after generation, our ancestors migrated ever eastward. They listened to the Tellers of the Tales and understood how deep the waters would fall and where new land would form. Finally, 36,133 years before our time, our revered Sea Floor King, the Morowan, reclaimed the lands of our forebears in the Plain of Sunda. At first, his people found vast shallow pools that remained after the sea had gone. Then the land dried, grasses grew, and forests flourished. The Sea Floor King knew the Geometry and the Tales, and thereby led his people to search for the Secrets of the Ages."

* * *

Darkness fell and Toth again took on the spirits of the Ancient Ones. Again the drums, the chorus, the priest.

"*Listen...*

Who is he?
He is the Morowan, lured from the north,
Named for that which draws him forth.
What says he, this Sea Floor King?
"The Sindwan's cave is dry again.
The Echo Trove lies deep within."
What claims he, the Morowan?
"The Secret Wall, I now can see,
Sacred source of Geometry,
Sindwan's gift to eternity."
What does he, the Sea Floor King?
Recalling the Tales of ancient terrain,
He surveys his flourishing, vast domain.
Fish are trapped in shallow pools,
Food grains thrive as weather cools.
What learned they, the Morowan's clan?
Seaside ways of game and trade,
Shellfish moored on reefs they made,
Crops that grow on salty land,
Glass reclaimed by fire from sand.
Who is he who stands beside the Morowan?
He is the Geometer, scientist wise,
Who fathoms the cycles of oceans and skies.
He measures the earth and sea and ice,
Checking each mark no less than twice.
What says he, the Geometer?
"Tilt!" he yells to men on shore.

"Seaward now!" he calls once more.
He taps a wedge and bends a stick.
He twists a cord; records each tick.
What calls he then?
"Back!" he orders and maps the tide,
Repeating each step till satisfied.
"For decades now, we've watched the fall.
No doubt, we've found the Secret Wall."
What does he, the Morowan?
With shard of glass and peace of mind,
He carves his staff to mark this find.
"Search this bluff," he calls aloud,
Commanding soldier, lord, and crowd.
What do they, the followers of the Morowan, this Sea Floor King?
Spreading out to left and right,
They scour this shore in dark of night.
First light finds each faithful soul,
Exploring and probing each unknown hole.
What say they, these searchers for Troves?
"Here!" calls a boy, too eager to please.
"False hope!" yells the captain who oversees.
"Take care!" a mother warns her flock.
"You'll bash your butt on that slick rock."
What find they, these soldiers of the Morowan?
A young lieutenant shouts the news,
"A cave's been found by distant crews.
Encrusted rocks beyond this cove,
Conceal the way to Echo Trove."
What does he, the Sea Floor King?
Arriving at the entrance late this day,
He calls for lanterns to guide his way.
Through earth and Ages he eagerly climbs,
Seeking all Secrets from ancient times.
What find they, the Morowan and his soldiers?
The Echo Trove lies safe and dry,
With mummies reposed and staffs piled high.
With leaping hearts, they scan the hoard.
Heritage lost has been restored.
What brings dread to this caring King?
Respectfully passing the silent throng,
The Morowan senses something's wrong.
"Where are the Secrets?" he asks in fear.
"The Tales insist they must be near."

> *What sees he now, this Sea Floor King?*
> A soldier points, in fearful trust,
> To rotted heaps of yellow dust,
> Wisdom saved through ancient deed,
> Forever lost to future Seed.
> *What says he now, this grieving King?*
> "My people will prosper along new shore,
> But the Sindwan's gift was so much more."
> Scooping some dust in the cup of his hand,
> The Morowan sheds a tear for his land.

> *Do not forget…"*

"Our people again understood their world and its workings, and the Morowan vowed that never again would our heritage perish. His descendants prospered, though their accomplishments never compared with what had occurred in the last days of the Time Before. He, his sons, and his sons' sons recorded all their history and science and gave to our people the Pyramid, the Trove, and the Geometry. Thus, always and forevermore, the Secrets of the Ages shall prevail against the Waters of Chaos."

Toth went on until all the stories of the Golden Age of the Second Kalpa were told.

The Rising Age of the Third Kalpa

"In Sunda, the people learned to live in villages like many Commoners today. Some lived near pools teeming with fish, others beside meadows rich with wild grain. The people built Pyramids and Troves on high ground, for they knew from the Secrets and the Tales that the Waters of Chaos would rise again someday. Over time, the people multiplied and divided into many nations, each ruled by a scion of the progeny of the Morowan. All lived peaceably until the Waters of Chaos came again, drowning the lower lands and beginning the Third Kalpa. Then, our people suffered grievously under the terrible reign of the Tirowan, the 'Rival King.' The Tirowan descended from the Morowan, but we are not of his line, and he had neither the Trove nor the Geometry.

"War began 30,991 years ago in the days of the Tirowan, and peace eluded mankind for 100 generations. Our people prospered during the Golden Age, and their numbers outgrew their land. In the Rising Age of the Third Kalpa, each year the Waters of Chaos stole more land. The Tirowan thus sought to seize our territory and enslave our people. He formed a mighty army and fought against his brothers and their people, his cousins and their people, all Tribes of the East and the West.

"The vanquished took flight in every direction—to the Eastern Ocean, to the Southern Ocean. Some even fled to the Lands of the North, which should have remade them to look and act like the primitives of that harsh land, but they learned to take with them the elements of the sea and forever after traded with our people on the coast. It was in this time that our close ancestors started their great westward journey out of Sunda, bringing with them the Secrets of the Pyramid, the Trove, and the Geometry.

"The Tellers of the Tales reminded them of a place in the west which had been their ancestral home in the Time Before. Thence, our people advanced for 350 generations, spreading along the shore of the Southern Ocean in their journey to the Valley Sea. Each generation fought, in turn, for new territory farther west. First, they came to the mouths of the rivers that fill the Southern Ocean. Then, they lived many generations on the Plain of Hormuz until that land also was lost to the Waters of Chaos. At each place, some people settled on good land, but there were too many people, and in each generation, the sea took more land. Finally, in the time of our people 26,902 years before the birth of Rahn Mennon, our ancestors, led by the Darowan, the Conquering King, reclaimed the Land of the Second Sunset, and again they lived as primitives. It was the Topping Age of the Third Kalpa.

"In the Falling Age of the Third Kalpa, the sea receded yet again, and our ancestors, led by the Latawan, the Claiming King, returned 16,000 years ago to the islands and coasts of the Valley Sea. The people again occupied its fertile plains and prospered until today. Others returned to former lands on the Plain of Hormuz and deltas of the east. Eventually, their descendants spread even to the Plain of Sunda." Toth paused and sighed at the passing of Ages. "But the Waters of Chaos now come again in the Fourth Kalpa, and the same exodus must be repeated even to the Land of the Second Sunset. The Beloved Land will be abandoned yet again because of rising waters, and we ourselves are threatened in this, the Rising Age of the Fourth Kalpa."

For an entire day, Toth looked back to the Third Kalpa and the rise and fall of sea level that defined each Age. He told of the days of the Moltawan, the Golden King of the Third Kalpa. At twilight, he concluded, "The Topping Age of the Third Kalpa lasted for a very long time, more than 13,000 years. In its midst the seas fell for a while, and the earth was destroyed by fire as if it were a Falling Age, but soon the seas returned, and there was little opportunity for our people to recover from the Fires and from the Waters of Chaos. That Kalpa was graced with little learning, and many people lived like primitives even in its Golden Age. This is not to say there was no learning at all. The people recorded the cycles of the seas and skies and many other valuable things, and the kings of those days preserved the Secrets of the Ages when the Waters of Chaos came."

He then told of the Rindwan, Nellawan, and Tattawan, all great kings of the Third Kalpa. "When the sea again receded in the Third Kalpa, our people recovered the Secrets of the Ages and so did not have to start over in their learning of history and science. When the Third Kalpa ended, the Trove was preserved."

Chronicle 18: The Fifth Moon
The Rising Age of the Fourth Kalpa

"In the time of our people 6,300 years before the birth of Rahn Mennon, the Waters of Chaos rose, and thus the Fourth Kalpa began. For many generations, the World Ocean crept upward ten manheights and more without affecting the level of the Valley Sea." Toth sensed that the cadets were puzzled, and he explained, "The Chasm of the Veil was not the gushing gorge we know today. This great divider of lands and seas was then a mighty cataract flowing downward to the Southern Ocean. Our kingdom and our sea thus were separated from the rest of the World Ocean by a long, arduous portage in the south then, as in the north today.

"In the Rising Age of the Fourth Kalpa, 4,867 years before our time, the Erawan, the Red King, led our ancestors to Erytheia, then a peninsula, but now the Red Island. He made it our greatest military stronghold and the center of his realm in every matter of commerce, administration, and religion. Not until 1,145 years before the birth of King Rahn Mennon did the World Ocean meet the Valley Sea and raise it one manheight. As the waters of the Valley Sea rose, the peninsula of Erytheia was severed from the mainland and hence it became the island you know today. All our cities lost land to the sea. Many of our monuments, temples, and pyramids, including this Sacred Pyramid, were inundated. Many people were deprived of their ancestral homes, fertile fields, and livelihoods. The displaced peoples of Berenicia and Erytheia formed a great exodus and, following the guidance of our priests, founded the remote colony of Egia.

"Before the rise, Berenicia was an important trade center. Afterward, with Erytheia cut off from the mainland, Berenicia became the most important city in the world, gateway between east and west, keeper of the key remaining passageway for all the world's trade. Erytheia withered in power and position. Berenicia grew stronger with each generation. Later, the Army and Navy of the Realm moved here to defend the trade routes. Now, Berenicia is the staging area for our campaign to build our next refuge in the Valley of the Great River, beyond the First Terrace in the heart of the Land of the Second Sunset.

"Erytheia remains the true home and sacred center of our people, but it no longer controls our commerce. Still, we answer gladly to our King who resides in Erytheia. To that great city, you will go after completion of your military training. There you will receive orders for further service and advanced schooling in the Sciences of Man, as befits your orders. There, in the Third Betrothal, you will at last select and be selected by your mates for life."

Toth described more of their history, omitting for now the troubling fact that recently the Realm had lost land previously claimed as its own.

* * *

As darkness descended on the Sacred Pyramid, in the eyes of his people Toth became the Red King, so called because of his marvelous copper-toned skin, unknown among earlier arrivals on the shores of the Valley Sea. The Erawan was the great leader of the Chosen Ones who was born 4,900 years before the birth of Rahn Mennon. He came from the east, descendant of kings forced, as so many times before, to abandon first the Sunda, then the deltas of the Southern Ocean, and finally the Plain of Hormuz. In his generation, the rising Sea of Hormuz had caused intolerable crowding on the remaining portions of its low coastal plain. Commoners stayed behind to fight for whatever land and resources remained, but the Chosen Ones moved on. To save the Seed was the Erawan's highest charge handed down from antiquity. The drums, the chorus, the priest.

"Listen...
>> *Who is he?*
>>> He is the Erawan, named by men,
>>> For earth and sky and sea and skin.
>> *From whence come they, this Red King's kin?*
>>> Early from Afar, then from the east,
>>> They follow the ocean's fickle feast.
>> *Where dwell they, the Erawan and his kin?*
>>> On Hormuz plain they long reside,
>>> Crowded by neighbors and rising tide,
>>> Forced to fight, then fought aside.
>> *What find they, these followers of the Erawan, the Red King?*
>>> Roving west, they settle this bay.
>>> Bluffs beyond now block their way.
>>> Brackish water spills and falls.
>>> Coursing deep through chasm walls.
>> *What soon befalls this restive clan, living now on bluff-bound land?*
>>> Each moon, the sea extends its reach,
>>> To flat and marsh and spit and beach.
>>> Waters soon flood this peaceful strand,
>>> Forcing this race to find new land.
>> *What lose they, the Red Ones, to this Fast Rise?*
>>> Beaches abounding with grains and fish,
>>> Mussels and clams in tidal swish,
>>> Marshes with seabirds, crabs, and shoots,
>>> Freshwater standing with cattail roots.

What fear they, the people of the Erawan?
    "The hills beyond are our last hope.
    Can we survive above this slope?
    We'll crave the elements of the sea,
    And face foul creatures behind each tree."
What answers he, the Erawan?
    "Scale these falls. They taste of brine.
    There must be sea above this line."
    Hoisting and climbing, the masses rise,
    Hauling the sick, the old, and wise.
What find they in these high hills?
    First they face a desolate plain,
    Devoid of sea and food and grain.
    Some suffer, some starve, some leave the band.
    Still onward the Erawan leads his clan.
Where go they, the Erawan's people?
    Northward they march beyond the pale.
    Through sweltering wood and mossy vale.
    Shadowed skies of birds in flight,
    Point to this insular seaside site.
What sees he, the Erawan?
    The Erawan gasps at the wondrous view,
    Of cliffs so red and sea so blue.
    "A welcome sight, this isle must be,
    Our long lost home on the Valley Sea."
What does he, the Erawan?
    Invading across a narrow strait,
    The Red King seals the island's fate.
    With threat and deed he claims this site,
    Where fish abound and seabirds light.
What proclaims he, the Red King, in celebration?
    Toasting this deed in feast and fun,
    He names his tribe for the Living Sun.
    He notches his staff and stakes his claim,
    "Erytheia, the Red, shall be thy name."

  Do not forget..."

  Toth became himself again, and explained in a steady voice, "Later the People of the Living Sun found even more land on many shores of the Valley Sea. The greatest of all was this land where Berenicia now stands."

* * *

  Near dawn, Toth took on the spirit of Keftan, the leader of a small band of the People of the Living Sun. He told of a time 983 years before the birth of Rahn Mennon when the people who would become Egians made their way through the Gorge of the Suas. It was an exodus provoked by yet another Fast Rise in the first Age of the Fourth Kalpa. Again the call. Again the answer.

> *"Listen...*
>> *Who is he?*
>>> His name is Keftan. He leads the way,
>>> To coasts recalled from an earlier day?
>> *Where lies this shore, if Tales hold true?*
>>> On the Midland Sea from Afar south,
>>> A delta grows at the Great River's mouth.
>> *Why go they there?*
>>> Chosen by lot, each pioneer,
>>> Trades his home for food and gear,
>>> And seeks new land, the next frontier.
>> *Why are they chosen thus to part?*
>>> The Fast Rise takes so many homes.
>>> The King of the Realm decides who roams.
>>> "Death's Shadow," they call the outbound trail,
>>> That weakens the strong and kills the frail.
>> *What happens now on Keftan's way?*
>>> The camels bray. The horses stall.
>>> They face a sheer, unyielding wall.
>>> "These brutes can't enter this tunnel pass.
>>> That hole's too tight for a full-grown ass."
>> *What commands he, Keftan, the pioneer?*
>>> "Slaughter every tall, ungainly beast.
>>> We'll serve ourselves a final feast.
>>> On bended backs we'll carry through.
>>> With calves and colts we'll start anew."
>> *What next awaits these pioneers?*
>>> Death's Shadow yields to harsh terrain,
>>> Then steeper slope and higher plain.
>>> Twice this night the sunset falls,
>>> Across, at last, a seabird calls.
>> *What sees he, Keftan, the pioneer?*
>>> Above twin falls, he stands aghast,
>>> At the ocean of water flowing past.
>>> Expecting pristine delta plains,
>>> Now shocked to see what yet remains.
>> *What does he now, this pioneer?*
>>> He calls a craftsman to his side,
>>> And points his staff toward the rising tide.
>>> With sharp bronze blade and talent keen,

The artisan carves this awesome scene.
What sculpts he now, this craftsman of old?
From end to end the Great River flows,
Egia spreads as the delta grows.
Pyramids dot the staff's bold shield,
Cresting over water and mud and field.

Do not forget...

Toth resumed his Tales. "From the beginning of the Fourth Kalpa to this day, 6,300 years have passed. The Waters of Chaos rose, and still they rise. Other civilizations have perished, first on the Plain of Sunda, then on the Plain of Hormuz. We enjoy prosperity because the World Ocean has reached only to the level of the Chasm of the Veil, portal to our Valley Sea. But the floods continue to rise. They will soon submerge the Veil's chasm and flood the Valley Sea. The time will soon arrive to abandon our cherished lands and find refuge above. It is your sworn duty to protect the King, make safe our escape to new lands, and preserve the Secrets of the Ages. And yes, again you must reclaim the Land of the Second Sunset. In this, you will not fail!"

Chronicle 19: The Sixth Moon

When the Sixth Moon came, Toth stood tall on the crest of the Sacred Pyramid. "Tonight, I will recite for you the Sciences of Man!" he began. "Heed me well, young men, for the best and brightest soon will move to the wondrous Red Island where you will be steeped in the Sciences of Man. Those who fail will go to lesser duties, but always you will depend on the knowledge I share with you tonight."

"The Geometry was the beginning of science, and all science today is based on the Geometry. As knowledge separates men from lower animals, the Geometry separates our kind from primitive tribes. The Geometry allows us to thrive in good times and survive in bad. It warns us of changes from time to time and place to place.

"First, I will recall the Geometry of Large Spaces.

"The Geometry of the Heavens reveals the relationships among our comets and stars, our sun and planets, our precious earth and the moon that revolves around it. It tells us when to plant, when to harvest, when grand celestial events will occur. By this science, we understand eclipses of the sun and moon and thus are not afraid.

"The Geometry of the Skies tells us the relationships among warm winds and cold winds, fast winds and still air, blue skies and white clouds, dark clouds and storms, rain and drought. The Geometry of the Skies tells us when the earth will turn cold and warm itself again. This knowledge helps our people know what to plant, which fruits of the land and sea will be abundant or scarce, and how much of the earth's bounty to store for the future. It allows us to plan for the rise and fall of the World Ocean's waters, both the Slow and Fast Rises. Without this knowledge our people would have been lost long ago to the seas or perished from thirst or starvation.

"The Geometry of the World Ocean is the dearest science, for we are a people of the sea. It is this science that permits us to sail the ocean and thrive on its coasts. It tells us the comings and goings of the currents in shallow waters and deep. It explains the saltiness of the sea and the warmth or coldness of its waters. It reveals the forces that cause freezing and melting of seawater far to the north and south.

"The Geometry of the Earth's Surface tells us the relationships among the mountains, valleys, and seas; the hills, plateaus, and plains; the deserts, forests, and ice. The military might of our nation derives from mastery of this most powerful of sciences. Yet we know far too little about the world outside our realm. We know only the lands beside the seas, the coarse features of other continents, and the huge Ice Masses of the far north and south.

"The Geometry of the Lands Beneath the Earth's Surface is the least known of the Sciences of Man. This science explains the earth's rocks, minerals, and sands; its ores of gold, silver, copper, iron, and redsilver; its veins of minerals that glow or burn. The riches of this treasure are scarcely known to the earth's people, but we know the storehouse is vast.

"The Geometry of the Earth's Commerce tells our people where to build cities and roads, pathways and ports, factories and markets. It is by this science that the great city of Berenicia was sited here and made great. By this science, our people knew where to place the colony of Egia. It allows us to thrive in times of plenty and survive in times of drought or devastation. By this science, our great military conquests are planned. You will learn much of this Geometry in the days ahead.

"The Geometry of the Earth's Living Things is the science that explains the domains of plants, animals, and people on the face of the earth. This science helps us know our allies and enemies. Through it we choose our leaders, and they, in turn, choose their followers and inspire them to do good."

Toth raised his hands high and spread his arms wide. Then, with a slow sweep he brought his hands together and extended his arms forward. "Now, I will recall the Geometries of Small Spaces.

"The first of these is the Geometry of the Elements. It tells us the compositions of the earth's substances. It tells of metals and minerals and what happens when they mix. Even in its infancy, this science now yields marvelous inventions and improvements. Without its benefits, our lives would be less pleasant and our military conquests would be few. Without this knowledge, no one could venture far from the sea without becoming sick and deformed. Your lives as warriors and protectors of the King will be greatly aided by the advances of this most promising of the Geometries.

"The Geometry of Stones and Structures is the most important of all the Sciences of Man for it is through this knowledge that we have the Pyramid. The Pyramid has allowed our people to preserve the Secrets of the Ages and thus to recover in each kalpa from the ravages of the sea. The Keepers of this Geometry are the most prized of our Geometers, and they are known by all as the saviors of our people."

The Pyramid

"In the Golden Age of the Second Kalpa, the Morowan and his successors made good on his pledge to protect our heritage from the Waters of Chaos. First, the Morowan instructed all his people to mark the highest point of land within the Plain of Sunda. Then, to each man, woman, and child, he assigned a number of baskets of soil to bring to the hill each year. In this manner, our first Sacred Mound was built.

"The Morowan was wise, but his efforts were small for he had no Pyramid, no Trove, and no Geometry. He did not understand the power of the sea or the strength of the rains. By the time of his son's son, the Utawan, which means the Stone King, the Sacred Mound had eroded so badly that only a small hump remained. When the mound was made full again with baskets of earth, the Utawan reasoned that stones would shield it from rain and surging waters. The Utawan was wise, for, in his life, the waters rose again, though only one manheight and for only a few seasons. The Utawan found sanctuary on the Sacred Mound and was saved. He made sacrifices to the Sun God Rahn and pledged to build an even greater Sacred Mound.

"The Utawan assigned each man, woman, and child a greater quota of baskets by tens and hundreds than his grandfather had assigned. The people obeyed and made the mound full. So great was the mound that its sides collapsed of its own weight, but the Utawan again ordered a solid wall of stone to enclose the mound and save it from itself. Late in the Golden Age, there was yet again a temporary rising of the sea, this time three manheights, a forewarning of things to come. The King took refuge on the Sacred Mound and was saved from the Waters of Chaos. From that time on, all kings, in turn, built mound upon mound of ever more grand design. Each king added height and more clever stonework to that which he had inherited."

The old man paused and peered at the horizon. He seemed relieved to see the first rays of sun above the earth's hazy rim. Soon the full disk of the sun would mount the heavens, and it would be time for morning prayers and chants.

The Trove

The following day the priest resumed with the lessons of the Trove. "By the end of that Golden Age of the First Kalpa, our ancestors created a solid stone treasury of the kind we call the Pyramid of the Trove. The Trove was invented by the Kondwan, which means the Wise King. Before his day, the Morowan, the Utawan, and others in their line tried valiantly to save the Secrets of the Ages, but each time the Sacred Mound was tested, some of the Secrets were lost.

"The Kondwan, whose name means the Wise King, was the last king of the Golden Age of the Second Kalpa. It was the Kondwan who decided the Secrets must be sealed beneath the waters so that, generations hence, his descendants might find them when the rising waters would once again fall. In this way, the Secrets survive each Rising Age to speed our regeneration in each new Falling Age.

"The Kondwan devised a scheme which we still employ. He ruled that each generation must protect and preserve the Secrets of the Ages that have been passed down from previous kalpas. In addition, the people of each Kalpa must inscribe a new version in their own best manner. The Kondwan ordered his people to build a sacred Trove deep within the highest pyramid and yet another near its top. In the Upper Trove, he placed all the Secrets of the Ages to be sealed until the next kalpa. In the Lower Trove, he placed certain Secrets that would be vital in the refuge. The Upper Trove was sealed for the Ages, but the Secrets of the Lower Trove went with our people when they fled the rising waters. The Benben, the Ark of the Trove, was stored in the Lower Trove. When the waters rose, this carved and gilded chest carried vital Secrets to the refuge and held them for safekeeping until a new pyramid could be built. When each exodus began, the last act of the nobles and priests was to restock the Lower Trove with cherished relics of their own Age, and these objects, like those ancient Secrets in the Upper Trove, were sealed for the next Kalpa.

"Here, as we stand atop our own Sacred Pyramid, we see the entrance to the Upper Trove which crowns its pinnacle. Already sealed inside are the Secrets of the Ages and the Royal Staffs which record the history of each owner from the Ancestor King onward. They will not be seen again until the Falling Age of this, the Fourth Kalpa. Beneath the waters lies the entrance to the Lower Trove. When the waters rose, its contents were placed in the Benben and moved to the new pyramid in Berenicia. In your own lifetime, the time may come when the Benben will again be moved to a new refuge."

"It was the Kondwan who decreed which relics and documents to place inside troves made of stone. Each trove's width is two manheights, its length four manheights, and its height one and a half manheights. The walls and floors are stone blocks the thickness of a man's body, and the ceilings are great sheets of stone. A massive stone seals the entrance." For the remainder of the day, Toth told of the Trove and the Secrets of the Ages that were contained within its walls.

The Geometry

On the third day, Toth proclaimed the highest achievement of the People of the Living Sun.

"Without the Geometry, our people would live in constant strife with the sea. Four times, the Waters of Chaos have come, and four times our cities have been destroyed. Each time, the Geometry improved as scholars learned from errors and made corrections. Each kalpa, the Pyramids were tested, and the Geometry of the Pyramids was improved. Each kalpa, the strength of the Trove was tested, and likewise improved. By the end of the Second Kalpa, the Pyramid, the Trove, and the Geometry reached the high forms we know today, except that there was no True Pyramid and there was still much Geometry left to learn. In the Third Kalpa, our people devised the True Pyramid, and the greatest Secrets of the Ages are kept there still.

"Today, the Geometry is our only true science, and the men and women we call Geometers are our wisest scholars and teachers. Wise Men predict that someday, if the Secrets are preserved, each and every part of the Geometry may become a true science in its own right."

For the remainder of that day and all night and following day, Toth taught the Geometry.

CHAPTER 9

Search Log 20: Cold Survival

Tuesday morning was bitterly cold—six degrees above zero then four, falling when it should have been rising. Ice covered all roads except the main highways that had been plowed and salted. Heavy snow covered ice except on tree branches where yesterday's bright, cold sun had left only glaze. Jared and Ellie stared from their bedroom window through a glistening forest, backlighted by the sun, and turned to crystal. *Like the inside of a chandelier,* he thought, *surrounded with piercing light reflected from every angle.*

For only the second time in Jared's career, Melton Valley Laboratory was closed. He reflected on the harrowing events of Sunday and Monday when he and Greg had been caught in the storm's full fury.

* * *

On Sunday morning it was two degrees above zero when they awoke. From his bed, Jared saw the Great Smoky Mountains capped with snow. They drove east toward the mountains stopping for a big country breakfast at Anna Lee's Hearthside Restaurant. It was nine degrees when they hit the trail at noon.

Cosby campground was covered with snow. They parked Jared's red Pathfinder near the closed gate, hoisted their backpacks, and headed for the trailhead. As they signed for permits, a park ranger warned of rough conditions with more snow and freezing rain expected. All afternoon they plodded up the mountain, higher and higher without a downhill break. Snake Den Trail led 5 miles up to the Maddron Bald Trail which then followed a knife-edge divide for half a mile before dropping down the back side. Soon they were coasting through a snow-covered rhododendron hell with close-up views of surrounding peaks. An hour before sunset, they reached Campsite #29. With practiced efficiency, they pitched camp and cooked a sumptuous meal. At sunset they crawled into sleeping bags and began the long night.

"What's the latest on your search?" Greg asked as he hung a candle lantern from the tent roof.

"I desperately need more information. You're studying marine biology. Have you learned much about coral formations? Besides fish and polyps, that is."

"Yes, we just finished a section. What do you need to know?"

"For starters, what kind of base does coral grow on?"

"The technical term is 'substrate.' Practically any rock will do, but, for certain, it has to be solid. Oh, I know where you're headed. Red Sea corals are presumed to lie on limestone, for the most part, but corals are too valuable to destroy just to see what's underneath."

"So how do they know it's limestone?"

"It's just a guess, based on the shape of the surface. Pits and mounds are typical of limestone on dry land. Red Sea corals grow in pits and mounds. Ergo, Red Sea corals must be growing on limestone."

"Wouldn't a city covered with coral also have pits and mounds?"

"Yes, but here's the difference, oh father of mine. People who believe in cities covered with coral are kooks, while people who believe in limestone are perfectly sane." Greg laughed as his dark eyes searched his father's face.

To Greg's relief, Jared laughed along with him and then asked, "Wouldn't a building, especially a pyramid, make a good base for coral?"

"Yes, excellent. I can't imagine a better substrate than a stone pyramid. Coral could easily attach and grow upward from each face. The mound would start out looking like a coated pyramid, but over time it would become a cylindrical column—a tower of coral."

"Why is that?"

"Well, it can't grow any higher than the sea surface itself. Corals growing from the tip would reach the surface first, but, given enough time, even the lowest tiers would reach the same level."

"I assume it can spread outward if more solid base surrounds it."

"Yes, I was talking about a nice clean pyramid surrounded by sand. But streets, buildings, temples, natural rock surfaces; all those would complicate the pattern."

"Like Foul Bay?"

"Yes, Dad, but don't jump to conclusions. There are other ways to create the same surface. Limestone terrain, or karst topography as you geographers call it, is the prime suspect in this case. In other regions volcanic terrain with lots of small cones could do the same thing."

"I need more. What controls coral growth? How deep can it be? How fast does it rise?" Jared spoke louder and sank deeper into his mummy bag as the wind's pitch rose and the tent's ripstop nylon flapped and snapped like a ship's flag in a gale.

"The expert on Red Sea reefs is an English geologist named Braithwaite. He says these corals started growing about 6,000 years ago and are about 10 to 20 meters thick in most places. Let's see." He paused for a mental calculation. "That translates to about 3 millimeters per year. But you'll have to explain pits, too. Braithwaite says the density of pits in some areas exceeds anything observed in terrestrial karst anywhere else on earth. Pits constitute as much as 60 per cent of the sea floor in some areas under Foul Bay. To be fair, those reefs could be called 'pitted' just as well as 'pinnacled.' That odd fact may lend itself to your odd thoughts about a coral covered city. Braithwaite admits it could be 'of some other origin,' but I doubt he was thinking of urbanization."

"Interesting! Imagine Washington, D.C., with a blanket thrown over it."

"Now there's a pleasant thought! Especially in this weather."

"There'd be pits all right...parks and plazas and all sorts of open spaces where buildings *don't* raise the blanket." Jared pulled his sleeping bag tighter around his face. "Oh, one other thing! Does Braithwaite say anything about tectonics? Even if we find a city, naysayers will claim it sank into the sea."

"You're in luck. That shore has been stable for at least 240,000 years. No uplift, no subsidence!" Now it was Greg's turn to snuggle deeper. He yawned. "I'm ready for some sleep."

"Hold on just a minute. What do you know about the Bahamas?"

"Patch reefs there are almost identical to those in the Red Sea, but the coral species are different, and the only pits are the famous Blue Holes. They're fantastic! Some are nearly 300 feet deep and connected through cave systems at great depth. They can suck a small boat under in seconds. Boaters know to avoid them, but it sometimes happens anyway. Bahamian lore says each hole contains a demon called the 'lusca.' A few divers have managed to go down by timing their descents with the tides. Any miscalculation, and the diver is dead!" He yawned again.

"Back to the Red Sea, I need ideas on how to examine those corals. Peek underneath their skirts, so to speak. Does that take you back to more familiar territory, College Boy?" Jared smiled.

Greg laughed. "You wound me so!" They both laughed. "Go east, old man, go east! That's the key. From what I've read, some of those patch corals are almost bare on their windward flanks. In Foul Bay that would be the eastward face. High energy currents constantly wash away any new coral that starts to grow."

"That may explain the photograph I found in *National Geographic*. Cousteau didn't say which direction the reef was oriented, but the coral was so thin I could see rock underneath. At least I think it was rock. It looked like the rounded capital of a stone column. And Sudanese pyramids always have stone columns on their eastern sides."

"Dad, you've got to find a way," Greg exclaimed as he blew out the candle. "See you in the morning."

That night Old Smoky decided to show them what a Southern mountain can do. First, the wind howled louder, and crusty snow fell from the trees, pelting their tent under a clear sky. Then, clouds moved in and fresh snow fell. Winds whipped over the ridges, dropping rain in some places, snow in others, and then turning into raging Chinooks. At times the tent flapped as if a huge beast knelt beside it, slapping their faces through the fabric.

After breakfast, they broke camp and headed back toward the ridge. The first half-mile was easy except where huge trees had fallen across the trail and occasional spots where slush or glaze slipped underfoot. The water-soaked tent and ground cloth added pounds to their ice-encrusted packs. Blowing rain dodged under, around, and through their ponchos. Turning a switchback, they reached the spine of the ridge and faced the full force of the furious wind they'd heard all night.

Maddron Bald was a white agony of blowing snow. Huge flakes whipped over the crest in waves. A river of snow, it seemed, except for scattered trees glimpsed through the blur. The rhododendron-lined trail was covered with several inches of new snow in thigh-deep drifts. Greg took the lead. Every step was an ordeal as snow tugged at boots, gaiters, and pants. They darted ten yards or more from one wind shelter to the next. Each time Greg went first, then waited for Jared. They timed each advance with the gusts. Once, Jared watched helplessly as Greg, darting from tree to tree, was blown over sideways to the ground. Fortunately, bushes blocked his fall and kept him on the ridge.

Finally across the bald, they rested, thinking the worst was over, for the downhill stretch lay just ahead. But they had misjudged the distance, and, worse yet, the drifts were thicker than below. Hurricane-force gusts burst through the trees. Alternating the lead, they finally reached Snake Den Trail with their last reserves of energy and will. Eventually they reached the cutoff.

The rest, as they say, was all downhill. Soon snow became rain, freezing on the foliage but not on the trail. Oddly, the temperatures grew colder as they descended. Rain turned to snow again and accumulated on the trail.

Cosby Campground was covered with downed trees and scattered limbs even worse than the slopes above. Their progress actually slowed on the camp road, as new snow and fallen trees blocked the way a couple of miles from the trailhead. Stiff and exhausted they finally reached the Pathfinder. A Park Ranger approached by car. "Glad to see you guys made it," he said. "Headquarters told us to keep an eye out for you. They were getting worried. You were the only guys on the mountain, you know."

"Thanks. We didn't know. But we fared okay, considering the conditions." Jared and Greg had kept warm as long as they were moving, but the temperature caught up with them in a hurry. "How are the highways?" he asked.

"I-40 is open, but slow going. Knoxville's a real mess; mostly ice. Highway 321 is open through Gatlinburg; lots of snow but not much ice. You should be able to make it in four-wheel drive."

"Thanks. See you next winter!" Jared yelled as he cranked the engine. The ranger laughed and waved a cheerful goodbye. Three hours later they were home.

* * *

Tuesday morning, it felt good to be inside the chandelier again, looking out, warm and rested though somewhat stiff. Beyond glistening trees, he could barely discern the mountains, their snowy outline only slightly whiter than the sky. Across the room, other windows framed the Cumberlands, also covered with an undulating blanket of white but more distinct because they were so near. *A perfect day to sit by the fireplace and read a good book*, he thought as he hobbled downstairs to start the coffee and build a fire.

Jared knew how to build a fire. J.L. had taught his sons the old ways hardly removed from their pioneer ancestors. As a child, he had admired old tools, old customs, old barns, and houses. The everyday item he liked best was an iron fire poker his great grandfather had made on an old fashioned forge. Later J.L made a forge for him, and with his own hands Jared hammered into shape a poker exactly like the one that hung by the fireplace during his boyhood. With his own hands, Jared carved boards and cut leather to make an authentic bellows for his fireplace. He was glad to have an iron poker and leather bellows as he stoked the embers on this cold morning.

Not long ago, he and the boys had cut truckloads of firewood each winter. For kindling they had pulled rich pine from stumps, split each thin log into splinters small and large, and kept a kegfull in the garage. From J. L.'s teaching, he knew to stack a fire with small pieces on bottom, larger pieces in the middle, midsize logs in front, and a huge backstick at the rear. He knew for sure that a two-stick fire would not burn. He knew how to bank a fire with ashes at night so there would be coals to jumpstart a new blaze in the morning.

Sitting on the hearth, Jared twisted Monday's newspaper into Tuesday's kindling, a rare concession to modern circumstances. As he headed outside for some larger sticks of real wood, Greg came down the stairs, hobbling on sore legs as he, himself, had done a few minutes earlier. "Oh. I'm sore," Greg groaned.

"Thank, Goodness!" Jared exclaimed.

"Gee, thanks, Dad!" Greg complained.

"Oh, no. Sorry, son. I thought I was sore because of creeping old age. If you're sore too, that means I still have a few years left. Well, both of us do. Say, I'm going out for firewood. How about hobbling down to the basement for more papers?"

When he returned, a stack of yellowed newspapers lay neatly on the hearth. As he reached for the first section and started to roll, he noticed the date—February 27, 1993. These are old, he thought, as he skimmed the headlines. Then, an item caught his eye.

"FREIGHTER SINKS IN MIDDLE EAST—Sabotage Suspected, No Survivors"

"Look at this!" he yelled to Greg. "This wreck happened in Foul Bay not long ago, and it may be our answer! This freighter hit something hard in open water. If that was one of our suspect reefs, the ship may have knocked enough coral loose to expose the substrate underneath. How quickly do you suppose new coral would cover such a scar?"

Greg carefully read the article, went back to his room, and returned with an open textbook. Jared frowned as he read the account of a ship that grounded in 1980 on Jackson Reef in the Gulf of Aqaba. Six months later, the reef's tip was bare, all color gone, all life turned to gray and white. Then a smile came over Jared's face. The authors were pleased to report that coral was beginning to grow two years after the collision and the site had completely recovered several years later. *So a fresh breach in the coral might still be visible, he thought. Now, if we can just get to Foul Bay.*

Search Log 21: The Ice-Dammed Bible

"GOOGLE," click.
"GLOBAL GEOMORPHOLOGY," click.
"UNIVERSITY OF EDINBURGH," click.
"DEPARTMENT OF GEOGRAPHY," click.
"SUMMERFIELD, MICHAEL A." click.
"jökulhlaup," click.
"Catastrophic draining of ice-dammed lakes . . .

"Modern-Vatnajökull reached 40,000 to 50,000 cubic meters per second at peak . . . Baffin Island release drained 5,000,000 cubic-meter lake in 30 hours.

"Late Pleistocene—Lake Missoula . . . northwest USA . . . volume 2,000 cubic kilometers . . . peak release 21,300,000 cubic meters per second . . . 20 times current discharge of *all* the world's rivers . . . repeated releases from 16,000 BP to 12,000 BP."

* * *

That night, Jared dialed Rick, "Hey, that question about fast rises still bothers me. I had a brainstorm, but it didn't pan out. Remember Lake Missoula?"

"Isn't that the Ice Age lake in Montana, the one that broke loose and created the Channeled Scabland. Were you thinking it might've caused the fast rise?"

"Well, sort of. I did a little browsing. It's like Hubbard Glacier...happened over and over. Experts say the ice dam periodically *floated*, releasing all the water at once. Then ice flowed in from a side valley, and the process started all over again. Sounds like a huge toilet that flushed automatically every time it filled."

"You're a true romantic," Rick responded.

"Okay. Time to find a new analogy. How about this? They've found *30-foot boulders* rolled along *like pebbles in a creek.*"

"Yes, sounds better, but surely that's not enough water to make much difference to the World Ocean."

"Nah. I did a back-of-the-envelope calculation," Jared said. "It works out to about a quarter of an inch vertical rise around the whole earth. Nobody would have noticed in Foul Bay. But it must have created quite a stir in the North Pacific. If my math is correct, the whole lake would have drained in just a few days. Now, listen to this. At peak release, if the entire flow exited intact through the mouth of the Columbia River, it would have made a column of water 50 miles wide and 900 feet high. That's a tremendous slug of H_2O, like suddenly dumping a bathtub into a swimming pool. I'll bet it launched a tidal wave that didn't play out until somebody yelled 'Tsunami!' in its native language."

"Japan? Maybe, but I doubt it. The mouth is 800 miles downstream from the dam. There must have been pooling and backflow along the way. Of course, a lot of debris would have been added, as well." Rick said.

"True. By the way, the lake site itself was discovered as early as 1880," Jared noted. "The Channeled Scabland is downstream, but no one made the connection. In 1923, a man named Bretz was trying to explain Scabland features called 'coulees.'"

"Oh, I know about 'coulees.' They're enormous gullies, more like canyons."

"Right. Well, he concluded that coulees were carved by an incredibly large flood racing across eastern Washington. Most scientists ridiculed him because no one could imagine where the water might have come from, but geographers liked his logic. In fact, one of his earliest articles on it was published by the American Geographical Society in its flagship journal, *Geographical Review.* At the time, he and his critics were unaware of glacial Lake Missoula. Years later, someone put it all together, and Bretz transformed from kook to genius, while geographers grew foresighted and wise."

"Fascinating!" Rick exclaimed.

"Encouraging, I'd say."

* * *

Three nights later, Rick called Jared. "Hot news! A Russian geologist named Rudoy and an American named Baker discovered another jökulhlaup like Lake Missoula. It's in Siberia, in the Altai Mountains."

"When?"

"1991."

"No, dammit, when was the flood?" Jared asked.

"14,000 BP."

"How big?"

"Enormous, though not as big as Missoula," Rick replied. "200 cubic miles of water compared to Missoula's 500. Peak flow was 640 million cubic feet per second compared to Missoula's 752 million."

"Neither seems big enough to explain the fast rise. I calculate a 25-foot rise worldwide would require 1,400 Lake Missoulas."

"That's as big as the whole U.S.–the 48 contiguous states anyway. No jökulhlaup could even come close to that size."

"I know, Rick. But step pyramids only make sense if the water rose fast enough for people to recognize what was happening."

"What about storm surges? They could add several feet to any gradual rise that had accumulated since the last major storm."

"Maybe, but I'd feel more comfortable with sudden sea level rises of a man's height or more."

"How can we find out?"

"I know somebody who may be able to tell me."

* * *

"Christ, Jerry, after all these years, don't you think we should be on a first-name basis? It's Kirk . . . Kirk. Try it."

At six-foot-five, Kirk Stone's lanky body could have made him a basketball star. At 81, his athletic days were over, but he still looked as bright-eyed as when Jared last saw him 20 years earlier. Soon it was obvious Stone was as smart and combative as ever. For months, Jared had looked forward to this visit. Despite his Ph.D., Stone insisted on being called "Mr.", even in academic circles. Now Jared's old UGA mentor was retired and living in Tucson, Arizona.

"Just habit," Jared replied. "I don't put much stock in titles." Privately he thought, *Stone could name himself after one of the seven dwarfs, and I'd still respect him for a career like his.* It was Stone who had enticed Jared into geography.

Caisson was on a tight schedule, as usual, and they locked in deep conversation for six-and-a-half hours without a lull. They recalled a few episodes from the '60s and '70s and caught up on happenings since, but nostalgia was minimal. Far from living in the past, Stone was anxious for the here-and-now, and Jared wanted Stone's advice on topics from Seagate to sea level. Stone was enthralled when Jared showed him what could be done with satellite imagery and GPS on a color laptop computer. "Christ!" he said. "What we could have done with equipment like that in my day!" Caisson lamented that all too many *young* scholars were less open to new ideas, new technologies, and good old-fashioned logic.

"Just a minute," Stone said, and he disappeared into his office. A moment later, he returned with a reprint from the discipline's premier research journal. It was an article he had written in 1962 encouraging geographers to use more remote sensing in their work and advising on how to do it. When the conversation resumed, Jared described what imagery had revealed about the ice dam at Yakutat. "Just a minute," Stone said again, and returned with another reprint from the same journal. It was a survey of ice-dammed lakes in Alaska, written by Stone in 1963. Sure enough, there on his map was Hubbard Glacier prophetically listed as potentially damming Russell Fiord. *I recall some forgotten scientist's remark that originality most often results from poor knowledge of literature. I, myself, was the guilty party this time.*

Discussing Lake Missoula, ice-dammed lakes, and jökulhlaups in general, Jared casually mentioned the catastrophic flooding that occurs when ice dams float.

"Ice dams don't float," Stone said flatly.

"Well, it's in all the literature," Jared replied lamely.

"I don't care if it's in the ice-dammed Bible," Stone said. "Ice dams don't float. Do you want to see pictures? I've sat for days watching them breach. When the conditions are right, water percolates through cracks and undercuts the ice above until the dam eventually washes out. It's that simple."

Jared felt silly. "Of course," he said. "You're right. All the water pressure is on one side of the dam. Nothing floats unless there's displacement, and there's no displacement unless the object is surrounded."

"Right. Precisely. Now, does that help or hurt your theories?" Stone asked.

"Hard to say. Everyone believes sea level rose gradually as glaciers melted," Caisson said, "but Rick and I have a nagging suspicion that it may have been rapid at times. What do you think?"

Stone looked up, while pouring two beers, and answered without hesitation, "If it's like everything else I've seen with glaciers, *it happens in fits and starts.*" The statement, itself, and the look in Stone's eyes reminded Caisson, once again, of the stark contrast between knowledge and wisdom.

Search Log 22: Seeking Culture

Rick Caisson had a love/hate relationship with libraries. He loved the mystery of unopened volumes and the excitement of discovery, but he hated the quiet, florescent monotony. Yet the hours he'd endured there as a student and professor were balanced by enough good memories to keep him coming back.

With only two hours available this afternoon, he resorted to a time-honored short cut. Dashing to the central Reference Desk, Rick approached a librarian. "Elena," her nameplate said.

"I've reached an impasse, and I wonder if you can help," he asked.

"I'll do whatever I can," she said. "What are you looking for?"

"Four topics. First, I need a compendium of creation legends for all the world's cultures. Second, the worldwide distributions of all types of pyramids. Third, an anthology of flood legends for all the world's peoples. And fourth, a flow chart tracing all the world's languages. I've exhausted every avenue in the automated catalogue."

"I don't think they're organized that way. You'll need to go culture by culture."

"Culture by culture? That could take months."

"I'm afraid that's the best way. Our automated index will speed things up."

Six weeks ago, he silently recalled, *I tried your damned index and found it to be cumbersome and possibly even slower than a manual search. But, nothing good will come of complaining.* He mentally summed up the effort and cast his complaint as a question, "A geography professor in Minnesota spent his entire career cataloguing barn styles of the Midwest. How come no one has catalogued the world's pyramids, which people generally find far more fascinating than Midwestern barns? And, no comprehensive compendium of cultures and architectural styles? Surely some enterprising scholar has done a cross-cultural comparison. It's a life's work on any one of those topics if I have to do it all myself."

"Not to my knowledge, but let's check the automated index just to be sure. Let's start with pyramids."

"I didn't find anything, other than Egyptian stuff and some New Age texts on pyramid power. Nothing global. Nothing cross-cultural, not even a comprehensive list of elementary info such as ages and locations worldwide," Rick said.

"Hmmm. Let's see. . ." She pointed to the response on her screen: "NO MATCHES"

"But there must be something. I ran across the term 'Pyramid Belt.' That alone suggests someone studied pyramids enough to know they exist in distinct belts."

"There . . . Pyramid Belt. No . . . wait . . . that's pyramids and belts, not Pyramid Belts. Maybe if we look in the index to the index. See, here it is, 'pyramids,'" she said.

"But it's all listed culture by culture. I need a comprehensive source."

"I'm sorry. We don't seem to have it."

"Okay, what about creation myths?"

"Did you look under folklore? Religion?"

"Yep."

"And you didn't find anything?"

"Sure, there's plenty of Adam and Eve stuff, but nothing global, nothing cross-cultural."

"Yeah. See. I think you'll have to go culture by culture."

Rick's face turned red. "That would take years."

She stepped back to her index of indexes. "Let's see. No. Nothing. Here is 'creation.' Oh, 'See: Genesis, Garden of Eden, Navaho.' That may help."

"But it isn't cross-cultural . . . comprehensive . . . analytical . . . comparative . . . global. In short, what's missing is a decent geography."

"Okay, here, try the BL224 through BL226 sections in the stacks. They're on the fifth floor. You can check book by book."

Rick spent almost an hour in a futile search of the stacks, then returned to the Reference Desk.

"How about languages?"

"No. Sorry, that's one I can't help you with. Maybe Linda here can help you. She's a reference librarian."

Linda pondered for a moment. "Probably have to go culture by culture."

"Is there anything comprehensive, any basic reference material that might be cross-indexed by culture."

Linda turned and walked toward the open stacks of reference books nearby. "You might try these," she said. Her hand swept past a well-worn set of 13 volumes. "*Mythology of All the World's Races.* It has an index." Linda kept walking.

Rick stopped in his tracks. He disengaged from the librarian as quickly and politely as possible, grabbed "Volume XIII, Index," and headed for a nearby table. Published in 1932 and written by several of those encyclopedic scholars who graced that era, it was a gold mine of information about creation stories and flood legends.

Like a man possessed, Rick copied page numbers from the index for 30 minutes. Then, in the remaining 15 minutes before closing, he made spot checks in Volumes I, II, and IX. Pay dirt, pay dirt, pay dirt. Again and again, culture after culture, region after region, the nuggets emerged. Flood legends or creation legends involving floods came from almost every culture on earth. Best of all, the legends were fortified with occasional analytical comments by the authors. He jotted furiously and would return later for more.

* * *

Picata's, Knoxville's finest Italian restaurant, had survived since the '82 World's Fair and now constituted a proper setting for a birthday celebration of the highest order. Rick and Anna, Jared and Ellie settled into comfortable, familiar conversation on this, the brothers' forty-ninth birthday—their real forty-ninth, not the fictitious repeat that everyone jokes about.

"I just need to tell you a couple of things," Rick said to Jared in a stage whisper. "It won't take long."

"No longer than the whole evening," Anna said ruefully.

"No, I'll just say what I found, and then we can get back to regular conversation." He scanned the menu, looking for his favorites. With a shrug, Anna yielded the floor, as Rick pulled a sheet of paper from his pocket.

"Listen to these quotes: 'Flood legends in the Philippines are common . . . Many legends there begin with such a tale . . . Deluge myths are well developed in Indonesia . . . in Greece, Zeus punished mankind with floods. He caused a great rain to fall and flooded well-nigh all Hellas and spared only a handful of men who had fled to the neighboring hills . . . Poseidon, angry at being dispossessed, covered the fertile plain of Attike with a flood.' So much attention goes to Atlantis, and yet the same flood theme ran rampant across the whole ancient world. And, those are just samples. But, let's enjoy our dinners. I won't say anymore tonight."

"You're going to leave us hanging?" Jared said.

"Yep. That's it for now. Call me tomorrow, and I'll fill you in on the rest."

"Go ahead. You know you want to tell it all." Anna protested, but she tolerated Rick's pursuits better than she cared to admit. Maybe even liked them just a bit.

"Well, if you insist. Stop me if I go too long." Drinks arrived. "I'll start with the Philippines. Their creation legends usually begin with a sister and a brother who were survivors of a major deluge. Everyone else was killed, and the two were stranded on separate mountaintops. As soon as the earth was dry, the brother went looking for other survivors and, finding none, told his sister they had no choice but to bear children to repopulate the earth."

The waiter stood unnoticed beside the table. "May I take your orders?" he politely interrupted just as Jared was forming his reply. Jared scowled reflexively, and they placed their orders.

Then, Jared picked up where he had left off. "It's always the same M.O., isn't it? Floods, pyramids, irrigation, incest."

What about Indonesia?" Rick asked.

"Similar story--including incest. Maybe it's to avoid the argument of ultimate source. Oddly, creation myths always assume that something was already here when the world was created. There's always a time before time. 'Re-creation' myths would make a better name. Often there are people before people. I'm sure you've heard about the Biblical enigma of who Cain's wife might have been? But there are more blatant cases. As you heard, the Philippine legends explicitly say that there were people who preceded their creation couple and that those people were killed off by the flood." "Why are Philippine and Indonesian legends so important?" Ellie asked.

"Because the Philippines and Indonesia were originally attached to Sunda, the largest sunken landmass in the world," Anna answered dryly.

"I take it you've heard this story before," Ellie said with a laugh as meals were served.

"Richard took me through half of the flood stories before I begged for mercy."

"There's more," Rick said. "Both cultures claim the sky was much lower before the floods came. Many creation stories claim someone forced the sky to rise."

"That's strange. Could Ice Age weather conditions have involved lower clouds in the tropics?"

"Hard to say," Rick responded with his fork poised over the restaurant's namesake dish. "I suppose there might have been changes in ceiling height as high-pressure belts moved equatorward."

"Back to the flood legends," Rick continued after the waiter finished serving. He pulled a slightly thicker pad from his pocket. "Quoting William Sherwood Fox, 1916, 'The Greeks shared with almost all other peoples the belief in a great flood, but the event—if it actually occurred—was so enshrouded in the haze of a remote past that all the accounts of it which have come down to us are plainly the products of the fertile imagination of the Greeks.'"

"Do anthropologists think the stories are real or not?"

"Again, the best comment comes from Fox. He says, 'Most scholars of comparative mythology now agree that the flood stories of the various peoples are germinally of local origin and in most instances consist of genuine traditions of a wide-reaching inundation mingled with pure myth.'"

"Sounds like a real flood. . .and global," Jared concluded.

"Does that mean you two aren't covering any new ground, or water, as the case may be?" Ellie asked.

"Yes and no. They were looking for a true flood—a terrestrial flood—like the one described in the Bible. Many legends claim water reached the tops of the mountains and then receded. That's the impression with Noah's flood, for instance. Even in the early 1900s, there were lots of scientific efforts to establish proof of Biblical events. Until recently, no one seems to have connected flood legends with global sea level rise. My guess is that all legends derive from local observations of the same global rise that's now well established in geologic literature. Noah's frame of reference must have shifted when he sailed onto a new, higher shoreline, and to him it appeared he had floated until the floodwaters receded. After all, he didn't have a global positioning system to confirm his new location or net change in elevation."

"Even today, GPS doesn't yield such a fine degree of vertical precision," Jared added.

"But the Philippine legend you reported doesn't say whether the waters went back to their original level," Anna said.

"That's right. Many legends refer to a drying-out after the flood, but they also refer to heavy rains. It isn't always clear whether the wet earth is from receded flood waters or from the rainfall."

"Why?" Anna asked. "I thought the rising seawater came from melting ice thousands of miles away."

"Dessert anyone?" the waiter asked cautiously. The four looked up, surprised they'd cleared their plates. Dessert orders were placed.

Then, Jared answered. "It did. Huge glaciers melted, but where precisely did that meltwater go? Sure, most of it flowed into the sea, but a substantial portion must have evaporated and returned to earth as rain."

"Maybe so," Rick said, "but it's possible rains were added to the legends purely to explain the rise. How else could listeners believe such wild tales?"

"How complete is the collection?" Anna asked, "Surely they don't have every myth ever told."

"No. A few legends don't show up. For instance, the Navajo account of waters reaching the peaks of the Superstition Mountains is missing. But it's pretty complete."

"So what conclusions do you draw from all this?" Ellie asked as dessert was served.

"Oral traditions are much older and more factual than conventional theory says. Our 'corporate memory' goes back much further than previously recognized. Human memory and awareness predate current sea levels. The possibility exists for more advanced cultural development prior to the flood than has been previously assumed." *There, I finally said it*, Rick thought. *I have no patience with fringe theories about human origins or lost civilizations, but, here's a solid hypothesis that must be tested.*

The others looked at Rick in amazement. Intellectual curiosity had turned to passion.

CHAPTER 10

Chronicle 20: Life in Berenicia

On their first liberty in Berenicia, Osi and Busah wandered about, gawking at palaces and palisades. Forts and temples, splendid as they were, paled in comparison to houses of commerce. Befitting the world's foremost port city, the most imposing monuments were dedicated to the munificent gods of commerce. Public houses for counting, trading, and storing lined portside plazas. Taverns, cafes, and barley houses lined avenues in every direction. The sheer number of businesses and frenetic level of activity, even on the streets per se, were awesome.

"Berenicia is the southern terminus and Egia the northern terminus of the most important portage in world history, but, *oh*, what a difference between the two cities," Osi said as the three youths stood beside a market stall.

"In Berenicia, the stakes seem so much higher," Busah added.

"Here, Tariffs of the Realm are collected on all goods entering or leaving the vital trade corridor," the merchant said. "Here, imports arrive from the north by caravan and are loaded on small boats for delivery to nearby cities or on huge freighters for long hauls to faraway places. Here, those same boats bring exports for transshipment overland to Kom Ombo and downriver to Egia where they will be dispatched to markets around the Midland Sea and beyond."

"And what goods!" Ketoh exclaimed.

"Yes. Jewels, spices, medicines, perfumes, incense, unguents, and delicate arts and crafts move north. Furs, meat, fruit, exotic woods, metal work, ivory, and horn move south. You'll find some in every port, and *all* in Berenicia."

"How long does it take goods to reach Egia from here?" Osi asked without expecting an answer. "Let's ask that man," he said, pointing toward a nearby building. "That's a shipping house. Maybe, he'll know." The young men crossed the street and approached the stranger.

"Yes, indeed. That's my job. I'm a dispatcher," the man said proudly. "Twenty days for outbound caravans to reach Kom Ombo. Depends on the Westerners, of course. Right now, we can't be certain of making it at all. Normally, our agents spend a couple of days at the caravansarai in Kom Ombo while the goods are transferred to boats. From Kom Ombo to Egia takes another 28 days by river. After Egia, who knows? It's my job to see that the goods reach Egia."

"Traffic must surely have slowed due to the hostilities," Busah said.

"Ah, yes. Traffic used to be heavy. At times the Garara Trail to Kom Ombo was as crowded as the streets of Berenicia. Since the trouble started, not much business. Luxury goods from the south pile up while necessities from the north are in short supply. Only the most valuable cargo justifies the risk. Business leaders and officials are worried. They blame the military and call for action."

"How long is it expected to last?" Ketoh asked. "Will your business survive?"

"We merchants must accept our losses, but there's consolation." He laughed wryly. "Good profits come from the influx of soldiers, the King's purchase of provisions, and construction of new roads and fortifications. Don't worry, lad, merchants prosper, war or peace, rain or shine. We just raise the price and keep on selling."

"As for what happens when goods reach Egia," Osi said, "I can tell you that. A sizable fleet delivers cargo to all the coasts of the Midland Sea, and huge freighters run to major ports on the Western Ocean. We're from Egia."

"Egians, eh? I thought you sounded funny. I'll bet there's not a decent ship in the whole Midland Sea."

"Well, not barquentines and transports like you have here, but . . ."

"Rubes!" The man spat, then quickly disappeared back into the shipping house.

Stunned by the insult, the boys slunk away in silence. Then, shaking it off, they ascended Berenicia with the new Sacred Pyramid always in view. Reaching the construction site, they watched massive stones rising from a water-filled shaft. One by one, rafts carrying giant blocks, two manheights long and one manheight square, floated to the top. "If I hadn't seen it for myself from aboard the *Ruby*, I would never have believed that such a simple operation could yield such monumental results. I always wondered how they moved such stones." Busah marveled at the ingenious apparatus delivering water to the top of the shaft. At each corner of the pyramid was a large water-filled tank. Smaller tanks sat on each stepwise level. Beside each tank stood two workmen and two shadufs. One dipperful at a time, these workmen passed water upward. At the top of the pyramid, the last shadufs emptied into a trough that flowed into a central vertical shaft.

"It's controlled by a complex arrangement of tanks and stone gates at various levels inside," said a construction foreman, who had been observing their amazement from nearby. "Those rafts arrive through a tunnel from the sea. Close the gates, and rafts rise up the shaft. Open the gates, water flows through side channels back into the reservoirs, and rafts descend."

"Ingenious," Osi said.

"Our little pyramid in Egia looks like a pile of bricks beside this marvel." Busah said. "Look at it, fellows. Every block is cut to such precision. Every stone interlocks with the next."

"It's hard to believe that our Geometers of Stones and Structures can design such an edifice and direct its construction without even seeing the pieces as they're cut," the foreman said. "Yet, everything fits together here as if it were carved by a single sculptor from a single piece of stone. It's a true pyramid, smooth-sided and sealed to withstand the rising Waters of Chaos for thousands of years to come. Both Troves are accessed through the main portico. The Lower Trove lies inside the main entrance. The shaft then angles downward past it and back up to the Upper Trove. That creates an airlock that keeps the Upper Trove from filling with seawater. It will be completed in the next few courses of stone."

"See how the four corners will part the waves," the foreman said, pointing proudly to the sharp angles of stone. "See how the smooth sides will resist the Waters of Chaos and mortar will seal the Trove. This structure surely can defy the sea for a thousand generations, holding safe the Secrets of the Ages until the sea again recedes." The boys thanked the foreman and headed back toward town.

"Where are the Secrets of the Ages kept while the pyramid is being built?" Busah asked.

"The Secrets of the Second and Third Kalpas have, of course, already been sealed inside other pyramids like the Sacred Pyramid of the Six Moons," Osi answered. "I'm not sure how many pyramids contain Troves, but it must take more than one, not to mention the lesser Troves in Egia and other parts of the Realm. Some date from the First Kalpa, some from the Second, and some from the Third. As you heard, copies of the Secrets of the Ages already are sealed inside the Upper Trove of this new one. The history and science of the Third Kalpa remains with the priests and scholars of our temples and academies. Geometers monitor the sea, and shortly before the Waters of Chaos cover the entrances of the new pyramid, they will sound a warning. A call will go out, and the Secrets of the Third Kalpa will be collected for safekeeping in the Upper Trove to survive the Rising Age of the Fourth Kalpa. Soon after, the call of 'Ma'at' will take us all to the new refuge. Copies of the Book of Truths will also go with us in the Benben, the Ark of the Trove."

* * *

Osi could barely bring himself to admit it, but he was beginning to like military life. He enjoyed workouts with stone weights, long swims and water drills, runs and forced marches, scaling cliffs above Berenicia. *Most of all*, he thought, *I love these mock battles, especially hand-to-hand combat. Warfare itself is changing. Just look at what's going on in the Land of the Second Sunset. This is a new order, a new way of fighting. No longer will military conflicts be won or lost through naval might and fortifications like Ollo-detu or Koro-nata. No longer will military objectives be limited to strategic control of sea routes, coasts, and portages.*

No, he thought, *we'll have to do that and much more. From now until the waters fall again thousands of years hence, we must seize vast territories for expansion and relocation of entire populations. As each homeland floods, its occupants will either take land from upland neighbors or perish. Seize or die! Henceforth, the battles that shape our future will be fought by foot soldiers on the move. Lines, columns, and phalanxes of soldiers outfitted for face-to-face battle against forces of superior number will be the rule, but we'll make hit-and-run attacks, as well. Superior training in the strategies and tactics of infantry will rule the battleground. Improved weapons, such as my own steel-bladed sword, will strike fear in the hearts of less advanced opponents. These are the factors that will decide between life and death for the People of the Living Sun. Seize or die! Yes. Seize or die!*

Most cadets dreamed of the day when they would command mighty barquentines on the open sea, serve in the King's garrisons, or, failing that, stand guard at the Royal Palace. Not one dreamed of Regular Army service in an urban garrison, such as the one in Egia or, least of all, frontier service at an outpost like Ollo-detu. Osi, on the other hand, dreamed of someday introducing his own brand of warfare. He longed to assemble a unit that could readily face a force ten times its own size. In the battlefields of his mind, he rehearsed and examined imaginary victories and defeats. Again and again, he played to perfection the strategies and tactics that would bring victory. Again and again, he reviewed historic battles and played them in his mind using his own revised tactics. Again and again, he agonized over never-tested theories of battles that might be won or lost.

Osi studied his comrades like a gambler assessing his hand. Here were his fellow Egians, gentle boys playing at games of war. They would make good soldiers; Osi knew he could count on them. Some, like his friends Busah and Ketoh and the cadet Sareem, were sure to become powerful leaders in their own right. They were men of conviction, intelligent and resourceful. Their heads would remain cool in the heat of battle, unaffected by the mindless ways of the old order.

But I don't know about these Berenicians, Osi mused. *I've tried to lay aside my misgivings, but I just can't ignore their flaws. They are soft young men with little or no experience in the real world. Many are the second sons of rich merchants and aristocrats and have never been challenged by so much as a toothache. They accept the Divine Right Order without question, whereas we Egians have learned to think for ourselves. It's a necessary part of living on the frontier. Free-thinking may once have been encouraged here, but it's become rare indeed. These Berenicians think the Divine Right Order is the only way to preserve culture in the Fourth Kalpa, and they've become slaves to custom. A rigid set of rules governs every aspect of their lives. Procedure has replaced judgment and reason. The strictures of the Divine Right Order long ago were formed by the King, or rather by his court, and now even he is bound to its rules. Each activity, each coming, each going, even each body function is regulated. Imagine the difficulties such people will face in battle on the frontier.*

And Setra, that Berenician aristocrat, the one all the Berenicians idolize. What of him? Maybe he's a nice guy beneath that brash façade, but he's dogged by uncertainty and false philosophy. He will make trouble for himself and for me. Setra is fanatically bound by the Order. Other Berenicians follow the rules but none so avidly as he. Setra acts out of blind ambition more than conviction. He wants to lead all the armies of the People of the Living Sun. Blatantly, Setra maneuvers for position among his trainers and fellow cadets, making no secret of his overreaching ambitions.

Like a cock crowing at dawn, he times every meal, every word, every act to the rising and setting of the sun. Others might begin eating when rations are offered, assuming it to be the appointed time. Not Setra. He makes a show of observing the angle of the sun and then refraining, sometimes until the others have finished, to start his own meal. Others may relieve themselves at the close of a drill. Not Setra. He declares the prescribed moment and relieves himself even in the press of mock battle. To Egians this is a laughable ruse, but somehow it increases the Berenicians' esteem for him. They even honor his act and forestall attack until the order has been satisfied. For my part, I'm not fully convinced Setra even knows how to read the angles of the sun.

"Tell me, Osi, what do you make of this Setra?" Sareem asked one evening as the officers returned late to their barracks because of an inordinate delay caused by Setra's posturing.

"He's a model for the Berenicians, isn't he?" Osi replied.

"No doubt, but I wouldn't want to serve under him. He doesn't understand the realities of warfare or life on the frontier. He's one of those extremists Priest Anbaht warned us about."

"What sort of fool would relieve himself in the heat of a real battle," Busah said.

"That's a good way to lose the better part of a soldier," Ketoh joked.

"He may not know the frontier, but he knows Berenicia better than we do," Osi said.

"He's a master of manipulation," agreed Ketoh. "Don't oppose him unless you're prepared to suffer the consequences."

"He's a lonely man who needs good friends with good advice. Perhaps if we could get past his pretenses, we would find something to like," Osi said.

"Well," responded Busah, "I know what I don't li . . ." Busah clipped his sentence short as Setra suddenly appeared beside him.

"So," Setra said, "you colonists are enjoying a quiet little conversation. Don't forget that quiet time comes in half a hand? Take care not to disturb those of us who faithfully follow the Divine Right Order."

"Quiet is a small matter for Egians, unlettered as we are, Master Setra, but we greatly admire the discipline required of one so eloquent as you," Ketoh flattered with more than a hint of sarcasm.

"Yes, Master Ketoh, I am completely devoted to the Divine Right Order, as are all learned men of the Realm. The appointed time for rest and quiet is almost upon us. I find . . ."

"We Egians sincerely desire that you be able to observe your customs undisturbed," Osi interrupted. "We, too, follow the Divine Right Order in our own thoughtful way. If we fail, it's because we're unfamiliar with your ways."

"Ignorance is no excuse. The Order is divine and right for all. You Egians are more civilized than the primitives of the west, but still you seem confused about the rules."

"Our people are your people, but we live in different worlds. We honor the customs that help us survive in the wilderness, but we are slow to adopt new ways that might lead to destruction."

"The Divine Right Order is the true and only way. There is no choice for anyone, especially colonials."

"When the cry of 'Ma'at' is heard, we will obey. Adherence to procedure will be essential, but surely it can be tempered with reason."

"By then I, Setra, will lead all the armies. You, cat-killer, and your fellow colonists will be assigned to the farthest outposts of the Realm. That is the way of the Divine Right Order. There can be no deviation from its laws."

"I trust our King will choose wisely when he selects leaders for the next generation," Osi said calmly.

Setra ignored Osi's evasion. "And what would you do to earn such leadership? Kill another kitten?"

"I seek only to serve my King. I will do whatever he requires...." Osi stopped speaking as the tolling of a bell signaled the time of quiet.

"Will you flash your tooth-handled sword?" Setra grabbed Osi's shoulder as he turned to walk away. "Are you afraid to face me?" Setra said, his voice softening. "I would be your friend, Dirk Slayer, if it were not ordained to be otherwise." The Egians silently walked toward their bedsides, strictly observing the time of quiet. Setra continued speaking to Osi, apparently failing to note the irony in his own behavior.

"Go ahead, colonist," he said. "Pursue your wild ambitions. The Order prevails, despite your best efforts. You will never lead an army in this Realm. Not because you are a colonist but because the Divine Right Order declares that only the devout shall lead."

Chronicle 21: The First Betrothal

Osi's unit reached the barracks amidst a flurry of activity as the first arrivals were already departing for the temple.

"Prepare, prepare," called Kanno, the major domo. "Tonight is the First Betrothal."

Everyone washed up and donned a clean linen habit. Orderlies directed them to the central courtyard where they assembled in ranks. Each youth carried a camphor bough, and the troop, now 20 columns wide and 25 rows deep, snaked through the ceremonial colonnade and into the broad avenue. The fresh smell of camphor, the rhythm of the march, and the cheers of gathered onlookers rendered the procession especially momentous. Palm fronds had first provided afternoon shade and now served as pennants to cheer the cadets on their sunset march.

"Hooray for our youths! Hail the Cadets! Blessings of Rahn!" the crowd chanted as the boys marched. Past the Governor's Palace and the Royal Garrison, past fine estates and shops, to the temple grounds they marched. "Hail! Hooray! Blessings!" the crowds yelled at every halt and turn. The boys were elated, energized by the tumult. They sang the songs of the faithful as they stepped in time.

When the column reached the street, Kanno signaled "column right" into the square. There, the boys dropped their boughs and stood among throngs of the faithful amidst massive monuments. The library, the court, and the academy stood on their right. The priest's quarters, the temple dormitory, and the mausoleum stood on their left, the temple straight ahead. Above these shrines of stone loomed the crowning achievement of the People of the Living Sun, their monstrous stone pyramid. This remarkable edifice stood like a watchtower of wisdom guarding the accumulated knowledge of the People of the Living Sun. At its base was the covered pit that held the Royal Barge.

The pyramid and temple stood as dual centerpieces in the monumental complex. On the far side, a grand ceremonial plaza with a sacrificial altar, now unused, faced the sea. Six tall columns supported a massive facade gracing the Temple Square. A glorious ceremonial balcony emerged from the center of the portico atop its famous 20 steps. On it, in stately silence, sat the Governor, and to his right the Commander-in-Chief of the Royal Army, and next to him, the Commander of the King's Guard. The cadets marched front and center to the steps where Kanno commanded an abrupt halt. Six wooden biers punctuated the perimeter of the formation, one at each corner and another midway on each side.

On the Governor's left, Toth, the Chief Priest, sternly faced the cadets as the Royal Musicians played an evening dirge. "Praise be to Rahn! Guard us through the night, oh Rahn, and defend us from the Waters of Chaos. Stay your winds and waves. Protect us from the loss of our land during the lives of our children and our children's children," Toth chanted.

"Praise be to Rahn. Light us through the darkness that descends when you depart, oh Rahn, and save us from the ravages of the sea. Shield us from your winds and waves. Protect us from the loss of our land during the lives of our children and our children's children," the people chanted in reply.

"May our strength be passed to each new generation. May the spears of our protectors be sharp and straight. May their shields hold firm against the stones of our enemies. May our sons and daughters be wise. May the path to our refuge be clear. May the Pyramid of the Trove protect the Secrets of the Ages. May the People of the Living Sun prevail." With these words, the priest lighted a brazier that would heat scented oil throughout the night.

The martial message impressed Osi with the importance of the role he and his fellow cadets were certain to play. Its meaning was clear: Fight poorly and the People of the Living Sun will perish. Fight well, and the people may survive and flourish again someday.

Ah, but there is more to the priest's message than talk of war, Osi recalled with a smile. *Just where are these wise daughters? When do we get to meet them?*

"Cadets of the Realm, cast off your robes of innocence," the priest commanded.

As Osi's robe struck the ground, it seemed strange that he should be so exposed, but the priest had timed the act so that twilight and shadows soon brought cover. Osi reminded himself that the greatest men of each generation had undergone the same ceremony. Priestesses next came forth with urns of olive oil, dutifully blessed by the Chief Priest. Infiltrating the columns and, using their hands, they coated each youth from head to toe with the sanctified oil.

"Where are our brides?" an anxious whisper spilled from the ranks. Ketoh giggled, breaking discipline. Several of the boys surrounding Ketoh reacted, some with hisses demanding silence, others with empathetic snickers. Osi held his bearing.

Kanno approached the section where Ketoh stood. "Report to me immediately when the column is at ease," he whispered authoritatively. No more words were spoken, but the matter was far from finished, and Ketoh knew it. Osi sensed his friend's apprehension.

The music stopped; a drum rolled. The crowd murmured, then roared as the doors of the temple dormitory opened. Two guards stepped forward and swung wide the mighty wooden barricade. A brief pause and the procession commenced. *Oh, dear Rahn,* Osi thought. Twenty-five columns wide and more than 50 rows deep, the virgins emerged from the dim, fire-lit interior of the massive sandstone dormitory. Through a deep portico, down the broad steps, out onto the open plaza. Slowly and gracefully they stepped into fading light.

In near darkness, the girls assembled on a square of polished stone immediately adjacent to the boys. Around them were six wooden biers arranged like the ones surrounding the cadets. On cue, soldiers appeared with torches and set all 12 biers ablaze. The masses roared with approval as light unveiled both formations.

"Maidens of the Realm, cast off your robes of innocence," the priest commanded, and the people cheered louder than before. The maidens cast off their robes and stood in the firelight, sheathed in shimmering diaphanous veils.

"People of the Living Sun," the priest continued, "the Elders of temple and state present to you the hope of our people, the Seed of our next generation, the vessels of our future. To you, I present the brightest, the strongest, the wisest, the most resourceful of our age. Behold and adore the protectors of our King and the Seed of our people forever. Tonight a new generation will advance on their journey to manhood and womanhood. Behold their betrothal. Behold the future of the People of the Living Sun." He raised his arms toward the heavens, lowered his head, and gazed earnestly. "Daughters of the People of the Living Sun," he said, staring at them and gesturing toward the young men. "I present the men who will become your husbands. They are the pride of your generation, chosen for special service to the King. They will become the defenders of your hearths, the fathers of your children. Be their wives, bear their children. Be faithful so that the People of the Living Sun may survive what is to come. Guide them with your wise council in every thought and deed and action. Be strong in all things."

"Sons of the People of the Living Sun, I present to you the women who will become your wives." Staring at the cadets, he gestured toward the square of polished stone. "Selected at a young age for their brilliance and resolve, they, too, are the pride of your generation. They will be your companions. Defend their hearths; listen to their wise council." Pointing column by column and shaking his finger, the stately priest seemed, for a moment, more like a wise, old uncle. "Woe be to any man among you who mistakes their physical stature for weakness. They are the keepers of our culture, the mothers of our future. They will decide the knowledge and values to be conveyed to our next generation. In the ship of our people, you are the bow, but they are the stern, and the bow must lead wherever the stern chooses to follow." Subdued laughter rippled through both formations.

"At ease!" the priest ordered. "Now, virgins, mingle among the cadets. Get to know them. Bestow your tokens if you wish."

Ketoh was as excited as the other boys, but Kanno silently stepped forward and motioned him and his fellow troublemakers off the field.

A few bold lasses took the initiative, stepping forward into the male formation. Osi's first reaction was an intense physical thrill, recalling his liberty in Wadi Jimal. *But no, the purpose here is too great. This is no time for fantasy. There is among these maidens one who will someday fill my life. But why did I say "one"? There's no limit to the number of women we may wed. Why would I not choose many? Too many decisions for now.*

Finally even the shyest of maidens browsed among the ranks.

They mill about like children on their first trip to the marketplace. Then he laughed to himself. I remember my own first trip to the market in Egia, he thought. *Now I know how the merchandise feels.*

Looking hesitantly at first, then more boldly, the virgins moved column by column, row by row, inspecting the merchandise. They were encouraged to introduce themselves, and many did so freely. After a brief conversation, each maid presented a token to any lad who pleased her, and she moved on. "I am, Nala, Interpreter of the Histories of the Eighth through Twenty-third Generations of the Third Kalpa," one said to a cadet standing beside Osi. "I am, Pranalat, Recorder of the Geometry of the Stars in the Southern Sky," another introduced herself to Osi and soon he had her token.

A pretty young woman glanced demurely at Osi as she ambled by. He didn't know whether she was shy or, perhaps, more selective than the others. For whatever reason, he noted, she still had all five of her tokens. "Who are you?" Osi whispered. It was a breach of protocol, but he couldn't let this one pass.

She hesitated, then spoke with a half-smile. "I am Bera, Keeper of the Equations of the True Pyramid."

The True Pyramid. This surely must be the most brilliant of them all. Small wonder she was reticent to reveal her status. Any keeper of equations must be exalted, and here before me stands the keeper of the highest form of the Geometry, the glory of our age. This girl will bear watching in more ways than one.

She stood a head shorter than Osi. Her smooth skin, accentuated by firelight, was golden brown. Her hair and eyes were the blackest of blacks. The lines of her thighs and legs, the triangle of her pubis, the circles of her breasts and nipples, the curves of her hips and abdomen—all perfect in Osi's eyes. And her face! Miraculously, Osi's boyhood faceless vision materialized before his adoring eyes. Under the force of his gaze, the girl moved on, leaving no token for her smitten admirer.

As firelight failed, an order went out and the maidens reassembled for an orderly recession to the dormitory. The cadets retreated to their own compound. On arrival at the barracks, they filed into cold baths, then retired to their sleeping quarters. When they tallied their tokens, Osi had eight, more than any other, but it was a hollow victory. Not one had come from the lovely Bera.

* * *

Morning came too soon. Osi expected to be tired after the festivities, but it was not fatigue that caused him to linger on this particular morning. It was heady memories of the night before. He wanted to savor every precious moment—the cheers, the crowds, the women, and, most of all, Bera and those alluring eyes.

As Osi rolled out of his cot, he was surprised to see Ketoh and the other delinquents entering the room. "I'm pleased to see you again, my friend Ketoh. We're lucky to have you with us after that breach of conduct."

"It wasn't me, Osi. Honest. I didn't say a word. It was a Berenician who stood next to me. I only laughed at his remark, but so did several others. Yet he let me take the blame. Commander Sennon didn't trust my word because I'm an Egian. Thank Rahn one honest Berenician interceded. Otherwise I'd still be under the lash."

"So, this fellow who spoke first must really be in trouble now. Breaking discipline and then failing to admit his guilt...those are serious offenses."

"That's the strange part of it, Osi. We Egians were forced to take ten lashes and stand guard all night, and Jumar, the Berenician who stood up for me, was punished most of all. He's still standing watch. Yet the Berenician who broke discipline was able to spend a comfortable night in his own bed. I saw him myself as I passed by."

"Who was this 'lucky' man? It sounds as if we will do well to stand clear of him."

"None other than your pal Setra. I don't mind the loss of a night's sleep. What I did was wrong, but the knowledge that he goes free makes my blood boil. He must have powerful connections in the highest circles of the Realm."

"If only you could have remained for the betrothal," Osi said. Ketoh first appeared to agree then, his pride mounting, he said with unconvincing defiance, "Who needs virgins? I can do without them."

"None of us can do without them, my friend. They're the hope and future of our people."

"Perhaps they're needed to bear our children, but why do our leaders teach them so much?"

"Now, Ketoh," Osi said. "Is this Egia's Great Lover speaking, or is it the voice of disappointment and defeat? You have no one to blame but yourself. . . and Setra, of course."

"It's easy for you to talk, Osi. You have your tokens and a full night's sleep. I have only lashes and labor," Ketoh said.

"How did you know about the tokens?"

"When they released us this morning, one of the soldiers told his mate that the 'Dirk Slayer' had received eight tokens. I admit I'm jealous."

"Don't envy these tokens, friend. I met my dream, and her name is Bera. She is the Keeper of the True Pyramid's Equations."

"So that's why you thought so highly of the Pyramid of the Troves," Ketoh said, laughing. "You must have had a vision."

"Perhaps she makes a marvel all the more marvelous, my friend, but who's to say?" smiled Osi. "Do its proportions not pale in comparison to those of its keeper?"

"No doubt, no doubt," Busah said.

"But there are plenty of other girls, Osi. Don't set your mind so soon."

"If I can't have her, I'll have no other. Take these worthless things." He handed all eight tokens to Ketoh.

"Can you do that? Can you just give them away to someone?"

"There's no rule against it. I saw some Berenicians throw tokens to the ground in front of the virgins who gave them. Other cadets, who weren't so lucky, bent down and picked them up. That's how the system works."

"But what will these virgins say at the Second Betrothal. They expect a second meeting with you, my friend. They've never seen me. Won't they be disappointed? Won't they complain to our commanders."

"Disappointed? How could they be disappointed with the Great Lover of Egia?" Osi said. "If they aren't disappointed in you, why then should they complain? But you'll raise suspicions if you have too many. Best to share them with a friend. That fellow Jumar who saved you might appreciate some of these."

"Tell me which to keep and which to pass on to Jumar."

"That's your job, my friend. Let fate make your choice. I've let fate make mine."

"You're serious, aren't you?"

"Never more so."

"Did you meet her, talk to her?"

"We. . .uh. . .exchanged greetings. . .but nothing more."

"Don't you think you should at least have a decent conversation with her before you decide to devote your life to her forever?"

"Oh, I'll meet her alright. Just give me time."

Chronicle 22: The Night of the Dark Moon

"No, Osi. You can't. It will destroy you," Busah said in hushed tones. "You've never defied orders."

"Others have, and they survived. Look at Ketoh. He's been caught twice. He still has a place in our ranks."

"That's different. Ketoh's offense occurred early in training when the officers expected less of us. A breach of discipline at this late stage will bring the wrath of Rahn. Besides, they expect better of you. You'll be drummed out of the corp."

"It doesn't matter, Busah. I have to know. I have to meet her, talk to her. Otherwise I'll be tormented for the rest of my life. Is she the girl in my dreams? Did I know her somehow, somewhere long ago? I have to find a way, but you and Ketoh should never have learned my plans. I hoped you could say truthfully that you know nothing if I'm missed."

Ketoh joined them. "Osi, we know you too well. You can't hide your excitement."

"I didn't realize it showed."

"Are you joking? You're acting like a five-year-old on feast day. Anyone could guess you're up to something."

"I'm going tonight."

"Tonight!" Ketoh said.

"Yes. One of the cooks told me the girls have liberty in the city. They're free on the night of the Dark Moon. They stroll the quay at dusk...*unchaperoned*. It's my only chance."

"Your only chance to destroy everything you have or ever hope to be."

"I know it's foolish, but I have no choice. I must go."

"Then we must help you. Otherwise you'll be caught."

"No, Ketoh. I'll do this alone. You can't risk being part of it."

"You will have our help whether you want it or not," Busah said. "We're your only hope."

"Then tell me your plan, friends, for I have none."

"You are a sick man, Osi," Ketoh said.

"Why do you say that?"

"Because that's what I told Kanno. You're confined to your sick bed for the night."

"But won't he see..."

"A writhing lump under your covers? Yes, that's what he'll see, alright. Take to your bed before Kanno arrives, and make sure he sees your face. After you leave, Busah and I will take turns lying there in your stead."

"What ails me then, if I may ask?"

"We've told Kanno you have a fever and a terrible cough. A friend in the kitchen warmed a stone in the oven. It's hidden under your covers so you can heat your hands and face for Kanno. We tried to do it all for you, but you'll have to cough for yourself."

"Quick, here he comes," Busah called from the corridor. Osi slipped beneath the covers and warmed himself till Kanno arrived at his bedside.

"Master Osi," Kanno said, "Ketoh tells me you're ill."

"I...I don't feel well," Osi said, peeking from beneath the covers. Kanno placed the back of his hand against Osi's forehead as the youth coughed vigorously and convincingly.

"My, my. You are a sick lad. But I brought you a wonderful remedy." He reached forward and placed a steaming earthen pot on the ledge beside Osi's bed.

"What is it?" Osi asked, with a guttural cough.

"Hot pepper soup! It works wonders."

"I...am...sure it does," Osi said. "But, do you really think I need such a drastic cure?"

"Can't ignore such a fever. Take it. You won't regret."

"Whatever you say," Osi said. "Just leave the pot here, and I'll drink as soon as I feel up to it."

"No, no. I must make sure you're properly treated." Osi spied Ketoh and Busah, grinning from ear to ear, over Kanno's shoulder as he poured the soup into a cup. They could hardly contain themselves as Osi took his first sip of the spicy hot brew. *I'll never survive this*, Osi thought. *This is the hottest stuff that's ever entered my mouth.* Kanno nodded sympathetically and placed another cupful to Osi's lips. He took another sip. And another. And another, until all was gone. "Now rest young man. You'll soon feel much better," Kanno said. Ketoh and Busah burst into laughter as soon as Kanno left the room.

I will never live through this. My lips are burning like coals. My mouth is on fire.

"Water! I need water!"

"Here, take this," Busah said, handing Osi a dipper of cool water from the nearby stone reservoir.

"Now be gone," Ketoh said, ignoring Osi's pain. "Dusk is approaching. You have no time to lose." Osi slipped from under the covers and started down the corridor.

"Be back before lights out, or we'll all be extinguished."

* * *

Osi hurried through the streets of Berenicia, wishing he could be invisible as he neared the scenic quay. This gathering place was especially popular at sunset when Berenicians put the workday behind them. Losing himself in the crowd, Osi walked northward past the docks to a small public park. There he saw a gathering of 50 or more young women. He moved close enough to see faces.

Pranalat! I remember her. She's pretty. I have her token, or rather I had her token. I gave it to Ketoh. She was near Bera then; maybe she's near her now. There she is!

Bera's face gleamed like amber above a pearl-white gown.

Pranalat looked in Osi's direction, and their eyes met. She whispered into Bera's ear. *Now what do I do?* he asked himself as both girls stared at him. *I've never been good at this. She's a highborn lady. I can't just blurt some stupid line. Something clever...but not too clever. Casual...but not too casual. What can I say?*

"Hello," he said. "Nice day." *Clever? Casual? Is this the best I can do? Now she'll think I'm dumb as a camel.*

"Well, if it isn't Master Osi," Pranalat said, blushing and smiling. "What brings you here, alone on this fine evening." She glowed, hoping she was the object of his attention, but Osi was oblivious to anyone but Bera.

"It's the Dark Moon. The scenery is lovely...at this place...on this night." *Now I'm getting the hang of it,* he thought.

"Is that a veiled compliment to the temple ladies?" Pranalat asked.

"It was intended to be." He stared straight at Bera, and Pranalat's heart sank.

"Then you've hit your mark. Thank you, Master Osi," Bera said. "We are honored by your presence and flattered by your praise."

"I am the one honored," Osi said, surprised by his own smoothness.

"I don't think you came to see me," Pranalat said graciously. "I'll step aside so you and Lady Bera can be alone."

Alone? Osi thought. *Am I ready for this?* "Will you join me for a stroll along the quay, Lady Bera?"

"I would be pleased, Master Osi."

"Call me 'Osi'," he said, offering his arm.

"Call me 'Bera'," she said, taking his wrist. The delicate touch of her fingers warmed first his arm, then his face, then his whole body. As the sun sank toward the horizon, the couple walked beside the bay. Palm trees lined the path, occasionally parting to offer unhindered views of the rippling water.

"I wanted to meet you. I hope you don't mind. I know it's against the Order, but I had to know more about you."

"There isn't much to know. I'm a Temple Virgin in service to our King. I keep the equations of the True Pyramid. I am pleased that you came but concerned. You must have taken a great risk to..."

"Don't worry. I'm not in trouble...yet." He smiled.

"Surely you must know that every virgin in the dormitory is in love with you. All have heard stories of the Dirk Slayer who led the Egian cadets to Berenicia. You are their hero."

"I'm flattered, but I don't care about the others."

"I know, Osi. I see it in your eyes. You love me, don't you?"

"Yes. I can't hide my feelings for you. But you, Bera? Could you ever love a simple colonial...Dirk Slayer or not? "

"I'm not free...to love any man. I'm promised to another."

"Promised? How can that be? What about the betrothals."

"I wish it were that simple, Osi. For some, it is, but I'm the daughter of...a very powerful man. Arranged marriages are...not uncommon. For me, the tokens are a sham. Otherwise I would have given you one . . . or. . .maybe. . . all."

"But surely you have a say in the matter. Surely you can give just one token. Surely you can tell your father..."

Bera placed her forefinger on Osi's lips and smiled tenderly. "Stop, Osi. I have no choice. I'm already betrothed. Please don't make it any harder for me."

"So you do...feel...something for me."

"I...please, Osi. Say no more." A tear formed in Bera's eye then rolled slowly down her cheek. Osi placed his hand beneath her chin. With his thumb, he wiped the tear away. She gripped his hand. "There is no hope for us, Osi. We must follow separate paths."

"We'll see, dear Bera. We'll see."

* * *

"Osi, up here," Ketoh called from the transom running beneath the barracks' eave. A rope dangled from the slit and down the outside wall. Osi quickly scaled the stone wall, grasping Ketoh's outstretched hand as he neared the transom. They dropped quietly to the floor inside. Ketoh drew the rope down and stuffed it under his mattress.

"Thanks, friend," Osi said. "I couldn't have done this without you and Busah."

"You would have thought of something."

A door clattered. Both boys dashed for their bunks. Osi jumped in fully clothed.

"What the...? Busah! What are you doing here?"

"Shhhh!" Busah said. "Kanno passed through for bed check. I rushed from my bed to yours while he was across the corridor. Barely made it in time. Must have fallen asleep."

"Thanks for your help."

"Think nothing of it."

"I'll be eternally grateful...*if* you'll vacate and let me have my bed back." He laughed as Busah trudged sleepily to his own bunk.

Chronicle 23: The Second Betrothal

The cadets assembled for the Second Betrothal. Osi and his comrades marched expectantly toward the central plaza as they had done a few months before. Again they marched to the temple for prayers and devotion, then on to Temple Square.

The betrothal routine was familiar, but the roles were reversed. This time the men would survey their potential mates, and the prospect was tantalizing beyond measure. The cadets waited on the plaza's perimeter while officials and spectators assembled. Again a whiff of camphor filled the air, emanating this time from the virgins' dormitory. Cheers rose as the mighty door swung open, and the virgins emerged. In steady procession, each girl dropped her camphor bough on an unlit bier and took her place in the center of the plaza. Cadets then formed rank and file beside them.

"Praise be to Rahn! Guard us through the night, oh Rahn, and defend us from the Waters of Chaos. Stay your winds and waves! Protect us from the loss of our land during the lives of our children and our children's children." Again the priest recited the ancient liturgy, and the people responded in kind.

As before, six huge wooden biers surrounded the men and six surrounded the women. In the dim shadows of fading sunlight, 12 soldiers set the biers aflame. The masses roared. The smell of camphor rose again, and sparks filled the night sky. The litany continued as in the First Betrothal.

"Temple Virgins of the Kingdom, cast off your robes of maidenhood," Toth commanded and the priestess in charge of the virgins repeated. Cadets thrilled to the sight as robes fell in twilight's last glow and again the maidens stood in diaphanous veils, shimmering in the growing light.

"Cadets of the Realm, cast off your robes of youth," the Chief Priest called and then invited the youths to mingle. No need for urging, as cadets quickly infiltrated the women's ranks. They wandered about, introducing themselves—some timidly, some boldly—to those unmet in the First Betrothal and searching anxiously for a selected few remembered from before. Each boy presented tokens to the ladies of his choice. Many a pretty young one tried to catch Osi's eye as he searched about, but he took no interest. Face by face, body by body, he combed the ranks looking for just one face, one body. A hundred faces passed as he wandered row to row, column to column. The night wouldn't last forever, and he must find Bera. Finally, he heard her name.

"And you are the Lady Bera." It was Setra who uttered Bera's name. Osi saw her stoically facing the Berenician.

"Ah, the selfish lady who hasn't awarded a single token, are you? That colonist Osi is one of your suitors, isn't he? You have chosen wisely, have you not, for I am Setra, son of Roton, Second Prince of Punt."

"Well, my betrothed. At last we meet." Bera said, her thin voice trailing to a whisper.

Setra! He's the one? She deserves better than him.

Osi approached, determined to press his own case and defend her against Setra's unwanted advances.

Or are they unwanted?

Osi puzzled as he watched the unthinkable. The goddess who filled his dreams placed a token in Setra's outstretched hand.

No! How can she marry such a loser? He is nothing but a vain child of privilege…though he does show himself well. How can she appreciate my clumsy advances if she is so easily fooled by false smiles and pompous ways?

Dejected, he turned to walk away.

"Make your move, Master Lover." The familiar voice came from an adjacent row where Ketoh observed Osi's crisis. "He's leaving now. Make your move, I say." Bolstered by Ketoh's urging Osi turned back toward Bera, but another Berenician had taken Setra's place.

"Who am I to win such a prize?" he questioned. "What makes me think she would defy the Realm on my behalf?" Osi turned to walk away.

"Osi!" Her voice was soft and lilting as he remembered it but strong and defiant, nonetheless.

Could it be? Has she broken protocol as I did after the First Betrothal?

Osi wheeled around and stared into her sparkling eyes.

"Cadets, fall in! Quickly!" the commander barked. The sudden rush of men swept Osi away. As he turned for one last glance, a passing cadet knocked him off balance. As Osi hit the ground, he realized it was Setra who had bumped him.

"No!" Setra said. "You will not seize my prize. It is ordained. This one shall be mine." A boot to the ribs left Osi writhing in pain. As he struggled to stand, he saw a slender hand reach through the passing crowd. Bera had broken ranks. Without a word she slipped a precious token into his palm. Joyfully, Osi looked longingly into her eyes, but there was no time to speak.

Ketoh grabbed his arm. They must rejoin the assembly or face stern discipline, perhaps even lose the tokens they had gained. Back in formation, Osi's mind flashed ahead to the Third Betrothal. Half a year hence, Osi and Bera would meet again on the Red Island. *There, in the sacred city of Erytheia, capital of our realm, I, Osi will claim Bera as my bride!*

Chronicle 24: Military Leaders of Berenicia

Another week ended, and the four comrades went out for their favorite meal—raw oysters, thin crisps of leavened bread fresh from clay ovens, and chalices of cool beer at the Harbor Cave Tavern. Following the meal Osi, Ketoh, Jumar, and Busah walked about at sunset, relaxing after an especially tough week. Osi led his friends along the quay to show them, more to his own interest than theirs, the park where he and Bera had met. Unexpectedly, on their return to the city, a great commotion engulfed the markets, streets, and alleyways. News from the north end of the Valley Sea told of a Royal Navy vessel attacked by mercenaries. At the straits called Tiran, which guarded the entrance to a bay called Akuba, several privateers had lain in ambush. Surrounding the anchored ship at dusk, rebels managed to set sails afire, then kill the crew as they abandoned the burning vessel. By this traitorous action, a warlord now controlled the lands surrounding Akuba.

"And were all killed?" a tradeswoman asked anxiously of the military spokesman.

"All are dead. Some refused to abandon ship and stood on deck while the ship burned," he said.

"My son was on that ship," mourned the woman. Concerned bystanders helped her to a nearby stall.

"We must retaliate," a citizen demanded.

"An armada sails at dawn. They'll put an end to these insurgents."

* * *

Six barquentines of the Royal Navy set sail, and three weeks later
returned. Not a single arrow shot. No territory regained. No insurgents
punished. Not a sign of the enemy.

"Have we won or lost?" a cadet asked Commander Sennon when word
reached the academy.

"We never found the enemy, and yet we know he is there. By the time
we reach a ravaged port, the vermin have already abandoned it. No sooner
do we leave one port than they attack another," he replied in frustration.
"They don't honor the conventions of warfare. Yet they achieve their ends.
We could defeat them if they would just show their faces."

"What can we do?" The cadets echoed their commander's frustration.

"In better times, we would return in force and occupy every port.
But...now...not enough ships, not enough soldiers."

Uncharacteristically, Osi expressed his view to every cadet within
earshot. "The only way to protect our ports is to invade the surrounding
hills. Clear the insurgents from their nests." No sooner had Osi uttered the
words than he regretted having revealed so much.

"That's not our way, Egian," responded Setra. "Soldiers don't fight for
empty hillsides. You colonists must learn our methods. We must not sink
to the low ways of our enemies."

Osi said no more.

* * *

Commander Sennon presided over a grand assembly on the main
parade ground of the Royal Military Academy. "Cadets of the Realm, it is
my great honor to present our King Rahn Mennon." The cadets cheered
uproariously, and the revered King stood to their ovation. Osi expected
flowing, royal robes topped with a heavy crown. Instead, the silver-haired
King wore military garb topped by a light, serviceable crown. A bright
steel sword with golden hilt swung at his side.

But he looks no less a King. No wonder our people revere him so.

Sennon went on. "Today our King and his high officers are gathered
here to plan the coming war. Listen and you will hear the Supreme
Commanders of the Royal Navy, the Royal Army, and the King's Guard,
and even King Rahn Mennon himself. As Cadets of the Realm, you are
privileged to hear these exalted leaders. Listen well, for our future depends
on their wisdom."

A chant of celebration and welcome rippled through the massed
cadets. Seldom did the King ever venture from the Red Island. His presence
in Berenicia was a once-in-a-lifetime opportunity filled with honor for all
present. Commander Sennon silenced the crowd, and each leader spoke in
turn.

First, Xenothon, Supreme Commander of the King's Guard, welcomed them to military service. He spoke of their grand mission and the personal sacrifice they would accept as part of their commitment. The man's delivery was impressive, but his speech was predictable. There was no mention of new strategies to counter new forms of warfare thrown against them. He spoke of monumental armadas, massive armies, and glorious past victories. He spoke of laying siege to enemy fortifications and they, themselves, surviving protracted sieges. *This is the sort of dolt who tackles new problems with old solutions,* Osi thought.

Second up was Admiral Vadic, Supreme Commander of the Royal Navy. He spoke of the need for faster vessels, greater mobility and flexibility, new armaments, and greater capacities for troop transport. He spoke of new frontiers, a need for greater knowledge of the Geometry of the Earth's Surface, and new alliances with other realms. He spoke of the need for creative thinking and new methods of warfare suited to the conquest of new lands. *This man grasps the new reality,* Osi thought, *but he has no idea what methods are required. The new warfare will be land-based. For the first time the Navy's role will be to support our troops, rarely to confront the enemy in battle.*

The cadets anxiously awaited the final presentation by Commander Ortilon, Supreme Commander of all the Armies of the Realm. Osi suspected the entire program would culminate in groundbreaking news from Ortilon. It all made sense: Xenothon's representation of the past, Vadic's ill-defined vision of the future. Surely, Ortilon would build on their speeches to announce major new policies, new methods of warfare.

"Cadets of the Realm," Ortilon began, "do not be alarmed by talk of change. We face an enemy of meager means. They can't pull together a dozen warships. It's a ragtag lot and a ragtag war."

Osi cringed at the familiar words. There's a rift among the leaders, he concluded. Hervov was right. Ortilon is out of touch. King Rahn Mennon is our only hope.

The King stepped forward to claim the podium. "Cadets of the Realm, take heart. We live in troubled times, but troubles always end. The People of the Living Sun have survived the rising Waters of Chaos many times, and we will do so again. The People of the Living Sun have conquered the warring hosts of the Land of the Second Sunset before, and we will do so again. The People of the Living Sun will have their refuge in the land above. The Divine Right Order will secure our future. We must live by its every rule. And you, my defenders, must preserve the military traditions that brought victory to the Realm again and again throughout history."

Chronicle 25: War Games

The troops in the field assembled for war games, stock-in-trade of Cadets of the Realm. This time the exercise would be more than simple mock battles typical of so many afternoons. Maneuvers would be massive and extended, and the entire academy would be divided into two opposing armies. On the waters of the Valley Sea and in the hills along its shores, two forces would meet on battle sites of their choosing for a fight to the finish.

War or no war, the games would proceed. Rules of engagement would be simple. Win the battle as if the enemy were real! Spare the honor of your enemy only if he fights valiantly and proves himself worthy. Each cadet would decide the fate of his vanquished opponent. Win or lose with honor, and stand to fight again. Fight without honor, and be banished from the corps…for many, a fate more dreaded than death itself.

Sennon, Supreme Commander of the Academy, took his place on the reviewing stand as the exercise commenced and cadets anxiously waited to hear who would lead each army. No one was surprised when the first commander was announced. "The Army of Setra shall assemble on the right." Sennon paused.

"The Army of Osi shall assemble on the left," he said flatly. Egians were pleased, Berenicians outraged, but all were shocked, for never before had a colonist been chosen to lead a student army.

Osi and Setra called out their chosen lieutenants. Then Sennon commanded, "Cadets of the Realm! Join your leaders." Half the remaining cadets gravitated to one end of the field, half to the other in accordance with previously selected lots.

"Proceed to battle!" the Supreme Commander yelled, and the contest between Osi and Setra commenced. The victorious leader would be named Commander of All Cadets, an honor that would guarantee top assignments and career opportunities. Osi's 12 lieutenants counted five trusted Egians, including Ketoh and Busah, plus seven men from Punt, including the Berenician Jumar, whom he had come to respect.

"Collect your equipment and weapons," the leaders commanded. The material necessities of warfare had been collected in two staging areas, one at each end of the field.

Osi responded promptly, "Busah, organize a supply corps. Load up and proceed to the ships."

Down the grand boulevard the student armies marched; past the Royal compound, military fortifications, the Royal Armory, and religious monuments; past warehouses, customs houses, trading houses, and factoring houses; past counting houses, taverns, cafes, and barley shops. Business owners, residents, and citizens rushed to view the young warriors on their way to battle.

Commander Sennon had already set up a command post in the harbormaster's tower where he could observe the performance of his student officers. Arriving at the port, Osi was surprised to find the *Ruby of Berenicia.* In the next berth sat her sister ship, the *Blaze of the Valley Sea.*

The *Blaze* was of the same class as the *Ruby* and newer, but somewhat less grand. Both ships' bows were clad with the same remarkable metal. *No wonder they call it redsilver,* Osi thought. *It gleams red like a torch reflecting on water, and it shines like the brightest silver, yet it wears far better than the strongest steel.*

Each of the student armies would have one of these vessels at its disposal for the duration of the exercise. On deck beside the gangway stood Captain Hervov, waving his welcome to the Egians. "Climb aboard," Hervov called. "My ship is at your command."

"So," Ketoh said, "again we board our favorite vessel."

On the dock between the two vessels, Setra had assembled his officers. "And which vessel might that be?" asked Setra.

"Why, the *Ruby,* of course!" answered Ketoh. "This is the vessel that brought us to Berenicia. Captain Hervov has invited us aboard."

"I see," snapped Setra, stalking off into the crowd as Osi's men prepared to board. In moments, Setra returned with Commander Sennon's written order granting him the choice of vessels.

"Take the *Blaze!* It's yours, Master Osi," shouted Setra, laughing as he directed his officers to the *Ruby's* berth.

From the bridge of the *Ruby,* Captain Hervov sized up the situation. With a wink toward Ketoh, he moved to welcome Osi's nemesis. "Welcome aboard, young man. My ship is at your command."

"My name is Setra, son of Roton, Prince of Punt."

"And you are a brave soldier, indeed."

"Ah, so you've heard of my valor in training," said Setra, beaming.

"No, lad, but I know you're a brave man anyway," responded Hervov.

"Is it evident in my bearing?" Setra swelled with pride.

"I know nothing of your bearing, lad, except that you are brave enough to defy the gods and that makes a man exceedingly brave in my eyes."

"What do you mean? I'm never one to defy the gods."

"Then why do you challenge the Divine Right Order, lad?"

"I observe the Divine Right Order in every possible way." Setra said, uncertainty showing in his voice.

"No, lad. You have transgressed, for the Divine Right Order assigns the newer vessel to the greater man?"

Setra flushed with anger, then embarrassment. "I'm not aware of such an Order."

"Little known by men of the land; well known by men of the sea. Did Sennon not advise you? Never mind, though, traditions are meant to be broken. Even on the lesser vessel, any man of Punt can best a colonist. Please board your men."

"You would defy the Divine Right Order?" Setra responded indignantly. "This vessel is unfit!" he proclaimed for all to hear. "Back to the docks! Let the Egian command this aging scow!" Setra stamped past the rival officers and grabbed Osi's shoulder. "Take your place on the *Ruby*. It befits a colonial army."

Smiling ruefully, Osi turned and guided his men aboard the *Ruby*. It felt good to renew old ties with the able captain. "Your rival does not approve of my scow," Hervov complained in mock offense.

"My men are tough enough to endure its hardships, Captain," Osi said with a wry smile.

"And have you prepared your battle plan?" the captain asked as the *Ruby* was towed to open water.

"Head for the breakwaters off Redsilver Point."

"Shouldn't we wait for Setra to reveal his strategy? Those waters are treacherous."

"My enemy will find me if he has a taste for battle. I know Setra. He'll think we're afraid to stand and fight."

"Currents and crosswinds are extremely hazardous this time of year."

"I trust your seamanship. You'll see us through. What can you tell me about the captain of the *Blaze*?"

"He's one of the brightest officers in the Royal Navy, but he's a brash young man."

"All the more reason to set a challenging course."

Capt. Hervov capitulated. "For the duration of this voyage, the battle plan is yours. My responsibility is to deliver your army safely ashore. I'll veto anything that puts the *Ruby* at risk. Otherwise, I'll take you wherever you choose to go."

"What do you think of my strategy?"

"It's a bolder plan than I would prefer. Most cadets fight their battles offshore and on the beaches less than a half-day's sail from Berenicia. Yes, Master Osi, it's a brilliant plan . . . but it does incur certain risks."

"Such as?"

"There's no escape from Redsilver Point. Cliffs block all routes to the north and south. And, of course, you'll have to avoid the ore mines, or you'll have a real army after your hide. I suspect you have considered that risk and have your plan in place. Am I right?"

"Yes, Captain."

"Then let's proceed. Hoist the mainsails!" The proud vessel took the wind to the north. After a full day under sail, the *Ruby* rounded the point at Wadi Jimal with the *Blaze* in hot pursuit. "No doubt the *Blaze*'s captain has decided we are daft by now," Hervov snickered as he ordered the sails struck for a turn into safe harbor for the night.

"Don't lower the sails. There is wind still, and the moon is bright. We'll reach Redsilver Point under the cover of darkness, then move closer to land in the first light of dawn."

"But Master Osi! No one navigates these foul waters by night. We'll run aground before we reach Redsilver Point."

"I remember the hazards here from our last passage and from our studies of this coast in the Geometry of the Earth's Surface. We'll find safe anchorage, and Setra will be confounded. This move will give us time to entrench before the *Blaze* makes landfall."

Sailing on black sea under a moonlit sky, the *Ruby* nudged ahead. A gentle breeze and the moon's beaming reflection brought freedom and exhilaration. Six hands later, the silhouette of Redsilver Point appeared on the horizon. Setting his course just east of the headland, Osi stood at the bow and directed the helmsman through a gauntlet of small islands and rocks awash. Turning toward the channel behind the headlands, Hervov ordered the sails struck, then lowered two boats. The landing craft, manned by regular crew and tethered to the *Ruby*, tugged the larger vessel into the narrow pass. When they found safe anchorage, the *Ruby* weighed in. Goods and equipment were lowered to skiffs. Busah and his men took over and rowed farther up the channel. Finally, the landing party maneuvered into a natural harbor near the base of Redsilver Point, arriving well before daybreak.

Busah's men hauled cargo to the beachhead and returned for load after load of cadets. As the operation progressed, Osi assembled his officers on an old beach ledge.

"How will Setra find us here? Won't he claim we're hiding and declare victory?" Busah asked.

"It doesn't take much to fool Setra," Osi said. "Besides, he'll need proof of his victory."

Osi handed Jumar a coiled rope and grappling hook. "Here, take this to the top of the headland. Build a fire at daybreak. Kindle it high when you see the *Blaze* top the horizon. Setra will know soon enough that we're here and ready to fight."

"Hervov said no one's ever climbed those cliffs," Jumar said.

"Maybe no one's tried." He slapped Jumar's shoulder. The cadet smiled, then charged up the slope.

Osi turned to his troops. "Find cover on this ledge. Sleep until the sun wakes you."

The day broke late as fog lifted and the headland's morning shadow peeled away from the sleeping army. Osi had been up for more than a hand checking Jumar's progress. Rope drooped from the cliff top down to the ledge above the encamped army. Already thin wisps of smoke rose up from Jumar's fire into the still morning sky. The sun's rays reflected off the smoke trail as Osi's men awoke. Another hand passed as Tanta fed the men and Busah inspected weapons and gear. Osi marched his men along the low ledge just above the waterline and around to the side facing the open sea.

"The *Blaze* will approach seaward. The Divine Right Order leaves no choice."

"But look at those rocks, Osi. Surely even Setra can't be that foolish," Ketoh said.

"Never underestimate the folly of your foes, Ketoh. Many a battle has been lost for less."

The signal fire flared high, and the *Blaze* maneuvered shoreward.

"She's in trouble already. They've hit the fouls," Osi said.

"Shouldn't we warn them?" Busah asked.

"No! They know the rules of engagement," Osi said.

The *Blaze* lurched violently. Even Osi was shaken by the sickening grind of metal against coral as its bow snagged a submerged reef. The redsilver cladding held, but the mainmast snapped at its base, and the sails cupped air over water as the tall timber cut the waves like a knife blade. Two men tangled in rigging and went under with the mast. Setra ordered the rest to abandon ship as the hull bulged and broke apart. Two skiffs, filled with provisions, were cut loose just as the gunwales sank. Setra's troops swam in disarray toward a tiny rock island that barely broke the surf.

Osi eyed the survivors as they regrouped. The ship's captain and crew formed two parties to row the skiffs toward shore. Setra boarded the foremost and barked orders to his men. In no time, the swimmers assembled and trailed the skiffs to the narrow beach.

When the ragged remnants reached the rocky shore of Redsilver Point, Osi's men were strategically pre-positioned and well hidden above the beachhead. "Let the main force reach shore. Strike before they get their land legs," Osi had instructed. "Yell when I yell and attack like savages. Give no quarter."

The boats landed, and swimmers crowded onto the rocks. In a shocking instant, Osi's raging hoard engulfed Setra's army. Wild screams shattered the murmur of wind and waves. Osi outwitted and overpowered his enemy before a single deathblow was dealt. Osi's soldiers quickly seized Setra's landing craft, then rowed the booty to base camp. Setra's army foundered on the beach.

Osi personally subdued his rival. "You have your victory. You may dispose of me and my men as you wish," Setra said.

"You won't get off so easy, Commander. You're going to have to work for your defeat. This little skirmish was nothing more than a warning. We will now meet for a real battle in the hills."

"What are you up to, Egian? You must have some greater scheme in mind."

"Yes, Setra, one you won't understand. I want a fair fight."

"A fair fight against unarmed men."

"Rest here on the beach. At dusk, move your men around to the opposite side of the headland. You will find your own weapons and provisions." Surprise rippled through both armies. Never had a student leader been so decisively victorious, and never had a victor been so generous.

Victory came too easy. My men haven't been tested. Better to face our challenges now than later at the hands of Westerners.

Back at base camp, Osi surveyed the huge stock of armaments and supplies. Here were all the necessities of conventional warfare—tents, pots, bedrolls. "The tools of modern warfare," Osi said to his lieutenants, shaking his head. "Trinkets! This garbage would be useful if our objective were to lay siege to an enemy stronghold—a city, fort, or strategic seaway. But it's worthless for us. We need to conquer and hold new territory. We must think like our enemy in the Land of the Second Sunset."

"But, Osi, aren't we supposed to fight more nobly than primitives? Won't we look crude and cowardly in the eyes of our foes?"

"Victory is our only goal," Osi said. "We'll fight the new war, and we will win. Anyone who disagrees can move to Setra's side. . .now." There were no takers.

Osi motioned toward the ship. "Dispatch the skiffs to the *Ruby*. Ask Captain Hervov to proceed to the first embayment north of Redsilver Point."

"Take only bedrolls, knives, swords, bows and arrows, and a few scraps of hard dough; we'll feed off the land. Leave this trash behind. Scale the cliffs. Ketoh, dispatch your hunters till dusk, then bring in whatever you have. Lorban, post a rear watch and keep your ears open. Take to the cliff when you see the enemy settle in. Pull the last rope up as you climb. Bring two cakes of dried seaweed." The lieutenants stared questioningly at Osi, and Osi smiled back.

The Army began its methodical ascent. One at a time, cadets inched up the ropes Jumar had secured. Above, the small force fanned out along a broad ledge of dry upland at the brink of the Land of the Second Sunset. Here they made camp.

Three hands past noon, Lorban scrambled over the rim. It came as no surprise that Setra had moved to Osi's abandoned base long before the terms of truce allowed. Shouting to his men that the Divine Right Order required him to make camp before dusk, Setra took possession of the abandoned supplies.

"The Divine Right Order made him break his word of honor!" Lorban said, rolling his eyes to the laughter of all. "Setra couldn't believe we left such valuable equipment behind. He told his men to break out the supplies and make themselves comfortable. He can't imagine where our troops have gone. He plans to search the shoreline tomorrow morning. He says we'll be desperate soon for want of supplies. 'Lazy colonials,' he calls us. 'Unwilling to carry a load,' he says."

"We too must rest," Osi said, "but we'll make good use of the time." They spent the afternoon fletching arrows, honing swords, and drawing battle plans. At dusk, Ketoh's platoon appeared with the day's kill, enough meat for a victory feast.

At daybreak, Jumar's scouts reported movement below. Setra's men probed the rockfalls and buttresses that blocked the shoreline in both directions. By two hands past sunrise, his scouts reluctantly concluded that Osi's entire army must have scaled the 'unscalable' headland, incredible as it might seem.

"Follow them," Setra ordered. "If Egians can do it, surely we can with ease." His soldiers gathered Osi's discarded supplies. After one hand, the little army, looking like ants lugging oversized morsels up a kitchen wall, were utterly exhausted and demoralized. In their disarray, each soldier had sought his own route, but no route had been found.

"Drop your loads. Reassemble at the base of the cliff!" Setra ordered. "From now on, think and act like our adversary. That bastard, Osi, behaves like a primitive. Match him wit for wit. Find him and destroy him."

The orderly assault commenced at daybreak. Setra himself found a route and led the climb. Hand over hand, they forged their way to the ridge crest where Osi's men waited. But this time there would be no surprise rout. This time Osi held back until his rivals were fully assembled. Osi wanted a fair fight with both armies on firm footing from the outset, and he set the terms of battle. Now he would fight as he knew his nation must fight for the remainder of his military life. Hand to hand, resourcefully, mercilessly, Osi's army would attack and triumph over a force now of equal strength, someday many times greater.

First, he allowed Setra's force to spread out over a sizable section of the ledge. Then, the wild cry of battle rose from Osi's lines. Screaming like savages and running maniacally toward the bewildered foe, Osi's force again surrounded Setra. This time, however, Setra's men did not quaver. They fought brilliantly and defiantly. For the rest of the day, the battle raged. Soldier by soldier, skirmish by skirmish, battle by battle, Osi's superior tactics won the day. Vanquished warriors were herded to a roped-off compound and declared ineligible for further combat. Only Setra and a small group of defenders still stood.

"Let's take him," Ketoh yelled.

"No," Osi shouted. "He's mine alone." Finally, the two leaders met face to face. A few thrusts of Osi's golden-hilted sword brought the exhausted Berenician to his knees.

"Go ahead, Egian. Mark me with dishonor," Setra said in resignation.

"No!" Osi said. "You fought valiantly. You learned from my lesson and adjusted a little. You will survive to serve the King."

"I am grateful," Setra said sincerely. "I have learned at your hand. I offer myself as your servant."

"I'm not a man who needs to be served, and you're not meant to serve. You will one day lead great armies. You'll rule the King's Guard."

"That honor would be yours...if you were more faithful to the Divine Right Order."

"I'll choose order *and* reason if the choice is mine," Osi said. "For now, take your men back down to the sea and wait for us there."

At nightfall and again at daybreak Tanta's men prepared hearty meals–sizzling skewers of ibex served with wild greens and a tea made from upland shrubs–like those on the trek from Egia. Lacking metal pots, Tanta steeped the leaves in ibex skins using hot rocks to boil the water, a trick Osi had learned from the Hill People. The following morning, Osi surveyed the terrain below. Alone, he spoke to the morning sky. "Oh, Setra, Setra. Why do you distrust me so? I would be your friend if you could be mine. How can you be so wrongheaded in your endless quest to do right?" *But, then there's Bera.*

"Now, let's get back to the *Ruby*," he said on his return to camp. "Lorban, where is your seaweed?"

"What does seaweed have to do with returning to the *Ruby*?" Tanta asked. "We should have eaten this seaweed with last evening's meal."

"You'll see," said Osi. Taking the cakes from Lorban's pack and ordering two of Ketoh's men to haul an ibex kill along with him, Osi walk slowly toward the First Terrace. He ordered the carcass deposited on the upper lip of the terrace, sent the two men back, and then wailed to the top of his lungs. After each call, he waited in silence for several breaths. Finally, a call came back as clearly as it had been sent. Back and forth, one after another the two voices echoed across the land. Osi withdrew from the First Terrace and stood in silence as two Westerners emerged from the bush. Cadets gawked at the near-naked savages.

Wearing crude headdresses and rough grass belts laden with axes and flint knives, the two proud warriors eyed their visitors. First, they inspected the ibex. Gift or trap? Inching ever closer, the two men poked and nudged the carcass. Rolling it over cautiously and finding no snare, they decided the gift should be taken at face value. A shrill call and three other warriors appeared to seize the animal and haul it back into the bush. The first two tribesmen remained behind as if trying to make sense of this strange visit from another world.

Osi edged forward holding a cake of pressed seaweed wedged between his body and his outstretched hand. Stepping up to the First Terrace, he gestured as if challenging the Westerners to meet him at the edge of their domain. Finally, one beckoned Osi to the spot where the carcass had lain.

Osi extended the seaweed till his arm ached, inviting the primitives to meet him face to face. Tension mounted. Beads of sweat rolled from the tip of Osi's nose and dripped on the seaweed, pooling in a rich brown circle. With a deep breath, the older of the two men summoned his courage and stepped forward. Slowly, purposefully he reached out and placed his finger in the pool of sweat. Wet, salty seaweed adhered to the tip. Touching his tongue, he gleamed a spark of appreciation as he confirmed this rarest of commodities. Without further hesitation he took the crust and returned to his fellow tribesman. After a brief conference, the two men stepped up to Osi, their hot breaths not a hand's width from Osi's nostrils.

Jumar held the second cake. Ceremoniously, he placed it in Lorban's pack. With a gesture over his right shoulder, Osi motioned for both armies to follow him into the Land of the Second Sunset. Slowly the entourage marched northward along the broad foreland. For most of the day, the strange procession progressed along the rim above the First Terrace. By midafternoon, they reached the head of the wadi leading to the embayment where the *Ruby* awaited. Osi and the two Westerners walked side by side, never looking eye to eye, until they reached their destination. Then, Jumar presented the remaining seaweed to the grateful primitives. This done, the armies walked north above the mines and began their descent to the water's edge. Hervov faithfully waited at the agreed rendezvous point. On the return voyage, they picked up Setra's army from the shore and the crew of the *Blaze* from their precarious perch off Redsilver Point.

As the *Ruby* sailed into Berenicia's harbor, Ketoh turned to Osi. "What more could a man ask of life than this sweet savor of victory," he said.

"A chance to see the Red Island," Osi said, looking southward toward the open sea. *And Bera again.*

Chronicle 26: War in the Valley Sea

Osi and a hundred fellow soldiers stood on Berenicia's wide dock awaiting transport to the famed Red Island. He gazed at the *Ruby* sitting idle nearby. Captain Hervov attended strategy sessions with the admirals. Setra stood aside speaking to no one.

Busah shivered in the morning cool. "The gods must be celebrating our victory," he said, pointing toward the spectacular mix of golden-yellow and rose-red dawn.

"Don't flatter yourself, Busah," Ketoh said. "The gods may be happy for some other reason, but they don't heed pimply cadets and silly war games."

"True, Ketoh, but maybe we're engaged in greater things," Osi said. "The King *did* head back to sea after a successful tour of the Realm. And the royal procession *is* on its way back to the Red Island. A modest celestial celebration may be in order. Now that you mention it, I don't know why the gods wouldn't celebrate our victory. After all, no one on earth thought you'd make it through training. Maybe they're as surprised as we mortals are."

Osi shook his head, then turned toward the sunrise. "What's that?" He squinted intensely into daybreak. Dark silhouettes paraded across the eastern sky.

"Three ships."

"I'm not blind. I mean the lead ship. What is it? Can it be the Royal Barque?"

"Red hull. High bow. Square rig. Slender lines. Must be. No common warship ever looked so fanciful. But why would the King return to Berenicia?"

Osi ran to the end of the dock for a better look. *Is the King in danger? Is my destiny at hand? Silly thought. Still…*

"Alert the garrison," he shouted, and Busah ran.

"You there," Osi yelled at an approaching coastal trader, "Make ready. Clear the way for the Royal Barque. You two, cast off. Make way." Two more vessels pealed from the dock. By the time the barque and escorts were within hailing distance, Osi had three berths open and men posted at duty stations along the dock.

"You there. Harbor guard," yelled the lead escort's captain. "Prepare to secure lines."

"We're just cadets, awaiting transport," Osi said. "But, nonetheless, happy to serve the King, Sir. May we join the honor guard?" *Maybe my time has come*, Osi thought.

The captain shook his head, then turned to Setra. "You there, soldier. Ten of your best. Join the King's honor guard. We're headed to the palace." Setra turned his back on Osi and started picking men. The captain wheeled back to Osi. "You're needed here," he said.

"But sir…" Osi said.

"You're the harbor guard now, whatever you may have been before. Take charge. Secure the dock. Guard duty until further orders. Sink that pretty sword into any man who nears the King's vessel."

"Yes, Sir!" Osi snapped. *Was Toth mistaken? Maybe my destiny is to watch Setra save the King.* He laughed at himself. *Patience, patience. All in due time.*

As the ships slipped in, Osi's men secured hawsers to wooden cleats. Even to the captain's practiced eye, it looked like a well-planned reception. "Guard these ships with your lives," he said as he rushed to the barque. With hurried formality he ushered the royal entourage ashore, then rushed the King past Osi toward the street. Busah returned, followed by a detachment of elite palace guards and a grand carriage.

"To the garrison," the captain ordered. Setra and his men rushed by.

"What was that all about?" asked Busah.

"Let's take a look from above," Osi said.

Osi, Busah, and Ketoh ran to the harbor light. They climbed the spiral stone staircase and joined the watchman on the circular balcony.

"Southwest. There's your answer," Ketoh said.

"Must be a hundred warships," Osi exclaimed.

"And the lead vessel must be the Black Ensign, for she flies the black flag of war."

"Ragtag war, eh?" Ketoh said.

"Ortilon claimed no enemy could amass more than a dozen. Now someone's floated a hundred, and no one knows who's behind it. That fleet is mighty enough to take Berenicia." The others looked on in silence.

The lookout blared his horn. Answers echoed back from the garrison, the academy, the palace, and coastal defenses north and south of the city. Warships sloshed from hidden harbors.

"We can't hold the docks," Busah said. "How can we possibly secure the Royal Barque?"

"They won't attempt a frontal assault, not yet. First, they'll flank and pick off the line," Osi said.

In time, thirty Berenician naval vessels took defensive positions from the quay north of the main harbor to the Coast Road well south of it. The approaching armada split into two forces, one arching northward, the other southward. The Black Ensign waited menacingly at sea, flagging orders to her split fleet. Soon lines were drawn, and the enemies stared each other down for a hand or more. Then a deadly dance began. Like daring swordsmen, the massive ships thrust and parried, sometimes charging at full speed, sometimes gracefully maneuvering for a crafty broadside ram. But no ship sat still long enough for such an easy charge. Again and again the combatants jockeyed for advantage. Soon, the enemy claimed the upper hand.

Osi, Ketoh, and Busah watched as seven enemy ships surrounded a single Berenician vessel. "What's going on? Why don't other ships help him?"

"Each ship is assigned a defensive position," Osi explained, "which she can't abandon for any reason. 'Vadic's Death Creed,' Hervov calls it, for the Admiral thinks it's a brilliant strategy. The attacking force has no such rule, of course. They gang up on our ships one at a time and gnaw their way toward the center."

"Vadic's Death is suicide."

"Its only virtue is that it buys time while our army readies for battle on land."

"Must our men die like lambs just to buy time? When can we expect them to land?"

"They won't reach the harbor. With Vadic's brilliant defense they'll seize beachheads along the coast, and we'll fight two battles, not one."

* * *

Immediately, Osi established a command center inside the lighthouse's greatroom. Quickly, his men erected a sturdy barricade between the lighthouse and the plaza.

At dusk on day two, Osi, Ketoh, and Busah watched from the top of the light as the enemy broke through coastal blockades north and south of the city. Twenty ships beached, and more than 3,000 seasoned troops emerged. Once the beachheads were secure, the Black Ensign and her fleet maneuvered for the kill.

Rebel troops advanced hour by hour, street by street fighting their way through the city. By noon on the fourth day, the two pincers converged at the garrison. All the while, Osi and his men waited patiently at the docks.

"Shouldn't we help?" Busah asked.

"No," Osi replied curtly. "We have our orders."

"Waiting is worse than battle," Ketoh said. "Still, Setra has his work cut out for him at the garrison."

At daybreak on the sixth day, word came that the garrison had fallen. "The palace is next. What now?" Ketoh asked.

"We hold our position," said Osi.

"But we can't just sit here," said Ketoh. "We have to do something, or they'll kill the King."

Yes and Toth prophesied that it is my destiny to save the King, Osi thought. *How can I fulfill my destiny when the King may die before he even makes it to the harbor.*

"Orders are orders. We will obey."

"You're right, of course, but I'm here to fight, not to stand around useless."

Angry shouts roared from the palace. Screams of the wounded soon followed.

"The palace guard can't hold out much longer," Busah said in despair.

Silently they waited. After half a hand of near silence, a shocking rumble sounded from the back wall of the greatroom. With a clamor of timber and stone, a hole a manheight high and twice as wide gaped open, revealing a hidden passageway.

Osi froze as a strange procession emerged from the dim interior. First came a torch-bearing squire of 13 or 14 years. Then, not the King, as Osi briefly expected, but a group of peasant children followed. Not one was older than ten years. Behind them walked a lady also dressed in servant's garb.

"I am Ammon," the boy announced with authority. He gestured toward his followers. "The children of the garrison are frightened. Please help us."

The lady hardly glanced in Osi's direction, so intent was she on protecting her wards.

She removed her cloak, and for an instant Osi and Bera exchanged tender glances.

"Rahn Mennon is surrounded," she reported solemnly, "with Setra at his side. The cadets fight well, but they are inexperienced. Our veterans are poorly trained, poorly conditioned, and now exhausted. I fear for them, King and all."

Young Ammon assembled the children, and Ketoh led them outside to the King's barque. One by one they filed up the gangway.

Osi and Busah remained on guard at the tunnel's mouth. For half a hand or more, they heard not a sound. Then came the clatter of running men and jostling weapons. Finally, hurried breathing and torchlight in the distance. Nearer and nearer the light and clamor came. Osi and his men stood ready for friend or foe. To Osi's relief, he spotted first the captain of the escort ship, then two officers of the King's own barque, and finally the King himself. Even without regalia, Rahn Mennon's stately bearing set him aside from other men. Behind them echoed sounds of rear guard action in the passageway.

A soldier ran in from the dock with a message from Ketoh. "Rebels over the barricade," he shouted. "Sixty or more. Well armed!" As he spoke, Setra and his men backed from the tunnel into the greatroom.

"Rebels in pursuit," Setra reported between breaths. Osi's men surrounded the opening as three more cadets emerged. Together they formed a staunch defense.

Winded, King Rahn Mennon leaned against a pillar. Osi quickly assessed the situation, then turned to the King's officers. *Many are severely injured, likely dying. They won't last another hand,* Osi thought. *Still, they did their noble duty, and the King is unharmed.* His first impulse was to bow before the King, but there was no time for ceremony.

Osi ordered eight cadets into a protective phalanx around the King. He maneuvered them onto the dock where hand-to-hand combat raged. Step by step they battled through an onslaught of rebel soldiers arriving from the city. Half a hand later the Royal Barque loomed merely two berths away. Injuries were slight amongst his eight, though not amongst the rest, and the King remained unharmed.

Meanwhile, Osi's cadets, under Ketoh's command on the dock, seemed certain to prevail. Better trained and better led than Setra's men or even veteran soldiers of the Realm, they felled five rebels to every one loss of their own. Soon, their enemy was down to fifteen able combatants, now retreating from the dock while begrudging every step. Victory, however, still lay at least one skirmish away.

Suddenly Ketoh saw what Osi could not. A dozen rebels crouched behind the gunnel of the ship berthed next to the Royal Barque. Down to the dock they sprang, from nowhere it seemed to Osi, and blocked his way. Others jumped down behind Osi and his men, now trapped.

Setra, arriving just in time, relieved Ketoh and held the rear. Ketoh attacked from behind while Osi charged forward. One by one the rebels fled or died as Osi and Ketoh lunged with vengeance. Finally the last man fell, and Osi motioned the King forward. *Old Toth was right,* Osi thought. *Now my destiny is complete.*

Suddenly, his reverie ended with a shout from above. "No!" Bera stood on the deck, roughly constrained by a rebel soldier, his arm around her chest and a dagger at her throat. "No!" she shouted again. "Behind you!" And she motioned sideways toward the crowd.

Osi realized too late that Bera screamed not for herself but for the King, as fresh enemy troops sprang from yet another berthed ship. He heard the thud of metal striking bone and turned to see Rahn Mennon fall, a spear embedded in his chest. *I've failed,* he thought. *Can Toth's prophecy have been so wrong?*

With Bera still in peril, Osi unsheathed his dirktooth dagger and darted up the gangway. A silent blur of redsilver flashed through the air and into the heart of her attacker. The rebel slumped silently forward, and Bera broke free. Osi ran past her, retrieved his dagger, and lunged onto the prow of the barque. Springing like a dirktooth tiger, he leapt into the mass below. Two men fell from a single swing of his sword and another from his dagger. Then another. . . and another. . . then two more. . . and another, until the last rebel lay dying in the collective pool of blood.

Osi rushed to the King's side where Bera knelt, his head in her lap. "I failed you, my sovereign," Osi said, more to himself than to the dazed king. Rahn Mennon gazed skyward.

"No, Osi," said Bera. "A friend has failed him, but you did not. You will one day be blessed, for what you did today."

"But I let harm come to the King."

"Not even a King can live forever," she said, but the pain in her eyes belied her bravado. "This battle was lost at the garrison, not here on the docks. You did all within your power." Bera stroked the King's brow as Busah pressed linen against the wound to staunch the flow of blood. "Forget me now. Find refuge for these children," the King said to Bera. He stared into Bera's eyes. She held his gaze, and gently patted his hand. Ketoh offered water, but the King refused.

"Now, I rest," Rahn Mennon said, as his eyes closed.

"A friend failed him." What did she mean? Osi wondered, but there would be no chance to ask.

CHAPTER 11

Search Log 23: Inquisition

On Monday morning, Jared sat at his desk and smiled as he recalled exchanging cards with Ellie before leaving for work. Valentine's Day was not his favorite holiday, but it meant a lot to Ellie, being a woman and all. For once, he'd bought her gift and signed her card ahead of time. He loved her for loving silly, romantic things like valentines...and forgiving his occasional thoughtlessness. For most of their marriage he'd placed Ellie and the boys above everything else, but recently work demands had grown out of hand. Last year, he missed both her birthday and their twenty-fifth wedding anniversary because of business trips abroad. She said she understood, as usual, but he couldn't bear knowing he had hurt her. After that, he resolved never again to let work take precedence. Thus far, he'd kept his promise and turned down some attractive invitations that would have conflicted.

Jared smiled again, imagining how she would look when she opened the gift that night, but soon his reverie was interrupted by a telephone call.

"Hello, Jerry! How are you?"

"Fine, Chuck. How are things at my favorite university."

"Oh, everything's fine. In fact, I'm calling to see if you can come over sometime. I'm in charge of the colloquium series this year, and I'd like to have you speak."

"I'd enjoy that. What do you have in mind?"

"Well, certainly we'd like to hear your latest thoughts on automated geography, but I have something else in mind as well."

"What's that?"

"Walde Peplies confided to me that you're working on Ice Age cultures. Our theme for this semester's series is global change. So far we've focused on physical change. I'll be letting the students down if I don't include human causes and effects. You're my best hope."

"Chuck, I'm not ready to talk about this research, and your folks may not be ready to hear it. Did Walde explain what I'm up to?"

"No, he said it was a bit hush-hush. He felt at liberty to mention the topic, but he wouldn't give any details. Is it really that sensitive?"

"If I'm right, it's a bombshell. If I'm wrong, I'll be called a kook. I have almost enough evidence to make a case, but fieldwork is absolutely essential."

"Okay, I'll tell you what! Come over and give a methodological talk. Say as much or as little as you like about your findings. We'll cover your expenses. How about it?"

"Oh, I suppose I don't have any problem with that. When do you want me?"

"Fortunately we've had a couple of cancellations. How about the first Monday in April?"

"Isn't that the day after Easter?"

"Oh, yes I guess it is. You'd have to travel on Easter Day, wouldn't you?"

"I'd rather not do that. Any other openings?"

"Well, I've got next Monday open, but that's awfully short notice. Maybe I can switch someone else around."

"No, I think I can make it. Will that give you enough time to set things up?"

"Sure, I just need to post an announcement. Fax me your vita and a paragraph summarizing the talk. You can drive over on Sunday and stay at our house. It'll take you, let's see…here to the state line, state line to Knoxville…and you're say, 30 minutes west of Knoxville. Why, you can spend most of the afternoon with your family and still make a late dinner here."

"Sounds good. I'll send the fax before I leave today and see you about 8:00 p.m. on Sunday. Thanks for the invitation. I look forward to it."

* * *

The Colloquium was scheduled to begin with refreshments in a classroom next to the big lecture hall where Jared would speak. Twenty minutes before the lecture time, two graduate students rushed in with bags of cookies and 2-liter bottles of Coke and Sprite. Another fidgeted with a huge coffee urn. As the young man plugged the cord into an electrical outlet, there was no chance whatsoever the coffee could brew before Caisson's talk was supposed to begin. Jared wasn't concerned about coffee, but he was concerned about starting on time. His lecture would be rushed even if he had the full allotted hour.

Jared was surprised when so many guests introduced themselves as archaeologists and anthropologists. He approached Chuck. "What gives?"

"Oh, yes. I should have warned you. I didn't recruit them. Someone picked up our announcement and passed it around the Anthropology Department. Ordinarily we try to get an interdisciplinary audience, but we're rarely this successful."

"Well, they'll be disappointed. I'm not about to spill the whole story until I have proof."

"I don't think any harm will come of it. Just be a little more cautious than usual when you get to that part of your talk."

Jared pretended everything was fine, but his nervousness edged up several notches. After further delay, everyone filed into the lecture hall.

He walked to a seat on the front row, a stack of viewgraphs under his arm, trying to appear totally at ease. Finally, Chuck stepped forward.

"Welcome, fellow geographers and honored guests. We present the fourth in our series of colloquia on global change. Our guest today is Dr. Jared Caisson, a Member of the Senior Research Staff of Melton Valley Laboratory. In his distinguished career Jerry has served as . . ." Chuck expounded Jared's credentials, ending with a list of topics on which Jared had published and the variety of journals in which they had appeared. An alarm flashed through Jared's mind as he realized Chuck hadn't understood how those seemingly diverse topics fit together. Chuck's well-meaning remarks inadvertently made Jared look more like an intellectual gadfly than a seasoned scientist focused on geography's main themes: spatial analysis, place-based research, fieldwork, and scientific integration.

"As you may have noticed," Chuck went on, "our colloquia so far have focused primarily on the physical aspects of global change. We've heard about past and present climates, and their observed and projected impacts on vegetation, the Ozone Hole, global carbon cycles, sea level, and other factors. I invited Jared Caisson to talk today about remote sensing and GIS and how they may be used to monitor and measure global processes. In addition, if we're lucky, he may say a few words about his newest research involving the human dimensions of global change. Jerry, welcome to our campus."

Jared smiled toward the audience as he walked to the podium. Inside, he was furious. How could Chuck set him up for such a fall? Now he felt obliged to say something about human dimensions whether he wanted to or not. Chuck meant well, but he just didn't understand the consequences.

Normally, he would have checked the room ahead of time. He didn't need much—just an overhead projector, a darkened room, a clear screen, and a pointer. Chuck assured him everything would be there. It was, but with a catch. In all his years he'd never seen such an outlandish projector. It was gigantic! It towered above his head, and the glass panel was high above his line of sight. The audience would see clearly what showed on the screen, but he couldn't see the viewgraph or the screen as he spoke. Ordinarily, he depended on that view to prompt every word of his talk. Now he would have to glimpse each viewgraph as he placed it on the panel, and remember every pattern he wished to discuss. It was a disaster in the making.

Jared surprised himself as he navigated the familiar terrain of Seagate and the geographic revolution in science. He spotted few signs of disagreement in the audience. When he came to sea level rise, however, the geographers grew still, and other faces turned pale, red, or grim. At first, he hoped they were interested and straining to understand his new perspective. Then he saw one face contort with an audible "Harumph!"

and knew he was in trouble. He added a few qualifiers to soften the blow of what he had already said, made a summary statement about the future of geography, and asked if there were any questions. Indeed, there were.

"Dr. Caisson," a graduate student began, "you spoke vaguely about the human dimensions of global change, and then showed us a map of sea level inundation over the past 17,500 years. What was your point?"

"Oh, I just think that, since the inundation is so thoroughly accepted by physical scientists, the inundated zone should receive more attention from social scientists."

Another student spoke. "But we do take that zone into account. The land bridge between Siberia and Alaska is central to our understanding of the early settlement of North America."

"There's a crucial difference between a 'land bridge' and a coastal plain . . ." Jared began.

"What do you mean?" a young woman asked.

"I mean ancient peoples didn't know which places would become important in the twentieth century, A.D." Jared responded. His audience looked puzzled. A few heads nodded agreement as he carefully explained the "Wallenda Vector," but others registered anger.

"Frankly, Mr. Caisson, where do you get off dabbling in our field for a year or two and then telling us what's right and wrong about it?" The harsh words came from a blond young man whose wholesome face seemed an unlikely source of such rhetoric.

Before Jared could respond, another student interjected. "What do you expect to find in the inundated zone that isn't already in the archaeological record?"

"What do you find in the Coastal Plain today?" Jared asked. "That's where most humans reside. That's where most cities are located. My guess is that there may have been a similar pattern in those days. Most of the population would have lived on Tropical coasts, and they would have been relatively more advanced than the people occupying the uplands."

"You think there were cities during the Ice Ages! That's heresy!" a student screamed as he slammed a book to the floor beside his seat.

"I didn't say that." Jared calmly replied. "I simply said they might be relatively more advanced than their neighbors in the hills."

"I heard what you said, but I know what you meant!" the student stammered.

"Don't put words in my mouth!" Jared shot back.

"Mr. Caisson, do you know how old the oldest city is?" The bright-faced student rejoined the fray.

"Yes, it's Jericho, and it's about 9,000 years old!"

"Do you know the age of the earliest evidence of human settlement at Spirit Cave? That's in northwestern Thailand, in case you don't know."

"I know where it is. But no, I don't know the exact age. Several thousand years older than Jericho. But what's your point? Both Spirit Cave and Jericho are in the uplands. They don't tell us much about the inundated zone."

"My point, Mr. Caisson, is that, if you don't know the age of those sites, you can't tell us anything about anthropology! Go back and do your homework!"

Another student mouthed "Kook!" to a friend across the aisle. Caisson looked around the room. *The young guns are blazing,* he thought. *The professors are holding back out of what passes for professional courtesy, no doubt, but they've primed their students to fire the shots.* If he hadn't known Chuck so well, he would have suspected he'd been set up from the start.

The geographers were, he sensed, somewhat sympathetic to his argument, but didn't feel confident enough to challenge the anthropologists on their own ground. Finally one geography professor spoke out, but her comment was patronizing, even apologetic. He stood alone in a room more hostile than he had imagined in his worst nightmare.

Then, "Atlantis lives!" someone cried in mock pain, and the room erupted in laughter.

Like the featured guest at a hanging, Jared thought! As with most hangings, there was no one to blame but himself. Afterward, Chuck tried to cheer him up, complimenting his courage but saying nothing about the idea itself or the reasoning behind it. Half an hour later, Jared headed home in utter despair.

The drive home turned out to be a blessing. Mile after mile, Jared reviewed the events that had led him to this low point. He reexamined every piece of evidence and logic that had caused him to suspect something so heretical that even the hint of it could evoke such anger and repudiation. He thought about what he had said, and what he meant, and what he would have said if scientists were truly open to new ideas. *Yes,* he concluded, *I still believe what I said, and what I meant is reasonable, and what I suspect is plausible, and I won't make any real claims without proof.* By the time he reached the Tennessee line, he felt better...confident he was no kook. Determined to find proof.

"How did the talk go?" Ellie asked as he slipped into bed beside her.

"Worst of my career," he said, "but it's alright. I know what I have to do."

Search Log 24: Back at the Lab

"What the heck were you thinking, Jer?" Ed asked, pointing to the newspaper in his hand.

"Ed, you know I didn't say all that. It's a crop of lies built on a kernel of truth."

"It's all the same now."

"So you think one sleazy yellow rag can cause problems in this great palace of science?"

"Think? Hell, I know! This thing is going to grow, Jer. It's going to grow."

* * *

A week passed and nothing happened. *Surely an ax will fall,* he thought. *If it blows up, I could lose the seed funds. Worst case, I could even lose funding for Seagate. But who knows? Maybe not.*

Two weeks passed, and Jared relaxed a little. Jabs continued from all angles, but Lab managers and colleagues still seemed supportive. Ed amassed a scrapbook of clippings—an op-ed here; a letter to the editor there; public sarcasm by a prominent scientist—all negative. Only the tabloids loved Jared's purported position "on Atlantis," but Ed didn't save any of those.

By Friday afternoon of week three, Jared was cautiously optimistic and allowed himself to daydream about the upcoming weekend with Ellie. He gazed out his window to the hill across the way, and that led his wandering mind to other hills beyond vision. *Ah yes, we'll head out right after breakfast and drive over the mountain toward . . .*

Suddenly his door swung open with such force that it slammed the wall behind it. Dave Halberd blazed purple and screamed like a frightened toddler, "What the Hell is this?" He slapped a tabloid on Jared's desk and jabbed the headline with his finger. "MVL SCIENTIST CLAIMS ATLANTIS FLOODED IN GLACIAL GUSHER."

"Who reads that trash?" Jared asked, but then he remembered seeing copies in Halberd's office from time to time. Next he recalled Ed Field once proclaiming that particular reading habit was the only outwardly visible sign of Halberd's inquiring mind. Halberd was their boss two levels up. Generally he was easygoing and congenial, rarely interfering with their work except to rake off his departmental overhead, objectionable only because, in Ed's words, "He served no useful purpose on God's green earth." *Nevertheless, he is my boss,* Jared reflected, *and he can make trouble.*

"Nobody here, of course," Halberd lied, "but lots of people on the street." He turned like a ricochet and disappeared out the door.

* * *

"Jer," said Ed. "If I were you, I'd clear my office of everything that has anything to do with this controversy. If there's no shred of evidence here, maybe you can claim it's part of your private life and has nothing to do with MVL. Thank god your seed money is strictly physical."

"Good point. I'll sort my files this week and clear out before the weekend."

"I wouldn't wait. I'd do it now."

"Now? You think it's that urgent?"

"Just a wise precaution. Yep. I'd do it now."

Reluctantly following Ed's advice, Jared spent the next hour sorting through files, mostly the ones relating to ancient populations and sea level rise. He gathered up several maps, a number of books, and sheaves of vital papers, and stuffed them into his now-bulging briefcase. He walked to his Pathfinder outside the gate and hefted them into the rear cargo space. *Now to get some work done!*

He reentered the main gate house awkwardly with an empty briefcase and a conference giveaway bag. Once inside, he selected the "fast lane" and inserted his badge into the automatic reader. His jaw dropped as the red flashing LED methodically spelled out:

"T-E-R-M-I-N-A-T-E-D"

CHAPTER 12

Chronicle 27. Return to Death's Shadow

"Twenty ships ashore, and the Rebels have at least that many more in assault formation," Setra said. "And no shortage of men. There must be a thousand still fighting in the city. You won't stand a chance in that old showboat," he said, pointing to the Royal Barque where the revered body lay in repose. "Take the *Ruby*. You'll have to run as long and fast as she'll go."

Can this be Setra speaking? thought Osi.

"What about Hervov? He'll want to pursue," Osi said.

"You know Hervov, Osi. He'd say the same. Load the Royals. Get them out of here. Most urgent of all, get Bera to safety."

"And you, Setra? Are you coming?"

"No. This enemy must be stopped, but this one I cannot face."

"What are you talking about? You fear nothing. You can't resist a battle like this."

"Not fear, but love keeps me from joining this battle. Besides," he said, "there's nothing more to be done for King Rahn Mennon."

Osi turned to his soldiers standing at attention on the dock. "Board the *Ruby*," he shouted.

Not fear but love? Osi thought. *What in Rahn's name can he mean by that? We can fight rebels whether in love or not.*

Osi's men loaded and launched in record time. Cadets seized the *Ruby*'s sheets and unfurled them in record time. The ship took wind. Osi again felt the cool breeze of the Valley Sea as it lofted the mainsail and rushed past his position at the whipstaff.

Bera leaned against him, touching but not facing him as he so wanted her to do. Instead, she stared astern for one last view of Berenicia. The massive lighthouse stood boldly with its gold and redsilver spire glinting in the midday sun. Slowly even the highest pyramids disappeared from view as the *Ruby* coursed northward, its wake obscuring more than a few sunken spires below. Finally, as the *Ruby* rounded Ras Banas, she turned to face him. She stared into his eyes with deep, abiding love revealed in the quiver of her lip, the sparkle of her eyes, the furrow on her brow. Then she went below to care for the children.

The *Ruby* sailed into night, then anchored off Wadi Jimal.

"Fond memories," Ketoh said as he and Osi rested on deck, beguiled by the city and its flickering firelights. Ammon and the children milled about aft. Bera remained in the Captain's quarters astern.

"Fond memories indeed," Osi echoed. "What boys we were. . . such a short time ago."

"You sound as if you believe *all* the good times are behind us."

"In victory or defeat, war takes a boy beyond his years," Osi said. "We'll get through this alright, but as men, not as carefree 'school boys.'"

"What's wrong, Osi? Don't tell me you're giving up, not the Dirk Slayer. He's the one who inspires everyone else. You can't succumb to this curse of false destiny. You didn't fail King Rahn Mennon. We failed you."

"I took my eyes off the King. I turned to Bera. I let my own selfish need take charge of my soul. I let Rahn Mennon die. Don't you see?"

"What I know for certain is that we would not be here without your leadership. Busah, Bera, the young squire Ammon, the children, I myself. . . . we'd all be dead. Look to the living. Dwell not on the dead."

"You are a true friend, Ketoh. I don't know what I'd do without you at my side, but nothing you say can erase my failing. Get some sleep, friend," Osi said. "We have much to do . . . tomorrow . . . and early at that." Ketoh scampered below. Osi lingered at the gunnel gazing into the night.

* * *

By morning, fog swallowed both sea and shore, and the *Ruby* embarked long before the bank burned away. "Due north. Lookouts beware," Osi barked as the giant vessel slipped silently, slowly across a nearly calm sea marred only by gentle ripples.

Bera emerged from below just as the haze began to lift. Osi's face brightened as she took her place beside him, and together they looked starboard toward the open sea. Sunlight reflected uniformly as from a perfect mirror except for sparkles and glints from rogue ripples here and there. Scanning the horizon, Bera turned slowly around until her gaze settled on Wadi Jimal. Gradually the town itself slipped below the horizon until only its harbor light remained. She turned again toward the south where a heavy fogbank still loomed.

Something caught her eye. *What is that? A lone pole thrust upward like a dagger though a pillow.*

"Osi, is that a mast?" Together they watched as sails and, finally, a high red prow emerged from the gloom. Square rig. Slender lines.

"The Royal Barque," she cheered, "they made it through."

But why, Osi pondered, *and who's in command? This wasn't the plan!*

Then another mast ominously rose behind. And more. And more. Into the sun sailed one rebel warship after another, the entire rebel fleet, with the Black Ensign in the lead, in hot pursuit of the Royal Barque.

"No!" Bera cried.

"You courageous fool!" Osi mumbled toward whoever steered the Royal Barge. "You can't outrun the whole fleet in a frilly barque. They'll have your ass on a skewer. I mean..." He glanced at Bera to see if she'd taken offense. A faint smile creased her lips.

It must be Setra, he concluded. *No one else would be so foolhardy. That's what he meant! He said he wouldn't fight. He meant he'd follow, "for love," as he said. But it is working. The rebel fleet is chasing him, not us.*

"He did it for you, you know," he said in disgust, cautiously testing his ground.

"I know, Osi. Not for his friends or fellow soldiers, not for the children, not for the King or for the Realm. He did it because he...loves me. He really does. Perhaps that makes his act less noble...but does it make him less heroic? I...I don't know. What noble purpose can it serve? Perhaps he deceived the rebels. Perhaps they think the King is alive onboard the Royal Barque."

"Possibly. In that case, he would have headed north to convince the rebels. They know the King would never head south. No refuge there. But to what purpose? With the whole fleet on his..."

"...trail..." Bera finished coyly. She grinned at Osi's timid blush.

"...wake." Osi finished for himself. He grinned too, then frowned once more. "He doesn't stand a chance. A barque does well enough on a straight course in open water. Its square sail runs like a jib downwind, but it can't run fast among the islands where we're headed. They'll run her down and ram her before nightfall."

"Is there nothing we can do?"

"They're three hands behind her now. The barque may be slow, but Setra knows these waters better than they do. We'll watch from a distance. If Setra opens his lead by five hands or more, we'll sweep in and evacuate the crew."

"And if not?"

"Setra is resourceful. He'll find a way."

"Do your best to save him, Osi, but don't risk Ammon and the children."

"Don't worry. I'll keep a safe distance, and there's more wind behind us now. We'll tack as far as Redsilver Point. If we can't make our move by the time Setra gets there, he'll be amongst the islands, and we'll have no choice but to disengage. There's open sea to the north, though I doubt he'll make it that far. The *Ruby* can outdistance those rebel ships easily enough."

"But, where will we find safe harbor?" Bera asked.

"Death's Shadow is our last hope. They'll find us, for sure, but we can defend against as many ships and men as they can send against us. It's far north, at the end of the Valley Sea. With luck, we can muster support from loyalists at Zafaga and the garrison at Gubal."

"You must have thought this out long ago."

"A plan for this, a plan for that, sooner or later you'll need one or the other. Toth said that's what it takes to master my duty and my destiny. But destiny? That's moot now that Rahn Mennon is dead."

"Who are we to question destiny? There is no pass or fail. There is sorrow, but no shame, Osi. Gods don't blame mortals for injustices done by others." She took Osi's hand in hers and squeezed gently. He looked into her eyes, with sorrow *and* shame in his own.

* * *

The *Ruby* reached Redsilver Point at sunset. Osi set his course squarely between the headland on one side and rocks awash on the other. He ordered the sails struck and lowered tugs. With the *Ruby* safely anchored in a hidden harbor, the tugs backed off with Osi and Jumar aboard and rowed them to shore. Climbing the cliff, Jumar led with rope and hook. Soon they were atop the headland with a panoramic view of the drama unfolding at sea. *It's over*, Osi thought, when he spotted the Royal Barque already among the islands. *Frequent short tacks are required, and the barque simply cannot perform them well, no matter how skilled the crew.* Three rebel ships closed within half a hand, and the barque's fate seemed clear.

"He's lost," Jumar exclaimed. "They'll sink him within a hand."

But, Osi sensed something unexpected. "Let's not count him out just yet. Watch his next move."

Suddenly Setra veered shoreward. Osi cheered. Jumar looked puzzled.

"He'll sink himself," said Jumar.

"Exactly," Osi said as the barque struck a massive rock awash. Boards splintered and ripped from the vessel's ribs. Instantly, it sank beneath the waves. The Black Ensign barely managed to stop short, but three other ships in hot pursuit were not so lucky. They crashed into hidden seccas not far from the Royal Barque. . .or what was left of it.

At least Rahn Mennon is properly buried at sea, Osi solemnly reflected as the King's sarcophagus, having slid from the Royal Barque, floated momentarily and sank beneath the waves. "Back to the *Ruby*," he said. "Setra knows these headlands. He'll elude the rebels ashore."

The remaining fleet first took Setra's bait, then caught on to his ruse. They paused dumbfounded for a hand or more, then regrouped and veered back to sea. Ships fore and aft broke from the line to patrol the coast for signs of Setra's men as well as their own survivors. It was only a matter of time until they would find the *Ruby* in its secluded cove. Never one to wait, Osi boldly drove the *Ruby* out to sea, and immediately the chase was on.

"The *Ruby* can outrun them all," Ketoh said confidently.

"But there's a risk," Osi said. "We must reach Zafaga and Gubal in time to mount a counterattack. Any later, and we'll simply be guiding these dogs to surprise our own forces."

"We're faster, but not that fast," Ketoh said.

"We'll have to sail..."

"...at night?" Ketoh interrupted. "Not again."

"We'll gain a day. That's all we need, and it's our only hope."

* * *

The *Ruby* plus six ships of Zafaga sailed into Gubal's harbor at midday with no time to lose. *Five rebel vessels are half a day back,* Osi estimated, *and the main fleet can't be far behind.* He surveyed the very docks where he once had bartered his precious sword for passage to Zafaga. Before the war, Gubal had been a bustling seaport, its streets full of life. Now, not a soul could be seen.

Each ship nudged the docks and secured its stout hawsers. Osi passed the command, "All ashore. Head to Koro-reni." He led his little army of fewer than 700, and Bera strode boldly beside him. Ammon and the children followed close behind, guarded by Osi's best men including Ketoh, Jumar, and Busah.

"Who is this boy Ammon?" Osi asked. "He seems noble far beyond his years."

"He is my brother."

"Your brother? I didn't know you had a brother," said Osi.

"There is much about my world you do not know, Osi."

And all the more I wish to know, thought Osi.

* * *

"Ketoh says this place holds hard memories for you," Bera said as they approached the fort.

Osi glared. "Is that all he said?"

"He said you endured a painful ordeal for the sake of your men. . . and won their eternal loyalty. He said Captain Arrak was a fool to…"

"Capt. Arrak did his duty. . . as he saw it. He was dead wrong, but hardly a fool."

"You forgive too quickly, Osi. What will you say to him now? How will you win him over to our cause?"

"You will be our emissary, Bera. As in Zafaga, you must bear witness that we are acting on orders from Rahn Mennon. . .last orders, but orders nonetheless."

"I will intercede as you ask, but you have to deal with this man on your own terms, Osi. Arrak is accustomed to unchecked authority. Only by strength of will can you prevail."

"Then, perhaps our best hope lies in an alliance among equals."

"Don't be naive. No alliance can succeed against such an enmity. Someone must be in charge, and it must be you."

"I will deal with that when we meet. . ."

". . .or not," he added. "Don't look!" he warned, as he scanned an ugly line of posts in front of the fort. Bera, of course, ignored his warning.

Lashed to each post was the mutilated body of a once proud soldier of the Realm. Captain Arrak's rotting corpse hung on the very same post where Osi had been flogged.

"Westerners," he blurted. "Those cowards are emboldened by the rebels' power. Now we face war in front and war behind. Shield the children from this horror," Osi ordered. Fifty men surrounded them while Osi led the rest into Koro-reni. Bodies littered the burned enclosure. "No survivors," he called. "Bring the others inside." Then, Osi climbed the ramparts and looked out to sea. At the long bay's entrance poked the tip of the mast of the first rebel vessel.

"Death's Shadow," Osi ordered, "Hurry!"

* * *

Inside the Gullet, Osi pointed to the sloping ledge he's wanted to explore when first passing through so long ago. "It must climb to the surface above. Too dark to tell now. but I'm sure of it. We'll bivouac here and check it out at first light."

"Yes, Sir!" Ketoh responded with a snappy salute. "Just like old times."

"Provisions. Water. Natural ramparts. What more does an army need?" Osi mused.

"Sleep," said Ketoh.

"Post sentries," Osi ordered.

Ketoh stationed men in front of the mouth, inside it, and on the rim above. Busah arranged soldiers in ordered lines across the chamber's floor. As bedrolls unfurled on either side of the gurgling stream, Bera and Ammon led the children to a protected balcony high up the cavern wall. Then he returned to his men.

"What do you think you're doing?" asked Ketoh, as Osi untied the straps of his bedroll.

"What does it look like? I'm bedding down."

"Not here, surely."

"Of course I'm sleeping here. Just like always."

"You can't. You're an Officer of the Realm. You can't bed down with your men."

"That's crazy. I'll do as I please."

Ketoh said nothing but, rather, pointed up to a tiny balcony beneath the larger one where the children slept. *Bera*. In the flickering torchlight, her diaphanous gown shimmered like the robes of an angel floating in shadows. Osi thought she glanced his way, but in the darkness he couldn't be sure.

Ever the conspirator, Ketoh whispered mischievously, "Now if I were you and an Officer of the Realm, that's where I'd sleep tonight."

"Perhaps you're right," Osi growled. "Bunking with common soldiers is beneath the dignity of an Officer of the Realm. I'll do as I please." With mock resignation, he ascended the ramp.

Stifling a laugh, Ketoh ambled to his own bed.

When Osi reached the balcony, he stared dreamily at last into those lovely eyes. He dropped his bedroll on the floor across from hers. "I'm here…if you need me," he said.

"And I for you," she said, moving ever so slowly until their bodies touched. Her arms reached out and drew him near. Her head tilted upward as Osi bent down. Their lips met fleetingly. Their embrace tightened. Her breath warmed the nape of his neck. His cheek touched hers. Her body melded to his, soft breasts against firm chest, warm thighs against hard muscle, each contour met. Every movement echoed from body to body as they became one. "Lie with me. Hold me. Love me," she said. She drew away just far enough to take his hand in hers. Then she retrieved his bedroll and led the way to hers. Together the thick furs made a luxurious soft mat. She lay down and pulled him to her.

"I'm here to protect, not to defile," Osi said nobly, reluctantly. "I hold a sacred trust, a command from our dead King. You also have your vows— sacred to all as well—against pain of death."

"We are here together. We find comfort in each other. Surely, we can find pleasure as well without violating your trust or my vows."

"May I kiss you?" he asked awkwardly, as if the answer weren't already known.

"You may." She whispered teasingly as she threw her arms around his neck and pulled his face again to hers. Their lips brushed, touched, pressed. Gently at first, then roughly as if they sought to devour each other's very souls. She laid her head back exposing the luscious contours of her neck. His lips moved downward. He pulled back to stare at her face again. His hand parted her gown from neck to thighs. Torchlight flickered sensuously on golden flesh, glimmering like the moonlight he'd seen reflected from the Great River when he first viewed it at Ollo-detu. He spread her gown farther. His gaze held fast on the perfect mounds of her bare breasts. Kiss after kiss, he descended from neck to breast to the enchanted triangle between her thighs. Bera quivered to his touch. Together at last, they found pleasure as she had promised.

* * *

Bera awoke when morning's first sunlight filtered down from the narrow slit above. Osi, already dressed and armed, smiled grandly. "Daylight, you see, my love. Did I forget to tell you? There is a way out." Then he added, "A blessing and curse, however."

"What do you mean, Osi. Are we trapped beneath the rebels. Can we defend ourselves?"

"I...I can't honestly say."

"But this place appears impregnable."

"And it is . . . almost. We call it a cave, but it's really a gorge. And that's the problem. The rebels would never be so foolish as to attack us directly through its maw. They'll block every portal and starve us out. We can last for a few days and no more. In retreat, our only hope would be to hike the full length of Death's Shadow . . . with not enough food to last one tenth of the way. That is, unless we find a means to attack these cursed rebels."

"Attack them? They have us surrounded . . . and outnumbered three to one."

"Sooner or later we must attack. Else we are doomed."

A runner arrived with the disturbing but expected news that the Black Ensign lay at anchor in the harbor of Gubal. Pair by pair, rebel ships were rapidly assuming positions in the narrow bay.

Wearing naught but a loincloth, Osi washed in the cave's chilly stream. He squinted into the shaft of light beaming down from the cave's split roof and followed it down to see Ketoh's silhouette blocking the entrance.

"Osi, look!" Ketoh yelled, "Soldiers of Gubal! Survivors of the massacre. And, what's more, they've ventured out for a morning hunt." A hundred men or more trudged into the Gullet, each with a carcass, or at least a haunch, of game slung over his shoulder: antelope, goat, mulia ibex. A cheer rang out. Fresh provisions for the siege, though even so much wouldn't last long with so many to feed. Ketoh led his guests to Osi. Each hunter proudly deposited his prize in the stream's cold water, saluted Osi, and took his place in formation behind their remaining officers.

Finally, Osi would get his answer. "Who attacked Gubal?"

"Westerners," one officer replied. "Our men fought bravely, but many died. We survivors rallied to protect the villagers who fled the city and now hide above the first Terrace. Four hundred have rallied at Koro-nata. We came back to see if Gubal is safe to return. We didn't expect to find anyone in Death's Shadow."

"We didn't expect to find such carnage. Our leader, Osi, brought us here to make our defense," Ketoh said.

"Osi! Did you say Osi?" another officer asked excitedly. "There is much talk at Koro-reni of a boy leader named Osi. Are you this man?"

At that moment, Jumar hailed Osi, who turned away instinctively, unintentionally exposing the lattice of scars that crisscrossed his back. The officer fell to his knees when he saw it, as did all the other men of Gubal. "You are the Dirk Slayer! You are Osi the boy leader who took 30 lashes for his men. You defied the tyrant Arrak. We will fight to the death for you."

"Rise," said Osi. "I am but a man. There is no need to bow before me...of all people. But your swords and strong arms are sorely needed. The Black Ensign awaits in Gubal. Send one man to Koro-nata. Summon your people to Death's Shadow."

* * *

Jumar ran to Osi's side while the lookouts under his command rushed in from the cave's mouth, and others called down from above. "The entire fleet is now in the harbor. They've boarded the *Ruby*. The attack force has landed. They've passed Koro-reni," he said. "A thousand men or more. They will strike within four hands."

"All men who stand with me," shouted Osi, "it's time to prove your mettle. Our time has come to serve the Realm." He stared solemnly into their faces. "Fifty volunteers . . ." He demanded, "Fifty men willing to fight and die."

"We are all willing to fight and die!" shouted one man. "Here, here!" resounded through the chamber.

"It is one thing to be willing and another to die. Who among you is ready to sacrifice himself, knowing he *will* die," Osi asked. "Before you volunteer, know that this is a mission like no other you have been asked to undertake. These rebels are not fools. They won't enter Death's Shadow to be slaughtered one by one. They will lay siege. They will hold us here until we perish. Our only hope is to draw them close. Your mission is to take up positions at the base of the cliffs on either side of Death's Shadow. This is a death watch. You will fight a losing battle to lure the enemy close to the cliff face. Few if any will survive." He paused to let the truth sink in. "Now, who will volunteer?" A hush fell over the crowd.

"We will!" shouted the men of Gubal in unison.

Soon every man in the Gullet joined the cry.

"And I will lead them!" shouted Ketoh.

No. Not Ketoh. Not Ketoh!

"No I will lead!" shouted Jumar.

Not Jumar.

"Draw lots," he ordered. And thus it was decided. Osi's heart sank as Ketoh "won" the draw. Fifty chosen volunteers stepped forward to receive orders and assemble at the cave's mouth. Ketoh led as they filed into daylight. *Come back, Ketoh, come back if you can.* Then Osi, tears secretly welling in his eyes, scanned the ledge that had intrigued him for so long. *Perhaps there is a way,* he thought.

The rebel army attacked at high noon. Ketoh's troops fought valiantly but, inevitably, were overwhelmed. One by one positions were lost as first arrows, then swords, met their marks. Ketoh, surrounded by a swarm of rebels, was the last man standing. The volunteers had made good on their pledge.

Plan or no plan, I can't let Ketoh die. He rushed headlong from Death's Shadow and fought his way to Ketoh's side. The two men carved a swath of death through the ranks of the enemy and back to the mouth of the Gullet. Fellow cadets fortified the entrance as the two bolted inside. *Mission achieved,* Osi thought, *we've drawn them close, alright.* Again he eyed the ledge. This time he issued orders, and scores of men scrambled up the ledge and through the slit.

An enemy force, a thousand strong, assembled around the opening, while their officers surveyed the battlefield. "Gather the dead. Lay them out for the sea," shouted the rebel commander.

"Strike!" yelled Osi on the cliff above. Two hundred archers sprang from hiding, and arrows rained down. By the hundreds the enemy fell while not one man was lost above. Osi led the way as sixty infantrymen scaled down the walls while the archers maintained their barrage. Osi and Jumar met the enemy in hand-to-hand combat. Soon Jumar was penned down directly in front of the cave's mouth.

"Stop!" yelled Bera as young Ammon charged from the cave. He grabbed a fallen sword and ran toward Jumar. Jumar broke free, but the boy was not so lucky. One rebel solder grabbed him from behind and held his head back while another drew his dagger to decapitate Ammon. In a flash, Osi picked up a dead man's spear and skewered both men with a single throw. Ammon broke free and calmly returned to an anxious Bera.

Next, Ketoh led a detachment downhill to flank the enemy and block escape from the narrow valley. In half a hand the rebel army was cut off from the sea. By dusk not one rebel still stood.

All that remained between Osi and victory was the Black Ensign's fleet in the bay. "A trifle," he joked, "with men like these at my side."

* * *

When the Battle of Death's Shadow ended, Osi walked solemnly to Bera and took her in his arms. He kissed her cheek and then her lips. Adoringly they stared into each other's eyes. "Mark the coming battle well, my love," he said. "For it will be my last."

"No. That can't be."

"I came to the Valley Sea to fulfill my destiny foretold by Toth, and I failed miserably. I failed myself. I failed you. Most of all, I failed our King. I am finished with war and so-called glory."

"Please wait, Osi. Decide later. Let this moment pass."

"First, I must defeat the fleet in the harbor. When that is done, I will return to Egia."

"If you have spoken, then so it must be."

"I have spoken."

Osi detected an unexpected smile at the corner of Bera's lips. *What can this mean*, he pondered. *What does she know, this woman who is so wise, so bold, and always one step beyond me?*

Chronicle 28. Long Live the King

At sunset, Osi stood atop the ruined stockade of Koro-reni. He surveyed the throng below. Bera, Ammon, and all the children had survived. Two hundred fifty of his men had survived. Four hundred villagers had returned safely to Gubal from above the First Terrace.

"We fought a great battle. We defeated an evil menace. The Battle of Death's Shadow is won." The crowd roared with joy and adulation. "But evil remains. Those rebel ships," and he pointed toward the bay, "are heavily armed and ably defended. Many men died at Death's Shadow. Many more will die tonight unless you choose to help. It is time for the people of Gubal to honor with your service the memory of all who died today. My officers will guide you."

As darkness fell and a crescent moon rose, Osi discerned the dark silhouettes of scores of vessels. From the hustle and bustle onboard, it was evident the rebels were preparing to attack at first light. Osi and Bera stood ready as, one by one, the citizens of Gubal arrived at the harbor. Without a sound, each man, woman, and youth laid sticks: one, two, or many according to his ability. As the pile grew, Osi's troops and villagers alike slipped into the water with hardly a ripple. Each one swam in darkness carrying only a single stick. Again and again they returned to the great stone dock. One by one the sticks disappeared until, late in the night, only a small bier remained.

Well before dawn, Ketoh lit the bier. *Those bastards will see it from their boats*, he thought, *but they won't have a clue what it's for.* And he chuckled.

When the bonfire glowed, each man and woman placed the tip of an arm-long stick in its coals. As soon as those, too, were glowing, each naked swimmer took one and wrapped its end in a thick ball of dry linen, tied tight with sinew, so air-starved that it couldn't flame. Each slipped into the water, black torch in hand. Near dawn, the wind picked up, Osi ordered the bonfire stoked to an inferno. On this signal, the swimmers struck, each one touching his torch to the dry wood placed earlier and stripping away its damper. Fires flashed ship by ship. Bright flames illuminated first the rudder, then the whipstaff, then the entire stern of every vessel. Rebels screamed as the flames grew higher. Soon, all the swimmers returned to the dock. By daybreak, not a ship stood above the water line, and any rebels who made it to shore were cut down by Osi's fighters or the waiting residents of Gubal.

Only the *Ruby* was spared, and she was easy enough to retake with the overwhelming numbers now in Osi's favor.

* * *

At dusk, the *Ruby* slipped into Berenicia's welcome harbor. On the way south, they had searched the shores of Redsilver Point without spotting any sign of Setra. *Sad,* Osi thought. *Was I wrong to leave him there? No, I had no other choice.*

Back in port at last, the *Ruby's* passengers debarked into throngs of celebrants, chanting praises and shouting for joy. Hoisting Osi, Ketoh, Bera, Ammon, and other favorites on their shoulders, the crowd whisked them through the streets. By the time they reached the new pyramid, practically the entire populace had joined in the melee. Among them stood Setra.

"How did you get here?" Osi yelled at the top of his voice.

"It's all in the distance between defeat and death," Setra said enigmatically. Osi tried to ask what he meant, but the crowd closed in around him.

"Osi! Osi! Osi! Be our king!" the people shouted as Osi, Bera, Ammon, and the children ascended the pyramid and stepped out on its portico. Berenicia's aging Agent climbed up to join them, so slowly in fact that Osi was fairly certain he stalled for dramatic effect. Eventually, the Agent held his hands aloft in a plea for silence. Soon the din subsided, and he was able to speak.

"Today the People of the Living Sun have spoken!" he shouted.

No, thought Osi. *Not this. He didn't ask, nor did he warn me. I can't accept. This was truly my last battle, my last war. I failed my destiny. I must return to Egia in shame.*

The Agent moved toward them. Osi pulled back. In his mind a thousand words flashed, but he was unable to say the ones that mattered: *Not me. Not me.*

"But we have no need of a new king!" the Agent shouted in exaltation. "Rahn Mennon lives!" The throng stood in stunned silence. "He was taken from the Royal Barge before it sailed. He has survived his wounds and now stands safely on the Sacred Pyramid." The crowd cheered wildly.

Bera burst into joyous laughter. "You didn't' fail, Osi. Rahn Mennon lives. Your destiny has been fulfilled! And well it may be again and again."

CHAPTER 13

Search Log 25: Revival

"T-E-R-M-I-N-A-T-E-D."

Jared gawked at the message. *What the hell?* The dreaded ax had fallen alright, bigger and harder than expected and double-bladed like a Middle Age pike. Undeterred, he changed course and tried a manned gate, hoping the guards had not yet received the message from Security.

Walk on by like a man on a mission, he thought. *Nod in a friendly way, but don't hesitate for a second.* He clinched his teeth and charged through with a slug of fellow workers.

"Evenin', Junior."

He smiled. "Evenin', Tom. Have a good afternoon. Weather should be nice."

"Yep. Should be."

* * *

Bright and early Monday morning, Jared called Personnel. Passed at first office to office, he eventually reached a conscientious bureaucrat honestly trying to do his job right. Minutes later an appointment was scheduled with Associate Director Walt Carlos who knew him well and, better yet, admired his work. A visitor's badge was ready when he got to the Lab.

"Walt, this just isn't right!" Jared protested.

"Didn't come from here," said Carlos. "Much higher. Seems there's a Congressman who complains that government is spending too many taxpayer dollars on airheads and ivy leaguers. Seems he's put you in the airhead category. Unfortunately, he's on the Appropriations Committee....and with the Lab contract coming up for review...."

"So the Lab folded."

"You might say so....I surely would."

"But I just need some time..."

"It's out of my hands."

"Isn't there something...."

"You didn't hear it from me, but firings like this are rare. Legal will carry the flag as far as they can, but they'll be nervous as a cat on a hot reactor dome. You can't change the decision, but you can force them to stick by the rules. If time is really what you want, insist on 60 days' notice. That's MVL's standard when legal misconduct is not alleged."

By the end of the day, his termination was postponed. Now, with two months to play, maybe he could get it reversed.

Search Log 26: The Geographers

A big brass plaque said, "BEER—IT'S NOT JUST FOR BREAKFAST ANYMORE!" The place was Brit's in Minneapolis. The five men around the table were old friends relaxing after an intense day at the annual meeting of the Association of American Geographers. Jared anchored one end, Walde Peplies the other. On one side sat Tom McCord, on the other Andreas Guttmann, famous for his work on global environmental hazards, and Dan Hinton, equally famous for his scientific advancements of remote sensing and photogrammetry. John Courage, a mug of John Courage that is, sat in front of each man except Dan Hinton, a devout Mormon and teetotaler.

"Hey, Caisson, you still bugging geologists with that continental drift malarkey?" This was vintage Dan, blunt but not malicious.

"The Australia manuscript is published, finally, but something else has come up. Now, I'm working mostly on sea level rise," Jared said, without acknowledging Dan's good-natured jab.

"And anthropology," Walde added.

"What does sea level have to do with anthropology?" Andreas asked.

"Oh, the connection may be stronger than you think. Sea level has risen about 400 feet since the Ice Ages. That's only 18,000 years." Jared said. "The territory exposed then but later inundated would have been the most favorable zone for human occupance during the Ice Ages."

"I assume you're talking Tropics," Andreas said, "since much of the high latitude portion would have been covered by glaciers or, in any case, would have been too cold."

"Yes, precisely. I suspect the Tropics were a haven for evolutionary advancement during most of the time humans were becoming truly human."

Andreas contemplated for a moment. "That would make sense. We are, after all, basically tropical animals. Otherwise, we'd be drinking our beers out there instead of in here." He pointed outside where the air was clear and cold, no more than 30° F.

"So what are you saying, Caisson? Do you think archaeologists may find ruins of an advanced civilization out there someday?" Dan and Andreas were the only ones at the table not informed of the theory. So far, Jared had handled the effort on a "need-to-know" basis. He hadn't needed their help yet, so he hadn't brought them into his confidence.

"Well, maybe."

"Oh, come on, Jerry. You can trust these guys," Walde insisted.

"Okay. Yes, I think there may have been settlements 10,000 years ago that were more advanced than anything we know about until, say, 1800. And I think I know where one or two sites may be."

"Jeez, Caisson! What are you saying? Are you sitting here, drinking John Courage, and calmly telling us you've made the greatest archaeological discovery the world has ever known? *Oh,* if you're right, I guess we can't say it that way anymore. . . the greatest archaeological discovery in 10,000 years."

"Yep."

" 'Yep?' Is that all you can say, 'Yep?' "

"Yep."

"Christ! Where is it? And why aren't you out there. . .in the field. . .excavating?"

"It's in the Red Sea. Tom can tell you why I'm not there."

Tom sloshed his mug and looked toward Andreas. "This guy has picked the worst spot on earth. There are no travel posters for this place. It's practically quarantined!"

"Because someone knows what's there?"

"I doubt that. It's just a coincidence, but there are serious security concerns because of its strategic location. Egyptian territory, next door to Sudan."

"I see what you mean. They haven't been the best of neighbors for a while."

"So how did you find this place?"

"It's a long story. I started with the fundamental question, 'How did we humans get to be so smart?' " Jared replied. "Think about it. Standard theory says we somehow evolved to the exalted intellectual state of modern humans at a time when we did nothing more than hunt and fish and gather. Why would we develop mental skills so far beyond what we actually needed? Ever since I was a kid, I suspected there had to be something more to account for it, especially the final organization of the brain in the last 100,000 years."

"Wait a minute! Did you say you thought this up when you were a kid?" Dan said.

"I asked the question back then, but I didn't find an answer until last year. Think about it. Hunting. Fishing. Gathering. That's what animals do. Why would we develop a brain capable of speech, great artistry, and advanced science if all we did was hunt, fish, and gather. That doesn't accord with my understanding of the normal process of evolution." Jared continued with hardly a pause. "Natural selection favors characteristics that fulfill a need. To me, even as a child, that suggests the archaeological record may be missing a civilized stage in which there *was* a demand for art and music and technology. . . if not high technology, then at least some sort of mechanical know-how."

Andreas reacted immediately. "An earlier source civilization could explain why we had such incredibly high peaks of culture in Greece and Rome before everything collapsed into the Dark Ages."

"Yes. There's no reason to believe culture always progresses upward. In fact, there is a continuing theme in ancient folklore suggesting an earlier decline of civilization, a sort of cultural entropy, that preceded the earliest known civilizations. There could have been many rises and falls, and the latest culture wouldn't necessarily be the greatest. In fact, if circumstances do push evolution as natural selection implies, then a very high culture would have occurred quite early in human development *before* the brain changed, not after. . . at least 50,000 to 100,000 years ago. That's much earlier than the one we think we've found in the Red Sea, and its memory could have been lost to them just as their memory is lost to us."

"We?"

"My brother Rick is up to his elbows in it with me."

"So human evolution and sea level rise set you two off! Get to the point, guy. How did you find this place in the Red Sea?"

"Well, when I mentioned my idea to Rick, he reasoned that sea level rise might account for step pyramids around the . . ."

"Pyramids! You've got to be kidding. How many families sit around the dinner table talking about human intelligence, sea level, and pyramids? And actually make a connection?" Andreas asked.

"Can't help it! That's my story, and I'm sticking to it. Anyway, I hadn't thought of anything more advanced than farms and villages until Rick said 'pyramids.' Then I started thinking maybe there had been some substantial stone construction, and maybe it was still there. I searched all the shallow tropical seas off Europe and Asia and found some very interesting features on bathymetric charts."

"Searched? You mean you eyeballed that many charts?"

"Yep."

"There's that word again."

"Yep."

"But wait a minute," Dan said. "If there are big old pyramids on the ocean floor, wouldn't somebody have found them by now?"

"Maybe they have and just didn't recognize what they were seeing."

"What do you mean? Pyramids are pretty distinctive."

"Hydrographic charts show coral reefs all over the tropics, and coral will *only* grow on a solid substrate." A wave of recognition coursed around the table.

"So you think they're coated with corals? That makes sense. But corals appear everywhere. How can you sort out the ones that contain pyramids?" Dan asked.

"Patch corals are the most likely," Jared said "They grow on sandy bottom, and they only occur in a few well-defined places. And, some of those locations appear interesting indeed."

"Alright, so you found this interesting sea bottom. What other evidence do you have? What makes those locations so interesting?"

Jared started to answer but glanced toward the door just as a striking young fellow entered. His wave caught the newcomer's eye. Dan also flashed a smile of recognition and beckoned him to the table.

"Hi, Matt!" Dan said. "Good to see you."

Jared turned to the group. "Tom, Andreas, this is my son, Matt. He's one of Dan's students at *the* USC. Matt, meet Andreas Guttmann. . ."

"It's a pleasure to meet you. I'm familiar with your work."

". . . and Tom McCord."

"Dad told me about your adventures in Czechoslovakia. Both of you were on that trip, weren't you?"

"Yes, but we won't talk about it. Suffice it to say the country broke apart immediately after we left."

"Walde, you remember Matt, I'm sure." Jared continued.

"Yes, but you've grown up. You couldn't have been more than 12 or 13 years old."

"You're forgetting our fieldwork in the Adirondacks. He was in college then."

"Oh, yes. How could I forget! You two were mostly way out in the wilderness on your own, but we did camp together for a couple of nights at South Lake."

"Ah, the Powderpuff Mountains!" Matt laughed and looked toward his dad.

"Must be a story there," Tom said.

"Well," Walde answered, "Jerry and I were studying acid lakes. We had gone up there over and over, and Jerry had survived some real adventures. It's officially a Wilderness Area, so backpacking is the only way to reach the most remote lakes. It seems he had been going home each time and telling his family how rugged the Adirondacks are. Finally, Jerry invited Matt along on one of the trips. Matt wanted to make everyone think his dad had been exaggerating, so ever since he's called them the Powderpuff Mountains."

"Can you imagine? We're hiking over a pass, four feet of snow on the ground, and dad stops and changes socks. He puts on gaiters, for Christ's sake. I didn't even own gaiters. What a wuss!"

Jared conspicuously changed the subject. "Not to change the subject, but I was just telling Dan and Andreas about my latest quest. They've agreed to vouch for every aspect of my argument. I've decided to base my case on their renown alone, no evidence needed."

"Oh, sure! I know Dr. Hinton will buy into that scheme."

"Matt, I regret to inform you that your father is a certified loony," Dan said with a grin.

"Actually, the idea sounds pretty reasonable so far. A plausible hypothesis, I mean," Andreas interjected. "But I am unclear on one point. I'm under the impression that sea level change comes ever so gradually over long periods of time. Are you suggesting a slow inundation or a catastrophic deluge of Biblical proportions?"

"Matt, tell them what you found," Jared urged.

Matt slipped into the empty chair. "I did my Master's degree in remote sensing and GIS, but my Doctoral dissertation is on climate modeling. I'm still in Geography, but I'm working a lot with the Geology Department and Computer Sciences Department, applying neural networks to ice core data from Polar regions. Records going back about 400,000 years reveal a distinct difference between Arctic and Antarctic cores. The impression of gradual change that you mentioned . . ." he nodded toward Andreas ". . . comes mainly from Antarctic cores that were the basis of most of the science until very recently. The problem with Antarctic cores is that snowfall there was light, and glaciers have been highly compacted. We're lucky to distinguish an individual millennium much less a decade or century."

"You've been holding back on me, man," Dan grumbled. "I knew what you were doing, but I didn't realize it had any connection to your crazy Dad." Still it was obvious he took pride in his student's work.

"Purely coincidental," Matt replied. "I was deep into this before I myself knew it related to Dad's work."

"So even if there were rapid shifts, we wouldn't know it from the Antarctic record," Andreas summarized.

"Exactly. But recently someone thought to take cores in Greenland where snowfall was heavier and compaction less severe. There, we can reliably distinguish a single year's snowfall. The result has been a dramatic turnaround in our interpretation of the rate of change. There definitely were some catastrophic changes in snowfall over very short time periods."

"So the rest of the story depends on how much *snowfall* reveals about *climate* in general?"

"Yes, to some extent, but I haven't limited my scope to snowfall. We also have chemical analyses of the ice itself, and that offers several indicators from which we can infer temperature, precipitation, and other climate measures. I picture a highly variable climate that can play some pretty nasty tricks practically overnight."

"Still, wouldn't it take quite some time for glaciers to melt, even if the air got warmer?"

"Melting, yes. But scientists now say there is a different mechanism that could raise sea level instantly. A major ice sheet collapsed about 20,000 years ago, filling the North Atlantic with icebergs, and it could happen again today. Coastal cities worldwide would be devastated."

"That's scary."

"The West Antarctic Ice Sheet is a prime candidate," Matt said. "Think of it as a gigantic basin filled with ice, always creeping to the sea. Today, its bulk is poised on solid ground. Beneath the ice, however, is at least one active volcano, maybe more. Meltwater constantly lubricates the base and helps dissipate the ice. If the sheet itself were to retreat upslope from those heat sources, the ice might build for a while, then catastrophically release into the Ross Sea. It would immediately add its own displacement to the volume of water and cause the World Ocean to rise. . . about 20 feet. . .instantaneously."

"Hey, what's this?" Andreas was staring toward the entrance with a bewildered look on his face.

"Oh, that's Rick. Hey, Rick, come on over. Pull up a chair."

Rick wedged in between Matt and Tom. "Hello, hello. I'm Jerry's brother, Rick."

"As if we couldn't guess. You guys look exactly alike." Andreas and Tom had never met Rick. Walde and Dan had known him for years.

"I didn't realize Jerry had a brother who was a geographer. So it's a real family business with you guys?" Andreas said.

"Well, sort of, but I haven't been to an AAG meeting in years. I'm not really here for the meeting this time either. I have business in St. Paul. Jerry mentioned that he would be here, so I moved the schedule just a bit, and here I am. After-hours only, though."

"Well, that's the best part a conference anyway. We were just rewriting the history of the world," Dan quipped. "Jerry tells us you came up with the idea of pyramids in the ocean. Pretty innovative! I thought you executive types were supposed to be conservative thinkers."

Jared could see the concern on Rick's face. "It's alright. You can trust these guys."

"Did you get them to sign a non-disclosure agreement?" Rick joked, referring to a common practice in his commercial high-tech field.

"Better! A 'non-derision' agreement."

"I didn't agree to that!" several voices protested in unison. They laughed, attracting stares from nearby tables.

Dan was anxious to resume. "What made you think of pyramids?"

"It just makes sense. Sea level threatens your hometown; build a platform. Sea covers platform; build a higher platform on top of the first. Sea covers second platform; build a third. Keep it up, every platform higher and smaller than the one beneath, and eventually you'll have a step pyramid, whether you wanted one or not. There are pyramids all around the tropical world, precisely where the bulk of Ice Age culture should have been. In fact, the Tropics plus a few degrees north and south are known as the 'Pyramid Belt.'"

"Also, as I reminded Jared, the Egyptian term for pyramid doesn't mean 'tomb,' it means a 'place of ascension,' precisely where one would go to escape a flood," Walde said in his firm, soft voice. "I used to assume the term referred to spiritual ascension into the heavens, but 'the Caisson heresy' has made me wonder if it's quite earthly. A place to ascend above rising water simply to keep oneself dry or, perhaps, to enter a boat moored there."

"Rick's been looking into the cultural aspects more than I have." Jared motioned toward his brother, "Tell 'em what you found."

"Oh, well, the other telltale sign is flood myths. Virtually every culture in the world has its own flood myth. They sound preposterous if viewed as floods that go high above the landmasses we see today, but they make a lot of sense if viewed as sea level rise inundating large segments of the old coast. We're assuming, of course, that there was some exaggeration in the retelling, largely because later storytellers didn't understand sea level rise any better than we ourselves did until just a few years ago."

"So the Biblical flood may be literally true but somewhat misinterpreted?" said the devout Mormon.

"We think so," Jared replied. "Try this little experiment. Go to your Bible and pick up any random verse that tells about the flood. Then read it again with sea level rise in mind."

"Oh, waiter, may I have a Bible please?" Matt said facetiously as an aproned young man zoomed past.

Matt looked as shocked as the others when the waiter reached behind the bar and pulled out a King James Version in tattered leather. The circular track of a beer mug stained its cover.

"I didn't expect you to actually have one." Matt mumbled, as he unceremoniously passed the book to Dan.

"We're not heathens, you know, just because we serve demon alcohol," the waiter joked as he headed for a new round of drinks.

"Thanks," Matt called to him.

Dan turned immediately to the concordance, picked a reference, and paged to the selected chapter and verse, "Exodus 15, Verse 4."

"Hey," Jared said, "how come you know how to use the concordance? I never could use that thing myself, and I certainly don't know my way around the Book of Mormon."

"We're not heathens, you know, just because we have a book of our own," Dan said, with his infectious grin. "Okay, now calm down and listen. Here's what the verse says. 'Pharaoh's chariots and his host hath he cast into the sea: his chosen captains also are drowned in the Red Sea.' I guess it could be taken either way. Oh, here's a better one farther up the page '. . . . and the Lord overthrew the Egyptians in the midst of the sea. And the waters returned, and covered the chariots, and the horsemen and all the host of Pharaoh that came into the sea after them; there remained not so much as one of them.' Sounds like a rescue attempt, I suppose."

"Wait a minute, Hotshot! That's not the flood, that's Moses crossing the Rubicon," Jared complained with satisfaction.

"Oh! Hold it! Here's one . . . Genesis 7, Verses 18, 19, and 20. 'And the waters prevailed, and were increased greatly upon the earth; and the ark went upon the face of the waters. And the waters prevailed exceedingly upon the earth; and all the high hills, that were under the whole heaven, were covered. Fifteen cubits upward did the waters prevail; and the mountains were covered.' Fifteen cubits! How long is a cubit. Let's see; weren't the dimensions of the ark prescribed in cubits. Yes, here. The boat itself was only 30 cubits high! Does this mean the water only rose half the height of an ark?"

"Andreas mentioned 'Biblical proportions' a while ago. Well, I checked after reading those verses last week. A cubit is about 18 inches, depending on the source, never more than 21 inches," Rick replied. "It comes to somewhere between 22 feet, 6 inches and 26 feet, 3 inches. *That*, my friend, is the 'Biblical proportion' of Noah's Flood."

"So there's a contradiction! Twenty-six feet of rise couldn't possibly cover mountains!" Walde noted.

"Yes, but notice that the first mention is 'high hills,' then later 'mountains.' 'High hills,' meaning the higher ground on low islands and coastal plains, might square with the 15-cubit figure."

"Coincidentally, it's also close to the worst case scenario for sea level rise over the next century of global warming," Matt said.

"I suspect it depicts one of the last major inundations at the end of the Ice Ages," Jared continued. "Noah was probably a real person who lived on an island or low coastal plain, probably where the Persian Gulf is today. A rise of 15 cubits probably covered most of the 'high hills' in his vicinity and forced him to move. He may have sailed northward toward Mt. Ararat, but he would have landed approximately on the southern coast of Iraq. Later, word got around that other low places had experienced the same problem, so everyone understood it was a worldwide event, but they didn't truly mean it had covered the whole earth vertically. That exaggeration probably came with retelling, and someone later mentioned covering mountains without realizing his error."

"I see what you mean. It's possible, I guess," Andreas said. "Maybe I better rethink the matter of global hazards from the oceans. I haven't considered anything that dramatic or that fast."

"Atlantis! Could sea level rise explain Atlantis?" Walde asked. Jared winced. *Don't go there, Walde!*

Jared looked around. *Kindred intellectual spirits,* he thought, *maybe I can hazard an answer.* "I won't go into details," he said, warming to the receptiveness of fellow geographers, "and please don't quote me on any of this Atlantis stuff. It's a lot like the Biblical account we just read. You can take it either way. The whole thing depends on the relativity of land and water. Everyone's taken Plato's account to mean that the continent sank, but it could just as easily be that sea level rose. In fact, a handful of writers *have* suggested the possibility. As to the question of whether such an advanced civilization actually existed, I can only say that Plato reports it in convincingly realistic terms."

"I thought he described earthquakes, too." Walde knew the story better than he'd let on.

"You're right, but I wouldn't rule out earthquakes happening in conjunction with sudden inundation. The added weight of water certainly could cause tremors. That's what eustatic pressure is all about—land being pushed down by the weight of water. Plato also mentions fires, and they too are quite common during earthquakes and floods."

"Sure, in San Francisco or LA with modern utilities pumping gas and electric sparks everywhere," Tom noted, "but would that have happened in ancient times?"

"There could be other causes," Jared said. "Eustatic pressure might cause geologic layers to rupture, and natural gas deposits might release and explode."

"Be careful, Dad. You're stretching," Matt cautioned.

"Well, I'm not claiming any of this...just exploring possibilities. Natural gas explosions *have* been observed in association with earthquakes."

"Wait a minute! "Come to think of it, Dad, there's another possibility that bears serious consideration. Methyl hydrates. Explosive gases that crystallize under tremendous pressure on the ocean floor. Really just methane in solid form. Even under thousands of feet of seawater, the stuff is so easily ignited that it's a deadly hazard for deep-ocean oil drilling. Release that pressure, and it turns back to a gas and floats to the surface. I can imagine a cloud of methyl hydrate floating balloon-like through the atmosphere. If it stays concentrated, especially over land, any sort of spark could set it off. That's a long shot with rising or stable sea level, but surely it could happen in spades when sea level falls and pressures drop across vast areas of sea floor."

"So, all this tells me we shouldn't dismiss the Atlantis story just because the topic has fallen into bad hands. It's an account written by one of the most respected scholars in history, and Plato carefully reported his source. He got the story from a pupil named Critias who got the story from his grandfather, also named Critias, who heard it from the Greek statesman Solon, who heard it from an Egyptian Priest in the city of Sais on the Nile Delta. Furthermore, Sais, itself, was not just any old ascetic monastery. It was an Egyptian center of learning, the most scholarly of its day, and its specialty was ancient languages. The priest is quoted in no uncertain terms as saying that, when Solon studied in Sais, its vaults still held records of Greek and Egyptian encounters with Atlantis' invading forces."

"Regardless, Atlantis *has* become the province of kooks. If you identify with it, you'll be tainted too. You'll have tabloidites on your doorstep quicker than you can say 'Global Inquirer.' " Tom said.

Tell me about it, thought Jared.

"What's even worse," Walde said facetiously, "is that we might be identified with you."

If you only knew, Jared reflected. "I understand. But look at what makes this stuff so kooky. It isn't Plato's account that causes trouble. It's silly garbage the fanatics throw in for good measure, stuff like harmonic levitation and psychic prediction and the Bermuda Triangle. Plato didn't say any of that. Some Atlantis books show legitimate evidence of inundated settlements in the Caribbean and Mediterranean Seas. If the authors would leave it at that and consider sea level rise as a possible cause, they might get somewhere. But that explanation only pops up in a couple of references, like Rachel Carson's 1950 book, *The Silent Spring,* and *The Mayan Prophecies* by Gilbert and Cotterell."

Rick leaned forward. "He's right. Geologists have solid evidence of sea level rise but little interest in who lived there. Conversely, Atlantis advocates have circumstantial evidence but terrible methods and theory. And the anthropologists and archaeologists, who could put it together, won't touch it with a ten foot pole for fear of getting in bed with kooks. I found a book that shows clear, convincing photographs of walls and building foundations underwater off Bimini...near the Bahamas. But the garbage that goes along with it scares off legitimate scientists. Without serious investigations, no one knows what to believe."

"Is that where you think Atlantis may have been? The Bahamas?"

"We're not sure. Plato's description fits the Great Bahama Bank in some respects but not in others. For example, he said Atlantis was a flat plain surrounded by precipitous slopes; that fits the Great Bahama Bank perfectly. At 17,500 BP, cliffs about 340 feet high would have surrounded virtually the entire island. The dimensions he gave are a pretty good fit for the land that would have been exposed. But he also mentioned high mountains, and that doesn't fit the Bahamas at all. He said Atlantis was an island in the Atlantic beyond the Pillars of Heracles and that it was next to the 'opposite continent.' "

"Heracles? I thought it was Hercules," Tom said.

"Not to Plato. It's Heracles in Greek, Hercules in Latin. Either name normally means the Straits of Gibraltar, but some authors even question that."

"He also said it served as a way to other islands," Rick added. "That fits the islands of the Caribbean to a T. He also mentioned an incredibly deep 'circular ditch' and a system of canals for irrigation and navigation that would be impressive even today. The most spectacular feature was a massive cut to the center of the island that was used for shipping. He said it was manmade, but it sounds just like Tongue of the Ocean in the Great Bahama Bank. I don't know any other place where a shallow island is cut to the core by a trench as deep as Tongue of the Ocean, and it ends in a circular embayment. At that time it would have been the finest natural harbor on earth. Atlantis or not, we suspect some substantial settlements existed on Great Bahama Bank and on some of the nearby islands, based on the patch corals we've located there."

"By the way, Andreas, if you want to visualize a world-class global hazard, just read Plato's *Timaeus*. The encounter between Solon and the Priest of Sais is a marvelous story. It seems Solon, a Greek, wanted to entice his hosts to talk about antiquity by mentioning some of the earliest history of his own land. The Egyptian priest replied, 'Oh, Solon, Solon, you Hellenes are never anything but children, and there is not an old man among you . . .'" Walde recited from memory, "'. . . there is no old opinion handed down among you by ancient tradition, nor any science which is hoary with age. And I will tell you why. There have been, and will be again, many destructions of mankind arising out of many causes; the greatest have been brought about by the agents of fire and water.' He went on to say that when the earth is destroyed by fire, 'those who live upon the mountains and in dry and lofty places are more liable to destruction than those who dwell by rivers or on the seashore . . .' Then he said, 'When, on the other hand, the gods purge the earth with a deluge of water, the survivors in your country are herdsmen and shepherds who dwell on the mountains, but those who, like you, live in cities are carried by the rivers into the sea.' "

"If he is talking about Ice Age cycles of sea level rise, he must have had a mental grasp of the last 50,000 to 60,000 years or maybe even 120,000 years of earth history. Explicit knowledge must have been handed down for millennia through records and teaching and oral tradition, a sort of corporate memory, you might say. The human dimension of global catastrophe couldn't be stated more clearly or elegantly than that!" Rick said.

"Oh, but it was!" Walde continued. "Next, the ancient priest said, '. . . if there were any actions noble or great or in any other way remarkable, they have all been written down by us of old, and are preserved in our temples. Whereas just when you and other nations are beginning to be provided with letters and the other requisites of civilized life, after the usual interval, the stream from heaven, like a pestilence, comes pouring down, and leaves only those of you who are destitute of letters and education; and so you have to begin all over again like children, and know nothing of what happened in ancient times, either among us or among yourselves.' Now, isn't that precisely what we fear today? Aren't we afraid of losing our history?"

"Well, I wasn't before, but I am now!" Andreas said solemnly.

Search Log 27: Office of the Damned

Ed Field grinned smugly as he entered Jared's office.

"Are you sure you want to be spotted in the Office of the Damned?" Jared asked.

"What kind of friend would I be?" Ed said absentmindedly while he counted the X-marks on Jared's wall calendar. "Forty-eight days down, twelve to go."

"That's the size of it," Jared said with a sigh. "And this controversy just keeps on going and going. I thought it would be old hat by now. You couldn't keep a legitimate news story alive this long. Not even if the future of the world depended on it."

Ed plopped a glossy science news magazine on his desk. "LINK FOUND BETWEEN SEA LEVEL RISE AND HUMAN CULTURE."

"Are you kidding?" Jared exclaimed, and he read a few lines. "Somebody else figured it out . . . and got published in a highly respected outlet. Maybe this guy won't lose his job over it."

"That's not all. Look at the citation."

Jared read the fine print. "Me? He cited me as his source?"

"Well, not the source, but the inspiration. Seems this guy's daughter was at your "Atlantis" Colloquium. Seems she really got into your theory. Seems she was horrified by the way you were treated, called her dad, who is a science writer, and told him the whole shameful episode. He investigated and saw a promising story. He interviewed the leaders in the field, item by item, and wrote this article. What impressed him most was that every one of those specialists knew part of the story, but only you, the geographer, put it together."

"Where did you learn all this background?"

"See for yourself. There's a sidebar on page three."

"Outstanding," Jared crowed as he skimmed the account. "But, will anybody read it in the next 12 days?"

"Look at the date. This came out yesterday. Today it's in just about every newspaper. There's a major international symposium on global climate change coming up later this month in Baltimore. As soon as this news broke, the conference organizers played it for all it's worth. Nothing draws a crowd like controversy. Better get your bags packed. I'll bet you get invited to give the keynote as a last minute addition."

"I meant Dave Halberd and anybody else in a position to reverse my termination."

"I may have scattered a few copies around for a few chosen managers to see. It pays to know the right secretaries." He smiled broadly and turned to leave.

Suddenly, Associate Director Walt Carlos burst in, crossed directly to the wall and ripped the X-marked page off Jared's countdown calendar. Chuckling, he tossed it in Jared's gray, military surplus trashcan and walked out the door without a word.

Search Log 28: City of Caves

Jared's phone rang as he sorted through a huge stack of mail that had accumulated while he was in Minneapolis.

"Hey, Jer!" Hinton said, "what's the name of that city you want to visit in Egypt—the one by the bay that has all those corals?"

"Berenice."

"I thought so. Do you realize there are three Berenices? Not just one!"

"No, that wasn't mentioned in any of the sources I found," Jared responded.

"Check the January issue of *Earth Observation Magazine*. The second one of three is called 'Berenice Epidire.' It's south of the Bay of Assab, wherever that is."

"Epidire. Bay of Assab. Got it."

"The third one is Berenice Pancrisia, a major center for gold mining and smelting," Hinton said. "This article is about how it was rediscovered using satellite remote sensing. According to the author, ancient Egyptians called the region Wawat. Wawat was famous, but its location was lost for centuries. It's like a lot of stories about lost gold mines, but there was plenty of evidence to prove this one was real. The discoverers were looking for the region when they chanced upon the city itself, Berenice Pancrisia."

"I wonder if my Berenice is the oldest, since the other two have second names to distinguish them from the port city." Jared stroked his chin thoughtfully.

"Oh, yours has a second name too. It's called 'Berenice Trogloditica.' "

"Trogloditica? That's odd!" Jared exclaimed. "Troglodyte means 'cave dweller.' That must imply that the occupants lived in caves or, at least, that the place is characterized in some way by caves. Yet the only karst topography mentioned in any of my references is beneath the sea. Does that mean the name predates current sea level?"

"Can't be. This article says all three cities were built by King Ptolemy around 270 BC and named after his mother. I doubt she was a cave dweller," Hinton said.

"It's the 'Trogloditica' part that intrigues me. I wonder if 'Berenice' was added to a preexisting name, maybe something translated into Greek from an earlier language."

"Oh, I see what you mean, Jer. Could be. You think that may mean the city is very, very old?" Hinton asked.

"Older than dirt! Well, maybe! I've read there's karst on the sea floor but not above current sea level. If caves aren't conspicuous above water, then the name must come from a time when the sea was lower. A settlement at that depth would be at least 5,000 to 10,000 years old."

"So what's your plan?"

"To see the terrain around Foul Bay. Caves? No caves? We have to find out."

Search Log 29: The Red Island

It was 10:15 p.m. but Jared had to alert Rick to a new finding. Rick answered his phone sounding considerably more energetic than Jared felt after an unusually strenuous day.

"Listen, I had to attend a symposium in Knoxville today. At lunch, I broke away and ran over to the UT Map Library," Jared commenced.

Rick interrupted, "I stopped by a few months ago, spent almost a whole day. They don't have any hydrographic charts. Did you find something else of interest?"

"They didn't have any charts when I checked before either, but now they have almost a full set of DMA's latest edition."

"Did you learn anything?" Rick asked.

"Surely did! Two things! Most important, I found a platform in the Red Sea that would have been an island not more than a few thousand years ago. You've got to see it! I'll drop a copy off at your house tomorrow after work. It's on the west side far south of Foul Bay, centered roughly on 16° North in Ethiopian waters. It's now called the Dahlak Banks, and even today a few protrusions touch the surface to make Dehalak' Deset and some other small islands. Most of the bank is so shallow that inundation would have occurred only in the most recent topping out. Even allowing for subsequent coral growth, it must still have been viable land, roughly contemporary with the settling of the Nile Delta."

"Well, we knew there were other areas where settlement was possible. Maybe this place was another province of the same nation that owned Foul Bay, but this one outlasted Foul Bay. Perhaps you've found the last stronghold of Punt."

"More than that! It's an island, Rick, an island! Do you see where I'm going? It's separated from the mainland by a deep, narrow channel called the South Mits'iwa Channel. Don't you remember the legend of the lost island? There are several explanations as to how the Red Sea got its name. One prominent legend, quoted by a fellow named Thomson back in 1948, is that there once was a red island, named Erytheia, which sank into the sea. The story says the island lay toward the sunset. That would be the western shore. This could be Erytheia."

"Oh yeah, you mentioned that. The Red Island. It's from the book on key environments of the Red Sea. I'm anxious to see the chart. What else did you find?" Rick asked.

"I went back to look at Foul Bay, and we have to revise the depth of its base. Remember I told you before that the rocks awash were in 30 to 60 meters of water. The new charts show a depth contour that the older maps didn't have. As far as I can tell, the general depth appears to be 20 meters or less in the zone that contains our suspected pyramids."

"That may mean all the settlement was at that particular platform level. Or it may mean they didn't build pyramids more than 20 meters tall, so those at the next lower platform just don't touch the surface. Anyway, we can only talk about those that show up on the chart."

"It moves the timeline, too," Jared reminded Rick.

"Yes, it means that the upper reaches of Foul Bay and the Bahamas reefs are precisely contemporary . . . say 6,000 to 7,000 years ago. If the basic premise of advanced culture is correct, then they may even have communicated with one another. Now that is an exciting prospect!"

"No kidding! But we're a long way from confirming either one ever existed."

"If one existed, then the other probably did too. The form of the corals is very similar—patch corals with grottoes, arches, and caves—in spite of big differences in species and ambient environments."

"And the vast distance between them."

"Hot damn."

CHAPTER 14

Chronicle 29: Erytheia, The Red Island

Three days at sea and not a ray of sunshine hit the deck as the reed boat plied southward from Berenicia. Low ceiling, fog, and drumming rain plagued the voyage from its outset. Sunless navigation was a constant challenge resolved only by keeping the vessel continuously within dim view of land. One afternoon, they almost missed the last safe anchorage for their nightly layover.

Suddenly, on the afternoon of the third day, the sky cleared. Osi marveled at the verdant mountainsides lining the western shore. *Like a thick green carpet, rich forest drapes to the sea's edge.* "I've never seen such beauty, such lushness, even in my homeland. Since childhood, I've heard of the dark-hued lands of Punt, but I couldn't imagine such splendor. These hills are greener than any oasis, greener even than the land of the Hill People, and yet they go on as far as my eyes can see."

"They say no man has ever climbed those peaks," Ketoh said, absentmindedly surveying cloud-topped pinnacles that seemed to collide with the heavens. Cadets stood silently at the gunwales staring at the spectacular panorama. Below the First Terrace, hanging gardens clung to every ledge and cranny. White-laced waterfalls dashed from the mountainsides to rocky beds below.

As quickly as the skies had opened, they closed again. Osi smiled as he likened the brief glimpse to a similarly tantalizing peek when in his youth a beautiful harlot had fleetingly opened her skirt.

Ketoh broke the silence. "Does rain fall here all the time?" His restlessness was apparent as the skies again darkened and the rumble of thunder shook him. Yet another storm, yet another lashing of rain, yet another punishing blow, and yet another soldier clinging to the gunwale seasick and wishing he could die. Three days at sea and three more to go.

"It's not like you to curse the elements, Ketoh. What concerns you so?"

"Maybe it's our mission in Erytheia. Two years of training in the Sciences of Man. To you, it's easy. To me it's pure hell."

"You'll do well. You're as smart as any man among us."

"I'm a man of action, not of learning, my friend. So far, the Sciences of Man have been only a small portion of our training, and I didn't like it. Now they're our primary duty, and the stakes are high."

"A proper career . . ."

". . . and marriage in the Third Betrothal . . ." Ketoh said.

". . . but you will not fail." Osi said. "Ketoh is the only person on earth who has such a low opinion of Ketoh."

"Is that a fact?" Ketoh asked, brightening.

"That is a fact!" said Osi.

The shallow-draught vessel shuttled passengers from island to island along the western shore of the Valley Sea. Cadets were packed among local travelers–merchants on their way to buy foodstuffs, wool, and piecework in coastal ports; local leaders heading to centers of power where they would appeal for the rights and privileges of constituents; rural poor freshly recruited to work in the cities; new soldiers not yet trained; old soldiers returning from service. These coastal freighters were the melting pots of the Realm, but they felt more like cooking pots at the time.

Ordinary citizens rarely traveled by sea, but few who were distinguished from the masses in any way could go through a year without several short voyages on the stout little vessels. Carrying 50 or 60 passengers and substantial cargoes of goods and mail, the stubby little reed boats were the camels of the coastal sea. For the price of an ordinary worker's daily wage in coin or kind, any man, woman, or child could hop aboard for a trip to the next port, half that amount for an able-bodied traveler willing to hoist a sail or manhandle an oar. Osi and his officers could easily pay the higher fare, but they welcomed the opportunity to flex their muscles and stretch their limbs as sailors and oarsmen.

On the fourth day, the weather improved, and they often saw land, occasionally highlighted by bright sunshine. On the sixth day, they awoke to sunny skies and a warm east wind, though clouds still billowed over coastal peaks.

"By noon, we'll round the northernmost point of Erytheia," Osi said. "By nightfall, we'll dock in the Holy City of Erytheia."

* * *

The low island crested on the southern horizon. Red cliffs rimmed its shores. "The ancient tales are true," Osi whispered to himself, holding up his arm to compare the island's hues to his own coppery red skin. Soon the Red Island lay to their starboard. A short time later, the boat veered southeast, then east to the main port. Finally, the Holy City's spires loomed before them.

Just as Osi had found Berenicia impressive for its mercantile glory, he now found Erytheia sublimely, almost ethereally, beautiful. The Pyramid of the Trove sat on high ground near the palace. Circular walls and domed seccas abounded. Metallic spires reached heavenward in a clear blue sky. Gold, silver, copper, and bronze adorned most of the stately buildings, and the capital could well have been called the "Red City" for its redsilver-clad structures alone. Beyond the city's walls and shoreward channel stood luxuriant green hills. "This must surely be the richest and most beautiful city on earth," Osi said to Busah as the vessel claimed its slip at the dock.

"That's what we thought of Egia as children," Busah said with a hint of irony.

"And what we said of Berenicia as young men," Ketoh added.

"Is it possible we will yet learn of richer, more splendid cities?" Osi asked, half seriously.

"Osi, you think too much," Ketoh said, shaking his head.

"You sometimes seek to know things that are best unknown," Busah said.

"I must know what lies beyond. It's that simple."

"Hold your tongue, and one day you'll lead all the armies of the Realm. Speak of what lies beyond, and you may be denied so much as captain of this coastal craft. That's the way such matters work, Osi. That's the way leaders are chosen."

"Then the price of leadership may be too high. You speak too cautiously. We can't give in to the malaise that grips Berenicia."

"Do as you will, my friend. But things are not so simple as in our youth. Then, you were able to draw your sword against the mightiest beast on earth. Now, you'll face enemies far more cunning…and they won't roar to warn of their approach."

Pages met them at the pier. They led Osi and his cohorts along a grand boulevard to the doors of the academy. Here, they would undergo general studies for a year, then move on to advanced work in special topics for yet another year. Military skills would be taught and muscles would be honed, but their main mission here would be to learn the Sciences of Man.

Time refused to pass quickly for the lovesick Osi. He, like Ketoh, would find the two years an eternity. Only at the close of the second year would he again see his beloved Bera. *She has my token, and I have hers, but what does it all mean? Will she defy her secret betrothal to Setra? With luck, she'll be mine at the Third Betrothal, but I won't know the answer for so long.* By day, he dreamed of that ultimate reunion with Bera; by night, he dreamed of their ultimate union.

* * *

After six months of training, the student officers were invited to a reception at the palace. The stated purpose was their introduction to members of the Royal Court, but Osi suspected it was, more than that, an opportunity for the nobles to evaluate future military leaders. The cadets gathered in the anteroom awaiting their appointed hour.

It's all so political. This single social function could have more to do with our future appointments than all the training and effort that brought us here.

"So, Osi, my friend, I hear that your work in the academy goes well." Setra's cordial tone caught Osi off guard.

"I'm enjoying my studies. And you?"

"I, too, but I'm not performing so well as you. Everyone says you are the best."

Is this the Setra I knew in Berenicia? Maybe he and I can make peace after all. Still, I'd be a fool to trust him.

"But I'm told that you are one of the brightest in the academy, Setra. Everyone thinks you'll be our designated leader," Osi said.

"No, no. It will be you who leads us, Osi." He laughed self-consciously.

"The King believes in strict adherence to the Divine Right Order. He will appoint a man of similar convictions...such as you, Setra. I believe in order tempered with reason, *and* I'm a colonist to boot. It won't be offered to me."

"If it were offered, would you not accept?"

"That is my..." Osi stopped mid-sentence. To his left was a large open corridor, and there, facing the nobles, stood Bera. Setra noted Osi's shock and was amused. For a while, Osi suspected Bera had come to Erytheia to teach in the academy, but he was surprised to find her in the Royal Palace.

What's Bera doing here?

As they spoke, Ammon, the young squire from Death's Shadow entered the anteroom. "I believe you know Prince Ammon, Crown Prince of the Realm?" Setra said, glaring smugly at Osi. Osi was speechless. *Bera's brother, a Prince of the Realm? But that must mean ...*

"And I see you have spied Princess Bera, who's visiting her father."

"*Princess* Bera?" Osi could barely speak. Bera was radiant in her golden jewelry, royal tiara, and flowing gown draped low to expose her breasts. She couldn't have been lovelier.

"Yes, *Princess.* She's the daughter of Rahn Mennon. Didn't you know?"

"No...it never occurred to me," Osi mumbled. *That Devil, Setra,* he thought. *He's known all along, and he's played me for a fool.*

"She's to become my wife!" Setra declared, as if Osi might welcome the news.

"But what about the Third Betrothal?" Osi stammered. Now Setra's game was clear.

"Don't be foolish, Osi. No one waits for ceremony. This was arranged before the First Betrothal. My father is a man of great wealth and influence, Prince of Punt, ruler of all the western coast of the Valley Sea. Several years ago, the King's Agent in Berenicia negotiated with my father on behalf of the crown. I was granted Bera's hand in exchange for certain benefits to the King and Realm."

"Have you spoken with the princess about this?"

"Why?"

"It's her life. Besides, she gave me her token. She has until the Third Betrothal to decide."

"She'll accept whatever Rahn Mennon commands. It's her lot." Princess Bera motioned to one of the servants, then exited without so much as a glance in Osi's direction.

It must be true, Osi thought. *Beneath my newly polished surface, I'm nothing more than a rube. I have fooled myself into thinking I could win the love of one so flawless as Bera. Now this boor, Setra, who seeks nothing more than her father's wealth and power, has outflanked me. I wish she were too poor for Setra's purposes.*

"Osi of Egia. Welcome to the Royal Court," said a soft-spoken old gentleman "Do me the honor of allowing me to introduce you to its members?" *Can this really be Toth, Chief Priest of the Realm?* Osi asked himself. *Yes, it surely is, but he seemed so...scary...when he spoke to us on the pyramid. Now he seems like a kindly old man.*

"Of course, sir, but the honor is mine." For more than a hand, Osi and the priest shuffled about the room meeting one dignitary after another. Conversations went smoothly but seldom ventured deeper than simple questions about Osi's studies. In the end, however, nobles and priests alike revealed their fascination with Osi's exploits, especially the death of the dirktooth cat and the victory at Redsilver Point. He responded politely and warmly, but he couldn't resist glancing frequently toward the corridor where Princess Bera last stood.

"I believe you have met Prince Ammon, Crown Prince of the Realm?" Toth asked as they neared him.

"Sire, I present to you Osi of Egia," Toth said to Ammon, bowing in deference to the young fellow.

"I am honored, my lord." Osi bowed.

"The honor is mine," Prince Ammon said with a sly glint.

"Surely you have heard, sir, of the one they call the Dirk Slayer."

"Oh, perhaps I have. Killed some sort of cat, I'm told," said the bemused prince.

"A dirktooth cat, no less," Toth went on. "No other lone man has ever done so."

"Then I am certain you will be a great asset to the armies of the Realm, Osi of Egia."

"It will be my pleasure to serve the King." Osi bowed deeply as the Crown Prince took his leave.

"You seem distracted," Toth said. "Is it possible you have an eye for a certain princess?"

"I...confess."

Toth shook his head woefully. "I know about your trysts. Osi, she is forbidden to you. She is of the royal house. She's secretly betrothed to another. It cannot be otherwise. Rahn Mennon would deal harshly with Princess Bera...and with any man foolish enough to defy his wishes. Don't wreck your future on such a gamble. She's bound to Setra. You must accept that."

"Why would Rahn Mennon force his own daughter to spend her life with such a tortured soul as Setra?"

"Setra is the son of Rotan, the wealthiest and most influential Prince of Punt. Without his support our kingdom would have split apart as soon as hostilities began. Rogue merchant princes of eastern Punt, across the Valley Sea, would have broken away. By now, Erytheia might be a vassal of *their* Punt."

"Still, how can Setra be so cruel?"

"He isn't cruel; he's weak. He's driven by his father's ambitions rather than his own. Endless bluster and confusion is the sad result. If he weren't your rival in love and war, you'd pity, not despise him."

"I know, Father Toth, and I wish we could put our differences aside. In many ways we're alike, and I think it might be possible for us to be friends. Not now, of course, not while he stands between Bera and me."

Osi's heart surged as the princess appeared again in the doorway. She glanced around the room, then headed back down the corridor out of his view. *Could she be looking for me?* Osi wondered.

"Speak to her, if you must, young man. She will tell you the same." Osi nodded his appreciation then shuffled through the crowd and slipped into the corridor. When he reached the doorway, Bera was 30 paces ahead, just turning into a side hall.

"Wait!" he called. "Bera, speak to me." She turned, then motioned and disappeared around the corner. When he caught up, she took his arm and guided him into a tiny sanctuary behind the throne room.

"I hoped you'd be here today, Osi. I must explain and beg your forgiveness. It is the least I can do. I should never have offered my token. I was weak. I gave false hope to both of us, when there's no hope for either. The scene is set; the script is written. I am betrothed, and my father will never relent. I've begged...pleaded...prayed."

"Stop! No more. Let me look into your eyes." He shushed her with his finger touched gently to her lips. "Tell me now. Say you don't love me." He lifted his finger. Bera looked into his eyes and started to speak, then turned away.

Grasping Osi's hands in her own, she nestled them tenderly between her breasts. "I do, Osi. I do love you. But it makes no difference. I would gladly suffer, but I *will not* condemn you. Father Toth says you're the only hope of the People of the Living Sun. I can't deny you that destiny. Nor can you deny our people."

"My fate will be fulfilled in ways as yet unsuspected by Toth or any other man. It isn't some mystical force that drives me, but the search for a new, wise order that will secure our future in the land above. I will find that order with or without your father's blessing. It will be founded on knowledge, wisdom, and strength."

"That's bold talk, Osi, and I want to believe, but no man alone can achieve so much in a single lifetime. You must have the King's support. Otherwise you're sure to fail."

"I'll take my chances, Bera, and I will succeed."

"You must go now. My father would not tolerate our meeting."

Osi bent down and kissed her trembling lips. She resisted, tears streaming down her cheeks. Then she relented. It was a sad, lovely, lasting kiss, a kiss goodbye that begged for a future *together*.

* * *

One year later, Osi was among a handful of cadets invited back to the palace to be interviewed by King Rahn Mennon's Agents. A selected few would meet the King himself. All in the chamber fell silent when Osi strode in. As an attendant escorted him forward, Toth entered the columned corridor. "Come, my son. You are to meet our King. Follow me!"

They entered the adjoining throne room, a stately chamber lined with massive columns. Each wall was adorned with splendid murals, etchings, and sculptures depicting episodes in the history of the People of the Living Sun. Osi first noticed a scene from the Topping Age of the First Kalpa when the Ancestor King led his little band of refugees out from the Land of the Second Sunset. Chased by a wall of fire, the tribe ran toward the rising sun. Behind them the old queen was engulfed in flames, her arm pointing eastward. Then a scene from the Falling Age of the First Kalpa. The Ondwan, the Star King, pointed eastward from the delta of the Indus. In other murals the seas receded even from the Plain of Sunda. Osi puzzled over an enigmatic mural containing mystically magical machines from the Golden Age of an unknown Kalpa even earlier than the Time Before. Next came a scene from the Rising Age of the Second Kalpa when the Sindwan, the Water King, secured the Secrets of the Ages inside the Echo Trove. Then a scene from the Golden Age of the Second Kalpa when the seas parted, and the Morowan, the Sea Floor King, discovered that same Echo Trove. There were well-known scenes from the Rising Age of the Fourth Kalpa when the Erawan, the Red King, established his throne on the Red Island and ruled his Realm from there. Images familiar and strange, too numerous for Osi to absorb, formed a diverse pantheon of revered gods and kings.

Osi glanced in all directions, but Bera was not to be found.

"Come. Stand before me," a voice commanded from a throne illuminated by a single shaft of light beaming down from a circular opening in the secca. Osi advanced into the lighted circle. The King sat in royal finery on a magnificent golden throne. Beside him stood his scored staff of office. An unwieldy crown, like an upturned vase, weighted his brow. Toth stood silently beside him. "So you are the Dirk Slayer. I have heard much. Are these legends true? Did you really kill the dirktooth cat?"

"Yes, Your Majesty, it is true."

"And you led the expedition of cadets from Egia to Berenicia?"

"I had no choice, Sire."

"And your remarkable stint at the helm of the *Ruby?*"

"Captain Hervov has been most generous, Sire."

"And your cleverness at Redsilver Point. Is that true as well?"

"We were successful in a mock battle."

"And the phalanx at Berenicia? For which I am most thankful, by the way, except for that nasty misstep on the dock."

"Yes. I failed you miserably, my King."

"That battle was lost at the garrison, not on the docks," said Rahn Mennon. "You did all you could. Setra's force could never have evacuated me to the Sacred Pyramid without your courageous defense on the dock. What's more, your voyage northward saved many children including my own Prince Ammon and Princess Bera."

"It was my duty, Sire."

"And then, your remarkable victory at Death's Shadow?"

"I am your loyal servant, my King. Nothing more."

"Now I am told of your mastery of the Sciences of Man. How can it be that you are able to do all these things so well."

"I am no better than any other man."

"Toth tells me you are no ordinary mortal. Reports of your birth under Sahu Orion, and your remarkable performance in training support his claim."

"I am but a mortal man, Sire."

"Mortal or no, you shall command a brigade of my finest Regulars in the Army of Punt. Do well, and one day you will lead all my military forces. Your grooming will begin with the next moon. Toth says this is an auspicious appointment, blessed by the stars. Anbaht, the chief Priest of Egia, did well to commend you even though you are a colonial. This day you must select your course of studies for the final year." He smiled broadly, expecting surprise and pleasure in Osi's eyes. He had, after all, just offered the most prized position in all the Realm. Toth beamed with anticipation and pride. *They aren't attempting to coerce me*, Osi thought. *They assume I will be overjoyed with this appointment. They don't understand what the Realm really needs of me.*

"I will do whatever you wish, my King, but this is not for me." Osi's words fell like stones dropped hard and loud on the floor. Rahn Mennon stared through him seeking an explanation of the strange declaration he had just heard.

"You refuse this most coveted of appointments?" Mercifully, the King's tone was more tinged with surprise and consternation than with anger.

"Do you not wish to serve your King as you have sworn?" asked Toth, likewise dumbfounded.

"I will serve in any post my King commands, but I respectfully suggest there is a different calling for which I am better suited, of greater service to the People of the Living Sun."

"How can that be?" the King asked. "I offered you the finest brigade of the finest army in the Realm. Surely you don't expect a larger force."

"I seek *no* army."

"What do you want then…the Navy, the Royal Guard? What appeals so to you?"

"Give me a ship and one hundred men . . ."

"But that is nothing," the flustered King said.

". . . and give me free range of all the earth."

"Free range of the earth? The entire earth? Why do you seek such a strange privilege?"

"I seek to know the earth itself."

"And to what end?"

"So that I may understand the Waters of Chaos and when and how high they will rise. So that I may help our Geometers sound the alarm. So that I may help your majesty prepare a refuge in the land above."

"But what can you do that our learned geometers cannot?"

"We face a new world order that requires new knowledge…new methods of science as well as warfare. Your majesty's commanders spoke of this in Berenicia. I want to find this knowledge and apply these methods." Silence prevailed as the King and Chief Priest exchanged questioning glances. A wordless exchange passed between them. Finally, Toth nodded. At last, the King spoke, shaking his head so that the cumbersome crown wobbled from side to side.

"We shall consider your request. Perhaps you ask too little…and yet too much." With a flick of his wrist, the King dismissed Osi. "Wait, cadet!" called the King as Osi walked away. "Do you have something else to say?" Osi opened his mouth to ask for the hand of Princess Bera. But he couldn't utter the words, knowing for certain what the King's answer would be, now sealed by his unusual request.

"No, Sire, nothing to add."

* * *

The hour of decision came. Osi would decide his course of advanced studies. He spoke to Calonta, his wizened mentor, Head Mistress of the Academy. "I choose the Geometries of the Skies, the World's Waters, the Earth's Surface, and the Earth's Living Things."

"By the Great Rahn, lad, that's too much for any man to grasp. Even a brilliant student and Dirk Slayer, such as you, would find it impossible to learn so much in a lifetime, much less a single year. You must choose *one* science."

"One science will do me no good, Teacher. My mission requires more than any one science contains."

"Yes, it would be a wondrous thing if one man could possess all these sciences. No one has ever attempted to learn so much," She said.

"Then I shall be the first."

"The King has ordered that I am to grant you your wish whatever it may be, but do you not know the price of such ambition? It surely will require every waking hour. You'll work night and day. No quarter will be given in any science, no failure allowed. You will distinguish yourself in each discipline as if it were your only one. You will live like a priest, apart from all others. I will personally oversee your studies. You will have the best teachers in all the sciences. In exchange, you must vow to carry your part to conclusion."

"On my honor, I will do so." *How else to divert my mind from Bera*, he thought, *how else to save my people.*

"Then let it be done!"

* * *

"You did what?" Ketoh yelled. "You rejected the King's offer? You chose, instead, a boat and an impossible course of studies. You should be restrained for your own safety."

"Come, Ketoh, it's not that bad. One year of hardship for a lifetime of adventure and service."

"You don't even know for sure the King will grant you a ship once your work is done. What if it's all for naught? Have you thought about that?"

"I plan for my dream, my mission, my destiny. You too long for more. I saw that yearning in your eyes as we passed those peaks beside the Valley Sea. Will you not choose to join me wherever I go?"

"Yes, of course I'll go. How else can you manage to come back alive?"

"And Busah? Do you think Busah will join us?"

"Yes, and Jumar and Sareem and Tanta, they will come as well. They've already said so."

"Then it's settled."

* * *

As Osi stepped into mid-morning light outside the academy, a servant girl approached, slipped him a note, and disappeared. He sternly resisted the temptation to read it, waiting until he could no longer be seen by peering palace eyes. In an alley a few hundred paces from the academy, he leaned against a cool stone wall and unfurled the message. It simply said, "Luska, noon, please."

Luska, of course, thought Osi, *the royal retreat of Erytheia. Bera!* he hoped with all his heart. *Where else can a Royal find privacy. It's rumored there is a secret path to a secluded lake at the island's crest. It must be true. But what can this mean? Has she changed her mind?*

In late morning, Osi was well on his way up the winding rocky trail. He crested a low ridge and looked down on a magnificent blue lake at the bottom of a cylindrical depression. *Must be at sea level,* Osi thought. *Like lapis set in a band of redsilver.* He negotiated the twisting trail to the water's edge. Rounding a bend, he saw Bera. Dressed in a diaphanous white drape, she sat alone on the sparkling, warm sand. She looked up, saw him, and waved a welcome. He ran to her side.

Osi touched her flushed cheek. A tear formed in Bera's eye as she spoke. "I love you, Osi. I don't want you hurt."

"I love you, too, Bera. And I'm fine. Don't worry about me. I can take care of myself. No one can hurt me." *Was there enough conviction in my voice?*

"I know you're strong, Osi. But you underestimate your enemies. You don't realize how treacherous a man like Setra can be. He suspects our love and knows your quest. He aims to stop you, and he's enlisted Roton and others who influence the King. Powerful forces are aligned against you."

"What can I do?"

"Tell me your plans. Arm me with every argument, every reason, every justification for your proposed mission. With Father Toth's help, I will become your eyes, your ears, and your voice in the palace. Toth and I will press Rahn Mennon to grant your request."

"I appreciate your help, my princess, but I had hoped for relief of a different kind. I hoped you had changed your mind...about the Third Betrothal."

"I can't, Osi. I'll destroy everything you hope to accomplish. It's not my choice, and defiance will only make it worse. We'll be denied a life together, and you will be denied your mission. If I comply, perhaps we can hope for your mission to be granted. Setra doesn't want to love me; he wants to own me. In that, he has won, but I freely give my heart to you. We must be content to love from afar."

As Osi reached to touch Bera, she stood, laughed, and ran. Before Osi recovered, she undressed and dove into the azure water.

My heart can't stand this, Osi thought. He shed his tunic and stroked to Bera's side. *Salt, not fresh,* he noted. At first, they swam side by side without speaking. Then they moved to shallower water and stood on the pebbled bottom looking into each other's eyes. Osi placed his hands on Bera's shoulders and drew her close. *My god, my god,* thought Osi. *I've never felt such love before. My heart pounds while I am with her...it will surely break without her. But for now...* They kissed, losing themselves in passion that transcended time and place. The two then swam to shore where they shared more of themselves than he could dream in a lifetime.

Chronicle 30: The Third Betrothal

Osi paced in the bright sun outside the palace awaiting his summons. *Do I get my ship or not?* he thought. *I've passed the final year with honors. Surely, with Bera and Toth on my side, the King will grant my request. Why is it taking so long? I've waited for three hands since the first cadets went in.*

"Osir of Egia!" yelled the Sergeant at Arms as the stout doors opened wide. *How odd*, he thought. *I'd almost forgotten my own name. It's been my formal name since birth, but no one has ever called me "Osir." Now that I'm full grown, everything will be formal, and I'll never be Osi again.*

"Osir of Egia!" the man yelled again as Osi, now Osir, mounted the steps and strode to the portico to be greeted by Chief Priest Toth, Head Mistress Calonta, and Ortilon, Supreme Commander of all the Armies of the Realm. The entourage turned and accompanied Osir in silence toward the magnificent throne room. His resolve wavered as the crucial moment approached.

"You are the strange one, the one who fights dirktooth cats." Ortilon's breath rumbled deep within his heavy chest as they walked the long hallway. Osir felt his displeasure.

"I am, sir!" responded Osir with appropriate military courtesy.

"And you say that even my job is not good enough for you?"

"Those are not my words," Osir said cautiously. He thought he caught the hint of a smile. *Is the commander toying with a young officer for his own amusement?* Osir could not be sure.

"We have with us Officer Osir, formerly of the Cadets of Egia," Ortilon announced to the King.

"Yes, I know this man," Rahn Mennon responded.

Ortilon shrugged as if to say, Of course, doesn't everyone? Resigned, he went on, "What is your pleasure for his future, Sire?"

"Osir, you asked for less than any other man, yet somehow more. You rejected our highest command, yet you ask for gifts I cannot bestow." Osir's heart sank at the words. "You asked for a ship, 100 men, and free range of the entire earth. These are not mine to give." Osir's spirit fell lower with each word. He stood in silence as Rahn Mennon went on. "The ships are not mine for they belong to their captains. The men are not mine for they belong to themselves. The earth is not mine for it belongs to all men. These are the gifts of the Divine Right Order. The Order is as it shall be, neither yours nor mine. You must earn your ship. You must inspire those who would follow you. And you must take the earth by the sheer strength of your will."

Can it be true? Osir marveled. *Have I been granted all that I asked? Yes! I can earn my ship. I can enlist my men. I can seize the world by my own hand. My wish is within my grasp.*

"Report to the *Golden Crown of Erytheia*, Captain Waleska in command. One month after the Third Betrothal you will board that vessel for a trip to our sister realm in the east. You will serve for one year until you have mastered the high seas of the World Ocean. Prior to departure, you are to enlist a contingent of 100 men, all volunteers. On return, you will be transferred to another ship for a two-year apprenticeship to a second captain. If you prove yourself worthy, you will then be commissioned to travel the earth at will."

"Thank you, Sire! You are most gracious." *And thanks to Bera*, Osir thought.

"These favors I grant because you have proved yourself worthy. You fought well, and you learned four times as much as any other man. But you must earn them again each day. Otherwise your wishes will be denied by men and fate beyond my control."

"I will be eternally grateful, Sire. I will prove the wisdom of your decision."

"There is no call for gratitude. The Divine Right Order ordains what I decree. Is there anything else you desire?"

"No, my liege," he stammered, but he couldn't hide his true feelings.

"You sound uncertain," the King said, incredulous at Osir's audacity, unspoken though it was. "What else is it that you want?"

"Might my final ship be the *Ruby of Berenicia*?"

"I will take your request under advisement." the King said shaking his head and smiling in disbelief. "Is there any other request?"

Osir noted bemused expressions around the throne. "Yes, Master. I ask only that Princess Bera be free to choose whom she will marry." He spoke casually as if asking for a piece of bread at table.

"Go!" shouted the King. "You ask too much!"

I've heard these words before, yet the King granted my request. But this time, there will be no easy victory.

* * *

Since leaving Egia, the boy *Osi* had looked forward to the Third Betrothal. Now the man *Osir* dreaded the fateful occasion. *Like it or not, the time has come, and the selection of mates will be complete. Only the best and brightest. I've heard that term again and again,* he thought. *Now its full meaning is clear. At the outset, I would have thought it impossible to work so hard, to learn as much as we have learned during our four years of training. Maybe I should have stayed in Egia. There I would never have known such impossible dreams.*

As before in Berenicia, the column made its way to the central plaza. Again the scent of camphor permeated the air evoking memories of the sensuous beauty whom Osir had come to love. Cheers again rang out as the procession of virgins, less one, entered the courtyard. The girls dropped their camphor boughs and took their places among the massive monuments of the People of the Living Sun. The Chief Priest recited the ancient liturgy.

Then, in dim shadows of fading sunlight, the men assembled. Six large wooden biers surrounded their column; six surrounded the women's. Twelve soldiers set the biers aflame. The masses roared. The litany continued as in the First and Second Betrothals.

Each virgin held the tokens she had collected. Each man did the same. On command, the men broke ranks and sought the virgins whose tokens they held. Most had several partners from whom to choose. Despite a wealth of tokens, however, Osir sought only one match. When he reached Princess Bera, there was but one other suitor standing near.

"And what brings you to this lady's side?" Setra asked. "She has found her match." Setra held up Princess Bera's token to prove his claim. Osir saw Setra's token in Bera's hand.

When their eyes met, Osir sensed her utter despair.

The time has come, and there is no hope for me. If she had chosen Setra of her own free will, at least she would be happy even if I were not. She doesn't want him; she, too, will live in misery.

Setra held out Bera's token to match his own. Once the tokens touched, their union would be sealed forever. Osir watched helplessly as the fragile clay symbols moved closer, ever closer. Setra's hand reached out to Bera as her hand reached out to him. In an instant, they would touch. Then it happened. First one, then several, then many shards of broken clay fell from Bera's hand. With the sheer strength of her grasp, she had crushed the precious token. Setra stared in disbelief. Bera quickly turned to Osir, and their tokens clinked. In an instant, she had claimed Osir as her groom, and he had taken her as his bride.

How much has this noble woman sacrificed to become my wife, Osir pondered as they embraced.

Setra glared at Osir in a sad mixture of pain and rage. "Thanks to you, I, Setra, Prince of Punt, am doomed to remain heirless. This union was ordained by the Divine Right Order. This woman should be my wife, mother of my rightful heir. Now, you've taken all from me. May your life someday be cursed as mine is now." He stalked away in despair and rage.

The priest confirmed that all matches were complete, then conducted the marriage liturgy. Osir saw that Busah and Nala had made their matches as had Ketoh and Pranalat.

"Cast off your robes of manhood," Toth commanded. The men dropped their clothing and stood naked beside their mates. Each held a small ceremonial dagger.

"Cast off your robes of womanhood." The women shed their outer garments leaving only a sheath of fine lace, the sensuous "outer" veil.

Each man drew his dagger, then rent his partner's veil and cast it aside. The biers were renewed, the flames roared, and the couples lay on conjugal robes to consummate their unions.

"Yes," Osir whispered to Bera, "yes, now it's all worthwhile."

The crowd stood in reverent silence, politely awaiting the proper moment; then roared its approval.

Chronicle 31: Piercing the Veil

The *Golden Crown of Erytheia* groaned against pilings at the naval dock of its namesake city. Osir examined the vessel, his new bride standing at his side. He looked into her eyes for a moment and lost himself. *No mortal should have the power to cast such a spell,* he thought. *Yet these are the eyes of an enchantress, who can indeed cast any spell she chooses.*

Disowned for insubordination, she was no longer Princess Bera. She was Osir's wife, his mate for life, and that meant more to them than all the royal lineages in the Realm. To their surprise, the King remained a man of his word and did not renege on his promises to Osir. Now, Osir faced the sea, savoring her love. He sniffed the salt air, then nodded toward the southern horizon. "We'll be in the Southern Ocean by the seventh day under sail." He glanced at Bera to catch her reaction.

Osir carefully avoided the words, "Piercing the Veil," because so many sailors had drowned in that dreadful passage at the southern tip of the Valley Sea. Bera, of course, knew precisely what Osir meant. One week later he would either be dead or alive, and she wouldn't know his fate for weeks.

"Don't worry, my dear. I'm blessed by the gods. Anbaht said so, and Toth agrees. I'll return safely." His mood was playful and his tone light, but Bera knew his heart was heavy.

"Father Toth is a dear old scoundrel, more predictable than prophetic, but you *will* return. I know it in my heart," she said bravely, "and that means more to me than all his priestly predictions." She smiled warmly.

"Goodbye, my bride." Osir stooped and kissed her. "I love you, Bera. I truly do."

"And I love you, too, my dear sweet Osir." After a long, heartfelt embrace, he picked up his pack of the Hill People and walked slowly up the gangplank. His golden-hilted sword hung jauntily at his side. Busah, Ketoh, Tanta, and Jumar, having said goodbye to their mates, were already on deck when Osir boarded.

The *Crown* pushed off and edged into the channel. Bera waved goodbye, then strolled purposefully toward the academy where she would teach the equations of the True Pyramid until his return. The current gently nudged southward as the vessel claimed its course. First, it pushed the stern, then ebbed as water spilled in from the World Ocean, then spilled back again. Several hands later, it shoved the bow, then ebbed again.

Thus began a pattern that would prevail for the next week. Twice each day, the tide-driven force reversed. Day by day, its thrust grew more intense as the walls of the Valley Sea loomed closer and closer to the *Crown*'s gunwales. At the outset, the winds easily pushed the ship along even against the inbound tide. By the third day, those same winds were barely able to counter the thrust of the bulging inbound sea.

Thereafter, tides grew even stronger, and the current increased. By the fourth day, heavy winds channeled into the narrow chasm, constantly blowing north or south in alignment with the gorge. Each shift of tide brought a new combination of wind and current, first against the bow, then against the stern. By the fifth day, the sails were struck. The *Crown* could make forward progress only by sweeping along with the outbound tide, anchoring fast, and waiting for the next favorable current. Even so, it was difficult to hold against the massive rush.

On the sixth day, the final challenge came. Before them stood the Veil, where opposing walls narrowed to a gap hardly wider than the beam of the *Crown*, itself. The Veil was aptly named for the constant cloud of spray and mist that shrouded its reversing falls. At the base of the Veil, hard rock formed a sill over which the waters gushed. As the tide rushed in, Osir saw a sizable waterfall tumbling over the sill and into the Valley Sea. At maximum force, the falls grew higher than the hull of the *Crown* itself. When the tides reversed, a similar waterfall would flow in the opposite direction. The outbound tide brought the *Crown* to rest less than two hands' drift from the awesome strait where the east and west walls nearly converged. Trapped between sheer cliffs, the *Crown* lay adrift, no safe anchorage to be found. Taking advantage of the temporary calm, Captain Waleska ordered his vessel lashed to the leeward side of a rock outcrop near the water's edge, 800 manheights from the veil. Another longer line was carried forward by a skiff with two daring oarsmen to a second rock, 250 manheights closer to the precipice. The lines to the first rock were loosed. Then slowly, arduously the crew turned the capstan to take up the slack, bringing the *Crown* itself alongside the farther rock. Again the vessel was lashed firmly to a nearby outcrop. Again the oarsmen moved the tether to a farther rock. Three times the maneuver was repeated, each time advancing the *Crown* closer to the gaping chasm. Finally the ship sat not 50 manheights from the brink. Waleska ordered everyone to rest for four hands while waiting on the tide.

With the next reversal, the time had come to pierce the Veil. Waleska's careful timing meant life or death. Cut the lines too soon, and the ship would founder on the sill. Her hull would crack like an eggshell. Cut too late, and the *Crown* would drop its own height on the ocean side, testing captain and crew and shipbuilders, too. Finally, all hands were ordered to their stations and placed at the ready. Each man lashed himself to a mast, bulkhead, or capstan. The countdown began as the current surged forward and mist welled up from the falls. The hull of the *Crown* crackled and groaned; its ropes stretched near breaking. The captain constantly watched the rising Veil to read its every mood.

Waleska watched with a vigilant, practiced eye as mist and spray arose, his hand held high while the rushing water built into a rising swell astern. The awesome current cut deep swirls seaward of the vessel's bow. Seamen stood poised with axes at each restraining rope. *Wait much longer and the current astern will take her down where she lies,* Osir thought. At the instant the roiling sea mist reached the chasm's rim, Waleska dropped his hand swiftly, and the seamen swung their blades. Like a stone from a slingshot, the ship surged forward. Teams of seamen held the tiller firm to keep her aligned with the current. In a breath, they careered at full speed through the treacherous gorge. To Osir, it seemed an eternity as the Veil loomed higher and higher. The vessel lurched and groaned, yielding to the will of the sea.

Suddenly, as in a fantasy, the mighty ship entered the mist. On either side, Osir could see only a mottled blur of rock as the *Crown* pierced the Veil. Instantly, the vessel cleared the dreaded sill and fell crashing to the watery base below. Their passage had come late but not so late as to spell disaster for ship and crew. Osir breathed relief as the *Crown*, freed from the Veil, rushed headlong toward the vast Southern Ocean.

Chronicle 32: Lands Across the Sea

The *Crown* skirted the scalloped coastline of the broad channel outside the Veil. They sailed within sight of the northern shore and anchored every night in sheltered inlets half-circled by grasslands. Moderate, westerly winds moved the ship at a good pace around the vast block of land east of the Valley Sea. On the seventh day, Osir spotted arid mountains, a landmark signifying that a strong current would soon quicken the *Crown's* pace considerably. By the eighth day, the current took hold and swept them far from land, out of sight for the first time.

That night, the moon, beaming brightly in a cloud-columned sky, reflected on gently rolling swells. Osir inhaled the salty air and marveled at the unimagined desolation of the open ocean. Not once from Gubal to the Veil had he lost sight of land. Osir stared into the void, overwhelmed by the immensity of the surrounding sea.

"Are you certain Captain Waleska knows how to find land again?" Ketoh asked half seriously as he, Osir, Busah, and Jumar leaned, elbows on gunwales, watching the unchanging horizon and savoring the night.

"We'll see land soon. The texts say that, after the eighth day at sea, a vessel will be swept due eastward by a current called the Monsoon Drift. Two days from now, we'll leave it and turn north. A day later, we'll make port in the Land of the Ziggurat Builders."

"What, may I ask, is a 'ziggurat,' and why would anybody want to build one?" Busah asked.

"Now, Busah, I urged you to take a different course of study," Ketoh said in mock disgust. "The Geometry of the Earth's Commerce leaves much to be desired. How can you understand commerce without knowing how people live?"

"So you studied the Geometry of the Earth's Living Things, and now you don't know how to barter for food in strange lands," Busah shot back.

"Osir, you learned it all. What's a ziggurat?" Ketoh asked as the others laughed.

"A peculiar form of pyramid with steep, almost vertical, sides. Actually, they're just step pyramids with a couple of huge steps rather than many smaller steps like ours."

"Steep sides? Will they hold as well as ours when the Waters of Chaos attack?" Jumar asked.

"Their design has survived two kalpas already. The plain is lower here than in Erytheia or Berenicia, but rock outcrops give them extra height. Most of the ziggurats are built on promontories heightened even more by the rubble of past ages."

"That's fortunate."

"Maybe, but many hills have already been flooded, and the Waters of Chaos may soon cover them all."

"Are the Ziggurat Builders aware of our Geometer's calculations?"

"Yes, but they stubbornly refuse to believe."

On their tenth day outside the Veil, the voyagers again caught sight of land, and a day later they resumed the familiar pattern of hugging the coast and anchoring nightly. Finally, the *Crown* rounded a sharp crook of land and entered a wide embayment. Inside lay the Sea of Hormuz—a wide, shallow basin stretching to the northern horizon.

"Take care," Waleska called to the helmsman. "Station watches on the bow! These old submerged seccas will rip our hull out from under us."

Osir saw no less than eight ziggurats of varying sizes on promontories, some barely above the water, others licked by surf. This, he knew, meant the sea floor beneath the *Crown*, not long ago, had been fertile fields and pastures. Some ziggurats had been completely abandoned, most likely because surrounding communities had migrated elsewhere searching for new livelihoods. Staring down into the clear water, Osir spotted a dark stripe that once had been a road.

Farther north, promontories stood high above the water. Farther still, they were surrounded entirely by sloped hillsides. Standing on the bow of the *Crown*, Osir scanned the new coast in utter amazement. Along the extensive shoreline spread a magnificent civilization. To the east and north lay flat lands with rich patchworks of irrigated fields. He felt a sudden tug of emotion as the familiar fields of Egia came to mind. He hadn't seen his home for more than four years, and there was no sight such as this in Berenicia or Erytheia. Now, more than ever, he missed his homeland and his family.

Osir's mood soon shifted from nostalgia to wonder. In the northwest lay a mighty city with massive fortifications and towering temples far greater than those of Erytheia. Here they would dock for several days to trade goods and replenish their food and water supplies. Most of the men would carouse in the city, but Osir would contact the Geometers of the Ziggurat Builders.

* * *

"My time is short," Osir said to the Central Council. "I want to discuss your calculations of the coming deluge."

"First, tell us your nation's projections," said Sikor, a learned advisor to the King of the Ziggurat Builders. Osir proceeded, but the findings of the Geometers of Berenicia were met with scorn. "How can you speak of a coming rise. Our Geometers see no such event. Your Geometers should reexamine these issues. We will be happy to tutor them."

"Very well. My mission is to gather information to improve our projections," Osir said diplomatically.

"But you have so much to learn," Sikor said.

"Our estimates need refinement. Hence, I seek your learned council. Please instruct me," Osir said. *It's a gamble,* he thought. *A straightforward request like this could flatter or offend such a prideful lot. Who knows how they'll react?*

The scholars exchanged glances. With a nod from D-El, the Chief Geometer, the council rose without speaking and turned to a large wooden archway in the chamber wall. Two armed guards unlocked its massive double doors. The Chief Geometer, flanked by council members, beckoned Osir into the second chamber. Inside were two massive hemispherical models, one of the Lands of the North and another of the South. Colors distinguished the land cover–blue for water, white for ice, and green or brown for land. At first glance, Osir judged the hemispheres to be consistent with similar models used in his training back at the academy.

"Your models are impressive. Please show me your levels." The models, of course, would be worthless without accurate measures of water, ice, and land. The scholars obligingly led Osir to a scaffold spanning the Lands of the North. He stood on a catwalk while the model rotated beneath him. Pegs dotted the surface at regular intervals. *Just like ours,* Osir thought.

The markers formed a dense grid over the spherical surface. Each peg was painted white and cut to represent the elevation of ice relative to sea level. The result was an abstract representation of height and horizontal extent, and thus the volume, of glaciers over the whole earth.

No one knew how the great glaciers were shaped or what lay beneath them, but they had been well observed from the sea. *I see no notable departures from the estimates of our own Geometers,* Osir thought. *Geometers everywhere must have refined these estimates to a uniform theory of ice volumes.*

"Now may I view your transforms?" The party moved to an enormous adjoining chamber. On the main floor were eight clay structures, each representing one-fourth of a hemisphere reshaped to a flat surface. A central water trough connected all. Water filled each transform up to the current level of the World Ocean, and the familiar pattern of pegs had been repeated. Osir suspected the most likely source of error would be here. If the transformed surfaces didn't represent equal areas on the earth's surface, any calculations resulting from them would be off. *I can't believe it,* Osir thought, when he found no significant departures from the forms he had used in Erytheia. *These models appear to be equal area transformations of the spheres and therefore reliable.*

"May I now see the basins derived from these transforms?" Basins consisted of inverted surfaces shaped so as to make the tops of the pegs level. The heights of the glaciers thus appeared as depressions in the clay rather than peaks above a level surface. In order to determine the volume of water represented by the earth's ice, the Geometers simply filled the basins with water. Next, they reduced the water by ten percent to adjust for the difference between the relative volumes of ice and water. Finally, they drained the remaining water from basins into transforms. The result was a prediction of the sea level rise that would follow from melting that much ice into the World Ocean.

Osir pulled a peg from one of the transforms. On it was a black band about the thickness of Osir's thumb. It was consistent with the findings of the Geometers of the People of the Living Sun. This band represented the amount of settling that could be expected of the ocean's floor due to the added weight of meltwater. Osir then pulled a corresponding peg from one of the basins. *There it is! There's their source of error,* Osir thought. *There's no black band on the peg from the transform. They haven't accounted for the corresponding rebound that occurs as ice is removed from coastal lands.*

"Is there no bending of the earth caused by the weight of ice?" Osir asked earnestly.

"Nonsense!" answered D-El emphatically. "Demonstrably impossible! Ice floats on water; it will surely float on land. It therefore must have no weight."

"But water floats on land, in a manner of speaking, and you have accounted for the weight of water as it flows into the sea. Can ice on land be so different?" Osir reasoned.

"Young Master, have you not seen that water always seeks the lowest point of land while ice always seeks the highest?" D-El grilled his guest. "Have you ever climbed a mountain?"

"No, Sire, hardly more than a hill."

"Well, you'll find ice at its top, not its bottom. Yet, crawl down in a cave, and you'll find more water the deeper you go. Without this principle, it would be pointless for thirsty men to dig wells. Why, the soil would get drier with each toss of the spade! I fear you have much to learn."

"But ice is made of water," Osir countered. "Surely it too has weight."

"Not so. Ice floats on water. I've heard your argument before, and I refuse to spend time considering it further, " D-El growled with a gesture of dismissal toward his young adversary. "Ignore this silliness," he ordered the rest of his council.

If they failed to adjust for this distortion, they've underestimated the impact of water held in glaciers. Without more evidence, how will they ever be convinced? I must get to the ice. "And where will your people go when the waters rise?" Osir asked the Geometers.

"Up the mighty river to the land of Dilmun near the confluence of its parent rivers—the Pison, Gihon, Hiddekel, and Euphrates. There we will find a new home. It's a lush, beautiful land inhabited by primitives. We believe we have the forces to take it when the time comes."

Osir reexamined the basins, then the transforms. According to them, Dilmun would be dry land. Yet, according to the calculations of the People of the Living Sun, all but its highest upland would be inundated. "Think also of Ur and other lands farther north," he said, pointing upriver on the center transform.

"Why?" Sikor asked. "To appease your worried Geometers?"

Chronicle 33: The Lands of the Indus

After four days in port, the *Crown* set out to sea. A day under sail brought them again into the eastward pull of the Monsoon Drift. Bobbing along for two days and nights, they at last came into view of the mouth of the Indus, where they would harbor for at least a week. The city of Lotar sat in a shallow estuary on the arrow-straight coastline that ran the entire length of the subcontinent. The *Crown* berthed, and Captain Waleska granted liberty.

Although less impressive than the city of the Ziggurat Builders, Lotar nonetheless contained remarkable structures—temples, fortresses, and trading houses—all adorned with intricate statuary. In the open market, hawkers of every sort of ware converged on the weary travelers. Strange wild animals were displayed in the bazaars. Naked acrobats performed to drums, cymbals, and flutes. Maidens paraded through the streets, beckoning men and women to their temples, first to participate in pagan ceremonies, afterward to join in sexual pleasure. The men of the *Crown* looked forward to several days of liberty in this exotic place. Everywhere, there was music and noise and clamor.

Osir, however, set out to learn all that he could of the Geometry practiced by the People of the Indus. Again, the relationship got off to an awkward start. The Geometers were friendly enough, but they took Osir's queries lightly and passed them off with shallow replies. The sharpness of his responses caught them off guard, however, and they took him more seriously day by day. They told him their plans to escape upstream to the interior valley of the Indus when the waters would someday rise. By the end of the third day, Osir had penetrated to the inner sanctum of the Geometers' laboratory. Here again, he saw the elaborate hemispherical models of the earth's surface. But there were no basins, no transforms.

"What do your models say about the coming rise?" Osir asked, perplexed by the lack of analytical tools.

"That the rise will come," answered the Chief Geometer.

"But will it be great or small? Will it be fast or slow? Will it reach the First Terrace?"

"The waters will come when the waters come. In any case, we have too little information. Only wild guesses as to the size of the ice sheets in our world and on the Opposite Continent across the Eastern Ocean. Your Geometers speak confidently of things they've never seen. We don't deal in such magic," he said.

"So you think our calculations are no more than guesses?"

"With all due respect, that is exactly what we believe. Not one of our Geometers has ever seen these ice sheets. The estimates on which you place so much faith must be verified by observation. We don't know how far east the vast ice sheets of the Northern Lands extend. If we but knew their general shape and extent, we could predict the deluge with more confidence. Of course, no man can venture far enough inland to observe the main ice sheet. That can never be, for the mountains are too high and the dangers too great, much too great." Osir's imagination took flight at the thought of these great, white, frozen monsters of the Northern Lands, all the more alluring because they were off limits to ordinary men.

"We shall see," Osir said under his breath. "We shall see."

* * *

The *Crown* headed southward toward the Land of the Drevids. Each night, they anchored in small estuaries within clear sight of the grasslands along the coast. In the evenings, Osir watched as animals of the savanna congregated wherever small streams brought fresh water to the sea. Elephants trumpeted. Cranes stalked amongst hippopotami, both giant and dwarf, sloshing in shallow streams. Geraffids loped across the plains. Shore birds of infinite variety filled the skies with silhouettes and music. Tigers slinked in stands of dry grass behind the beach.

Farther south, savanna gave way to rich jungle, and the *Crown* reached a trifling port in the Land of the Drevids, a scattered population of coastal fishermen and hunters. The Drevids once had possessed a great culture and mighty cities, but everything had been demolished repeatedly by the rising waters of the past 4,000 years. War destroyed most of whatever the floods did not. Now they possessed no Pyramid, no Trove, no Geometry, and their heritage lay sunken beneath the waves.

"With the next rise, they will have no refuge. Their numbers will be reduced, their remnants scattered," Osir told Ketoh. "It's painful to think of such sad prospects, but that's nature's way. Some flee; others perish. It's been that way for thousands of years and will continue until the oceans are drained again."

There was little to be done in Drevidia except to restock foodstuffs and effect minor repairs of the vessel. Osir went ashore to walk on land and eat fresh fruit and seafood bought from street vendors. The Drevids held no council to discuss his mission.

* * *

Traveling for five days on open sea, the ship plied first southeast, then due east to a big peninsula that hung off the subcontinent. Densely settled and heavily tilled, this lush land supported a highly developed and sophisticated civilization rivaling the People of the Living Sun.

These were an industrious but fun-loving people whom Osir and his fellow adventurers quickly befriended. Their society had benefited early on from the domestication of animals, especially the ox and the elephant. They followed the predictions of Geometers elsewhere but had no such science of their own. They were simple agriculturists who took the word of others as to the rising and falling of the sea. Osir found no additional information to enhance his understanding of the Waters of Chaos.

* * *

"It's Triple Point," the captain said as they pulled into deep water far off Drevidia's shore. Looking just beyond the ship's bow Osir saw the strange pattern. The *Crown* floated on deep blue water. To the east, he saw dark green, to the north, dull gray.

"Where three oceans meet," Osir said, as the captain changed course and headed southeast toward the Sunda.

Chronicle 34: The Sunda

The next leg was the most adventuresome to date, taking the *Crown* out of sight of land for six days. The ship sailed east to the subcontinent of Sunda, thence southeast along its coast to the Sunda Kelapa pass, gateway to the Plain of Sunda. Osir's party debarked from the *Crown* and went ashore in a tiny inlet at the base of a volcanic peak called Krakatau. North of it lay a coarsely etched pass between the Sumatra Mountains to the west and Java Mountains to the east. As soon as his troops landed, Osir gathered them on a grassy meadow beside a rocky cove. For the first time, he briefed them on their mission.

"We will cross Sunda. From this place, we will proceed northward between those mountain ranges. We will enter the lowlands beyond and cross to the river of our ancestors, the Chao Phraya. We'll build boats on the river's edge and float downstream to its confluence with the River Mekong. We'll sail to Mekong City at its mouth. We will converse with the Mekong Geometers concerning their studies of the coming rise."

After giving orders for the day, Osir assembled his officers to answer any questions they might have.

"It is a great challenge," Ketoh said.

"It's a tremendous undertaking, Ketoh," Osir replied, "but this crossing is only the beginning of our true mission."

"Isn't our mission to visit the world's centers of science so that we can compare their predictions?" Busah was not one to question Osir's wisdom, but surely the time had come for a better explanation.

"That and more. It is also to visit the Ice itself and measure its volume so that we can predict how high the Waters of Chaos will rise . . . and how soon . . . and how fast."

"But, Osir, that's impossible. No man in one lifetime can possibly visit the Ice in enough places to understand it," Jumar said.

"If we understand the process, how the Ice forms and melts, we won't have to see all of it. Our first objective is to learn as much as possible from the world's Geometers so we can plan our travels wisely. A few sample observations then will serve us well."

"You really intend to do this, don't you? You plan to lead us to the far edges of the earth." Ketoh was both amazed and amused by his friend's audacity.

"Are you certain this can be done?" Busah asked.

"Our exploration is sound. We must learn about the Ice...in time to help King Rahn Mennon plan our people's refuge."

"Why must the prediction be so precise? Won't any place above the First Terrace serve the purpose?" Jumar asked.

"We must choose wisely. A haven too low might save a few generations but condemn the rest to repeated struggles with the sea. Our line would be diminished like the Drevids. No nation of perpetual refugees—without cities, livelihood, and learning—can maintain its wealth for generations.

"A haven too high would be even worse. We can't live apart from the sea. Our bodies demand its elements. Our children would die at the hands of the primitives or perhaps live like primitives themselves. No, the key to survival is to choose the time and place precisely so our descendants will survive for Kalpas to come. Time and place are everything."

"I never thought of it in those terms, Osir. The King is wise to support your mission."

"And, I'm fortunate to have you as my army," he said. "Together we will accomplish much."

"The first thing we need to accomplish is a fast run to those rocks," Ketoh said, thumbing over his shoulder at a black rhinoceros ambling out of the brush. Suddenly, the rhino charged and Ketoh led a hasty retreat. The near-sighted behemoth passed by harmlessly.

Later, when the troops were assembled for departure, Osir spoke. "You've seen the black rhino. He's just a hint of what is to come. We will trek through wilderness unlike anything we've encountered before. No one can ever be caught off guard. Is that clear?" Osir then ordered his men to lash their gear and prepare to march.

When the officers reported that all was ready, Osir gave the command, and his troops formed into four columns of 25 men each. The young leader smiled fondly as he remembered their passage from Egia to Berenicia four years earlier. *Many of these men are fellow Egians, veterans of that passage. Will this expedition have similar risks and rewards?* Osir wondered, as the column trod from the beachhead toward the pass.

Plants, stung by salt winds, were scrubby at first. Only a short walk inland, however, a dense canopy covered the land. Osir led them alongside a sleepy stream that drained the shallow divide. The men reveled in the freshness, the bright hues, the heavy scent of moist humus, the sights and sounds of abundant life. Vines drooped from a scaffold of huge trees that reached for the sky. Most of the path lay in dark shadow, but stark beams of light pierced the high canopy wherever one of the giants had fallen. Senses stirred to the mixed fragrances of wild flowers and musty, steaming detritus as 100 men trampled the mossy carpet of the open forest floor. They rejoiced in the cacophony of shrieks and calls and laughed at the antics of monkeys and birds high in the trees.

Osir's men found special delight in one treetop acrobat they called the Old-Man Ape, for it was about the size of an overweight human, and its comically large face looked like an aging man. Its arms, dangling at its sides or suspended at odd angles above its head, were completely out of proportion to the rest of its body. These apes lived together in small groups and appeared to have tender relationships with their offspring, much as humans do. The silhouette of an entire family, backlighted in the morning mist, was a rare thrill. Their graceful movement from vine to vine, treetop to treetop, was breathtaking.

Funniest of all were times when the man-like creatures came to ground, approached the encampment, and snooped through soldiers' belongings. Once one of the males made off with a sash, and the owner gave chase to no avail. The Old-Man Ape then swung from the trees with the treasure draped around his body to taunt the poor fellow. The soldier, of course, became the object of ridicule among his brothers-in-arms. For the remainder of the trek, he had to replace the lost sash with wild vines —a constant reminder to his tormentors.

From the pass, for the first time since leaving the seashore, Osir saw the forest through which they marched. It was a fierce and beautiful land, green to the sea and to the horizon in every direction, except for the blue of distant mountains and, in the east, a massive circular lake. Every ironwood tree could be spotted easily, even on distant hills, by its blotch of red-yellow-orange, the only tree in the tropical forest that changed color from season to season.

Osir found himself falling under the spell of this stunning, fearsome terrain. *No,* he heard himself say, *Don't do it. Don't believe it. This land is too dangerous . . . too treacherous to be trusted. The next weeks will prove just how dangerous.*

After a day's rest, he led the column down into the jungle, their course again set north-northeast toward a lone peak standing like a sentinel above the interior valley. This leg of the journey would take them across the upper reaches of the Javan River. Twice they had to ford its tributaries only to emerge, leeches and all, back to the black organic muck of the flat terrain. By the time they reached the second peak, his troops had suffered severely from the combined assaults of insects, poisonous snakes, tropical fevers, and animal attacks. Osir himself suffered a thigh wound from a broken tree branch. Festering wounds complicated their plight as the animals of the forest took up their scent and stalked the weakest men.

Ketoh slapped a mosquito on his neck. "One more bite and my neck will swell as big as a Westerner's," he said.

They pressed on, through sheer willpower, to the next summit. Osir was determined to find a place where they could recuperate in comfort and safety. Finally, Ketoh reported that a perfect spot had been found—a high, clean platform with its own pristine waterfall a little below Natuna Besar Peak. Red soil replaced black as they climbed. Reaching the site, his men were jubilant at the prospect of rest. Considering their physical condition, however, many would have preferred a longer rest than Osir could allow.

"We can't stay long, a couple of days at most, for the rains come soon, and we need at least two weeks to build boats. To cross the swamps in high water would be impossible, and to navigate the Chao Phraya and Mekong at flood stage would be suicidal."

On the morning of the third day, Osir ordered Bracon, one of Ketoh's scouts, to climb to the top of the low cliffs that framed the falls. "There it is. That must be the Chao Phraya," Bracon yelled. "I see the dark line of trees that lines its course. It slithers through the valley like a viper, about ten days walk to the northeast." On Bracon's return, Osir ordered the men to pack up and move on. For four days, they trekked across the seemingly endless plain. With luck, they would find a navigable tributary of the Chao

Phraya long before reaching its main stem. Each day, Ketoh dispatched scouts to the north and east looking for suitable streams.

* * *

Slogging through hauntingly beautiful but pestilent swamp, Osir was relieved to hear Ketoh's scouts report a promising channel. Noon next day, he was standing beside a lazy stream, staring into black water. Fish swarmed in the upper layer, which was strangely clear despite its tannic tinge. *Here on the bank, we'll build big wooden boats. The bulk of my force can cut and hew trees while a smaller detachment shapes paddles and rudders from its limbs.*

They felled the giant trees using the ancient method of slow burning. Small pockets were sculpted all around the base of the trunk. Each hole was stuffed with sun-dried moss that was then ignited by sparks from hard struck flints. The niches gradually expanded as ever-larger charges of moss and sticks were inserted. Steam constantly issued wherever fire met sap. Eventually, the holes became hearthlike in size until finally they met near the center with dramatic effect.

"Most beautiful sound I've heard in this cursed jungle," Ketoh said as one of the mighty behemoths crashed to earth. With skill and luck, the tree would fall headlong into the river flowing past its stump.

"Great!" yelled Busah as the falling mass found the channel. Immediately, several men crawled out to clear limbs and carve the boat's rounded exterior while others set a row of fires lengthwise on top of the trunk. By this time, two more giants had fallen upstream, and the same procedure was underway at all three locations. Gradually each tree assumed its final form, a giant canoe that would transport more than 30 men. Each one slowly began to float as ashes and air replaced solid wood inside.

It took less than the allotted two weeks to sculpt the boats. Before dark on the final day, most of the equipment and personal gear were loaded for departure. At daybreak, Osir ordered his men to board and launch. At first, the going was slow in the narrow meandering stream. Gradually, the course straightened and flow increased as two other tributaries joined the first.

Half a day's float with vast swamplands on both sides convinced all of their good fortune in finding a suitable stream. "How can anything be so beautiful as these wetlands and yet so frightening as these swamps?" Ketoh asked without expecting an answer.

"Thank Rahn, we're not trudging through that soggy mess," Busah said. "Surely, many men would have been lost. Even with these wooden hulls, I don't feel safe." Three times snakes dropped from overhanging limbs. Two men were bitten and lay writhing in pain for days. Another died from suffocation before his comrades could pry the constrictor, two manheights long, from his torso, neck, and head.

Dropping the body overboard demonstrated the fate that would befall any man who toppled in. Giant crocodiles slithered gracefully alongside, then gracelessly seized the floating corpse. Thrashing their mighty tails, they writhed and sounded. Hidden in the murky depths, the unseen monsters seemed somehow more frightening than in full view.

Near the main stem, the tributary broadened like a coastal estuary. "The Chao Phraya must be near!" one of the men yelled as standing waters appeared beside and below the main stream. Those who had studied the Geometry of the Earth's Surface knew to expect such a natural levee and backwater basin formed by perennial flooding and deposition of silt and debris. Here, the basin's level was half a manheight below the river and would remain so for a few more weeks until the river overflowed in its annual cycle.

On the morning of the third day, lookouts yelled, and two hands later, they discharged into the giant river. "Holy Rahn!" Osir said, as the scale of it took his breath. *Even here, so far upstream, the Chao Phraya is as large as the Great River of my homeland. And we still must converge with the River Mekong! Together they must look more like an ocean than a river. The green-shrouded shore, the giant strands of water lilies floating in placid backwaters, and the swells and swales of the stream itself are awesome,* he thought. *Surely no one can swim in such a river, for the current is much too swift, and crocodiles lurk under every wave.*

* * *

Three days on the Chao Phraya brought them to the Mekong. Osir, standing in the bow of the lead canoe, was the first to spot the massive vortex formed by conflicting currents. "Hard to port! Hard to port!" he yelled as his own boat veered toward the enormous souse hole. Realizing it was too late, he reversed his strategy. "Full speed ahead!" he ordered. In a heartbeat, oarsmen assumed the new cadence—balanced, strong, constant— and the vessel lurched forward. Osir crouched as the prow first went airborne, then plunged into the gaping maw. "Keep the cadence. Keep the cadence," he yelled.

Momentum carried the massive hull across the void and into the wall of upwelling water on the other side. Suddenly, Osir was immersed in the murky water. He gasped for air as the bow broke free again. "Row, row!" he yelled as oarsmen, two by two, reappeared above the waterline.

Osir looked back at the other vessels. The third boat had successfully steered away from the vortex, but the second was not so lucky. They watched in horror as it fell into a deep trough leading straight to the souse hole. The canoe still floated, but only heads and shoulders appeared above the near-vertical walls. Then the trough gave way and filled the boat from bow to stern. For an instant, the bow plunged downward, throwing the stern high. Two men flipped skyward, and the boat dropped out from under them. In moments, the entire vessel and all aboard were sucked beneath the swirling waters. The boat resurfaced with seven men missing. The rest clung desperately to the gunwales, gasping and retching, but alive.

Maybe the boat will right itself, Osir hoped. *With luck the missing ones can grab on and survive.* But the rogue current held its grip, and the river had taken its toll.

"Help! Save me!" came a feeble cry. An oarsman spied the source and pointed. Osir's crew sprang into action, rowing toward the screaming man. Just as quickly, hope turned to despair. Not five manheights behind the swimmer, a crocodile glided in for the kill. Osir looked into the swimmer's face. It was Salacoa, a faithful friend since the trek from Egia. "Swim, Sala, swim!" he cried as the croc drew ever closer. With superhuman effort, Sala at first outpaced the patient reptile. With only ten strokes to go, the beast disappeared beneath the surface.

Sala's face contorted, and he went under just as the boat arrived. At the last instant, two men grabbed his shoulders and tried to pull him aboard, but their combined strength was more than matched by the powerful croc. Osir drew his redsilver dagger and dived overboard. Plunging beneath the surface, he groped about until he felt the animal's knobby hide. *The neck,* Osir thought. *That's my only hope.* He searched for the soft underside and quickly sank his blade to its hilt. Blood gushed into the water, but moments passed with no release of the vicious grip. Finally, the men above pulled the flailing soldier aboard, and the cause of his release became clear. Sala's leg was severed at mid-thigh. The croc had taken its prize.

Osir quickly recognized his own peril. *Blood in the water! More crocs. No time to waste.* Grabbing the tip of a paddle, he pulled himself against the hull and swung over the gunwale. Rock hard snouts banged the dugout as hungry crocs, cheated of a meal, vented their rage. Sala nodded silently to Osir.

Nearby, swirling and thrashing drew Osir's attention. His stomach turned as Sala's leg broke the surface suspended between two crocs, then disappeared with the victor. For two hands, they searched, and for three more, they watched, but six men were lost, for no other survivors were found.

After their turbulent introduction, the two rivers settled into a more congenial relationship. Osir looked across the broad expanse.

Ocean indeed! Look at that. The surface even bulges upward in the center. It never occurred to me that a stream could be so broad as to curve like the sea itself.

* * *

As the expedition continued downriver, the first signs of human habitation appeared–fishermen afloat in reed boats and shallow wooden canoes, reed houseboats, bamboo shacks on natural levees, houses on stilts in the shallows, and even houses perched high in treetops. Floating markets clustered at the water's edge, a sure sign of even larger populations nearby. The forest, which had towered behind the levee, abruptly disappeared, and the levee, which had been covered with dense shrubs, turned mostly bare. Soon, the watery plumes entering from side channels shifted from blackish blue to reddish brown. Villages of tall buildings on manmade hillocks could be seen in the distance.

"Take her to starboard!" Osir commanded. Oarsmen veered, and the other vessels followed. Putting ashore in a backwater cove, the troops jumped into the shallow water, then quickly sought solid ground on a natural levee. Two men with an improvised litter helped the injured Salacoa ashore, the stump of his leg medicated and bandaged heavily by soldiers specially trained in field medicine.

"It's a land of plenty!" yelled the first man to reach the levee's top, excitement and disbelief evident as he saw the lush plain of the Mekong delta. Carefully tended fields stretched to the horizon. Dikes and canals divided family plots of rice and vegetables. Raised platforms, drier than the land around them, held swine and fowl. *Surely*, Osir thought, *no other land on earth could support such populations. This is truly the Chosen Land as our ancestors have told us.*

"Look, Osir!" Ketoh whispered. "We're being watched."

Out in the paddy, a farmer unbent from tending rice. Soon others joined him in amazement. The farmer spoke to a boy standing nearby, and the boy scurried in the direction the farmer pointed. Unable to take his eyes off the strange spectacle on the levee, the boy stumbled twice, almost falling into half-filled paddies. Reaching a larger berm, he ran toward a distant compound distinguished by a tall turret. Osir judged the structure to be three or four manheights above the surrounding fields. "We'll wait here," he decided.

"What if they're hostile?" Busah asked.

"Then their leaders in Mekong City will be hostile as well. If we can't make peace here, we'll surely suffer at their hands farther downstream. I'd rather face them where the odds are better matched." The men prepared their midday meal, a jerky of wild game plus fruit and nuts, all gathered in the jungle. "Stay vigilant. Keep your swords handy," Osir ordered, and his words passed quietly along the levee.

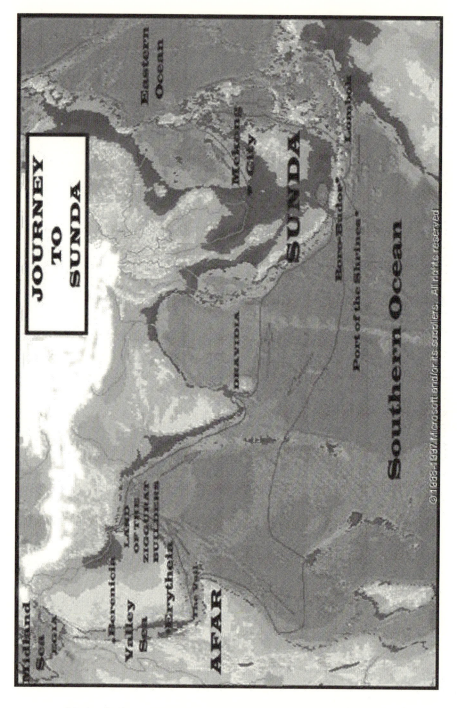

[Color images available at **www.thewatersofchaos.com**]

"Here they come!" one of the lookouts warned as dust rose near the village. The men watched as the powdery plume progressed steadily toward the river. Half a hand later, a cavalry unit arrived. "Greetings, friends!" Osir said to the soldiers, knowing his words would not be understood. His bold stance and friendly tone served him well, however, for the approaching guardsmen immediately relaxed, viewing their visitors with curiosity more than concern. The unit's commander spoke authoritatively, and Osir guessed what he meant. "Stand still!" he ordered.

The cavalry, about 30 in number, dismounted from their horses and surrounded Osir's men. They walked about curiously, studying the foreigners from every angle. One ventured forward and touched the fabric of a soldier's tunic; another pinched between his fingers the linen of Busah's singlet; another fondled Ketoh's brightly colored sash. *What are their thoughts?* Osir pondered. *Given the sophistication of their own brightly colored fabrics and well-crafted linens, they're probably just curious.*

Amid a flurry of unintelligible banter, the cavalry commander finally spoke above the others. Come with us, he seemed to say as his soldiers descended the embankment and nudged Osir's men back into their dugouts.

As Osir stood ready to board, the commander's eyes fixed on the fabled dirktooth sword. Slowly, cautiously, the man reached out but could not bring himself to touch the exquisite weapon. Osir slowly pulled the knife from its scabbard. Seeing its grand design and shining redsilver blade, the commander knelt at Osir's feet in a gesture of profound respect.

The foreigners' status quickly transformed from invaders to honored guests, and the cavalry commander held a brief conference with his men. "You! And you!" he apparently said, appointing a soldier to each boat. He himself then took a position beside Osir in the lead boat's bow. Thus, it was settled. Whatever the commander's initial intent, the dirktooth sword guaranteed a friendly escort to Mekong City.

* * *

As a brilliant sunset formed in the west, the gleaming seccas and spires of the mysterious city came into view. Soon the three canoes entered a grand canal, the central thoroughfare of Mekong City. *An urban marvel surpassed only by its own glorious past,* Osir thought when he spotted scores of older seccas in deep water, barely beneath the surface.

So greater empires do exist beyond our realm. Erytheia may be the greatest city to those who have never ventured beyond the Veil, but this spectacle is unsurpassed—unless there is yet another greater world beyond!

Oarsmen guided into vacant slips at the city wharf. Crossing the levee, they found an enclosed market filled with stalls, each lighted with lamps beneath a covering of loose palm fronds. Salacoa and two other injured men were rushed to an infirmary. The remaining troops were free to explore the market. On many tables were soft goods and light household items. One particular soldier rushed in a beeline to a clothier's stall for a new linen sash.

Vendors sold an exceptional variety of fruits and vegetables, most of which Osir had never seen before. Jackfruit, rambutan, guava, mangosteen, and lychee lay in piles on tabletops and shelves. Durian, a strange fruit with a tough green shell studded with hard spikes, lay in pyramidal piles on the ground beside stalls outfitted for splitting its hard shell and serving its meat. Osir's escort smiled and gestured to offer him a heavy durian. Holding his fingers together in midair, almost swooning, the commander looked heavenward, then fell silent still searching for words. Osir and his men laughed at the man's struggle to describe the fruit's ethereal delights.

"Its taste must be beyond description," Osir said, and the men laughed again.

"Must be better than sex," Ketoh said. This time the commander joined in the laughter, though certainly he didn't understand Ketoh's joke.

Osir signaled that he was willing to taste the fruit. He quickly regretted his decision, however, when a hand ax split the tough hide, and the stench of rotted meat filled the air. "Perhaps another will be better," he said to the commander without effect. "Surely they can tell it's spoiled." Osir said helplessly to his men as they turned away in revulsion.

The commander, however, appeared unaffected by the scent. Smiling broadly, he handed a section to his guest. Osir couldn't help wrinkling his nose as the fruit neared. "Foul. Rotten. Sour. Bad!" he said to the commander, his voice escalating.

Understanding full well Osir's reaction, the commander shook his head and laughed. Grandly, he reached for one of the large pulpy sacks poised loosely on a thick rind. In a move of pure passion, he thrust it into his mouth, then beamed in ecstasy.

"Apparently, it's supposed to be eaten this way," Osir said, wrinkling his nose as the man spat a large pit from his mouth. Remembering the foul brew of the Hill People that he had accepted as a boy, Osir yielded to his fate and grimaced. Peals of laughter came from his men and a growing throng of onlookers. The commander wheeled about and offered Osir a fresh section. Holding his breath, Osir followed the commander's lead and thrust the sack into his mouth. Instantly, he experienced a strange fetid delight. The same flush of pleasure that had possessed the host now overwhelmed his guest.

The audience first cheered, then stood in curious silence as Osir reacted favorably. "There must be a magic potion in this fruit," one Egian said to his comrades as silence turned to banter. In moments, several men lined up to try it. Some had the same reaction as Osir; others were repulsed. A pail of fresh water sat nearby so customers could wash the sticky juice from their hands and cleanse themselves of the odor. Even so, one soldier vomited.

Emerging from the market into the central plaza, Osir was dazzled by bright lights beaming on the massive white facade of the King's Palace. Fully ten manheights tall and stretching far down the main avenue, the walls of the palace were impressive. The commander guided them to the main gate where guards screened visitors. After a brief exchange, the watch chief granted permission to enter. He escorted them to an open barracks to wash up and relax before heading back to enjoy the city.

Osir was overwhelmed by the vastness of the compound with its open courtyard and massive temples. He was ushered to a large building on the eastern end. Above its entrance more than 20 lines were carved in different scripts. Coursing down, he found one line of familiar script. It read, "Hall of the Emissaries." Inside the great hall, he was motioned to wait in a theater-like atrium while his hosts summoned a dozen or more dignified gentlemen wearing monk's garb. Through signs, they urged him to speak, then listened keenly.

An elderly gentleman stepped from the group and interrupted Osir in mid-sentence. "Welcome to our realm," he said, then turned and dismissed the others, whose services were no longer needed once Osir's language was known. "How may we be of service to you?"

"My mission is to learn all that can be known of the coming Waters of Chaos."

"You are welcome to hear our findings. Our Geometers will be at your disposal. We ask only that you share your own knowledge in the same manner."

"Gladly!"

"Our Geometers will convene at noon tomorrow. You may remain in this hall as our guest." The old man then led Osir to a private chamber. He surveyed the apartment, a comfortable room with seating for three or four guests and, on either side, a bath chamber and a bedroom. The old scholar clapped twice, and servants appeared with food and drink. He then left Osir to eat in private.

Shortly, Osir heard a soft knock on the apartment door. He stared in surprise as a lovely young woman clad in loose white silk pants, a matching bodice, and sandals entered the room. Clean towels and a fresh robe draped over her right arm. "Come," she said, "you may wish to bathe." *The lines are well spoken,* Osir thought, *but I suspect they are newly learned under the monk's tutelage.* He found her gentle voice, smooth brown skin, and sensuous body exceedingly appealing. The maiden took Osir's hand and gently tugged him toward the second door where a large pool of steaming water awaited. The girl immediately untied the sash that held his sword in place. She removed his boots, tunic, singlet, and breechclout. She then emptied a pot of salts into the water along with a vial of scented oil. *Jasmine,* Osir recalled.

He stepped into the pool and looked into the girl's questioning gaze. "Yes!" he said, trusting the monk had provided her with such basic words. The smile on her face proved that she did indeed understand. She removed her sandals but otherwise remained fully clothed. Slowly, sensuously the courtesan advanced into the pool. One step at a time, she slowly immersed her silk-covered body in the steaming, scented liquid. Touching water, her garments instantly became translucent, revealing no less of her than if she had completely disrobed. Without protest from Osir, she began a methodical massage that left no part of his body untouched. Osir's thoughts turned to his home in Erytheia and his lovely bride Bera.

Should I take pleasure with this young lady?

Men of his realm were expected to do so freely, and surely Bera would have no objection to his needs being met. But his love for Bera, so fresh in his young heart, was overpowering in his loneliness.

Now I understand why she remained clothed. The choice is mine, and she has sensed how it will go. My thoughts are of Bera, my need is for Bera, and no other woman can fill that void. I will feel pleasure, but there will be no love between us.

At peace with his world, Osir lay back in the steaming water and relaxed for the first time since piercing the Veil.

CHAPTER 15

Search Log 30: The Coastal Imperative

Rick leaned back in a comfortable old armchair, savored a fine cigar, and faced Jared with a thoughtful scowl. He picked up a salt shaker and sprinkled white grains on the back of his hand. "Iodine could be the key."

"Iodine? Key to what?"

"To the big question we've been asking from the start. If a more advanced civilization lived down at the old coastline, why haven't archaeologists found traces of it in the land above?"

"Or, to put it another way, what geographical factors might differentiate coastal populations from interior populations?" Jared recalled many hours of discussion and many guesses but no firm answers.

"Right. Iodine may be the answer. We humans are highly dependent on iodine. Why is that?"

"I don't know . . . because our ancestors put too much salt on their fries?"

"Natural salt doesn't contain much iodine. We add iodine to table salt because it's essential to human health," Rick said, ignoring Jared's failed joke.

"So where does it come from?"

"Three sources: seafood, seafood, seafood! Actually, that's a slight exaggeration. I should have said seaweed, saltwater fish, and shellfish–all of them from the sea."

"Nothing in the interiors?" Jared asked.

"Hardly anything. I'm not certain whether freshwater shellfish concentrate iodine or not, but they're not a big part of the diet in continental interiors anyway."

"Unless you happen to be a Tennessee pearl diver," Jared joked, referring to the huge Tennessee River mussels harvested commercially– not for food but for their exquisitely contorted pearls. "Or a Cajun."

"True, true. I've indulged in fantastic crawfish boils, myself. I guess we better check that out. Fieldwork in Louisiana will be just the ticket. And forget about your garden. Vegetables don't contain much iodine in the first place, and many, like cabbage and kale, block the beneficial effects of iodine consumed from other sources. Hard to guess where it could have come from in prehistoric diets."

"They must have eaten a lot of meat."

"I've done some reading over the past few days. Meat and eggs are decent sources of iodine, but it takes a lot of meat to reach the minimum daily requirement. Besides, iodine content is dependent on the amount of iodine consumed by the animal, which in turn is dependent on the amount of iodine in soils and groundwater. Except for rare mineral springs, groundwater is a weak source in most interior regions. On the other hand, rainwater drifting in from the sea often contains more than enough iodine to replenish coastal soils. That helps boost levels in some plants and animals, but it's spotty, and it diminishes quickly with distance from the ocean."

"So most interior populations would be iodine deficient if they didn't import seaweed, saltwater fish, or shellfish purposely, either as food or medicine. Go on," Jared urged.

"Here's my question. If modern humans evolved on interior savannas as conventional theory has it, why would we have developed an overwhelming dependency for an obscure substance that doesn't exist there in quantities sufficient for human health? That just doesn't make sense."

Jared sipped a peaty 21-year-old Scotch and matched Rick's scowl. "Sounds like anthropologists and medical scientists should get together on that one."

"I gave Kent a call. He confirmed that the dependency is universal. All races get goiters and life-threatening diseases if they don't regularly consume iodine. Some family lines are more susceptible than others, but everyone has a threshold requirement. There you have it . . . from our very own medical scientist, you might say."

On a nearby sofa, Ellie and Anna sipped Chardonnay and chatted as the two couples waited for a dinner table in the Smoky Mountain Brewing Company, Knoxville's newly opened microbrewery. The restaurant's Cigar & Scotch Lounge was a relaxing haven for patrons awaiting seating. Throughout the room, guests were engaged in easy conversation, even among strangers. A walk-in humidor at one end contained an assortment of rare cigars and aged, single-malt Scotches. Both brothers had stopped smoking pipes and slowed down on cigars years earlier for health's sake, but the temptation here was too great. On the other hand, neither had found any good reason to forego the occasional shot of fine Scotch.

"Goiters aren't life threatening, are they?"

"They can be, but it's rare. The big problem is disfigurement and discomfort. Goiters don't usually affect human reproduction . . . physically, that is," Rick said.

"So there's nothing except social distain that would eliminate them from the gene pool?"

"That's right. Still, it seems strange that a bad trait, like goiter, would persist solely because of a deficiency in the very environment where the population is supposed to have evolved. Surely, that means anthropologists are missing a crucial episode in human evolution. A major biological leap must have occurred in the coastal zone where iodine was always abundant."

Both men paused for a while, savoring their cigars, and listened to a young woman telling Ellie and Anna her candid opinion of the pub's four brews. Given the typical American taste for light beers, they were surprised to hear that she actually preferred a stouter brew than the pub offered.

"What about salt domes? That could account for deposits in some interior areas, couldn't it?" Jared asked.

"Nope, even sea salt itself is a poor source. Most people associate iodine with salt, but that's purely because, in the first half of this century, most modern societies decided salt was a good medium for administering the iodine supplement that good health demands."

"So where does goiter occur?"

Rick held his own neck like a noose. Jared ignored Rick's antic.

"According to encyclopedias, the general rule is mountains and formerly glaciated areas," Rick went on.. "*Most* of the world's mountain zones are Goiter Belts. The Great Lakes Region of the U.S. is another stronghold, not because of mountains, but because it was so heavily glaciated."

"When you ran the idea by Kent, did he think it made good medical sense?"

"Our brother says evolving organisms develop such dependencies only if ample quantities are available in the environment. We humans didn't develop the ability to produce certain necessary proteins, for instance, because they are ubiquitous in available food sources. Of course, we couldn't manufacture an element like iodine per se, but we might have evolved along different lines that wouldn't require that specific element. If a substance is universally available, no selection will occur to breed the deficiency disease out of the population. Goiter may be a prime example of that biological principle."

"In that case, the remaining question is *when* the dependency developed. Was it in primeval times when reptiles emerged from the sea? Was it when hominids split off from other primates? Was it when *Homo sapiens* split off from *Homo erectus*, or when *Homo sapiens sapiens* split off from just plain old *sapiens*?" Jared asked. "That's a tough one."

"Well, perhaps not. A little evolutionary logic could help narrow it down."

"Such as?"

"First, how prevalent is iodine dependency among non-humans? Not many animals have the luxury of importing seafood. How many have goiter? For that matter, how many have thyroids?"

"Yes, but let's not focus on goiters alone. Maybe there are worse symptoms of iodine deficiency that do affect natural selection," Jared said.

"Good point. I'll call Doris Pickard. She's a friend of ours and a medical librarian over at UT hospital. I'm sure she can point me in the right direction."

A waiter politely tapped Rick on the shoulder and announced that their table was ready.

* * *

A week later, Jared called Rick at home. "Any luck with iodine?"

"Doris came through with some good references. She searched the MEDLINE system and found a World Health Organization study done in the sixties and a follow-up in 1980 by Stanbury and Hetzel. Your hunch that there might be other, more serious symptoms was right. There's a doosie."

"Oh?"

"How about endemic cretinism?"

"As in *cretin*? Serious business, I'm sure."

"It is. Severe mental retardation and physical deformity. Dwarfism. Distinctive physical appearance. Characteristic gait. Drooling. Can cause total dysfunction. Can be fatal."

"And iodine deficiency is the culprit?" Jared asked.

"Yes, dietary deficiency . . . or faulty thyroid. Either way the iodine doesn't get where it's needed."

"Is it common?"

"Yes, in certain regions. That's really what 'endemic' means. . . a disease that happens throughout a region because of environmental conditions, not by the spread of germs. Can be as high as 10 percent of the population in low-iodine environments when there's no artificial iodine supplementation."

"What about goiter?"

"Can be as high as 80 percent in iodine deficient regions."

"Eighty percent! You can't be serious," Jared exclaimed.

"Eighty percent goitrous. Six percent severely disfigured and retarded. If humans really evolved in a low iodine environment, goiters would have been their natural state and lack of goiter an oddity. That's absurd."

"Impressive figures! Still, investigators must be counting some rather mild symptoms to get such high numbers."

"These were scientific studies with well-established criteria. The definition includes any enlargement of the thyroid. But no one can miss a 15-pounder," Rick said.

"Fifteen pounds!"

"That's right. The most severe cases include *children* with goiters that big. The implication is clear. Modern humans desperately need iodine. Iodine comes from the sea. Ergo, we must have dwelt mostly in or by the sea until we developed physical and cultural mechanisms that would allow us to import iodine."

"Mechanisms such as?" Jared quizzed.

"Trade with the coast would be my first guess. Of course, anyone living on a salmon stream might get home delivery."

"So when did the dependency develop?"

"My instincts tell me it must have happened not long before the dawn of modern humans. Otherwise, every ape would have the same dependency that we do."

"Are humans the only creatures who have iodine dependency?" Jared asked.

"No, there are others. Goiters can be induced experimentally in mice and monkeys, for instance. I don't know whether or not the symptoms occur in the wild. I seriously doubt it, but I'll keep looking."

"It's getting late. I have to hang up, but, before I do, just give me some quick answers."

"What's on your list? I'll give them my best shot."

"Okay, is the dependency unique to *Homo sapiens sapiens* or did *neanderthalensis* have it, too? And what about archaic *sapiens*? Did they have it?"

"It's all very sketchy, but my personal guess is that it was present in the ancestral lines. Next!"

"Were other sources of iodine available in prehistory that are not available or not exploited today?"

"Unlikely. In fact, glaciated areas must have been super deficient, even worse than today. Next!"

"Are there other dietary markers that would serve as similar clues to human origins?"

Rick replied, "Just check out the side of a cereal box. The nutrition label, I mean. Take Vitamin C, for example. Does our dependency on it mean we originated in a tropical area? There aren't many indigenous sources elsewhere. You can get it from conifer needles, but, believe me, that's no way to sprout a new branch of the family tree. I had pine needle tea in Navy survival training. It was awful! I had spruce beer, too, in Alaska. Captain Cooke made spruce beer to avoid scurvy when he wintered over in Cooke Inlet—the anchorage for which the city was named. He had to flog his men to make them drink it. It's vile stuff, certainly not worth evolving for."

"But we already know humans have tropical origins. That's standard theory. Maybe iodine explains those origins and a whole lot more. Maybe it explains why later humans, even in the last Ice Age, would have stuck close to the seashore. Maybe it explains how an advanced culture could have existed for millennia without leaving traces on the higher lands we see today. Now get some sleep and check out that cereal box in the morning. Keep searching."

"I will."

Search Log 31: The White Buffalo

"It just doesn't get any better than this." Ben Carter slouched in a rickety swivel chair with feet propped on the johnboat's gunwale. Blue skies reflected off the swiftly flowing water; midsummer leaves draped high cliffs along the north bank of the White River. He and Rick Caisson had caught and released more trout in the past three days than most folks catch in a lifetime. Ben jerked his line again. This was their annual retreat to the Ozarks. Six guys in two cabins by the river…two rivers actually, for their fish camp sat beside the confluence of the White and Buffalo Rivers at Buffalo City, Arkansas. Their fishing hole consisted of a three-mile stretch of river in a setting so idyllic it once appeared in *National Geographic*. For an avid trout fisherman, that's sort of like dating a former Playmate, and theirs was the July '79 centerfold.

Almost annoyed at the pesky fish for disturbing his rest, Ben trailed the tip of his rod back and forth giving the trout every opportunity to break free. "Get off now. Go on," he said. Finally, it let go. He cast again. "So you think you and your bro have solved the age-old riddle of the universe?"

"Nah, but we've got a good start at it."

"So the ocean rises 400 feet. Big deal! I say you're making too much of it."

"Maybe, but I don't think so. Four hundred feet is a lot of water."

"Roscoe, the guy at the camp store, said that cliff over there is 660 feet high." He gestured toward the highest point of the bluff.

"Yep. That's the gospel according to Roscoe," Rick said, "not counting the cross on top." He laughed to himself. Confounding Carter was one of his favorite pastimes.

"So, if we were floating here at sea level and the water rose 400 feet, we'd only rise two thirds of the way up. Big friggin' deal! Any self-respecting caveman could climb that in half an hour and move his belongings to a new cave farther up."

"Speak for yourself, Carter. You'd rather drown than climb a cliff."

"You're right, I'd just stay here at this trout motel, and let this old rowboat float me to the top."

"Trout motel? Fish check in, but they don't check out? Right?"

"You got it! But seriously, shouldn't you rethink this deal before you stake your reputation on it?"

"Ben, how far do you think we are from the ocean?" Rick asked.

"I don't know. Four, maybe five hundred miles. Why?"

"See that boat ramp over by the meadow?"

"Yep."

"I checked Roscoe's map," Rick said. "That boat ramp is 381 feet above sea level."

"Are you kidding me?"

"Nope."

"So if the ocean rose another 400 feet, for real . . ."

"We'd dock at our front porch up on the meadow."

"And everything from New Orleans to here would be gone."

"Plus all the Coastal Plain from here to Washington, D.C. Wiped off the map."

"That does sound serious."

"You'd really miss Bourbon Street, wouldn't you? And what about your home in Houston?" Rick asked.

"No, that's okay. I've got homeowners insurance."

"Now there's a man who plans ahead," Rick deadpanned.

"Still, if reasonably advanced civilizations existed back then, why hasn't someone found solid evidence?"

"Let's move upstream." Rick cranked the outboard while Carter hauled in the anchor. "Take a look at that field . . ." Caisson yelled over the motor's drone, ". . . where the farmer was shooting crows yesterday."

"It's lovely," Carter responded uncharacteristically, and Caisson sensed a hint of sarcasm. Carter continued after a dramatic pause. "We just about got our heads blown off, and now you leave a perfectly good trout motel to go sightseeing at the killing field. Sometimes I wonder about you, Caisson."

"Roscoe told me something else, Carter. That's where Buffalo City was at the turn of the century. Two thousand people lived on that meadow! What we call Buffalo City was then just a suburb across the river. There was regular ferry service crossing the river, and a scheduled steamboat brought passengers and freight up the Arkansas River from Little Rock to a sizable hotel next to the camp store. Never guess it now, would you?"

"No, you're probably right. But a trained observer would."

"Not under 400 feet of water."

"Okay, so 400 feet of water *is* a big friggin' deal."

Search Log 32: Tel Aviv to Athens

Desperate for English after 16 days abroad on business, Rick dashed into a used bookstore on Tel Aviv's Diefendorf Street. A "recycler" specializing in used English language books was beyond Rick's best hope, but there it stood. A quick run through HISTORIES, AUTOBIOGRAPHIES, and ROMANCES turned up nothing of interest. *Something on ancient sea levels would be too much to expect*, he thought, as his impatience mounted. How about *DOCUMENTARIES AND CURRENT AFFAIRS*? As he turned to do so, however, his eye caught an intriguing title, *Cold Sea Rising*, by Richard Moran. *Has someone else put two and two together*, Rick asked himself. *Have we been scooped?* He reached for the book, eager to read, yet afraid of what he might find. He would read it on the plane to Athens.

His concerns were unfounded. Set in modern times, the book foretold an imaginary set of events including a volcanic eruption and a nuclear holocaust that would break loose the Ross Ice Shelf and send it floating northward. The great threat lay in public fear that the rogue iceberg of near-continental size might float into tropical seas where it would melt and flood the world's seaports. The novel's central drama lay in the attempts of mere mortals to direct the berg back south to keep it cold.

Moran had indeed made some valid points regarding sea level change and had done his homework on the geography of Antarctica. Unfortunately, however, as Rick later told Jared, "the guy missed the boat when it comes to the physics of ice and water." *The simple experiment of dropping an ice cube into a glass of water would have set him right. Once an iceberg floats, its effect on sea level is immediate. The buoyancy of ice is determined by the weight of water it displaces, and a floating object must displace its full weight. Hence, the same volume is added instantaneously, with or without melting.*

Earlier, Rick and Jared had noted this point of confusion even in serious literature about the Ice Ages. Most accounts, including some from scientists who should have known better, assumed that the water's rise would always be gradual because of the slow rate at which melting occurs. Most forgot that glaciers poised near the coasts or on shelves extending out from the coast, and ice mountains resting on the ocean floor have the potential to float free at any time. If lots of them did so at the same time, the impact on sea level would be immediate and catastrophic. Furthermore, the effect could be amplified as each event triggered another. A chain reaction thus could be set off, and the result would be *monumentally* catastrophic.

* * *

Rick stood atop the Acropolis staring at a postcard sunset above the rooftop jumble of Athens, an out-of-the-way but necessary stopover. His itinerary called for business meetings in Tel Aviv, then Saudi Arabia. The Saudis, however, won't admit travelers whose passports show they have visited Israel. In the standard charade, Israel issues disposable visas, and passports aren't stamped. Or rather they are stamped, but on a sticky note pasted to a page in the passport. No Arab country will admit anyone, however, without a stamp indicating place of origin. A stopover in any other nation willing to ignore the missing Israeli stamp satisfies that demand.

Rick chose Greece. *All my life I've longed to see these ancient ruins,* Rick thought. *Earlier, I would have envisioned the glory of Hellenic Greece like Jared did when he came here in '68. Now, I want to look past these crumbling ruins, past the ancient temples. I want to see this rock itself in an ancient time before human hands blemished or embellished its natural wonder.* The crest was remarkably level, and its white stone shone brilliantly. He walked to the apron in front of the Parthenon. To the south spread the blue waters of the Aegean. To the north stood the dramatic capstone of Lykavitos and majestic distant

Olympus. Below, spread the picturesque Plaka filled with taberna, shops, and rooftop gardens.

Imagine life in the land now beneath the waves off Piraeus. Would this imposing mass of stone have been visible from that ancient shoreline, Rick pondered. *Would Homer's ancestors have been tempted, like later Greeks, to deify this place? Would they have stared from this rocky crown toward Olympus and declared its pinnacle the dwelling place of gods? Did learned men and women bear witness to the deluge as it unfolded? Did their traditions become the mythology we know today?*

Esteemed writers such as Plato described forgotten times and places. Myths tantalizingly depicted gods pestered by floods on the plains of Attica, yet there are no plains to speak of there today. How could they have known? What truths gave rise to the legend of Elysian Fields on islands lost to the sea?

In popular culture, Atlantis overshadows flooded Greece. Yet, the old priest of Sais who told of Atlantis also gave a fascinating account of Athens before the flood. Plato's rendition is judged to have been politically motivated and therefore of doubtful authenticity, yet its description of antediluvian Greece is hauntingly accurate when compared to modern profiles of the Aegean floor. How did they know what lay beneath hundreds of feet of water? How could a myth cut from whole cloth correspond so convincingly with the now-verified sea level rise at the end of the Ice Ages?

Perhaps Plato merely repeated an eyewitness account flavored with 9,000 years of embellishment. Perhaps Greek gods were mortal men who ruled this land before the flood just as the old priest told Solon? Perhaps illiterate shepherds in the hills were the only survivors left to tell of Elysian Fields and halcyon days. We may never know, but the rationale seems clear. Someone noticed when this homeland shrank to a narrow strand, and someone else thought it worth repeating generation after generation. Hesitantly, Rick turned to the gently winding path. *How could the ancients have known so much,* he pondered, savoring a last view of the teeming, twilight-shrouded city below?

CHAPTER 16

Chronicle 35: The Geometers

Sultry morning air poured through open windows and penetrated the fine lace netting of Osir's bedchamber. Birdsongs brightened the Sunda day. Scents of gardenia, jasmine, and rose resurrected delightful memories of the previous evening…and the never-to-be-forgotten pleasures of the Mekong bath. A knock on the door signaled the ritual of food, drink, and bath that erased all thought of the rough transit that had brought him here. After his bath he asked the maiden to summon the interpreter.

"How is it that you speak our language?" Osir asked, trying not to sound overly impressed by the man's skill.

"We are the parents, and you are the children," the old monk explained. "It's our duty to attend our offspring. We know the languages and cultures of all nations that grew from our clan. For thousands of years, our grand library has trained two monks of our order to speak the language of each realm. You People of the Living Sun are but one of many peoples. I am Butyeh, interpreter of the languages of the Valley Sea. In my youth, I was chosen to speak your tongue."

"But languages change over time. How do you know our language today?"

"Each generation, your king provides our court a temple virgin who speaks your language well."

"And how is it that your people are able to move so freely from your land to ours? The journey across Sunda decimated my small army."

"Our Geometers of the Earth's Surface have charted passages around the Kalimantan between Sunda and Sahul. Your sailors don't know these passages. You are welcome to share this knowledge with your people."

"Our leaders and scholars must know the splendor of this place. What other worlds are omitted from our Geometry?" He paused. "And do our emissaries visit here often?"

"You are the first in recent times, Commander Osir. But your King Rahn Mennon, knows much about our realm."

"But how . . ."

"You ask, of course, how we acquire the maiden," Butyeh interrupted. "It is customary for our ships to meet your ships on this side of the Veil. The exchange always occurs on the morning of the High Sun Solstice every twentieth year. You may meet the virgin who was most recently brought here, if you wish."

"Perhaps before my departure," Osir said politely. As a child, he had accepted as noble and worthy the loss of his twin sister, Isas, to some unknown place. Later, when Mira was taken to the temple dormitory in Egia (or Berenicia or Erytheia, he might never know which), he questioned the custom. He would meet with this woman if it pleased the monk, but he did not look forward to it. "First we must see to the Geometry."

"Certainly, I had no other intention," the old monk said with a touch of embarrassment. "One should never put such a trivial matter above one's supreme mission. This great building is the Hall of the Emissaries where delegates from each tribe come to work and study with us for months, sometimes years, at a time."

"Are delegates here now?"

"Only one, Master. The distinguished Emissary of Cha, the yellow tribes of the east, is in residence. You will meet him today. He is an expert on the Mystery of the Cauldrons and will make a special report for your benefit."

"Mystery of the Cauldrons? I'm not familiar with this mystery."

The old man registered shock at Osir's ignorance of this basic tenet of the Geometry. "You have much to learn," he said.

"Then shall we proceed to the Hall of the Geometers?"

"At your pleasure, Master Osir."

* * *

At the far end of the compound stood a stately building with a towering temple-like structure at one side. The carved teakwood entrance dwarfed every other doorway Osir recalled from Erytheia and Hormuz. He noted the now familiar array of scripts. The one he could read said, "Hall of the Geometers."

Inside, the sergeant-at-arms conducted them to the main assembly floor where more than 100 Geometers had gathered. In a conspicuous place of honor sat a wrinkled little man with narrowed eyes and saffron skin unlike any human Osir had seen before. Even the whites of the Yellow Emissary's eyes looked like yellowed ivory. All heads turned as Osir and Butyeh were announced. Butyeh then stood before the council and spoke at length of Osir's origin and his mission. The council clapped a warm greeting.

Osir reported the findings of his people and the other councils he had visited. At first, Osir presumed he was delivering new information regarding the flaw in the models used by the Ziggurat Builders. The Geometers of Sunda, however, were already aware and had been similarly frustrated in their attempts to correct an emissary from that land who had appeared before them many years earlier.

"Some people will never change!" concluded Sutallee, the Chief Geometer. "You may continue."

Osir then told of the complaint he had heard from the People of the Indus that too little was known of glaciers in the far north and south. A string of loud words, at first expressing annoyance, then anger, rumbled from the Yellow Emissary. Then came a lengthy discourse only slightly less intense than his opening outburst. Finally he fell silent.

Now the stooped, spindly fellow spoke softly. His interpreter followed suit. "The People of the Indus are correct."

The entire council laughed more loudly than before. The Yellow Emissary first scowled, then smiled in resignation and laughed gamely along with his hosts.

Sutallee reclaimed the floor. "Indeed they are correct, as is the distinguished emissary from the Plains of Cha beside the Yellow Sea," he said, as another flutter of friendly humor echoed through the chamber. "We must explore the Ice. We know little about the causes of the Slow Rise and less about the Fast Rise. We especially want to solve the Mystery of the Cauldrons."

"And what of the Drevids?" the Chief Geometer asked. "You made no mention of their science."

What about this Mystery of the Cauldrons, Osir thought. But a question had been asked, and protocol demanded that he answer before pursuing his own question. "They failed. They lost their heritage. They have no Pyramid, no Trove, no Geometry. They seek only to survive." His listeners shook their heads in pity.

"Such is the way of the world," spoke one of the councilors. "Knowledge, like the flames of a night fire, must ever be rekindled. Never are we more than one generation from the dark ages, if only we fail to teach our children. The tragedy of the Drevids is a powerful reminder of our own obligation to learn more about the Waters of Chaos, protect all knowledge, and pass it on to our children."

When Osir finished, the Chief Geometer spoke. "Thank you for sharing your knowledge with us. Your people have learned much. Your scientific work is well conceived and carefully conducted. The Ziggurat Builders are...making progress." Earlier the assembly had withheld its laughter during Osir's straight-faced account of D-El's arguments concerning the weight of ice. Now they laughed heartily. "Tomorrow we will share our knowledge as well."

* * *

Next day, Butyeh joined Osir at the appointed time, and they returned to the Hall of the Geometers. On arrival, Butyeh led Osir to the council chamber for Sutallee's introduction. "You are now at the center of all Geometric learning among the Chosen People. We honor you with admission to our sacred chambers. You are solemnly obliged to use this information to the betterment of your people and to the furtherance of Geometric knowledge. Will you swear to so do?"

"I swear, Teacher," answered Osir, using the title of utmost honor.

"Then you shall be admitted." The Chief Geometer motioned grandly to the sergeants-at-arms who then opened the inner chamber doors. Council leaders rose from the dais, and everyone entered. Osir found familiar models, transforms, and basins, easily ten times the size of those in Erytheia and Hormuz.

The Geometers conducted a tour for Osir's benefit. "Here is the Ice of the Southern Continent . . . the Ice of the Opposite Continent . . . the Ice of the Northern Lands . . ."

Such detail, such precision. Each coastal margin so well defined. But look to the interiors. Nothing but broad, wavy bands, uncertain strokes. Nothing but crude guesses. Probably hearsay from coastal tribes who've never even seen the Ice. Yet, here are three features I've never seen before.

"These are mere tools," the chief Geometer said. "The center piece of our Geometry is the hydraulicon." He opened yet another set of doors and led the party into a chamber cluttered with mechanical devices. Osir's jaw dropped in amazement. In the center spread a massive, detailed model of the Sunda. Mekong City appeared in minute detail. Every building, every hill, every wall or roadway occupied its proper place.

"How does this machine work?" Osir asked.

"Geometers theorize the behavior of ice in northern lands. Then we release the reservoir's gates, so that water flows across the model land and into the model sea. Using this technique, we predict the effects of sea rise on every piece of our land."

"And what have you determined?"

"Nothing. We have too little information about the ice to use the hydraulicon effectively." Sutallee shook his head sadly as he spoke. He then led the group back into the main chamber. "For now, we must be content with these." He waved his hand toward the large-area basins and transforms. "Someday we hope to gain enough understanding to employ the hydraulicon." Osir looked at the models with renewed interest.

At the poleward extremes of the World Ocean were continuous lines of white. He pointed curiously to the feature. "Ice shelves discovered by Sundan explorers," Sutallee explained.

"Then Sundans have actually seen the Ice?" Osir asked.

"No, no. We only know it from the tales of natives on islands between here and there. They describe shelves that extend far from land."

Osir then pointed to scattered white blotches spreading from tidewater glaciers across adjacent stretches of ocean. "And these?"

"Here islands of ice float continuously on ocean currents. Their numbers and sizes change from time to time. We believe they tell much about the Ice, but we have so few accounts. Perhaps someday we'll have sufficient observations to predict when collapses will occur," a councilor said wistfully.

Osir pointed to the third feature. At three map locations, blue lines extended from continental ice sheets down to the sea. One line lay on the western edge of the Opposite Continent near the southern boundary of the Ice. Another lay on the eastern edge of the Northern Lands. A third one lay on the low divide between their own Northern Lands and the Opposite Continent. At the origin of each line was a patch of blue paint. When Osir switched to the transforms, he found in each of those same locations a cauldron suspended on a rod.

So that's the Mystery of the Cauldrons! Well, they certainly are a mystery to me.

The Yellow Emissary spoke. An interpreter repeated every word to Butyeh, who then conveyed them to Osir. "Good friends, fellow Geometers, Distinguished Emissary of the People of the Living Sun. Allow me to explain the Mystery of the Cauldrons." He pointed to a giant chart above the transforms. "In the past 6,000 years, we have continuously experienced the Slow Rise of the Waters of Chaos. On five occasions, the Fast Rise has occurred. On each of these occasions, coastal natives near the places marked in blue describe a freshwater flood of incredible magnitude gushing from the interior. Many villages are destroyed, and many people drown. Each spill brings a wall of water great enough to make its own mighty winds so that no man can stand even if he is far from the water's path.

"Our explorers never observed these floods, but they have seen the aftermath—land scoured to bedrock by rushing water, deep pools of water remaining after the floods have gone, boulders as large as pyramids tossed about like pebbles. Geometers have measured watermarks as high as 100 manheights above the valley floors. These watermarks lie many days walk from the streams that formed them. What's more, we know these floods happen repeatedly. We sometimes find as many as 100 separate layers of soil deposited wherever floodwaters were impounded by natural blockages. Native legends hold that the gods of the Ice have overturned their cauldrons in anger, over and over again. Thus, we call these the Valleys of the Cauldrons." He slapped each blue splotch with his pointing stick.

"We believe these great floods flow into the Eastern Ocean and create walls of water that reach across the ocean even to the land of Cha. They inundate our coastal lowlands and destroy villages and towns. For years, our Geometers have believed these floods are the sole cause of the Fast Rise. However, my calculations prove that, despite the great volume of water released, each cauldron by itself is capable of raising the World Ocean no more than the height of a man's ankle." A collective murmur coursed through the room.

"Clearly, the spilling of the Cauldrons is a harbinger of the Fast Rise but not its only cause. Keep in mind that the Fast Rise always begins with a sudden tidal wave, but it continues in stages for months thereafter, sometimes reaching a manheight or more. Three times, to our knowledge, the Fast Rise reached four manheights. Tribes were lost, civilizations destroyed, lands covered forever. Now we know the sequence of events, but that is not enough. Our purpose is to discover the reasons these Cauldrons spill. If we know this, perhaps we can determine how long it will be until the next Fast Rise and thereby know when to flee to the lands above."

"Are any unusual conditions associated with the Cauldron floods?" Osir asked, still awed by the old man's insight and masterful presentation.

"According to coastal tribes, streams in the Valleys of the Cauldrons barely flow for many years prior to each spilling."

"And has this occurred in recent memory?"

"I regret to say that it is so. Even now, some great rivers have almost ceased to flow."

"And observations from warm lands where no Cauldrons exist?"

"Our brothers on the island continent of Mindanao, northeast of here, were first to record that tropical skies sometimes rose to new heights in earlier kalpas."

"The skies rose? What does that mean?" Osir asked.

"In most ages, clouds meet the mountains on lower slopes. Yet, in the rising age of each kalpa, the age when Cauldrons empty, these same clouds strike the mountains only on upper slopes. Late in the Rising Age, clouds even soar high above the mountaintops so that the land is visible from bottom to top. We have no explanation, no theory, but always the Fast Rise occurs when clouds rise and rivers cease to flow."

"And has the sky now changed?"

"Yes, I sadly report that clouds began rising three generations ago. Now they rise ever more swiftly."

"So, you conclude that the Fast Rise will come soon. Is it possible that the spilling of the Cauldrons somehow unleashes water from another source in quantities much larger than the Cauldrons themselves?" Osir asked.

"Yes, that must be it. But how? Where? Where would that much water be hiding?" The old man gestured toward the model, then threw his stick in frustration.

Now I know where my next adventure must be.

Chronicle 36: The Virgin from the Valley Sea

One morning in the fourth and final week of Osir's stay, Butyeh knocked at his chamber door. With reluctance, Osir extracted himself from his daily bath. The girl, still dressed in silk, emerged from the warm waters and dried him. He dressed quickly and answered the door. Butyeh's initial conversation centered on matters of business and Geometry. Something in his demeanor, however, belied an unspoken agenda.

"So tell me Butyeh, what do you really want to say?"

"Why, nothing, Sire. Is there something you would like me to say? I will be happy to say whatever pleases you."

"No, Butyeh, there is nothing I want to hear, but your manner suggests more than your words. Is there something I can do for you?"

"Perhaps. I would like to discuss with you, once again, the forms and uses of the action words in your language which describe the movements of the tides."

"We've already covered that sufficiently, and you never forget a rule of tongue, Butyeh. There must be something else."

"Perhaps, perhaps." Butyeh gave an air of unconcern, but Osir sensed that something remained unsaid.

"Have you forgotten the words? Can that possibly be?"

"I want to review them with you *and* the Virgin from the Valley Sea."

"You don't need my help."

"Yes, I'm certain you're correct. Nonetheless, it might be best if you could join me."

"Ah, so that's it. You want me to visit the virgin. You've been steering me toward her for the past week, haven't you?"

"Not to my knowledge, Sire."

"Oh, Butyeh. Don't take offense. I don't mind, really."

"But you seem reluctant, Sire."

Perhaps, Osir thought, *but I don't know why. Maybe it's guilt. After all, I have given my life to a social order that forces these young women to serve in captivity and subjugation. I can't think of anything sadder than a child torn from her family and forced to spend the rest of her days in a foreign land. Yet I've never taken a stand to oppose this injustice.*

"Why do you want me to meet this lady?"

"I have no reason, Sire, only my inner feelings to guide me."

"And your feelings say it is important."

"Indeed, Sire."

"Alright, Teacher. Take me to the virgin!" A walk across an open courtyard brought Osir and Butyeh to a quiet garden outside the Hall of the Linguists. A matron met them at the gate, listened to their request, and disappeared into the building. Soon the girl's footsteps could be heard in the hallway. Moments later a delicate, dark-haired maiden, dressed in a white silk gown, stepped into the dappled sunlight and shadow of the garden. Osir looked into her deep, brown eyes and a tremor rocked his soul.

"Mira!" he gasped.

"Osi!" She ran to her brother and threw her arms around him. "Can it really be you? Am I dreaming?"

"None other than your favorite brother."

Butyeh stood in shocked silence. For all his scheming, never had he guessed they were brother and sister. At last, he understood his own purpose, though he would never understand the intuition that guided him. Befuddled but pleased, the old monk ambled off to a far corner of the garden.

"Are . . . are you well?" Osir's mind immediately turned to ways he might end Mira's enslavement.

"Yes, yes! I'm fine."

Osir looked into her eyes. *Still the same sparkle that I remember from our childhood in Egia,* he thought. *No hint of pain or deception. Can she really be happy as a captive in this foreign land?*

"Tell me your adventures," she urged. "You must have done well to travel so far from our homeland."

Osir sat down beside her and recounted his experiences since their last parting so many years ago.

"So *you* are the legendary Dirk Slayer. Your encounter with that cat is famous far and wide. The virgins of my order spoke of nothing else. They imagined you the handsomest man in all the realm. . . and perhaps they were right. Many dreamed they would someday marry the Dirk Slayer."

"And one of them did... the most beautiful of the temple virgins. Her name is Bera."

"Princess Bera, adopted daughter of King Rahn Mennon? I know her well . . . I . . . I love her dearly." A frown flashed across her brow, then disappeared so quickly Osir wasn't sure what he had seen. "She is said to be the most wonderful woman in the Realm. You...must be a...very happy man."

"I am indeed most fortunate."

Mira's lips shifted to a pleasant smile. "And so is she."

"Tell me, Mira, in the temple dormitory did you ever hear any word of our sister, Isas?"

"I know nothing of her whereabouts." Mira shuffled nervously and avoided Osir's eyes.

"What is it, Mira? Is there more to this than you are telling?"

"Perhaps there's more than you should know."

"What is it? Did you meet Isas? Do you know her fate?"

"She was . . . adopted."

"Adopted! By whom?"

"By . . . King Rahn Mennon, Osi." Mira avoided Osir's glare.

"That can't be true. Bera has no sister!" Osir shrugged. *Oh...oh, Great Rahn. It can't be.* His face hardened. "We . . . we talk too much of the past."

How can my love for Bera be woven with guilt so powerful and fear so great.

"Now, let's speak of your future. I must return you to our homeland."

"No, Osi, that cannot be. I am destined to serve my realm as Linguist to the People of the Mekong. There is no other way for me. You must accept that."

"But I can help. I'll speak to the court. If that is unsuccessful, my men can help. We'll save you from this place. You deserve to be with our own family...in your own world."

"No, Osi. This *is* my world. You have your mission in life, and I have mine. Don't risk either for the sake of a foolish dream."

"But, what happens if you stay?"

"I will be married to a prince of the Mekong and treated as a royal. I've met him. He is an honorable man, handsome . . . and nice . . . and we love each other."

"Is that what you want? Can you really find happiness here?"

"Yes, Osi. I'm not needed in Egia, or Berenicia, or Erytheia. I was trained as a linguist, not a Keeper of the Secrets. Besides, I was sent here before the betrothals. I'll never wed if I go back now."

"If this is your wish, I will honor it. But you must be honest. I must know your true feelings."

"I will remain."

"So shall it be."

Chronicle 37: The Yellow Emissary

Osir returned to his quarters. "Butyeh, we must leave for home immediately. Please have your runner assemble my men."

"Which route will you take, Master?"

"As we came, Butyeh."

"But, Sire," Butyeh protested, "your numbers are already reduced. Your force cannot endure another crossing of Sunda. Surely our King will provide an armed escort."

"No, Butyeh, that's too much to ask. My men are seasoned now and recovered from their wounds. We'll rendezvous safely with the *Crown*."

"If it is your wish, young Master."

"Now, Butyeh. Don't worry so. I appreciate your concern. You don't want us to take chances. But, we can handle it. We'll be alright."

The next day, Osir received a message from the Yellow Emissary requesting a meeting at his convenience. Osir rushed immediately to the renowned Geometer. Conveniently, Butyeh was already there to translate. "Young man," the Emissary said, "you are a brave man and a great leader. I can see it in your eyes. Your daring will take you far, but you must first live so that you may dare. Don't take the land route back to your ship. It is too dangerous . . . and unnecessary. You and your men must join me aboard my ship."

Osir had seen the *Eastern Star* in the harbor. It was a tall ship with ungainly lines. To Egian eyes, it appeared top heavy and unstable. But Butyeh had assured him that it was, in fact, quite seaworthy. "Captain Chou and I will take you as far as the Mindanao. From there, you can hire a coastal trading vessel back to the Bay of Sunda."

"But . . ."

"Enough said. There is no reason for further discussion. We leave two days hence."

On the afternoon before departure, Osir walked alone for one last look at Mekong City.

This place is even larger than I had thought. The press of humanity is overwhelming. People are packed everywhere, every street, every dock.

Shacks of wood and bamboo cluttered the riverbank and spread across the delta. Flatboats laden with farm goods served as permanent floating markets in side channels. High above the rooflines of ordinary homes and businesses towered the temple spires singularly characteristic of the Mekong. Osir could see the strength of design in these remarkable structures. Wide at the bottom like giant bells, they narrowed quickly tier by tier to delicate, pointed peaks, some of them more than 20 manheights tall. Like pyramids, these buildings were built to withstand the ravages of a rising sea.

The Geometers of the Mekong had concluded that much of their land would be inundated in the next rise. Sadly, their homeland would soon be nothing more than a lost subcontinent awash in the World Ocean. The Rising Age would be cruel because their population was great. Soon, only scattered remnants of their people would survive in the low hills to the north where a new coastline would form.

Doomed but undaunted, the people of the Mekong were remarkable for their cheerful outlook on life. Osir found himself buoyed by their high spirits. *I would like to have stayed longer to learn more about their ways*, Osir thought. His men, of course, would sorely miss the fair maidens of the city. Their physical beauty and sexual talents would grow legendary as stories of love and adventure, already remarkable, were enhanced in the retelling. Osir, for his part, would remain forever silent about the pleasures of the Mekong bath.

* * *

The morning of departure arrived balmy and overcast. The voyagers boarded the *Eastern Star* before daybreak and cleared the river's mouth in two hands. Butyeh would accompany them as far as the Mindoro Channel and return by commercial vessel. Gulls swarmed the beaches; pelicans guarded docks and jetties as the rotund ship carved its way into deep water. After they had been at sea one hand on a bearing of north-northeast, clouds lifted to reveal clear skies over deep blue water. Schools of fish, porpoises, and the occasional gray whale passed in clear view. Great flocks of birds darkened the skies. Two hands outside the channel, a cluster of spires pierced the surface, marking the site of old Mekong City, already lost to the Waters of Chaos. Osir, and his soldiers were happy to be back at sea.

"It's remarkable, is it not, this land of our forebears?" The Yellow Emissary smiled as he looked across open waters to the verdant shore. Butyeh translated.

"That this land should be so rich? That our ancestors should have been so fortunate to find it and claim it as their own? It is truly remarkable," Osir replied.

"Yes, but the richest land known to man will soon be lost to all men. This nation that begot so many nations will be lost from earth and from the minds of men for hundreds of generations."

"Lost to man, perhaps, but surely never lost from the minds of men!" Osir was shocked by the old man's assertion. Had not the Chosen Ones and the nations fathered by them taken every possible measure to ensure that the heritage of the people would survive the Waters of Chaos even if the people themselves were to perish?

"You are naive, my son. The powers of nature are too great, and the minds of men too small. The ages of forgetting are upon us. The waters will cover all beneath the sea. The corals that coat all ocean-covered stone will one day encrust all of Mekong City. Only when the age of learning arises again may our descendants realize who we were and what we accomplished."

"But the Secrets of the Ages, the Geometry, the Trove, the Pyramid?" Osir grasped for words to rebut the old man's claim.

"Five thousand years from now, they will be told as nothing more than myth."

"Why do you say this? What is your reasoning?"

"Observe the land. It's like a mother who nurtures her children and then devours them. Observe the sea. It's like a dragon that swallows all in its path. Nothing can survive forever. Nothing we build can truly withstand the forces of time and nature." In Osir's own land, this sort of talk from one of high estate would have been heresy. Were all men in the land of Cha so fatalistic? So outspoken?

"Then why do you take such earnest steps to preserve your heritage? Why do you maintain your temples and your troves?"

"Not for our children or our children's children but for the children of all time. All nations wax and wane with the coming and going of ice and water, but the cycles are different. You People of the Living Sun are like the lilies of the north that lie dormant in winter and thrive in summer. Hormuz is like a desert flower that blooms once every year when rains come. Our people are like that rare tropical flower that blooms for only one day in a hundred years. Consequently, each of us even has a different concept of time itself?"

"Ah, but the Yellow Emissary spins such eloquent parables of ice and water and flowers. Please tell me more about your world."

"We are many people in Cha. We live in lowlands on the eastern edge of our continent. We live off paddy rice and the fruits of the sea."

"How do you know about the Cauldrons of the Opposite Continent?"

"Our ships are great. We ply the waters of the Eastern Ocean. Our traders course the islands and shores of the Opposite Continent."

"And have you, yourself, seen that far-off land?"

"As a youth, I once sailed its tropical waters and visited our colonies there. As an adult, I have, more than once, seen the far ends of the Opposite Continent, north and south, where darkness prevails almost half each year."

"Survival must be difficult in cold lands like Beringia."

"In the far north natives live well despite harsh conditions. Seals, otters, fish, and thick-shelled crabs are abundant in the sea. Mammoth, elk, bear, and moose are abundant in the forest. Farther south the land is warm and lush. In the far south the lands are cold, too. Yet the wildest tribes of the far south live like swine. They wear no clothes in spite of the cold. Some nest in their own filth."

Osir was appalled. "Few animals will tolerate their own filth."

"Among the beasts, we stand alone in many ways, my young friend. Few animals will kill their own kind."

"We kill only to defend ourselves," Osir said.

"Osir, Osir, you People of the Living Sun are such children compared to the old men of Sunda and Cha. You have the Secrets of the Ages, as we do, but your Secrets are young. No ancient wisdom has been passed down to you, and you have forgotten the science of old. You know each kalpa begins with the destruction of mankind by the rising Waters of Chaos, but you don't know the greatest destruction of all." The Yellow Emissary paused.

"We have heard of the great fires that chased our people from the Land of the Second Sunset," Osir offered feebly.

"Fires? Yes, many lands have been devastated by fire, especially during the Falling Age of each kalpa. Sometimes the sea boils like a pot. Ships sink, and birds fall from the sky. An invisible cloud drifts until it meets fire, then explodes like a thousand bolts of lightning. We know this happens, but we do not know why. Yet, once there was a conflagration greater even than these."

"Greater than fire? I...I don't understand."

"Oh, fire it was, but your fires of Afar were nothing compared to the one of which I speak. In the Golden Age of an unknown Kalpa deep in the Time Before, mankind reached a peak of culture and science that has never been equaled. There were many things too wonderful and too terrible for us to understand. In spite of their good fortune, the citizens of Sunda grew more arrogant, greedy, and vile than any animal." The Yellow Emissary's face contorted. "In the Ancestor Queen's day, Sunda and the land of the Indus were destroyed by fire from a weapon of man's own making. In our

Tales, the flying chariots called Vimana dropped iron thunderbolts with the power of ten thousand bolts of lightning."

"No! That can't be," Osir said. Incredible as it seemed, something in his gut told him to believe the old man.

"Those who dwelt on the mountains and other exposed places were consumed without so much as a warning. Some were seared like meat over a cooking fire; others turned to vapor and ash. Still others who lived in valleys or along the shore survived. But for what? Their science, indeed all learning, was lost more completely than when the Waters of Chaos come. They made a pact to remove the threat from all the earth, but soon the Waters of Chaos came, and all was lost again."

"How was this terrible fire created? How was it spread?"

"You are not ready to know," the Yellow Emissary replied.

"How do you know these things?" Osir asked.

"You are right to question, for I know the truth is hard to believe. Our Tales say this disaster was described in the Secrets of the First Kalpa, which were lost in the Rising Age of the Second Kalpa. But, our people told these Tales by mouth from generation to generation. In the Falling Age of that same Kalpa we were again provided with letters and other requisites of civilized life. We recorded the Tales, and they are preserved in the temples of Sunda and Cha."

Osir decided to say nothing of this to his men but to write it down and include it in his report so the old man's startling account could be considered by the Geometers of the Realm.

From the ship's bow, Osir and the Yellow Emissary watched as the great landmarks of the Eastern Ocean hurried past. First came the Mountains of Sibu and Sabah, then a string of small islands in the center of the open sea. To the south were occasional glimpses of the high ridge of Kalimantan. "I love this sea, old man...I love this life."

"But it is a burden, is it not?"

"You've paid its price, haven't you?"

"Just as surely as you pay it now...to know so little of those you love. To lose them all and not even know. It is a hard life."

"If I could but be with Bera...to protect her from whatever might befall her in the capital." The Yellow Emissary looked at Osir with amusement. "If she is all you say, who's to say which of you protects the other?"

"Perhaps so. I know she takes care of me, but do you think a woman can take care of herself as well as a man?"

"Osir, Osir," the sly old man shrugged. "Which is stronger, the lock or the key?" He paused a moment to let Osir conjure the proper image, then added, "Yet neither is worth much without the other."

*　*　*

Finally, the Mountains of the Mindoro Peninsula, the northeastern extreme of the great continent, came into view. As the ship slipped gently into Mindoro's harbor, Osir summed up his first impression. "This little village reminds me of Zafaga," he said, with a hint of disappointment.

"Only smaller," Busah said.

"Only dirtier," Ketoh added.

"Only busier," Osir said, "but that, after all, is the reason we're here. This busy outpost connects the islands of the east and south along the Mindoro Channel."

"I've never seen sorrier vessels," Jumar said. "These foul freighters are floating pig sties."

"True, my friends, but they probably smell better than we do after so long at sea."

"Speak for yourself, Busah." Ketoh shot back with a sly glint.

"Why are these people so horribly impoverished, Osir," Busah asked.

"Sad, isn't it?" Osir said. "These lands once had a wide shelf of lowlands stretching from the base of those mountains to the sea. There were hundreds of villages and a few larger cities. They lost their lowlands a thousand years ago. Tragically, they had no place to go due to the steep mountains that flanked their lands. Some fled to the sea in search of sanctuary, but most of the nearby islands faced the same problem. More and more people were crowded into ever shrinking lands."

"Didn't they have Geometers to tell them where to go?"

"There is no place to go that is not already occupied by stronger tribes, and the problem will only get worse with each generation."

"No place to go?"

"None within reach of their resources."

"Did they not have cities, armies, navies?"

"They did."

"But to no avail?"

"None."

"What separates us from them, Osir?"

"Land, Busah. We have land for a refuge; they don't. And time. In the cycle of the kalpas, because our land sits high in the seabed, we are always the last to go and the first to return when the waters rise or fall."

Once the ship was berthed, Osir, Butyeh, and the Yellow Emissary searched diligently for a suitable vessel to take them back to the *Crown of Erytheia*. Luckily, they were able to charter a tolerably sound boat. As part of the bargain, however, locals worked for three days scrubbing, repairing, caulking, and painting. Osir personally inspected the rigging and insisted on repairs to the rudder. By the fourth morning, the little privateer was a spotless marvel, seaworthy and ready for duty. Its decks gleamed white, its hull bright red. Topped by crisp linen sails, the vessel was a fit conveyance for any army. Porters brought stores aboard, and Osir's men trimmed the sails. "Here, my friend, we must part ways," the Yellow Emissary said to Osir.

"We may never meet again," Osir said, "but I will always have fond memories of our days aboard the *Eastern Star*. You have shared so much knowledge and speculation about the world. Your views are of inestimable worth. Now I know where I must go and what I must do to unlock the mysteries of ice and water."

Butyeh added a kind farewell of his own, then placed in Osir's hands the charts needed for safe passage. "Here," he said, giving Osir a small scroll. "You'll need this." To Osir's puzzled look, he explained, "It's a lexicon of our language and yours—simple words only, but all you will need at sea. Learn it and, without my help, you will be able to converse freely with the captain, pilot, and others along your way." With that, the voyage was underway.

* * *

The first two days were spent in an uneventful eastward drift along the mouth of the channel. Turning south, they found themselves swept at a fast clip through the Mindoro Channel, one of only three passages between the Eastern and Southern Oceans.

"This current is terrific," Osir said to Ketoh. "Yet the Yellow Emissary says it flows ten times faster when the Cauldrons spill."

"Can that really be true, Osir? He also claimed great waves sometimes swallow their harbors, cover their lands, and recede again in the course of a single day. He even said great blocks of ice sometimes float into shipping lanes that cross the Eastern Ocean. I sometimes wonder if the old man is exaggerating just to make us think the Cauldrons are important, though I can't imagine why."

"He's a man of his word. All the Geometers of Sunda respect him and believe him. You can trust what he says. I'm sure there are sensible explanations for all these mysteries."

"If you say so, but I still have my doubts," Ketoh said.

"Can anything be more strange than the Cauldrons themselves?" Osir asked.

"If you ask me, they sound like the imaginings of ignorant natives, who often believe odd things about gods and nature. I wouldn't be surprised to learn that the entire story is fantasy."

"The Yellow Emissary says his people have seen the scoured lands after the Cauldrons have spilled," Osir responded.

"Perhaps." Ketoh said.

"You won't have to wonder forever, my friend. You'll get to examine the evidence for yourself."

"So it's true? We're headed for the Cauldrons?" Ketoh laughed. "What a pity no one would take my bet."

"There's no other way to settle the issue."

"I'll bet the Cauldrons don't exist! One full year of servitude against your sword?" Ketoh said.

Osir smiled at the prospect of having Ketoh as his manservant, but he wouldn't risk the sword for anything less than the welfare of his men. "Not the sword! A month's wages against a month's labor, shall we say?"

"Done," Ketoh said. "If I can't have a golden-hilted sword dangling on my sash, at least I'll have gold coins jingling in my purse."

Chronicle 38: Sula to Lombok

Tropical winds built to a fury as the bright-hued vessel approached the narrowest strait between Sunda and its island barricade. The hired captain had chosen the shortest, most direct route from Mindoro to Lombok, famous for its swift current and staunch tailwind. Here, the Eastern Ocean traded waters with the Southern Ocean, bounded on either side by Sunda and the island continent of Sahul. Like boulders in a mountain stream, islands served as precarious steppingstones for travelers moving through the straits. Through a tangle of confined channels passed all the flow of one great ocean to another. And here at the Sula Strait was the most restricted passage in the entire chain.

"This course is always a gamble because the same current that rides so fast and steady in good weather becomes an absolute terror in bad. Look at these charts, Ketoh. Threading the Sula's needle in a storm must be almost like Piercing the Veil," Osir said. As the storm raged, the captain sought safety in a lagoon on the outer rim of the strait.

"Take her to port!" he ordered, but rain whipped the helmsman's face and obscured his vision. "Now!" the captain yelled again over the howling winds. Osir sensed the captain's panic as he squinted into the stinging rain, trying in vain to read the roiling sea.

The vessel lurched violently to starboard as a wave slapped her broadside. Another such blow and she would surely swamp. "Take her in!" the captain almost pleaded, but the helmsman still couldn't find the narrow pass. Grabbing the whipstaff, Osir took control as the bewildered helmsman knelt with hands upturned in prayer.

As soon as the whipstaff cut to port, the vessel righted and found its course. Osir fought the winds with all his strength and guided the vessel into a lagoon more deftly than he had berthed the *Ruby* at Ras Abu Uwayd. Once inside, the craft immediately came to rest on protected waters. One sail was ripped and the rudder was damaged, but the boat was still seaworthy.

The lagoon's waters may have been calm, but the wind and rain continued unabated. Captain, crew, and passengers sheltered below decks.

Osir fell asleep in a wildly swinging hammock. When he awoke next morning, the ship was steady as a rock.

"All's clear. Storm's passed," one of the crewmen shouted upon opening the hatch and peering skyward. Each man unfurled himself from his hammock and rushed to assume his duty for the day. Ketoh ran, as usual, to be the first man on deck with the start of a new day. He bounded up the ladder through a shaft of morning light. In an instant, before even putting a foot on deck, the athletic young man came sliding back down, a look of shock and amazement on his face.

"It's a war party! Nothing less!" he said, slamming his back against the bulkhead and calling all to arms. In two breaths, the crew assembled behind their leaders.

"Ready and hold!" Osir called before he and Ketoh rushed up the ladder. Once on deck, the seriousness of their plight unfolded. Brightly painted war canoes surrounded the privateer, and three heavily armed outriggers blocked escape. Osir led his men on deck and shouted defiance as they assumed defensive positions. The ship's 97 men were outnumbered five to one. From the lead war canoe, the tribal chief stood waving a feathered spear. Each face shone bright with the color of war paint. An attack was imminent.

"They're ready for war alright," Osir observed calmly. "And so are we, but for what purpose? We have no quarrel with these people." In the language of the Mekong, Osir said, "Captain, tell these noble warriors we are friends."

The captain spoke in a language understood by the natives. Louder, angrier cries resounded from the throng of warriors.

"It's good he didn't say we're enemies," Ketoh said in a half-hearted attempt to lighten the moment.

"Tell them we came in peace and want to leave in peace," Osir ordered. The captain spoke. The chief replied.

"They have no quarrel with us. It's tribute they want!" announced the skipper. The chief suddenly belted a command, and the captain relayed his message. "He says, 'These are our waters. Your gold or your lives!' " Osir translated for the benefit of his officers.

No man owns the world's waters. How can he make such a claim? "Ask by what right he claims these waters."

The captain complied. The chief thumbed downward into the water, casually at first and then emphatically, as if that were explanation enough. Then he spoke with conviction.

"He says the home of his people lies deep beneath our hull. They cultivated these shores long before the waters rose. Now, there is little land left to support them. When their fields were lost to the sea, they turned this little haven into a livelihood."

"He has a point," Osir said. *Yes, in his view, it was theirs before and still theirs now. What difference does a few manheights of water make?*

"But surely we can't honor such claims," Ketoh said.

"Not when we have a choice," Busah said. "By that measure, few coastal waters would be free for the passage of commerce."

"Still, you have to admire their resourcefulness," Osir said with a smile. "Or perhaps 'piracy' is the better term."

"Shall I translate?" the captain asked obligingly.

"No!" Osir snapped. *They wanted to attack when I called them noble warriors. It won't help matters to call them pirates.* "Busah, what tribute have we to offer?"

"None. We have just enough provisions for our own needs. We have no gear to spare, no gold. We can't give up our weapons."

The pilot made an impassioned plea, saying the travelers had nothing to give. Whereupon, the chief hocked and spat as if to say that he would brook no claim of such poverty. At first, it appeared he would order an attack, then he paused to give peace just one last chance. "Have you nothing else?" he snapped toward the boat. "Is there nothing you can think of?"

The crewmen looked to Osir. "What about our sashes?" Osir asked. "They're wearing such drab garb. Maybe these bright colors will satisfy them. Hand me a sash," he said turning to his officers. Busah complied. Osir removed his own sash, as well, then held the two outstretched. The chief grunted, then nodded and pointed all around the deck. Osir motioned for each soldier to follow suit. Scores of sashes fluttered over the gunwale like streaming ensigns.

The chief's outrigger edged closer. Soon its prow bumped solidly into the boat, and a rower stepped forward to retrieve the goods. One by one, the sashes disappeared into a basket in the center of the canoe. When the last sash slipped downward, the victorious warriors roared in celebration.

"That solves one problem," said Busah. "Now if we can just get this broken rudder back in service."

No sooner had he spoken, than the war canoes aligned themselves bow to stern in an arc leading from the crippled privateer's bow toward the nearby inlet. Each lead rower seized a rope trailing from the stern of the next outrigger and snagged it on the prow of his own. A man in the hindmost canoe tossed a weighted line into the bow rigging of the privateer. A drum-like cadence rumbled from the outriggers as boatswains beat time on gunwales. Quickly the now friendly rowers, laughing and shouting, pulled the privateer into the narrow inlet.

"They'll probably cast off once we clear the channel," Osir said. "We'll row into still water to make our repairs."

"Nice of them to give us a tow," Ketoh said.

As they exited the channel, Osir's troops waved a hearty thanks, but onward the oarsmen rowed. Like village children on a romp through familiar streets, the rowers threaded the currents and eddies of the Sula Straits.

"Where are they taking us?" Busah asked.

"One guess is as good as another," Osir said when the canoes kept towing well into the main channel.

Finally, the warriors veered eastward into a channel on an adjacent island. Osir's first impulse was to order the line cut and the sails unfurled. Seeing no immediate danger, however, he let the little drama play out. Red mangroves hovered over the channel, marking the seaward extent of barrier islands. As the final outrigger rounded the turn into a natural harbor, Osir saw the destination of this comical maritime parade. Across the bay stood a cluster of longhouses made of bamboo and thatch. Surrounding hillsides were dotted with half-completed pyramids of stacked stone. Interspersed among them were monumental stone sculptures, many toppled on their sides, which Osir took to be their gods. "Ask him about the sculptures," Osir instructed the captain.

"He says, 'They are worthless. Our gods are no good. They failed to protect us from the ravages of the sea.' "

"Why have they abandoned the pyramids?" Osir asked.

"He says the seers instructed them to build many pyramids, and his people expended such energy that they were left starving. Now, they know for certain that the next rise will cover their refuge, but they have no resources left to rebuild at a higher level. They have no dream of escape. They take their livelihood from the sea. They will follow it and do whatever they must to survive. They are determined to find joy in life and let nature take its course."

Dragging their guests to a bamboo pier, the rowers beamed as if the boat were a war prize. The entire village poured out to greet their returning heroes. Osir burst into laughter at first sight of the villagers. Sash after sash in every color of the rainbow adorned each man, woman, and child.

"We're not the first to fall for this chief's bluster," Osir said to Busah who stood beside him, blushing at his own gullibility.

"Are we captives or guests?" Osir asked. The others replied with uncertain nods. Islanders clambered onto the docks, their intentions still unclear. When the crowd reached the boat, however, only young women came aboard. Bare breasts bounced as maidens bounded over the gunwales. Grass skirts were quickly discarded, and each woman grabbed a crewman by the hand. Gaily, they tugged startled men across the docks and into nearby longhouses. Osir, Ketoh, Busah, Butyeh, and the captain were left to deal with the chief who now spoke grandly from atop a bale of goods.

"They offer to repair our ship," the captain reported.

"They're most generous. But we can fix our own rudder and sails if only he'll let us use his dock."

"To refuse his offer would be an unpardonable affront, Sire. Do you wish to risk that?"

"No." Osir shrugged. "He has us at his mercy. Tell him we'll accept his kindness."

"We are invited to feast until the vessel is repaired," the captain translated.

"Surely, he doesn't mean we'll feast the entire time!"

"I believe, Sire, he means precisely that."

"Our men can eat and drink with the best, but this repair could take days."

The first week passed with hearty food, boisterous music, and rousing sensual diversions for travelers and natives alike. Each night they drank. Each day they slept until noon, then feasted again. "The only thing missing is progress on the repairs," Osir complained.

"The chief says 'Enjoy yourselves. Your ship will be whole soon.'"

"Tell the honorable chief that we appreciate his hospitality, but we must be on our way as soon as possible. If we're not back to the Sunda Kelapa by the full moon, we'll miss the monsoon winds, and we'll have to wait another year before returning home."

"He says he'll have his men complete the work as soon as the feast is finished," the captain said, with an impatient shrug.

"And when will that be?"

"When all the food and drink are gone."

"We have no choice but to take the matter into our own hands." Thus, Osir and his officers hatched an intrigue worthy of a royal court. Drinking a sour brew of fermented fruit juice, the islanders had hosted feast after feast of roast pig, baked fish, steamed tubers, and assorted fruits. On this particular night, by appearing to be in an especially celebratory mood, the visitors encouraged their hosts to drink more than usual while only feigning to partake themselves. As a result, the natives fell into a stupor early in the evening, and their guests remained sober. Rushing to the harbor as soon as the last islander passed out, one team hoisted the rudder and another collected the sails. Hacking, sawing, binding, and stitching went on well into the night. Night after night, they repeated the routine until the rudder and sail were good as new, but furled and hidden so the natives had no inkling of their progress.

On the day following completion, Osir announced his intention to depart. Glibly, he discussed plans for reaching the Straits of Lombok, their next landmark on the way home.

"But we haven't fixed your vessel, yet. You'll surely perish at sea," the chief said.

Osir, diplomat that he was, tried to think of a way to avoid offending the chief, but his mind went blank. Ketoh came to his rescue. "Captain, tell the chief we will pray at sunset. Surely their gods can heal the wounds of our faithful ship. I will be honored to conduct the service." Osir and the other officers almost laughed aloud.

At sundown, the nightly feast was immediately transformed into a session of prayers and supplication as Ketoh stepped forward and assumed control. The normally jocular young officer assumed the solemn demeanor of an Anbaht or a Toth. Again, his friends could scarcely avoid snickering. Osir recalled a time years before when Ketoh had danced at the tip of a pyramid's shadow. A contingent of Osir's men slipped away from the festivities and raised the repaired equipment into place.

Ketoh's rendition covered their sacred mission and sorry predicament, adding a most sincere appeal for the islanders' gods to heal the wounded vessel. In closing, Ketoh thanked the bewildered natives for the blessings of their gods as if his prayers had already been answered. The chief himself, though skeptical, suggested that the congregation should inspect the vessel.

"Your gods are great!" shouted Ketoh as the mended rudder emerged from dark waters to glowing torchlight. Islanders gasped in disbelief at the unexpected sight. They drew back in shock when the fully repaired sails were unfurled. Others then joined Ketoh in thanking the islanders for their gods' assistance. Finally, convinced of their gods' power, the villagers resumed the feast to celebrate a miracle. The travelers were on their way again at dawn.

* * *

"Islands ahead. Mountains on the southern horizon!" All free hands rushed to view the fabled islands of Lombok and Bali. "Thank Rahn, the sighting confirms my dead reckoning, but we're two days behind schedule. We'll have to pass up Lombok."

"Fine," groused Salacoa. "First I lose my leg; now I miss a once-in-a-lifetime stop in paradise."

"Sorry, Sala," Osir said with a laugh. "It was a difficult decision, but we really don't have much choice. After we pass the Straits of Lombok, we'll know whether the monsoon's east winds still blow strong. If they're strong, we can stop for a day at Bali and still make our rendezvous."

Among the world's most challenging stretches of water was the treacherous Strait of Lombok, worse even than the Sula Strait, which they had already negotiated with difficulty. Here the channel was narrower, and because there were fewer alternative channels, far more seawater rushed through. Horrendous currents required deft handling at bridge and helm. As they neared the passage, Osir convened his officers to rehearse the operation with the ship's captain. Every rock, every shoal, every known wave pattern was discussed in detail. Each contingency, each response was pondered, and final decisions were made. Emergency procedures were planned.

Careering through the narrow channel, the little boat seemed tossed in every direction at once. Creaks and groans rose from boards and beams. Waves crashed against the bow with frightening force. Occasionally giant surges crashed over the bow and the deck. Busah's men constantly bailed to keep afloat. "This old boat may not be up to the challenge, Osir," Busah said, showing concern more than fear.

"These little tubs don't look like much, but they can take punishment. Those creaks and groans may sound like weakness, but they're really the sounds of forgiveness, for the hulls are built to bend with every wave. We'll just hold the bow into the swells and set a constant heading in center channel." As he spoke, waves shot the vessel a full manheight to starboard. Busah and two of his men were tossed into a heap against the capstan. Osir, lashed to the whipstaff, stood firm.

Busah shrugged and pulled back to his previous position. "Just get us through this as quickly as possible. That's all I ask."

"You have my word on it. It'll be quick or not at all." Busah was pleased at first, then troubled by Osir's response. Osir smiled with satisfaction as the vessel responded to his control. Half a day's sail brought them through the strait and into open sea. Their passage had shown them a quick view of the most beautiful islands in the tropical world. With volcanoes, rich green slopes, pristine beaches, and swaying palm trees, Lombok and Bali surely were among the most scenic spots on earth. Their people were renowned for their beauty and hospitality, a point to which Osir's men frequently referred.

Finding a small harbor on Bali's western shore, Osir directed the captain into port. Islanders rushed to meet them at the landing. The captain bartered with local vendors for food and other supplies, while Osir's men swam and consorted with native girls. One night in port, and the travelers were again at sea.

Chronicle 39: The Port of the Shrines

"The winds and currents are friendly, indeed." Osir summarized his calculations as the privateer bobbed along on the westbound current. "Five days ahead of schedule. We'll have free time at the Port of the Shrines."

"No stop at Lombok. Less than a day at Bali. Yet several days at a bunch of boring shrines. You're a master at boosting morale!" Ketoh's jibes were unrelenting.

"You know Osir made the right choices at Bali and Lombok," Busah said. "We didn't know whether the currents would work with us or against us. Now we know, and the news is good."

"Don't prejudge this place by its name," Osir said. "You may find it one of our best stops."

"Sure, Osir, you know me . . . Ketoh, Lover of Knowledge. Learning, scholarship, contemplation. That's what I yearn for. Let's hang around and ride next year's monsoon home."

"As you wish," Osir said with a smile.

The steep-sided bay housed one of the most advanced communities on the Southern Ocean. Stone buildings–two academies, several temples, and a monastery–lined the shore. His troops might prefer beaches and island ladies, but Osir had his mission, and he sensed that the Port of the Shrines might hold some hidden key to the world beyond. The sides of the boat scraped as it glided into an open slip at the wharf.

"Look at this place. Looks like it comes from the Time Before." Ketoh gawked at the crowded cobblestone streets.

"Almost makes me homesick," said Busah. "This place is more like Berenicia than any of the cities we've seen since Piercing the Veil."

"Everything here looks old: buildings, walls, terraces. Look at these cobblestones. It must take thousands of years for hard stone to wear flat and smooth like that. None of the other cities look this old." Ketoh shook his head in amazement.

"Every city we've visited outside the Veil was built after the floods of the Rising Age," Osir said, "but this one must have been built long before this Kalpa even began."

"How can that be? Why was this city alone built so high above the ancient water line?" Busah asked, as the group ambled within earshot of scholars milling about the city's amphitheater. One scholar took note of their language and dispatched a runner. Within a few fingers of time, a frail young man trotted into the square to act as translator. The question was repeated and relayed to the scholars.

"Most of the world's cities were occupied in previous kalpas," the interpreter said, "but few signs of those earlier times remain. Their old streets lie on the ocean floor under ten manheights of water. The Port of the Shrines is unique. None of its structures have been lost to the rising seas."

"Why?" Osir asked.

"The world's cities are built by commerce," a nearby intellectual responded through the interpreter. "They reflect the material needs of man. Our city alone was built solely for the human spirit and intellect. Our forefathers were scholars and priests and explorers who retreated here to form a place of learning, meditation, and contemplation–a beautiful place where men could feed their minds and souls as well as their bodies. Here were built shrines to knowledge as well as to gods. We were called the City of the Shrines for ten millennia. Now the waters have risen, and we are called the Port of the Shrines. So we have been for a thousand years, but our explorations have ceased. We remember the wisdom of before, but we know little of today's world."

"How did your ancestors support themselves so far from the sea?"

"This was a school for the children of nobility, of merchants, of soldiers, and for young men and women who would be teachers or priests. Our ancestors were paid handsomely for their services. Their world was prosperous and good. They had no need of ordinary commerce, no need of the sea, except for its essential elements, like seaweed, which were brought in tribute by students and their families."

"And for what wisdom did those sons and daughters come?"

"Our scholars traveled all over the world. Our Geometers mapped and studied the entire earth, except for areas covered by the Ice, of course."

"And then the waters rose?"

"Yes, to our doorsteps. Irony of ironies! Our little village, which had shunned the sea, became known as a great port, while all those cities that loved the sea were destroyed by it. Our little place of knowledge became a place of commerce while the great commercial cities became centers of learning . . . of necessity . . . so as to avoid being destroyed again. Our mariners no longer sail the World Ocean in search of knowledge, but young cultures such as yours now explore the world we once knew. Our city, once like a child among the world's great, became the oldest among them, and the oldest cities were rebuilt as newborns. Now we, like our sister cultures, seek refuge in the mountains. It is an endless cycle for which there is no end."

"The great stores of knowledge that your people claimed . . . What happened to them? Where are your maps, where are the fruits of your labors? Are they here?"

"Oh, we have them. We have thousands upon thousands of books and scrolls and hundreds upon hundreds of maps, but they aren't here. Our ancestors moved them to a sacred place in the mountains for safekeeping."

"Mountains? Where?"

"A mount called Boro-Budor. There, many years ago we established a refuge where we started building a great shrine to protect all knowledge."

"No one could desire more than I to see these treasures. I have no riches, but I pledge to take your knowledge and magnify it many fold for the betterment of humankind, if you will share this great gift."

"Don't worry, young man. You have touched on yet another irony. Once, our leaders hoarded knowledge like a miser hoards his gold. Now, we are rich from commerce, as rich as those who used to pay us for our words, and our people no longer care. Even those of us who value knowledge share it freely. As our guest, you will be supplied with everything you seek. It will cost you nothing."

"First tell me of these maps. May I see them?"

"Our Geometry of the Ice will be yours for the asking. Prepare for a trek into our mountains. You'll be gone four days, and you'll find the scholars at Boro-Budor most helpful."

* * *

Soldiers from the Port of the Shrines conducted Osir, Ketoh, Busah, and two aides, Thronos and Phrate, toward the crest of the Javan range. The interpreter accompanied them, though Osir feared the frail fellow wouldn't survive the trek. Snaking through the hills, the trail seemed to rise over layers of landscape as it repeatedly advanced, switched back, then advanced again. The air became cool and misty at elevations greater than Osir or his men had experienced before. As the interpreter ascended the steep trail without faltering, Osir upgraded his appraisal of the man.

For a day and a half, they wound upward. Then, breaking through a tight gap, the trail opened into a broad valley surrounded by four distinctive volcanic peaks. The river split into two courses, one to the east and one to the west, each hugging the base of the mountains that rimmed the valley. The valley was remarkably flat except for a massive low peak standing north of its center apart from the surrounding ring of mountains. The two rivers converged at the base of the central peak.

"Boro-Budor," said the guide pointing to the mist enshrouded peak.

"I can see why the ancients considered it sacred," said Osir as the clouds momentarily parted. "Its flat crest is ideal for worship and sacrifice . . . and refuge."

"Welcome to our refuge," the dean of the sanctuary greeted them at sunset. A courier handed a pouch to the dean, who paused to read the instructions sheathed inside. "So, esteemed scholars, I am granted the honor of bestowing to you the knowledge accumulated by our ancestors. We don't get many callers here at Boro-Budor. It will be my great pleasure to assist you. We shall commence when the sun rises tomorrow morning."

Osir and his men were taken to a dormitory for the night. When they awoke, their hosts served a light meal and soon ushered them to a spacious chamber in the sprawling temple complex. Thirty or more maps of varying antiquity were laid out for their inspection. "Where shall we begin?" the scholar asked.

"Tell me first of the world's known lands."

"Certainly, Sire. See here. One vast landmass stretches, unbroken, from southernmost Afar north to the Ice, across the Northern Lands, through the Opposite Continent, thence southward to the Southern Ocean. We call this great land 'Gai' after the Earth Mother. See here. Many islands stretch in an almost unbroken chain far into the Eastern Ocean. Two smaller continents lie south of Gai. They are the Sahul, which is only a short distance southeast of Sunda, and the Frozen Continent. See here. These maps show the contours of those lands as our Geometers knew them six millennia ago. Since then, the Waters of Chaos have covered many of the peninsulas and some of the islands. In other cases, they have turned hills into islands."

"I'm familiar with much of this Geometry, but I've never before seen maps of such antiquity. Now, tell me, please, about the people of the earth."

"A greater world than ours was destroyed when the Waters of Chaos rose in this, the Rising Age of the Fourth Kalpa. People have inhabited the shores of continents for tens of thousands of years, but few have lived in the uplands. Many settled in coastal cities."

The scholar moved to another table. "See here. These maps show where the main cities were located in the Golden Age of the Third Kalpa. There was fabulous commerce among them, and the greatest port of all lay just outside the Veil. The Valley Sea and Great River route is the key to world commerce because, when the world's waters are low, winds and currents and ice make the Southern Passages between Afar and the Frozen Continent almost impossible, even worse than Piercing the Veil."

"Can this be true?" Osir said.

"Yes, in each Golden Age not one ship in a hundred can make it through those treacherous straits."

"Please go on."

"Here you can see that most of today's cities are the daughters of older cities which now lie beneath the waves. Our city and the cities of your land are among the few to survive the deluge. The greatest city of the Third Kalpa was called Aztlan, but we do not know whether it survived or perished. See here. It lay on a distant island east of the Opposite Continent. Other cities lay on the shores of the Opposite Continent itself where no man of our realm has ventured since the most recent deluge. If these cities found refuge, their scholars will hold many secrets of winds and ice and seas."

"Now, tell me, please, the history of the Ice," Osir requested.

"See here," he said as he switched to a third collection of maps. "The Ice came from the north and covered the Northern Lands where in previous millennia only scattered settlements existed, crude villages possible only in the Rising and Topping Ages, when the Ice was gone and men lived almost like animals. When the Ice returned, rich hunting grounds became frozen wastelands, including vast areas covered by ice many manheights deep. But the Ice also consumed the oceans, and the shorelines receded. So people advanced from the uplands leaving behind only a pitiful, scattered few who lost the struggle for warm coastal lands. For thousands of years, there were many advances and retreats of the Ice and of the sea, but the greatest occurred 7,500 years ago when the lowest sea levels occurred. See here the extent of the Ice at that time. With the aid of these maps, one need observe only a few select places to learn its behavior."

"How may I obtain duplicates? Perhaps some of my men will be allowed to remain here and copy these priceless maps? Later, they can procure passage on a commercial vessel back to our Realm."

"That won't be necessary. Our scribes routinely make copies from the originals so that the information can never be lost. You may have copies of any you desire."

"Thank you most sincerely. These maps will form the basis for our future explorations. With them, I trust we will unlock the secrets of the Ice." The rest of the morning was spent selecting maps and preparing for transport down to Osir's waiting ship. By noon, the party was back on the trail, and by sunset of the following day, they reached the port. Osir could scarcely contain his excitement as the treasures were loaded. They sailed at dawn of the following day.

Chronicle 40: Lost *Crown*

Osir's ship slipped past the moorings and into the swift westbound current. Tropical winds bathed the boat in pleasant warmth while low-hanging clouds hid the tropical sun. For five days, they ran with the wind, and late one afternoon, they entered the Bay of Sunda. Navigating the final turn into the bay, everyone cheered as they sighted the *Crown*.

"No watch posted," yelled Bracon, and jubilation turned to alarm.

"Come alongside! Stand ready!" Osir's men armed themselves while he guided the privateer into position, gunwale to gunwale with the larger vessel. "Boarding hooks!" shouted Osir, as his boat settled beside the derelict. "Prepare to board! Advance!" The party clambered aboard and cautiously entered every room and finally the hold.

"Abandoned! No sign of struggle," Ketoh yelled. "Not a trace of our men."

"Transfer to the *Crown*," Osir ordered. "Take special care with the maps. We'll search ashore."

"Can't remain here long. We'll miss the Monsoon Drift west," Jumar said.

"Our shipmates deserve no less." Osir took command of the *Crown* while Busah remained on board the privateer.

Busah ordered torches made of sticks and discarded sailcloth, soaked in tallow. A search party, headed by Ketoh, quickly set out. Arriving ashore in the dark of night, Ketoh divided his men into three groups of six each. One unit headed east along the beach, another west. Ketoh led the third group inland along the trail that had taken them to the interior six months earlier. Each party used the system of birdcalls employed by the military wherever enemies might reside. Throughout the night, they searched the forest floor and called without answer.

Near dawn, a faint call came back, and an answering call was made. Silence followed, then finally came the answering signal. Following the familiar drill of search and rescue, Ketoh advanced 200 paces to the west of the trail, then called again. A weaker response came back. The party reversed, trekked 400 paces east and got a stronger response this time. They moved another 200 paces farther eastward. The call went out. The reply came back stronger than ever. Through massive tangles of vines, over the spreading roots of standing trees, the soldiers advanced. Every 200 paces, a new call went out. After a thousand paces, the sounds were distinctly near. As the torchlight penetrated past a blind of rotted tree trunks, Ketoh gazed into the wild stare of a lone crewman from the *Crown*. The emaciated boatswain stood like a statue in the hollow base of a fallen forest giant. Ketoh stepped cautiously into the clearing.

The man, despite his dutiful response to the military calling code, appeared addled.

I remember him from Waleska's crew, but he doesn't recognize me. "Raelan, it is I, Ketoh of Egia. We've come to help. We'll take you back to the *Crown*." The sailor shook violently. He had no obvious injuries but suffered grievously from hunger and fear.

It was late morning when the search party reached the shore, and Raelan, now fed and calmed, reported his ordeal to Osir. "After disembarking your Excellency and his honorable men on this shore, Captain Waleska set course for the Sahul as planned. Not a day out of this anchorage, a horrible storm overtook us. Waves broke our whipstaff, and we hobbled back for repairs. We anchored in this harbor and started work. When the ship was complete, we began provisioning. All was calm the night before we were to depart." The man fidgeted nervously.

"Go on," insisted Osir. "What happened next?"

"A hoard of natives had gathered daily on the beach to watch our progress. We thought their curiosity was amusing. On our last night, native girls came along as if to see us off. When they invited us to join them, our captain granted one last night of liberty. Because the natives appeared friendly, only officers were left on board to guard the vessel. Onshore, we paired off with the girls and were engaged with them when the attack came. At our weakest moment, the warriors came after us with torches and clubs. They brandished fire in our faces and blinded many, bashed the heads of those who became helpless, and skewered others with lances. They boarded the *Crown* and slaughtered Waleska and his officers. A handful of us escaped to the forest, but they hunted us down one by one until only I remained. I escaped by hiding in the hollow tree where you found me. Daily the hunters searched. Again and again, I heard them pass within a few paces."

Osir settled up with the captain of the privateer and wished him a safe voyage home. He ordered a quick departure, and the *Crown* exited the bay in less than a hand. The rescued sailor fell silent on the deck as the barquentine found its westbound current. Osir's sea legs trembled at the awesome responsibility he now faced without the experienced Waleska to serve as leader, teacher, and guide.

Chronicle 41: Southern Crossing

The first crossing of the Southern Ocean with Captain Waleska had been the experience of a lifetime for Osir. His love and respect for the sea had been honed by constant battle with winds, waves, and currents. This time was different. The way west was *his* responsibility, and at its end loomed his greatest challenge ever–Piercing the Veil.

From Sunda, their best course was to ride past the southern edge of the great continent, Gai, then island-hop westward across to Afar, and thence along its eastern coast back to the Veil. Osir prevailed, but not one sea league came easy. When the *Crown* neared Afar, the currents shifted, and he faced unfavorable winds pitted against unfavorable currents. Remembering his first sail on the Great River, Osir began to tack and come about, tack and come about, a seemingly endless chore. Through it all the massive barquentine held its westward course despite the currents that pulled and winds that pushed ever southward. Progress was slow but steady, and on the forty-eighth day a lookout shouted, "Land ho!"

Osir strode forward and scanned for safe harbor. Eventually, he eased the vessel into an inlet with singular peaks framing its opposite shores. He dispatched a survey party in the landing craft to test the 'longshore waters for depth. Soon the cry came back, "Five manheights deep all the way to shore. Safe harbor 40 lengths ahead."

Osir ordered the vessel turned and maneuvered into the cove. He needed provisions, but no traders could be seen, and, according to Waleska's charts, none would be found. *Tomorrow we'll form scouting, hunting, and foraging parties. Ketoh and his archers will hunt for meat. Busah's and Tanta's men will harvest the sea and pick wild greens and fruits along the shore.*

The crew debarked and made camp on the beach. For the first time in all their travels, Osir couldn't tell them where on the face of the earth they had landed. How could he plan the next leg if he didn't know their current position? Astronomical observations would be essential.

Darkness fell quickly while the mariners deployed their instruments. "Tilt!" yelled Osir with his hand held high in the air. "Seaward!" barked an assistant. "Back!" said a second. With each instruction, skilled navigators carefully adjusted their instruments–a tap on a wedge, the bowing of a rod, a stick-turn that tightened a twisted sinew. Each movement brought greater precision to the calibration. "Tilt!" Osir said again, this time with his hand only partially extended. For much of the night, this ritual was repeated in different locations with one variation or another until Osir was satisfied.

"Mount Zanzibar!" Osir announced next morning to his men after numerous crosschecks. "That northern peak must be Mount Pemba." All had heard of fabled Mount Zanzibar, but no one from the Valley Sea had returned with an eyewitness report. The lack of objective information, of course, did nothing to diminish legends of a strange world inhabited by creatures found nowhere else on earth. For the most part, scholars throughout the Realm had dismissed such reports as nothing more than sailors' lore. Like stories of strange serpents at sea and beautiful sirens who lured men to their deaths on rocks awash, these reports were judged to arise more from what men drank than what they saw.

CHAPTER 17

Search Log 33: Teotihuacan

El Principado Hotel, Londres, Mexico City, beside the Zona Rosa.

The bellman was reluctant to provide directions. *Fodor's* wasn't. "Take Linea Nuevo to Autobuses del Norte; from there, take the local bus to Teotihuacan." The trip took almost two hours, but it was well worth it. Rick, traveling on business in this part of the Pyramid Belt, hoped to answer two questions. First, were Mezzo-American pyramids simply large piles of mortared stone with temples on top, or were they, like Egyptian pyramids, penetrated by shafts and troves? Second, how might these magnificent structures look encrusted with coral under seawater?

The bus stopped at an entrance flanked by two rows of shops, tasteful by tourist standards. He walked quickly past them into the temple complex. From a high rock wall, he saw the main plaza and massive works in every direction. Two temples dominated the far side, and a small enclosure sheltered an archaeological dig. He headed for two side-by-side pyramids. A walkway wound behind the first and into a small chasm. Inside was a cramped amphitheater, whether part of the original structure or added in recent times he couldn't tell. Neither pyramid showed any sign of an entrance shaft.

Rick returned to the sunny central court and couldn't resist climbing its sacrificial altar. *Thousands of victims died here, their hearts excised by Aztec priests,* he thought. *Imagine the spectacle—a priest holding the bleeding heart aloft to the cheers of 200,000 spectators!*

Time was short, and Rick was far from the Pyramid of the Sun, the greatest of the monuments at Teotihuacan. He ran across open ground, then turned to face the 210-foot pyramid.

That answers my first question.

Rick peered into a low shaft at the pyramid's base. Iron bars blocked entry, and the passage disappeared into darkness.

Above, hundreds of tourists wound up the steep stairs from platform to platform. Ten minutes later, Rick was at the top. The massive temple complex spreading before him held both excavated and unexcavated ruins.

Lost for centuries? So massive. So obviously pyramidal in shape. Its camouflage composed only of vegetation and slumping earth. If people missed such obvious pyramids in plain sight on dry land, surely they could miss them under water. Submerged, this complex would look like a series of conical peaks scattered across flat ocean floor.

His mission accomplished, Rick turned to the darkening sky. *Enough men and women have died here. I don't want to be standing on this fateful altar when that storm hits,* he told himself. Quickly maneuvering around the peak,

Rick queued into the line of tourists poking around the crest and down precipitous steps. The storm passed long before he reached the plaza below.

"What are these?" asked a lady on the four o'clock bus back to Mexico City.

"*Obleas,* I think," her husband replied. Placing two pesos in the onboard vendor's hand, the man reached into a tray and pulled out a brightly colored treat with the texture of Styrofoam. The lady followed suit, and so did Rick. The treats, two purple crepes sandwiching a layer of caramel, were delicious.

"Thanks for the tip," Rick said. He was glad to hear English after a week in Latin America. "Been in Mexico long?"

"Only two weeks," answered the husband.

"Actually one week on land," the wife corrected. "We spent one week on a Peter Hughes live-aboard dive cruise."

"Then we came by car from Campeche to Merida to here. We've seen as many pyramids as possible. They're scattered all over the Yucatan."

"See any while diving?" Rick felt safe asking for he knew the question would be taken as a joke.

"No." The man laughed. "But we saw some beautiful corals."

"Any unusual seamounts or spires of coral?"

"Not this year."

"You've seen some in past years?"

"Last year. Bay Islands, off the north coast of Honduras."

"What were they like?"

"A series of small volcanic peaks covered with coral. They rise abruptly from a flat plain. It's remarkable. They were discovered by satellite. Now everyone wants to go there."

"So they're islands?"

"No, that's just the name of the islands where we were based. Darnedest thing! All those conical little seamounts. All about the same size, rising about the same height above the ocean floor, and yet not one of them reaches the surface."

Like what I just saw from the Pyramid of the Sun. Like Teotihuacan flooded with seawater.

"How deep?"

"Oh, diver's depths, a hundred feet or so below the surface. Do you dive?"

Rick wished he could say yes. "No, I started taking lessons last spring but sinus problems stopped me. Now business travel keeps me from starting up again. Guess I'm destined to stay a wannabe."

Search Log 34: Contact

Jared was in high spirits. A year of persistence was beginning to pay off. His plan for getting to Foul Bay was falling into place. Three events had turned the tide. Most important was the small cache of Seed Money that arrived in mid-January. Then South Florida was picked for the next Seagate site. Not long after the decision, Wade Onover called.

"Jerry," he began, "how good a swimmer are you?"

"Oh, we'll still need a boat, if that's what you mean."

Wade laughed, "No, no, you'll have a boat. You just can't stay in it. Glenn Jamerson needs some help with sea grasses. I know you're used to handling the uplands and wetlands while he does the sea grasses, but in Florida there's a lot of shallow sea, and Glenn can't do it all by himself."

"But I don't dive."

"I know. There's a NOAA diving course in Seattle in May. I want you in it. I'll arrange everything." By summer, Jared would be a NOAA-Certified Diver qualified down to 160 feet. It was the best training available, and it could mean the difference between life and death in Foul Bay.

The third lucky event was an invitation from the International Space University to speak at its summer course in Brno, Czech Republic. Jared would spend a week there in late summer. By combining the ISU travel funds with frequent flyer miles, he would reach Egypt without bankrupting his Seed Money account.

At the same time, Rick would visit his company's branch office in Milan, and the brothers would converge on Egypt in the first week of September. "We have six months to establish contacts in Egypt," he told Rick. "We can rendezvous in Cairo, meet with them, and head overland to Foul Bay. On the way south, we can observe pyramids, temples, and other structures and sketch out what they might look like under thick blankets of coral."

"That's good. The Red Sea coast will be hot in September but not as bad as July or August."

"Let's hope so," Jared said.

"We should keep it simple, though. If we try to do too much, we'll get overwhelmed."

Jared passed Rick a handwritten note.

Six Steps to Glory

Step 1: Learn everything we can about the situation in and around Foul Bay. My security clearance is more than sufficient for updates that Tom McCord can provide.

Step 2: Find a contact in Egypt. You exploit your business contacts in the Middle East while I check out university and government channels. We need someone who can open doors *and arrange travel permits. A university professor would be more likely to understand our curiosity without suspecting an ulterior motive, military or political.*

Step 3: Communicate directly with the Egyptian government.

Step 4 Go to Foul Bay!

Step 5 Dive Foul Bay!

Step 6 Document, Document, Document!

"I hope to delay Step 3 as long as possible," Rick said.

"Me, too. Don't invest much in it now, and pull back at the first sign of trouble."

"Success depends on finding good contacts in Egypt."

"Sink or swim, so to speak."

" 'Fraid so."

"Oh, and, since you're going to the Czech Republic . . .I have just one word for you."

"Yeah?"

"Macocha Ravine."

"That's two."

* * *

During spring break, Hesham Saad stopped by to visit Greg Caisson on Beaver Ridge. In high school, the boys had been best friends. After two years of college, this was their last chance for a reunion before Greg left for an entire school year abroad. Hesham's parents had grown up in Egypt, and he had accompanied them on several family visits.

"I'm going to visit your homeland," Jared said.

"Great. I can recommend some good restaurants in Cairo."

"Thanks, but we won't spend much time there. Have you been to the Red Sea coast?" Jared asked.

"Just to the beach a couple of times."

"Hurghada?"

"Yes, I think so. I'm pretty sure that's the name. It's been a while."

"Egypt has fantastic coral reefs. Did any of your family dive?"

"Ah, no, sir. We just swam at the beach in front of our hotel."

"I'm particularly interested in the corals farther south. I need to contact someone who knows about them before I go."

"Ah, we have a cousin who teaches at the American University in Cairo. Maybe she can help."

"Is she a marine biologist?" Jared asked hopefully.

"I don't know what she teaches. But she will surely know someone in the right field."

"That would be great. Give me her address, and I'll write her."

"Sure thing. I know Mom has it."

Two days later, Hadi called. "Well, Jerry," she said in her distinctive accent, "I do not have an address, but I do have telephone numbers for you, one at home, one at work. It is difficult to get through, but you are welcome to try."

"Thanks. I'll give it a shot. Do you know what department she's in?"

"No, but I think it has something to do with the environment."

"That's good. Maybe she knows the area that interests me. At least there's a good chance she can direct me to the right specialists. Plus, if she can help me contact government officials, she will be of great help."

After innumerable tries and language problems with operators and secretaries, a woman's voice finally answered, "Salam aleikum." It was afternoon in Cairo, early morning in Tennessee.

"Is this Professor Bassily?" he asked.

"Na"am," she answered, then caught herself and switched to English, "Yes, yes, it is. May I ask who is calling?"

Jared explained his connection to the Saads, then stated his purpose quickly and concisely, all in his best international English. Listening to her replies and questions, he gradually perceived that something didn't add up. At first, he couldn't put his finger on it. Then he realized it was her accent. He wasn't surprised that she spoke English quite well. She was, after all, a professor at the American University. But her accent was American—Northeastern to be exact. "I expected British English. How did you get a Standard American accent?" he asked.

"Oh, didn't Hadi tell you? My parents went to the U.S. when I was very young. Most of my education was in Boston and New York."

"In that case, I repeat: How did you end up with a decent American accent?"

The gambit paid off. She had been in the U.S. long enough to know its regional rivalries. "What do you mean?" she laughed. "We talk just like they do on TV!"

"Ah," Jared said, "you know us well. Even some Americans don't recognize that red herring. But go on, what took you back to Egypt?"

"More personal commitment than anything else. When I completed my Ph.D. at Hunter, I considered teaching at an American college. Then I thought maybe I could do some good over here. I've been back five years, and I love it."

"I admire your decision. I enjoy talking with you, but I better wrap up before I run the national debt too high. Do you think you can help me?"

"Yes, I think so. There used to be some marine research along the Red Sea coast, but I haven't heard of anything lately. I'll check around."

"Do you know anyone with expertise in corals? At American University? Anywhere in Egypt?"

"Not really, but I'll ask. I'll write you if I find anything. Or I can send a fax. Our departmental budget won't allow transatlantic calls."

"What about e-mail?"

"We have it on campus, but the cable hasn't reached my building yet. I'd rather fax."

"Thanks. I'll wait for your letter. If you need to talk with me, just fax me, and I'll call you."

Later that morning, Jared placed a call to Tom McCord. "Hi, Tom. I'm going to be in Washington later this week. Will there be a convenient time to show me those internal documents you mentioned? Say, 9:30 Thursday?"

"Sure. Come on by."

* * *

On Thursday evening, Jared called Rick from Washington. "Well, I've seen the documents, and I know what's going on in the Hala'ib Triangle."

"What is it?" Rick asked.

"I can't tell you."

"Why not?"

"Because it's classified. I thought I told you."

"Yeah. I just forgot for a moment. Is there anything you can say?"

"Actually, a few key questions are answered in unclassified documents. For example, how long has it been since civilian divers or researchers were able to go there?"

"So what's the answer?"

"The conflict began in the early 1950s, and fighting has erupted several times since then. That's crucial! It means diving has been discouraged ever since scuba came into common use. I doubt anyone would have been poking around earlier. World War II would have sidetracked half the previous decade. So, even if there are buildings beneath Foul Bay, it's unlikely anyone would have found them."

"I thought you said someone had done quite a bit of research on those reefs?"

"Some research, but not a great deal. Plus, I'll bet there's been hardly any pleasure diving or treasure hunting."

"Anything else?"

"Yes, I know what type of project Egypt is attempting, but I can't tell you anything more than we already knew from the guidebooks."

"Okay. Tell me this. After reading the classified stuff, do you think our chances of getting in are better or worse than before?"

"Worse. Definitely worse."

"Can Bassily help us?"

"She sounded enthusiastic. I have some doubts, but she's our only hope."

CHAPTER 18

Chronicle 42: Home to Erytheia

The coastal route from Zanzibar back to Erytheia was in many respects the most spectacular leg of the entire journey. Lush cliff sides like those that rimmed the Valley Sea were visible most of the way. Behind them, higher mountains rose, touching tropical skies in the distance. White sandy beaches fringed the wave-cut cliffs often enough, but safe harbor was difficult to find. Anxious to be home, Osir kept moving as if he were on the open sea. By the middle of the sixteenth day, the *Crown* reached the wide seaward end of the Chasm of the Veil and headed due west for the Veil itself.

Anxiety reached a fever pitch three days later as they neared the feared obstacle. "Stop here, and we'll rehearse the drill during today's tides," Osir ordered. "We'll commence Piercing the Veil at high tide tomorrow!"

"Every seaman knows the risk," Busah said. "Yet, to a man, they trust you to get us through, Osir."

"Don't confuse confidence with bravado, Busah. At the very least, their trust isn't justified by my experience or proven ability. We have to duplicate, in reverse, a feat we have seen performed only once. Every man must hold his position and perform with breath-by-breath precision." Osir sighed mightily. "So let's get to it."

Movement by movement, his men rehearsed the actions that would spell the difference between life and death. Despite his private self-doubt, Osir spoke with unwavering authority. He hoped to feign enough confidence in himself to instill real confidence among his men. Rehearsals proceeded from slow, stylized motions to realistic precision and timing. After timed drills on the incoming and outgoing tides, Osir declared, "Men, we're as ready as we'll ever be. Tomorrow is the day."

Soon after dawn, the high tide rolled in, and the crew executed the tactic of advance and secure, advance and secure that had worked so well on their outbound way. Three days of battling tides took them to the very lip of the infamous Veil. As before, they lashed the ship to a boulder. After a fitful sleep, the crew arose to take advantage of the next rising tide. The veil of mist rose higher and higher until Osir judged it to be right. After wrenching themselves to the brink, at Osir's order, a crewman cut the ropes; the *Crown* rushed headlong through the channel and into the mist. When the fate of the ship was out of Osir's hands, he held his breath and waited.

Whoosh, the ship plunged over the raging torrent! Osir's timing was near perfect. To his amazement, despite a momentary crabbing and list to starboard, the vessel righted itself, plowed through the Veil, and emerged on the far side with scarcely a nick.

* * *

Six days later the *Crown* faced heavy rain and blustery winds as it cut the waters of Erytheia's channel. At dusk, Osir took the whipstaff and steadied the rolling ship on its final tack into the harbor. When they reached the calmer waters of the inner harbor, he relinquished the helm and moved to the bow to direct docking operations. Once the vessel was securely moored, he immediately shifted his attention to the crowd of onlookers gathering at dockside to celebrate their homecoming. Word spread and, despite the rain and winds, families and friends came to greet their loved ones. Cheers of celebration rang out from the crowd and crew. Standing on the foredeck, his back to the wind, Osir anxiously searched face to face, eye to eye with every individual in the crowd. To his dismay and utter disappointment, there was no sign of Bera.

"Where can she be?" Osir pondered as the gangplank was laid out, and his crew debarked. It was his sad task to inform many of those waiting on the dock that their husbands or fathers or sons had died in the line of duty. Finally, the crowd dispersed leaving only Osir and a few sentries.

Puzzled and deeply worried over his wife's absence, Osir stepped down from the foredeck and visually surveyed the barquentine. Memories of the past year's adventures flooded over him as the huge vessel slowly bobbed in the lapping waves. Tomorrow, he would offload the treasures. Tomorrow he would submit his reports to superiors. Tomorrow, he would contact the King's Geometers and schedule a symposium on his maps and other findings. Tomorrow, he would reassemble his men to arrange for the orderly watch of the ship while in port. Tonight, he must find Bera.

Osir walked briskly toward the little house that he and Bera called home before his departure. In darkness and rain, he entered the officers' compound and approached the closed door. His heart pounded as he grabbed the latch and stepped inside.

"Bera," he called. "Bera!" No answer. Fumbling through the darkness he sought the customary door side lamp and a striking stone with which to light its felt wick. Slowly, then rapidly, light spread across the room. Everything was in its place, but still no sign of Bera. The same was true as he searched the next chamber, which contained the sitting and cooking areas, and finally their cozy bedroom.

He rushed outside holding the lamp, not knowing where to turn. A light in a nearby cottage offered hope. Osir darted to its stoop and knocked on the door. A woman came out.

"No one has lived there as long as we've been here, half a year at least!" she responded to Osir's urgent inquiry. "Maybe you're at the wrong house," she ventured in a kindly attempt to calm him.

Osir shook his head. "It's my own house," he said, and the woman touched his arm in consolation.

At the same instant, a runner emerged from the dark street and pounded on Osir's door. "Master Osir of Egia!" he called.

"Here, man! Here I am. It is I, Osir!" he shouted anxiously, and the messenger ran quickly to his lamp's glow. Shaking rain from his hair, the runner joined them under the tiny portico.

"Please come with me to the palace."

Osir stood quietly, expecting the runner to say more. *Will Bera be there? Is she an outcast? A guest? A prisoner?* The man stood silent, awaiting Osir's compliance. Despite his lowly station, he represented the house of the King and was accustomed to higher men of the Realm snapping to his word. Osir bristled at the insolence.

"Why?" Osir asked. "Does this have something to do with my wife?"

"I believe so, sir," the chastened servant said, yielding only a hint of his precious information.

"And is she at the palace?"

"I believe she may be, sir." The messenger's resentment mounted. To surrender information was to relinquish a good portion of what little power the man held.

"For the sake of Rahn, man, tell me the news. Is she in good health?"

"I believe she is, sir." His power spent, the servant softened. "She is well and waiting. Will you please come now for an audience at the palace?"

"Let's go," Osir said, and immediately the two were on the run. They raced through the streets for half a hand until, dripping wet, they reached the palace gate. A footman met them at the entrance and rushed Osir to an antechamber where towels and dry robes awaited them. Down the massive corridor, past the court chambers, past the Agent's Hall, past the throne room, past the priest's quarters, the footman led the returning explorer. Soon, he stood before the double door of a private suite immediately adjacent to the King's personal quarters. The footman departed. Osir knocked softly. The door slowly opened, and Bera's face appeared. Her delicate hand extended and tugged him gently into the dimly lit room.

Osir entered in a trance. Bera appeared in a soft flowing gown. Even in the faint glow of the lamps, he could see her beautiful skin, her nipples, her pubis through the filmy whiteness of finest linen. She stood before him, a vision of perfection. This was Osir's dream, the fantasy that haunted his early years, the once-faceless form that had awakened him so often in boyhood, the specter that had comforted him through years of tough training in Berenicia and Erytheia. Now she had a face, the loveliest in the land. He rushed to enfold her in his arms. Her hand fell against his chest.

"One moment. Just let me look at you," she said, circling 'round so the light at her back would fall on his face. Bera paused for a moment as if to absorb every detail of his weathered visage, then stood back in the light.

Slowly, sensuously she loosed the sash, and her delicate robe fell softly to the floor. This time, Osir advanced without resistance as he encircled her with his arms and pulled her body to his own. Lowering his head, Osir met her lips and lost himself in passion.

"My beloved," she said. "I've missed you so much, so much. It's been so long. Tell me you still love me."

"More than my life!" he responded. He raised his head and oriented himself in the dim light of the room. Guessing where the bedchamber lay, he motioned toward the arch.

"No, silly warrior," Bera said with a grin. Delicately, playfully she nodded toward the opposite wall. The lovers advanced slowly, arm in arm, toward the open door. Once inside the ornate chamber, Osir saw the ample folds of covers on the downy bed. Bera lay down as Osir removed his tunic. He placed one knee on the bed beside Bera, then slowly lowered himself to her.

This is the moment of truth that has haunted me ever since Mira's revelation. He told himself it wouldn't matter, but it did. Now the conflict that had seethed within him would be resolved not by high principles but by overpowering lust. Bera thrust her arms upward, clasped her hands around his neck, and pulled him down. His qualms melted in her embrace. Their lovemaking lasted until dawn penetrated the high windows that separated the chamber's walls from its roofline.

With the golden sunlight, Bera's dreamy smile returned. "I have something to show you," she said, taking his hand in her own. She pulled Osir to the central room, across its smooth stone floor, through the arch he had spotted the night before, and into a smaller room. There, on a bed inlaid with mosaics of fine wood and tiles, lay a tiny baby with copper skin and coppery hair. "Horesh. I named him Horesh. He's three months old," she whispered as the proud father stared in amazement. Osir smiled with love and beamed with pride as his wife reached down, picked up the still-sleeping infant, and placed him in his father's arms. No man could have been more pleased. No moment of his life had brought greater joy. He held his son until the babe began to squirm, then gently placed him back in Bera's arms. She embraced him, soothed him for a moment, and tucked him back in bed.

"Horesh, the falcon. A fitting name. Well chosen."

"It is his sign."

Osir and Bera moved into the bath chamber where they soaked and showered and groomed. Bera answered a knock at the door, then backed away to make room for servants bearing trays of food and chalices of cool fruit juice. The two dressed, then sat down to eat. "When were you invited back to the palace?" Osir asked.

"In my sixth month, as soon as my brother Ammon learned that I was with child."

"Prince Ammon? Why was his decision of importance? It was your father's edict. Did he find it in his heart to forgive you for breaking his pact with Roton, Prince of Punt?"

"My father…is no longer making decisions, Osir. He suffered a seizure not long after your departure. He hasn't been the same since. He is paralyzed on one side of his body, and he can't speak. My brother Prince Ammon now rules as his Regent.

This tragedy makes a mockery of my lifelong mission to save the King, thought Osir.

"But surely your presence here in the palace must infuriate your father, despite his diminished state."

"He's not a hard man, Osir. He loves me very much, and I love him. He respects you more than you know, my love. And he gazes at Horesh with the same deep love as you and I. His anger toward me was due more to a father's pride than a king's concern."

"But he disowned you."

"He knew he had been unfair as soon as he acted, but his pride wouldn't let him recant. He would have found a way to restore my title sooner or later, but now it's out of his hands. Prince Ammon has come to power before his time, and he restored my royal name at his first opportunity. The pending birth of a nephew prince served his purpose well. My brother will be crowned King Rahn Ammon, but still my heart aches for bad news comes with the good. Father will die soon."

"But there was no word of all this at the docks."

"This secret is unknown outside the palace. The alliance with Punt was endangered enough when I rejected Setra. If the rogue princes of Punt had known my father's weakened state, they would have assumed power months ago. They still regard Prince Ammon as a mere child. They don't know him as you and I know him. My brother has sought to strengthen his ties with Setra and to prepare Punt's leaders for the news of my father's passing. Above all, in this time of war, he must be decisive and cunning, else our dynasty will end. Our plan is proceeding well. We brought Setra into our confidence, and, despite his allegiance to Punt, he sits at Prince Ammon's right hand."

"Am I, too, welcome in the royal house? Is Prince Ammon aware of my presence here, or must I come and go in secrecy?"

"He readily welcomes you to the royal household. He asked to see you privately—about other matters," she added.

"Other matters? Now you make me curious."

"Matters of state."

"Is there a problem?"

"We are always at war with the Westerners, Osi, but now it is more serious than before. Our trade routes are under siege. Several garrisons have fallen. Egia is safe for now but virtually cut off from Punt. The

Westerners are enraged by our attempts to establish a refuge in the Land of the Second Sunset. They will stop at nothing, and our armies seem helpless."

"But that's not all, Osi. The Divine Right Order causes terrible dissention in our ranks. Some factions want rules to replace all reason. Others want no order at all. Both have become bolder in their intrigues. Radicals have infiltrated the ranks of the Divine Right Order and recruited key commanders. No one knows whom to trust."

"Prince Ammon seems capable of handling such challenges."

"Ammon *is* wise. He will be a good leader. But he is young, and he needs help."

"What does this have to do with me? I have my mission. The commanders have their armies. Can't they restructure their forces to preserve both order and reason?"

"That's why Prince Ammon wants to speak with you."

"He's going to deny my mission, isn't he?"

"Perhaps it will work out for the best. I'm certain Prince Ammon will want you to succeed, once he understands the purpose of your mission."

"You're right. I'll present the findings from my travels and convince him to let me continue. The Waters of Chaos are coming, and we must know when."

"Osi. Help him in whatever he asks. Life in the Realm has become unbearable for the people grow viler each day. We drown in chaos, whether or not the waters come."

"But what about my destiny? I may not have saved the King, but I still must find a way to help preserve our people."

"Surely you understand, Osi, that your mission to save the King has been fulfilled."

"Don't mock me Bera. Sadly, there will be no saving of this ill-fated King."

"Not this King, Osi, but the next. Did Toth ever give your King a name? Your brave defense at Death's Shadow fulfilled your destiny. You saved Crown Prince Ammon. Your destiny is fulfilled. Prince Ammon has so declared it."

"Prince Ammon is smarter than I," Osi said with a wry smile.

* * *

Osir walked the hallway to the throne room. The giant doors opened. Prince Ammon sat on the throne. Beside him stood Setra. The Prince greeted Osir more warmly than he expected. Setra, too, went out of his way to make Osir feel welcome.

"Welcome home, Osir of Egia. Welcome to the Royal Court of Erytheia. Praise be to Rahn!" Prince Ammon said in the traditional blessing before important proceedings.

"Praise be to Rahn!" echoed Osir and Setra.

"It is my great honor to stand in your presence, Regent."

"I am in your debt ever since we fought together at Death's Shadow."

"Oh, yes. I believe you may have saved the Regent's life, or some such thing," Setra interjected.

"He did indeed," said Prince Ammon. "Your men tell of your greatness. They declare you a hero. General Setra tells me your fame is spreading throughout the land."

Setra nodded.

"News of heroes travels fast in troubled times," said Prince Ammon. "You have heard, no doubt, of our growing war?"

"I have, Your Excellency."

"It is not going well, Osir." Setra, for once, was humble.

"So I've heard," Osir said.

"Our old generals made no headway in this war. I've retired the fools to bungle their own affairs, and I've promoted your friend and fellow soldier, Setra, to lead all land and sea forces from here to Gubal."

"You have, no doubt, chosen wisely," Osir said graciously.

"Your service is needed," Prince Ammon said flatly.

"My allegiance is yours, Your Majesty. I will do whatever you command."

"You are my sister's mate. You are thus my brother. I will not force you to act against your will."

"Tell me your wishes, Excellency. I ask for no special treatment."

At the Prince's nod, Setra laid out his plan of attack. "We have two strategic objectives. First, our Navy must maintain control of all coastal garrisons from here to Gubal. Second, we must regain control of the trade route along the Great River. To that end, I ask you to fight, garrison by garrison, from here to the Midland Sea. As you take each garrison, establish a new front from which to stage the next campaign. Siege and hold, hold and advance, that's the key. It may take years to reach Egia, but it can be done."

"Are you willing to lead this force, Commander Osir?" Prince Ammon asked. "You will be granted whatever you ask for the campaign. When your mission is accomplished, in gratitude for your service, I will provide whatever you need to complete your global exploration as promised by my father."

"I am willing to accept this post, and I will obey your every command. If I am to succeed, however, I must be allowed to determine my own strategy."

"Granted!" the Prince said. "You will report to Setra and no other, and you'll have the freedom you seek in your own theater of war." He glared at General Setra as he spoke the last words.

"And what *is* your strategy, Commander Osir?"

Osir ignored Setra's tone. "I'll lead a large force, but we'll travel light and fast. We'll strike vicious blows on a broad front. We'll reclaim the garrisons alright, but, more than that, we'll take land. We'll cut a swath from Berenicia across to the first cataract and down the Great River to Ollo-detu. We'll move as swiftly as a desert wind and strike as fast as lightning. When this war is over, the Westerners will know the fearsome might of the People of the Living Sun. Never again will they stand in our way. Thus will land be secured for our refuge."

Setra looked doubtful, but Prince Ammon was unrelenting. "It's a bold plan. I ask only for your word of assurance that you *can* win."

"I can, and I will!"

"There is one other condition." Prince Ammon's determined words took Osir by surprise. "I want Setra to observe and advise during the first days of your mission so the two of you can learn together, much as I watched and learned your ways at Death's Shadow."

"I am your servant. I will do as you wish...but no army can have two masters."

"The leadership is yours. You have my word. Setra will go only as far as the first garrison. He will then return to the naval campaign. Is this agreed?"

"It is, Sire," Osir said.

"It is, Sire," Setra agreed.

"And your other mission? I'm told you want to see the Ice."

"When the trade route is secure, and we reestablish contact with my Beloved People, I ask that you allow me to find the Ice."

"First retake Egia. If you are successful, I will consider your request." As Osir left the throne, the Prince picked up his royal staff and carved a small nick into the main body of its shaft.

"Wait!" hailed the Prince as Osir opened the door to leave. Through a deft hand signal, he communicated with a nearby servant. From an anteroom near the throne, the servant emerged carrying a strange-looking staff. Unlike the King's Staff, which was straight and only chest high, the staff presented to Osir was tall, and its top was curved like a shepherd's crook. The Prince smiled at Osir's puzzled look.

"This shall be your staff of office. It will proclaim your authority, and its height will render it clearly visible in the field. Its crook of lowly origin will remind you that you serve your King as humbly as any shepherd."

Osir grasped the staff firmly, turned, and departed the throne room.

Chronicle 43: The Land Campaign

In all the chronicles of the People of the Living Sun, no commander had ever mounted a land campaign so ambitious as the one now planned. To clothe, arm, and feed such an expeditionary force taxed the wealth and strength of the Realm in its now reduced circumstances. Osir's army was doubly spectacular to the citizens of Berenicia, for it was equipped to travel fast, strike hard, and advance relentlessly in a manner totally unfamiliar to the entrenched armies of its day. In three months' time, his quartermaster, Colonel Busah, became the Realm's foremost master of military field supply. Colonel Ketoh alone commanded an unprecedented mobile force of more than 400 archers. All told, more than 1,000 men served at Osir's command.

To those who watched and prayed for Osir's success, the task was fearsome. "How can any man lead such an overland campaign?" some asked.

"If anyone can, Commander Osir is the one," others declared.

"I can't imagine what it will be like to be part of such a force," one soldier confided.

"Nor can I, but I am proud to be so," his friend replied.

Day by day, men gathered, and stockpiles mounted on the grounds of the academy. Crowds gawked as soldiers scrimmaged and equipment was prepared. Day by day, item by item, man by man, the troops were readied, and the expeditionary force was fully mobilized. Osir would deploy early on the morning of the ninety-third day.

The full moon provided an auspicious setting for prayer and supplication on the eve of their departure. Priests kept the ceremony brief to allow a good night's sleep. Men said goodbyes to loved ones and moved to a temporary encampment on the parade grounds. Having left Bera and Horesh in Erytheia, Osir had no goodbyes to say.

Osir rose early. He toured the camp for more than a hand, reviewing the state of preparations one last time before departure. The call was sounded, and the men rose. After breakfast, a second call pierced the morning air. Soldiers grabbed arms and gear and mustered to assigned ranks—swordsmen up front, archers next, supporting units behind. For the first time, Osir commanded a force large enough to take an entire land, though not everyone agreed with that assessment. His army would be difficult to control, difficult to motivate, difficult to lead. Setra and his entourage, eight guardsmen and four servants, were the last to arrive. Fog hung ominously heavy and gray on the parade grounds.

"Forward, march!" barked Osir, and the expedition was underway, Commander Osir at its front, General Setra at his side, Osir's lieutenants next, and a thousand men behind. Eight abreast, they marched down the thoroughfare to the temple complex, up the winding road past the new pyramid, then up the new roadway toward the interior.

During his three months in Berenicia, Osir had confined himself mostly to the military complex and saw little of the city. As his column wound through the business district, the war's cost became apparent. Stores, clearinghouses, and warehouses were closed, their docks piled high with exports once bound for the Midland Sea. Shops were shuttered.

Workers who had been the lifeblood of a bustling economy now loitered on street corners or wandered aimlessly. Children played on stockpiled goods. Weeds grew in potholes and street cracks throughout the commercial district. Signs of decay were everywhere.

The new pyramid was the only site that reminded Osir of the bustling city he had known just a few short years before. Contrary to the rest, its construction had been accelerated. The site was busy as an anthill, and the main structure neared completion. Precision-cut triangular capstones were set from the base upward to provide a smooth exterior face against the rising waters. At the top, workmen hustled in and out of the open apex, suggesting that finishing touches on the Upper Trove's vault were underway.

Upward past the bluffs, past the reservoirs, up the long valley, the column reached the Land of the Second Sunset late that day. Only a handful of men, mostly Egians, had ever risen to this level before. Osir watched the others closely as they observed the first sunset, which was especially pronounced on the east-facing wall of the Valley Sea, where it came half a hand earlier than at sea. Osir smiled as he listened to conjecture regarding this strange behavior of their otherwise predictable sun. The experience brought back fond memories of his first trip with his father.

Setra caught up with Osir. "Observe the sun, Osir. It's time for Sunset Prayers," he said.

"No, Setra, this is the false sunset. We are at the First Terrace, in the land of the enemy. We must abide by their rules, and they will not honor this illusion. Remain vigilant. The second sunset will come soon enough. Then it will be safe for your men to pray. Westerners won't attack after their own sunset."

"That's foolish, Osir. The Divine Right Order knows only one sunset. It is time for prayer."

"We can't stay here in this exposed position. We must keep moving."

Defiantly, Setra mounted a boulder and lifted his arms to the sky. The men, confused by the false sunset and thinking Osir had sanctioned Setra's action, dropped to their knees in prayer. Osir yelled to warn them, but not in time. A hail of arrows rained suddenly from the cliffs. He watched helplessly as more than a score slumped forward, faces in the dirt. At least 200 Westerners lined the escarpment, their bodies eerily silhouetted in the golden sunlight.

"Gods!" more than one man yelled, "Gods of Gold! Golden bowmen! Gods of the Sunset."

Troops panicked and cowered in disarray. When the first volley ended, Osir stood. "An illusion. It's just an illusion," he yelled. "It has no meaning. The real sunset is yet to come." But few heard, and fewer still would listen.

"Then, we too shall be gods!" Osir screamed as he charged the slope. Soldiers understood and rallied to his command. Scores of Westerners scampered back behind the rim.

Osir was first to reach the brow. Seeing him bathed in sunlight like the fleeing Westerners, the rest of his force rose from their hiding places and followed in a frenzy. "We too shall be gods," one repeated, and others took up the call.

"Not gods, perhaps, but brave men bathed in sunlight," another answered.

Setra himself never cowered, but he was slow to act and found himself lagging behind.

Soon order was restored, and the Army took defensive positions at the brow. No second volley came, but a single arrow arced through the air. Suddenly, Setra fell flat on the rock-strewn slope. A primitive arrow stood like a tiny flagstaff above a spring of blood issuing from his thigh.

"Get your man off this hillside," Osir said to Setra's aides while Ketoh's archers secured the rear. "Take him to the city for treatment. Here, take this message to Prince Ammon." Osir handed Setra's aide a parchment containing a hastily written account of the incident.

"I'm sorry, Osir. I never meant to hurt anyone." Setra's apology came as Osir stooped to crop the arrow near its base. "The Divine Right Order has failed me, Osir."

"Yes, Setra. A failure of judgment. Your ordered ways aren't suited to such wild places. You would do well to remember this lesson."

"I have learned a lesson alright, Osir."

Osir stared at Setra. *Let's hope the lesson you learned is the one you've been taught.*

Setra's men placed him on a makeshift litter. Soon, the embarrassed commander was on his way to Berenicia where surgeons and medicines waited. Setra would soon heal. Due to his bungling, however, 24 good men were laid out for the sea.

Suddenly, the miracle of the second sunset commenced, and everyone understood what had caused Setra's confusion. As they marveled, Osir recalled his first night at Koro-detu with fellow cadets naively embarking on the adventure of a lifetime. Just like these soldiers tonight, the youngsters had marveled, recounted lore, and engaged in unfounded speculation as to what strange forces of nature could produce two sunsets in a single day.

Under Osir's sole command, any man could say his prayers on the march, and every man was encouraged to do so. Thus, quickly the column advanced, and soon the dim outline of an abandoned garrison loomed stark against the fading glow of the second sunset. Westerners seldom occupied sites after overrunning them. On the other hand, it was possible that a trap had been laid, making approach in darkness an unnecessary gamble. The troops would bivouac in a defensible position, then take possession at dawn. The night was peaceful, however, and the weather was pleasant. With increasing elevation, the river they followed had dwindled to a peaceful brook above the First Terrace. Its water was cool and refreshing.

"First garrison unit, prepare to advance!" Osir called out the following morning. The Army carefully surveyed the deserted fort. Their uneventful entry contrasted sharply with Osir's arrival at Ollo-detu so many years before. Yet, the sights and scents of the sacked fortress brought back buried memories of that ruined fort and its charred defenders. Osir assigned a contingent of 50 well-armed men to remain behind and hold the garrison. Colonel Busah stocked its larders quickly, and the Army was underway again.

To their south extended a vast rainforest. To their north lay open savanna. But here, threading away to the Great River and far beyond, stretched a band of upland forest. Huge ancient oaks, maples, and poplars formed the canopy while holly, willow, alder, and scraggly bushes formed the understory. Occasionally, the Army had to climb over or crawl under decaying hulks of fallen giants.

The trail to Kreim Pass etched snugly into the sinuous contours of the high valley that would take them much of the way to the Great River. According to plan, they would spend five days traversing the valley, then turn westward, climb a steep slope to the pass, and finally descend a broad downhill grade to a line of low hills bounding the Great River. Later still, they would camp beside its waters.

Before ascending to the pass, however, Osir took one look at the exposed trail and declared, "This won't do. We're waiting prey. Divide the force. Colonel Ketoh, take half your archers to high ground on our northern flank. Lieutenant Jumar, take the other half along the high ground on our southern flank. Colonel Busah, lead the supply caravan up the trail, but stay behind the main force. The rest will march with me. We'll meet where the valley becomes level at the headwaters of the River Hodein."

"Sareem, take 30 foot soldiers along the main trail well ahead of Busah's men. Lances only." Osir looked into the shocked faces of Sareem's troops. "Advance casually without regard for personal safety." Lieutenant Sareem smiled as Osir's strategy became clear, but his soldiers were not so reassured.

Trekking off-trail, it would take an extra day to reach Kreim Pass, a saddle ridge notching the mountains that ran parallel to the coast. Open forest covered steep terrain. Thickets of dense brush made passage difficult in places, but broad expanses of open ground allowed troops to fan out for the first time since leaving Berenicia. In ranks of 20 men abreast, the Army was much less vulnerable to attack. Osir instructed Lieutenant Jumar to be especially vigilant on the inner flank lest the decoy platoon be attacked and annihilated. The Army moved steadily forward.

Three days later, shouts rose from the inner flank, "Ambush! Westerners beside the main road! Sareem's unit pinned down." Stealthily, Lieutenant Jumar led his archers in a sneak attack against the unprotected backs of unsuspecting Westerners. Three volleys from high ground were sufficient to annihilate the enemy without a single casualty among the decoys. Osir's unorthodox tactic paid off in this skirmish and twice again as they advanced up the eastern slope.

* * *

The stream dwindled at each fork as the troops forged westward. Osir watched carefully for the turn that crossed the drainage divide between the rivers Hodein and Garara. "Encourage your men," he advised his lieutenants. "This leg will be the most demanding." The men had indeed begun to grumble and press their platoon leaders for rest as hot sun drained what little energy the steep trail left in them. "The top of the pass by nightfall," Osir ordered. "We aren't far from the crest. We'll rest tomorrow at the pass."

With promise of rest, spirits rose, and the final ascent was completed by late afternoon. From a lofty vantage, Osir gazed toward the setting sun. "Reminds me of the view from Ollo-detu," he said.

"Such a vast land!" Jumar exclaimed. "I've heard about the animals of the plain, but I never thought there would be so many . . . all at once. It's beyond belief."

"True," Osir agreed. "I've never seen anything like it."

"These plains, if made secure, can feed our people for centuries. It's unfortunate we left such abundance to the Westerners for so many thousands of years," Sareem said.

"They, on the other hand, don't have the bounty of the sea. It would seem to be a fair exchange." Jumar said respectfully but somewhat defensively. The others looked at Jumar. "I see no reason to envy the ways of the Westerners," he said.

Sareem agreed. "I, too, would find it hard to give up the sea and live like these Westerners, though I wouldn't mind leaving the city. I enjoy these open lands, but I couldn't live for long without swimming in the sea or eating its bounty."

"If you did, Sareem, you'd soon have a neck as big as a Westerner's." Jumar laughed at the thought of Sareem with a huge distended goiter about his throat. Travelers along the interior portion of this route who had seen Westerners up close reported this strange condition, derisively called 'bigneck.'

"Westerners are born with those!" Sareem said. "A man of the Realm couldn't get the bigneck without having Westerners' blood in his veins."

"I wouldn't be so sure about that, Sareem. Remember the children of our kind who were kidnapped and reared by Westerners. When found years later, three of them had the bigneck," Jumar said.

"That's just a folk tale to keep children from venturing into the woods. My mother told me that story when I was a boy."

"What do you think, Osir? Is it true?"

"Yes. Geometers can't explain how it happens, but they believe it's true. It must have something to do with the Land of the Second Sunset. Westerners who live close to the shore don't have the bigneck. Surely we need the sea's elements, but we simply don't know what happens if we can't soak in the sea and eat its fruits for long periods of time. We season our food with cakes of dried seaweed; perhaps that's enough. Still, we can't take the risk. That's the main reason our refuge must be well chosen. If we plant ourselves too far from the sea, we may get the bigneck or even worse."

"Worse?" Sareem and Jumar spoke in unison.

"It's been said . . ."

Conversation stopped as Ketoh's force caught up with the main army. They had been detained in a minor skirmish not far from the rendezvous point. Archers had been deployed, and the natives were easily dispatched.

"We've been fortunate. Our losses to battle and predation have been few. And yours?" Ketoh's pride at a safe arrival was evident through the cover of his military bearing.

"Few as well," Osir said. "So, we're ready to descend into the valley . . ." Osir realized he had lost Ketoh's attention. This was his first view of the immense valley, and he had succumbed to its beauty, its majesty.

"Col. Busah!" Osir called toward a group of men gathered behind him. Out of their midst emerged the master of logistics. "We'll bivouac here. Go ahead and make camp," Osir shouted to Busah over the din of the troops.

"Already underway, sir," he responded with a broad smile. In two-and-a-half hands, the camp was set up, and a feast of wild boar, deer, and mulia ibex was served. Osir marveled at the practiced efficiency of their encampment. With Ketoh's and Jumar's offensive forces and Busah's supply lines, he felt his army was invincible. Starting tomorrow morning, they would cut through the heart of the Westerners' territory and retake the trade route to Egia. They would subdue the primitive population and, for the first time this kalpa, establish control over a wide expanse of ground within the Land of the Second Sunset.

Osir stood on a promontory overlooking the vast interior. "Our victories in this place will be crucial," he said quietly, almost to himself, as he watched a stunning lilac-tinted sunset. Ketoh, Sareem, Jumar, and Busah sensed, however, that he had left something unsaid. Looking up from his reverie, Osir snapped back into conversation. ". . .but it is the battle we now learn to fight that will be of utmost importance."

"What do you mean, Sire?" Sareem asked.

"Sooner or later, the battle for uplands will begin in earnest. Our old ways of battle weren't suited for taking vast tracks of land. On this mission, we'll perfect new ways of waging war. When the Fast Rise comes, we must be ready with strategy and tactics to seize and defend our refuge in the land above."

As he stood above the vast frontier, Osir was reminded of another day many years earlier when he had stood on a promontory and surveyed the vastness of the Beloved Sea. His thoughts went back in time to the closeness he had felt with his father. He was reminded also of the dangers in this wild land, for in that distant memory his own mount had been attacked by short-face hyenas. Only now as an adult could he appreciate how narrowly he had avoided becoming their meal.

Osir lingered at his lookout well after the other officers had retired to their bedrolls. He peered into the heavens. *I wonder what lies ahead*, he thought. *These skirmishes are hardly more than practice for battles yet to come. Westerners maintain no strongholds in these mountains, just scattered tribes and clans poorly organized, with little allegiance to the land. They're hunters and nomads and certainly no match for us.*

Tomorrow we descend into their heartland. From these mountains to the Midland Sea, the enemy holds sway. Our mission is to break their power and secure the Great River for travel and trade. Each day will take us deeper into native territory. Soon we will face the hostile forces that hold the river. Those tribes can hardly be said to form a kingdom, but they can muster an able force if they choose to unite. Soon we will know how formidable that force can be.

Osir imagined beyond the looming battles to a coming day when he would march triumphantly into Egia and learn the fate of his family and friends. No word had arrived from them for half a year. *Are my father and mother alive? Are my brothers and sisters safe and well? These must be hard times for Egians. With trade routes open, the city prospers. Without trade, who can say?*

* * *

"This must be the place they call 'the Animal Garden.'" Sareem said late next morning as he scanned the vast herds of wildebeest, elephant, rhinoceros, and ostrich.

"No," Osir said, "these animals are wild. The Animal Garden is quite different. There, herders drive animals they've tamed while warriors fend off lions, tigers, hyenas . . . and other warriors, of course."

"Let me guess. The warriors who protect cattle from other warriors . . . they're the ones we'll meet in battle?"

"Right you are," Osir answered. "They're better organized than the tribes we've encountered thus far. Their numbers are greater, and they are . . ." He paused, ". . . well armed."

"Well armed? What do you mean?"

"They've stolen modern weapons in recent raids. They may even have copied them, though iron not steel, of course."

"So we have serious work ahead, eh?"

"Our next encounter may be the greatest battle yet known to the People of the Living Sun. How many warriors can they muster? How good are their weapons? Let's hope we have answers before we have battles."

Deeper in the valley, they reached the real Animal Garden and sought cover among dense thickets along the Garara River's slender flood plain. At regular intervals, scouts penetrated the brush to check for settlements and evidence of herders or warriors on the move. Cautiously, methodically, the army traversed more than half the Animal Garden without incident. Within the small strip of forest, game animals were abundant, water was plentiful, and trees provided ample shade. The men ate well under constant guard.

Near Bir Qulaib, as soldiers lounged and chatted on bedrolls, eerie echoes disturbed the quiet of the night. Noises like the chanting of men, yet louder than any voice, penetrated the forest from unknown distances across an unseen plain. Replies reverberated from distant hilltops.

"Slit gongs!" Osir shuffled apprehensively at the unnerving effect on his men as the cacophony of call and answer continued without relief—call and answer, call and answer. He summoned his officers. "That's the signal system of the Westerners. They pound on those infernal slit gongs to communicate from village to village."

"So, what do the bignecks find interesting tonight?" Busah asked, knowing full well the answer but hoping against hope that he was wrong.

"Every Westerner within ten days walk must know we're here. They're gathering for an attack. We need to reach the wide plain where the Garara meets the Atmur Nugre. There we can fight on our own terms."

Again the next evening slit gongs chattered loudly and continuously—call and answer, call and answer all night long. Again the constant pounding upset the troops. "It's nothing more than a split log struck by a stick. Remember that, men. Don't let mere sounds spook you." Osir passed these words to his lieutenants who passed them on to their men. "Besides, we've reached the plain. We are in position to strike at first light." At daybreak, the men appeared rested, calm, and ready. In perfect battle formation, they emerged through shadowy mist.

As soon as sun cut fog, Osir's first question was answered. Army faced army on the open plain, and his force was outnumbered ten to one, perhaps even worse. Osir stepped to the fore and raised his sword. Its steel surface glistened like polished glass in the morning sun.

The opposing chief, dressed in a feathery crown and loincloth, likewise stepped forward, raising his own sword in direct imitation of Osir. Then, to everyone's dismay, each Westerner on the front line drew a saber and waved it from side to side in a blusterous show. Osir's second question was answered, and it was not to his liking. He didn't understand how the Westerners could have acquired such an arsenal. Yet the glittering weapons were in plain view. *Can my own army's superior training offset the superior numbers of men and swords we face?* Osir's forces stood resolutely with swords still at their sides. No bluster for his men! The two armies began a slow, steady march, then halted no farther than 100 manheights apart.

"Charge!" shouted Osir, and his army's wild cries jolted the morning air.

Shock registered in the chief's gestures when he realized his show of force had failed to intimidate the invaders. "Charge!" he shouted, but panic seized his troops. One by one, then by the hundreds, the primitives dropped their weapons to the ground. *They're giving up.* Osir thought with relief, but to his bewilderment they continued their charge into his own advancing lines.

Picking up stones, they proceeded into lethal range of first Sareem's spearmen, then Ketoh's archers, then Osir's swordsmen. A self-inflicted massacre thus unfolded, as Westerners died by their scores, first by arrows, then by spears, then by swords as Osir's army gained momentum.

Osir watched the native chief take his first arrow, a damaging strike to his left side. Yet the man stood firm. A hail of arrows struck his body, more than enough to kill any man, yet the chief remained standing. A spear struck him in the groin, then another in the ribs. Still the man stood. Swordsmen advanced. The chief didn't move. The first slash scored deeply into his left arm. He stood firm. The second slash cut deep into his abdomen, another into his chest. The chief still stood.

In awed respect, invaders and natives alike pulled back. Despite the raging battle, they cleared a circle of open ground around the incredible sight. Only as life spilled from his veins did the warrior chief relax his rigid stance. Finally, his body leaned, then fell upon the pile of weapons that had robbed him of his life.

The spell broke, and Osir's swordsmen ran like madmen headlong into the stunned force. Superior training overcame sheer numbers. By the hundreds, Westerners fell and died. By the thousands, survivors turned and ran. Osir's troops pursued for a distance, slashing and killing until the victory was complete.

"Assemble the troops. Count the dead." Stepping respectfully around slain Westerners, Osir puzzled over their strange behavior. *Why would anyone choose stones over swords?* he asked himself. When the army reached the line where the weapons had been discarded, his question was answered.

"Great Rahn!" Ketoh said. "Would you look at that?" On the ground lay the shattered remains of more than a thousand imitation swords. "Clay! Can you believe it? Clay."

"These innocents," Busah said. "They have no place in war. They must have thought our own swords were nothing more than talismans to ward off evil. They were dismayed when we didn't panic."

"Well, we called their bluff, and now they know better," Ketoh said, shaking his head. "They won't make this mistake again."

"Let's get moving," Osir said. "We still have 13 days' march before Ketoh can dip his toes in the Great River."

* * *

Along the way to the Great River, the army passed through four abandoned villages. In places, inhabitants ran desperately before them, forsaking the remnants of their simple lives—grass and mud huts, cattle pens, fire pits, and hide kettles. Invariably, near the center of each village was an enclosure consisting of four posts and a thatch roof, and inside was a smooth section of log with a long slit down its center. Beside each gong lay the hefty wooden rod used to pound out the haunting sounds of the night.

In each village, Osir ordered a soldier to pound the drum for more than a hand. "Westerners will hear and know that we now claim their prized possessions, their symbols of power. This battle will be won not only on the battlefield but also in their minds." Like a voice from another world, the plaintive moan of each slit gong rang out as if to mourn its fallen defenders.

Chronicle 44: Beside the Great River

"Beautiful." Osir stood atop a ragged escarpment, staring across the wide valley. Deeply incised, the Great River wound northward like a monstrous slithering python. Galleries of lush forest circumscribed each meander. On the opposite side of the floodplain stood low hills that mirrored the ridge on which he stood. The army had crossed overland from the plain of the Atmur Nugre to this point, well downriver from Biga Point where the usual trade route met the Great River.

* * *

Soldiers boarded a hundred clumsy gufas, eight men per boat. It had taken less than a day to gather willow withes for the ribs, weave reeds for the shell, and cover with skins and resins, plus another day to assemble and test. A rudder pole guided each boat while two poles, one on each side, propelled it forward. The poles were pushed along the bottom in shallow water or rowed as spindly oars in deeper water. Rudder men struggled to maintain control. In spite of their best efforts, however, the round, keel-less craft twirled at times like children's tops. Laughter rang out as boats bumped into boats and oars became hopelessly interlocked. Gradually, they yielded to the unrelenting force of the river.

Order emerged from chaos as each crew righted its course and headed down the open waterway. The scattered fleet remained in the river's powerful grasp for five days. On the sixth day, they entered the broad floodplain that extended all the way to the Great Gorge. Finally, they stopped at the mouth of the Fayuum Channel, a spur of the Great River that flowed into a huge inland lake west of the river. Stashing their gufas in a swamp, the army assembled and marched west into the Fayuum Basin, heartland of the territory of the Westerners. Here, it was said, the natives prospered, and the bigneck was rare.

When they reached the lake, a show of force was all they needed to spread panic among the Westerners. Village after village fell to the conquering army without resistance. Droves of desperate natives fled before the army's arrival, and those who remained bowed down in subservience. Five days later, Osir's men had returned to the mainstream and again bobbed peacefully downstream.

At a safe distance above Twin Falls, Osir led his men ashore. He stood on a jutting mound above the riverbank. "Men, we have come far. We've fought only a few real battles, but our campaign has filled the enemy with fear. We subdued this land, not with the wanton shedding of blood but with boldness, resolve, and overpowering might. We taught the enemy to quake at the sound of our footsteps. We resisted the urge to kill and plunder in ways that would slow our advance and cause lasting hatred among our neighbors. Yes, these Westerners will be our neighbors for thousands of years to come, as they step aside and we occupy their present lands. Our foes will remember your valor. More important, the wisdom of our battle plan will live long in the minds of our own people. I salute you. You honor our King.

"I've heard your words, and I know your fears. Westerners have fled by the thousands, but where are they now? What are their plans? Bracon's scouts have found their paths to the north, and they are still a formless mob. Now, they're trapped between our own force and the defensive lines of Egia. Surely they'll turn and fight somewhere between here and Twin Falls. With any leadership, they may rally and form a mighty army. Prepare yourselves for the greatest of all battles.

"We'll march day and night. We'll eat on the move. We'll seize the high ground and make our stand before the Westerners gather."

The men looked at one another. Two days of forced march into hard battle was well within their endurance, but even the most zealous would not relish such an ordeal. All eyes faced the northern horizon as the column, now again 20 men wide, settled to a brisk cadence. They set a beeline course due north along the river plain. The first day passed uneventfully along the age-old land route to Egia. Late on the second day, the silhouette of a low ridge appeared on the northern horizon. Osir knew its outline only too well. Before them stood the forbidding fortress of Ollo-detu and, below it, the mystic Lion Rock, oldest shrine in the Land of the Second Sunset.

Osir halted the column. While the troops rested, he wandered up a hillock for a better view of the plateau. Ketoh and Busah joined him, and each, in turn, grimaced as he scanned the upland. Westerners swarmed by the thousands across the plateau.

Osir shrugged. "This place holds hard memories for me. The massacre lingers as if it were only yesterday."

"You've never spoken much about that night, Osir, and I've never asked," Busah said.

"It was as savage as anyone can imagine," Osir said.

"Tomorrow morning, you will have your revenge." Busah's words were harsh, yet his voice compassionate.

"No, Busah. We'll teach the Westerners there is no place for such barbarity. Ketoh, order our men to kill no more than victory demands."

The army formed its defenses and made camp for the night. Eight hands later, a sentry awakened Osir in the predawn light. The man was clearly shaken. "Come, Sire, I have failed on my watch. You must see what the Westerners have done."

Osir and his officers accompanied the guard to the forward perimeter. Suddenly, their collective laughter awoke men nearby. During the night, Westerners had stealthily penetrated almost to the edge of camp. A short distance away stood scores of comely, naked maidens bound to trees and saplings.

"Are those bastards sacrificing virgins?" Sareem asked.

"No, it's a trap! They think our troops will fall for such a stupid trick. Our men are better than that!" Osir spoke through laughter.

In moments, the entire camp was ablaze with the news: "Women. Women for the taking." Men came running from all directions.

"Stop," Osir yelled. It was the first hint of panic he had ever shown. "Head them off!" he yelled even louder to his officers, as the rush became a stampede. "Stop!" he yelled over and over. The men kept running, their minds set on the favored spoils of war, an obvious sign of surrender, they thought. "No!" shouted Osir above the din. *These men don't hear. They don't want to hear.* Jumping onto a nearby boulder, he drew the dirktooth sword and flashed it high in the air.

"Stop!" he yelled again as he struck the sword's blade broadside against the rock. The sudden clang of steel against stone startled a few men at the front. Officers with drawn swords blocked their way. Finally, the stampede slowed as, one by one, the dazzled troops came to their senses.

"Not one maiden is to be touched," Osir shouted. "Arm yourselves and fall in," he said. Disappointed, the men reluctantly complied. "Expand the perimeter," he ordered. Debate ensued among the officers, but Osir knew what had to be done.

"Secure the line!" he shouted. A quickly assembled troop of seasoned soldiers rushed to make it so. "Loosen their bonds. Escort them to camp," he ordered. The army packed up and commenced its march to battle. A hand-picked detachment of mature, trusted soldiers guarded the maidens and herded them along behind the advancing army.

As the sun disk broke from the eastern horizon, a scene of monumental pathos unfolded. From the extensive flood plain to the rolling upland to Ollo-detu and in every direction as far as the eye could see, the mass exodus of Westerners converged on a single point. Thousands on thousands of fleeing primitives crowded around the giant lion-shaped rock at the base of the plateau.

"I thought they considered this place taboo," Ketoh said. Throngs already mounted the sides of the rock. Others amassed at its base. Vast numbers still surged onto the crowded plateau.

"Desperation!" Osir said. "Don't forget, they twice attacked Ollo-detu in spite of their fears. They may be superstitious, but they're not fools. They know the value of high ground in battle..." He looked at the crowded old garrison ". . . and fixed fortifications," he added. "Attack!" he yelled. "Attack Lion Rock!"

In precise formation, the troops stepped up their cadence, then accelerated to an all-out run, heading for the base of Lion Rock. Their path cut a wide swath through the mass of humanity as Westerners scattered to each side. At first, panic reigned. Then a solid corps of Westerners reached the base of the rock and turned to stand firm, each wave buoyed by those who had already made their stand. Weapons—clubs, spears, and a few swords—appeared everywhere. Osir's troops suddenly faced a mass of warriors outnumbering them 50 to one. Osir rushed headlong into the throng at the base of the sacred rock, followed by his officers, then by the mass of troops. Slashing and hacking, they penetrated successive lines of defense and advanced steadily to Lion Rock. Over its haunch, along its back and mane, finally to the crown of its head, the vanguard forged its way to victory.

Distrust of the rock now reconfirmed, thousands of Westerners fled before the final advance, many leaping to their deaths from the lion's brow or from the rim of the adjacent escarpment.

Osir stood triumphant on the crest, his dirktooth sword slashing victoriously skyward. A hush fell over the Westerners as they watched in wonder. Osir surveyed the masses, then ordered the maidens brought forth. As his officers led a few to the precipitous brow of the rock, a blend of cries, wails, and moans rose from the vanquished. Osir himself led some girls to the very brink. Then, to the surprise of the masses, he stopped his charade. He ordered the maidens escorted back down the lion's shoulders and returned to their people. At this dramatic act of mercy, the crowd bowed down before him as if he were a god.

Osir then turned his attention to the fortress atop the ridge. Ollo-detu had been taken by brute force a second time and remained even now in the hands of diehard Westerners. His mind churning with stark memories, Osir led his men up to the protective outcrop where he had hidden in moonlight years earlier.

"Take the sentries,' Osir whispered. Ketoh's archers snapped into action, and three silhouettes fell silently from the ramparts. Soldiers advanced to the fort. To their surprise, the wooden gate swung freely open. Stealthily, Ketoh and 20 handpicked volunteers slipped through the gate and into the interior courtyard. It was abandoned.

"Ketoh…to the left toward the quarters…Sareem…with me…to the right…," Osir ordered. "Watch above," he said, pointing to the rampart. "Find torches, men! Search every nook." With Sareem at his side, Osir led a party of five into the dank hold beneath the fortress. He reeled at the sight. "They could have lived," Osir said, shaking his head. In a perfect circle lay the lifeless bodies of more than twenty Westerners, each slain by his own hand.

"Cowards," Sareem accused.

"We know how to behave in victory, Sareem, but who knows how we ourselves might handle defeat?"

Chronicle 45: Return to Egia

With the last opposing Westerners defeated, Osir divided his army. He left the main force to hold the valley from Lion Rock to the Animal Garden and dispatched another contingent to defend the crossing from Kom Ombo to Berenicia. Ollo-detu and Kom Ombo would become the hubs of mobile networks of movable outposts and roving squads, unlike anything the Realm had established before. About 100 Egians would continue with him to their homeland. Soon a steady stream of commerce would follow in the wake of such good news received at both ends of the trail.

At dawn on the third day, the familiar path toward Egia steepened downward beyond the First Terrace.

"Great Rahn!" exclaimed Ketoh. "There's been a major battle!"

"These bodies must be Egians. Westerners burn their dead or leave them where they lie," Busah said, pointing toward an orderly row of a hundred skeletons or more.

"And it was a victory of some degree," Osir said, "for enough survived to lay these men out for the sea." He studied the scene reverently, then ordered the march resumed. Soon he found himself on hauntingly familiar ground as he and his fellow Egians neared the site of the legendary dirktooth kill.

"Show us the spot, Osir. Tell us how it happened," Ketoh said.

"Aw, fellows. You know I don't like to…"

"You have to show us, Osir. It's part of our heritage."

Everyone talks about the dirk kill. Sometimes I wish the story had never been told, but now it belongs to my people. I suppose I have no choice but to share it.

Osir first led them to the spot where the giant deer had lain. After describing the scene, he returned upslope to the rock from which the cat had leapt. He ended beside the trail, chuckling as he described his predicament, hanging from the precipice merely by his sash. He laughed. "Geb, have you not taught this boy how to ride a camel?" He quoted, imitating Hano's booming voice. Then, he sobered as more solemn memories surfaced as well. *Now, I'm a soldier like those I admired so much that day. I swore I would honor the sword of Phanus, and I have kept my word.*

They descended to the valley floor in view of the barracks beside Twin Falls. Osir whistled, but no response came. Cautiously, his troops entered the compound and found it truly deserted. He ordered camp for the night inside its walls. More than ever, Osir feared what he might find in Egia and whether, indeed, the city still stood.

He would know soon enough as they tackled the final leg. "The trail itself was little traveled before the uprising, but river traffic was always heavy," Osir said as they walked. "Now, both river and trail have been abandoned."

"Abandoned! It's as if there's never been a trail at all," Ketoh said while hacking his way through thick foliage. For two hands, they fought unrelenting tangles of vines and trees until remnants of the old trail appeared. After half a day's walk, the forest canopy thinned. Where magnificent groves once had reigned, now ragged, untended patches of upland rice grew in an otherwise charred landscape of girdled trees and fallen limbs. A little farther on, the trail breached the tattered edges of orchards and fields. Bushes and weeds encroached where, not long ago, neat crop rows had once flourished.

"Look! There . . . in the road. I see children." Ketoh yelled.

"They remind me of the three of us when we played together as boys! How long it has been!" Busah exuded.

Children darted repeatedly into the ditch and back up to the roadway. An abandoned shaduf was the focus of their frenzy. Each time they emerged from the pool at its base, they placed something in a small basket sitting on the bank.

In an instant, Egia's desperation was apparent to Osir. *These children aren't playing; they're foraging for food. No adults around. In my youth, no child would have gleaned from roadside pools. No child would have wandered here without a well-armed escort. Times must be hard, indeed.*

Anxiously, they approached the children. "Hello!" Osir called in a friendly tone, then issued the traditional greeting, "Hail, Children of the

Beloved Land!" The startled children panicked. Screaming and gesturing wildly, they stumbled to the roadway and ran frantically toward the city. One boy dropped his basket and sprawled on hard-packed earth. Jolted from panic, he assessed his pursuers. Despite his fears, he dashed for the fallen basket, then turned toward Egia and caught up with his companions. Five tiny tadpoles squirmed where his basket had lain.

"Wait!" Osir yelled. "We're friends! Egians! I'm Geb's son." He broke into a sprint, but the boy was too far ahead. He halted as the frightened children disappeared in the distance.

Osir drew his men into an orderly formation. "This is a bad sign. Be prepared for anything." In late afternoon, they spotted the distant rooflines of the city, capped by its magnificent but still unfinished True Pyramid. Half a hand later, they would reach Busah's family estate, then Osir's, then Ketoh's. Anticipation rose with every step.

Finally, an encouraging sight! Familiar fields with hundreds of harvesters among the rows. Warily watching his advancing unit, workers dropped their baskets and gathered beside the road. Osir calmly raised his bright sword skyward. "Osi! It's Osi, the Dirk Slayer!" yelled a villager. Others ran forward to confirm with their own eyes. Soon a multitude came to watch the surprise parade. Searching expectantly for family and friends, the troops marched home through roaring throngs. As the column passed Busah's gate, a shrill shout caught his attention. Joyously he broke ranks and rushed to his mother. He embraced her, then his father, then his sisters and brothers, nieces, nephews, and total strangers. His relief was obvious.

"Your family has fared well," Osir whispered when Busah rejoined the march.

"Did you see the pride in their eyes?" Busah asked, looking back over his shoulder at the aging couple. "They managed to keep the estate, and now they even feed others. I haven't seen them so happy since I was a boy. If not for my pledge to the Realm, I'd stay here. One day they'll need me more than ever."

Now it was Osir's turn to learn his family's fate. As he turned into the gate, he abruptly found himself trapped in his mother's arms. At Nuuti's side was Hammon's boyish face now gracing the lanky frame of a proud teenager. Osir beamed as he stared *upward* into his brother's eyes. One by one, Thalan, then Rannah, then sister Imea appeared. "Father! Where's father?"

"He's . . . no longer with us," Nuuti said. "Your father was a courageous man, Osir. When the Westerners took Ollo-detu and closed the trail to Berenicia, Egia was open to attack. Geb organized a force to meet them at the First Terrace. Our men prevailed, but he and other heroes are laid out for the sea above the First Terrace."

"I saw the men laid out for the sea." He shivered, recalling sun-bleached bones and knowing now that Geb was among them. "They saved Egia," he said simply, and no other obituary was needed.

Nuuti nodded. "The Westerners saw only a valiant defense. Fortunately, they didn't know this costly victory left too few men to mount another attack or even to defend our city. But it seemed only a matter of time until they would learn of our weakness. For more than a year, our people have lived under constant fear of a second attack. Now we are saved by my own beautiful son." The crowd pressed inward. Torn with emotion, Osir looked back at his men, then at his mother, brothers, and sister.

"March on, my son. Our people need your strength. Your triumph will inspire and encourage them. Go, Osir. Go quickly. March proudly into the city. It is yours."

* * *

Reunions followed, one after another, until everyone located his family, though all too many loved ones would be missing forever. The celebration continued ever more riotously down the main boulevard. . . past the academy where they received their first military training. . . past the Agent's Palace and grounds. . . past the garrison, now in disrepair, and fine estates, now overgrown. . . past small shops, many abandoned. Osir cringed at the ungroomed temple and idle pyramid.

Liberated Egians gathered in the market plaza, each vying for a glimpse of the victorious army and its fabled leader. The best of Egia's remaining food stocks materialized from hiding, and the celebration ran long into the night with Musicians, acrobats, and dancers. One after another citizens offered testimonials to their liberators. Nobles, Chosen Ones, and Commoners alike paid tribute. Gifts, both simple and extravagant were laid at their feet. Never before had the staid little city thrown such celebration.

Anbaht and his priests led an all-night vigil to offer thanks and praise. The ceremony, however, seemed more for Osir than for Rahn. Following the obligatory prayers and chants, speaker after speaker gushed with praise for the Dirk Slayer. Finally, Osir was invited to address the multitude.

"Friends of Egia, Beloved People, People of the Living Sun!" he hailed to tumultuous applause. "Today we proclaim a great victory. For the first time in the history of the People of the Living Sun, an army of the Realm has prevailed in a land war against the Westerners." Osir paused and surveyed the crowd. "The sons of Egia, as well as of Punt, make up this army of deliverance. Here stand the Egians. Others guard the way from Lion Rock to Kom Ombo and on to Berenecia.

"The citizens of our Realm face new dangers, new challenges. Our age-long idyll at this beloved seaside city is over. Our truce with the

Westerners is no more. Our ability to protect all within these walls is gone forever." Osir warmed to the crowd, and they to him.

"We achieved an overwhelming victory, but it is temporary. We built the greatest land army the world has yet devised, but that is not enough. Under Geb's leadership, you proved you can fight. Now you must do so, over and over. . . first to defend this land as long as it holds. . . then to seize new ground in the Land of the Second Sunset. For this purpose, I will assign 50 soldiers of Egia to remain here, to train you and lead you. They are the finest soldiers in the Realm. Colonel Busah, proud son of Egia, will be their commander." He gestured grandly toward Busah and the soldiers surrounding him. Busah's pride, surprise, and elation were evident in his broad smile. The crowd cheered. "They will train you to fight the battles yet to come."

Osir stood silent as the rumble of adulation swelled to a roar. "Osir! Osir! Osir! Hero of our people! Dirk Slayer! Leader without peer!" the crowd yelled. "Be our leader!" they chanted over and over.

He raised both arms to quiet the growing din. "My mission lies elsewhere. You will be safe in the hands of Busah and his soldiers. Follow their lead. Prepare yourselves for the struggle to come." The crowd quieted only when Osir stepped down from the podium and departed the square. The heroes slept at the Agent's Palace, bedding down just in time to miss the dawn.

After the festivities, Osir, Busah, and Ketoh returned for warm reunions with their families. Ketoh's parents hadn't escaped all hardships, but they had managed to live comfortably on a diminished share of produce from their vast holdings. Osir was pleased to learn that his own brothers and sister had done their part to help the community survive. He told them about his meeting with Mira in Mekong City, emphasizing her contentment and omitting his doubts. He said nothing about Isas and loathed his own weakness as he shrank from the truth.

CHAPTER 19

Search Log 35: Sea Tech

The night was warm and clear as Jared drove toward Knoxville. Rick was beside him in the Pathfinder's front seat, and Curt Stratton was in back. Curt, an old college roommate of the Caisson brothers, had called earlier to say he would be in town and hoped they could get together Saturday night. Jared had other plans, but a night out with Rick and Curt was not to be missed.

They headed straight for Tomo, the Old City's sole sushi bar. Curt had been to Knoxville's quaint downtown before but never to the part called Old City. He was surprised to find it so lively. Rick liked to say it was "a century long and two blocks deep but well worth the visit." Curt had no idea how large or small the revitalized district, actually no more than four blocks, might be. As he reached for Tomo's door, Jared held him back and pointed toward the heart of Old City, half a block away. "Now, Curt, just so you'll know what to expect, I want you to look up the street. You see all that excitement. Well, it just goes on for blocks and blocks, and gets better all the way," he said, as if he meant it. "Stay sober, and we should be able to see it all by daybreak."

"Well, hot damn!" Curt said, as if he meant it, too. "Let's get on with it!" He wrenched the doorknob, and the three of them walked briskly toward the sushi bar. "That felt odd!" he said, once they had settled in. "I had forgotten what it's like to walk through a crowd with you guys. Everybody stared at you, then looked at me as if to say, 'What doesn't belong in this picture?' Just like old times." Curt was a big man capable of attracting a few stares of his own.

An easy banter developed at the bar, and eventually a fellow diner asked, "Are you twins?" Curt and Jared leaned toward one another in a brotherly sort of way and said, "Why, yes we are. How kind of you to notice." Rick sat quietly to one side.

"No, seriously. You two, pointing at Rick and Jared, look just alike. Are you brothers or twins?"

"Both, actually," Rick said, drawing a laugh.

"We haven't pulled that trick since college," Curt said, when the moment had passed.

"No, but we did it enough back then to last several decades."

"We should write a book about those days. It would be a long one."

"Yeah, but we'll have to use pseudonyms."

The sushi looked good. The service was unhurried, leaving plenty of time for conversation. The two brothers earlier had confided their ideas to Curt, and he was fascinated. Waiting for the first course, Jared described the difficulties of traveling to Foul Bay.

"So, can this Egyptian professor lady get you in or not?" Curt asked.

"Her last message sounded hopeful. She talked with some low-level bureaucrats, but she needs to go a lot higher. She's pretty astute, though. If anybody can do it, she can. I lucked out finding her so easily."

"Piece of cake!" Curt pronounced with a flourish.

"Not exactly! Even if we get permission, logistics are difficult. I don't know what services to expect in Berenice. The best case would be a local diving service that would take us out and provide support. I doubt we'll be so lucky, however, since it isn't a tourist destination. Guidebooks don't mention any such services. We may be stuck on dry land."

"Why not carry equipment with you?"

"We'd need Sherpas to carry that much stuff."

"Maybe not. All you need is scuba gear. It's light and fairly compact."

"We don't even know whether boats are available. What if we have to stay within swimming distance of the beach?"

"Carry an inflatable raft."

"That's so crazy it just might work," Rick said in the same facetious tone Curt had used earlier. "Let's think about it. But we'll need a compressor to keep our tanks charged and plenty of water if we stray very far from land."

"We can buy collapsible plastic jugs from REI, but what about the water itself? We won't want to run back to Berenice every time our supply gets low," Rick said. "A few wells are marked on the map, but the reefs are a long way from land. That may require more water than a small raft can hold."

"Buy a desalination pump. They're in all the sailing magazines."

"Oh, I forgot you're into sailing! What are those pumps like? How big are they? How heavy? How do they work?"

"Not very big compared to a boat, but bigger than hell compared to a suitcase."

"Assume the worst case, zero local support. What do we need?"

"Definitely a lot of stuff. You're talking about freight, not baggage."

As they waited for dinner, the "roomies" reminisced about their travels through New England in the summer of '65. They worked at New Hampshire's Camp Takodah, where they had barely survived the season hanging on the hairy edge of the camp's strict rules. "Takodah will never be the same," Rick said. They had topped off the summer with a stop at the Newport Folk Festival where they witnessed the birth of rock, when Dylan went electric.

The sushi arrived, and the conversation returned to their glory days at the University of Georgia when they and four friends had rented an old dilapidated house they named "Shadowdale Lodge." Years later, friends from high school and college, some of whom had visited only once or twice, proudly professed association with the legendary "lodge."

In recent years, the three veterans of Shadowdale Lodge had managed to reunite two or three times each year, and recent meetings had become adventures in their own right. The Old City was just the beginning of a night that would take them to five different establishments where they would eat and drink and laugh and banter with strangers. Of course, everything was scaled down from the old days, especially the drinking. At the last saloon of the night, Curt recalled something he'd meant to bring up earlier. "Speaking of Egypt, do you guys remember what we heard at Camp Takodah?"

"About Egypt?" Rick asked.

"Yes, indirectly. One of the counselors said some Indians over in Canada speak a language virtually identical to ancient Egyptian. Don't you remember?"

"That explains it!" Jared exclaimed. "When I read Barry Fell's book about pre-Columbian contact, I knew I'd heard that somewhere before. He says the Micmacs of New Brunswick and Nova Scotia had a language identical to ancient Egyptian. It's only the written version that's Egyptian, I think. A French missionary, Father Maillard, wrote translations of Micmac hieroglyphs in the 1700s. Fell claims Maillard's dictionary could have explained Egyptian hieroglyphics 60 years before Champollion deciphered the Rosetta Stone, but no one put the two together."

"As I recall," Curt said, "they claimed it was taught to them by a man who came from the east in a stone boat. They called him 'trickster,' because he was so clever."

* * *

Jared didn't mind going to work on Monday morning after a good weekend. Friday night, the whole family had gone to Little Joe's for pizza and beer. Saturday, he and his sons had cut firewood all day. As the boys grew older, they finally understood why he enjoyed hard work with his two favorite people. The boys left on Sunday morning. By then, the mild weather had turned cold again, but Jared and Ellie liked nothing more than a day at home with the fireplace glowing.

On Highway 95, Jared passed through the I-40 intersection mentioned in Tom Clancy's *Debt of Honor* and mentally offered thanks that its "15 minutes of fame" hadn't spawned souvenir shops and fireworks stands. *How odd*, he thought, *that Clancy moved the famous fog-bound stretch of interstate from its actual place to a different highway 50 miles away.*

I guess all novelists do that. But the real fog bank on I-75 is more interesting than Clancy's fantasy. I wonder if it's possible to write a novel based mostly on fact. Probably not.

Caisson parked his Pathfinder in a gravel-surfaced lot that looked more like a trailhead in a National Forest than a parking lot at a National Laboratory. He walked the tree-covered path, wishing he were carrying a backpack instead of a laptop slung over his shoulder. He watched the Lab's resident flock of Canada geese fly over in their characteristic V. Some landed on the swan pond, others on the main parking lot where they would leave fitting mementos for employees lucky enough to find spaces there.

As soon as he settled into his office, Jared called Glenn Jamerson. "Glenn, I need a favor, but I'm hesitant to ask."

"Good, then let's just leave it at that." He paused. "Seriously, Jer, what can I do for you?"

"I'd like to borrow the underwater camera you use in your sea grass work...for a trip overseas. I don't want to interfere with your work schedule, though. Just say 'no' if I'm out of line."

"Well, we can probably work something out if you really need it, but this thing we use is old and cumbersome. Can't you just buy a new camera? You can get a good one for less than a thousand dollars."

"Not really. This is on internal money, and my budget is too tight as is."

"I'll tell you what! Buy yourself some disposable cameras, as many as you need, then buy an underwater cover for about $20. Lots of sports divers say they're satisfied with the results. Just about any camera shop will have them. The results won't be magazine quality, but they'll be plenty good enough for identifying corals. Best of all, the equipment will be lightweight and cheap."

"The price is right, but I need incontrovertible documentation. I can't risk blowing it with less than professional quality photos."

"Have you considered underwater video?"

"No. I assumed the cameras were too bulky and too expensive."

"They get smaller and cheaper and better every year. We're switching to video in our sea grass mapping, and we've bought several cameras. With a little advance notice, I can lend you one for a few weeks."

"Great. Thanks. I'll send a memo to make it official."

Before Jared could hang up, Walde Peplies knocked on his door and peered inside. Jared motioned to Walde as he said goodbye to Glenn. They started chatting, but Jared hadn't had coffee yet. After first trying not to let on, he suggested a stroll to the coffee room. It wasn't really a room but rather a big open space surrounded by all sorts of machines and electronics housed in wire mesh cages to prevent accidental contact. One of the cages actually had a sign, presumably intended to console the wary, that said, "FUMES FROM THIS DEVICE ARE NOT HAZARDOUS." It was the kind of lounge only an engineer could love.

Jared recapped the travel plans he and Rick had made, as well as Curt's and Glenn's advice on gear. *Sounds more and more like a real expedition like old time geographers used to make,* Jared thought, as he listened to himself talk. *Move over, John Wesley Powell.*

"Rafts make a lot of sense," he said, "but I'm concerned about weight. The only ones I'm familiar with are those seven-man monsters used on rivers like the Ocoee. We'll probably need something like a two-man Zodiac, but they're expensive and heavy."

"Take my Folbot!"

"Fold boat? Oh, Folbot! Your folding canoe! I didn't think of that. Sure. It worked pretty well in the Adirondacks. Your students ferried Matt and me across South Lake and back without mishap. But Foul Bay and South Lake are entirely different situations. Besides, as I recall, that thing weighed a ton, and it was cumbersome as hell."

"No, no. That was the old model. I have a new one now...a kayak. Remember what happened! My students strapped mine on top of their truck, and it blew off on the way back. The skin was badly damaged so I tossed what was left."

"Well, I understand. What good's a boat that can't slide down an interstate any better than that? Did you say the new model is lighter?"

"Much lighter. Only 62 pounds. They replaced the wooden frame with anodized aluminum tubing and all sorts of exotic materials. Much easier to assemble, too."

"Can it take saltwater and high seas?"

"My two-man version is actually designed for ocean kayaking. Canoe magazines describe good performance in tough sea expeditions. Alaska, British Isles, places like that. It works great as long as you buy the optional foot rudder kit, about 90 bucks in their list of accessories."

"That's reasonable."

"There's an optional sail, too."

"I'm not a sailor. I can paddle all day and most of the night, but I don't trust myself with a sail. When Greg and I canoed in Canada, we made 72 miles in six days, and 12 of those miles were portage. In contrast, my one experience with sailing was a disaster."

"What happened?"

"I visited a family at their summerhouse on a lake in Canada. I was 21 at the time, and their sixteen-year-old daughter took me out for a sail. She won a big race the year before, so I assumed she knew what she was doing. Then, the wind picked up, and she panicked. She handed me the tiller and ran forward to take in the sheet. I did what seemed natural, and it was precisely the opposite of what I should have done. We capsized before she reached the mast."

"That doesn't sound like you. I've never known you to be scared off by something like that."

"Not fear, just embarrassment. And I would have been happy to try it again, but I moved in other directions, like backpacking, and the opportunity never arose again. But that incident convinces me not to try sailing on Foul Bay without a lot more experience."

"Probably wise."

"Your first boat was open from gunwale to gunwale like a canoe. What's this one like?"

"You have a choice. Its cockpit is open, but a spray skirt snaps to the gunwale. It cinches around your waist, like the outfits Eskimos wear...should keep everything dry inside."

"Load?"

"600 pounds max."

"Wow, let's see. Rick and I are about 180 pounds each. That leaves more than 200 pounds for gear. That's a gracious plenty. Airlines! How big is the carrying bag?"

"That shouldn't be a problem. Two bags, one about the size of a suitcase, the other about five feet long, but quite narrow, not much bigger than a golf bag."

"One last question. How tough is the skin? That's the one big advantage of rafts. They're made to take a whacking and keep on tacking."

"The deck is waterproof, and that's all you need on top. But the hull is made of precisely the same material as those rafts you trust so much. Still, don't slide it down the highway."

"Live and learn, huh? By the way, what color is it?"

"Dark blue deck, black hull. Does it matter?"

"Great camouflage! They'll never find us if we get washed out to sea."

"Red would be better! They'd never find a red boat on the Red Sea."

"Good point! And you don't mind if we take your prized possession to Foul Bay, named for its singular effect on shipping, with mines on land, mines at sea, under threat of terrorist attack, and with no experience whatsoever?"

"I trusted my students, didn't I?"

"Some people never learn."

Search Log 36: Version 2.0

The Bell 206 B III helicopter skimmed over Alaska's North Slope. Jared sat in the navigator's seat, an updated fieldstation in his lap. His job was to navigate, pick sites, and direct the pilot. Ed sat in the rear seat calling out land cover types. A fourth man recorded Ed's observations. Vast tundra stretched to the horizon, and a herd of caribou darted away beneath the chopper. Seagate had expanded to the far north, and Caisson and Field were there to define training samples, just as they had done at Yakutat the year before. The fieldstation performed flawlessly.

A week later they were back at Yakutat for a final check of its database. Matt Caisson joined them, compliments of Jared's frequent flyer miles, to help in the work and to see Alaska. The Seagate team retraced every mile of road in the Yakutat Foreland, then took to the air in fixed-wing aircraft. On Monday, they flew west as far as Icy Bay. On Tuesday, they flew south past the Dangerous River, then inland to Russell Fiord and Hubbard Glacier.

Late in the final afternoon, Chris Ojala led them to the local cannery where, for a dollar a pound, they bought whole salmon, "round fish" in fisherman's parlance, caught in the Situk River that very day. Later the entire team sat on the beach, cooking fish and remembering the week's events. Mount St. Elias, a distinctive landmark for early explorers, and Mt. Logan, the second highest mountain in North America, stood like silver sentinels across Yakutat Bay. A huge bonfire cut the chill of the long evening as two big salmon sizzled and dripped and scented the cool, salt air. In native fashion, two alder-woven rackets stood upright around the fire, each holding a splayed salmon and silhouetted like a talisman against the backdrop of ocean, beach, and old-growth forest.

Jared leaned against a driftwood log. *I feel like a shaman overseeing a pagan ritual,* he thought. The scene grew ever more surreal as fog drifted in from the sea, alder smoke rose from the fire, and Alaskan Amber flowed amply.

Chris stepped away from the firelight and walked over to the beached log. "It's amazing how much that fieldstation has improved since last year."

"Yep, the Shroud of Tourin' is the biggest advance of all," Jared said. "Gone is the old cardboard box technology of Version 1.0, replaced by advanced black felt and coat hanger technology in 2.0."

"That's probably true," Chris laughed, "but overall performance seems smoother this year. That goes for everything from power supply to GPS link."

"Well, experience makes a difference, and we've had lots of experience with it since September. We used it in Maine and New Brunswick, Oregon and Washington, the North Slope, and here. So far, we've deployed it in automobiles, helicopters, and fixed-wing aircraft. The only thing left is boats, and we've played around with them a little. And, yes, we've customized the flimsier components."

Kinski joined them. "Of course, it doesn't hurt that Ed produced a near-perfect database. Watching the screen is almost like walking through the landscape itself," he said.

"Ed and I were both relieved when we spotted those bogs up by the fiord," Jared said.

"Me, too," Matt said. "On the image, it looked as if they were hanging on the side of a mountain, suspicious as hell. But there they were, in a little swag about halfway up the slope."

"And what a slope! That mountain must rise 5,000 feet directly up from the fiord to the ice field," Chris exclaimed.

"5,520 feet," Ed said.

CHAPTER 20

Chronicle 46: The Lands of the North

On their ninth day in Egia, the *Ruby of Berenicia* sailed into the harbor. Captain Hervov brought news that Rahn Mennon had died and Rahn Ammon had been crowned King of the Realm. True to his word, the new King had dispatched the captain and his vessel to support Osir's expedition to the Ice.

Osir could hardly imagine how difficult the Southern Passage had been for the storied vessel. Only Hervov could make the uncommon voyage seem a sane thing to do. It was fortunate that Rahn Ammon had sent him, trusting Osir to reach Egia by land, for spring was near, and they would need the entire summer to accomplish Osir's next objective—to view the Ice.

From Egia, the *Ruby* would sail to the lowlands of Etrusca. An elite force of 50 soldiers accompanied by three Geometers, who had arrived aboard the *Ruby*, would trek over mountain passes to reach the Ice. In late autumn, if all went well, they would rendezvous with Hervov at the northern tip of the Midland Sea.

On the day of departure, Busah escorted them to the harbor. "Take care," Busah said. Despite his carefully clipped phrases, Busah's affection for his lifelong friends sounded in his voice and showed in his face.

"We will," Osir said. "You, too, Busah. We'll both face our share of danger before we next meet."

"Take care," Ketoh said. "Busah, the time will come when . . ."

Busah interrupted, knowing what was on their minds. "Say no more, friends. The duty and the honor are mine. I'll care for your families as my own. If we survive the Waters of Chaos, you will meet your loved ones again in the land above."

Catching a break between late winter storms, Hervov quickly set sail. Within two hands, they were free of the harbor and riding a strong west wind. Osir welcomed the long-overdue reunion but felt an inward pain as he studied his aging mentor's wrinkled face. Hervov had said a day would come when he and Osir again would sail the World Ocean. Osir was pleased that day had come. But Osir felt a pang of fear when he recalled that Hervov had also foretold a time when Osir himself would command the *Ruby*.

Soon the sails were trimmed and a northbound course was set. Osir questioned Hervov. "Tell me again of Bera and Horesh. Are they truly well? Have you hidden anything from me?"

"They are well," Hervov smiled. "Horesh speaks your name like an orator. He's a fine young tyke. He'll make you proud."

"And Bera?" It pained him to ask again of Bera's welfare, wishing he were the one who knew, the one who would answer rather than ask. "Is she also truly well?"

"She is truly well. She sends her love. Read her letter again if you don't believe an honest old man." He chuckled.

Osir walked slowly to the bow, away from pathways and duty posts, where he could concentrate on the letter, now worn and supple from numerous readings. He sat astride a gear locker and weighted the sheets side by side on its lid.

"My dearest Osir . . ." the letter began. He felt a drop form in the corner of his eye and roll down his cheek. He wouldn't call it a tear. Red ink pooled where the non-tear hit papyrus. Bera first affirmed her love for him and then for their son, Horesh. She recounted the boy's childhood progress since his father's departure.

"Horesh hasn't learned to walk . . . he only knows how to run. This way, that way, everywhere. He's learned to make full sentences and never stops talking. Last week I took him to the docks to watch the ships come and go. "Aba's ship!" he proclaimed every time a boat of any sort sailed by. I told him your ship would have a red bow. That seemed to help him understand. Then he saw the *Ruby* and screamed with joy. He was terribly disappointed when I told him you weren't aboard. We went to the market and bought sweets. He entertained the shopkeepers with his babbling. I can't wait for you to see him again.

"Life in the palace is lonely but never dull. There is so much intrigue, and I have become quite an observer of the court...more than an observer, actually. Many nobles have grown to respect my council. They sometimes seek my advice, and I am not above giving it. Rahn Ammon is no fun. He takes his 'kingness' too seriously if you ask me, but at least he appreciates having Horesh and me at the palace.

"Toth remains my most loyal friend. He appears stodgy at a distance, but he's really a much kinder man than either of us had taken him to be. Sometimes he calls me 'Little Isas' which means 'light' in the tongue of the ancients, I am told. He says he has known me since I was a little girl, even before I came to be Rahn Mennen's daughter. He admires your father, Geb and your mother Nuuti, and respects you highly, Osir. He continues to speak well on your behalf to Rahn Ammon.

"I am anxious to hear your version of the skirmish at Wadi Hodein. Rumors in the streets say Setra foolishly endangered your men, but that's not what he told Rahn Ammon. He said you failed to post watches so that the faithful could pray in safety and 50 men died in the breach. Toth vowed to get to the bottom of it, but for now that is the only official account presented to Rahn Ammon. Setra claims he reprimanded you at the First Terrace and expects you to perform better in battle now. I'm sure that's a lie. Rahn Ammon still believes in your mission and thinks you will succeed."

So my first report never made it to Erytheia. Probably not even to Berenicia.

Finally, Bera turned to matters of state and the public clamor that followed news of his victory at the first garrison. She told of improved morale around the Valley Sea in hopes that the trade route to Egia would be open again. Already, she said, signs of new commerce abound as hopeful merchants prepare their wares for export. She repeated how much she missed him and longed to be in his arms again and ended, "Give your family my love. I hope to meet all of them someday."

I'm indeed a fortunate man, he said to himself. After half a hand, Osir returned to the helm where Captain Hervov still stood. The captain placed a fatherly hand on his shoulder.

"You're lucky, Osir. No woman can love a man more than Bera loves you."

"And no man can love a woman more than I love her."

"Then why do you have such a heavy brow, my friend?"

"Because I shouldn't be here."

"What do you mean, you 'shouldn't be here.' This is your mission."

"I should be home with my wife and child. I should be there to protect them. Instead, Bera has to risk herself protecting me. It isn't right. I should be there."

"This is foolish talk, Osir. No one serves a greater purpose than the Dirk Slayer." He smiled gently and set his hand on Osir's shoulder. "Bera is doing a fine job with Horesh, and she's a natural at all this palace intrigue. You're needed at home but *not* for politics. You'd set the whole kingdom on end, and poor Bera would have to set it right again." Both men laughed. "I've heard how you shocked the King with your brashness. No, Osir, I think you'd best leave politics to politicians."

The two men dodged into the captain's chambers and conferred for the remainder of the afternoon. They were still browsing through maps and documents when dinner arrived. During the meal, Hervov explained what Bera had left unsaid. The new King's authority had been eroded by the poor performance of regular forces under Setra's command. Setra had been discredited as well.

"Watch your back, son." Hervov said without further explanation. "Setra is an unduly proud man. He will not take failure well."

At the whipstaff, sighting low across the bow, Hervov again ordered the sails trimmed and the rudder set due north. With currents pushing westward and winds pushing eastward, constant corrections were needed to counter the drift. Still, they spied land on the north shore of the Midland Sea after only four days under sail. Another day and a half on the leeward side of a stubby, boot-heel peninsula brought them to the broad, low-lying basin of Etrusca.

* * *

The Po River estuary offered ample anchorage for the fleet of vessels that regularly plied the waters of its bay. Sun shone through drifting cloudbanks as the *Ruby's* passengers looked shoreward. Small vessels worked upriver beside dormant fields. Intricate canals permitted access to the city and farmlands, protected from the sea by low barrier islands.

Nowhere else in the Lands of the North could such an expanse of productive lowland be found, but human hands had altered only a small fraction of its land. Inland, at the first hint of a slope, sat the town of Etrusca that dominated the fertile valley, politically and economically. The *Ruby* could navigate to Etrusca but no farther. The river beyond was broad enough for tacking but too shallow for the ship's deep draft. Here Captain Hervov and the explorers parted ways after agreeing to meet again hundreds of leagues to the east.

Etrusca was called the City of Love, for its people were open, generous, and loving. Openness and generosity were fine qualities, the travelers agreed, but it was the legendary loving that made Etrusca a favored stop for mariners. Osir granted liberty to his men as soon as Captain Hervov completed the skillful docking maneuvers required in Etrusca's riverside harbor. Into the streets of the city poured the rested and restless crew.

Street-side taverns were clearinghouses for a wealth of goods and services. For Osir, information was the most valuable commodity. Officers scoured the city seeking expert advice on what lay to the north. What will we encounter? How can we prepare? What must we carry? Where can we find provisions? His Geometers interrogated Etruscan Geometers, asking questions and purchasing updated charts of routes to the interior.

Colonel Sareem, now in charge of logistics, inquired about supplies and interviewed guides. "Packhorses are available only in the lowlands," one man said. "Tribes of the north manufacture the best winter gear. Best get your heavy clothes just before reaching the mountains," someone else advised. Sareem would have preferred to purchase all necessary supplies at the outset, but too many specialized items were needed. Better to wait until they reached expert craftsmen in villages within sight of the Ice. After two days of bargaining, Sareem's unit spent an equal time stocking dockside sheds. Osir's final act before leaving town was to hire an Etruscan named Nicco as interpreter and guide. Finally the expedition was ready.

Fifty four men and ten horses stood by as Osir surveyed the graying skies. A stiff breeze heavy with cold light rain foretold the misery to come in the land of ceaseless winter. Four horses were laden with trade goods, particularly sea salt, smoked shellfish meats, and dried seaweed, part for their own use and part for barter. The other six would be packed along the way as necessary goods were acquired in trade.

Osir addressed his officers. "Soon we will face mountains completely covered with ice. Farther on, the frozen stuff will build its own mountains—masses of ice so great they've piled and plowed and bent and gored the earth. Our chosen course will take us up the Po River two day's trek to its confluence with the Tagliamento, up the Tagliamento to the Isonzo, then over a series of mountain passes into the upper valley of the Sava. From there, we will follow well-worn trade routes that skirt the headwaters of the Sava, the Drava, and the Mura. On the seventeenth day, we'll cut through a low pass to the Marcal, down to the Donau, and up the Dyje. If all goes well, within a month we'll be in the upper valleys that recently broke free of the Ice. Beyond lie the dreaded, frozen lands where none of our kind have ventured."

* * *

Two days on the trail, as if to further warn of things to come, a bitter blowing rain stung Osir's face. "So this is what they mean by 'cold weather,'" Jumar said. "I thought the winds on the Valley Sea were bad enough." As he spoke, the rain turned to hard pellets of ice that bit into a man's cheeks like hard-blown desert gravel. Already, some voiced fears, and Osir felt the strain.

I've heard stories about extreme cold, but never did I imagine this. I never imagined the physical effects on a man's body. Pain, not just discomfort...and the way it plays on a man's mind. Fear, self-doubt, desperation, despair—I feel them all.

"I've never been so cold in all my life," Ketoh said.

"We haven't seen anything yet. This is just a hint of the cold that lies ahead," a Geometer said with scholarly detachment and little concern for morale.

"We'll soon reach the Tagliamento," Nicco said. "A village sits nearby. The natives there will exchange fur parkas and hide boots for blocks of salt and cuts of seaweed."

* * *

Villagers gawked upward from their handiwork as the soldiers cautiously explored a street leading to the village center. Crude huts lined the rambling thoroughfare. Farther on, a clearing was filled with the odds and ends of subsistence. The circular council house at its edge consisted of a high pole with hide-draped saplings radiating outward. An earthen berm surrounded the entire structure, except for a front opening curtained with a hide flap.

Outside the council house, rugged villagers sat on piles of mammoth bone, blocks of wood, or crude stools. Some sold ibex and saiga antelope meat; some sharpened stones; some worked hides; others sewed leather garments of the type Osir's troops needed. A few words from Nicco convened the entire council. "Lay meat here...." Nicco pointed to a huge flat stone stained red with blood. ". . . clothes here." He pointed to a rare clean spot in the common. Tribesmen shuffled to comply. Nicco then pointed to a soldier holding the reins of a pack animal. "Show your goods," he said to Sareem. Sareem motioned to one of his men.

Untying a pack, the soldier produced a pressed block of seaweed and laid it on the rock with a flourish. Stepping forward, one of the elders bent over the precious commodity. Sensing its thickness and compaction between his outstretched forefinger and thumb, the elder nodded with obvious pleasure. Murmurs of satisfaction rumbled through the assembled villagers, some of whom suffered grotesquely with the bigneck. A quick exchange between the council and the guide ended in curt nods. "A quick bargain has been struck," the interpreter informed Sareem.

Orders were given, and the village came alive. Men, women, and children bustled from building to building gathering well-worn garments from their huts and depositing them on outstretched hides.

"Wait," Sareem called out. "We want new garments, not used ones off their backs."

"No choice," responded the interpreter. "You are fortunate they have enough to spare. Tailoring new garments would take too long."

"Then, we'll move on to the next village," Osir interjected, sensing the mood of his troops. "Our men can bear the cold a while longer. Let's warm ourselves by their fires, then we'll be gone." The interpreter passed Osir's words along to the council. Instantly, their mood changed. Villagers retraced their footsteps, returning the worn garments to their dwellings. Osir secretly shivered, but passed word along that no soldier was to let on that he felt the cold.

"Now food!" Osir ordered, and Sareem instructed the interpreter to bargain for yet another luxury. Villagers served hot antelope stew and wild grain bread, for a price, of course, and the men feasted to contentment.

Meanwhile, a nearby doorway swung open, and out stepped a young lady laden with new parkas. Others soon followed, and a pile of exquisitely tailored garments covered the ground where grubby ones had lain. "Ha!" Osir laughed. "These people aren't simple, Sareem. They know how to bargain."

Osir savored the earthy scent of newly-tanned leather and the gaminess of heavy fur. Slipping his arms into thick sleeves, he felt a rush of warmth. Sliding first one foot and then the other into mukluks, he almost swooned as feeling returned to his feet. In moments, hot blood coursed to his ice-burned cheeks. Looking across the firelight to the glowing faces of his comrades, Osir watched the same transformation as each man wriggled into his own new garments.

Officers were invited to sleep in the village's longhouse. Other soldiers pitched camp just outside the village. The following morning, they awoke to clear, frosty air and a magnificent view of snow-capped mountains in the distance. Rested, well fed, and wrapped in warm furs, the expedition struck out again with high hopes and improved dispositions.

Leaving the Isonzo River, the men of the south at last entered the mountains of the north. From the last vestige of flat land, Osir scanned the mountains and marveled at their sheer heights.

"This is not as I had imagined," Osir said, his gaze fixed on the towering cliffs.

"Where in Rahn's name are we?" Ketoh asked. "I've never seen so many slopes and peaks and ridges."

"How can we find our way through this maze of stone?" Sareem asked.

"Follow the terrain with your eyes. The landmarks must be nearby." Obeying his own advice Osir traced the river's course across the plain, then raised his eyes. There, splitting hilltops, was the faint outline of a steep mountain pass. "Now let's get on with our business," he said. Hastening to a knoll and unrolling charts on a boulder, the Geometers deployed equipment and began taking measurements—sun angles, levels, known landmarks, unknown peaks. No Geometer could resist the urge to add to the growing slate of charted lands. For several months they would fix positions, trek deeper into uncharted lands, then fix positions again and trek farther. If Osir got his way, the slate would expand beyond their wildest dreams.

Chronicle 47: The Ice Mountains

Continuing upward for leagues on end, they followed the Isonzo's winding course, just a few manheights above the stream. The river diminished at each turn as it split into smaller and smaller branches until it was little more than a trickling mountain brook. Ice-covered slopes towered above until there was nothing but ice. Osir grimaced at the prospect of their first ice crossing with no comforting reference to land. "I've led men into the unknown before, Ketoh," he said, "but the risks of solid ice are greater than any other. If the weather's still clear, we'll ascend at dawn."

Sareem's men made camp between scattered patches of crusty snow beside the icy stream. As night fell, only a few faces peeked from bedrolls. Guards paced the perimeter, dressed in warm parkas with loose shrouds draped over their heads to ward off sleety rain mixed with snow. With Osir's rare permission, the second and third watches were canceled. Even wild animals would hardly attack on such a bitter night.

Osir awoke the next morning unable to move his legs. An enormous weight penned him to the ground, and he could hardly breathe. He squirmed until his arms were free. With great effort, he maneuvered his hands to his face. Slowly, carefully Osir peeled back the thick hide from his head and neck. Suddenly he was blinded by a bright glow of bluish-white light. Cold shock struck as ice and snow tumbled down his collar. He bolted upright. His face, neck, and ears were bathed in frozen crystals. Looking about, he saw no signs of the army that slept beside him the night before.

Fully awakened by the shock of ice and cold air, Osir finally realized his predicament. He sat in knee-deep snow, and snow covered every other man in his party. *This is the opposite of those sweet mornings in Egia when I was awakened by a beam of sunlight,* he reminisced. Back then, his vague precognition of Bera was only a dream. Now he knew the missing face, and he longed to share this amazing white scene with her.

"Hello!" he yelled at the top of his lungs. No answer came. "Hello!" he repeated, louder still. A muffled groan came from a nearby lump. Soon a head popped out of the whiteness. First came Jumar, then Sareem. Next Ketoh, emerging from the snow like a hatchling. "Rouse your men," Osir ordered.

Five, then ten, then 20, then the rest of the men popped up. Laughter replaced shock as each man overcame his rude awakening, and each in turn saw what had happened. Looking to the ridgetop, Osir was pleased to spy its crisp outline against an azure sky. "The time is right," he declared. "Hustle, men! Get on the trail."

One hand later, the climb was underway, and for the next six hands, they trudged through knee-deep drifts of cold, dry snow. In late afternoon, they crossed the pass. Near sunset, they reached a stream on the northeastern slope and began a tricky descent into the alabaster valley beyond. Two more days of hard trekking brought them to the Sava's main stem.

* * *

The central valley of the Sava was clear of snow by the time the explorers arrived. Never having witnessed a northern spring, they were astounded by the vitality of what most men considered mere frozen wasteland. On grassy plains roamed vast herds of antelope, deer, musk ox, and mammoth. Blossoms of red, yellow, and blue carpeted the low valley. Meadows of deep, rich green, and trees festooned with white and pink clusters skirted the streams. Osir ogled the scene.

Prettier than Egia in spring. I never thought it possible.

"Beware the cave bear and cave lion," warned Nicco, "they're awake now, freed from the bonds of winter."

Standing on a slight rise, Ketoh pointed northeast. There in plain view was a living testament to Nicco's words. A pride of cave lions stalked a musk ox herd, chasing and parrying, attacking and evading. The ferocious cats culled weak quarry from the herd and finally snagged a sluggish old bull.

By midsummer, the expedition reached the central valley of the Donau, and scouts brought news of a settlement on the upper reaches of the Svitava River, halfway to the last mountains before the Ice. They bore an invitation from Stallof, the local chief. "His village is known for its magnificent well," said Nicco. "...and it's on our way," he added. Two days later, the explorers entered the orderly village.

"Does this place seem strange to you?" Ketoh whispered to Osir after a short time there.

"Yes, everywhere else, feasts and ceremonies prevail. This place is somber, not cold but...empty...lifeless."

"It's depressing, if you ask me."

"These people survive on the very margins of man's domain, and their lives must be hard. I can do without the feasts, but the silence gets to me. Even when they sit around the fire, they speak quietly or not at all."

"You'd think they would seek some relief from their daily routines. Hunting, butchering, tanning, sharpening. That's about all they do."

On the third day, however, Stallof was suddenly inspired to lead his esteemed guests to a nearby wonder.

"He's taking us to Macocha Ravine," Nicco said. "It's legendary."

Stallof led them on a sandy trail up a slow rise to a high plateau. The trail leveled and opened onto a grassy meadow with a thin wall of trees on the opposite side. Stallof urged everyone to use extreme caution as he crossed the meadow and led them into the trees. Now Osir understood the chief's concern as he glimpsed the immense pit not more than 20 paces from where they stood. He had no idea how deep it might be. He would have to lean over the edge to see its bottom, and surely no sane man would lean that far over such an abyss.

"How deep is this thing?" Sareem asked.

"No one knows," Stallof answered. "We have no rope long enough to reach bottom. Even if we made such a rope, it would be so heavy it would break of its own accord."

"The top must be 100 paces across," Osir said.

"Yes, and the bottom is even wider," Stallof said.

"Bottom? I don't see any bottom. Wider? How do you know what's down there?" Jumar asked. The rim was irregular, sloping gently to the vertical wall in some places, abruptly in others.

"Once the men of my clan tied a rope to my waist, and I climbed down far enough to see over the edge." He grabbed a fist-sized rock and hurled it as hard as he could toward the center. It quickly disappeared from view. He motioned for quiet, and they waited. Many breathless moments later they heard a small "kerthunk," the obvious sound of rock striking water. "That's what's at the bottom. But listen." Suddenly, the pit reverberated with a thunder louder than any sound that ever came from the sky.

"You've struck the bowels of the earth itself," a hardened soldier yelled as he trembled from the impact. The thunder gradually reduced in volume but went on in a low rumbling echo.

"No. I've seen what's below, and I can explain," Stallof said. "The sides are not truly vertical, and they are coated with ice, even in the summer. Side caverns lead deeper into the earth. How far they go, no one can tell. Water collects in the basin. On its surface, a whisper becomes a roar. Each roar echoes through the caves, and, when it comes back, it's like the voice of the thunder god himself. Like a man's cupped hands, the hollow walls cause the sound to boom like thunder across the land."

"Rope or not, no one could make me climb over the edge as you did," Sareem said.

"It was for good reason," Stallof said, his mind straying into remembrance.

"Nothing could be that important," Jumar said.

"Something was," the chief mumbled. Reluctant to say more, he turned abruptly and headed home.

At the campfire that evening, Stallof was more withdrawn than before. When the coals died, the two leaders and Nicco, acting as translator, sat alone. Stallof opened his mouth to speak, then paused. After a seemingly endless wait, he began again. "They call the pit 'Macocha.' In our language, it means 'the Stepmother.' I was there when it earned its name."

"She must have been very close to you."

"She was my sister."

"She fell? How did it happen?"

"No. She didn't fall." He paused, sighed, and started from the beginning. "She was married to an older man whose first wife had died. She loved his children and was happy to raise them as her own. One spring day, she climbed to the meadow, bringing their little boy with her to pick herbs and flowers and lingonberries. She warned him to stay at her side, but suddenly, as little boys will do, he bolted through the trees and into the pit. Fortunately, it was at a place where the edge sloped steeply for many paces before dropping. He would have fallen except that his clothes caught on brambles far down the slope."

"I know that feeling all too well," Osir said, remembering his own brush with death on the trail to Ollo-detu.

"She loved him so much," Stallof said, "that she risked her own life to climb down and rescue him. All the way she watched as the uncomprehending child tried to free himself from the brambles. She hurried, fearing he would break loose before she could reach him. She screamed for help, knowing that the pit would amplify her calls."

"Did she reach him in time?"

"Yes, in time to save the boy but not herself. Hunters heard her call and arrived just as she pulled the boy free."

"Were they able to help?"

"Oh, yes. They helped both mother and boy. When they returned to the village, however, they testified that she had been caught trying to throw her stepchild into the pit."

"How could they do such a thing?"

"They honestly thought that's what they had witnessed. But it never made sense. If she had wanted to kill the child, she could have thrown him from a safer place . . . and she wouldn't have called out for help."

"And she was condemned to die?"

"Yes, in the same manner they thought she had intended for the child. I myself bore witness."

Osir thought of his own sisters and thanked the darkness for hiding his face.

"I walked by her side to the edge. I spoke words of comfort to her and sang with her a chant of our people, one that brings solace in times of great sorrow. Then she turned from me and leapt willingly into the pit. She sang as she fell through the cold void. Her voice was lost to the sound of thunder. We were certain she had died, but miraculously her voice, loud as thunder but sweet as heavenly music, came echoing from the deep. She had survived the fall."

"Did the villagers then relent?" Osir asked hopefully.

"No, young man. They did not. Her celestial song haunted our land for more than a day. Slowly, on the second day, her voice weakened. It was then that I suspended myself over the ledge. I couldn't see her. By the third day, no sound could be heard. Yet, sometimes when the winter wind blows and the heavens cry out for her soul, we still hear her sweet voice singing."

* * *

I haven't been this excited since I was a kid. Two-and-a-half months in hard country, and today we reach our goal. Today we see the Ice!

Under a cloudless sky, Osir addressed his crew. "You boldly endured and bravely overcame ordeals never before faced by our kind. Today, we climb Mount Tatra, the most difficult passage of our lives. Nicco will return to Etrusca with the horses. No need for interpreters where we're going."

As if for battle, Osir wheeled and faced the ice field that led to the top of the mountain. He and a handpicked squad of soldiers and Geometers would attempt the final ascent. Despite a blistering summer sun, the land was chilled from the sheer volume of ice. Onward they climbed into never-ending winter where ice completely capped the high peaks.

New-fallen snow exhausted them as their leggings met constant resistance in deep powder, but cleats purchased earlier from clever natives enabled them to get purchase on packed snow underneath. Osir followed a draw upward, hoping to avoid slicks that occasionally peeked from the blanket of new snow.

Slow, steady progress brought them close to the summit just before noon, and they faced slippery glaze for the last thousand paces. Taking turns at the front, the lead man gouged footholds with an antler pick. A rope connected him to the others. All or none would make it to the top. At last, the terrain leveled, and the going became easier, though breathing was difficult.

"Osir, no!" But Ketoh's words were in vain. Osir untied his rope and broke into a full run across the remaining stretch. Suddenly he stopped dead in his tracks.

No teacher could have prepared me for this moment. No man could imagine the grandeur of this magnificent ice mountain. To the east, to the west. The ice rises higher and extends farther than ever I thought possible.

In the deep valley that separated the Ice Mountain from Mount Tatra, the chasm swirled and steamed like a boiling pot where warm air met ice. Rivers of mist flowed down the mountain's face. Here and there, storms formed as cold air spilled into the valley, suddenly forcing captive warm air violently upward. Everywhere, the sound of fierce winds and thunder echoed from the endless chasm below.

The team stood in silent awe. Ketoh was first to break the spell. "It's my privilege to stand beside you at this historic moment. It's a spectacle few men have witnessed or even imagined!"

"Geometers! Set up your gear! Work quickly while the weather's clear." Winded from their climb and stunned by the view before them, they stood motionless despite Osir's commands. "Now!" yelled Osir. "Work quickly and be gone!" The urgency of his tone awakened the scholars to action. Packs were tossed on the ice and opened with labored breathing. Instruments were unbound and deployed, and the maps from Boro-Budor were spread on the hard-frozen surface. Geometers assumed their posts and went about their business.

"Tilt!" yelled one.

"Level!" yelled another as instruments found their footing.

"East horizon fixed!" yelled one.

"West horizon fixed!" yelled another.

"North declination fixed!" yelled another.

"That was quick!" Osir said with pleasure. "Now the rest of us can get to work!" Measurements of the ice itself were the most demanding task and would take the rest of the afternoon. By noting reference points on the ice and calculating angles to them from this known point, the Geometers could create a crude three-dimensional profile. By moving east or west and taking more sightings, they could improve precision. A third set of sightings would further increase accuracy while extending the observation area. Finally, they would estimate thickness based on assumptions regarding the rock surface beneath and the depression caused by the weight of ice. When the Geometers were satisfied, ice volumes would be noted on the maps from Boro-Budor. Osir recalled D-El's foolish arguments as he observed that here, where cold was all around and ice abounded, the stuff seemed to spill downward like syrup from an overturned bowl.

By nightfall, sightings were finished, and their mission on the mountain was complete. "Camping on the peak will be difficult, perhaps even deadly, but descent in darkness is unthinkable," Osir said.

"I can't wait to get back to the summer below!" Ketoh said, shivering from the cold.

"Something's wrong," Osir added thoughtfully.

"That's for sure, Osir! We're freezing to death!" Ketoh shook even more violently to make his point.

"No, I don't mean cold. I mean warmth."

"Warmth! I haven't felt any. Have you been holding out on us?"

"You saw it from the peak...those clouds and storms at the base of the Ice. Something strange is happening, though it's impossible to know from here. Something's amiss in this land of ice, and we must find out what it is."

"But Osir, the only way to find out is to cross over into the Valley of Mists. No one is fool enough to . . ." Ketoh stopped short, suddenly realizing what he had just called his commander. He looked Osir in the eye and smiled a silly smile. ". . . I hear the Valley of Mists is delightful this time of year."

"We have to go, Ketoh. It's too important to ignore."

"What about the time?" Ketoh asked in a subtle appeal to reason. "We're already short of days before hard winter hits the valleys below. If it's this cold in summer . . ."

"We'll make skin boats and float downriver to the Inland Sea. That will be faster."

With no appeals remaining, Ketoh resigned himself to the new adventure.

* * *

A cold, blistering wind whipped up in the early morning. Osir called out to his reunited force at the first hint of light, "Muster and move out. We'll freeze if we stay here." His order came too late for two soldiers and one of the Geometers. Their lifeless bodies lay stiff in the snow. "Lay them out for the sea," he directed. "Let's get out of here."

Skirting the snow line, they proceeded from valley to valley for three days until they sighted a low pass into the Valley of Mists. Again, Osir selected ten of his best men to accompany him. The weather had cleared somewhat, creating a strange vision of sky on sky—a dome of clear blue above, a massive veil of sparkling white below. It was as if this wondrous land, like the whole world in the coming Chaos, had been turned upside down by the all-powerful Ice.

Beneath the pass, a steep ravine led to a rock-strewn slope. Down, down they clambered until they themselves were concealed within the shroud...cold mist...dim glow...eerie sky, lit only by blue-filtered light, and all beneath it unearthly. Hardy bushes and low vegetation dotted the open plain. Red berries proved a tart treat for the men whenever they stopped to rest. Larger bushes filled the narrow ravines that etched nearby slopes. A shallow stream braided and meandered through the valley. They camped beside the stream and continued, refreshed, the following morning. By noon, or the time they guessed to be noon, they reached the Ice.

In front stood a towering wall of ice interleaved at lower levels with rock and grit. Glimpsed a few manheights at a time as the shroud occasionally parted, its dark surface glistened with the unmistakable sheen of water. Water gushed from every crack and crevice. Here and there, waterfalls poured off the massive face, and springs gurgled from beneath. Cold winds drained down, and rain clouds formed wherever warm air rose to replace the falling cold.

Fascinated, they ambled laterally along the base, encountering Dall sheep, Arctic wolf, Arctic fox, lynx, and brown bear. Arctic terns flushed, and Arctic hare skittered. Elk grazed in shallow eddies of the stream. A cave lion dashed over a pile of rocks and disappeared.

Every few hundred paces, a milky green creek gushed from beneath solid ice. Most of the gushers were perched high on piles of rounded stones, and all spread quickly so that they could be crossed easily in front of the Ice. Shedding their hide pants, the men waded cold streams up to their waists.

"I fear my manhood is lost forever," Ketoh groaned, half seriously.

"Ketoh," Sareem said, with a devilish glint, "how can you fret? You're the only one among us whose equipment suffered no damage from the cold?"

"What do you mean?" Ketoh asked. "It's tiny."

"Yes," Sareem said, "but no smaller than before. The rest of us shrank from the cold."

"Ayee!" hooted Ketoh, slapping his forehead.

Osir gathered the Geometers and officers to discuss the Ice. A ridge of jumbled rock ten-manheights high formed a low fortress-like pediment in front. "Kerchoong...kerchoong...." A strange sound echoed periodically from its far side. Osir climbed the fortress and found a basin filled with loose stone and blue meltwater. He stood entranced, then descended and crossed a narrow gravel spit.

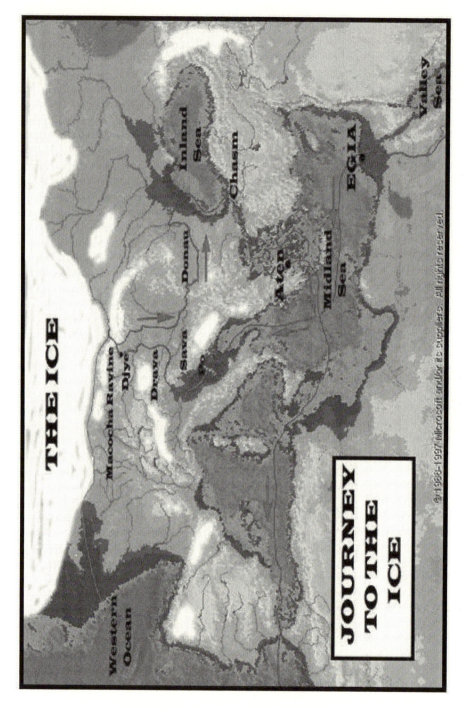

[Color images available at **www.thewatersofchaos.com**]

Beyond the lake, an ice cave gaped beneath the main block. The dark interior spiraled out of view. Inside, large chunks fell one after another, each with a crashing rumble that built to a muffled roar as the tunnel amplified and echoed the eerie sound. "Kerchoong…kerchoong…" In front, successive linear mounds of boulders, rocks, and gravel, dropped from melting ice, clearly showed how far the glacier had receded in recent years. It shook Osir to his very being. He stood in silent contemplation, then faced his men and signaled back toward the mountains from which they had come.

At the pass, Osir turned for one last look. A momentary break in the clouds allowed sunlight to reach the bottom, and a beautiful rainbow appeared. "The Ice is dying!" he declared. "A sign of what is to come!"

Chronicle 48: Return from the Land of Ice

The remaining ice sites were no easier to reach than the first, but observations were accomplished ever more efficiently. Within a month, the expedition headed homeward at last. The Vah River was navigable farther upstream than expected, offering quick progress toward their rendezvous with Captain Hervov. On a plain beside it, they built five bowl-shaped frameworks of willow, lashed together with mammoth sinew and covered with untanned hides. Inside each hull, they lashed a second framework, covered with hide, which formed a floor large enough for ten men. At villages on the Vah's banks, Osir and his men joined friendly natives to hunt and slaughter mammoths, five in all, and kept a fair share of the meat for themselves.

With the expedition's goals fully accomplished, everyone relaxed and enjoyed a peaceful float down the mighty Donau, the Mother of Seas. The hide boats were a marvel to villagers along the way. Good workmanship paid off as the expedition sailed through the ferocious gorge of the Donau. One month later, they reached the marshes at its mouth. There, they exchanged winter furs for lighter clothes and, with the help of local craftsmen, fitted their clumsy vessels with rudders and crude sails. They crossed the western end of the Inland Sea and made port at a village near its outlet. Aided by an interpreter from Aten, Osir met with locals to discuss the next leg.

"What will we find in the chasm?" Osir asked in the last village before the ferocious cataracts.

"Death!" answered the man emphatically.

"But we must pass through," Osir said.

"Then you must die!" the man said.

"Has no one made the passage and lived to tell of it?" Osir asked.

"Only a few fisherman to whom the gods owed great favors."

"So someone did survive?"

"Yes, but only one who is still alive today. I beg you not to follow his path."

"Let me speak with him so that I can hear for myself."

"As you wish."

After a short walk Osir found himself waiting outside a crude wooden shack with the interpreter. A weathered old fisherman emerged and sat, cross-legged, beside the door.

"Tell me, old man, what's inside the Chasm?"

"All that is death, nothing that is life," answered the fisherman obliquely. Then he paused, reflected, and spoke of the waters that flowed from one great sea to another. "The chasm contains two steps. First, a fearsome river of seawater pours from the Inland Sea to a giant lake at the midpoint of the chasm. The waters of the lake are swift, but smooth. Then there is a second river that flows from the lake to the Midland Sea." He described every current and shoal, every rock and eddy of note in the immense gorge.

"Can it be done in boats such as ours?" Osir asked, pointing toward his little fleet.

"If you must. Keep your ballast well centered and steer to the west bank. Use sails only on the lake. With the gods' blessings, you may survive as I did. One mistake, and you will never surface again."

"As you advise," Osir said and bade him goodbye.

As predicted, the cataract was swift and dangerous. It was not, however, as harrowing as the men had led them to believe, not for seasoned sailors who had mastered the Veil, navigated the Chao Phraya, and survived storms on the open sea.

"This is fun!" Ketoh said as they dropped into a souse hole, struck a wall of water, then bounded upward. ". . . even more fun than Piercing the Veil." Whooping and yelling, the youthful, exuberant sailors rejoiced in the adventure...and relished the water's fury.

* * *

In a rocky bay at the mouth of the chasm stood the tall mast of the *Ruby*. Captain Hervov, faithful as ever, greeted the returning adventurers with a hearty smile and grand salute. Over the next few days, however, Osir noted that Hervov was far from youthful or exuberant. His look was sallow, his breath short, his hands weak. Sometimes he leaned on a bulkhead or half-sat on a crate. Once, he clenched his fist against his chest, then removed it when Osir looked in this direction. On another occasion, he grimaced and rubbed his left arm.

"Are you ill?" Osir asked.

"No, I'm fine," the captain insisted. "Just a touch of indigestion."

The city of Aten lay six days west across a sizable gulf of the Midland Sea. Islands directed the placid surface, many with broad fertile plains fanning outward from rocky backbones. "It's unbelievable," Osir exclaimed as the *Ruby* passed close.

"These must be rich lands," Ketoh added, as they gazed at lush fields spreading in every direction. "Have you ever seen so much land in cultivation? We were taught that Egia was the leading center of agriculture on the Midland Sea. Until now, I assumed Elysia to be a backward place. Yet I've never seen more prosperous lands than these."

"Nor such a harbor," Sareem said. They had visited the somber gray cities of the east, the deep red of Hormuz, the bright red of Erytheia, and the buff-yellow bastions of their own land, but nothing compared with the dazzling white of Aten. "White stone. It's everywhere." He gazed at luxurious wharves, graceful monuments, majestic estates, magnificent temples. The city gleamed in late summer sun as the *Ruby* glided into the harbor.

When docking was complete, Osir wandered into the city. Draped in flowing white robes, citizens of Aten strolled their central plaza. Learned men sat on marble steps beside the market place engaged in heavy conversation.

"We're a bit underdressed, don't you think?" Jumar said, looking down at his drab uniform.

"Nightshirts in daytime, if you ask me," Ketoh said, rankled by the arrogance he observed.

"This city is surely among the greatest we've seen." Osir was amazed by its opulence and sophistication. "Their farms must be highly productive to create such wealth. How else could they afford to loiter in such numbers discussing lofty ideas?"

"Snobs, if you ask me," Ketoh said.

"Don't be critical, Ketoh. Such wise men may know more than we do about the coming Chaos. I'm anxious to meet their Geometers." To Osir's disappointment, hardly a Geometer could be found. He managed to engage them in a discussion, but they knew little about land, ice, or water. They had given little thought to the Chaos that would come.

"Tell me, citizen of the Realm," one scholar said to Osir, "How does it profit a man to know what is to come? We are children of the present. Are we not therefore born to a prescribed destiny with neither past nor future?"

"The future is what we make it," Osir responded. The scholar sneered, then turned to his companions and laughed.

"So our present is what someone in the past made it to be?" he scoffed.

"Yes. That's also true," Osir said with less certainty than before.

Apparently satisfied that his trap was set and bait taken, the scholar glanced about and smiled ruefully. "Then certainly our fate has been set by those who came before, and we have no choice in the matter." The entire assembly broke into laughter.

"Each generation has its say. Soon the Waters of Chaos will come, and your land will be gone," Osir said. "What then of your philosophies, sir?"

"Fate leaves us no choice but to perish," the scholar answered.

"Or to survive!" The voice flowed like muffled thunder as a man of common stature but uncommon bearing entered the plaza. Frowns appeared on every face as the bold man of Crete stood to speak.

Right or wrong, that man clearly stands alone in this court of opinion.

"You're precisely correct, foreigner," the arriving scholar boomed, more to the men of Aten than to Osir. "Indeed, we control our own fate, and actions determine destiny. Elysia is a great nation with vast lands, productive fields, and powerful armies. Yet, we've grown soft. We have forsaken the Pyramid, the Geometry, and the Trove. We have forgotten the call to order. Once lions. Now sheep. We are prey to the lion . . . and to the rising Waters of Chaos. Surely the reckoning will come."

Derisive calls echoed from every quarter. "Hiss! . . . Hiss! . . . Be seated! . . . Speak no more . . . You bore us . . ."

"Back to philosophy. End this debate," said the officious scholar to whom all others acquiesced. The outburst ended.

"Epistemology is the essence of knowledge . . ." the next speaker intoned.

The lone dissenter left his seat and tapped Osir on the shoulder. "Failure is the essence of persistence, Commander Osir. Let's leave these men to persist in their self-chosen failures. Wisdom such as yours and mine can only be a hindrance to such weighty deliberations," he said. "Come with me. I'll take you to a place of greater meaning than all the words spoken here."

The two men walked through the city and into the countryside. For three hands, they ascended a rock-strewn path through wheat fields, olive orchards, and vineyards. As the terrain lifted gently above an azure sea, green fields and grazing sheep came into view, and finally, their destination–a towering monolith. Despite its gargantuan size, the mount seemed more approachable, more welcoming than other nearby peaks. Its flat crest loomed like a massive table made ready for unexpected guests. Natural rock steps led from tree-covered slopes to rock-crowned crest. Halfway up, they stopped to drink from a gurgling spring beside the path. On top, Osir squinted from the brightness of exposed white rock.

"This, Commander Osir, is our refuge."

"I thought you had no refuge."

"The intellectuals ignore it, sir, but this mount, in truth, is our natural refuge, our god-given place of ascension. When the waters rise, the people of Aten will flee here because they have no other place to go. Most will perish, but some will survive."

"Enough to carry on?"

"No, good captain. In your realm, the survivors will include leaders, skilled artisans, scientists, farmers–Chosen Ones who have been trained to preserve your culture in the lands above."

"And in yours?"

"See those shepherds tending flocks below? Those humble men will inherit this land. They will be left to tell our story." He laughed at the thought. "And the fools who led us in this folly will one day be called gods!"

CHAPTER 21

Search Log 37: Swimming the Distance

Arriving in Seattle just in time for dinner, Jared knew precisely where to go. Exiting I-5, he headed across University Bridge and down through twists and turns to Ivar's Salmon House. Posts and lintels of big round logs lined the walkway. Carved and painted totems on pale-brown clapboard festooned a wooden door that seemed unimposing despite its heft. The building resembled a Tlingit longhouse and fell short only because the surrounding neighborhood was so patently commercial.

Alder smoke permeated the interior and with it the promise of salmon and halibut grilled to perfection. *I've spent enough time in Alaska to know good salmon fresh from the river*, Jared thought. *Ivar's is as good as it gets outside Alaska.* He took a seat, satisfied that here he could relax, take in the view, and contemplate the arduous diver training that would begin on Monday morning.

The first order of business, of course, was to order alder-smoked king salmon. He decided against the heavy appetizers and chowders in favor of clam nectar, more like a hot drink than a soup. And, finally, which beer? He skimmed the list and picked Pyramid Wheaten Ale, because he always chose whichever beer he hadn't tried before. He was well into his meal when the irony hit him as he noticed the ale's two golden pyramids in the midst of a fir forest. *Odd coincidence,* he thought. *I wouldn't be drinking this if it weren't for those damned pyramids in Foul Bay.* The fascinating quest had grown into a burden. *Here I am for two weeks of hard labor away from home and the wife I love. I can't afford the time, and I'm not entirely comfortable with diving.*

Caisson glanced up at three dugout canoes, suspended upright from the dining room ceiling as if floating on a lake. He smiled. *Ah, that quaint Tlingit custom,* he thought, *of labeling each canoe with its construction material (CEDAR) and length (26 FEET, 27 FEET, 52 FEET).* Then a slight shiver coursed through his body. The sight reminded him of an incident when he had almost drowned trying to swim too far across New Hampshire's Lake Takodah. *That's how Camp Takodah's canoes would have looked as they circled above, searching for my body,* he reflected.

Caisson visualized the initial diving tests and was pretty sure he could pass. *First, we'll swim 50 feet underwater. That shouldn't be a problem. Last fall, I swam the full length of a motel pool with air to spare. Next, we'll tread water for 30 minutes. I haven't done that in years, maybe never, but I'm pretty sure I can. The test that really concerns me is the 1,500-foot free-style swim. It will require both strength and endurance, especially in arms and upper body.* Running, his usual exercise, didn't help in those parts. *Still, my arms feel strong from cutting and lifting firewood.*

After dinner, Jared drove to the cheap motel that would be his home for the next two weeks. He settled in as best he could and, in a final act of commitment, shaved his mustache to ensure a tight seal for the scuba mask. Before going to bed, he stared at the unfamiliar apparition in the mirror. The upper lip seemed thin and the skin pale. "Don't he look purdy?" he mouthed spontaneously, with a hollow laugh. Only an upland Southerner would have caught the macabre twist of that grammatically flawed but otherwise well-intended phrase. *One great mystery of my homeland is that a man can live his entire lifetime thinking himself handsome, and no one would dare call him pretty. Yet, when he dies, more than one good woman, who knows English perfectly well, will walk up to his casket, take a long, sorrowful look, and say, "Don't he look purdy?"*

Caisson stared at the mirror for another moment. *Maybe I'm more worried about this training than I thought.*

* * *

Skipping breakfast, Jared headed out Sand Point Way, allowing more than enough time to locate the NOAA facility. At precisely 8:00 a.m. Cliff Newell swept into the classroom, said "Hello," and took charge with a vengeance. His manner, part swagger and all competence, generated instant trust. *I know I'm going to like this guy,* Jared thought. *No actor could fit the part better.*

Everything was in order. Manuals, notebooks, and pencils had been placed at each table, 13 student positions with all but one occupied. "Mr. Webb will be joining us shortly. He's flying in from the *Relentless,*" Cliff explained. *A NOAA ship,* Jared reflected, prompting him to look around and take stock of the class. Cliff asked each of them to state his or her name and affiliation. Some were from NOAA, some from the Environmental Protection Agency, and some from local police forces. Jared felt a little relief when Cathy, an attractive, blond woman at the far end of the front row, named a NOAA sanctuary instead of a ship. *Ah, good,* he thought, *another beginner.*

"How many of you have previous diving experience?" Cliff asked, and all but three raised their hands. Cathy waved more vigorously than the others. At the first break, Jared spoke with her and learned she was in charge of a new dive-oriented sanctuary on the Great Lakes.

* * *

"Been practicing for the swimming test?" an instructor named Steve asked on the way to the pool.

"Nope," Jared replied brusquely, expecting Steve to take the answer more lightly than he did. Steve frowned, so Jared bluffed, "But I could do most of it the last time I tried. I'm just a little rusty."

"Well, I hope you can handle it," the muscular fellow said, offering more challenge than encouragement.

With seven lanes, it would take two heats to get everyone through the long-distance swim. Caisson wanted to get it over, but he would be slow and didn't want others waiting while he struggled to finish. He counted laps for Gayle from EPA as she completed the course in short order. When she climbed out, he splashed into the water without a second thought.

The water felt wonderful, and he felt strong. Smoothly, swiftly he glided toward the midpoint of the first lap. His overhand stroke was clumsy but powerful.

Slow down, jerk! You can't keep this pace for more than a lap or two. A novice would know better. Find a reasonable pace. But what would that be? After two laps, I surely know what it isn't.

When Gayle called out "Five," he rejoiced just a bit, exhausted though he was, until it occurred to him that he still had that same distance to go. "Six." "Seven." Late in the lap, he began to feel a little weak. He felt himself sinking a little deeper into the water after each lazy stroke. "Eight."

He smiled and spoke to Gayle, as if everything were fine. Halfway back he slid under, gulping water instead of air.

"Nine." *Great,* he thought, *one more lap to go. Now, I know I can make it.*

Then a terrible thing happened. With the best of intentions, everyone stood around the pool and yelled encouragement. The other lanes were empty. Pride turned to embarrassment as he saw himself in last place. *The same kind of failure that I've pitied in others so many times, so long ago.* Turning for the last time, he carefully estimated how far he could make it at full power. Then, with two-thirds of the last lap remaining, he defiantly shifted back into the exhausting overhand stroke and plowed toward the end as fast has he could.

"Wow," he heard someone say. "Great finish," another exclaimed as he climbed the ladder. But to him, the effort still seemed a poor token of what a man ought to do.

Caisson tried to catch his breath as he rushed around to the side where Steve was giving final instructions for the next test. Just as Jared arrived, everyone suddenly hopped in and began treading water and he plunged in too. Soon there was no way to hide his exhaustion. Then, the instructors tossed in a two-pound rubber brick and had them pass it around. Each time the brick reached Jared, he churned his legs, expending the last of his remaining strength.

Keith, another swimmer, was first to mention time. "Steve, I calculate five minutes to go. That about right?"

"No way," Steve replied. "By my watch, you guys started at 2:00 p.m. You're halfway."

"Fifteen minutes! No way."

"That's according to my watch," Steve said, and Steve's watch was right, of course, because he was in charge. The final minutes were an endless, painful, gasping blur. When Steve finally blew the whistle, Jared struggled like a beaching seal onto the cold concrete slab. He was still out of breath when he got to the bleachers, and his arms and legs were weak from 40 minutes of treading water.

Surely we'll get a break before the final test.

Without fanfare, however, Steve quickly recited instructions for the underwater swim. "Who wants to go first?"

Gayle ran to the far end of the pool, with others following closely behind. She lowered herself into the water and skimmed beneath the surface. Jared watched admiringly as her shimmering form glided from shallow to deep. In the final stretch, she sank so far beneath the surface she almost disappeared, then her face broke through only inches from the wall. A splendid performance!

Jared stalled till he could stall no longer. Only he and Mike, a sheriff's deputy, remained. *I should have caught my breath by now, but I feel as if I just finished a quarter-mile sprint. Maybe I'll feel better when I get in the water.* He lowered himself into the pool. *Something isn't right, and I don't understand what. Maybe I'll feel better when I get moving.* He breathed deep a couple of times and plunged.

His third futile attempt caught Steve's attention. "Your arms and legs aren't synchronized."

"Maybe I'm just tired. I still haven't caught up after the distance swim," Jared said, not as an excuse but simply wanting to understand and hoping the cause could be remedied with time.

"We've got to move on. You and Mike can try again first thing tomorrow. We've got lots of other things to do this afternoon," Steve said.

Snorkel . . . fancy name for a drain pipe, Caisson mumbled as he realized state-of-the-art snorkels were no better than the toy he hated as a child. Over and over, the class plunged in and thrashed about, each time learning some new technique for dealing with masks, snorkels, and fins.

Steve headed his way. "Submerge. Pull your mask forward enough to break the seal. Replace your mask. Press your hand against the top front. Breath out through your nose." He followed the directions precisely and was surprised that the rush of water didn't bother him. When the mask was back in place, he breathed out just a little. Some water remained inside, just enough to cover his nostrils, but that didn't bother him either. He simply repeated the effort with a small puff of air and the mask completely drained. *That worked well,* he thought. *I'm not sure why I dreaded it so much.*

"Now, get accustomed to water in your mask, because it's going to happen a lot. Stick your head under water. Pull your mask forward and replace it. Then come back up, and I'll tell you what to do." When they were all back up with water in their faces, Steve continued, "Keep your eyes closed and breathe through your mouth until I tell you to release the water."

Let me out of here. Why am I panicking? This should be a breeze. What's the problem?

Screaming inside, Jared held the position as long as the others.

"Now we'll practice strokes."

The third stroke was the porpoise kick, continually plunging and thrusting the upper body, each stroke so powerful it was impossible to control the snorkel. He coordinated his breathing with the influx of water, and again he was surprised that he handled it so well.

"Look. You did pretty well out there today," Cliff said at the close of the day. "You're in good overall condition, a runner, I heard you say. I've seen young men do a lot worse. You passed everything except the underwater swim, and I'll bet you pass it tomorrow. Hell, I've had people who didn't pass it till the fourth day. All you really need is 50 feet. We just tell 'em the whole pool to challenge the better swimmers. Hell, I'll pass you if you're on top of the water as long as your face is down."

"Thanks, Cliff. I'll make it tomorrow. I'm sure I will."

* * *

Jared called Ellie as soon as he reached the motel. "Well, I made it through the worst part," he began. "I still have to swim 50 feet underwater, but I'm adjusting fairly well. I think I'll make it." After the call, he lay down and tried desperately to relax, but his mind again slid into a state of near panic. His heart beat wildly. His face flushed red. *I've got to control myself,* he thought. Eventually, he gave up and went out for a quick meal.

Later, Jared completed Cliff's homework assignment and went to bed still exhausted. Immediately, the panic set in again. All night long, he slept in fits and starts. He rolled and tossed and gasped for air. His head pounded. His heart raced so fast he thought it might fail. *Why am I here in the first place,* he asked? Seagate needed divers, it was true, but it was those "damned possible pyramids" under Foul Bay that justified this agony. *I know it's the right thing. Yes, I'm sure it's the right thing. I know I can do it. But what's wrong. I still don't understand what's going on inside me. Surely I can reason this out. Sleepless in Seattle,* he thought in a rare moment of comic relief sometime near dawn.

The second morning's lectures covered diving physics. Cliff made Boyle's Law and Charles' Law sound so matter-of-fact. "If you take a good deep breath at one or two atmospheres pressure and then rise more than a few feet without breathing, bubbles will form in your brain and you will die. That's called an embolism." He described the bends, along with other lethal possibilities. *Why is it,* Jared wondered, *that these things don't faze me, yet I can't escape this horrible dread that's dogged me ever since I got here?*

Finally, it was time to swim. Jared and Mike jumped in ahead of everyone else for another try at the underwater swim. Mike went first and failed. Then Jared took a couple of deep breaths and began his first attempt. It was just like the day before. No matter how deeply he inhaled, his chest seemed half full, and the supply took him nowhere. Mike tried again and made it to the 50-foot mark. *Once again, I'm in a class by myself, so to speak,* Jared thought, *and it's not a pleasant spot to be.* He tried again with the same result. Finally, Steve came over to advise him again about the infamous, unsynchronized use of hands and feet.

"I'm trying," Jared replied. "I just can't seem to get it right." He didn't mention that he was also having trouble inhaling sufficient air to make the distance.

"Well, you'll just have to wait till tomorrow," Steve said after several more tries. "We're already behind." He turned to the class. "Let's get going. Just like yesterday."

As a swimmer passed by, Jared was obsessed with the possibility that one of them might bump his facemask and cause it to flood. After they pulled away, he paddled along in relative peace.

Get control of yourself. What's wrong, what's wrong? I feel trapped. I feel like I'm in a closed pipe breathing stale air. That's what it is. I'm scared! I've never known this feeling before, not like this. But what am I afraid of? He ripped off his mask and reveled in the rush of fresh air. *It isn't the water. I've been swimming since I was a kid. I'm not afraid of water, not even deep water. It's more like...like claustrophobia. It's this mask. It's this damned tunnel vision. I'm not just tense. Not just apprehensive. I'm gripped by cold, irrational fear. I've heard others describe it, but I never thought I'd experience it myself. Maybe I can conquer it now that I know what it is.*

"What's wrong?" Cliff asked.

Jared sloshed to the side. *There's no option but to tell the truth and see what can be done,* he thought. *Surely these schools have standard procedures for dealing with such problems.* He looked up, and Cliff knelt at the edge. "I've got some kind of problem dealing with the mask and the water. It's sort of like claustrophobia. Any advice?"

"Claustrophobia? At this stage? We've had lots of people who felt it on a deep dive, but I've never seen anyone experience it at this stage."

Jared's hopes came crashing down, and it showed in his face.

"Look, Caisson, diving isn't for everyone. Maybe you should hang it up," he said almost kindly.

"No, it's too important. I need it for my research."

"Well, the only thing I can tell you is to go back and try again. That's the only cure." He watched as Jared returned to the circuit. From Cliff's viewpoint, the lap looked fine. But it wasn't. On the next round, Jared swam to the side.

"Still the same problem?" Cliff frowned.

"Afraid so."

"Just sit out for a few minutes and think about what you want to do."

Jared removed his flippers, climbed out in the prescribed manner, and walked to the nearest bench. He sat quietly for a moment, devastated, almost in a daze.

"Caisson, I'll bet you've never failed at anything before. Have you?"

He looked up and saw the tough old diver staring down at him. "No, that's not true. I've failed at a few things. But, I recall every one of them as if they happened yesterday. Failing is hell. But this thing that's happening to me now, it's real. I didn't climb out to quit, though. I came out to see if you had a solution."

"No, I don't."

"It's not just the mask and snorkel. It's water and hardware combined, and the anticipation of all those additional layers of equipment that will be coming in short order."

"Caisson, let's see if we can get to the bottom of this."

"Shoot."

"Everybody has some secret fear of dying. Down deep inside, what is the most horrible way you can imagine to die?"

"I remember seeing war movies with sailors trapped inside sinking ships. That haunted me for a long time. Especially the idea that water would gradually fill the air space."

"What about now?"

"Oh, I don't think about it much, but, when I do, it still seems like a terrible way to go."

"If you had to choose today between fire and water, which would you choose?"

"Fire, no contest."

"Okay, now tell me this. When you imagine what it's like on the bottom and you imagine getting into trouble, how do you imagine getting out?"

"Bolt to the surface . . . fast as I can."

"Now, think hard. Do you imagine yourself breathing as you head for the top?"

"No, I always hold my breath the whole way."

"Everybody talks about the bends, but that's nothing. We can cure the bends. What I'm talking about is embolism. If you hold your breath on ascent, those bubbles are going to pop up in your brain and you'll never live to see the bends. At best, you'll be brain-damaged for the rest of your life."

"So what am I going to do."

"To be honest, Caisson, I can't let you back in. I'd never forgive myself if you panicked down there, came flying to the surface, and had an embolism. Command decision, pal, you're out of the program."

"Just like that!" As the realization sank in, Jared's expression shifted from shock to despair.

"Just like that."

* * *

"It's no big deal," Rick insisted when Jared called to report his failure.

"That's not how I feel right now," Jared said.

"Don't you see? This is exactly what we've been talking about. Human adaptability. You and Greg survived the high mountain blizzard. Your dive school classmates will survive the flood. That's how human adaptation works. For survival of the species, it's not necessary for every individual to survive every challenge. The key is that, for every type of adversity, lots of us may fail, but some will survive."

"Nice theory, but not much consolation on a personal level."

"Shake it off, Jer. Shake it off."

"Rick, I still kick myself for quitting track in high school. That was 35 years ago, and I became a respectable runner in later years. I won't forget this defeat anytime soon."

"Don't kid yourself, big fella," Rick cracked. "You may be a halfway decent runner, but nobody would ever call you 'respectable.'"

Search Log 38: Echoes of the Past

Delta, Delta, Lufthansa. Jared's itinerary read like a new fraternity. Knoxville to Atlanta, Atlanta to Frankfurt, Frankfurt to Vienna, a grueling night, but he managed to get six hours of sleep and two of dozing. Vacation season was over, so open seats were plentiful. Boarding in Atlanta, he went straight to the middle section in back, flipped up a row of armrests, and stretched out. He sat up just long enough to satisfy FFA, then fell asleep before the aircraft reached cruising altitude. Choosing sleep over food, he didn't rouse until tires screeched on German concrete.

He passed through Customs and boarded a "domestic" flight to Vienna. At least he thought he remembered passing through Customs; it was all such a haze. He accepted a solid German breakfast on the Lufthansa flight, drank several cups of strong black coffee *mit Krem*, brushed his teeth and shaved in the tiny restroom, and arrived in Vienna refreshed enough to enjoy the drive to Brno.

This was not new territory for him. In April 1991, just after the fall of Communism, Jared had driven through Czechoslovakia from west to east, passing Prague on his way to Brno and Bratislava. He talked with Czechs and Slovaks, including former Communists, who said, "We know we will have to pay for the mistakes we made." *There must be a point at which stupidity becomes criminal*, he thought while viewing the sad, monotonous landscape of factories–rusted and abandoned or belching black smoke–side by side with dilapidated apartment houses. When he returned for a second visit in September of that same year, he saw people working, cleaning, painting, remodeling, and full of hope. It was good to see how far they had progressed.

* * *

The International Space University is a real university that began as a faculty without a campus. Each summer the participants, primarily managers in the space programs of 29 nations, met for ten weeks of intensive course work at one university or another anywhere in the world, but the rest of the year they telecommuted. Ultimately, a permanent campus was established in Strasbourg, France, but, true to its origins, summer sessions continue to be held off campus in a different city each year. Telecommunications remain a vital link for students and faculty all over the world.

As a Visiting Lecturer in the Space Applications Department, Jared had taught at previous summer sessions in Kitakyushu, Japan; Huntsville, Alabama; and Barcelona, Spain. This year's meeting was in Brno, and its quarters were at Impuls House on Dominikánská. Jared drove into the old city center, around on the broad avenue Kolišt, then left on Husova. At the top of the hill, he turned left again and spotted Impuls House on the corner ahead. He parked on the sidewalk directly across from the entrance. Everyone was at lunch, no doubt, so he was on his own.

Jared strolled down the alley, searching for a particular tavern remembered from his previous visit. He found it quickly and chose a seat among locals at a communal table. It was pleasing to listen to their friendly banter even though he couldn't understand a word. They quickly noticed that he was a foreigner and nodded a welcome. He ordered beer and schnitzel. He smiled partly because Czech beer is so good and partly because schnitzel is so inevitable. If a Czech or Slovak menu contains eight items, six of them will be schnitzels—all fried of course. Some come with cheese and a fried egg on top, all with fried potatoes, finely chopped. *I grew up on a Southern diet and appreciate fried foods as much as anybody,* Jared thought, *but I can't imagine eating fried foods every meal or the same food of any type, for that matter. I'm used to lots of vegetables. These tiny piles of beets and carrots are little more than condiments.*

At one o'clock, he retrieved his computer and briefcase and entered Impuls House. It was good to see the familiar faces of Siammak Khassam and Scott Mabry. Within minutes, they were immersed in ISU activities as if they had parted only a few days ago.

In one room, students were linked by satellite to Biosphere 2 in Arizona. One of the students, on leave from his regular job as construction manager of Biosphere 2, was engaged in casual conversation with the biospherians he would replace inside at the next crew change. In another room, an engineer was remotely extending and retracting an experimental space station antenna. Jared sat for a while with a group planning an advanced telecommunications system, ultimately intended to link space stations and colonies on other planets. On the following day, he joined a different class, exploring technological options for drawing energy from space. At breakfast, quite by accident, he found himself in an engrossing conversation with Russian Cosmonaut Oleg Atkov and U.S. Astronaut Bruce McCandless. The American discussed his part in the mission that launched the Hubble Space Telescope, and the Russian described his 237 days aboard the Soyuz-Salut-7-Progress space complex in 1984. Jared was astonished to learn that Atkov's 12-year-old daughter didn't know her father was a cosmonaut until she saw him peering from the spacecraft on TV.

On the third day, he joined a field trip to Macocha ravine, a huge pit more than 450 feet deep that resulted from the cave-in of a monstrous domed cavern in the famous Moravian Karst, north of Brno. As Caisson stared at the incredible hole, he compared it with every other karst terrain he had seen, including the hills and valleys around his home in Tennessee, and he thought how different they all were from what had been interpreted as karst topography beneath Foul Bay. He would need to see Foul Bay himself before he could accept that it was really natural karst.

Their guide explained that Macocha meant "stepmother" and came from local lore about a cruel woman who tried to throw her stepchild into the pit. Local villagers rescued the child and threw the woman in, instead.

Standing near the edge, the guide yelled and his voice returned like booming echoes of the past. Later that afternoon, the visitors went by boat through natural caverns and recently carved tunnels to the bottom of Macocha and looked upward between its towering, moss-green walls.

With such activities, Jared's days in Brno passed quickly. Soon it was time for his lecture. As usual, he hinted at some of his latest interests but held back anything that might cause students and fellow faculty to brand him too radical. He showed the latest maps of sea level rise in timed sequence from 17,500 BP to the present. He discussed their relevance to biophysical processes but carefully avoided any mention of cultural implications. Jared was pleased with the give-and-take that followed, but none of the discussion dealt with the topics that intrigued him most.

At dinner that evening, Vladimir Anenkov, a Russian faculty member, politely asked if he might join their table. The restaurant was a grotto originally built as an arsenal of Brno's ancient castle still situated high on the hill above. "Beats schnitzel!" an American scientist said as the main course was served.

"When I came back from Africa in '82, I couldn't donate blood because I'd been in a High Malaria Zone." Jared said. "Now I won't be allowed to donate because I've been in a High Cholesterol Zone."

Jared had met Anenkov earlier but hadn't engaged in substantive conversation. The Russian looked nervous, though he smiled and laughed at all the right times. During coffee, Jared suddenly remembered that he had often seen Anenkov with a cigarette in his hand. Smoking at dinner would not have violated his own country's customs, but the cautious young scientist refrained in deference to his American colleagues. Taking pity, Jared asked if the others would mind, and the guests collectively granted permission. Anenkov thanked them profusely and sighed after his first long drag on a harsh Russian cigarette.

Later, as the others left the table, Anenkov turned to Jared. "Excuse me, Doctor Caisson, but there is something in my laboratory that I think you should see. It has to do with your work on sea level rise."

Words such as these were guaranteed to attract Jared's interest. "Oh, really. What is it?"

"Photographs from space. You Americans and the French have the best digital imagery, but we Russians have the best photographs."

"Yes, I know. Five-meter resolution, I believe." Jared also knew, but didn't mention, that they were only black and white glossies, and poorly registered to real-world coordinates.

"When can I see them?"

"Come by my laboratory in the morning. Please."

* * *

Next morning, Jared arrived an hour early, hoping to catch the Russian before class. Anenkov was alone and already busy. Across two big tables, he had spread 40 or more highly detailed photographs. One makeshift mosaic covered the Middle East and another covered the Caribbean. Two magnifying glasses lay at Anenkov's side. "Look at the shallows," he said.

Jared grabbed a glass and eagerly scanned several Caribbean coastlines. Sure enough, he saw details far more precise than Landsat's 30-meter resolution or SPOT's 10-meter resolution. Small features, including patch corals, virtually jumped out of the picture. He rushed over to the other table and zeroed in on Foul Bay. The deep portions were dark and unfathomable, but the shallows were etched in exquisite detail. Indeed, the reefs were precisely as he had imagined them, except for a few features that made Foul Bay more exciting than ever. In practical terms, the photographs simply confirmed the hydrologic charts that Jared had already seen. In the arcane language of science, however, the patterns rejected the null hypothesis that Foul Bay's bottom was not a city. In other words, it could well be a city.

* * *

Later that day, Jared returned to Frankfurt and used his personal frequent flyer miles to reach Tel Aviv, Delta's closest destination to the place he really wanted to go. From there, he would travel to Egypt and return again via Tel Aviv. In this way, only the Middle Eastern portion of the trip would be charged to his dwindling Seed Money account. Anticipation grew along with exhaustion as the flights followed one after another, but he patiently endured the ordeal, inspired by what he had seen on the Russian photographs.

CHAPTER 22

Chronicle 49: Across the Western Ocean

Captain Hervov's mood was grim as he read Osir's sealed orders that arrived on a ship from Egia. "Take the remaining troops. Go as far as you wish. Stay as long as required. The *Ruby* is at your disposal."

"I can't believe it," Osir shouted. "The King has granted everything I asked. Now we can sail the Western Ocean . . . *and* explore the Opposite Continent."

"There must be more to this than meets the eye, Osir," Hervov said. "I want to know what's behind such generosity. Maybe Bera knows what's going on." He handed Osir a sealed leather pouch.

Osir read silently, then reread parts aloud for Hervov. "Tales of your military successes finally reached Erytheia, my darling," the letter said. "My brother's advisors now fear the people will shift allegiance from Rahn Ammon to their new hero, the Dirk Slayer. He can't allow that."

"So that's his game! The King wants you out of sight for as long as possible."

Osir laughed. "The King's advisors fear success. Now we'll learn what this Ice is all about!" Osir finished reading.

"And Bera? You seem disturbed. Is all well?"

"I...I don't know. She closes on a strange note. She says, 'Setra has become possessive of Horesh. Sometimes it frightens me.'" Hervov shook his head silently, but didn't reply.

"Come, Ketoh," Osir yelled, shaking it off. "Let's see this world of ours. You will, indeed, have an opportunity to lose your wager regarding the Mystery of the Cauldrons." Ketoh leaned against the door frame, feigning ignorance of any bet. "I believe I recall, Colonel, a pittance waged that the spilling of the Cauldrons is pure myth," Osir said.

"And the stakes?" Captain Hervov inquired.

"Ketoh volunteered to be my manservant for one month if the Cauldrons really exist."

Hervov laughed deep and loud.

"Oh, *that* bet!" Ketoh said. "Perhaps I'll win a little gold of my own." He pointed toward Osir's purse.

"Look at you. You know you're going to lose."

"I have spoken, and I stand by my word."

"That is your way," Osir laughed.

Ketoh took the diplomatic pouch and read the decree in its entirety. "'General Osir!' You've been promoted."

"Oh, did I forget to mention that?" said Hervov with a broad smile.

"Let me see that!" Osir exclaimed. He turned to Hervov. "You knew all along."

Hervov nodded. "Everyone knows it's your due, and Princess Bera is quite the magician when it comes to politics. I believe the King still trusts you. After all, he granted your promotion even against the counsel of his advisors. Enlarging your mission may be his concession to those vultures, more to protect you from them than himself from you. Setra must be miserable. He's failed in the field. Now surely he must be bitter at your success."

"Let's set sail," Osir said, staring vacantly toward the horizon. "Get out the charts, Ketoh."

"We must pass through two narrow straits to get to the Western Ocean. You see them here," Hervov said, pointing to the chart. Tight passages flanked on either side by high cliffs. 'Pillars of the Gods,' they're called. This will . . ."

Hervov froze in mid-sentence, then grasped his chest with his right hand. His left hand jerked as pain shot through his shoulder and arm. In dire agony, he slumped to the deck as Ketoh and Osir dashed to check his fall. Gently, they laid him on his back.

"A litter, a litter for the captain," Ketoh yelled. Hervov raised his head to object but closed his eyes in resignation. Crewmen carried him to his quarters.

* * *

Osir assumed command of the *Ruby*. Ample charts allowed him to guide the ship easily south and then west. After his worst pain subsided, the veteran captain, incapacitated but alert, advised Osir when to tack, how to exploit outbound currents, and where to come about.

On the thirty-fifth day of sail, a cloud of mist concealing the sea for more than a day, then lifted briefly. Silhouetted against a gathering dark sky stood the mighty gate to the Western Ocean. The south pillar formed dramatic high cliffs backed by mountain peaks. The north pillar was even more spectacular, with steep cliffs rising to a stone pinnacle overlooking the straits like a sentinel.

Osir entered Hervov's stateroom. "Captain, we've sighted the pillars." There was no answer. "Captain?" He gently nudged. Hervov stirred slightly. "Captain!" shouted Osir.

Hervov wearily turned toward Osir. His eyes opened weakly. "My end is near, Osir!" he whispered. "You'll make this passage on your own, my son!"

"You will again take the helm of the *Ruby*, Captain," Osir said. "I can't sail this water on my own."

"It's your sea to sail, my son. If not, then make it your own." His voice grew weaker.

"But I'm not worthy, Teacher. The honor should be yours."

"No man deserves this passage more than the Dirk Slayer." He smiled gently, then closed his eyes in final rest.

Tears welled in Osir's eyes. "I am Osir, the Dirk Slayer!" he said, looking to the heavens. "I will do honor to this man as to the father of my house," he yelled to the growing wall of clouds between the *Ruby*, the pillars, and the open sea. "No man, no fault, no force of nature will deter me from this mission." Abruptly he strode from the stateroom and across to the helm. Rudely shouldering the helmsman aside without a word, Osir seized the whipstaff and commenced his personal battle with the raging sea.

"A noble star has returned to the heavens!" he yelled to Ketoh across the deck. "Return his body to the sea!" As Ketoh and two of his men commenced the ritual, the storm's first assault struck. Seawater crashed and spilled across the deck. The surge struck the startled pallbearers. In an instant, the swirling waters collected Hervov's lifeless body and swept it overboard. "An omen," Osir smiled. "The sea is anxious and proud to claim its own."

Crosswinds tossed the *Ruby* perilously close to the vertical walls of the watery canyon. A gust of wind hit broadside, knocking the ship violently starboard into a trough. A massive crest threatened, dashing the gunwales ever closer to the cliff.

Adroitly, Osir swung the whipstaff with all his strength while the ship's sisal-bound boards creaked and groaned. One broken rope could rupture the hull's fragile bastion against the sea, but the *Ruby* stood firm. Another wave, then another and another, bolted over the gunwales. Each time the *Ruby* rode higher in the water. Two more hands of sailing finished the gauntlet of wind, water, and stone. The storm passed, and Osir stared in awe at the Western Ocean, its waters deeper and darker, its powers greater, than any he had seen in the east.

* * *

Ketoh reviewed Hervov's directions. Forty-two days had passed since they cleared the pillars, and the crew was restive. "Osir, are you sure this Aztlan exists? Some say it's only a myth."

"It's real, Ketoh. Hervov knew. He spoke with men of Egia who made the crossing, and Hervov could tell the difference between liars and dreamers and honest men."

"Still..." Ketoh thought for a moment to recall the captain's precise words, *Yield to the trade winds. Thirty days out, you'll spy seaweed afloat in deep water. Better yet, hang a rake from your bow. Whenever it fouls with the cursed stuff, veer south. Be quick about it. Stray north, and the Sea of Kelps will ensnare the Ruby till its timbers rot. Once in the trades, stay the course. You'll strike Aztlan whether you want to or not.* He frowned. "We've done all that he said, Osir, and still no sight of Aztlan."

"As the old sailors say, 'Give the winds time to work their magic.'"

"I wonder if it's true, as the old sailors also say, that derelict barquentines lie befouled in the Sea of Kelps with skeletons clinging to their rigging." Ketoh shuddered at the thought. "It all sounds fanciful."

"I don't doubt it. We've seen the cursed stuff drifting in loose patches. It's fouled our rake easily enough. But let's hope we don't get close enough to the Sea of Kelps to find out," Osir said. "I'm more interested in finding this bottomless channel called Tongue of the Ocean that cuts to the heart of Aztlan. Hervov said it was as deep as the ocean itself, yet flanked by pleasant lands atop high cliffs and at its end the most spectacular city on earth. He spoke of elaborate canals, some big enough to accommodate barquentines, and a fabulous inner harbor that holds a thousand warships. It's sure to be there alright."

"Then why haven't we yet felt the lick of the Tongue?"

"Look to the horizon, Ketoh."

"Land ahead! Land ahead!" a lookout shouted. Osir dashed to the *Ruby*'s high bow. On the far horizon, like an emerald on a silver ring, stood the mythic land of Aztlan.

"Hervov was right, wasn't he! Aztlan exists," Ketoh exclaimed.

"Did you ever doubt him?" Osir asked.

"Only a fool would doubt Hervov," Ketoh replied.

Osir smiled. "Quite a fortress, isn't it?" he said offhandedly as he scanned the bluffs.

"A little sea rise will do them no harm," Ketoh said, "for the shores are steep. If the rise is great, however, this land will disappear. All we can see of the island sits no more than 60 or 70 manheights above the sea, and the plain no more than 40. Where can they go for refuge?"

Without effort, the *Ruby* soon drifted into the channel. "We've entered the mouth of the Tongue," Osir said, trying to top Ketoh's earlier pun. "These are the most majestic cliffs imaginable," he said as the ship rounded the Tongue's first sharp bend.

"But nothing can contend with that!" Ketoh said pointing toward a magnificent arched bridge that spanned the chasm, more than 40 manheights above the sea.

"The Geometers of Aztlan must be wizards. That's a marvelous feat of engineering." Above them stretched the mighty structure of iron, redsilver, and stone over which men and animals passed from side to side—a bridge so high that even the mightiest warships and merchant vessels scarcely reached one third its height. Tall guard towers stood beside the anchoring pylons.

At the end of the channel lay a spacious harbor with a forest of tall masts, hundreds of ships by Osir's reckoning. A boat with 20 oarsmen rushed out to meet the *Ruby*. "Drop sail. We'll come alongside," a man called in the tongue of the People of the Living Sun, to Osir's surprise. Osir complied. The *Ruby*'s boatswain tossed a rope, and the tug took the huge barquentine in tow. To each side of the harbor's mouth lay deep-cut canals leading inland.

A dock had been carved into the cliff beneath the fortified acropolis. There, on a wide platform, dignitaries awaited. After formal introductions, Osir followed them into a tunnel, then up a cavernous, spiraling stairwell. They surfaced in a courtyard just outside the city wall. Finally, Osir saw the extended city, its circular harbor, and its fertile plain with well-tended fields and orchards spreading southward into the distance. It was more wondrous than the legends had foretold. The island was circled and crossed by elaborate canals for drainage, irrigation, and transportation unlike any in the east. Berenicia's extensive canals were impressive, but mere ditches compared to those of Aztlan.

The enormous city gate opened slowly, and a stout hand beckoned Osir to enter. He was astounded by the grandeur within. Circular temples domed with beaten gold filled the lower ramparts. Lush gardens covered the slopes. A line of fine palaces and stately public buildings stood on each side of the promenade that wound to the even grander stone temples—some white, some black, and some red. Several buildings, like the hull of Osir's ship, were leafed in redsilver, the most precious of metals. Bronze ornaments emblazoned their opulent designs.

"Our Geometers are anxious to greet you. They know you have come a great distance, and they have many questions to ask. You will do us honor," said Mixtla, leader of the guards.

"The honor is mine," Osir said. "There is much for me to learn as well."

"It shall be arranged." Mixtla disappeared into the impressive Academy of Geometry. Osir was ushered to a castle and invited to a warm steam bath. *What a clever invention,* Osir thought as he examined the workings. A metal tube bore water from a hot spring high on the hillside. The luxuriant bath reminded him of Mekong City. *But where,* he asked himself, *is that pretty young lady who comes with such baths?*

Two hands later, Osir answered a knock at the door and greeted a distinguished young man of the court. "Come, please. We are prepared to convene," the man said.

Osir followed him to the same building into which the guard had disappeared. "Welcome, visitors from Egia!" hailed the sentry as Osir and his guide passed through the giant doors of the academy. There, assembled about him, were 20 or more scholars of all ages and both genders.

"Welcome, General Osir," their moderator said. "We have long hoped for a visit by a scholar from your realm. We are eager to hear of your travels."

"In what regard, sir?" Osir asked, fearful of some underlying warlike motive.

"As you may guess from the geometry of our island, we fear rising waters. You do have knowledge of an impending deluge, do you not?"

"That is the purpose of my voyage, Sires. I have seen the Ice Mountains in the Northern Lands. I now seek to see the Ice of the Opposite Continent."

Pleasant smiles, cautious frowns, doubtful smirks popped like bubbles throughout the room. "Tell us your findings."

"I am pleased to do so. In exchange, I ask only that you share with me your knowledge of the Ice."

"We will respond in kind," the leader said. "Do you require specific information?"

"The Mystery of the Cauldrons." Expressions of surprise appeared about the room. "So, you too know of this strange phenomenon!" Osir observed.

"We know. But how do you know? You've never seen our ocean?"

Osir told of meeting the Yellow Emissary and the old man's account of strange events preceding the wall of water that devastated his land so many times. Each giant wave, he recounted, had been followed soon by a Fast Rise of the World Ocean. Not every Fast Rise could be so explained, but enough had been linked to suggest a connection. "He says the Cauldrons sit among the high mountains on the western side of the Opposite Continent," Osir added.

"It is edifying to know what others have seen. Our records show that great waves have come many times over the past 6,000 years. Few have come in the past 1,000 years, but we fear that the Cauldrons are filling and another spilling is imminent."

"And were the waves then followed by Fast Rises?"

"Yes, many were, but other Fast Rises came without warning. Perhaps, your Yellow Emissary holds one piece of the puzzle, and we hold the other."

"You mean the spills he observed may explain some Fast Rises while the ones you observed explain others?"

"Precisely. Do you know the times of the yellow man's spills?"

"I do, indeed. They are recorded on a calendar stick aboard the *Ruby*." A runner was dispatched. The assembly waited impatiently. When the stick arrived, Osir rushed to place it beside Aztlan's corresponding calendar stick. Each covered a period of 4,000 years. Short notches marked the spills, and long ones marked Fast Rises. Every Fast Rise matched a Spilling of the Cauldrons on one stick or the other. Silence held momentarily, followed by loud applause, for together the two sticks told a single tale.

"We must know more of these Cauldrons, Master Osir. But first, tell us what you observed at the Ice Mountain. We need to know its behavior, as well."

"We expected perpetual winter in the land of the Ice," Osir said. "What we found instead was summer on the Ice. Storms attacked its face, and great falls of meltwater plummeted from its heights to the ground below. Mounds of boulders fringed its front, clearly marking its retreat."

"We suspect that is happening at both ends of the earth," remarked one of the experts.

"But what does that have to do with the Spilling of the Cauldrons?" Osir asked. "If the Ice is melting, why doesn't it simply flow to the sea?"

"Gradual melting explains the Slow Rise, but something else must cause the Cauldron's to spill. We must solve this Mystery of the Cauldrons, if we are to unravel the riddle of the Ice."

"I welcome your assistance."

"We will provide experts who know the Northern Lands and the legends of its peoples. They will guide you to the land of the Micmac. We sail at dawn plus one day."

Chronicle 50: The Cauldrons Revealed

After eight days on a warm ocean stream, the *Ruby* nosed into a sizable bay guarded by two scrawny peninsulas. "I thought pirates and raging seas were hazardous enough, but we've never faced anything so scary as these huge floating blocks of ice. Our Aztlan mentors came here before, but they never described anything like this."

Monstrous icebergs barricaded the strait, blocking their entry for almost a week. Osir drew the coastal outlines on a chart. The round bay looked like a crab with pincers ready to clutch a baited cord. Twice each day, the *Ruby* played the bait as incredible tides, more than five manheights, tossed ships and bergs back and forth like gaming sticks on a tavern floor. Finally, a favorable wind pushed the larger blocks out to sea, opening a path for the *Ruby*. Once inside, Osir tacked repeatedly to avoid floating chunks of every size and shape, some white as polished ivory, others blue-green like gemstone, still others gray like tarnished silver, some layered with shades of gray and dark as soot.

The ship docked in an inlet formed by the river of the Micmac. Within sight was the glacial front from which the river poured, making the entire stream visible from beginning to end. More than 100 manheights wide, the milky green stream was studded with icebergs rushing to the sea.

Look at that ice with its gnarled and broken faces. No words could describe the blue-green glow emanating from crevices within. Like glowing embers–except that blue cold replaces red heat.

He watched silently as an entire ice column separated and collapsed into the river. He stood awestruck as water splashed and surged downstream. A moment later, he heard a boom like Macocha's wet thunder. Later still, he felt the *Ruby* stir.

The metal bow of the *Ruby* clanged hard into the horizontal monolith that formed a natural pier, and the sound echoed across the valley. Warriors leapt into the clearing, spears in hand.

"We come in peace," an Aztlan guide called.

Oklit, leader of the Micmac, spoke, and the guide interpreted. "He asks where you come from, Strange Traveler?"

"I come from the east, from the lands across the Western Ocean."

Unfamiliar words were exchanged. "He says you need a better navigator. This is the Eastern Ocean."

How could I be so stupid. Of course, he calls it by a different name. Mixtla should have warned me on that one.

"Everything is relative. Use whatever name they call that water outside this bay." He pointed his thumb dramatically back over his shoulder past a small armada of bark canoes.

More words followed in Micmac. "He says you are welcome, Strange Traveler," the interpreter smiled in Osir's direction. Oklit spoke again. "He says they do not understand your magic."

"Magic?"

"He doesn't understand how any mortal man could make a stone canoe float on water. His people make fine canoes of bark, he says, and they are light as down."

"I don't suppose he would understand that it's simply wood sheathed with redsilver?" Ketoh said.

"Tell him we come to learn about the Ice."

The interpreter complied, then turned back to Osir. "He wants to learn your magic. For that, he will tell you all he knows of the Ice."

"But I don't have any magic."

"Then teach him something that is not magic," Ketoh suggested.

"Do these people know how to raise grain?" Osir asked.

"No, they live by fishing, gathering shell fish, and hunting." The guide pointed toward a sheltered clearing where wooden racks held clams and fish for drying. "Their land has always been too cold to grow grain. But now...I don't know. I've never seen it so green here."

"The time is right for planting. We'll show them our magic. Sareem, bring seeds from our hold. The grain we acquired in Etrusca should grow equally well in this cold land. Summon our best men who know the Geometry of the Earth's Living Things. Help these primitives prepare new ground and plant seeds. In return, they can teach our men to build bark canoes. You will become our master builder." Sareem and his men snapped into action. Oklit ordered his warriors to assist. By late afternoon, a plot of ground had been cleared and prepared.

"They raise no cattle. There's no dung to fertilize the growing plants," a soldier said as planting commenced.

"They must have plenty of fish, though."

A spark lit in the soldier's eyes as he caught Osir's meaning. Baskets were brought from the village and planting resumed. Handfuls of tiny fish were tossed in each row and covered with soil. "Watch the field for 12 days," Osir said. "You will have your magic. Tomorrow morning, we will convene to discuss the Ice."

Mixtla whispered to Ketoh. "Chief Oklit wonders how this ritual can cause a stone canoe to float."

Ketoh laughed. "That's alright. By summer's end, he'll wonder how it turned fish into barley."

The following morning was misty and cool. Osir rose early and joined the tribal council in the sweat lodge. Wearing only breechclouts, six men sat cross-legged on supple hides that covered the floor. Heat radiated from a stone-filled fire pit in the center, and a clay pot filled with water, sat next to Chief Oklit. Steam filled the dim lodge as the chief slowly dipped and poured water over the hot stones.

"Do you know of the rising waters?" Osir asked.

"Our people have known for hundreds of generations," Oklit replied.

"Do you know of the Fast Rise?"

"Yes, our people know. The old ones repeat the stories to each new generation."

"What do they say of the water's rise? Do any strange happenings foretell its coming?"

"They tell of the Giant Wave Person who churns the sea. Many die. Lowlands and rivers are flooded from the sea."

"Then what happens?"

"Then the Ice Person moves."

"The Ice moves?"

"The Ice Person always moves. When the great wave comes, many large chunks break off and float out to sea. Our river and bay become clogged with floes."

"Of course," Osir said thoughtfully. "It's not just meltwater, but ice columns that break away from glaciers all along the coast. That has to be it!" Osir quickly grabbed his pouch, removed a quill and a scrap of papyrus, and jotted some notes.

"Whatever you say, Glooscap," Oklit responded, puzzled by Osir's strange explanation that made no mention of spirits or persons. "Now, what are you doing?" he asked, pointing at the pen and papyrus.

Osir explained the concept of writing and reading as a means of recording knowledge. "Like you preserve food gathered in summer for a meal next winter," he concluded.

"Whatever you say, Glooscap," Oklit said again.

"Why does he call me, 'Glooscap?'" Osir asked the interpreter.

"It is an honor. It means the Trickster, the Deceiver."

"That's an honor! Why does he call me a trickster? I'm an honest man!"

"Because you tricked the water to float a stone and then tricked the papyrus to remember words for you. Soon he will say you tricked the soil into growing grain. He says you will be a legend for many generations, if only you will teach his people such wonderful tricks."

"Perhaps I will return someday to teach his people. Meantime, I must inspect the Ice. Ask the chief to provide a guide, and we'll have a fair exchange."

"Chief Oklit agrees. He will accompany you himself. He knows the Ice."

"Does he know the Spilling of the Cauldrons?"

Oklit laughed at the thought of a cauldron spilling. "His people say 'the gods must do their wash,'" the interpreter repeated straight-faced.

Osir chuckled at the thought of gods washing their own clothes. "When did the gods last do their laundry?" he asked.

"He can speak with certainty only about the Cauldron at the head of a particular river that lies southwest of here. It last emptied 200 generations ago."

"Does he know when this Cauldron may spill again?"

"He says the god's clothes must be filthy by now, but the river still flows."

"The river still flows?"

"First, the river must die. Then, after a time, the Cauldron will spill. He will take you there."

* * *

Osir selected nine men plus the interpreter to accompany Chief Oklit and himself. Several canoes were strapped onboard the Ruby, and the expedition sailed west. At Oklit's direction, they entered an estuary, lowered canoes, and set out upriver. Along the way, Osir was astounded by the richness of the murky river teaming with trout and salmon. Moose, elk, and deer grazed at the river's edge or browsed in shallow marshes.

Eventually, the boats reached impassable rapids. Grounding the canoes in a grove of birch trees on the southern shore, Oklit led the party up a well-worn hunting path into lush, damp forest. After three days' walk, the splendid mountain of ice appeared. Osir directed a Geometer to take measurements.

Granite cliffs bounded each end of the Ice Mountain, a wall of ice fully 100 manheights high. From the basin at its snout, a river of meltwater flowed smoothly toward the sea. Sparkling reflections of late morning sun backlit the intervening forest.

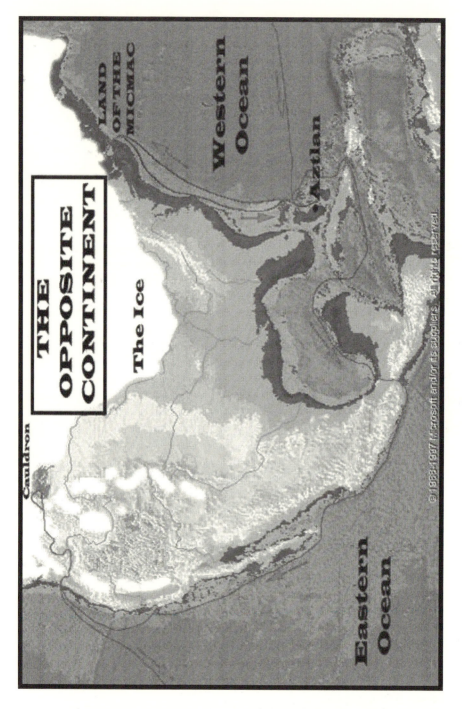

[Color images available at **www.thewatersofchaos.com**]

Oklit directed the party to a high overlook, and the Mystery of the Cauldrons was revealed. Downstream from the massive glacier, two opposing tongues of ice issued from valleys on each side of the channel. Like enfolding arms, the ice tongues almost touched. A deep ice gorge separated them at the point of intersection, where the river still flowed freely.

"Ah," Osir exclaimed. "If 'the Ice Person moves' as Oklit says, the two arms eventually close to create a massive dam." Osir folded his arms to mimic the moving ice. The guide translated, and Oklit nodded knowingly. "An enormous lake forms in the valleys upstream." The chief nodded again. "The lake fills to overflowing." The chief nodded again. "The waters breach the dam, cutting it down to the valley floor." The chief stopped nodding and stood, arms crossed, smiling approval as Osir jumped from insight to insight. "The flow will be disastrous, flooding the valley until the lake is drained, and the cycle begins anew." Oklit nodded yet again and beamed with pride. He had pleased the Trickster. In turn, his people would now learn the ways of the East.

* * *

The Geometers of Aztlan hastily convened a special meeting. "We saw a spilt Cauldron. They are real," Osir said. A low murmur rumbled through the assembly. "The Ice moves!" he further declared, and a hush fell as he told of all he had seen.

"But how does this Spilling of the Cauldrons cause the Fast Rise," the Chief Geometer asked.

"The chief of the Micmac explained it thus: Ice always flows into the sea. When the giant wave comes, huge chunks break away. Sometimes entire slopes of the Ice Mountain slide into the sea."

"But the Cauldron is empty. How can it cause harm?" one Geometer asked.

"Not through our own ocean, perhaps," the Chief Geometer said. "But we don't know whether the other ocean's Cauldrons are full or empty. We must send an expedition to learn where and when its Cauldrons will spill again."

"No," a Geometer shouted. "Aztlan can't waste scarce resources chasing after Cauldrons. What can one more ice pot tell us that we don't already know?"

"It may reveal when the waters will rise and how high," another argued. "If the Geometry means anything, now is the time to use it."

"Silly arguments, if you ask me," another said. "We can't act quickly enough to do any good anyway. Might as well stay home and take our chances."

"I'm prepared to go!" Osir said. "My mission continues."

"Enough," yelled the Chief Geometer. "One of us must accompany this man. Remain here, and ignorance will be our reward. He will need our help. Men among us know the way and speak the languages of the primitives."

"I am pleased to accept your help. In turn, I will leave copies of my earlier measurements. You can calculate for your own satisfaction how great the rise may be."

Chronicle 51: The Opposite Continent

The *Ruby* sailed directly westward through a chain of verdant islands, thence through a channel separating the largest of the islands from a huge peninsula to its north. The channel opened into a broad gulf, where they faced another peninsula. They skirted its shores first north, then west, then south, then west again. They kept in good position to dart shoreward in case of foul weather.

"You may wonder at our willingness to accompany you so far, my friend," said Quixtl, Osir's new translator and guide, as the *Ruby* found refuge from a fierce tropical storm.

"I presume you have good reason," Osir responded.

"This land is our refuge. We need to know more about it."

"But it seems so far from your Aztlan homeland."

"Primitive tribes occupy all the lowlands surrounding our Tropical Sea. They'll flee inland in large numbers, then turn and fight to hold the new shores. But here is a promising upland with no lowland between it and the sea. We'll get our ships here first and defend it." Quixtl paused. "Besides, we are an island nation. Our people can escape only by boat. Once afloat, there's little reason to stop short of the best lands."

"And what steps have you taken to secure this new land?"

"We established a small colony and built this harbor, some roads, and, of course, a pyramid. You will see them when the storm abates."

The *Ruby* moored in a crude harbor carved into an embankment surrounding a tiny bay where the ship rocked and bobbed for half a day. Except for a sloping path, Osir saw no sign of civilization. As the rains subsided and tall trees whipped in the wind, Osir caught fleeting glimpses of a step pyramid at least ten manheights tall. "It's an impressive structure," Osir said once the weather cleared.

"We're proud of its design. It will tower above the risen waters," Quixtl said. "Follow, and I will show you our refuge." Osir and the crew scrambled more than 50 manheights up the slope onto a level plain. When they reached the village, Quixtl called out, and its citizens quickly appeared.

"Games. We will hold games to honor our esteemed guests!" said the governor. The villagers prepared a feast and led their guests to reviewing stands. Contestants entered the court and commenced a fierce contest. The objective was to deposit a small rubber ball into a basket suspended from a pole in the center of the field. "The first team to score ten balls wins," Quixtl explained. "It's a marvelous sport, a great diversion for our people."

Indeed, the game did provide lively entertainment. At first, with the game's fast pace and the strong drinks they served, Osir enjoyed himself as seldom before. Two teams of seven men each were marked with colored dye on naked skin. Osir bet on Blue, Ketoh Red.

"These men are captives taken in war," Quixtl told Osir.

"They have taken well to the spirit of the game," said Ketoh.

"Yes, they do put their souls into it, don't they?" said Osir.

A raucous roar rose from the crowd as the Blue team scored its final goal. The victors, panting from the effort, stood joyfully in the winner's circle. The exhausted losers lined up in front and prostrated themselves before the victors. A runner brought a club as long as a man's arm. The Blue captain had first honors. He raised the club high and swung its bulging knot to the base of the Red captain's skull. In turn, each victor held the club above the head of his counterpart on the losing team. The crowd signaled with shouts for mercy or death. Only two were spared. The crowd roared approval as fatal blows fell.

Osir left the stand in disgust. "Let's get out of this place," he said.

* * *

Heading directly west from Aztlan's refuge, Osir, Ketoh, Sareem, and Quixtl commenced the rugged crossing of the Opposite Continent. As they topped a low ridge, Quixtl turned east and squinted into the haze-cloaked horizon, searching for one last view of the Tropical Sea. Through a break in the haze, he watched the *Ruby* sail eastward. "Are you certain your man is capable of taking the *Ruby* to our rendezvous?" he asked. "If he doesn't make it, we will be stranded in the autumn at the river's mouth."

"Jumar's spent many days at sea and is prepared to command. He'll discharge his duties well. Besides, it's only a short distance across the gulf." Osir sensed Quixtl's fear. "Don't worry. He'll arrive in time." *I hope I've made the right decision,* Osir thought. *Returning by land across the Opposite Continent has its risks, but the maps show great rivers flowing from the mountains to the north coast of this gulf. By the time it reaches the coast, it is one river, more massive than the Mekong. He can't miss it, and it will be easy enough for us to find the Ruby.*

* * *

The inland trek passed without incident, but Quixtl was worried. Not a single hazard hindered their progress, and that seemed too good to be true. In the quiet darkness between supper and sleep, Quixtl leaned back against the gnarled roots of a banyan tree and peered past the campfire into darkened rainforest. He sniffed the air. "Stinking Giants," he said absently.

"Stinking Giants? What are they?" Sareem asked.

"Lumbering prowlers of the night...three, maybe four manheights tall...heavier than 50 men. They terrorize our settlements. It's worse to encounter them in forests like this. We can't protect ourselves because they see in the dark when men are blind. They eat every plant a farmer puts in the ground and trample houses."

"As large as mammoths and able to turn night into day!" Ketoh said. "Are you sure these things are real?"

"Oh, they're real alright."

"You've seen one?"

"Well, no, I haven't actually seen one, but . . ."

"So you don't really know, do you?" Ketoh said, smug now, thinking he had gained the upper hand.

"Well, yes, I know they're real. I spoke to settlers who saw them in the refuge."

"Quixtl, has no one taught you that words are poor witness to things unseen? Even in our homeland, which surely is among the most learned places on earth, still there are myths that can't be trusted. No, I'll have to see one of these Stinking Giants to believe."

"Where did these pests . . ." Sareem froze as a flutter of insects invaded the camp.

"Stinking Giants!" This time Quixtl trembled as he spoke. "These tiny moths are harbingers." Abruptly the sickening smell of rotting fruit permeated the camp. "They're nearby, that's their stench," Quixtl said with alarm.

"Nothing but smelly flies," Ketoh said. "You place too much faith in Aztlan myths."

"Thwack!" rang the sound of breaking limbs. "Thwack!" Still louder.

Ketoh looked around, wild-eyed. "What in the name of Rahn is that?" he asked.

"Aztlan myths!" Quixtl snapped back.

Ketoh's expression quickly changed to abject fear as he spied two, then four sets of gigantic eyes sparkling with the campfire's reflected glow. "Stinking Giants!" he yelled.

With no place to run, every man wedged himself deeper into the curtain of banyan stilts. The lumbering behemoths stomped slowly through the camp. While they watched, one of the beasts stretched to its full length up the side of a tree—four manheights at least. Towering into the night sky, it reached out with immense arms and methodically stripped succulent leaves from the limbs. Its dagger-like claws, three on each paw, made easy work of the crown. One by one, it removed the bushiest branches and drew them through its pendulous jaws, shredding and chewing. In short order, the once lush crown stood as a single spike, pointing heavenward.

"I've never seen anything like this!" Osir whispered, as the beasts finished off one tree, then another.

"Let's get out of here!" Ketoh whispered too loudly. Suddenly, the animal turned and peered in his direction.

"It sees us!" Quixtl coughed in panic.

"These stems are no protection from a beast that size," Osir said. "If it heads our way, wait for my order, then spread out and run for your lives. It can't chase us all."

The animal lowered its hulking front quarters, then loped noiselessly, deliberately toward them. "Run!" Osir yelled. In three measured strides, the Stinking Giant reached their hiding place. Only Ketoh failed to extricate himself in time. With a wide sweep of its paw, the creature splintered the limbs where Quixtl had stood. Raising its head in the air, it looked about, then sniffed the still night air. After a moment's hesitation, it reached for Ketoh.

"Help!" Ketoh yelled. In a panic, he stumbled backward, tripped on a root, and hit his head against a rock. He lay unconscious on the ground, less than three strides from the Stinking Giant.

Osir, Quixtl, and Sareem yelled and beat the bushes as they tried to reach Ketoh. Osir was first to arrive. "Here! Chase me, you reeking hulk!" He tossed a heavy stone at the beast's flank. Unfazed, the creature crouched above the fallen warrior. Ketoh would surely be crushed. Miraculously, the giant sloth stopped short. With the tenderness of a mother helping a fallen child, it extended a taloned paw. Ketoh lay as still as death.

"Yeiiii!" yelled Osir, trying to distract the beast. "Yeiiiii!" he yelled again, but to no avail. "Ketoh's helpless. We must save him."

The beast slipped its immense paws under Ketoh's back and gently lifted his body. It then cradled Ketoh against its chest, stroking him carefully and rocking gently. The beast seemed intent on nursing the injured man back to health. Ketoh roused. Suddenly overcome by the odor, he sneezed into the Stinking Giant's face.

That's it! Osir thought. *No beast will suffer that indignity.* But the giant was forgiving. She patted Ketoh on the back as any mother would and stroked and rocked until he was again at ease. Then she set him down, patted him on the rump, and sent him on his way.

What a story! We'll never let Ketoh live this down.

* * *

From a high ridge, Osir and his party viewed the vast blue expanse of the Eastern Ocean. "Seems odd," Ketoh said, "calling it the Eastern Ocean when our first view of it is to the west."

Osir laughed, for the same thought was on his mind. "Everything's relative," he said, remembering his conversation with the chief of the

Micmac. Still smiling, he turned to Quixtl, "Do you really expect to find transport so quickly when we reach the sea?"

"No problem! Coastal freighters work these waters all the time. They're crude tubs, made of thatch, but, if we're lucky, a ship of Cha may happen along. They're fine vessels, almost as good as your *Ruby*."

"Yes, we once sailed on such a vessel."

They made camp at the shore and waited. Two days later, a fishing boat made of reeds put into the bay and offered a ride. Three days at sea brought them to the sizable village of Tehuantepec where Quixtl inquired about northbound vessels. He returned, excited, with the news that a ship of Cha was expected within the week. The ship arrived precisely on schedule, and Quixtl arranged passage.

"Ask the captain if he knows the Yellow Emissary," Osir directed the interpreter.

Quixtl was relieved that the natives spoke a smattering of the same language as certain primitives of his own Tropical Sea. "He knows well the *Eastern Star* and its famous Geometer. He says they are presently based in the Land of the Fuming Mountains 25 days sail to the north. Odds are, we'll meet up with him there. He believes the Yellow Emissary will be exceedingly interested in your mission."

"I hope it can be arranged. He will provide greater insights when I tell him about the Cauldrons."

* * *

The merchantman plied north to the port where they hoped to find the Yellow Emissary. "No, he's not here!" the port's master replied. "He and Captain Chou took the *Eastern Star* north to Beringia. If all goes well, they should be back any day."

"We'll wait," Osir said. The little port was in a pleasant valley running parallel to the coast. High ridges formed a barrier broken only at the harbor's entrance. Far to the east was another ridge of snow-capped peaks. The village offered little entertainment. After their gruesome experience in Aztlan's refuge, however, Osir and his crew were satisfied to enjoy a quiet break.

Soon enough, the port's master summoned Osir. "The *Eastern Star* has been sighted at sea. The Yellow Emissary will arrive straight away." Osir readied himself. He had much to tell the legendary Geometer and didn't want to waste a moment. Finally, the ship arrived.

"Greetings, my son," the Yellow Emissary said, as the *Eastern Star* docked. "How fortunate." Osir sensed a warm welcome beneath the guarded expression.

"We visited the Ice of the Northern Lands that drain into the Western Ocean. I myself have seen its Cauldrons!" Osir said. "I understand the

Spilling. Now we seek the Ice of the Northern Lands that drain into the Eastern Ocean. Can you point us to its Cauldrons?"

The Yellow Emissary paused for a moment. "Let us sit and talk. I'm eager to learn your findings." The two men conferred in earnest for the remainder of the day. "It is, as you say, imperative to see the Cauldrons. Perhaps, in fact, one particular Cauldron is all you need, General Osir. The Beringians say this mightiest of all Cauldrons is full and soon will spill. There's no time to waste. I am too frail to trek inland, but I'll deliver you to the river where the Mountain Cauldron spilled in past episodes. We'll resupply here and outfit your men for the cold. Be ready to sail tomorrow morning."

* * *

The *Eastern Star* plummeted over a wall of water extending from shore to shore across the vast estuary, then sailed upriver, fighting huge swells with every tack. Dense conifers lined steep bluffs on both sides. Long dugout canoes worked the main channel, while smaller ones, similarly made from cedar logs, plied a wine-dark tributary. Twenty Tlingit longhouses clung to the right bank. In the east, ice-capped mountains reached for the heavens. Through these mountains Osir would pass to find the source of a now-empty stream channel that once contained massive flows of meltwater. As soon as they docked, the party set out.

"Goodbye, my son. Good luck. You'll need all the strength and courage you can muster to reach this mighty Cauldron. May the gods be with you . . . " the Yellow Emissary said. ". . . and strong legs and mighty arms."

A Tlingit canoe, nearly nine manheights long, took the explorers past the Coastal Mountains and far inland to the head of navigation. A Tlingit guide joined the overland trek. Crossing a high plain for days, they marveled at cone-shaped peaks in the distance, some still belching smoke from recent eruptions. Mantles of ice and mud flowed down their sides and clogged valleys below, the guide explained. From a rise near the edge of the plain, Osir surveyed the terrain ahead. One low ridge followed another to the horizon. At great distance, white-capped peaks formed a solid wall.

Three weeks later they reached the last ridge before the Cauldron. There the Tlingit led them along the once mighty stream, now little more than a trickle, occupying a deep, wide gorge. Huge scoured pits, 50 or 60 manheights deep, scarred the earth. Progress was far slower than Osir had imagined: scrambling over boulders, miring in sand or gravel, slipping on occasional patches of ice, dodging around sculpted cliffs. Jagged peaks, cloaked in snow and ice, hovered like frozen waves over valley walls. One shout too loud might set a snow cornice tumbling down a bluff, engulfing entire forests. Hurricane force winds driven by the plummeting snow mass then lashed up canyon walls, destroying forests well beyond the reach of the mass itself. Eventually, the Tlingit spied a sloping tongue of ice sprawling down a side canyon and led his party to the ice field above.

"Water!" shouted Ketoh, as he crested a knoll on the fifth day atop the ice. Extending to the northern and eastern horizons was the largest freshwater lake anyone had ever seen or ever would again. Its width and breath were like a sea, and its blue water seemed as bottomless as an ocean. It was bounded by ice, but here and there along its southern shore stood outliers of hardy vegetation, mostly birches and willows, clinging desperately to the shore.

"Look at that!" Quixtl said. "The lower branches grow beneath water like the mangroves of Aztlan."

"Trees can't live like that for long," the Tlingit guide politely informed him.

"So the water is rising!" Ketoh concluded. "This Cauldron is filling rapidly. It can't hold forever."

"Down to the water," Osir said after surveying the area. "Build birch bark canoes as the Micmacs do. We'll paddle till we find the ice dam."

The icy waterway was a pleasant relief from overland travel. Cold breezes lashed the canoes from time to time, but the sun was bright and warm. Each night they put in near shore and camped on rock outcrops or gravel strands. They built driftwood fires to warm themselves and cook trout and small game. On the sixth day afloat, the blue of the lake came to an abrupt end against a white wall of ice. They maneuvered closer to the wall and around its right end and found no apparent outlet.

"There, over there! A channel to the left. Follow it!" Osir ordered. They paddled through a slender corridor walled by cliffs of ice. Its surface was a flat, calm extension of the lake itself. Before they rounded the bend, Osir already knew what he would see, for they heard the eerie "kerchoong-kerchoong-kerchoong" of dying ice. Blocks fell from the roof of an ice cave into the tongue of frigid water inside. Again and again, the quiet reverberation built to a terrifying roar. Beside the cave, the ice dam had thawed into a low saddle glistening with meltwater–a paltry bastion against the rising mass of water behind it.

For five days, they camped on a knoll overlooking the 80-manheight-deep gorge and measured the ice. On the final day, new cracks appeared. "It can't hold much longer," Osir declared.

While he spoke, the familiar "kerchoong" was overwhelmed by a horrendous bellow from the valley below. A mighty crescendo started loud and bounded beyond the range of human hearing. Ultimately, they felt it more than heard it, and it seemed as if the ice had consumed itself from within. A column of vapor and white mist shot upward like a heaven-bound river. "This dam is breaking from bottom to top," Osir yelled. "The Cauldron may spill before we reach the sea."

* * *

Thankful for clear skies each day and a bright moon each night, Osir and his party trekked heroically with fewer than four hands of rest per day and six per night. Slipping and sliding, they made their way across upland ice fields, down ice canyon walls, around gaping pits, then across the rolling hills of the high plateau. Retrieving the stashed canoe, they paddled swiftly through the coastal ranges and back to the estuary where the *Eastern Star* lay at anchor.

"To sea, get this vessel far out to sea!" Osir yelled as the exhausted men clambered up the ramp and collapsed on deck. The Yellow Emissary started to demand an explanation, then saw Osir's eyes. "Aweigh! Haul anchor!" he yelled to his captain. "Haul away, Captain Chou. The Mountain Cauldron is spilling. There's no time to waste."

A stunned Captain Chou managed to carry out the emissary's orders. His men loosed lines from stumps on shore and tugged the vessel from the bank. The Tlingit guide nobly had chosen to return to his people, and already families could be seen scrambling up the south bluff. Sails lofted, and the ship made a hasty retreat into open ocean, then southward along the coast. As soon as they cleared the channel, Osir motioned toward a bay that cut deeply into the coastal bluff. Here he hoped for a better chance of survival than out on open sea.

They maneuvered the *Eastern Star* to the center of the half-moon bay and set its prow seaward. Each makeshift anchor of ballast stone had 50 manheights of line coiled and ready to pay out as needed. The crew dropped anchors to port and starboard. They then battened down the vessel and abandoned it. Making camp on the crest of a high ridge, the men settled in to wait.

On the third day, Osir rose early and stared east. The time was near; he could feel it in the pit of his stomach. Then it happened. A horrendous blast resounded from the mountains and echoed through the valley. Like the dawn of creation, it racked Osir's body. Frantically, he covered his ears with the palms of his hands, but the deafening roar was more than mere sound, and there was no stopping the pressure against his chest.

Then he saw it! A massive pile of water, mud, boulders, trees, and ice surged down the valley. *My god. Great Rahn*, Osir thought. *Even the whole Eastern Ocean can't handle that much water.* Ketoh quickly appeared at his side. Suddenly, the air that had filled the valley blasted across the ridge in its own frantic attempt to escape the onrush. Hurricane winds lashed and whipped the camp, dislodging men from their bedrolls. Leaves, limbs, and even whole trees broke and scurried across the ridge. Holding desperately to the bare trunks of two surviving trees, Osir and Ketoh took the full brunt. Suddenly, Ketoh's tree was wrenched from the ground and swept from view.

Through howling wind, Osir heard his friend's faint cry, "You . . ." His voice faded.

"Ketoh, are you alright?" Osir yelled. "What did you say?"

"I said . . ." Again his words were lost.

"Ketoh, Ketoh! Speak to me!"

Finally Ketoh's voice broke through. "I said, 'Manservant at your call! Would you like your slippers now, Sire?'" On a calm day, Osir's laugh could have been heard throughout the camp.

The winds slowed, and both men regained their footing. Standing together once again, they watched the deluge stampede downstream. A wall of water 100 manheights high rushed by and churned out to sea. When it hit, the watery front seemed to hesitate as if it had no stomach for the mayhem it would cause. For an instant, the high front hovered surreally over a calm sea. Suddenly, the wall gave way and fell over itself, crashing and roiling. The ocean itself then bulged in every direction.

Osir quickly turned to the *Eastern Star*. The surge appeared at first to spare the little bay. Then a vast swell raised the anchored ship more than 20 manheights. He cringed as the ship tossed about like a jackal thrown up in the air by a bull elephant.

Did we leave enough slack? Will the anchors hold?

The vessel heaved and lurched upward, then miraculously rode the crest and hovered in position as the great wave passed. Osir watched the wave hit the shore, reverse course, and head back for the ship.

But can it survive the echo? No, it can't sustain such a surge to its stern.

As the wave neared, the ship miraculously swept around and met it, bow first. This time, there was no doubt the *Eastern Star* would prevail. Osir's mission would succeed.

"One question remains," a suspicious Osir pondered. "How did the *Star* manage to turn itself so easily, almost knowingly, to meet the reversed surge?"

"Luck, I suppose," Ketoh said. "Never look good fortune in the eye."

"Yes, but I know someone who never trusts fate to fortune." Osir eyed the *Star* as he spoke. From its deck, the Yellow Emissary's spindly arm waved triumphantly. His other hand rested firmly on the tiller.

Chronicle 52: Return to Erytheia

The reunion aboard the *Star* was joyful but short-lived. Even in their jubilation, they knew what was to come. "The Cauldron has spilled. The Waters of Chaos will wreak havoc around the whole world," Osir said to the Yellow Emissary. "You must return to your people immediately, and I to mine. Will you first take us back south where we can find a quick path back to the *Ruby*?"

"You won't make it home in time that way, young man," the Yellow Emissary said. "Crossing the Opposite Continent and rounding the horn of

Afar will take too long. We must travel together in the *Eastern Star* all the way to Erytheia. On our way, working as one, we can calculate the rise that is to come."

"But you must return to your people and flee with them."

"I'm an old man, my son. I've spent my life on this ocean and have no desire to die on land, with or without my people. Yes, of course, I will see to their safety, but after a lifetime of seeking, I must finally know what you and I alone can discern. We will require the instruments of your people-the models, transforms, and hydraulicon. At Mindoro, we'll encounter many ships of Cha. Through them, Captain Chou will warn our people. He'll warn Sunda and the eastern lands. Erytheia can be saved only if I take you there immediately."

"But I still have men aboard the *Ruby*, and Aztlan must be warned as well," Osir said. He tried not to think of Mira, his sister in the Sunda, but he fervently hoped she, too, might be saved.

"Your officers can return on their own. You've taught them well; now trust them. Meanwhile, the currents will be with us, and we'll reach Erytheia within five months at sea."

"Erytheia by spring equinox," Osir said with a hopeful smile. "Sareem!" he called, and the young lieutenant appeared at his side. "Return to the *Ruby* on our planned route. Rejoin Jumar and take Quixtl back to Aztlan. Spread the news there. Then return to Egia as fast as you can. Order Busah to declare 'Ma'at' immediately and lead the people upriver. Tell them to bring the seeds of their fields and all essentials specified in the Divine Right Order. Their survival depends on you. I'll ride the *Eastern Star* and warn the King that 'Ma'at' must be declared in Erytheia and Berenicia."

"But what about Ketoh? Will he not lead in your stead?" Sareem asked.

"You will be in charge on the overland trek, Jumar at sea, and Busah in the Beloved Land. I need Ketoh in Erytheia. There is much to do."

Sails went up, and the *Eastern Star* raced into open sea. Looking northward, Osir saw blocks of ice as large as the temples of Erytheia floating where ice shelves previously had formed the shoreline. It is beginning, he said to himself as the *Star* turned south.

* * *

The *Eastern Star* maintained a southwest heading until it reached a powerful current flowing due west. The route, just north of the Equator, was strung with islands like stepping-stones. Hopping thus from island to island, the adventurers had no difficulty navigating or restocking supplies.

On a featureless day like so many others on the long crossing, Ketoh joined Osir on the deck. He was more serious than Osir had known him to be before. "Why must we endure these cycles, Osir? I know it is nature's way, but why must our people suffer so? Why can't we just have peaceful oceans that hold their own levels? Peaceful and unchanging. That's what I want."

"A dream we all share, Ketoh, but it is not to be. These cycles have long been our lot and forever will be."

"But why? Does anyone know why they occur?"

"The Geometers speak of the Fullness of the Waters. When the oceans are full in each Topping Age, something causes the Ice to grow. When the Ice is great and the oceans are low again in each Golden Age, something causes the Ice to wither away."

"So the Spilling of the Cauldrons isn't the real cause of the rise?"

"No, Ketoh. The spilling only hastens a change already underway. If the Ice weren't moving and melting, the Cauldrons couldn't fill."

* * *

Fifty-one days on open seas brought the *Star* to the familiar harbor of Mindoro. Osir and the Yellow Emissary immediately encountered ships of Cha and the Sunda, whose captains readily volunteered to spread the alert. Captain Chou surrendered the helm to Osir, and his crew gratefully accepted passage back to Cha.

Down the Mindoro Channel, past Sula and Lombok, Osir coursed, this time without the complication of a tropical storm. Stopping at seductive islands only long enough to resupply, they sailed swiftly along on the channel's fast flow.

"Hard to tell if there's any rise yet," Osir reported to the Emissary as the *Star* cleared the Strait of Lombok.

"Don't rush the waters, lad. They will rise soon enough. These banks will be scoured, and some stray icebergs may even reach here. Meanwhile, we've taken our calculations as far as we can without benefit of models or hydraulicon. It is time to discuss our findings."

"The ice is melting. That much is clear." Osir restated the foundation of all their discoveries.

"Causing the Slow Rise," the Yellow Emissary said.

"The Ice Mountains then create ice dams that impound vast stores of water . . ."

". . . creating the Cauldrons."

"Melt waters then fill the Cauldrons . . ."

". . . causing the ice dams to fail and Cauldrons to spill."

"The Cauldrons then pour out to sea..."

"...causing huge columns of coastal Ice to break away . . ."

". . . and adding ice as well as water to the World Ocean . . ."

". . . thus causing the Fast Rise."

"It all sounds so simple."

"So why aren't we satisfied?" The Yellow Emissary asked, then answered his own question. "Because the volume released by each Cauldron, though great, is tiny compared to the floods our ancestors observed."

"Precisely! There simply is not enough water to account for the rise that occurs."

"So where does this mysterious water come from?"

"Let's review the possible sources," Osir said.

"Cauldrons spilling . . . ice melting on land . . . ice columns breaking from the coastal Ice. We've observed the first two . . ."

". . . and we've estimated the third. Yet it's not enough!" Osir struck his fist on the table in frustration.

"True, but what about ice shelves that lie in the water, yet are still half supported by land? Remember those that went to sea after the Cauldron spilled? What if that happens all over the world? A little sea level rise might float them all."

"The total would be enormous."

* * *

For two days, the Yellow Emissary worked alone, calculating and recalculating the volumes of the world's ice shelves. The *Star* sailed through the Sunda Pass and on to the Port of the Shrines. Still the Emissary had no answer.

"Too little is known of the Southern Continent," the Emissary complained as Osir docked the *Star*.

"Geometers here at Boro-Budor know those coasts," Osir said.

After landing, Osir announced the coming deluge. Quickly, runners summoned the Geometers of Boro-Budor. On the third day, they arrived with their precious maps. Osir conducted a hasty conference.

"Ice islands!" the head Geometer declared. "Maps of the Golden Age show continuous shelves of ice spanning fully one quarter of the Southern Continent. But, according to primitive lore, these broke away and floated out to sea in the Rising Age. Later maps show those shelves have reformed. Take as many maps as you want, early and late, the more the better. See what you can learn from them."

The *Star* again set sail, armed with key new information. A day later, the old man called Osir into the chart room. He pointed toward two ancient maps of the Southern Continent. One showed a shoreline rimmed with ice shelves and a vast ice sheet sloping inland. The other showed bare shore and an empty basin dotted with volcanoes where the ice sheet had been.

"Yes, my son, the Ice moves . . . not just on the coast, but everywhere. A vast nation of Ice can slip into the sea, and that is surely enough volume to cause the Fast Rise. Now we must hurry to the hydraulicon and put these numbers to the test."

* * *

"Such a smooth crossing is unheard of," Osir said as they approached the infamous Veil. Sailing west to Afar and north to the Chasm of the Veil, the *Star* had followed the same course taken by the *Crown* just two years earlier. "It's as if the elements want to fool us into thinking all is well. But now, my well-traveled friend, the sea will test our seamanship as never before. The Veil is one of the greatest challenges faced by any seaman. This afternoon, we'll have it in sight. Then we'll anchor and let the tides shoot us through. It's quite an adventure."

We made it before, but what about the Star? *These ships of Cha weren't built with the Veil in mind.*

"I'm sure I'll find it…exciting!" the old scientist said as Osir explained the procedure for clearing the reversing falls.

As the *Star* rounded the last bend, Osir's jaw dropped in surprise. No longer did a column of mist hide the narrow gorge. Not a ripple remained to mark where the famous falls had been.

"The water is rising faster than expected." Osir said, his heart in his throat. "Are we too late?"

"This is only the first small rise, a harbinger of what is to come. We may still reach your people before the Chaos comes."

CHAPTER 23

Search Log 39: Entry

The big El Al jet landed on schedule at 9:00 a.m. Cairo time. Jared felt tired and grungy even after shaving and brushing his teeth in the lavatory. He had been flying since the previous afternoon, with no time for sleep on three separate flights. It was a relief to hear tires screech on the runway and know the ordeal was finally over. On the ground, he faced new ordeals, and he couldn't relax until he reached the hotel. Professor Bassily offered to meet him at the airport, but that seemed too much of an imposition to place on her. Now he wished he had someone to usher him through the hubbub of Cairo International.

Passage through Immigration was slow and tedious. Labels read: "EGYPTIAN CITIZENS," "ARAB LEAGUE," "FOREIGNERS," and "AIRLINE CREWS." He chose "FOREIGNERS," of course, but the lines didn't match up with the counters. Jared stayed in one for a while then realized it veered off toward the wrong shingle. He moved to another. Attendants directed him to another, and he realized the labels meant nothing at all. Finally, he maneuvered in front of a desk at Passport Control. There he learned he should have purchased a visa stamp at one of the "Bureau de Change" windows on his way in. He went through yet another line, paid $3.00, and returned. By then, he was the last passenger in line.

The agent glanced perfunctorily at his visa and slammed down the necessary rubber stamps. *Thank God and Jimmy Carter Egypt doesn't care about Israeli stamps*, he mused, *and even allows this direct flight from Tel Aviv.* Passengers shuffled into a large bay where bags awaited. Chaos reigned. Jared raced quickly through jumbles and heaps of luggage, searching intensely for his own. *I'll be astounded if every piece made it here*, he thought. The bright blue Folbot bag was easy to spot, then the duffel filled with electronic gear and miscellaneous equipment. Finally, miraculously, the green suit bag materialized, just barely visible under a pile of luggage.

Passing through Customs was slow. Inspectors frowned as they spotted the computer slung over his shoulder. He would have to pay a Customs deposit to ensure that he didn't sell it within the country. They frowned even more at the bag of electronic gear and half a folding boat. None of it was illegal, but they pretended to bend the rules just so a very welcome 'khawaga' could enjoy his vacation without having to rent video equipment in Cairo. Mr. Jared's equipment was so much better than the poor quality merchandise available in Egypt. Wouldn't it be a pity if he had to leave it at the airport until his return? A little baksheesh appeased both agents, and the weary traveler stepped through yet another door, mercifully released from the eternal limbo of international travelers, into the main terminal of the old airport.

"Dr. Caisson . . . Dr. Caisson . . . Dr. Caisson." Not expecting to hear his own name, Jared at first failed to recognize the repetitive call. Alert at last, he searched the crowd and spotted an Egyptian woman calling, one hand cupped beside her mouth, while staring at the door behind him.

"Yes," he replied, stepping nearer, but she continued to focus on the Customs door. Caisson needed to move directly in front to catch her attention. Before he could do so, however, another woman stepped forward.

"Hello, Dr. Caisson," she said quickly. "I am with the Egyptian Chamber of Tourism." Her brass badge indicated that she was, indeed. Still Jared was suspicious. He couldn't imagine how the Egyptian Chamber of Tourism would know he was arriving and why they would send anyone to meet him. Professor Bassily was the only one likely to meet him, and she must be the woman still standing over there calling his name. This other woman must have picked up on his body language in response to Bassily's call.

He played along. "I'm honored," he bluffed, "but I do hope there won't be any official ceremonies. I am so very tired. Just take me to my hotel. My secretary booked it and will discuss reimbursement with you later."

"Oh. No, sir," she said in a fluster. "If you already have a hotel, you won't be needing my service." And she melded back into the throng of impatient greeters. Jared smiled at his successful ruse.

Pressing into the horde, Jared abruptly found himself beside the first woman just as she called, "Dr. Caisson," for the umpteenth time. Her voice was husky, almost hoarse, from calling.

"Hi, I'm Jared Caisson," he said, mindful that this, too, might be some kind of ploy. Then, looking directly at her face, he was stunned. She was beautiful . . . and taller than anyone else in the crowd, including the men, except for Jared himself. Glistening black hair peeked from beneath a pure white scarf. Blue eyes blazed like gemstones set in coppery brown cheeks.

"Welcome to Cairo. I'm Sari Bassily."

It's so good to meet you, finally," Jared managed to say without stammering. "I didn't expect you to be here. I could learn my way around, given enough time, but you are a welcome sight." He hoped she hadn't keyed on "sight," and he tried to change the subject. "Right now I just want to get into bed as quickly as possible." No, that was worse. He flushed.

"I know what you mean," she laughed without embarrassment. "May I take one of your bags?" Chivalry never entered his mind as he handed over the heavy duffel.

When they separated from the crowd, it became painfully obvious that the rest of her didn't match her face. She wore a drab, loose-fitting dress.

Being generous, he labeled it "sedate," but "frumpy" would have said it better. With each sideways glance, his assessment of her imposing figure gradually turned from "tall" to "large."

"It's about 25 kilometers downtown. We can take a service bus for 50 piasters or a cab for about 40 Egyptian pounds. The bus terminal is right outside."

"Let's take a taxi just this once. I'd rather not carry all this stuff through the public transportation system. Too much hassle." Emerging from the building, they were assailed by a score of eager drivers vying for business. "How much downtown?" Jared said to the nearest one.

"70 pounds." the man answered.

"20," Bassily said firmly.

Hearing Arabic, the man quickly changed his tune. "50," he offered, "Many bags." Ultimately, they agreed on 40 pounds. He grabbed *many bags* and eagerly stuffed them into the trunk, with the Folbot sideways atop the load. The trunk lid he left unsecured, free to flail about on every start and stop.

The drive down Sharia Al-'Urubah was like nothing Caisson had ever experienced. "My previous Third World experience was in Liberia. But, they were too poor to own this many cars," he said, as they rushed headlong into the congestion.

"Best not to use that term here," she warned. "The *in* phrase is 'developing nation.' "

"Oh, I'm sorry. I forgot. 'Third World' was already out of vogue when I was in Liberia 12 years ago. The preferred phrase then was 'less developed nation.' I'm not big on tokens and symbols, but I try to comply for the sake of those who are."

"I guess we're all searching for a better way to say 'poor.' It's easier to change the name than to solve the problem," she said with a sad smile.

Drivers from both directions swerved in and out of their respective lanes, occasionally facing head-on until one or the other chickened out. Their own driver seemed more aggressive than most. He passed at every opportunity, and twice when the way was hopelessly blocked he turned right, darted through detours of several blocks, and eventually returned to the main Sharia. The side streets had fewer automobiles, but they were just as congested with carts and pedestrians. Somehow, the most likely casualties moved aside just in time, and the taxi hardly slowed. On the main thoroughfare, pedestrians occasionally waved and called out destinations. The driver seemed tempted to stop and once angled to the curb hoping to pick up another fare. Bassily protested. He argued. She handed over an Egyptian five-pound note, and his black-and-white Lada rejoined the fray.

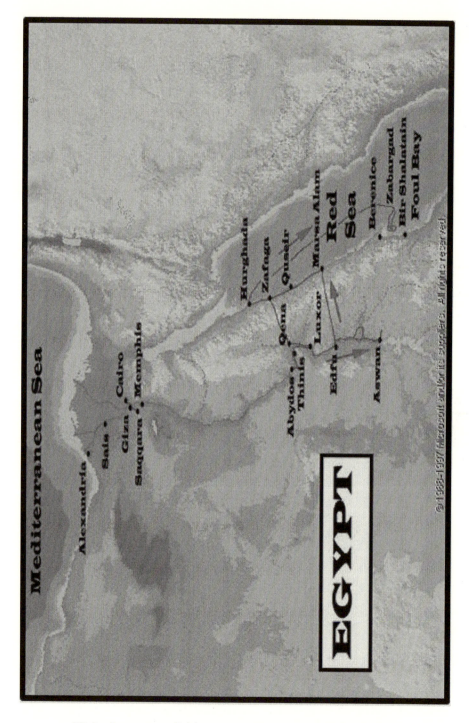

Mediterranean Sea

Red Sea

EGYPT

Alexandria

Sais

Giza
Cairo
Saqqara
Memphis

Abydos
Thinis

Qena
Edfu

Luxor

Aswan

Hurghada

Zafana

Quseir

Marsa Alam

Berenice

Zabargad

Bir Shalatain

Foul Bay

[Color images available at **www.thewatersofchaos.com**]

Ignoring the driver's wild antics, Jared turned to Bassily. "Were you able to arrange a hotel for us? My brother and me, I mean," he stumbled.

"Yes, that's the main reason I came out to meet you. Our departmental secretary was late making it. I sent an e-mail, but you didn't reply, so I assumed you missed it."

"Thanks. I planned to call your office on arrival."

"I didn't want to take any chances."

"Where's the hotel?"

"Downtown near the University . . . overlooking the Nile. I'm sure you'll like it, but there may be a problem."

"What's that?"

"Well, I forgot to ask your preference, and I didn't say anything to the secretary, so she booked you at the Semiramis Intercontinental. It's plush and very expensive. Native Cairenes always assume Americans want all the comforts of home."

"Actually, I prefer local color, and I'm on a limited budget. A night or two won't hurt, but I'll need something cheaper after that."

"Shouldn't be any trouble to move. When does your brother arrive?"

"Tomorrow, from Riyadh. We'll spend three or four days visiting the ruins here, then head south. What's the latest on Foul Bay?"

"Your approval is almost ready. I got as far as the Deputy Minister of the Interior. He says the minister will sign but first wants to meet you and your brother."

"Excellent! Can we arrange a meeting for day after tomorrow? That will give Rick time to recover from his travels. He says he finds Saudi exhausting."

"No problem. The minister's in town all week."

"But I'm surprised the decision is being made at such a high level."

"Oh, this is sensitive. Few foreigners are allowed to visit Foul Bay, and hardly anyone gets into the Hala'ib Triangle per se. Plus, you don't just want to see it; you want to explore it. I've been asked at least 20 times why those corals are so important. The minister will ask again, and I hope your answer is better than mine."

The driver resumed his artful dash through crowded streets and grid-locked intersections . . . past Baron Empain's palace, past the Sinai Bus Terminal, right on Sharia Sikkit, then left on Sharia El-Geish at Ain Shams University. Denser and denser the congestion grew as, angle by angle, segment by segment, the street's name changed from El-Geish to Abdel Aziz, Aref, Abdel, and finally Tahrir. The climax came as the driver bluffed and edged and yelled his way through Midan Tahrir, a huge square where every mode of transport in Cairo seemed to converge. Taxis of all kinds, private autos, and pedestrians scrambled together in a clamorous concoction of sound and color, dominated by overstuffed buses heading in and out of smoke-filled terminals.

They passed a man in black uniform standing on guard with rifle and bare bayonet, "Why so many soldiers in the city?" Jared asked. "There's one of these guys on about every second or third corner. Is trouble brewing?"

"These aren't soldiers," Sari replied. "Just city police. They look military and act military and bear the same arms."

"Well, it's an armed city, just the same."

Jared and Sari chatted nonstop throughout the hour-long ride. She was eager for news from America, tidbits that wouldn't make it onto CNN. For his part, Jared was eager to learn more about the exotic culture he saw on every street. "It's not much farther now," she said in a consoling tone. Two blocks more, and the Nile came into view; another block, and the taxi stopped in front of the Semiramis Intercontinental Hotel. When they stepped from the car, he felt he knew her well. She was congenial yet totally professional. *A wonderful combination*, he thought.

"You probably stay in places like this all over the world," Sari said, with a hint of longing in her voice.

"No. Not often." He surveyed the towering hotel. *Rich Americans pay good money for hotels like the Semiramis*, Jared thought, *but I can take it or leave it. I want to see Egypt up close, not from this luxurious viewpoint like any other city on the planet.*

"It's a far cry from Mammy Toe's Motel," he said absentmindedly.

"Mamitoze?" she asked.

"Mammy Toe's . . . Toe, as in 'foot.' It was her motel . . . in Ganta, Liberia. Dirt floors . . . hand-dug well . . . outdoor toilet . . . all conveniently located just a few steps from one another. Not comfortable, but surely memorable."

"Not much to remember about posh places like this, huh?"

"Oh, they have their charms, too . . . often memorable . . . in their own way."

The check-in went well with Sari's help, and the bellman took Jared's bags. When Sari followed the cart without hesitation, Jared wondered what local custom allowed. *In Saudi Arabia, women aren't permitted to check into hotels without a father, brother, or husband as chaperon. Egypt is more lenient. But how much?* Sari followed all the way to the room and stayed when the bellman left. She removed her scarf as soon as the door closed. Her hair was longer than Jared had guessed. *Coal-black. Uncommonly beautiful.*

Not bad for a "developing nation," Jared thought, after scanning the room. Clean, roomy, well furnished. The bathroom sparkled at a distance, and the windows were huge. Caisson walked over and looked down at the Nile. A floating restaurant, the Scarabee, occupied a slip on the bank below. Surprise registered when he looked back at Sari. She began removing her dress as casually as if it were a coat and she'd come in from the cold. He watched in wonder as she undid a long row of cumbersome buttons.

Unbelievable, he thought, as she stepped nimbly out and threw the dress on a nearby chair. A pretty sundress remained.

Sari saw his reaction. "Oh, I didn't mean to startle you. I wear this horrid old thing when I ride the bus or walk on the street." She pointed to her discarded outer dress and shuddered. "It's my concession to local custom, and it helps keep men in check. Egyptians think any woman in western dress is a whore. Combined with a dark scarf, it's almost like an abayya, the traditional outfit that covers a woman from head to foot."

"I saw several on the street. I've heard it defended as a mark of special respect for women, but I find it very disturbing."

"Respect? Are you kidding? Even Arab men call us 'BMOs' for 'Black Moving Objects.'"

Jared laughed uncomfortably but continued to gawk just the same. With the disguise removed, she was "tall" again, not "large," and her proportions were perfect. The wispy sundress bounced and swished as she walked toward him. He watched without pretense as she looked at the river, conscious of his stare.

She pointed below. "Those riverboats are feluccas. They've plied the Nile for thousands of years. We're looking across the Tahrir Bridge to El Gezira. It's actually an island, though you can't tell it from here."

"What's that building?" he asked, pointing to the upstream end.

"Oh, that's the new El Gezira Sheraton," Sari answered. "The other one is the Cairo Tower. It has a rotating restaurant and offers the best possible view of Cairo. Perhaps we can go there sometime." The tower's design combined delicate white filigree with a bullet-shaped top that was anything but delicate.

They stared for a few moments in silence, then sat down in front of the window. She talked about her teaching interests, living in Cairo, plans for the week. Try as he might, Jared couldn't resist staring at her coppery brown legs, exposed at times almost to her hips. But he was equally drawn to her face and gentle cleavage. His roving glances didn't seem to faze her, and they conversed with an intensity otherwise reserved for young lovers, though they weren't lovers and Jared wasn't young.

Finally, Sari looked at her watch and said, "I have a class. Sleep for now, and I'll come back in the afternoon. We'll explore the city, then go for dinner."

"Sounds great," Jared replied. "I feel fine now, but I'm sure to crash soon."

Sari recovered her frumpy dress, latched its frumpy buttons, and knotted her scarf. *The scarf itself is actually quite pretty,* he thought, *but it plays a spiteful role, diminishing beauty and denying innocent pleasure.*

Jared relaxed in a steaming tub of water, then slept much of the afternoon. He smiled as he drifted off because the bed was cool and soft, because Sari had been so delightful, and because his life was full.

About 4:00 p.m., Jared awoke from a deep sleep. As his eyes focused, he recalled the morning and smiled again at the prospect of Sari's return. Then he frowned. He wasn't supposed to feel that way about anyone but Ellie. Still, it was good to remember the single man's quest. Surely it wouldn't hurt for his imagination to roam as long as his actions didn't.

By the time she returned, he was dressed and reading a book, his bed remade for propriety's sake. His imagination indeed had roamed, but now he was back in the real world where men and women of professional measure conscientiously abstain from experiencing too much pleasure. Her knock brought him back from the safer fantasy of a mainstream novel. He answered the door with no illusions about her or himself.

"Hi," Sari said. "Did you sleep well?"

"Marvelously," he replied, using a word he never ever used in normal conversation. He watched as she removed her garb and guessed that meant she planned to stay for a while. "Are you hungry? I don't have anything to offer. Where would you like to go for dinner?"

"No, I don't usually eat this early. Let's wait 'til sunset when the streets are clear at prayer time. Then we can walk about freely. Shouldn't be long. We can watch from here."

"Good idea." Staring straight down at the bank of the Nile, he saw a row of boats, each about 20-feet long, moored against the narrow shore. Most were covered with plastic or canvas, and many seemed too rickety for a placid pond, much less a mighty river.

"Those aren't fishing boats," Sari said, pointing to the fleet. "They're housing for the poor. Cairo has a terrible shortage of living space."

Jared looked closer and saw children skittering over the bows. The shore served as a backyard littered with discarded cans, old tires, and miscellaneous debris. Smoke curled from oilcan stoves where squatting women prepared the evening meal. Men straggled home from the day's work. "Mostly odd jobs," Sari said.

When almost every boat had its man, the street was nearly clear. "Ready?" Jared asked.

"Ready," she answered. On went the disguise, and out went they.

The street itself gained a semblance of order—not like Europe or America, of course—but enough to avoid the constant jostling of workday traffic. A few cars passed, but not in a frenzy as before. The low sun sent its silent red glow across the Nile. Thanks to smoke from the houseboats, the place smelled as exotic as it looked. They crossed over to the embankment and strolled northward along the Corniche El-Nil. When twilight fell they were still heading in that direction.

It's fine with me if she wants to walk all the way to the Med.

From a distant minaret, a muezzin called the faithful to prayer. In the dim light, Sari stumbled at the edge of a pothole. Jared grabbed her hand, just to steady her at first. He resisted a fleeting urge to hold on . . . just a moment longer.

Blue Nile. *White* Nile. And yet the river was black as ebony when the wandering couple returned to Tahrir Bridge. Hunger had kept them from reaching the Med. Well, that and 100 miles of delta. Only 6,000 years ago the Mediterranean lapped the Giza Plateau. Then, the river built its delta, and today the sea is far away.

"What would you like to eat?" she asked.

Jared forgot about food when they left the hotel, but he hadn't eaten since arriving in Cairo. Sampling the local cuisine would require just the right kind of native restaurant.

"Let's go on the Scarabee," she squealed girlishly, tugging his arm. Without waiting for an answer, she pulled him toward the landing.

"But there's no boat here," he protested, trying to avoid the touristy fare typical of floating restaurants.

"It's out on the river. But it will return soon and go out again at 10:00 p.m. You'll see."

"But I'm starving," he grumbled, still hoping for an authentic Egyptian meal.

"Oh, it's not long. We wouldn't be served any sooner at a regular restaurant. If you're too hungry, you can try some street food." She pointed toward a vendor's grill. The man stirred a heap of steaming peanuts.

"Looks like a wok," he said, handing the vendor two Egyptian pounds for a scoopful. He took one bite of the salt-encrusted nuts and shuddered. "Too salty for my taste. I'll pass." He handed the bag to Sari. She passed it to a beggar and guided Jared back toward the Scarabee. Her smile said she had wanted to do this for a long time. *She's probably had her fill of authentic Egyptian food*, Jared reasoned, *and working long hours for days* on end.

"I promise, tomorrow I'll take you to the best neighborhood cafe in Cairo," she said.

"Okay. It's a deal. The Scarabee tonight...tomorrow a place so Egyptian it won't even serve Coke."

"I don't know about that. Would you settle for one without a Coke sign?"

"If such a place exists." He bought tickets, and they waited on the quay. The boat returned at 9:30 and pushed off behind schedule at 10:15.

Once on board, she disappeared to the ladies' room and returned wearing the sundress. The scarf, spread over her shoulders, "dressed up" enough for the cruise. They enjoyed ordinary Middle Eastern fare served in grand style. Skipping the Oriental floorshow, they ambled the deck enjoying the lights of Cairo. "A thousand and one Arabian lights," he joked, as silly as a schoolboy, and she laughed. When they heard the band start playing, they returned to the main lounge and danced until the boat landed just after midnight.

Climbing back up to the Corniche, Jared looked across at his hotel and wished the evening didn't have to end. He was still going strong, but now it was Sari's time to tire. She said nothing as they stepped across the street and headed toward the hotel. Jared thought perhaps she had left something in his room, books or notes maybe, and needed to retrieve them before going home. He wondered how she planned to get back to her apartment, but he wasn't going to be the one to bring it up. Probably a taxi; if necessary he would pay for one of the "specials" she had described earlier, a bit pricey but perhaps the only taxis available and safe so late at night. She knew her way around, and he didn't even know where she lived. Into the lobby, up the elevator, into the room, and still no indication of her plans. He closed the door behind them and laughed.

"Did you see that desk clerk's face? His frown practically screamed 'Whore!'"

"To hell with him!" she said, then laughed at herself for being so harsh. "I cover up to keep men from pinching, but I don't care what he thinks. Of course, he may think I'm a non-paying guest, and that would upset any hotelier."

"No, I've paid for two people, two beds. Rick was supposed to be here tonight"

"Really?" She thought for a moment. "Do you mind if I sleep in the extra bed. I have a class at 8:00 a.m. I can get two extra hours of sleep and avoid the Metro so late at night."

"Sure," he stammered. "I mean sure, why not? The hotel staff can't hurt your reputation at the university, can they?"

"No. I doubt they have any idea who I am or where I work. I'll just leave a tip for the maid, and nothing will come of it."

"Great. Pick a bed."

Sari showered and reappeared wearing a half slip and bra. Jared had removed his shirt. She walked purposefully toward him and said, "Goodnight," standing only inches from his chest.

The impulse was automatic. Caisson reached out and took her in his arms. He hugged her affectionately, kissed her on the lips, and said, "You're neat." Suddenly, he thought himself the silliest grown man on earth. If she had felt any passion, the brotherly hug and outdated phrase would have doused it in an instant. *I've been out of action far too long,* he thought. *Hell, we didn't even say "neat" when I was single and young enough to do this for real.*

But Sari hugged, too, every bit as affectionate as he. "You, too," she half-whispered.

* * *

Morning, sunlight, a slight ruffling of covers. Jared watched as Sari retrieved errant lingerie from the floor. After more stirring and a soft grunt or two, she emerged in slip and bra as she had been the night before.

Soon she returned from the bathroom, fully dressed in the abominable pseudo abayya. "I have class most of the morning," she said. "I'll be back before noon prayers. As soon as they're over, I'll keep my promise. You'll have your authentic Egyptian meal. What time is Rick arriving?"

"About 5:00 p.m."

"Perfect. After lunch, we can visit the Khan el-Khalili bazaars. We'll leave for the airport a little before 4:00."

* * *

Rick's arrival was almost an exact repeat of Jared's except that the plane was a little late and Customs took a little longer. At 5:45 he stepped into the main terminal. Sari was astounded at how much the brothers looked alike. She couldn't help staring. Rick stared back at her scarf-covered face. *Why would anyone hide such beauty,* he wondered. *Still, it's better than the veils in Saudi.*

Heading into Cairo, the streets were less crowded than the morning before but harrowing just the same. Jared anticipated Rick's reaction as the driver wove from lane to lane, but he was disappointed. Rick, who had taken wilder rides in the streets of Jakarta and Bangkok and Calcutta, was unfazed.

They told Rick about their afternoon together, interrupting at times to explain places along the route into town. They described the loose collection of bazaars that made up Khan el-Khalili: goldsmiths, coppersmiths, spice sellers, an entire section of fragrances from Sudan (most with bootleg labels), a maze of streets and passages with everything imaginable from antiques to fruits and flowers and tiny sphinxes and enough pyramids to house all the tiny little secrets of the ages.

"Did you buy anything?"

"No. You know I hate to shop. I just enjoyed the sights and sounds and smells of the place."

They told him about their lunch in a fatatri and their coffee at Fishawi's. "It was great." Jared exclaimed. "Fatatris are cafes named after fateers–pastries with fillings–falling somewhere between a pizza and a pancake, sweet or not, depending on your taste. We had peppers, white cheese, and olives, a lot like a Muffuletta sandwich except they use filo instead of French bread."

"And Fishawi's? Is that a coffeehouse?"

"No, it's a cafe, but lots of people go there for coffee or mint tea. It's full of smoke, but that's part of the charm. The place is more than 200 years old, and it shows. Real people sitting around chatting, laughing, drinking coffee, drinking tea, and smoking sheesha in a waterpipe. A young woman selling jasmine. You would have liked it a lot."

"And best of all . . . no Cokes," Sari added with a giggle.

In less than an hour they were at the hotel. The clerk frowned when Sari appeared, dressed now as a modest Moslem woman. "Double or nothing," she taunted in Arabic.

"Nothing," Jared said nonchalantly as he handed over a tip large enough to soothe any man's righteous indignation.

She bade them goodbye in the lobby. "Don't forget. Our appointment is at 9:00 tomorrow morning. I'll be here at eight sharp. It's just a short walk."

* * *

As soon as the door closed, Rick confronted Jared. "What was that about? What's going on between you two."

"Friendship!" Jared snapped back.

"That's not what the clerk thought. Something happened here last night."

"She stayed over, but we slept in separate beds."

"Think of Ellie. You're married, and you know the rules."

"Sorry, Rick, I'm a poor student of Ma'at. Society's rules were written without my consent. Besides, they keep changing. In the '50s, sex was wrong. In the '60s, sex was good, though not always convenient. In the '70s, sex was liberation. In the '80s, it was degrading. I didn't sleep with Sari . . . because I love Ellie . . . and it has nothing to do with silly rules. Most of all, I don't ever want to lie to Ellie. If I ever cross that line, lying will be my only choice because the truth will hurt her too much."

"So what happened with Sari?"

"Nothing either of us should feel guilty about," he said stubbornly, recalling the scene—her panties washed and hung to dry over the tub, her bra and slip lying on the floor. In the dim light, he had barely made out her sheet-draped form in the bed opposite his own, but it was exciting just to know she was there. Her shadowed face and innocent breathing were exhilarating. Yes, a bond formed in one short day, but it wasn't lust, and it wasn't love.

"She's a remarkable woman, the most natural human being I've ever met."

"How about her feelings? Does Sari see it the same way?"

"You know, in books and movies the guy always knows exactly what the woman wants. As for myself, I've always been completely inept at deciphering women, even the ones I like best or love most. I'm not sure how Sari would have reacted if I had slipped into her bed, but I suspect we could have remained friends either way."

"Don't forget AIDS. Add this to your list: In the '90s, sex is dangerous."

"Right. I have no right to risk Ellie's life or health or happiness, no matter how small the odds...nor how great the temptation."

"So it wasn't society's silly rules; it was the harsh realities on which those silly rules are based."

"I'll grant you that. In the end, though, I know my decision had little to do with reason. Years ago, I would have rationalized until hopping into that bed was absolutely essential, the only reasonable course. And I would have tried even if she had thrown the lamp at me. Today, I can say 'No' of my own accord." *But I can dream, by God, and last night I dreamed the dreams of a younger man.*

Search Log 40: Passport to Nowhere

Sari, Rick, and Jared were in good spirits as they approached the Ministry of Interior on Sharia Sheikh Rihan. Their walk from the hotel, seven blocks, had been pleasant, though the streets were already crowded. Sari, wearing a western style outfit, businesslike and modest, led the way as they entered. Speaking Arabic, she addressed the receptionist in an authoritative tone, mentioning their appointment with the minister.

"No, madam," the woman replied in English. "Your appointment has been changed. You will be meeting with the deputy minister."

"That will be fine," Jared said, though he wasn't entirely sure that was true.

"Please be seated. I will escort you when he is free."

They ambled to the opposite corner and sat down. "What do you suppose this means?" Jared pondered.

"It could be good or bad. The minister may have signed already...or he may be sending somebody else to deliver bad news. We'll just have to wait and see."

It was impossible to miss yet another troubling sign of Egypt's uneasy truce with itself: At one end of the waiting room was a desk. In front it was an endless queue of plainclothes policemen filing in from one door and out another. Each man waited his turn, signed his name, drew a semi-automatic pistol from the clerk, and inserted it in a holster concealed beneath his coat. The trio sat waiting for forty-five minutes, and the line never faltered. *So, maybe ten concealed weapons for every rifle and bayonet we saw on the street,* Jared thought. *This place must be a powder keg. How long can Mubarak stand?*

Finally, across the room, the receptionist called, "Please follow me." Down a long corridor, they saw the minister's door at the end, but their escort turned left into the deputy's office. Once inside, the deputy greeted them effusively.

"Pleasant morning, Professor Bassily. It is so good to see you and to meet your American guests." Here Sari's western image was an asset, for he would not have treated a traditional Arab woman with such professional respect.

Sari relayed the formal introduction. "This is Mr. El Baz, Deputy Minister of the Interior."

He turned to the brothers. "You look very much alike. Are you brothers or twins?"

The temptation was almost overwhelming, but Jared answered simply, "Twins."

Each extended his hand as she said, "This is Dr. Jared Caisson of the Melton Valley Laboratory in Tennessee . . . This is Dr. Richard Caisson, president of Caisson Systems, Inc." Hearts sank as Mr. El Baz shook each hand with a lifeless enthusiasm that could only be a prelude to rejection.

"May I offer coffee?" he said. They chatted inanely while a servant prepared four cups. El Baz flitted from topic to topic, obviously avoiding the subject at hand. Every minute or so, his eyes darted back toward the monitor beside his desk. Rick noticed that the computer itself was an old IBM-XT from the early '80s, but only El Baz could see the screen.

"Mr. El Baz, my brother and I need to visit the corals of Foul Bay," Jared said. "We come in the interest of science, but our research will benefit Egypt, as well."

"We welcome your interest and wish you well in your research. Let me suggest the beautiful corals of Ras Muhammad. People come from all over the world to visit there. There has been much research. Many articles have appeared in your *National Geographic* magazine."

"It is very important for us to visit Foul Bay. It contains a special type of patch coral that is essential to our research."

"Our scientists tell me that we have also such corals at Nuweiba and Hurghada. Perhaps you can visit those, instead."

"No, sir. I am sorry, but those will not serve our purpose."

"Hurghada is a popular resort. Many people go there to dive with the scuba. There are many types of corals in the vicinity. Perhaps some of them will serve your research needs."

Jared realized he was becoming too argumentative, and diplomacy was in order. "Hurghada seems interesting. Perhaps we could visit there first."

"Yes, yes. You could visit there first. From there, you could then sail along the Red Sea coast." This sounded promising.

"Toward the south?"

"Yes, yes. Toward the south."

"As far as Foul Bay."

"Yes, yes. As far as Foul Bay."

Sari, Jared, and Rick looked at each other and breathed a sigh of relief. Sari addressed the deputy, "Thank you so much, Mr. El Baz. I am sure the minister will not regret his decision. Please thank him for his approval."

The deputy squirmed. He faltered for a moment, then said, "I am sorry, Professor Bassily. The minister has decided to deny Dr. Caisson's request."

"But you said they could go to Foul Bay. I am confused."

"No, no, Professor Bassily. I said the gentlemen from America can sail on the Red Sea as far south as Foul Bay. Entering the bay itself is a different matter. From Hurghada, many cruise boats sail the coast. One of them is very luxurious, more like a yacht, you see. It caters to divers and sails almost to our border with Sudan, stopping at many islands along the way, but it does not enter Foul Bay. Unfortunately, it is not convenient at this time to allow foreigners there, due to many improvements that are underway. We have to repair much damage caused by the illegal Sudanese occupation of our territory. My assistants have been documenting these damages for many months." He couldn't resist looking at the screen. "At this moment, I am retrieving important data files which they have placed in my computer." He pecked at the keyboard with his index fingers and hit the return key several times. Frustrated by the computer's response, he slapped his palm onto the desktop.

"Is there a problem? Perhaps, I can help," Rick offered sincerely, a habit from years of work in computing.

"No, no," El Baz replied. "I can manage. The minister urgently needs this information, and I will provide it to him momentarily." A poor liar, he was worried and it showed.

"I am certain your development projects are extremely important, but, sir, surely you could make an exception in our case," Jared insisted.

"Excuse me Dr. Caisson, but the minister has asked me a question and I must ask you. This Melton Valley Laboratory, is this not the place where the atomic bomb was invented?"

So that's it. The minister thinks we're plotting to drag Foul Bay into somebody's nuclear fantasy.

"Melton Valley was one of the principal facilities involved in developing the atom bomb during World War II," he replied. "However, today barely one-tenth of the Laboratory's budget involves nuclear research, and that's mostly for energy, not defense. Personally, I have never been involved in any nuclear programs, though I take pride in what our institution did to support Egypt and Britain and our common allies in the terrible days of World War II."

"I own my own company," Rick said. "I've never worked at Melton Valley and have no dealings there."

"Very well. I am certain the minister will be pleased with your answers."

Their hopes rose again. "Is it possible the minister will reconsider our guests' travel permits?" Sari asked.

"Yes, yes. I will ask him. I am certain he will reconsider the matter." Again his attention drifted to the computer. He punched a few keys and accidentally shifted the monitor toward Rick. The message "FILE NOT FOUND—foulbay.rpt" was displayed prominently on his screen.

"Thank you for your help. Thank you so very much." Sari spoke for all of them. "Should we wait here or come back later? Perhaps this afternoon?"

"Unfortunately, the minister is very busy." He stared blankly at his own calendar. "As you leave, please ask my secretary to make an appointment for two weeks from Thursday." He returned to his screen, desperate for the file but too proud to ask for help.

His message was clear. Interview over. Request denied. Silently, solemnly they filed out. As an afterthought, Rick leaned back through the door and advised in a pleasant voice, "Have you tried the [Format C:] command?"

"But . . !" Sari's puzzlement suddenly transformed to pure glee, and she said no more.

El Baz looked up, his face flushed. "Thank you, sir. It was a minor problem, however, and it has been solved," he lied again.

They ambled down the hall. Just short of the exit, they heard El Baz scream.

* * *

The trio strolled aimlessly along Sharia Sheikh Rihan. With no conscious decision, they headed toward Abdiin Palace, then north toward downtown. They chatted as they walked, but mostly they just contemplated the dismal turn of events and mulled their options. More than once, they laughed at Rick's revenge. "Can you imagine El Baz's face when he realized he'd wiped his hard drive clean," Sari said, her mood lifting.

Twenty minutes later they wandered into Azbakiyyah. "Let's discuss alternatives," Rick said as they entered the old gardens. "If we can't enter the bay itself, maybe we can find some good candidates elsewhere. El Baz mentioned two possibilities in the north end of the sea."

"I was surprised when he mentioned those," Jared said. "Maybe there's something important at Nuweiba or Hurghada; maybe there isn't. The problem for us is that the patch coral distribution in those spots is so limited. Big area, few sites, little chance of a hit. Besides, all our research has centered on Foul Bay. It would take weeks to catch up anywhere else."

Sari looked puzzled. "What exactly are you looking for? I get the feeling it's something very specific."

Jared wanted to tell her the whole truth but felt honor bound to clear it with Rick first. "Well, yes, we're looking for indicators of processes already underway when these areas were inundated by sea level rise at the end of the Ice Age. Timing is absolutely crucial, and location is a precise measure of time. By location, I mean vertical and horizontal zones corresponding to specific stages in sea level rise. We can tell a lot about the coral formations themselves from certain indicators within the 3-D form of each column."

Sari accepted the explanation, as far as it went, but still looked perplexed. "There's more to it, isn't there?"

Rick stepped in. "Yes, we need to understand the precise interface between the coral and its substrate. We need to know what material makes up the substrate and its shape in 3-D."

"Why is shape so important?" Sari would not be satisfied easily.

"So we'll know where to start our measurements of coral growth," Jared said. "The height of the column, minus the height of the foundation, divided by the estimated growth rate per year yields the time elapsed from initial inundation to the present. That's how we know when the inundation occurred."

"But you said you already know the relationship between sea level and time. Sounds like circular reasoning to me. You're going to great lengths to calculate something you already know. Am I missing something here?"

"Got me there," Jared admitted.

"Look, I know I let you down with the ministry, but I did go out on a limb. If you two are hiding something, I need to know. This is beginning to sound creepy."

Rick and Jared looked at each other. Jared had no doubt she could be trusted. He nodded, and Rick described what they were looking for. Together they explained the logic behind their quest. Sari's eyes grew wider as the story went on. ". . . and so you see, we told the truth. We just didn't mention that the processes are human as well as physical."

"Okay," she said, "it sounds outrageous, but it makes sense to me. I understand why you were reluctant to tell the whole story. But from here on, no secrets! Either I'm part of the team, or I'm not. Which will it be?"

"You're in, if you want to be, and no more secrets. Agreed?" Jared turned first to Rick and then to her. They nodded. "Good. Now, what are we going to do?"

"I still don't understand why you're pessimistic about Hurghada and Nuweiba. If pyramids existed in the south, why not in the north?" Sari asked.

"Oh, pyramids may exist in lots of places, including the sites El Baz mentioned. But the probabilities are different. Really, it's a matter of efficiency. We might search those scattered patches for months and find nothing. Maybe we hit a place with natural rock and no pyramids. Or maybe the pyramids are there, but none exposed enough to be observed. And scattered sites mean we'll have to spend way too much time moving around. In contrast, Foul Bay offers hundreds of possibilities highly concentrated in a small area. Plus, some of the patterns there appear geometric, more like human settlement patterns than natural features."

"And don't forget its strategic location. If inter-ocean commerce existed 10,000 years ago, that's where the greatest port in the world would have been." Rick said.

Sari immediately recognized the geographic significance of Foul Bay and gasped at the implications. "What about farther south?"

"It's possible. We've also evaluated a concentration of patch corals off the Sudanese Coast."

"Plus the Cousteau site at Sha'ab Rumi," Rick added.

"Yes, I suppose we could make good progress there. Still, anywhere else but Foul Bay is a huge disappointment. It's like prospecting for scattered gold nuggets instead of mining the mother lode."

"I'm sure you'll find diving services in Port Sudan," Sari said.

"How does this sound? We'll visit the ruins around here, then work our way up the Nile Valley into Sudan."

"I like it. We can visit the Sudanese pyramids at Meroë. It's really the Sudanese form that we expect to find in the sea." Jared added.

"You'll have to go first to Khartoum and then to Port Sudan. Otherwise, they won't issue a travel permit."

"Okay. Are we agreed?"

Rick concurred. Sari said nothing.

"Sari, do you want to go? We can use your help."

"Let me think. Yes, I can be gone for a few days, if I find someone to cover a couple of my classes. Dr. Hassan owes me a favor. I'm sure he'll do it. Yes, I'll go, but I may have to return before you do."

"Fair enough. I'm sure we'll need visas. Where do we get them?"

"Easy. The Sudanese Embassy is between here and your hotel. We can spend an hour here and reach the office just after noon prayers."

* * *

At one o'clock, the trio stepped briskly from Sharia Qasr Al-Aini into the well-worn foyer of the Sudanese Embassy. Sari spoke with the receptionist in Arabic and, after some confusion, obtained directions to the office where visas would be granted. They walked to a waiting area, little more than an alcove in one wall of the corridor, and joined a line of foreigners, mostly Arabs. Thirty minutes passed with little movement, though there was always a lively exchange at the teller's cage. Harsh words sometimes drifted back, but applicants invariably left with papers and smiles.

When their time finally came, Sari spoke at length with the clerk. Turning back to the Caissons, she translated, "He says the normal time for approval is three weeks. However, if you can bring him a letter of recommendation from your American Embassy, it can be done much faster, perhaps in a day or less."

"I'm sure we can get a recommendation. Please tell him we'll return tomorrow morning."

She spoke again in Arabic, then whispered, "He strongly hints that you will need a little baksheesh along with the letter."

"Oh, certainly. We want to obey all local customs," Rick panned.

The clerk spoke to Sari again. "He wants to see your passports."

Both men handed over their booklets with little thought for what the pages contained. The clerk officiously opened each and handed it back without smile or frown. He spoke what sounded like a single, declarative sentence in Arabic, and Sari's face fell.

"You will not be permitted to enter Sudan because you have been to Israel," she told Jared. "Worse yet. He denies both requests because you look so much alike he can't tell which passport is which."

"What?" the brothers groaned simultaneously.

"It was just a layover. I was there for only three hours, and I never left the Tel Aviv airport," Jared said.

Sari relayed Jared's explanation.

The clerk retrieved Jared's passport from Sari, held it in front of her face, and pointed to the blurry stamp.

Another brief exchange, and Sari resumed in English, "It doesn't matter when or how long. No one with an Israeli stamp is allowed to enter Sudan. It's the law; no exceptions, no appeal." They were the first applicants of the afternoon to leave with neither papers nor smiles.

"Damn! I could have avoided Israel if I had thought ahead. I knew it would be Okay with Egypt but didn't even think about Sudan, mainly because we didn't plan on going there. I only went through Tel Aviv to save the project a little money," Jared grumbled. He turned to Rick, "Wait a minute. Weren't you there before Saudi?"

"I didn't let the Israelis stamp my passport. Common practice is to put their stamp on a throwaway sheet, then return through a country that's willing to ignore where you've been. I went to Athens on my way to Riyadh. I didn't warn you because it never occurred to me either that we might go into Sudan."

"Can you get a new one from the U.S. Embassy here in Cairo?" Sari asked.

"Hey, that might work," Rick said. "I got a new one in Bangkok once when mine was stolen. It didn't take long."

"It won't take much to find out," Sari said. "The Embassy is only two blocks from here."

"What are we waiting for?"

Ten minutes later, they stood at a counter similar to the one they had just left, only newer and cleaner and maybe a little taller. This time the conversation was in English, though the young woman behind the counter was Egyptian. "Hello," she said with a helpful smile. Jared returned her greeting, then stated what they needed and why.

"A letter of recommendation may be granted, but new passports are a problem. Officially, we only issue new passports when there is an urgent need due to a missing item," she explained. "Of course, we serve American citizens, and we do not investigate the circumstances when someone tells us a passport has been lost or stolen. Unfortunately, however, a new passport will not help in your case. The Sudanese will not admit anyone with a fresh passport issued in Cairo, because they always suspect it was done to dispose of Israeli stamps. Your only hope will be to fly to another city, Rome or Athens, for example, but even that would not guarantee entry." They left their third meeting of the day more dejected than before.

"Terrible! What are we going to do?" Sari said as they stepped to the street.

"Let's find a place where we can think. There has to be a quiet corner somewhere in this town," Rick said. Sari walked purposefully west, and beckoned the brothers to follow. After four blocks of congested sidewalks, they came to the Corniche. Soon they settled on a low stone wall overlooking the bustling Nile.

Rick kicked off. "Maybe we should reconsider El Baz's suggestion. Nuweiba's no good; it's way too far north, but Hurghada has possibilities. We may find something interesting in the patch corals near town. Or, we can take a cruise south. Or, we can try to reach Foul Bay overland along the shore. In Saudi, I spoke with an Egyptian businessman who claimed to know the Red Sea coast. He said it would be easy to hook up with a tourist group and ride south to Foul Bay. I even saw a tourist map that showed symbols for sailing and snorkeling at Berenice. Often in these centrally controlled countries, it's hard to get permission at headquarters, but there's little enforcement in the boonies."

"The problem I see is time," Jared said. "We can explore as long as we want in nearshore patches, but the most interesting sites will be well offshore, and no cruise boat will hang around in one place for long."

"Good point. Plus, at this moment, we don't even know how far south the cruise goes."

Sari looked troubled, "I have a couple of problems with the cruise. For one thing, I don't dive." She blushed ever so slightly.

"Neither do we," Jared and Rick said in unison.

"You don't? Then how will you examine the corals?"

"Underwater video . . . and geographers' magic. You'll see," Jared said.

"And . . . uh . . . those cruises are expensive. I just can't afford it."

"Don't worry about the cost. Rick and I will take care of that."

"No, no. I couldn't let you."

"Don't take it personally," Rick said kindly. "This is work and your expenses are part of the cost of doing business, a small part of the total, I might add. We need a native speaker on our side."

Jared patted her hand, and it was settled. "Now, let's find out about cruises. The hotel will have brochures, won't it?"

"Yes, I recall racks of tourist propaganda against a back wall. And your concierge will have some, too. He can tell us where to buy tickets."

"I think there's one of those MISR Travel Agencies in the hotel lobby," Rick said.

"MISR?" asked Jared.

"The Egyptian word for 'Egypt,'" responded Rick. Sari nodded.

They lingered for a while, their gazes following the steady pace of the river. Buff and blue—the scene could be described almost entirely with only those two colors. Deep blue water. Bright blue boats. Buff brown buildings with an occasional splash of white, edging the water and penetrating the heart of the city. A meager band of green separated blue from buff along the river's bank, not a deep green, but rather the dusty pale shade so typical of dry lands everywhere. A felucca drifted toward them, its crew motionless. As the boat neared shore, a few deft motions of tiller and sheet sent it off on a westward tack. On the path beside the stream, a sailor, dressed all in black except for his dirty-white sailor's cap, ambled by. Jared noticed a bandage and wondered how the man had hurt his hand. The river smelled foul and the scene could hardly be called quiet, but its tranquility somehow enticed the watchers to forget the day's disappointments.

By evening prayers, they were well supplied with brochures and price lists. Soon afterward, the faithful resumed their usual activities, and the three conspirators sought dinner. *How different from my evening with Sari two nights ago*, Jared thought, as they sat down to eat. But the topic on everyone's mind was Hurghada. Rick was the first to speak. "There's no contest as I see it. This dive cruise boat called the -*bella* is head and shoulders above all other options. It goes farther south, stays out longer, and offers all the services we need. It's posh but still within budget, and a little luxury won't hurt us."

"No question. That's the way to go. Sari?" Jared said. She nodded, and he continued, "The next cruise starts Sunday. That gives us two days in the valley and one at Hurghada. Does that sound Okay?"

"Well, I'd like to have more time to inspect the pyramids and mastabas and temples around here, but we have no choice," Rick said. "We can't afford to kill a week waiting for the next cruise."

"Seeing ruins here will help us recognize ruins under the sea, but it's more of a refinement than necessity. We already have a pretty good idea what to look for, the shape of the coral, I mean. Ultimately, we just have to recognize the difference between a rock and a block," Jared said.

Sari resumed her role as chair and lone member of the Local Arrangements Committee. "Where do you want to start?"

"I say Saqqara. It's the oldest one on land and therefore most likely to resemble the earlier undersea pyramids."

* * *

At midmorning on Thursday, Sari led them to a rise overlooking the step pyramid of Djoser. "This is where it all began," she said. "Saqqara . . . a trendsetter if ever there was one."

"Amazing, isn't it. Today it's hardly more than a crumbling mound of brick-like stones, but 4,600 years ago, it was the most imposing building on earth. If we're right, it was the true phoenix, a monument to the eternal hope of people who had passed the brink of destruction and survived, though much diminished. It was a tangible new beginning for a nation determined to regain its former glory. The construction probably took every skill they had preserved and every resource they could muster. The outcome still didn't measure up to what they had lost, but they did it anyway. A century later they were back on their feet."

"Even if you're wrong, it's still an important building, the start of something new versus the revival of something old. Either way, this place is awesome," Sari said.

Rick soon switched to the pyramid's construction. "I doubt they considered it inspirational at the time. Maybe they just wanted a safe vault for their most prized and perishable possessions. Maybe this pyramid was just one in a sequence of vaults built at successive levels as the water rose. They didn't know where the sea planned to stop, so they just kept on building pyramids, always preparing for the next rise."

"True. But I suspect this one was special, because they'd already lost their battle with the sea. They had so little left. It must have taken tremendous will to start anew." Jared cupped his hand above his eyes and stared at the pyramid's crumbling peak.

A local guide droned in the late morning sun. Now and then came a tidbit relevant to their quest, but most of it was commercial hype. *Roman tourists probably heard the same lies 2,000 years ago.* Jared listened out of one ear and barely heard the guide say, ". . . this primitive pyramid was begun shortly after the Egyptian capital was moved from Thinis to Memphis."

He jerked his head and turned to Sari. "Did he say there was a capital earlier than Memphis?"

"Yes, Thinis. It's way up the Nile Valley near Luxor."

Caisson jerked the map of Egypt from his rear pocket and studied it quickly. "We *have* to go there immediately," he said. He motioned to Rick. "Did you hear what he said? Thinis was the original capital. That's what we need to see. The buildings there should be closest to what we can expect at Foul Bay. I'm impressed that it's not on either coast. It's about halfway from Foul Bay to the delta. That could be significant."

"Makes a lot of sense. The current delta wouldn't have formed for several centuries after the final rise. Do we have time for Thinis before we sail?" Rick asked.

"It's a little out of our way. We can manage, but we'll have to leave Cairo a day early. We can fly to Luxor, then decide whether to cross over to Hurghada by air or hire a car.

Search Log 41: First Capital

Friday was almost a repeat of the day before. Since arriving at Luxor, they had shuttled from site to site, in and out of tourist vans. A plentitude of empty seats eased the uncomfortable ride ever so slightly. Recent terrorist attacks on sightseeing vans such as these had scared off most tourists.

Yet again, they stood in the hot sun listening to a glib guide. Surrounding them was a broad flat plain, so green it could have been the Tennessee Valley. But palm trees, ruins, and red cliffs confirmed that it was, indeed, the Nile Valley.

Before them stood all that was left of the tomb of Djer, a First Dynasty king who ruled after the capital moved to Memphis and kings were returned here for burial. Later, the local "Chamber of Commerce" claimed that the tomb was actually that of Osiris.

"Djerry, did you hear that?" Rick joked, then finished seriously, "This place was dedicated to Osiris, God of the Underworld."

"That's too good to be true!" Jared whistled.

Sari overheard. "Why is that significant?"

"Well," Rick explained, "Jerry and I have long suspected the Egyptian Underworld may have been misinterpreted. Maybe it was the land that was lost to the sea. Maybe Osiris, God of the Underworld, was the king who led his people to refuge in the Nile Valley."

"Or helped prepare the way, at least," Jared said. "Of course, the original Osiris probably lived centuries before Djer. Maybe several millennia. Djer just benefited, posthumously, from the old boy's reputation."

The guide droned on, "The cult of Osiris replaced a funerary cult dedicated to a local god known as The Foremost of the Westerners . . ."

"Whoa! Another hit," Rick whispered. "Why would Egyptians think of locals as Westerners, unless the Egyptians themselves came from the east? Foul Bay? The Arabian Peninsula?"

"Unless the locals migrated here from farther west," Sari said.

"Good point. Everything is relative."

They listened carefully from then on, but the remaining spiel was a humdrum rendition of stories for tourists.

The next stop sounded as if it might shed a little light on the God of the Underworld, himself. The Temple of Osiris was built in the Thirtieth Dynasty near a funerary complex predating the First Dynasty. Its walls were made of mud brick, and it was a likely precursor of the first step pyramids. Nearby was a site of unquestioned antiquity, known as the

"Mother of Pots" for the tremendous, mysterious quantities of potsherds found there.

"Here we go again," Jared said. "Refugees have to carry their goods in some kind of container. These very pots may have come from the Underworld, like packing crates that pile up when you move to a new house."

"A bit of a stretch, don't you think? They could have been traveling from anywhere, not necessarily from the drowned lands of the Red Sea," Rick said. "Or it could have been a bakery or even a pottery factory, for all we know."

"Okay! Sure, there could be lots of other explanations, but I'm encouraged that all the evidence, so far, is consistent with the hypothesis. It all fits so well, but nothing seems to seal the deal."

"Only one way to be sure," Rick said.

"How?" Jared asked.

"Check for those little white, numbered stickers. I still find them from my move to Knoxville sixteen years ago."

* * *

The last site of the day didn't sound very promising, for it was built almost 2,000 years after the capital left town. The agenda simply listed the stop as "The Temple of Seti I near Abydos." A new guide joined them, and she seemed more professional than the others. Only then did Rick and Jared realize the entire complex was dedicated to Osiris rather than to Seti I himself. It seems Seti I lived in the Nile Delta. To rule both the Lower and Upper Kingdoms, he needed to prove himself upriver. That was no small feat because he worshipped Seth, the typhonic God of Chaos, mortal enemy of Osiris and his son Horus. Local folks worshipped Osiris. This was no friendly Baptist/Methodist "feud", because sometime in antiquity Seth had killed Osiris. Finally, Seti I bought his way into their hearts by constructing an elaborate temple to honor the slain god.

"Seth, the typhoon god who symbolized the Waters of Chaos, killed Osiris, God of the Underworld? That's perfect!" Jared said, when she finished her lecture.

Next, the guide stopped at a mural and explained its meaning. "Here Seti I offers Ma'at to Osiris and two other gods. The God of the Underworld represented order and was the author of Ma'at, the Divine Right Order. It was this conflict between order and chaos that caused the people to distrust Seti in the first place."

They crossed the temple grounds and overlooked the Osireion. "This enormous hall," the guide said, "is named after Osiris. Much older than the temple itself, it's one of the greatest puzzles in Egypt. Here a rectangular island is surrounded by canals continuously fed by an elaborate system of springs and tunnels. It does not appear to be a bath, but rather something more formal, probably ceremonial. Experts believe it may represent the primeval mound, or place of ascension, from which the people of Egypt were said to have come."

Wow! Rick and Jared instantly understood the symbolism of the structure. The island, surrounded by water and red granite pillars, surely must represent Erytheia, the mythical red island from which the Red Sea got its name. "Look at this place," Rick said. "It's not a temple; it's a working hydrologic model."

"Many scholars believe the real Osiris may have lived on the Indian Ocean or Red Sea south of Egypt. His beard is depicted in the style of Punt," the guide droned on. "Residents of the Underworld are signified by pale green skin, as opposed to the red or black of ordinary people."

"Pale green. Just like real people viewed under water," Jared said excitedly.

"Or corpses," Sari said flatly.

Search Log 42: Coming Down in Egypt

Luxor creaked with age enshrined in decadent splendor. Streets, crowded with cars and scooters, carriages and donkeys, horse-drawn carts and an occasional camel, were powdered with dust and dung. Yet here was the splendid Winter Palace Hotel where Agatha Christie penned *Death on the Nile*, and the movie was filmed. Rick entered a bookstore just down the street from the hotel. He perused the used book section and bought a hardbound volume called *The Riddle of the Pyramids* by Curt Mendelssohn. He would have plenty of time to read it during the coming week.

Back at the Arabesque Hotel, the Matterhorn on the wall of Room 302 appeared incongruous against the city of Luxor and its "main street," the Nile River. Rick sat at a tiny desk, Sari lay on the bed, and Jared lounged in an easy chair. Jared spied Rick's book on the nightstand.

"*The Riddle of the Pyramids?*" he said. "That's an appropriate title. Does it say anything we don't already know?"

"It's mostly about the construction of pyramids. Not the architecture, but the actual construction effort. Mendelssohn contends that pyramid construction was primarily an end rather than a means. He says pyramid-building absorbed excess seasonal labor when the Nile flooded the fields. It also provided a justification for food distribution during the off season. The result was a nation-building exercise that led to greater unity for Egypt's rural populace."

"So it was a public works project like our Civilian Conservation Corp during the '30s."

"Or like Vista is today—a means of distributing wealth and training workers."

"But that doesn't speak to the original reason for picking the pyramid as the nation's target project."

"No, that he leaves to speculation."

"Egyptian pyramids, I assume?"

"Not necessarily. He's discusses both Egyptian and American pyramids. He thinks they both served the same purpose, but he dispels one notion I got from my trip to Mexico. That shaft in the base of the Pyramid of the Sun wasn't original equipment after all. It was an exploratory tunnel cut in 1917. They didn't find any chambers inside. In fact, only one American pyramid is known to have a chamber inside. The rest were solid stone and mortar."

"Chambers are crucial," Sari interjected. "We've got to get to Foul Bay. It makes even more sense than ever."

"I agree," said Jared. "A cruise may work, but then again it may not. We could be trapped in nothing more than a sightseeing excursion."

"If you still want to find a way into Foul Bay under our own power, I'm game."

"We'll improve our chances if we split forces," Jared said. "How about this? Sari and I take the train south to Aswan, then head east overland by car on the old caravan route through Wadi Hawdayn. Meanwhile, Rick hires a car and driver in Luxor, heads straight east for the coast, and approaches Foul Bay from the north. We can pass messages through the front desk here at the Arabesque. If both teams succeed, we'll meet in Berenice. If only one gets through, the losing team will reroute and follow the other in."

"So we totally abandon the idea of a cruise?" Sari asked. "What about the tickets you bought?"

"Hold onto them as backup," Rick said. "I'll call and reschedule the cruise. If both teams fail, we can still make it to Hurghada for departure on the following Sunday."

* * *

Nearby, a driver from Luxor Airport was about to embark on the adventure of his life. Abdullah Ghorimi had never been south of Marsa Alam on the Red Sea, east of Edfu. Now, he and Rick would undertake the 300 mile trip to Berenice and hopefully beyond to Bir Shalatain at the old administrative border with Sudan. Rick wanted to go all the way to the southern end of Foul Bay. He would be lucky to make Berenice, though. Security forces surely would block the way beyond.

Rick's greatest concern was the tread-bare tires on Abdullah's tourist van, a ramshackle once-white box of questionable vintage. A notepad in Rick's hand listed "food and water," enough to survive several days in case of breakdown, and "blankets and bedding." That was all part of his bargain with Abdullah, for no accommodations would be found south of Marsa Alam. If necessary, they would sleep on the van's blue kitchen-vinyl floor.

To make matters worse, recent floods had knocked out several desert roads. The trip would have been difficult under normal conditions. Now, it was unclear how far they could go or how long the trip would take. "I will go no farther than Bir Shalatain," Abdullah announced at the outset. "The Hala'ib Triangle has been closed for years. It would be foolish to go there." He looked askance, embarrassed by his own boldness. "And we must first register with the tourist police," he said.

Sounds like a perfunctory precaution, but I see concern in his eyes. He doesn't believe permission will be granted freely. Yet he still seems confident we'll get in. I wonder if he really knows what we're up against. He certainly wouldn't be optimistic if he knew what Jared and Sari and I went through in Cairo.

The shabby headquarters of the tourist police was an easy walk from the Arabesque. "The chief is not here. Come back at 1:30." At 1:30: "You must have photocopies of all required forms." Abdullah hustled to the Arabesque, copied the forms and returned to a lengthy discourse in Arabic. No translation was needed as his face signaled defeat.

"What's the problem?" Rick asked.

"Some recent difficulties. Attacks on tourists."

"By whom?"

"Sudanese terrorists. Trouble on the border."

Rick had heard rumors of secret military operations but no word of active terrorism inside Egypt. He wished he could ask Jared, but Jared couldn't reveal what he knew from the classified reports anyway.

"He says, 'Go to Hurghada. Join a tour group and drive south in convoy.'"

"That would add 300 miles to the trip and leave no time for Marsa Alam, much less Berenice."

"I know," Abdullah said. "Besides, he doesn't know whether any tour groups are heading that way or not."

"What do you think?"

"Most doubtful. I haven't heard of any in years."

"So he's passing us to another command, and we still get 'No' in Hurghada."

"But that is no problem. No problem." Abdullah tore the agenda to shreds, then took on new resolve. "We only need their permission because I drive a tourist van. My friend has a taxi. I will borrow it. Tourist police don't control taxis. I will pick you up at five o'clock tomorrow morning."

At sunset, Rick stood on his balcony while the eternal prayers of Islam resonated across the Nile. The gigantic pillars of Luxor Temple, among the most ancient of monuments, contrasted starkly with the pale-rose hues of the western sky. The West Bank and its high cliffs, home to the Valley of the Kings, created a noble backdrop.

The kings of 36 dynasties must have stood in awe of this very scene. One minute the sun's disk sat on the horizon, and next it was gone. For eons, the desert had swallowed the blazing orb each day.

* * *

Awakened at 4:30 a.m. by a servant bearing tea, Rick rose quietly and readied himself for the trip. Jared and Sari slept peacefully in separate rooms down the hall. At least, Rick assumed their sleep was peaceful and separate. He still found their friendship troubling, but he had begun to accept Jared's "not guilty" plea. Rick stepped out on the night-dark balcony, enchanted as always by the predawn pageant of starlight and street life and muezzin's chant. Sunrise was an hour away, yet the city was vibrant. Five times a day, the faithful knelt—near dawn (fajr), just after noon (dhuhr), in the afternoon (asr), just after sunset (maghrib) and around nightfall (isha'a). Yet, as Abdullah attested, the faithful call it a privilege rather than an obligation.

Rick arrived a few minutes after the appointed hour of his rendezvous with Abdullah. *Today sunrise prayer is at 5:00 a.m. Yet Abdullah set our meeting for exactly that time. It's a curious thing,* he mused. *Prayer times are fixed, yet Muslims often set appointments at prayer time. Tacitly, by common agreement, 15 minutes is added to any such an appointment. By this strange reckoning, Rick arrived early at 5:05, and Abdullah arrived precisely on time at 5:15.*

"This is a good car. A very good car." Abdullah said, trying to convince himself more than Rick, it seemed. Indeed, it was a good car though its best qualities were cosmetically obscured, to say the least. It was an old Peugeot stationwagon, workhorse of the Egyptian taxi fleet. Dents, dings, and scratches testified to 12 years of faithful service. Thankfully, its tires showed more tread than the van, but its speedometer must have been transplanted from a newer car. Like the far-flung travels of Osiris, its actual mileage had been lost in antiquity.

The first morning was a blur of exotic adventure. Two hours upriver to Edfu . . . guards waving them on to Marsa Alam and claiming passage to Berenice was possible, beyond there difficult. Three more hours across the Eastern Desert and Red Sea Hills, and over to the sea . . . Bedouins trekking the desert . . . military guard posts on the Desert Road . . . dust clouds hanging over phosphate mines in the distance.

At the coast they tried turning south, but guards stopped them in their tracks. "No passage beyond Marsa Alam," a guard flatly decreed in Arabic.

"Why not?" Rick asked Abdullah.

"Some recent difficulties. Even if *he* lets us pass, other guards will stop us short of Berenice."

"Perhaps we can speak with his superiors."

Another exchange in Arabic. "Seven kilometers north. We can speak with his commander." After a much-needed tea break, the two-man expedition arrived at a desolate compound. It was 11:30, and hot sun sparkled off machinegun barrels aimed at the taxi. The commander, wearing a day-glow orange exercise suit and dime-store flip-flops, squinted as his eyes adjusted to daylight. Another hail of Arabic, and Abdullah grimaced.

"No one goes south of Marsa Alam. We must speak with his commander in Quseir for special permission."

"But that's 80 miles north," Rick complained.

Abdullah shook his head knowingly. "It is no problem! We will go to Quseir." Rick was impressed by Abdullah's never-say-die attitude. Even with an extra 160 mile roundtrip, they could still reach Berenice by late evening, so off they went. The rickety Peugeot clipped along at more than 75 miles per hour. Portions of the Red Sea Road were in good shape, except for washouts from recent floods. In places, undercuts left pavement suspended as high as six feet over thin air. Collapse of an overhang would spell disaster. Still Abdullah pressed on.

The beat-up Peugeot raced past the bluest water Rick had ever seen and stopped at 1:00 p.m. in the seaside town of Quseir. It was considerably larger than Marsa Alam, but that wasn't saying much. Its jumbled streets fell sadly short of the quaint seaside town Rick had envisioned. It was a poor native village far off the beaten path.

They quickly found the commander, and Abdullah pled his case. Suddenly, he led Rick from the dilapidated headquarters to a plywood kiosk nearby.

Instantly, the proprietor dashed off to the main compound with Abdullah's papers. Rick looked puzzled. "Photocopies. They want photocopies of my license," the driver explained. "This man will help…for a small fee." Soon the man was back with the necessary copies.

The proprietor served Mirinda Orange sodas from a galvanized pail filed with filthy ice water. Rick wiped the bottle with his handkerchief and popped the cap. Pursing his lips, he sucked from the bottle's rim as if through a straw.

"I see, Dr. Rick, that you have learned the Mirinda Kiss," Abdullah said. "To you the water is dirty. To me it is clean." He laughed heartily as he took a mighty swig. Rick waited at the kiosk while Abdullah went next door for the final signoff that now, at last, seemed imminent.

When Abdullah returned, his face told a different story. "Hurghada. We must meet his commander there. Only the highest officer can grant permission. Recent difficulties."

Why no warning in Luxor or Edfu? Obviously, someone wanted to keep a lid on the uprising—if there is one.

"But that's 75 miles," Rick said. "Did you tell him how far we've come?"

Abdullah nodded.

"That I've come all the way from America?"

Another nod. More Arabic. Then, "There's nothing this man can do. If we reach Berenice without proper papers, they will say, 'What are you doing here?' They will arrest us."

"Can't we phone Hurghada?"

"No, the commander there must speak with you in person. He has questions."

Sounds ominous, but I can talk my way through just about anything if given half a chance.

"Okay," Rick said. "Let's hightail it to Hurghada." Abdullah was confused. "Let's go for it!" Rick translated, and Abdullah smiled.

At two o'clock, they reached Zafaga, a processing center for ores mined in the Eastern Desert. Its new railway provided a vital link between the Nile Valley and the Red Sea coast. "My dream is to live here," Abdullah said as they passed through the town. On second look, Rick realized it was indeed a quaint little city by developing world standards. "I like it because it is quiet," Abdullah said, while blasting his horn at every passing car and pedestrian.

"You can cure that, for sure," Rick cracked. Abdullah smiled, then laughed as he caught the irony.

In midafternoon, gleaming condos blocked Rick's view of the Red Sea. In recent years, Hurghada had become a major resort for sun seekers and scuba divers. Finding the command post could have been difficult, but a pedestrian graciously jumped in and guided them right to it. A lively discussion with a guard ended with Abdullah's familiar look of disappointment.

"Ask him to let us meet his commander!" Rick demanded, showing the frustration that had been bottled inside for three hours.

"I did," Abdullah said. "Let's go."

A winding lane led to the heart of the compound, and Rick realized the distinction between the "military" and the "army"—two separate organizations in Egypt. The military is an internal security agency charged with enforcing a state of near-martial law. They operate on a miniscule budget, living in compounds more like refugee camps than military posts. Yet Hurghada's concrete-block building held an air of casual authority. The military commander for Red Sea operations—wearing a flowered shirt, "pedal pusher" length slacks, and flip-flops—was indifferent but gracious. He appeared open-minded as Abdullah again pled their case, and Abdullah looked hopeful at first. By degrees, the familiar furrow returned to his brow.

"He says there's no way. Too many difficulties. The order comes from Cairo. We would be arrested even if he gave us a pass. It's all military, no civilians from Berenice to the border. He would not go to Berenice himself...even if he had the chance."

"End of the road?"

"We have no choice." Abdullah's head lowered and his voice dropped.

Back in Hurghada, Rick called the Arabesque's front desk. No word from Jared...command decision. "I'll go back with you," he told Abdullah.

"We must leave now to pass Qena before dark." Abdullah appeared uneasy. As they headed south, he unexpectedly turned into the parking lot of an elegant new mosque and cinched the brake. In an instant, he was out of the car and inside. Fifteen minutes later he emerged.

Finally, there was time for a late lunch of sesame breadsticks and bananas packed by Abdullah's wife. *This food is outstanding,* Rick thought as they shared a giant bottle of warm Sprite. A tea break at a roadside "cafeteria" and the homeward dash was underway. Sunset fell somewhere in the Eastern Desert, thwarting Abdullah's plan to clear Qena by nightfall. On the outskirts of the city, he pulled off the road.

"We must wait for a military escort," Abdullah said. "It is for your protection. They will make the way safe."

"Safe?" Rick asked.

"Yes," Abdullah said. "Very safe. Extremists have bombed several tour buses in recent weeks. They have nothing against tourists. They just want to embarrass the government by disrupting tourism."

"That's comforting," Rick said. "Why Qena? My guidebook says the problems are at Asyut."

"Oh, no! Qena is the worst. It's the university." Abdullah was surprised that Rick was unaware of "recent difficulties."

"Fundamentalists?" Rick asked, echoing the official explanations reported by U.S. media.

"Some," Abdullah said, "...but not all."

"What do you mean?"

"The young people. They want a better life. They go to school and get a degree. Then they wait ten years for a job. They want a better economy. They want more freedom."

"We don't hear about this in the U.S. Are the people against Mubarak?"

"They want to choose. They want more than one name on the ballot."

"That seems reasonable."

"Yes, but killing is wrong. I am embarrassed for Islam. Allah does not condone killing. It is forbidden in the Quran. The people who do these things don't know what Allah wants. They are wrong."

"How do the people feel? Do the terrorists act with popular support or on their own?"

"In one village, the people told the terrorists, 'We will forgive you if you kill Mubarak, but don't touch the tourists. They are our lifeblood.' "

"That bad, eh?"

"It is very serious, but mostly from Qena to Asyut. All the country wants change, but there is not so much violence elsewhere." Both men climbed out of the Peugeot to stretch their legs. For an hour and a half, they chatted in darkness with a carload of Italian scuba divers. Finally, guards arrived in a pick-up truck, two up front, four in back with automatic rifles aimed in all four cardinal directions. For the rest of the way, that's how it was: tourists in convoys, one guard post after another, one pick-up or jeep after another jockeying to lead. Guardsmen in traditional robes, toting World War II vintage British Enfield rifles, stood at every major intersection. Altogether, they passed through more than 45 checkpoints, most with some delay for clearance. Closer to Luxor, Rick was disturbed to learn such precautions had commenced on the very same roads he and his partners had traveled only two days earlier.

* * *

Back at the Arabesque, Rick awoke late on Sunday morning, rested from his ordeal but worried about Jared and Sari. Why hadn't they called? He doubted they would make it all the way to Foul Bay. Probably they'd reach Aswan with relative ease, only to be turned back immediately when they headed east. In that case, however, they should have called back to the Arabesque by late Saturday or early Sunday. He checked with the front desk yet again, just to make sure. Still no call.

Rick spent the rest of the day bored, anxious, and restless. Standing on the balcony, watching the sunset and listening to the muezzin, he resolved not to endure another day in such a miserable state. He caught Abdullah after evening prayers.

On Tuesday morning, commencing with a 5:30 a.m. rendezvous, they joined a convoy back to the temples of Abydos and Dendara. Rick wanted more information on the legend of Osiris. His first stop was the Temple of Seti I where they had toured the previous week. Dating from around 1,300 BC, it was started by Pharaoh Seti I and completed by Ramses II as a tribute to Osiris, first pharaoh and greatest of all the Egyptian gods. The temple itself was spectacular in both art and architecture. Its walls told and retold the story of Osiris–half-man, half-god–who rose from the primeval Waters of Chaos to lead the rebirth of his people. He was credited with bringing agriculture to the Nile Delta. After stabilizing Lower Egypt, he was said to have gone abroad to other lands to share with them the benefits of agriculture, as well. The story of Osiris' gruesome death–his body cut into 14 pieces and scattered throughout the region–*and* his resurrection dominated Egyptian faith and lore for thousands of years.

Rick's objective was to photograph the Osireion in greater detail. Again he inspected the sunken chamber immediately behind the inner sanctuary of Osiris. Again he found neither tomb nor temple nor fortification but rather a complex feat of hydrologic engineering, once covered by slabs of stone and layers of earth. From the now-exposed rim, he stared into green waters that filled the base of the chamber. Tall pillars of red granite, which once supported massive ceiling slabs, surrounded a moat. A central mound of earth had washed away, thanks to inept British and French "conservators." According to his guide, the only explanation was a hinted connection to older legends that Osiris was born on an island that rose from the Waters of Chaos. As for the hydraulic system itself, no practical purpose had ever been proposed. *Yes*, Rick thought as he stared at the odd structure: *This is an invention—a machine, a model, not a building.* He dedicated an entire roll of film to it and recalled a similar device used by the U.S. Corps of Engineers to study the Mississippi River's antics.

Dendara, on the other hand, was a straightforward temple built by occupying Romans. It was well preserved and not ravaged by "conservators." Rick was drawn to a sunken stone-walled structure called the Sacred Lake of Dendara. Once used for ritual ablutions, it was now a dry pit filled with camel fodder.

Rick descended its weathered steps and stood among towering palm trees now growing from its dusty floor. He held his breath momentarily, imagining how it would have been with cool water inside. Admiring the impressive architecture, he noticed a stairwell that disappeared into a wall. Entering it, he encountered ankle-deep water on the third step down. Around a corner, the stairwell disappeared into darkness. *It's surprising*, he thought, *how close this desert soil lies to such abundant water beneath.*

Rick recalled a similar feature of temples upriver. "Nilometers," as they're called, are stream gauges dug deep into the earth some distance from the river's edge. Situated where the river's seasonal rise and fall is dampened through a sandy gravel bed, they provide accurate measures of seasonal changes without confusing daily fluctuations caused by local rain or drought.

Of course, he suddenly realized, *that's how the ancients would have measured sea level. With "oceanometers" as sea gauges carefully placed in coastal aquifers, hydrologists could have monitored long-term rise and fall, while ignoring the temporary effects of storms, tides, and seasons. Clever, indeed!*

* * *

Luxor is the kind of place that makes people say, "Nice place to visit, but I wouldn't want to live there." Rick agreed. By Thursday night, he felt as if he had taken up residence. With still no word from Jared and Sari, he had to decide whether to remain in Luxor or head back to Hurghada for their prearranged rendezvous. Friday would be his last chance to leave for

Sunday's cruise. For all their careful planning, no one had foreseen a situation in which the two teams couldn't communicate at all. Surely telephone or telegraph lines reached even to the troubled region around Foul Bay. He was worried and puzzled.

Friday at 5:00 a.m., he was awakened from fitful sleep by the stutter of the old-fashioned telephone beside his bed. It was the front desk. "Mr. Caisson, I have a call for you."

Rick hoped it was his brother, but it might well be someone back home who had miscalculated the time by an hour or two. An awkward pause was followed by static peppered with a dash of English. He couldn't recognize the voice. Eventually, he heard a click, indicating that the clerk had completed the connection. Finally, Jared's voice.

"Rick, Rick, is that you?"

"Yes. It's me. Where the hell have you guys been?"

"Apt description, but it's a long story. The whole south is a mess right now. Floods have devastated roads, railroads, telephone lines. We made it to Aswan on the train. No cars for rent, but Sari talked a former student who lives there into lending us his Land Rover. We tried to go up the old caravan route, but Security stopped us even before we left the valley. I guess the same thing happened to you."

"Military everywhere I turned. I saw signs of flooding, but nothing like you describe."

"We tried to find another way in, but no luck." The phone crackled menacingly.

"And you managed to get stranded, even with a Land Rover?"

"It was awful! We sloshed through a congested little town, and guards stopped us as we entered the desert. The wadi flowed like a flume, and there was no chance of going any farther even if the guards had been willing. I heard a train and looked back as it crossed the wadi at the edge of town. It was like watching an old movie in slow motion. The bridge slumped, and cars toppled one by one. We knew everyone on the train would drown, but we weren't prepared for what came next." He paused.

"It took a second for me to realize the train was mostly comprised of tank cars. Some sank immediately; others drifted on top. Then fuel spilled and spread across the floodwaters. It was just a matter of time until the slick found a fire of some sort, and the whole town went up like a torch."

"My god! How many were killed?"

"Nobody knows. We hung around and helped, but we left long before authorities arrived."

"Listen, we can discuss this when we get back together. Right now, we have a reservation in Hurghada. Can you get back here?"

"Yes, we're at the railway station in Aswan. Can you meet us at Luxor station?"

"What time?"

"I'm not sure. Just check with the ticket office. It's the one leaving Aswan at 6:20."

"I'll be there."

CHAPTER 24

Chronicle 53: A Message for the King

The *Eastern Star's* arrival created a commotion in Erytheia long before the ship reached port. Lights glowed through early morning mist, and daybreak struck as the *Star* slipped into an open berth. It was two days before the spring equinox, and revelers still frolicked from the night before. With word that Osir was aboard the strange vessel, the hubbub turned into near-riot as Erytheians rushed to hail their hero.

"Take me to the palace," Osir commanded the King's Guards, and immediately they obeyed. At his approach, the palace gates sprang open. There stood Bera and three-year-old Horesh. Osir could contain himself no longer. With tears in his eyes, he embraced Bera, then fell to his knees before his little boy. "My son, my son!" he wept.

"Aba?" The boy smiled, then giggled.

"Look how tall you've grown, how much of your life I've missed. I'll never again leave you for such a long, long time." Lifting Horesh to his chest, he rose and stared again at Bera's face. "And you, Bera, henceforth you will always be at my side. I will never leave you behind. Now, we must talk privately."

With her arm around Osir's waist, Bera led her family to their quarters. The couple bantered lightly, occasionally tickling or teasing Horesh, as they walked the long corridor past the King's apartments. Once in chambers, however, husband and wife turned serious. "The Fast Rise has begun," Osir blurted. "The Waters of Chaos will soon surround the Sacred Pyramid. The end of Erytheia is near. Rahn Ammon must decree Ma'at. I will tell him so, but you must guide me. You know him and all that has transpired in my absence."

"Your news will not be welcome," Bera said. "Setra is insanely jealous of your successes and shamed by his own failures. Watch your every step. He hoped you would die on your journey . . . and even spread rumors that you did."

"So that's why everyone was so thrilled at the docks!" He laughed. "I thought they were glad to see me. Instead, they came to view my corpse." Again he laughed. "But surely he'll put aside such petty thoughts when he learns of the impending deluge."

"Setra is a changed man, Osi. He convinced himself that rumors of your death, claims of his own successes, and lies about your actions at the First Terrace would turn the people to him. But his ploy failed miserably."

"Why should I worry? They can see I'm alive. Can't I present my own case and be done with him?"

"No, Osi. Setra still has the King's ear. Rahn Ammon tries to play the bold, decisive king, but he doesn't fit the part. He has isolated himself from the people, the court, Father Toth, and even me. He's become Setra's dupe, and Setra has poisoned his mind against you and the Divine Right Order."

"Setra? Against the Devine Right Order? That's crazy. He's the one who carried the Divine Right Order to such disastrous extremes."

"But look at it through his eyes, Osi."

"That has never been my strength, Bera. You must be my sight through the eyes of others."

"In Setra's mind, the Divine Right Order failed him at Redsilver Point. It failed him at the Third Betrothal and at the First Terrace; and it denied him a rightful heir. Now he says, 'What good has come from my devotion to these silly rules?' All that's left is his power over Rahn Ammon, and your news will threaten that too. Your words will fall like seeds on rock-hard ground."

"Seeds of reason, well grounded in truth."

"Oh, Osi. You fight armies and conquer worlds, but you are such a babe. Setra will twist your words. He has already sown doubt, warning that you may spread panic for your own selfish ends. Plan your moves carefully. Be certain of your findings. Be ready to demonstrate them to the King, priests, Geometers, and Setra himself. Use your allies; Father Toth speaks with me often and secretly has committed to help."

"Is the hydraulicon ready?"

"Yes, built to your exact specifications. I've overseen the work myself. It's a masterpiece of art and science."

"And the sea gauge?"

"Precisely as you ordered."

"First, an audience with the King."

* * *

"The time has come, I vow, to make known the coming flood. The waters now rise, and Chaos soon will reign." Osir's practiced description of the Ice and careful explanation of the Cauldrons took more than two hands of time, during which the King spoke hardly a word. Toth sat in respectful silence throughout the afternoon as the frightful story unfolded. Setra smirked skeptically. At the end, Toth and the King sat in silent contemplation, and Setra left in disgust.

"You understand what this means, don't you, Sire?" Osir stared intensely into the King's eyes as he spoke. Rahn Ammon remained trance-like, staring at Osir, yet beyond him. "You must declare Ma'at!" Osir shouted, louder than he had intended.

Unnerved by Osir's outburst, the King shook his head doubtfully. "Interesting adventures, Osir, but they hardly herald the end of our world.

There is too little information. You must bring proof if you expect me to make a decision with such dire consequences. I will confer with General Setra. Together we will decide what proof is required. You may go now."

"But, Sire!"

"I said you may go!"

Toth stared impotently as Osir backed respectfully from the throne.

* * *

Osir stalked out of the palace in frustration and despair. Toth caught up as he left. "You made a case any fool can understand, Osir. Now we must build one that no fool can misunderstand. Where is this expert from the east?"

"The Yellow Emissary. He's aboard the *Star*, and we agreed to meet at the sea gauge at sunset. Come with me." A brisk stroll brought them to the beach and a roofed turret rising more than a manheight above its sands. The scholar waited beside the sea gauge.

Steps spiraled up the outside of the structure. Inside, a second set, mirroring the first, curved down into its depths. Osir grabbed a flickering torch from the inner wall and led the way. Reaching a platform at ground level, he peered deeper as more steps disappeared into the blackness. One step, another, and another. Eventually his leading foot sank into cool water.

"I've reached the waterline. Hand me the pegs." Toth removed ten metal pegs from a niche in the wall. As Osir knelt at the water's edge, torchlight fell on a vertical line of holes punched into the wall. Scores of holes stretched from beneath the water upward for a manheight or more. Osir inserted one peg precisely at the waterline and others in the next nine holes above.

"We'll check back tomorrow at sunset," he said, and the others nodded. "Now, to the hydraulicon. We must get to work."

The peculiar structure sat in a swale behind the palace. Like its Sunda prototype, the hydraulicon was a masterpiece of hydraulic geometry. A long, arched tunnel provided its only access. Water flowed from a subterranean reservoir into the hydraulic chamber. "Its level can be controlled precisely by a gate that allows water to flow into the pool on demand," Osir explained to Toth as the Yellow Emissary demonstrated by releasing a small quantity of water. "A similar outlet can be opened when the water level needs to fall."

"I doubt we'll need that part." Toth laughed dryly.

The central chamber consisted of a sizable pool surrounded by two colonnades of massive pillars on which rested massive stone slabs forming a roof covered with clay. A stone walkway gave access to all sides of the central pool. In all respects, this was an exact copy of the hydraulicon Osir had observed in Mekong City, except that the original contained a model of Sunda, while Osir's version featured Berenicia and, in the center of the pool, an exact replica of Erytheia. Every contour, every building, every pyramid was faithfully rendered in miniature.

"I see how the chamber works," Toth said, "but how can it predict the coming floods?"

"The hydraulicon's waters now strike the shore at the same place as in our real world today. Releases from the reservoir simulate the Waters of Chaos. Our measurements of the Ice tell us how much water and ice will be added to the world's oceans. When we add that amount of water, the pool's level rises to indicate the new shoreline."

"When will the test be completed?" Toth asked.

"There's much to do. If all goes well, we will finish tomorrow afternoon." Osir looked to the Yellow Emissary for confirmation, and the Emissary nodded.

* * *

Setra sneered as Osir commenced his demonstration for the King. "The Fast Rise has begun. The First Surge came from the Spilling of the Cauldron on the Opposite Continent. Immediately, the Eastern Ocean poured through Sunda Pass and around Sahul. The World Ocean rose no more than the height of a man's ankle." Osir signaled, and the Yellow Emissary raised the control gate. Water coursed into the pool, but the rise was barely perceptible. Even Toth was unimpressed.

Unfazed, Osir went on. "The Second Surge occurred when rims of coastal ice broke free all over the world." Again he signaled the Emissary, and water poured from the reservoir. "It covered the Veil and now lifts our Valley Sea." This time the hydraulicon's rise was more dramatic, first covering Erytheia's docks and low-lying settlements, then major streets in the heart of town. Even in Berenicia, which generally sat higher, many seaside buildings were swamped. Osir's audience seemed surprised but hardly alarmed.

"So we abandon some fields and rebuild a few docks." Setra winked toward the assembled officials, convinced he was discrediting Osir's science. "Hardly reason for panic."

"And, still, the Third Surge is to come," Osir continued. "At this moment, the Second Surge shakes gigantic ice shelves loose from all the earth's cold coastal lands." The Yellow Emissary released more carefully measured water. The onlookers squirmed when it sloshed over the low wall that protected Erytheia's marketplace.

"And how soon will this come to pass?" Toth asked earnestly.

"When crocodiles fly!" responded Setra.

"Within days!" responded Osir somberly, ignoring Setra.

"How bad will it be?"

"Exactly as you see here, if our calculations are correct. But, still, the Fourth Surge comes."

"Another!"

"Our models and transforms say the worst will come when a vast ice basin slides from the Southern Continent into the sea." The Yellow Emissary opened the hydraulicon's main gate allowing water to flow freely. Toth, priests, and Geometers gasped in unison as water rose three manheights, in miniature, and breached the palaces of both cities. Among major structures on Erytheia's waterfront, only the Sacred Pyramid remained dry, and waves lapped against its portico.

"I fear there's more you have to tell, Osir," Toth said.

"The Fast Rise finishes here, but the Slow Rise continues. All the ice mountains of the world are melting, and that will go on for centuries, even millennia." He nodded. The Yellow Emissary slowly lowered the reservoir's gate, and released a relentless flow. One village, town, or city after another was inundated. Finally, the Red Island itself sank beneath the waves.

"The First Terrace?" shouted Setra. "You contend the Waters of Chaos will reach the First Terrace? Where then can we find refuge?"

"The Valley of the Great River is our only option. We must claim the land from Kom Ombo to Lion Rock and make our home at the great bend known as Thinis." He pointed dramatically to a map unfurled on a stone table. "If we seek refuge below the First Terrace, our cities and lands will be covered again and again by rising waters. In the East, we saw how such miscalculation can ruin a nation. Now it is *our* Realm's turn, and we must choose wisely. It is better to build a lasting refuge than to be refugees forever. Even so, our descendants must remain vigilant in future millennia, always ready to build higher pyramids on higher ground, for there is much ice left in the world's cold lands."

"But Thinis is far from the sea. How will our people survive?" Toth asked.

"We must change our way of life. Like Egians, we'll plant crops beside the Great River, and its floods will nurture them year after year."

"And we'll all get the Big Neck!" laughed Setra, holding his hands beneath his chin to mimic a huge goiter.

"Traders will bring a steady supply of seaweed from the coast," argued Osir. "We'll need salt, too, but river navigation will be clear for moving goods since the sea will soon cover the rapids at Twin Falls."

Setra shrugged. "We've wasted too much time on this idle show. The festivities of the equinox are underway. I've seen enough." He stalked from the hydraulicon. Osir looked to the King, who should have been upset by Setra's disrespect for him, if not for Osir.

"This is nothing more than wild speculation!" the King said, then exited in Setra's wake. Osir looked to Toth in despair.

"May the gods help us!" Toth said as the other officials left the hydraulicon.

Osir, Toth, and the Yellow Emissary stood in silence, perplexed by the King's intransigence. "What more can we do?" Osir asked.

"Perhaps the sea gauge! If a second peg has been covered by water, Rahn Ammon may reconsider."

Osir and Toth walked to the shore at sunset. Kneeling at the water's edge inside the dark turret, Osir looked for the pegs, but found none.

"Someone has stolen them!" Toth said.

Osir stepped into the water and felt the wall. Placing his fingertips into the holes, he worked his way down. Elbow-deep, he suddenly exclaimed, "I've got it! I've found a peg. No," he said, reaching deeper, "I've found ten pegs. They're all here. The water has risen the height of a man's knee in a single day. That's more than we predicted. Clearly, the end is near."

"We must convince the King, but even this may not be enough." Toth thought for a moment. "If he won't heed your science, perhaps he will heed my sorcery."

* * *

Toth eyed the night sky as he and Osir ambled to the Sacred Pyramid. Broken clouds drifted over the Great River, but not enough to obscure Toth's cherished constellations. "The heavens have changed. Almost as long as our people have studied the skies, the Virgin has marked the coming of spring, just as your likeness, the swordsman Sahu-Orion, heralds the coming of winter. Now the Lion, to which Lion Rock is dedicated, rises later each year. Today is the equinox. Let us see which constellation hails the dawn."

From atop the Sacred Pyramid, they stared at the predawn sky. "It is time," Toth said with longing in his voice, "and where is the Virgin, our guide to the heavens?"

"Nowhere to be seen," Osir said. "There!" he exclaimed. "What is that?" A single sparkle of light in a different constellation appeared, then disappeared immediately behind a passing cloud. It was the brightest star of the Lion.

"That's it!" Toth shouted. "The end of an age. Surely Rahn Ammon will pay attention to such an auspicious sign. We must alert him this instant!" Then, he smiled wryly and confessed with a wink. "Celestial changes take place gradually. I've watched this star's precession for most of my life. Dawn, too, comes gradually, and timing is crucial to every illusion. What Rahn Ammon doesn't know won't hurt him and indeed may help our cause. Already I've sent word to the palace guards to be on watch. Surely they have reported this new harbinger of spring to General Setra by now."

Osir and Toth rushed to the sunken, stone-walled Sacred Lake where the King performed his regular morning ritual. Bathing in hallowed waters, the King looked up and made his annoyance known.

"The skies have changed!" Toth boldly proclaimed. "The Virgin abandons her house. The Lion now heralds the Sun."

"Nonsense!" the King said. "Surely someone would have informed me." He gestured toward Setra, who knelt in prayer beside the lake. "Is there any truth to this, General Setra? Has the Lion replaced the Virgin?"

"No," Setra said. "Surely I would have been informed."

"Perhaps we should question the palace guards," Toth suggested.

Setra blinked. "Oh, perhaps a guard did mention some odd celestial illusion."

As he spoke, the intervening cloud drifted, and the bright eye of the Lion sparkled low on the horizon. Then, suddenly the sun burst behind it.

"Indeed, the Lion now heralds the sun!" shouted Toth.

"You knew of this portentous event, Setra, and didn't inform me?" the King shouted.

"There was no need to trouble you, Sire," Setra said.

"You deliberately withheld vital information because it would prove General Osir correct. Now, you lie to hide your deception."

"No!" Setra shouted desperately. "I withheld nothing. The Lion is unimportant."

"You deceived me. I should never have trusted you. How many lives this delay may cost! You are relieved of your command." Rahn Ammon turned to Osir, "Henceforth, you are in charge. Declare the Divine Right Order. Issue the call of 'Ma'at.' Lead the exodus. So let it be done!"

Setra left, seething at his own undoing.

"Exhume the Royal Barge," General Osir commanded.

* * *

As soon as his orders were issued, Osir ran to warn Princess Bera of the coming Ma'at. He entered the palace and rushed down the dark corridor. At the doorway of his family quarters he heard hushed voices.

"You shouldn't be here, Setra," Bera said. "You must go. Osir will…"

"Osir be damned. I'm here to…" He stopped mid-sentence as Osir stepped into the room. Bera held Horesh tightly to her bosom.

"Don't let me interrupt you," Osir said sarcastically. "What do you want?"

"I'm here to claim my rightful heir."

"What! Your heir?"

"Bera should be my wife and Horesh my son.

"You have no wife, no heir. Horesh is my son."

"You stole everything that is rightfully mine. You won every triumph that belonged to me. Through Toth's sorcery, you destroyed Rahn Ammon's faith in me. The Divine Right Order has failed. You need no longer fear my devotion to its folly. Henceforth, I'll live by no man's rules. Chaos shall be my guide."

"It was your deceit and blind faith in the Divine Right Order that denied your destiny, Setra. I played no part in your downfall."

"Don't renounce all that is good in the Divine Right Order, Setra," Bera pleaded. "Tempered with reason, it is our only hope. Without it, we'll perish like Drevids."

"Join us, Setra. Forget the past and make a new future with us," Osir said.

"No, Osir. My fate is sealed. I can't turn back." His voice quavered as he spoke.

"Then we'll next meet as enemies, never again comrades as before."

"So be it," Setra said. He touched the little boy's shoulder, looked sadly into Bera's eyes, then stalked out the door. His footsteps echoed down the long corridor like nails hammered into a coffin.

Osir turned quickly to Bera. "The Ma'at has begun. Prepare to depart Erytheia. I must go to the harbor and summon all ships to assist in the evacuation."

* * *

Moored boats pounded the docks. Waves crashed the seawall. As Osir leaped aboard the *Eastern Star*, the seawall breached, and seawater flooded the streets. Finally the disaster was clear to all, and ships at sea headed to port. Seasoned captains knew they would be needed when Ma'at was declared.

"Where's the Yellow Emissary?" Osir asked the *Star*'s first mate.

"He's doing more research. Left before daybreak."

"The hydraulicon!" Osir exclaimed, and he bolted through the streets. Panic seized Erytheia as Chosen Ones rushed to escape, and Commoners realized they were not included in the evacuation plan. *How sad*, he lamented. *There aren't enough ships on the whole Valley Sea to evacuate this island's entire populace.*

It's odd, Osir thought as he watched the lucky ones pass by, *what people consider important when their world is about to end.* Despite the tragedy, he almost laughed at the sight of a man running with a large pack on his back topped by, of all things, an old wooden chair with one leg missing. Soldiers cordoned the harbor and repelled hoards of desperate Commoners, often with deadly force.

Near the palace, Osir saw first-hand the orderly evacuation readied for the King and his protectors. Priests and soldiers had rapidly unearthed the Royal Barge and reassembled it for the ceremonial exodus. Already, Toth had prepared his Book of Truths for its journey. Faithful followers assisted and awaited orders. Osir recognized the King's silhouette as Rahn Ammon knelt atop the Sacred Pyramid in prayer for his people one last time. Bera and Horesh stood among the Chosen. Osir hugged her and held his son's hand.

"Rahn Ammon is distraught," Bera said, worry showing on her face.

"Go to him," Osir said. "Come with me, son. Your mother is needed here."

Delaying the Ma'at cost many lives. Now guilt weighs heavy on Rahn Ammon's heart.

As Osir neared the hydraulicon with Horesh on his arm, he glanced back at the pyramid. The King supped the ritual sacrament. The Royal Barge maneuvered into place on waves that lapped near the pyramid's base.

Osir and Horesh entered the apse, poorly lit with a flickering torch. He called out, but no answer came. He called again. No answer. Moving close to the pool, he searched its dark waters. There, at the edge, floated a lifeless body. Blood oozed from the Yellow Emissary's scalp and darkened the model sea around him.

True to his vow, this man of the sea has returned to the "sea" in death.

Chronicle 54: The Chaos

"Don't look!" Osir commanded Horesh. He set the child down. "Run! Run to your mother! Go quickly!" As he tugged the emissary's body, Osir heard the clink of iron at his back and felt a slash in his side. He turned as the assailant swung again, this time sinking the blade deep in his right arm.

The chamber dimmed as Osir's torch fell to the floor, nearly extinguished. He reached for his sword but found in horror that he could no longer lift his arm. Grabbing instead the dirktooth dagger, with his left hand he blindly slashed the darkness. The redsilver blade met no resistance. Through blinding rage, he spotted a dim form lurking in shadow. He retrieved his fallen torch, fanned it back to life, and faced his attacker. Finally, Setra's contorted face moved into view. "I have a new destiny!" Setra screamed. "I'll lead the Commoners abandoned by their King."

"The Chosen can survive the exodus, but Commoners cannot, not on their own. No training. No Secrets of the Ages. No Divine Right Order. Would you deny refuge to all the People of the Living Sun merely for you own false glory?" Osir said in disgust.

"Yes . . . and you and the man who stood beside you and all the King's men...if that's what it takes."

Osir struggled to remain conscious and make sense of Setra's strange words. "There was no man beside me. I faced you alone."

"Another soldier ...a second man...I struck him in the dark?"

"No, Setra. There was only Horesh." The realization hit both men at once. "Horesh! Where are you?" Osir yelled. Swinging the torch frantically, he found the little body face down on the floor.

"I...didn't know. I wouldn't have hurt my little Horesh. I didn't know," Setra babbled. A pool of blood, mingled with clear liquid, formed beneath the boy's face. Before Osir could reach him, his own injuries won out, and he fell headlong into the water.

* * *

Bera watched her brother complete his last ritual act in Erytheia. Alone at the summit, Rahn Ammon emptied the sacramental cup. Slowly, laboriously he descended the steps. Bera met him at the base. "Are you ill?" she asked when she saw his halting steps and pale countenance.

"Take me to the palace," he said feebly. She signaled for Ketoh to join them. In the short walk, the King became noticeably weaker. Once inside, he collapsed. "Poison," he whispered, ". . . in the sacrament. Take me to my throne...the only fit place for a King to die. Carry on, beloved sister," he said as she placed him on the throne. He looked deeply into her eyes one last time, revealing a brother's love for the first since childhood. "My body must ascend the Sacred Pyramid, board the Royal Barge, and be borne away by it. The rightful King must be with his people when Ma'at is declared. It is my destiny. It is the Divine Right Way."

"It was Setra, wasn't it?" she said. "He's crazed."

Rahn Ammon nodded. "Yes," he said. "The Divine Right Order must be enforced. Ma'at must be called as soon as the new King is anointed. Crown Osir in my stead, and you will be his queen. So let it be done." He closed his eyes in death.

Bera embraced him and sobbed with a sister's love that had never faltered.

* * *

Ketoh grabbed four loyal guards and ran to warn Osir of Setra's treachery. Inside the hydraulicon, he found the carnage. They pulled first Osir and then the Yellow Emissary from the pool. They heard soft moans in the darkness.

"Aba...Aba."

"Look here," a guard called, and Ketoh saw Horesh. Turning the little boy over, he recoiled at the sight. A vicious gash claimed the child's right eye. With Osir borne by the guards and Horesh held against his own chest, Ketoh ran to the palace. "Take them to our chamber," Bera cried as she and Toth rushed to assist. They placed them on the bed, both barely breathing, and sent the guards to their posts. "How did this happen?" Bera cried out in grief. "How could Setra have done this?"

"He's deranged. He must be stopped!" Ketoh raged.

"So try and stop him!" a voice boomed from the doorway behind Ketoh. The grizzled soldier, one of Setra's inner circle, raised his sword and lunged for Osir. Ketoh drew his own sword and blocked the assailant. Ketoh's slash stopped the man cold.

"Behind you!" Toth yelled as two more rogues entered. Lunging and parrying, hacking and slashing, Ketoh set upon them. Soon, both men, their sword arms severed, lay in lifeless heaps.

"The struggle has begun," Bera said. "They won't stop until my beloved Osi is dead."

"They think he is," Ketoh said. "Setra left him for dead, and now these thugs can keep a secret as well as any." He nodded toward the dead soldiers.

"In that case, Setra will seize a ship and head for Berenicia," Bera said. "He'll claim the crown as soon as the Chosen Ones of Erytheia land. We must stop him."

"You must lead in Osir's stead," Toth said. Bera winced, and Toth added, "...until he is well again."

* * *

"If only we can reach Berenicia ahead of Setra," Bera said. "Osi is revered there, and Setra has not yet spread his poison." She examined her unconscious husband. Would he live to become King or die of his wounds? She examined her young son. The eye was lost, but his life did not appear to be in danger. Horesh slept peacefully, one hand resting on his father's arm.

"I have a plan!" Toth said. He bolted from the room and rushed to his chambers.

Horesh roused and stared at Osir. "Is Aba...sleeping?" he asked, ignoring the bandage that covered half his face. A tear rolled down his other cheek.

"Father is sick, but he won't die." *There! I've said it. I've promised my son that his father will live. Now it must be true.* She embraced Horesh.

"Mommy! Where is my eye?" Horesh asked, feeling the bandage.

"Setra took it," Bera said bitterly. The boy started to cry, and she realized she had spoken too harshly. "But Toth now holds it for safekeeping," she said to soothe his fears.

Toth strode back into the room. "I have a plan for Berenicia," he said, "but timing is crucial. We must work quickly before Setra learns what we're up to." Toth opened the small ebony chest he held under his arm. Taking a vial from the box with one hand and opening Osir's mouth with the other, he placed a tiny drop of liquid on Osir's tongue.

"May I help?" the child asked.

"Here, little man, take this flint. Place it between your father's teeth." Horesh complied, gently guiding the smooth stone into place. Toth turned to Bera, "I've given Osir some herbs that will help him rest. The stone will keep him from suffocating."

"Please give him my eye to watch over him until he is well."

Toth was visibly touched by the youngster's request. "Certainly, my child, I'll see to it." Toth reached into his ebony box and pretended to pull the boy's eye from it. "Here, Osir, take this token of your son's love for protection in your travail." He pried open a clenched fist and placed his own sapphire ring in Osir's palm. Toth held Osir's hand as he prayed.

"Berenicia?" Bera asked. "Do you really think we can go there. Setra's men are sure to watch our every move."

"He knows Rahn Ammon's body must be taken to Berenicia. He won't try to stop it, else the people would know he killed the King," Toth said. "Bera, you must accompany the King's sarcophagus to Berenicia."

"But I need to be near Osi," she protested.

"Perhaps, my dear, perhaps," Toth replied, smiling enigmatically.

* * *

The King's body reposed in a finely carved sarcophagus beside the throne. In the chamber next door lay the modest coffin of the fallen hero, Osir. The rising waters left no time for embalming and little time for ceremony. As the abbreviated ritual began, Bera and Horesh stood by the King's sarcophagus while priests and Geometers paid their last respects to the King. Each mourner then passed through the adjoining room and paid final tribute to General Osir, as well.

Ketoh and other faithful officers formed an honor guard to watch over the King's remains. Dressed in his royal finery and wearing the crown of the Realm, he looked somehow more a king in death than ever in life. "A good man brought to power too soon," Bera said as she viewed the pall.

Ritual blessings and prayers were spoken and, one by one, the last guests filed out. Finally only Toth, Bera, Horesh, and Ketoh remained for an intimate farewell. Guards kept watch outside the door. All doors were closed, and the coffin's lid was sealed.

* * *

The Royal Barge awaited. "Make way! Make way!" shouted the pallbearers. "Make way!" they insisted as they penetrated the mob. Water stood knee deep in the marketplace. Carts and stalls sloshed in splintered heaps against abandoned shops. Bodies sloshed, too, some drowned, others trampled. Warily, Ketoh surveyed the scene, constantly on the lookout for Setra's men. Rising water surged over the docks with every incoming wave. As they watched, a small boat crashed through the crowd and dashed to pieces against a temple wall. "Lucky wretches," Ketoh said of the five or so Commoners in its path. "Better to die quickly than to perish in the coming Chaos."

Once aboard the Royal Barge, Bera stood stoically beside the coffin. Ketoh and Toth stayed beside her, and Ketoh held Horesh's tiny hand.

Trumpets blared and drums pounded as the barge set sail. Off shore, the fleet of the faithful awaited the Royal Barge. Ketoh counted at least 20 vessels, but the *Crown of Erytheia* was not among them. "The *Crown* is missing!" Ketoh whispered to Toth. "Setra is well on his way." The wails and pleas of doomed Commoners lasted long after the fleet pulled into open sea.

* * *

The docks of Berenicia were a welcome sight after the sad journey from Erytheia. Hundreds of vessels, large and small, crowded the bay. Many had been scuttled to form a temporary breakwater. Others bobbed and thrashed in the Waters of Chaos. Passengers jumped from gunwale to gunwale, some crossing ten or more decks to reach shore. With each wave, the thump of wooden hulls met the clang of redsilver as barquentines jostled helplessly in the surging sea. As Ketoh predicted, the *Crown* had already arrived. "Setra and his cronies are here. You can be certain they announced the King's death and blamed Osir. Trust no one," he warned, but thousands awaited their King's remains.

"Make way!" barked soldiers guarding the port.

"You there!" called one of Setra's thugs. "Wait up! My orders are to inspect everything. I must open that coffin."

"Surely you won't dishonor our King," Toth replied.

"Orders., I must look inside every container, coffin or not."

"Let the King rest in peace!" cried Bera. "Have you no respect?"

"This coffin must be opened, King or no King," he said firmly. "Lift the lid."

Bera nodded to Ketoh. When the lid was barely raised, the blusterous bully gagged at the stench of decay.

"Seal it!" he yelled between coughs. "I've seen enough!" But he had seen nothing.

The honor guard eased the sarcophagus onto its caisson and began the final procession to the King's mastaba ready and waiting beside the Sacred Pyramid. The throng in the plaza pressed forward until progress was no longer possible.

"Something's wrong!" Bera said. "The faithful would never block their King on his way to the grave."

Ketoh agreed. "This must be Setra's doing."

"He must be stopped!" Toth said.

"No one can stop me now!" Setra's voice sent chills up Ketoh's spine as he turned and met the angry eyes. It was the mad, cold voice of a man without conscience. "Seize them!" Setra commanded. "Teach them what happens to swine who poison our beloved King." Setra's squad separated from the crowd and surrounded the royal party. Rough hands grabbed

Bera and Horesh. Sword tips nudged Toth's and Ketoh's backs. "Where is Osir?" Setra asked.

"He's dead, you fiend! Killed by your hand!" Bera shouted.

"Dead because he killed our King!" Setra retorted.

"Dead because of your iniquity!" Bera screamed.

"Then where are his remains?" Setra asked. "My men searched the Royal Barge. He wasn't aboard."

"He was entombed on Erytheia!" cried Bera.

"Don't lie to me. I know you too well, and this I know: Neither you nor Ketoh would have left his body behind."

Setra looked about. "Give me my sword!" He stared suspiciously at the funeral caisson while an aide presented a leather bundle. He theatrically unwrapped the sword and sheath.

"You bastard!" Ketoh yelled when he saw the dirktooth sword in Setra's hand. Lunging toward Setra, he tried futilely to break away from his captors.

Setra cast an evil smile as he grabbed Horesh's arm and raised the sword above his head. "Deliver Osir's body to me, woman, else here and now I will claim my rightful heir."

Bera jerked free and ran to her son's side. "I'll tell, but first you must vow by all that is sacred never to harm my son again."

"I love Horesh. He's my heir. I would never hurt him. You have my word!" Setra smiled tenderly as he tousled Horesh's hair and wistfully nudged the boy toward his mother.

"Let Ketoh and Toth go. They have no reason to fight you anymore," Bera said.

Setra nodded to his henchmen. Toth and Ketoh moved to opposite ends of the ornate coffin and opened its stone lid. There, in the overpowering stench of decay, lay not the King's body but Osir's.

"And is he dead?" Setra stood aside as wary as a man who thinks he may have killed a serpent.

"Do you fear this man even in death? Can't you look inside?" Ketoh asked.

"Don't you trust your own senses?" Toth asked.

"This corpse looks too fresh to cause such a smell of death! I want proof!" He mounted the caisson and poised to plunge the dirktooth sword into Osir's chest.

"Here," Toth yelled, blocking Setra's move. "This is your proof . . . if you have the stomach for it." He reached into the coffin, pulled a severed arm from the body, and dashed it at Setra's feet. Setra's stomach churned as he recoiled from the putrid limb. He slipped Osir's sword into the scabbard at his waist and jumped down from the caisson.

As if unsure of his own emotions, Setra paused for a moment then again unsheathed the sword. Ketoh readied himself. In a final show of contempt, Setra tossed the sword into the coffin. "Here," he said. "I have no need for this trinket."

CHAPTER 25

Search Log 43: Deception

Every moment in Hurghada was a frantic rush of planning, purchasing, and preparation. Cash-on-hand was running low, so first thing Saturday morning they cashed in one of the three cruise tickets bought in Cairo.

Rick in jeans and Sari in skirt and blouse boarded the cruise boat with almost no sleep or rest since Friday morning. Still, her dark eyes sparkled as she untied her scarf and stuffed it in Rick's pocket. "For safe keeping," she said, "I won't be needing it for a while."

A porter met them, examined their tickets, and ordered two stevedores to fetch their luggage. Young and strong though they were, the workers frowned at the huge pile and grumbled bitterly when they spotted an enormous trunk underneath. Rick and Sari watched from the deck as the baggage came aboard, and Rick followed each item to a fancy stateroom. Sari watched anxiously as they tried to lift the trunk, called for help, and finally lugged the monstrous thing aboard. Once inside, Rick stood in a corner of the stateroom, and Sari followed behind while four men maneuvered the box awkwardly through the hatch. Everyone, especially the stevedores, gave a sigh of relief when the trunk cleared its final obstacle. At that moment, however, the purser stepped inside and politely asked to see the contents.

They hoped this wouldn't happen and thought they'd almost made it. With no alternative, Rick unbuckled the straps and let their buckles clank to the sides. He searched his pockets for a key and unlocked the two big latches in front. Then he opened the lid, chatting all the while. The purser stared quizzically at the contents. Inside was the skin and frame of the folding boat, tarps, assorted jugs, a swim mask, snorkel, tire pump, Rick's venerable SVEA backpacker's stove, and enough video equipment for a Japanese safari–everything, it seemed, but scuba gear. On top of the jumble lay five kilos of rice and a half-liter bottle of something that looked like motor oil. He picked up a battery pack for a portable computer, started to speak, then shifted his attention to a stack of heavy objects wrapped in black plastic.

"Extra weights . . . going deep," Rick explained casually in response to the purser's glare.

The man handled it well, in spite of his consternation, for they were his customers, after all. "This isn't a freighter," he joked. "Won't this be in your way?"

"Oh, we'll make do," Rick replied. "We plan on camping and sea kayaking after the cruise, and we have nowhere else to store our gear." The purser looked back at the stack of batteries.

"I'm a writer. I need power for my laptop," Rick explained. "I didn't know whether your ship would have DC outlets."

"Of course, we have outlets . . . but we don't have much storage for passengers. This box will have to stay in your stateroom, and it will be very difficult for our crew to clean your quarters."

"Oh, that's alright," Rick said, maybe a little too eagerly. "Just have them leave fresh linens outside the door each morning. My wife and I will take care of the rest." Rick conspicuously closed and locked the box as the men departed. When the door closed, he quickly reopened the box and began stowing the gear in a closet-like cabinet, the stateroom's only concealed storage space.

Sari then left the boat, alone and unnoticed, heading into nearby shops as if she needed to purchase some last-minute items. Shortly before departure, she returned with Jared on her arm. "Welcome back, Mr. Caisson, Mrs. Caisson," the purser said.

Sari presented her passport and stamped ticket, Jared presented Rick's passport and stamped ticket, and they walked on board. Meanwhile, Rick lay quietly in the trunk, empty except for himself and a soft pillow. This was only the second "twin trick" of their lives, and so far it had gone perfectly.

Finally, as the *Lali-bella* pulled away, Sari and Jared strolled on deck with abandon, meeting fellow passengers, who were polite enough but clearly shocked at the mismatched couple, while Jared enjoyed a couple of beers. After little more than an hour, they disappeared, presumably to do whatever couples do on second honeymoons.

"Where the hell is Rick?" Jared asked. He searched the closet, then opened the box. In it lay Rick holding a wooden tent stake to his chest as if impaled. *Ah, clever. This way no one could spot him when we walked in.* They needed rest more than laughter, however, so Sari climbed to the fold-down bunk, and the brothers sprawled on the double bed below. Exhausted, they caught their first real sleep in almost three days.

They awoke in time for dinner, and a glance out the porthole confirmed they were far out to sea. This time, Rick went to the lounge with Sari, letting her do most of the talking until he had picked up on names and faces. Having been too busy to notice as he supervised the loading, Rick was truly impressed by what he saw. The yacht itself was more than 100 feet long, and every inch of it said luxury. From hull to bridge, the entire craft was made of wood, and yet every fixture and feature was obviously brand new, a rare combination in the modern era when most boaters opt for fiberglass. Real wood and brass brought a sense of quality, stability, timelessness.

In the main lounge, a lavish dinner had been laid out for all comers. The alabaster top of the dining table glowed with soft light from fixtures imbedded in the parquet floor. Seafood, steaks, and local delicacies piled high in a presentation worthy of haute cuisine. Famished from hard work and long sleep, Rick and Sari mounded their plates in presentations anything but elegant and moved to the comfort of thickly padded sofas. Placing their dishes on coffee tables, also alabaster and glowing with muted light from the floor, they ate their fill and chatted with fellow travelers. Sari delicately managed the difficult task of eating beneath the black veil.

"Excuse me. I'll only be a moment," Rick said and returned to the stateroom. He handed a wrinkled napkin to his brother and summarized the conversation underway. A few minutes later, Jared emerged wearing identical clothes for the first time since age ten when they rebelled against the "twinsy" cuteness imposed by their parents.

"Hon, I think I'll have a second helping," he said nonchalantly as he passed Sari. "Want anything?"

"No," she said, "but please watch what you eat. This trip lasts a week, and they'll be overfeeding us all the way." He returned with his plate piled as high as Rick's had been. Passengers gawked as their new acquaintance devoured bite after bite of the rich food. Sari ignored them. When Jared finally set his empty plate aside, she looked at him and said with a straight face. "That's better, dear. At least you didn't overdo it the first night."

As they lingered over coffee, a tanned gentleman rose from his table and sauntered over. "Hello, I'm Jean Claude Allard, your dive master and instructor. I'm sorry you missed today's dives. The dive deck will open at 8:00 a.m. tomorrow. We should be anchored off the Brothers Islands by then. If there is anything I can do to make your dive more enjoyable, please don't hesitate to ask." His accent suited the posh surroundings.

"My wife doesn't swim, but I'll be there first thing. I look forward to it. I wasn't able to participate this afternoon due to extreme exhaustion."

"A Frenchman understands such matters," he said with a knowing smile. "I'll see you in the morning."

* * *

They awoke to find two low, stark islands on the starboard side. Rising more than a mile from deep sea bottom, the Brothers would have been little more than jagged rocks if not for the old British lighthouse declaring them an outpost of the civilized world. Peering from the upper bunk, Sari suppressed a giggle as she named one of the islands Brother Rick and the other Brother Jared. "I'm going to check out my namesake," Rick boasted as he rose to take the first dive. A few minutes later he appeared on deck at 8:00 a.m. sharp. The dive deck, however, was already crowded with eager divers, and he couldn't take the plunge until half an hour later. When he did, it was the bluest world he had ever known.

Sari enjoyed a leisurely breakfast, then took coffee and food back to the room. "I just love breakfast," she said to fellow passengers, who seemed surprised that she wanted more after eating plenty in their presence. Jared, famished by that time, appreciated every bite, knowing he couldn't go out until Rick returned from Brother Rick Island.

After reboarding the *Lali-bella*, Rick hung around to exchange stories with fellow divers. Finally near noon he returned to the stateroom. As the door closed behind him, Sari gushed, "How did it go?"

"It was hilarious! I jumped in last, so it took them a while, but you should have seen their faces when they learned I was only snorkeling. And when it was over, I hung around like a 'poser' and traded stories as if my dive had been on par with theirs. It was all I could do to keep from laughing."

"Did you find anything?" Jared asked.

"Oh, yeah. Two remarkably well preserved ships. The sea was beautiful, the fish fantastic, and the wrecks interesting as hell. But there's nothing out there that looks like a pyramid...nothing I could spot from the surface, at least."

"Just as I expected. I don't think we'll find anything until we get into patch corals. The Brothers are just small islands with fringing reefs. There must be a fascinating story explaining why such pinnacles rise from so deep, but it must be geologic, not archaeological."

"Is that why you let me take the first swim?" Rick asked.

"No. We'll take turns. I'll go out this afternoon, and you can dive at our next stop. But I'm not expecting much there either. It's another mid-sea reef."

"Oh, I'm not complaining. The *Aida* was spectacular, even from far above. It's resting on a slope, in two pieces but mostly intact. Everyone else is here to see fish and corals, so they're more than satisfied with shipwrecks. Of course, that's what separates us from most divers...other than not diving, that is."

"For us, that's the problem with dive cruises like this. They go to offshore islands because fringing reefs have everything sport divers want and are a lot more approachable than patch reefs in places like Foul Bay. The Cap'n can anchor in deep water right next to some of the most spectacular sights in the sea. It's less risky. I don't blame them, but it works against us," Jared complained.

"You're right, but keep your eyes open. These islands were here through the Ice Ages, too. They may have served as stopovers on Red Sea voyages or as havens in storms. If so, they may have had harbors and buildings, if not pyramids."

"True. But harbors and buildings may be impossible to recognize under coral."

"Depends on how big they are . . . and anything else that may distinguish them. Long walls, for example."

"Granted."

* * *

Early in the week, Jared broached the touchy question, "Who will do Foul Bay?" Both brothers desperately wanted the job, but the issue would be decided by one consideration. "Who stands the better chance of coming back alive...with the data?"

"Age will be a factor," Rick argued, for he was 22 minutes younger than Jared.

"Yes," Jared quickly retorted, "maturity is essential."

"Seriously," Sari said, "who's the better swimmer?" Rick won that round.

"Who knows computers?" Rick added, and he won that round.

"But this is mostly about geographic information technology–GIS, GPS, remote sensing, depth finders. Who knows how to operate that particular type of electronic equipment?" Jared countered. He won that round.

"There's still time to learn," Rick countered.

"Who knows the data?" Jared asked, and he won again.

In the end, it was a draw.

By midweek, after several more rounds of discussion, debate, and argumentation, the decision was made, and all three swore never to reveal the answer.

* * *

The rest of the week was an unbroken string of pleasures. Each meal was excellent, each swim magnificent. For Sari and the active "Brother on Deck," whichever that might be, evenings were filled with conversation and laughter and holiday goodwill. Sari, especially, delighted in the charade as she switched from one escort to the other. With a few notable exceptions, their fellow passengers turned out to be full of life, as much fun as any group they had ever encountered. It reminded them of a college spring break, except that conspicuous affluence had replaced student poverty. "The Caissons" were accepted as good company, if somewhat quirky for having paid good money to snorkel among real divers in the best diving waters on earth. Their presumed status as constant lovers, however, did wonders to bolster respect among the crew and passengers.

Even the "Brother in a Box" was in Sari's company much of the time, since she didn't go out to swim, and that would have been a treat under any circumstance. Even when she wasn't there, Jared didn't mind the isolation of the stateroom. In that quiet, restful time it was pleasant to think and dream and let his mind wander home to Ellie. Still, there was no denying he liked the times when Sari was there, constantly but unconsciously reminding him of their first evening in Cairo. Best of all were the hours when all three of them holed up in the cramped stateroom, just killing time and making jokes and laughing at the jokes they made.

* * *

Then, there was that afternoon...

Rick sat with three men playing backgammon and drinking strong sweet mint tea, his back to the staterooms. Suddenly, all play ceased. The other players stared behind him, transfixed in shock and awe. He wheeled around. There stood Sari in a stunning one-piece swim suit. A vivid royal blue--sensuous--not revealing by Western standards but sensuous beyond measure in the middle of burqa land.

Winking toward Rick, Sari smiled and mouthed, "No mo' BMO." Then she moved on to the sun deck where she joined other sunbathers and engaged in lively banter.

* * *

At week's end, after rounding Ras Banas, the cruise reached its southernmost point and anchored for the night off Zabargad, also known as St. John's Island. As the sun sank low in the west, Jared stood on deck and faced the desolate mainland. After nearly two years of planning, scheming, working, and dreaming, he finally stood before Foul Bay, the ageless body of water that held the key to ages past. Sari stood beside him. Together they stared, entranced, watching a sky almost as red as the thin line of hills surrounding Foul Bay. Soon water, land, and sky merged in a single redness and finally into black. He hugged her and gently kissed her hair.

"Tonight?" she asked.

"Tonight," he answered.

Search Log 44: Sailing the *River Styx*

As the sleek ivory yacht faded into darkness and distance, the designated Caisson recalled his surreptitious departure and breathed a long, slow sigh of relief. In the planning stage, it seemed easy enough to say, "We'll assemble the kayak in early evening and slip it into the water as soon as things quiet down on board." But quiet is a relative term on a luxury cruiser loaded with vacationers bent on partying. The plan demanded absolute quiet, everyone asleep, and that seldom came before three or four o'clock in the morning, sometimes not until dawn. Finally at sea, Caisson estimated about an hour left before daybreak to paddle out of sight and find a hiding place on Zabargad. He wouldn't know until morning if there were boats nearby or people ashore who might spot his tiny craft in daylight. He would, of course, assume the worst until he could scout the island and scan the sea in full daylight.

From here, he judged, the tip of Ras Banas must lie about 30 miles to the northwest and most of Foul Bay's shore no more than 50 miles distant in the west and southwest. Not that he expected to reach the mainland. Zabargad would be his base of operations for the next two weeks, and the nearby reefs he'd studied for so long would be his domain. All open water crossings would be at night, but the actual work over each reef would require daylight. Then, he would have no choice but to stay alert and take his chances. Patrol boats near shore and gun emplacements on the coastal hills were his greatest concerns. Caisson figured he could cover about 30 miles a day stroking hard in the open sea, but he hoped that wouldn't be necessary.

He knew the layout of rocks awash in Foul Bay almost by heart, but there was no need to rely on memory. Weeks before, Ed Field had scanned topographic maps and hydrologic charts and stored all those minute details in Jared's laptop. Every shoreline, every navigational feature was there, carefully registered to precise geographic coordinates. What a pity Ed couldn't be here to see the system in action. The computer, now stowed in a drybag beneath the kayak's deck, would enable Caisson to view the map on screen in full color. The GPS, also onboard, would tell him precisely where he was on the earth's surface and on the chart. He had spent hours charging extra batteries from the yacht's DC power system. As long as the electronics held up, he would always know his exact position and could navigate from reef to reef, even at night, without the navigational skills that sailors have relied on for millennia. On the other hand, if either the GPS or the computer were to fail, he would have to guide on shore features, a prospect that was difficult at best, unreliable in foul weather, and impossible at night. What a pity Ed couldn't be on hand to fix the damned thing if it broke.

His immediate objective, however, was to find a sheltered spot on Zabargad where he could conceal himself and his kayak. *A cave is too much to hope for*, he thought. *A ravine leading up from the sea will suffice. Even in daylight I can creep up and reconnoiter without risk of detection. But, there'll be precious little time to find the right spot between dawn's first glow and full daylight, when I'll become a sitting duck.* He paddled forcefully in a wide arc around the island. He doubted the *Lali-bella* would circle Zabargad on its way out but wanted to be far away and hidden just in case. After 45 minutes of hard paddling, he stopped to catch his breath.

Caisson reached under the deck and removed the fieldstation from its cubbyhole. Both the computer and the GPS had been running on battery power since his departure. The screen, automatically suspended to conserve power, popped to life as soon as the lid was open. The first image centered on Zabargad. The GPS, set to record a new position every ten seconds, had marked the location of the yacht with a congestion of red "plus" marks. His subsequent route had been etched as a C-shaped trail of crossmarks. Where he had stroked hard and fast, they were far apart; where he had slowed, they were close together. The pattern showed that his navigation had been erratic at best. What had seemed like a smooth arc, showed up as a jerky, angular bow around the island. His current position, gaining a new cross every ten seconds, quickly became congested. *Better move on*, he thought. *Another hundred yards or so should do the trick.*

When the trail arced almost 180°, Caisson stopped paddling and placed his finger on the rubber-tipped pointer in the center of the keyboard. He double-clicked on an icon shaped like a magnifying glass and zoomed in. Holding the left button down, he selected a rectangular stretch of shoreline. When he released the button, that part of the island jumped to fill the entire screen, and he saw far more detail than before. Sure enough, not far ahead was a promising little indention in the shoreline, probably the mouth of a small ravine. He picked three more sites and ranked them in order of potential.

A hint of daylight silhouetted the island as Caisson reached site A. He didn't need much light to see white waves crashing and boiling in the throat of a jagged crevice.

It's hidden alright! No one will ever find my body inside that churning hell.

He headed for site B, stopping first at site D because it was on the way.

Promising, he thought as he focused on a shadowy wedge cut into shore. Moving closer, he saw seawater lapping gently against a jumble of boulders. Steep banks converged at the rear. A slight overhang offered shelter behind the boulders where runoff would pour from the gully above. *This is it*, he decided. *It has shelter of a sort in the rare event of rain and a ravine with access to higher ground. No need to look farther, at least not for now.*

Caisson broke through a line of surf and scraped bottom, then extricated himself and tied a line to the nearest boulder. The shelter turned out to be larger than he had guessed, ample for a tightly organized campsite. Fine smooth sand, slightly above waterline, made an ideal sleeping place. There was just enough room for the kayak, as well, but no way to drag it in without unloading. Immediately, he began ferrying equipment, all four hundred pounds of it, from "ship to shore."

After piling his gear in loosely ordered stacks, he slid the kayak into the hiding place. Just to be sure, he wrapped the boat in buff-colored canvas to hide its blue deck and black hull. The kayak, which Sari had christened the *River Styx*, thus served double duty as a blind for part of the camp. After a short rest, he collected rocks and constructed a wall in front of the gear. Once that was done, even a beachcomber strolling 30 feet away might not spot the camp. His bed lay immediately behind the boat, where he could peer through the boulders, revealing no more than a watchful eye.

Now I can relax, Caisson thought, as he inspected his lair from every possible vantage point. Only then did he feel safe firing up the backpacker's stove for tea. Flavored with honey and powdered milk, the hot brew warmed his throat and lulled tired muscles. After a second cup, he nestled into his sleeping bag against the morning chill and drifted off.

As the day wore on, the sleep that had begun so well grew fitful. Before noon, Caisson awoke to find himself drenched in sweat. Frantically, he unzipped the bag and bolted upright. That brought some relief but not as much as expected. Heat had begun in earnest and wouldn't let up till sunset. His only relief came from an occasional sea breeze, but the same terrain that made him safe blocked that breeze most of the day.

Sari had packed a bag of stealings from the galley. For one day only, he had plenty of good food prepared by an expert chef. Croissants, creamed eggs, and caviar. He chuckled at the irony of such dainty fare in such a rugged place. He brewed strong coffee and devoured the feast with all the enthusiasm it deserved.

After his elegant brunch, Caisson scouted the land immediately above camp and several hundred yards along the shore. Observing not a single sign of human life, he returned, washed his plate and utensils in a bubbling surf, and stashed the gear. Retrieving a military-style folding shovel, he chose a small ledge high beneath the overhang, dug an arm's length deeper into the wall, and cached his food supply. As a final precaution, he blocked the hole with stones to fend off marauding animals—just in case. Dripping with perspiration and smeared with dirt, he charged over the boulders and into the surf.

Ah, cool relief, at last.

With the noonday sun beaming on his face and chest, he floated in the gently rocking waves for 20 minutes or more. *Moments like this are always short-lived*, he thought, even alone in pristine wilderness. *It's time to search the island.*

Unfortunately, the best time to search fell precisely when the sun was highest. *If anyone lives on Zabargad, they will surely take siesta. If not, at least they'll be dulled by the heat. At the very least, they'll be blinded by sunlight reflecting off this bare ground.* With food, water, and gear in his knapsack, Caisson scrambled out of his pit and into the ravine above. Even wearing a cap and sunglasses, he groaned when the sun hit his face. The ravine's black rock radiated like baking stones.

From the sea, cone-shaped Zabargad could easily pass for an aging volcano. The narrow ravine snaked upward from the beach to the summit, inscribed four to 12 feet into the rocky slope. In the deep portions, Caisson walked upright for several yards at a time, then climbed the banks to look around. In the shallow portions, he crawled steadily upward, stopping every few feet to check his surroundings. Never did he spot a sign of anything that caused alarm. *But this place is miserable. God, is it miserable!* The heat came on like a sickness, and the rocks seared his hands. *Like a kiln*, he thought, and from then on that was the gully's name.

Zabargad was mean enough to kill a man but fortunately not big enough. In less than an hour, he reached the summit. In the face of a merciful breeze, he scanned the shore. The *Lali-bella* had left its morning dive site. Now it was a white speck on the northern horizon riding the blurred line between water and sky. All around was a sea of deep blue that gradually faded in every direction, even west where the land was lost in haze. Caisson turned full circle and saw no other vessel. He cautiously repeated the turn one sector at a time, carefully eyeing anything that stirred the still waters. Nothing appeared except the jagged outline of Rocky Island, which he knew already from the chart. Safe from the sea . . . at least for the present.

From the highest rocks, Caisson peered over the edge and down the slope. *Nothing to the north. Nothing to the east. Nothing to the south from which I climbed. Nothing to the west.* White sands fringed the island like the lacy hem of a dancer's whirling skirt. *Clogger Beach*, he thought, and gave it that name. Finally satisfied that all was clear, he spread a sky-blue poncho over a natural pit among the rocks and settled in. *I'll remain at the summit until nightfall, just to get one final view when any accommodating resident may reveal himself with a flash of light. When it comes to waiting and baking*, he reasoned, *one place is about as good as another.*

The poncho reflected most of the sun's rays, but too much light and heat still got through. Meanwhile, surrounding rocks radiated heat and blocked any hope of a breeze. *The Crucible*, he thought, and that's what he called it for the rest of his stay. Water every hour on the hour was life-giving, but never refreshing. His canteen started out tepid and grew hotter as the day wore on. He crunched the imaginary ice of winter. He swam in the chilled whitewater of his precious Smoky Mountains and drank to his heart's content.

Sleeping fitfully for the second time that day, he longed for night. When it came, he crawled out of the Crucible and stared into uninterrupted darkness in every direction. Satisfied, he descended through the Kiln, its rocks still warm to the touch but radiating little heat, like any potter's kiln at the end of a long day's work. An hour later, he reached Clogger Beach.

In starlight, Caisson loaded the kayak with precisely what he would need at sea. He slipped into the cockpit, strapped the computer beneath the deck just above his knees, and secured the palm-sized GPS antenna on top. This sensitive part of the fieldstation would thus remain dry and visible for navigation. Red crosses formed a ragged scatter as he maneuvered out of the cove, then a fairly straight trail heading out to sea.

Stroke, stroke, stroke. Each pull of the paddle drew him closer to the place that had occupied his mind for nearly two years, perhaps to answer the question that had plagued him since childhood. The reefs lay far ahead and wouldn't be reached until dawn. In the featureless watery night, there was little to be gained by watching the sea. Instead, Caisson watched the screen and soon learned to steer by it as well as any pilot with sextant and chart. Once each hour, he stopped to rest. Early on, the air grew cooler with every stop and the breeze more welcome. Later, it became so cold and his clothes so wet from perspiration that he had to move on before the end of each break. Two hours before dawn, he stopped. His anchor held at 62 feet, and the screen accumulated a mass of red crosses 100 yards away from rocks awash. He turned off the fieldstation, covered himself with the sky blue tarp, and fell fast asleep.

At daybreak, the boat's gentle rocking and the sun's soft warmth awakened him. Faraway red and yellow cliffs marked the coast of Foul Bay. Nearby, whitecaps disclosed a reef, barely discernible beneath the sea. Finally, as Caisson focused on the shoal, an awesome realization struck home. After years of anticipation and months of preparation, his quest lay within reach, just beneath the sea. Weeks before, he had picked this spot because its coral configuration suggested human design. Try as he might, Caisson couldn't see any other shoals, but he knew the reefs were there, each spaced one-and-a-half to five miles from its nearest neighbor.

Suddenly recalling his vulnerable position, Caisson searched the sea in all directions. Seeing no threat, he quickly ate the last crumbs of yesterday's bread, weighed anchor, and resumed paddling. When the *Styx* lay as close as he dared to the submerged reef, Caisson dropped anchor again. Strapped atop the deck was a drybag holding more electronics. Among its contents were a video camera hardly larger than a man's thumb, a compact video recorder, a viewing screen, and several rechargeable battery packs. Earlier in the week, Rick had carefully waterproofed the camera and attached a nylon cord and coax cable.

Like a marionette, the device would respond to the movement of his hand, controlling tilt, depth, and direction. The camera itself was attached to a 20-inch long dowel, and a diver's weight swung beneath as ballast. The cable, rising from the camera's end of the stick, served as a fulcrum, and the nylon cord provided control. His hand held a similar dowel to which the cord and cable were also attached. With this homemade device, he could tilt the camera vertically 180° and rotate horizontally 360°. Both cable and cord, marked with white paint at one-foot intervals and red paint at ten-foot intervals, slid through metal rings at each end of the upper dowel. It was possible, though not always worth the trouble, to lock the top bar so that it mimicked the bottom bar and showed the vertical angle as well.

Soon the viewer sprang to life with an awkward sideways image, half deck and half water. Then he saw his own face. He dropped the camera overboard and peered at the screen. First came a seagreen glow with the boat's silhouette above and bright light all around. As the camera descended, the light became uniformly blue, and a dark mound materialized. For safety's sake, he had to avoid the reef that made the shoal for it would shred his hull. An experienced diver could have anchored nearby, swum to its base, and searched for telltale signs, but Caisson relied on the video camera suspended beneath the kayak. Orienting the camera forward, perfectly level, at a 20-foot depth, he paddled first in a tight circle, then an ever-widening spiral, around the shoal. He paddled vigorously until the tip of another reef appeared in his screen. Shifting to the fieldstation, he clicked to record the reef's precise geographic coordinates and typed the depth into the database. Fifteen feet, he measured on the marked cord. A portable depth finder agreed and gave a wider view of the surrounding terrain. As the search continued, he learned to coordinate the two instruments, but he dearly wished for a hardwired connection to enter the depth finder's measurements automatically into the computer. *Maybe next time*, he thought.

The spiral search pattern might have appeared odd to someone accustomed to search and rescue at sea. A linear pattern of back and forth passes would have been more efficient and easier to control. But this was not a normal search. It was geographic science, agreed on with his brother and Sari before he left the yacht. It was painstakingly designed to avoid error and bias. A rectangular search pattern might have skewed the results to look more rectangular, and that in turn might have made the reefs appear more human in origin. From the standpoint of spatial statistics, a random search pattern would have been ideal, but that would have required an outrageous amount of roaming to and fro. A spiral pattern offered the best balance between objectivity and efficiency.

Parking the *Styx* directly over a submerged reef, Caisson explored its coral. Maneuvering the boat and cables, awkwardly at first, then deftly as he got the hang of it, he examined the formation from every possible angle. In particular, he watched for cracks and openings and zoomed in for any hint of masonry underneath. With the camera hovering inches from the bottom, he recorded its depth again. *Sixty feet*, he noted. Thus the formation itself was about 45 feet tall.

By midmorning, the center of the screen was filled with a coarse spiral of red crosses. Here and there red blotches marked places where he had stopped to observe the bottom more closely. Together, the two patterns reminded Caisson of a spiral galaxy, like the Milky Way, spreading its tendrils across a scaleless sky. On that celestial note, he stopped to rest and began preparing his noon meal. First, he poured a cup of rice into a ziplock bag. Then he filled the bag with seawater and placed it on the deck, hoping the sun would cook rice at least as well as it cooked his own sweltering body. He slathered every square inch of his exposed skin with 30 SPF sunblock and resumed paddling.

All morning, the spiral expanded. Caisson's forward progress continued unabated, though his radial expansion showed as the circumference grew. Each pass was carefully spaced one-tenth of a mile farther out from the central shoal. He planned to extend the survey a little more than halfway to the next shoal. Thus, the first pass with a radius of one-tenth mile would be only 0.6 mile long, while the last pass with a radius of two miles would be 12.6 miles long. A complete pattern of 20 concentric circles around a single shoal would have been 130 miles, about six days work, so he needed a way to reduce the effort. Ultimately, he decided to complete the first mile as full 360° circles, less than two days' work, then zigzag laterally to cover only 90° arcs on the rest of the passes. *I'll orient the 90° arcs so they meet in the middle and provide some overlap. Let's see, three days to complete the survey around each shoal, and I can afford to devote nine days. That's enough time to cover three shoals. That leaves six days, one of which I'll lose resupplying myself from Zabargad.* Last, he recalled that some of the territory was too deep for reefs. That part could be bypassed, saving some time that might permit coverage of another shoal or two if the need arose.

At noon, the first shoal lay precisely one-half mile away, and Caisson stopped for lunch. He dropped anchor and rested for a few minutes, then donned a mask and snorkel, tethered himself to the Folbot, and slipped into the sea. Below, the water teamed with shimmering, darting, living color. A column of coral lay only a few yards away. Remaining on the surface with his face in the water, he swam to a point directly over the reef. *A veritable fish market,* he mused. No sport and little skill was involved as he selected a likely fish, aimed his spear gun, and fired. Silver walls of glassy sweepers parted only briefly as he reeled the line in, his easy prize struggling until death ended its fight.

Soon Caisson sat upright in the *Styx* again with a fresh coat of sun block, carefully filleting a small gray reef shark. He tossed the remains overboard and washed his cutting board, deck, and hands in seawater. *The world is my sushi bar,* he thought, as he reached for the bag of rice and began his meal. Sushi 'a la Foul Bé was the first installment of an unvarying diet that would sustain him for the next two weeks. Relishing the first bite, Caisson voiced "Thanks" to a family of Japanese campers back in Hurghada who had unwittingly contributed the essential bottle of soy sauce and ten tubes of genuine wasabi.

An hour after the break began, Caisson lowered the bill of his trusty Vols cap and returned to his meticulous, ever-widening search. During the break, he had been tempted to call the data onto the screen. The urge was especially strong as he shut the system down, replaced the batteries, and rebooted to full power, but he resisted for fear of biasing his results. All in all, it would be best not to see the pattern until all the observations had been entered. *Ten days? I'm not sure I can wait that long*, he thought.

The screen showed his path and stopping places but no indication as to the depth of the reefs, general bottom, or pits. All that information was stored in the database and would be processed and displayed when the time was right.

The sun painted the western sky crimson for yet another gorgeous twilight, and Caisson stopped, exhausted from 12 hours of strenuous labor. Before sleeping, he repeated the mealtime ritual, returning this time with a three-pound grouper. The texture and taste were excellent—whiter and flakier and sweeter than the shark. There was plenty of rice, but the soy sauce must be rationed sparingly to last his whole journey. At lunch, he had eaten with his fingers, washing them often in the sea. At dinner, he dug deeper into his bags and came up with a pair of chopsticks, compliments of those same Japanese campers. After dinner, he washed everything, tossed the scraps overboard, and paddled a hundred strokes away just in case local sharks shared his taste for sushi.

Just before dark, Caisson removed an inflatable two-man raft—compliments a ship's chandler in Hurghada—from beneath the deck and inflated it with a plastic hand pump. When the sturdy raft was pumped full, he laid it in the water and strapped one side to the Folbot. The sides of the raft were dark enough to avoid easy detection, despite its bright yellow bottom, thus colored because of a later-discredited notion that bright colors repel sharks. He didn't need the optional tent-like cover, but it was good to know it was there in case a rogue wave came along. *Floats me like the waterbed I owned in college. Rides like a bareback Pinto pony.* After a full day crouched in the kayak's cockpit, it felt good to stretch out, but he wasn't quite ready to sleep yet. As darkness fell, he spotted the running lights of a vessel approaching from the northeast.

Undoubtedly she's heading into Berenice at the northern end of the bay. Yes, undoubtedly, but still I have to treat her as a threat.

He watched impatiently. To his relief, the ship followed precisely the course he had predicted. Then Caisson cherished a brief, silent respite and lamented that the rest of the night couldn't be the same. He wrestled a portable generator from behind the seat, placed it on deck, and lashed it from gunwale to gunwale. With regret, he jerked the cord. The sound wasn't excessive, certainly not a deafening roar, but any noise at all was a far cry from the quiet he had known ever since leaving Zabargad.

All day, I've enjoyed the benefits of modern technology. Now, I'll suffer the consequences while my batteries recharge overnight. Worst of all, I'll have to wake every couple of hours to exchange batteries and watch for patrols that may hear the generator.

The weary explorer then shifted over to the raft and wriggled into his sleeping bag. Before reclining he again tethered himself to the gunwale, and before sleeping, he reflected on what he had seen below. All day long, in addition to mapping coral formations, Caisson had meticulously watched for telltale signs. Most of the mounds were so luxuriant with coral that any architectural form would have been covered many times over. Before noon, however, he had found three reef columns with prominent humps on one side. By late afternoon, he had seen so many of them, always on the eastern face, that he doubted the hump could be accidental. Of course, that didn't prove they were of human origin. Plenty of alternative explanations existed in the natural world, as well. The hump, for example, could be due to more abundant growth in the direction of the prevailing current. *Still,* he reflected, *I can't help but remember those Sudanese pyramids with their offertory chapels consistently facing east.*

Search Log 45: Discovery

The second day started much like the first except that genuine excitement replaced beginner's angst. Eagerly, Caisson resumed mapping where he had left off the day before. Frequently, however, the camera captured one thing or another that teased his curiosity and tempted him to abandon the tedious survey. He would have preferred to search directly for reefs that offered a glimpse of masonry or some other sign of construction. But no, that would have to wait. In this geographic analysis, empty spaces might be just as important as the reefs themselves.

Shortly before noon, the search was completed for the first shoal, and he headed for the second. Soon whitecaps confirmed the location of rocks awash targeted on his screen. Caisson paddled in to get a closer look, then backed off to the first ring, one-tenth of a mile out. It was time to eat, so he donned his diver's mask, tethered, slithered over the gunwale, and plunged. At first splash, the water felt refreshing, so clean and cool. Crusted salt dissolved from his skin, and heat dissipated as he stroked downward.

Wham! His face struck something hard, and his mask flooded with water. Startled more than injured, he resurfaced and quickly replaced the mask. Peering down, he found the bottom a lot closer than expected. Five feet below lay the tip of a rectangular coral mound. Circling, he surveyed its triangular vertical profile on all four sides. Every facade was covered with coral, little more than a veneer, and all about, the coral was stunted. Suddenly remembering what he knew about coral growth, he looked over at the slack rope drooping from the kayak to its anchor, 60 feet below, yet clearly visible.

Clear water. No current. That explains it. These corals don't get much nourishment. Too slow and coral won't grow. Too swift and it can't stick to the substrate.

Ignoring his private sushi bar for the time being, he climbed back into the *Styx* and reactivated the video. Positioning himself directly over the summit, he began a methodical examination from top to bottom. The top itself was flat and round like a disk, less than four feet across, and the sides sloped away at steep angles, all of them the same. Knobs of antique yellow interlaced with dark shadows and purple velvet. Sunlight diffused through plates and clumps of green and lavender pastels, teasing like a sheer blouse and revealing no more. Each nook and cranny, it seemed, might open a window to the substrate, but no opening came. Unlike the overgrown mounds of the day before, this one couldn't be caused by coral growth alone. *There must be a hard substrate near the surface,* he reasoned, *and it has to be shaped pretty much like what I see.*

Caisson understood the reef diver's fascination with colorful tropical fauna. In his mission, however, fish were a constant nuisance. Ubiquitous and dense even on this impoverished reef, they often blocked the view as he tried to peer under the plate-like shelves. An emperor angelfish, midnight blue with zebra-like stripes of white and sky blue, hovered in front of his camera, only to be replaced by a clownish Picasso triggerfish, yellowish gray with stripes of black, gold, and royal blue. Slit after slit, hole after hole, he patiently waited for the fish to clear, searched for an opening, and yet found none. At about 42 feet, the camera abruptly stopped its descent, and jagged fans of coral appeared on the viewer.

Bottom already? That can't be. I distinctly remember paying out more than 60 feet of anchor.

He checked the depth finder. Yep, general bottom of 62 feet, then the sloping side of the mound with a tiny blip about 40 feet down. A sudden recollection led him to check his compass. Yep, eastern face! He raised the camera a few feet, then tilted the rod in his hand so that the lens peered straight down. There in stark outline was a rectangular shelf extending outward from the face precisely as a chapel roof should appear from above. *Thank you, Jacques Cousteau,* he thought, recalling the photo from *National Geographic.*

Excited, Caisson secured the rod and paddled out a few yards. Lowering and leveling the camera, he watched intensely as the front of the shelf came into view. Blocky! He lowered the camera to 50 feet. An inverted triangle of pale light appeared. Too close, he guessed, and backed off a little. As the lens refocused, the triangle appeared to be a shadowed opening formed by the convergence of two cones. He moved to one side and saw what surely must be the covered grotto of an offertory chapel, but still no masonry appeared. Thin though it was, the coral concealed its substrate.

Caisson moved in and scrutinized the formation from every possible angle. He zoomed and panned to no avail. He peered under the shelf, as best he could. Still nothing. Having no alternative, he backed off a few yards, moved the camera out of harm's way, raised the anchor to 45 feet, and prepared to ram it into the lintel. He stroked with all his might. Just short of the portico, however, he stopped. He simply couldn't bring himself to destroy the coral or damage the lintel. When Caisson stopped paddling, the *Styx* jerked swiftly backward as the anchor did what anchors do. It hadn't budged. He sat for a moment to reconsider his strategy.

This whole area seems rich with possibilities . . . mostly because of puny coral growth. Perhaps I'll find other formations with even less coral...or some that have lost their coverings for one reason or another. At any rate,
using the stored coordinates, I can check back here on my way "home" to Zabargad.

He continued searching the other three sides but found no portico and no opening to anything more solid than coral. Finally, he resigned himself and resumed mapping.

Elated from the previous find, Caisson was halfway into the third ring when he suddenly remembered how vulnerable he was. Squinting against the sun, he turned slowly, scanning for patrols. *Just in time!* Two fast-moving boats were heading south. Rounding Ras Banas, they curved in a wide arc before entering the channel that led west to Berenice.

Just like last night's patrol, but I'll have to lie still at least until they reach the harbor entrance.

Without concern, Caisson sank back into his seat. Unexpectedly, both boats suddenly turned 90° south, straight for his position. His first instinct was to flee, but he knew there was no escape. As soon as their turns were complete, both boats kicked into speeds that would close on him in a matter of minutes. Rooster tails of water, exhaust, and spray flared from their sterns.

Did they spot me? Either they know these waters well or not at all. No one in his right mind would run Foul Bay at such speeds.

The instinct to run seemed silly, but it caused him to glance toward shore and that turned out to be fortunate. There, in the distant south was a large boat with no clear markings. Apparently it had come from Hala'ib or maybe a Sudanese fishing port farther south. Caisson understood, with relief, that it was the trawler, not his tiny craft, that had attracted the patrols. He wasn't out of danger, though, for the patrols were bound to notice him as they passed by. He envisioned one boat speeding on toward the trawler while the other broke in his direction with guns leveled. But that hadn't happened yet, and maybe it could be avoided.

Caisson and partners had anticipated such an encounter, but the plan they devised now seemed paltry in the face of real danger. With no other choice, however, he grabbed the sky blue tarp and a bundle of folding tent poles. Spreading the tarp over the *Styx* and extending it smoothly over the water, he leaned as low as the boat would allow and yelled, "I'm a shoal. I'm a shoal. Believe me, you bastards, I *am* a shoal."

The suspense was agonizing. Blinded by his own disguise and sweltering in the midday heat, he listened helplessly. His only relief was the occasional spray of seawater splashed in from an oblique wave. He couldn't guess how soon they would reach him, but the sound left no doubt they were heading his way relentlessly at full speed. Then a second horrible thought occurred.

What if the camouflage works too well, and they don't see me? As far as I'm concerned, an accidental death is just as bad as an intentional one. No time to worry, though. I can't do a thing about it anyway.

The high whine of each powerful engine, sounding more like a cigarette boat than PT-109, grew ever more intense. Finally, the boats seemed only a few yards away from colliding with his silly little blind. That impression lasted for at least ten minutes, growing ever more convincing each second. *How long can this go on?* he wondered.

Finally, Caisson convinced himself the boats' proximity was just an illusion and relaxed his grip on the gunwale. At that instant, one of them passed to starboard so close that water surged over the tarp, and the *Styx* spun like a turnstile. Someone on the first boat screamed, "Secca!" and the second boat's whine shifted ever so slightly. The driver must have reacted on instinct rather than his comrade's warning, for the word itself came too late. Caisson grabbed the tarp, and, before he could catch his breath, the turnstile reversed as the second boat skimmed by on the opposite side. The tarp held, mostly from the weight of water that splashed over it from both sides, and the danger passed as quickly as it had come.

"Excuse me!" he yelled through ripstop nylon, "I meant 'secca.' I'm a secca! I'll never make that mistake again." Then, he laughed aloud at his own joke. Later, however, when he reviewed the affair in minute detail, it didn't seem so funny. The adrenaline ebbed, and heat pushed him to the edge of physical collapse. After forcing fluids and taking a quick plunge to cool off, he assessed his situation.

The afternoon was shot. Time had been lost evading the patrol, and another three hours would be lost watching them board and inspect the trawler, then monitoring all three vessels as they headed home. When his strength returned, Caisson became ravenously hungry.

No wonder! I was so excited about the pyramid I forgot to eat lunch. At least I can swim and eat in peace as long as those damn boats hold their distance.

Chewing his sushi a bit less enthusiastically than before, he watched as the trawler disappeared southward. To his relief the patrols took the inshore boat channel home to Berenice. His hunger satisfied and the "dishes" put away, Caisson took one last glance back at the spot where the trawler had first appeared and mentally recalled the path taken by the two fast boats. "Follow the dotted line," he whispered to himself. *Now why did I say that*, he wondered, still staring at the path the boats had followed. Suddenly, he realized the path wasn't imaginary at all. It was marked by two lines of dots on either side, barely visible above the surface— red to starboard and green to port. Each line grew less distinct with distance as they converged toward a vanishing point on the distant shore. Outside the lines, however, were two parallel lines of spheres, dark in color, with irregularly spaced spikes. *Guide buoys! Safe channels. My God, this place is mined*, Caisson realized. *A corridor lined with mines! That's why those boats passed so close as they buzzed through here. I can pick my way out if I'm careful. Question is, how the devil did I get here without blowing myself to smithereens?*

* * *

Halfway point. Time to resupply. For seven days, Caisson hadn't touched land except, that is, to bash his face into the top of a pyramid. It would be a long night's journey back to Clogger Beach, for the survey had led him many miles closer to the mainland. In his favor, however, was a full week of continuous paddling that had conditioned his muscles and quickened his stroke.

So far, he had been blessed with monotonously fine weather, though miserably hot in the daytime and cool at night. Best of all, winds had been calm and his journey safe. Once or twice there had been a stout breeze, but he steadied himself with the anchor and held his position with ease. Not once had his seaworthiness been tested by the elements, though his patience had certainly been tried as cables and connectors corroded in saltwater. Fortunately, the partners had anticipated such problems, and he was able to repair or replace each damaged piece with time-consuming, but not debilitating, disruptions.

This night, however, showed signs of rain, and he was glad to be heading for Zabargad. He left a few hours early, hoping to beat the storm. As darkness fell, the screen showed his position about two-thirds of the way between the westernmost crosses of his survey and the easternmost crosses at Zabargad. The island, visible on the horizon at twilight, was now dark. Onward he paddled, guiding by the image on his screen. When not looking at the screen, despite the darkness, he stared forward purely out of habit. For some reason, his body tingled with an odd sensation that he had felt before, but couldn't place just where or when.

Suddenly, the night took his breath away and triply blinded him with light and water and darkness. Lightning struck directly in front of the *Styx*, close enough to throw seawater at his face. He felt the spray, a gust of wind, and then a vacuum that sucked the air from his lungs. It was a near miss, if ever there was one. When the initial shock passed, however, he laughed. After too many days of raw fish, it occurred to him that there must be cooked fish floating somewhere nearby. *Too bad I won't be able to retrieve them*, he thought.

Batten down the hatches, he remembered as soon as his eyesight returned. Earlier he had formulated a contingency plan for storms at sea. Perhaps it would work, perhaps not. First, he placed the fieldstation in a drybag and lashed it to the underside of the deck forward of its usual nook. Then he inflated the life raft and lashed it securely to the stern of the kayak both port and starboard. He did not deploy the tent, but he would if needed. Partially filled with sea water, it would serve as an effective sea anchor holding the Folbot steady in pounding surf. Finally, he covered the whole boat with a tarp strapped tightly to the gunwales from bow to stern, and, working underneath the tarp, he snapped the Folbot's watertight spray skirt in place.

High seas may beat me to death, but I doubt they can sink me.

He was right, but what a ride! Like a Tilt-a-Whirl at a county fair! Seas bucked and mauled. Winds blew first one way and then another. Waves thundered against the tarp, but the Folbot held straight with the wind. Never before had he been seasick, but this was the ultimate test. An hour into the storm, he suspected he would fail this test. Two hours into it, he was sure he would fail. Three hours into it, he didn't care. At times, the air grew stuffy, held in by the wet tarp, and then a refreshing blast would hit as a bucking wave threw the boat upward and the tarp billowed like a parachute on its way down. After five harrowing hours, the wind abated without notice, and the sea regained its composure. Still, he never got seasick.

Caisson waited to be sure the storm was over, then anxiously removed the spray skirt and tarp. Above was a clear sky, with stars shining brighter than on any previous night and a new moon low in the sky. Last of all, he bailed the life raft. On reflection, he remembered the tingling sensation and recalled when and where he had felt it before. It was at 12,500 feet on a mountain in Arizona. As he reached the summit, lightning was hanging fire, and his hair stood on end. *Too many near misses*, he reflected.

Casually, as if dreadful storms at sea were an everyday occurrence, Caisson stowed the still wet tarps and rafts, then restored the fieldstation to its mount. When the screen came back to life, red crosses appeared in strange places. The flashing blue dot indicating his current position was closer to Zabargad than before but miles north of his planned course. Stroking vigorously to overcome a mild current, he set out on a new heading and reached the island well before dawn.

Navigating by the fieldstation's bright screen, Caisson moved into position offshore of his makeshift base. Waves crashed into the little cove, a pounding backwash driven by the spent storm that had mauled the *Styx* earlier in the night. Fearing another vessel might have sought refuge in the island's lee, he watched closely for signs of life.

Should I move in now or wait till dawn? In full daylight, I can spot any signs that my camp has been disturbed or, worse yet, is being watched, perhaps by a patrol like the ones I saw earlier. In daylight, however, anyone on land, friend or foe, can spot me. In darkness, I can slip in without detection, but I'll face a greater risk of ambush. And how about negotiating the surf in darkness? The high seas may abate by morning. On balance, however, daylight is too risky. I'll opt for a quick beaching.

Waves converged in the cove and crashed on boulders with a fury that would tear the kayak's rubber skin to shreds. Ultimately, he chose to hit Clogger Beach about a quarter of a mile eastward where conditions seemed more favorable. He paddled into position, secured his gear, and charged toward shore. His plan worked but not without some anxious moments. High seas repeatedly lifted the *Styx* and threw it back down again, and he had no idea what might lie underneath. If rocks, he was fortunate enough to miss them. Finally, a long, slow wave sprawled forward, and the *Styx* scraped bottom on soft, white sand.

By midmorning, Caisson had explored every direction and felt confident that the camp had not been compromised. From the Crucible above, he spied no sign of life on land or sea. Not until then did he feel safe to cook and rest and sleep. Back at camp, olive oil quickly boiled in a little pan suspended over the SVEA, its flame cup glowing like a hot red tulip. Fillets had been marinating in a bag of seawater all night. *Well shaken*, he thought. Soon they sizzled in the pan. He ate the first few bites while the crisp pieces were so hot they burned his tongue, and the taste was worth the pain. *I'll never eat sushi again*, he said to himself, knowing the vow couldn't take effect for seven more days. When the meal was over and the campsite back in order, he slept soundly.

The long day ended uneventfully, and he was oblivious to its passing. A cool breeze woke him. Vaguely, he remembered times when heat, rather than cold, had disturbed his sleep. Wrapping himself in the sleeping bag on which he had lain all day, Caisson savored the night like a cold Beamish Stout, at once both bitter and sweet. Unfocused, his mind wandered over the territory that had been his playground for the past week. Underwater scenes were etched in his mind as clearly and permanently as their videotaped images, now stored in a drybag stashed against the wall. His mind cleared, his mood changed, and he reviewed the week's findings with cold realism.

"What does it prove?" he asked aloud, inquisitor questioning heretic. "You've mapped a few coral reefs, but who knows what the patterns will turn out to be. You've shot footage of coral, but it's no more convincing than a nature photographer's stash for a PBS show."

"But lots of those formations looked like pyramids, and some had porticos," the heretic answered.

"Fantastic!" an imaginary biologist interjected without a trace of sarcasm. "Caisson's discovered a species of coral that grows in a pyramidal form in response to light and current. Exciting, yes, very exciting . . . if, of course, his discovery stands up against the observations of real biologists."

"You see, Caisson. There's nothing here to suggest human origins," an archaeologist scoffed.

"Okay," the geographer replied feebly, "but isn't there enough evidence here to make you curious?"

"No, we don't need outrageous cities under the sea to clutter our literature."

"...or your minds," Caisson rebutted.

Well, maybe the imaginary skeptic is right. I won't really know until the spiral survey is complete, and that will take another two days of hard work.

He cooked another meal, then headed out to sea in darkness again.

* * *

The *Styx* rocked gently on a tranquil sea. As evening passed into night, Caisson excitedly scanned the fieldstation screen to ensure that every secca had been covered, every arc traversed. When that was done, he relaxed his grip on the keyboard and rejoiced. Finally, after ten days of constant labor, the survey was finished. With practice, his technique had improved daily. The weather had cooperated and so had the charts, one might say, for part of the bottom was so deep it would surely have been covered with water, even when sea level was lowest. Due to these breaks, he covered more territory than anticipated. In addition to the original plan of three seccas, he covered the extra two in his most optimistic scenario, plus two more for good measure—seven in all.

With nimble fingers maneuvering the pointer and clicking keys, he rushed to clear the screen. Now it was time to examine the hard-won data.

At first, red crosses cluttered the screen as thick as tomahawks at a Braves game. With a single click they dutifully disappeared, saved for future reference. With several more clicks, the software that served the survey so well was replaced with other, more-analytical software programs. With the final click, a 3-D image of the bottom of Foul Bay began forming at the top of the screen. Steadily, tier by tier, the mesh-like drawing progressed down the screen.

Abruptly, the display went blank before Caisson could absorb its meaning. He knew immediately what was wrong. Engrossed in the task, he had missed the computer's beep. Its batteries were low when he started. Now they were dead. A quick inventory confirmed that the drybag that usually held his charged batteries was empty. Disheartened, he rigged the generator, made his bed, and went to sleep without supper.

At 11:00 p.m. and again at 12:15, Caisson's wristwatch sounded, and he woke to switch batteries. In the familiar nightly routine, he reacted like an automaton and quickly fell back to sleep. At 1:30, the alarm sounded again. This time he stirred more, and curiosity returned. He reached into the cockpit, changed the battery, and tried to sleep. But sleep was not an option. Curiosity got the best of him, and he stayed up to see the survey's results. Minutes later, he lay crossways on the raft with his upper body stretched over the gunwale. Peering down into the cockpit, he repositioned the screen, fumbled with the switch, and booted the system.

He held his breath as the 3-D image again formed from top to bottom. When the screen was filled, he adjusted the contrast and stared. The eerie specter was a jumble of lines–lines of only one color, an unpleasant bright yellow–against a black background. The database and the drawing were completely unbiased by theory. Yet, there was only one word to describe what he saw, and the word was *"city."* Not just any city, but a great city! Its street pattern resembled modern places like London and Philadelphia, but its three-dimensional form looked more like Washington, D.C., with all but the tallest monuments restricted to a few stories in height. Its vast expanse reminded him of LA.

Meticulously, he identified areas that would have been water even when sea level was low, and he painted the background there light blue. Then, he identified streets and plazas and painted them red. He painted the lower ground dark green, the middle ground light green, and the higher ground an earthy ochre. The new image might easily have been mistaken for the caricatures, half map and half art, so often published by tourist bureaus or Chambers of Commerce. This he saved as a separate file while keeping its image on the screen for further examination.

Broad avenues fanned outward from the rounded tip of a channel. A chain of vertical spikes outlined what surely must have been the waterfront of a bustling port. The chain broke only once for a broad depression that must have been a marketplace or ceremonial plaza. A single spike just north of there must have been a lighthouse. Along the avenues, tall buildings and pyramids stood at major intersections, often flanked by depressions that must have been parks or plazas.

Still, something seemed amiss. Caisson puzzled for a moment, then snapped his fingers as he recalled. With a few belated clicks, he retrieved a separate file containing the locations of the rocks awash themselves.

And there it was! With the missing pieces inserted, the city center transformed into a plaza so grand it could only have been a center of empire.

Now everything fit. There was the port with its sprawling complex of two- and three-story pinnacles, most likely ship's chandlers, warehouses, and stores. An abrupt wall more than 30 feet high swept around the old water's edge, marking a quay. Just inland was the central business district with its large, orderly buildings where finance and commerce were conducted. Next came the plaza, with enormous structures, widely spaced. To the west, a grand avenue wound upslope toward the present-day shore. To the northeast radiated a dimpled sector of pinnacles and pits, row after row, presumably homes of the rich and famous. Off to the southeast lay a disorderly maze of humps and mounds typical of working class neighborhoods in today's large cities. Closer in, a concentration of low mounds and narrow slits surely must have been the ancient equivalent of a modern-day slum.

And, through it all, a river ran. At least, that's my best guess for that swath of low-lying, featureless terrain that dissects the city from east to west.

Click. Zoom. Click. Zoom. In fine detail, the display that had looked so real turned surreal. Buildings became haystacks, many of them flattened at their tops. Even the widest boulevards now looked like ditches with slumping banks. Pits, even the broadest and deepest that had looked like plazas, now looked like . . . like . . . well . . . like pits.

Click. Pan. Click. Pan. As the view shifted from one neighborhood to another, the blanket thickened or thinned depending on amounts of coral growth. One sector still looked like a real urban landscape with well-defined streets and buildings, but most looked like one of his mother's thick quilts draped over a cabbage patch.

To a geographer, the shape itself was compelling. To most others, however, it would mean nothing. *It's disheartening,* he thought, *that geography's precious, hard-won data are dismissed so often as mere circumstantial evidence. These shapes are every bit as real as the chemists' flame or physicists' mass.* Of course, no respectable geographer would argue that form alone was sufficient proof. For that, he would need physical artifacts or, at least, a close-up view of something that revealed the underlying process, human versus physical. Masonry joints would do nicely, and that called for a window through the curtain of coral.

But that would have to wait. Click. Click. Click. He turned off the power and closed the laptop's lid, then exchanged batteries so another set could charge while he slept. Finally, he pulled the blue tarp overhead, planning to sleep late for the first time on Foul Bay.

Search Log 46: The *Tress* and the Trove

Caisson woke slowly. The sun was high, and he was ravenously hungry. The first order of business was shopping in the sushi bar below. When that was done, he prepared the fish as usual and devoured several pieces along with rice that had been soaking in seawater since the day before. He skimped on the soy sauce, for it was running low.

Reflecting on the city he'd seen in the night, Caisson satisfied himself that the survey was finished, then turned to the next phase. His goal was to find a specific reef and attempt to peer beneath its coral. Just before he left the yacht, a fax had arrived from Ed Field. It was a handwritten note containing more digits than words. "UTM coordinates of sunken freighter, *Tress of Berenice*," Ed had scrawled without revealing his source. *Maybe the highjacked freighter that sank last year struck a reef and chipped off enough coral to reveal nature's stone or mason's block,* he thought.

Ready for departure, Caisson reconfigured the computer to fieldstation mode. Then, a different idea struck. Why not do it without GPS coordinates to guide him? Click. Click. He abandoned the fieldstation software and returned to the 3-D image. More than a stunt, it was a test to see if he could navigate old Berenice just as if it were a modern city. He entered the freighter's coordinates and recorded his current position from the handheld GPS. He stashed the unit below. He then counted the streets in a grid stretching out from the central port . . .40 . . . 41 . . . 42 . . . 43. *Got it. Corner of Western Boulevard and 43rd Street.* Finally, he noted a prominent landmark and closed the lid.

Paddling with a burst of energy and pleasure, Caisson headed west, this time guided by video and depth finder alone. The depth finder showed bottom at 325 feet in a broad arc that once must have been shoreline. Spikes dotted the upslope side. At 300 to 250 feet, their density increased so that no smooth bottom could be found. From 225 feet up, their numbers declined, and by 100 feet the walls of the ancient valley were mostly bare.

This time no red crosses marked Caisson's progress. It was, in fact, more like finding an address in Washington or Cairo. His first objective was to find the landmark plaza beside the pyramid on Western Boulevard. Occasionally, the trench became obscure, and he reverted to the GPS unit, though not with its coordinates displayed on the fieldstation screen. One by one he counted streets until he reached 44th. He checked the GPS again as he neared the site of the wreck, and the coordinates didn't match. Somewhere along the way he had miscounted; the crossings weren't as distinctive as he had hoped. He paddled until the coordinates matched the ones Ed had provided. He watched for the wide plaza on his left, and there it was, spreading all the way from 43rd to 44th.

"Times Square," he said with a smile.

Suddenly, an awesome sight loomed in his video lens. There at 200 feet lay the sunken freighter, like an iron sculpture with a statement to make, on the edge of the plaza. Closer still, the viewer showed a barnacled hull with scattered wisps of new coral growth. Fish of all sizes and shapes and colors swarmed over, around, and through its twisted beams. Peering inside a gaping hole, he saw a sprawling mass of rifles and, amidst them, one white skull. But it was what lay behind the stern that stunned him, for there, toppled on Times Square, was an enormous chunk of broken coral.

His first view was the familiar flat bloom of a patch reef top, this time facing sideways rather than upward. Flushed with excitement, Caisson paddled to the opposite side, taking care not to place himself too close to the secca itself. When the *Styx* was perfectly positioned between freighter and secca, he refocused, and there it was. The proof he had sought for so long! Inlaid in the coral was a jagged square of flat rock, then another and another. Zooming closer, he found slivers of mortar joining rectangular blocks. Each block bore the unmistakable geometry of hand-carved stone, and every one of them contained a glyph that must have been a maker's mark.

Can this be the apex of an ancient pyramid? On second thought, how can it not be? Physical evidence! Confirmation! What more can anyone want?

Engrossed in the discovery, Caisson was slow to take the next logical step. Finally, he turned impulsively toward the enormous pyramid and maneuvered into alignment. He then recalled, just as abruptly, that he must approach the reef with caution. Halting his stroke, he wheeled back to inspect the fallen apex one more time. He carefully estimated its height. *Roughly 15 feet...plenty of clearance above the remaining structure,* he reckoned. On a hunch, he circled behind the apex. He was elated to see that the outer course was comprised of multiple blocks held together by dabs of mortar, while the center stone was a single plug, many times larger than the outer ones and finely finished on its underside. *Perhaps capstone or hatch for an underlying chamber,* he reasoned.

Caisson pulled the camera within a yard of the surface and tilted it downward. Then he paddled into place directly over the pyramid. On the way, he was gratified to find the standard profile of a Sudanese pyramid, the familiar portico discernible on its eastern face. Otherwise, it was a true pyramid in the Egyptian style, like Cheops' or Kephren's except for steeper sides and shorter height. At its tip was a gaping wound where the massive capstone had been.

Once in place, the camera quickly revealed a low rim of serrated coral outlining a hollow square of stone. In the center, a black void beckoned. A hidden chamber, he decided. It must have been a ceremonial pyramid of some note...perhaps more sacred than the others.

Not in his wildest dreams had he expected such a golden opportunity. Looking inside was almost frightening. Even if the contents were as ordinary as a child's toys tossed in the corner of a messy room, they would still hold the key to an age that no living person had seen and few had dared imagine. He shivered as he planned his next move.

No question, he had to see inside, but the interior was dark, a problem he hadn't foreseen. *My camera has no light. I can lower it inside and take all the shots I want, but it won't show a thing,* he lamented. *There's a flashlight below. Maglites are supposed to be waterproof. Maybe, just maybe.*

He considered swimming down to explore the interior, but the opening lay near the limit of his diving range; going inside would definitely exceed it. *What would that accomplish, anyway? Still my word against the world.*

He pulled the camera up and ducktaped the Maglite beside the lens. When everything was ready, he twisted the Maglite's head to turn it on and slipped the apparatus back into the water. Anxiously, he watched as camera and spotlight slithered into the chamber. First, a bare rock wall. Turning the camera, he found walls on three sides and a stairway on the fourth. When the camera had descended about a man's height, the stairway opened into a vaulted room.

Murals! Oh, my God! Murals...and hieroglyphs. And wood? Long, skinny sticks? How could they have survived? This chamber must have been sealed tight for 10,000 years or more. Thank God I beat the shipworms, but Teredo navalis won't wait long. Murals I can understand, but why preserve a pile of sticks? They look so ordinary...but wait, what the hell is this?

CHAPTER 26

Chronicle 55: Revival

From the funeral caisson, Toth stared at the ground and checked his shadow while waves pounded the plaza. He glanced into the heavens and checked the sun's position. Satisfied, he pulled a delicate vial from the inner folds of his cloak. Bending over Osir's body, the old priest surreptitiously poured its contents into Osir's open mouth. Again he checked the sun. Setra and his men stood bewildered.

The crowd grew deathly quiet as a fearsome shadow swept across them. The People of the Living Sun watched their sun die, its life-giving rays blocked by a monstrous dark disk in the sky. Amazement gave way to abject fear.

Suddenly, a burst of light spilled from the shadow's edge like the sparkling set of a gigantic ring. "Perhaps there's hope for renewal . . . rebirth," some said. Then darkness came again. "Perhaps this is the end!"

As darkness deepened, Toth cut through the crowd. Reaching the Sacred Pyramid, he mounted its portico and prayed loudly, "Deliver us, oh Rahn! Deliver us from this darkness, this unholy night." In darkness he prayed for guidance . . . deliverance . . . justice . . . refuge. When the sun burst again from its ring of fire, he yelled with a flourish, "Oh Rahn, Great Rahn! Show us the Divine Right Order! Give us one who will lead." Toth's prayers were answered as daylight returned to the People of the Living Sun. He swept his arms dramatically downward and pointed at the caisson below. "Behold! He is risen!" From the coffin, Osir slowly rose and stood majestic, arms stretched heavenward, the dirktooth sword gleaming in his hand. "Behold!"

"Behold! He is risen," echoed the people. "Behold!"

Osir climbed to Toth's side. "I, Osir of Egia, will lead you to the refuge. Let the Chosen Ones pray for the deliverance of all in the coming Chaos." Only Setra and his supporters stood defiant as Toth and the Chosen knelt in fervent prayer.

Osir spoke again, "Who challenges my right to lead the People of the Living Sun? Let any man who seeks Rahn Ammon's throne step forth. Declare yourself to me and the Beloved People."

And Setra did just that. "I, Setra, son of Roton, Prince of Punt...and all my legions . . ." he added, gesturing toward the tiny band beside him.

Catcalls rose from the crowd, "Traitor...fool...filthy rabble." Citizens surged forward surrounding the rebel and pummeling him to the ground. As the crowd became a mob, most of Setra's men cast down their arms, though a handful held out and were beaten into submission. Finally, Setra stood alone, spared only by rank and lineage. Arrogantly, he walked to the portico and stood beside Osir.

"Who speaks for this man?" asked Toth. He pointed toward Setra, and the crowd remained silent.

"Who speaks for this man?" He pointed toward Osir, and the crowd roared approval. Screams rang out as surging water forced onlookers to higher ground.

"You have your General," said Setra. "But I will have...," his voice trailed off as he turned and stalked into the pyramid. A great wave sloshed up the steps and spilled through the open entrance.

He's heading to the Upper Trove. He must be stopped.

Osir followed Setra inside, grabbed a reed torch, and lit it from a flaming sconce. Peering down the shaft, he saw no sign of Setra. In the bottom airlock, he found seawater chest high and rising fast. From there, he looked up the sloping shaft and saw Setra's torch bobbing high above. Near the Upper Trove, Osir drew his dirktooth sword. Bursting from the tunnel, he faced his foe.

"Ah, the Colonist who would be King," Setra said. "Shall we celebrate with a little bonfire?" He stabbed his torch into the darkness, illuminating first the staffs, then the Secrets of the Ages, and, above them all, magnificent murals depicting the history of the People of the Living Sun.

"Put down your weapon, Setra."

"And which weapon would that be? This paltry sword, which can kill a man? Or this glowing torch, which can purge generations?" He lowered his torch to the nearest bundle. Osir lunged. Setra dodged and shook the torch. Sparks flew, and fire flared wherever they fell.

Setra fought with an axelike swing, while Osir thrust and parried. Osir stepped aside, just in time to save his hand, and Setra's blade struck stone.

"Your silly heroics are over, Colonist. No miracle can save you now. I'll prove myself the better man at last," Abandoning all caution, Setra raised his sword for one final blow. Osir made his move. The gleaming red blade slashed at Setra's heart, but his parry deflected it, and it cut deep into his groin. Setra screamed in pain, dropped his sword, and clutched himself with both hands.

"First you stole my wife and child, then my kingdom and crown. Now, my manhood." Setra stumbled and fell backward down the shaft.

Osir frantically extinguished the flames, ending at the altar, but the entire Trove was engulfed in smoke and darkness. Exhausted and choking, he fell forward to catch better air down low against the altar.

Is this the end? Will I never see Bera and Horesh again? If I were a praying man, I'd pray...Save my people, oh Rahn. Lead us to the land above. Help us secure our refuge.

"This sword shall be my offering," he yelled, reverently placing it on the altar. He recalled every battle against the primitives and imagined those to come. *No, on second thought, this dagger will be my offering,* he decided, retrieving the sword for better use.

Osir found a wall, then worked his way around to the exit and began the long descent. Water now filled the airlock. He plunged in and swam for his life.

How far must I go?

Downward...downward...downward. Each stroke ended with the scrape of stone above. *No turning point yet!* Finally his hand felt water, not stone. *Time to turn!* He swam upward.

My lungs will burst if I don't get air now.

Long after he thought his lungs would explode, his head collided with a soft, floating object.

Setra, he guessed. *Claimed by the Waters of Chaos. Even in death he blocks my way.*

He shoved the body aside and burst to the surface. Gasping for air, he ran the final stretch. Waiting priests stepped aside, and when he had passed, they sealed the pyramid. *Now, Setra,* Osir thought as the huge stone fell, *you have your monument...fit for a king...the grandest tombstone of all.*

CHAPTER 27

Search Log 47: Confirmation!

Muscles stiff and sweat beading, Caisson hunched beneath the nylon tarp. Floating in the same location since dawn, he repeatedly scanned the horizon for any speck that might be a boat. Watching for the *Lali-bella*, he was alert to any craft that might betray his presence. *I can't get caught now*, he thought. *I'd be accused of spying, and I can't deny it...not with all these data onboard. In any case, I'd never see these tapes or artifacts again. Then it would be my word against the world, and only my closest friends and supporters would believe me.*

The sun was high when he noticed a gray-white blotch approaching from the north. *It's moving too fast for a guard boat on routine patrol*, he thought, *and too slow for one closing in on a target. Probably a pleasure craft. With luck, it's the Lali-bella.* Finally, the familiar profile came into focus, and he rejoiced. Caisson had placed himself well off the island, fearing the yacht might steer too close. When the crew cut power, the big boat settled down precisely where he had guessed. He reclined as best he could and drifted into fitful sleep.

Caisson awoke toward evening. He heard a few sounds and saw passengers moving on deck. He drank some water, dozed again, then heard a faint splash. A second diver went over the rail, but that didn't worry him. *It's impossible to spot this kayak from underwater at such a great distance*, he reasoned, *and it's too late in the day for a long swim.* He drank again from the canteen, then reached into the food pouch and pinched a bite of fish and rice. *I'll never eat sushi again*, he swore for the umpteenth time. *Patience, patience. If I can board unseen, I'll have eggs and toast and Turkish coffee come tomorrow morning.*

If my shipmates thought my appetite was voracious before, just wait till then. Caisson laughed at the thought, and his mouth watered. *I'll insist on fried eggs. Maybe schnitzel, too. Maybe schnitzel with eggs and cheese on top.*

A warm, dry breeze ruffled the tarp at twilight. Peeping from beneath the edge, Caisson finally decided it was dark enough to uncover. Every motion was calculated in advance and cautiously rendered as he folded and stowed the tarp. Item by item, he jettisoned all unnecessary gear. For the rest of the night, noise was his principal concern and greatest enemy. An oar bumping a gunwale, for instance, could send an alarm much farther than the distance between the two vessels. Judging from the previous night, he estimated eight hours between the last glow of twilight and the rising of the moon. If passengers turned in early, darkness would be his ally. If not, moonlight would work against him. The call was his, but everything hinged on the erratic habits of passengers and crew. His parting instruction to his partners was to signal when everyone was quiet, then watch the sea toward Zabargad. He would approach when the time was right, and they would pull him aboard.

When darkness came, Caisson dipped his paddle and eased forward. Guiding on the deck light but safely skirting its glow, he paddled with a steady J-stroke, taking more than half an hour to reach the first perimeter. Suddenly, light from the *Lali-bella's* party deck reflected off the kayak's forward deck. *Too close*, he thought, and reversed his paddle, still without stirring more than a tiny ripple. Soon the night sky reached a deep, penetrating purple. Zabargad disappeared . . . no Kiln, no Crucible, no Clogger Beach. *All that remains is a yacht at the center of the universe with a trillion stars above.*

Five hours after dark. *Those passengers have been at sea for nearly a week*, he thought. *They probably aren't as rambunctious as they were the first few nights, but any sailor worth his salt will stay up for another hour or two. Maybe it's wishful thinking, but I believe activity has begun to subside a little.*

Caisson caught a glimpse of his partners on deck.

Days on the boat. Two weeks in Hurghada? More days on the boat. That's a lot of time—and that's a pretty small cabin. Then he laughed. *Bet the Lali-bella's crew was surprised to see those avid snorkelers back on board for a second cruise.*

A passenger arranged a table and chairs on the rear deck.

Look at that bastard. He's dealing cards. A card game can last all night. Oh well, might as well relax.

Six hours after dark. *The wind has picked up. Rough seas will make for a bumpy, and noisy, rendezvous.* His kayak drifted seaward. He tried to hold steady, but the effort was excessive and the risk of noise too great. Finally, he settled into a routine of drifting for several minutes, then paddling carefully back to his correct position. The tactic worked and also helped relieve boredom.

Seven hours after dark. The game was still on, but everyone else had turned in. Then some cards blew across the deck, and the dealer cursed. He retrieved them and started to deal again. "To hell with this!" another player exclaimed, "I'm going to bed. Can't discard without showing! I'll see you guys in the morning."

The wind has repaid me for the inconvenience it caused. Still, better watch to see if they head for the bar or down the passageway to their staterooms. Even a long shower can upset my plan now. Time is growing short. I need at least 30 minutes to board before the moon rises.

Deck lights finally went out, and he moved closer.

* * *

Eight hours after dark. Slowly he circled the yacht, and all was quiet. *At least ten minutes since the last cabin lights went out. A couple of lights remain in the lounge and galley, but those rooms look empty. No sounds, no movements.*

The moon was still down, but a barely perceptible glow hovered on the horizon. A cabin light flashed in the pre-agreed pattern. Caisson cautiously aligned his compass so that its mirror reflected the boat's lights back at his own stateroom. For a moment nothing happened, except cold shivers at the thought of signaling the wrong cabin. Then Sari's silhouette appeared in the porthole, and the cabin light blinked again in acknowledgement.

Caisson moved the *Styx* to the side opposite the moon, well behind the rear stateroom. When both partners reached the deck, he edged closer and whistled softly. Sari waved, and he edged closer still. Rick Caisson leaned over the rail, more than ten feet above the water, and reached out, swinging a rope above the place where he wanted the kayak's bow. Sari followed suit at the stern. Cautiously Jared aligned himself with the yacht and cut deep with his paddle. While they fumbled to lasso each end, he secured the paddle under its usual strap and tried to stand.

My legs won't move! For 28 hours I haven't left this boat, except for nature's call. My legs are so numb I didn't realize they were numb. I can't call for help. They'll hear me inside.

He spotted a hawser line slumping over the rail and just barely reached it with his outstretched fingers. He pulled both ends until one of them became taut. Then he pulled himself up, thankful that paddling had done for his arms quite the opposite of what it had done for his legs. Inching up the smooth white surface, he was able to grab the rail and lift himself over, rolling onto the deck with a controlled thump. Sari dropped her rope and helped him stand while Rick held the boat steady.

Silently she extended her hand and gently touched his forehead, then abruptly withdrew. "Welcome back, stranger," she said with a forced laugh. Jared grabbed hold of the rail and pulled himself upright.

The three of them leaned over the handrail and lifted the kayak's bow. Slowly they pulled the keel up and over. Ultimately, the kayak rested on deck, and Jared worked to restore his legs to service. Holding on to Sari, he walked across the deck and back. Eventually, full motion returned. He was good as new.

In two quiet trips, all the kayak's deck gear was delivered to the stateroom. They cleared the hull, starting with the cockpit and working forward, and made two more anxious trips down the corridor. They tackled the section from cockpit to stern and made another cautious trip. Finally, they released the center hinges and removed the frame. Piece by piece, they disassembled the kayak and placed each part in its carrying case. Tiptoeing back into their room with the last load, they felt like shouting as Rick eased the door shut and latched it tight.

Quietly, ever so quietly, they hugged in silent reunion. "What did you find?" Rick whispered, his excitement barely in check.

"Pyramids!" Jared replied, "Lots of them. What's better, I poked inside the one breached by the freighter. It has fantastic murals that show a civilization beyond anything we imagined. A city! I mapped a city far larger than we imagined. We weren't even in the right league! No bodies, though. No sarcophagi. No ornaments. No machines. But these…" He handed over a long drybag.

"What are they?" Sari asked.

"Sticks!" He opened the bag, and three wooden shafts fell out. "I don't know what to make of them. The chamber is stacked with these things. Not like shepherds' staffs, more like hiking sticks, but they all have slashes or glyphs carved on their shafts. If they can be translated, maybe they'll tell us something. In any case, I got some good video. Shots of murals, masonry joints. Lots of hieroglyphs on the walls."

"That's it?"

"And these…" he said with a grin, drawing two waterlogged scrolls from his pack. One appeared scorched, but both were intact.

"And this…" he said, reaching again into the pack, showman style. The dagger's grip was a single spectacular tusk. Its hilt was burnished gold. Its red metal blade was iridescent and shiny as new.

CHAPTER 28

Chronicle 56: The Cry of "Ma'at!"

"Behold the eye of Horesh," Toth called, and he held the sapphire high. He placed the ring on Osir's finger. Bera then presented her brother's crown to Toth who placed it on Osir's brow.

"I crown you Osiris, King of the world above, Lord of the world below," Toth said. Then he touched Bera, "And your name shall be Isis, Queen of our refuge, consort of the Underworld. Osiris will conquer. Isis will lead."

"Ma'at! Ma'at is decreed! The Divine Right Order will be our guide for thousands of years to come!" Osir shouted defiantly toward the sea, and his own words shocked him. He had long imagined the King's decree with trumpets blaring and drums sounding. In the end, it was just a few simple words that changed the world forever.

* * *

Order amidst chaos! Under somber skies troops by the thousands formed a phalanx around the Seed and their new King. In the ranks, every person maintained a precise position assigned by the Divine Right Order. Every Chosen One knew what to bring and when to march or stand. Each obeyed without question. Even the King and Queen walked because every beast of burden was needed for hauling freight.

All eyes focused on the Ark of the Trove, front and center behind the first column. Flanked by swordsmen, followed by archers, its standard would be their guide every step of the way from Berenicia to the refuge. Only Toth could look inside the ark. Drawn by horses on the same caisson that had carried Rahn Ammon's coffin, the Ark was hidden by shrouds. Each night, it would be stored and guarded with utmost care. Soldiers would protect it with their lives, not just from enemies but from anyone whose curiosity got the best of him.

Inside the Ark were the Secrets of the Ages thoughtfully selected by Geometers and priests and reverently packed by Toth himself. What he alone saw was the iridescence of redsilver and gold, inlaid with finest ivory. The Ark was the highest art and strongest vessel, and it contained the Realm's most cherished relics and precious knowledge. Inside were the Geometries of the People of the Living Sun, exact copies of much that had been sealed inside the Sacred Pyramid. Included were histories, maps of all pyramids abandoned in the sea, instructions for building new pyramids, and plans for the hydraulicon that would be their guide to future rises. Inside was the text of the Divine Right Order, meticulously stating its laws and instructions, and beside them, Toth's Book of Truths.

Outside the phalanx, madness reigned as Commoners sought salvation. Some scurried for the First Terrace. Others pleaded with troops. Many tried to force their way in and were killed without reservation.

Osiris surveyed his people. The contrast between the fates of the Chosen Ones and Commoners was heartrending. It pained him to see the masses abandoned, but that too was decreed by the Divine Right Order. From his vantage point, Osiris watched them flee toward certain death. Word had come of a battle raging beyond the First Terrace to the south of the River Hodein. Westerners, overwhelmed by fleeing masses, had reacted violently in self-defense. A massacre of Commoners was underway. Hardly any would survive, but a fortunate few might someday create a lesser Punt along the shores of the risen sea.

Osiris looked back at the coast and pitied those who would stay. Fires, reportedly caused by lamps and stoves overturned in panic or desperation, spread from house to house. Most of the city would be destroyed by fire, if not by water. He spotted a wondrous conflagration in an unguent factory. Huge vats of oil had spilled, and burning oil floated on rising seawater.

Even for the Seed, despite their preparation and order, the exodus would be hard fought, and many would die along the way. Osiris walked among them with Toth at his side. First, came officials who would establish a new government in the refuge. Then, followed Keepers of Knowledge, close to their husbands stationed in the phalanx. Next, were essential artisans and craftsmen.

Osiris stared at the Seed. "Who will survive?" he asked, without expecting an answer. "Will there be enough good administrators to run a government? Will goldsmiths and makers of redsilver ply their trades above? Will brewers and potters ply theirs?" He contemplated the staggering, inevitable loss of Geometry, history, and culture. "Will the Keepers of the Knowledge of the Second Kalpa, the Geometers of Living Things, and the Geometers of Small Spaces survive?"

"The Divine Right Order will preserve much knowledge and skill," Toth said, "but only for a time. As before, necessity will pry us from our learned ways. Thinkers and creators may tag along, but their days are numbered. From now on, hunger will be our guide, and winds and rain will be our teacher. We'll hunt and gather food . . . like animals. Later, we'll tend herds and raise a little grain. Thousands of years will pass before we prosper again. Only then can we rebuild what we have lost."

They walked past the carriers of tools and seeds for food and grain. Rows of horses, then camels, were laden with jars and bundles. Finally, they came to the rear phalanx. Just in front of it were the Geometers. Osiris was saddened by their bright, eager faces. "Where are the teachers we once knew, Toth? Must we start so soon anew?"

"Anew? There's nothing new here, my King," Toth said sadly. "These youngsters were chosen for their memories."

"Even so, is it wise to place them all together in the order of march?" Osiris asked.

"The Divine Right Order is essential but not always wise," Toth replied.

Osiris set his jaw and strode to the front. Isis and Horesh appeared at his side. "Let the exodus begin," he said to *General* Ketoh.

* * *

The coastal highway had become a marsh. Before the tail of the column turned west, many of the Seed drowned when the sea surged. The news was relayed from back to front in the system Osiris first learned in Death's Shadow. "One hundred soldiers and 80 Geometers laid out to the sea," the message came. Isis touched Osiris' arm when she saw the look in his eyes. Both knew how few Geometers remained.

At midmorning, they reached the ravine that led to the Land of the Second Sunset. As Osiris watched the column snake up the newly completed road, an arrow fell from the rim above and struck an artisan within the ranks. Ketoh quickly dispatched a squad to sweep the hillside, killing every defender of the pass. Osiris reached the man's side as he died. It was the very same master, he was told, who had forged his own redsilver dirk and the *Ruby's* redsilver prow. "How long will it be till such mastery is restored?" he asked himself.

Sunset fell as the column approached the First Terrace. Many argued for rest as the sun disappeared over the horizon, but Osiris urged his people onward. "We must reach level ground before we camp," he said.

Farther along, the terrain flattened, and spirits revived. Mysteriously, daylight returned. The people gasped as, for the first time, they beheld the Second Sunset. Many fell to their knees in awe. Osiris turned, arms outstretched against the brilliant sky. With Isis and Horus at his side, he spoke to the People of the Living Sun.

"Our new home lies beyond this strange horizon. There, in fertile land, we'll meet the Egians and turn our backs to the sea. Never again will fickle ice and ocean determine our fate. We will rely instead on the Great River's bounty and its annual rebirth. Now, we must fight to secure our refuge. Many will die, but those who survive will be the Seed of a new generation. Someday our children will become a great nation again. I brought you here to witness with your own eyes the first wonder of our new home. Like this second sunset, the People of the Living Sun will someday be reborn."

King Osiris turned to the west. Taking Isis by one hand and Horesh by the other, he resumed his march into the Land of the Second Sunset.

THE END

Epilogue

Satellite surveillance now provides precise measurement of sea level change. From 1993 to 1997, while we wrote the first edition of this book, global sea level rose about eight millimeters (.3 inches. Between the two editions of this book (1997 to 2011), it is roughly estimated to have risen another 44 millimeters (1.7 inches).

For a more thorough review of sea level change see "The Rising Seas: How Much of a Threat," *Scientific American*, Volume 276, No. 3, March, 1997, pp. 112-117. For a more recent look at global sea level changes, see the Climate Institute website:

http://www.climate.org/topics/sea-level/index.html#.

For a more detailed look at the complicated issue of localized sea level rise, see the National Oceanographic and Atmospheric Administration's website:

http://tidesandcurrents.noaa.gov/sltrends/sltrends.shtml.

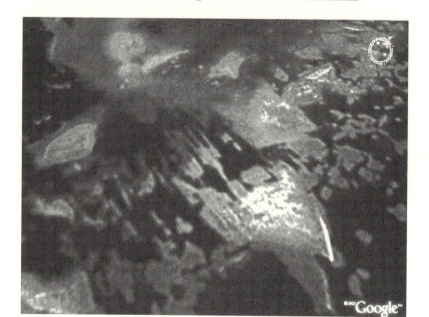

In 2008, Jerry Dobson discovered this image of what surely looks like a coral-shrouded, submerged port city in one of the sites predicted in The *Waters of Chaos*.

Nature gave us the greatest story our earth has ever told. We hope we retold it in a way that informs and intrigues.

Jeff Dobson
Jerry Dobson

The Authors

Jeff Dobson heads a firm specializing in communication systems for collaboration during emergencies. He lives in Knoxville, Tennessee, and travels extensively worldwide. He previously headed an international computer firm and has served on the faculties of the Ohio State University, the University of Illinois, and the University of Alaska. Jeff served several terms as an alderman in the town of Farragut, Tennessee. He holds a Ph.D. in geography from the University of Georgia. He has conducted fieldwork in the Arctic regions of Europe and North America as well as deserts in the southwestern U.S. His business travels often take him to the Middle East. He served as a Lieutenant in the United States Navy.

Jerry Dobson is an innovator and popular writer in the fields of geography and geographic information science. He is a professor of geography at the University of Kansas and president of the American Geographical Society, America's oldest geographic association. He previously worked at Oak Ridge National Laboratory and the U.S. Department of State. He has published more than 200 professional articles, editorials, and reports on geographic information systems (GIS), continental drift, coastal change analysis, and human evolution. Jerry led the development of the current world standard for estimating populations-at-risk in disasters of all kinds and the current world standard for cartographic representation of land mines and minefields. He holds a Ph.D. in geography from the University of Tennessee. He has conducted fieldwork throughout North America, especially Alaska, Mexico, and the Adirondack Mountains of New York, plus many faraway places: South America, Liberia, East Africa, the Middle East, East Asia, and Australia.

Jerry and Jeff have collaborated on research about ancient sea levels since 1993. *The Waters of Chaos* is an outgrowth of their real world research into the physical and cultural evidence of global sea level rise that occurred at the end of the Ice Ages. Like Jared and Rick Caisson, Jerry and Jeff are twin brothers who lived in the Knoxville, Tennessee area during the writing of *The Waters of Chaos*.

Made in the USA
Middletown, DE
07 February 2022

60482174R00333